THE NEW YORK TIMES BESTSELLER

D1052442

Praise for *The Secret Place*

"*The Secret Place* may be French's best novel yet and that's saying something. She's that good."
—*New York Daily News*

"Rendered vividly, with sharp dialogue and finely observed detail."
—*The Wall Street Journal*

"*Gone Girl* fans will revel in this enthralling thriller."
—*People*

"[Tana French's] mysteries are less procedurals and more thoughtful, smart, stunningly clever, and well-written literary yarns."
—*USA Today*

"A twisting, teasing, and tense murder mystery that, while impressive in the matter of whodunit, soars on the psychological insights of whydunit. *The Secret Place* rips you to shreds, too, but in all the right ways. While channeling teens and cops alike, Tana French has—OMG, like, totes amazeball—written a novel that seems all but certain to be among the best mysteries of the year."
—*The Christian Science Monitor*

"*The Secret Place* is Tana French's latest extraordinary procedural. . . . French's plots are inventive and her prose is elegant, but she's always been more interested in character development. Here, her steely gaze brilliantly nails the baffled and baffling emotions of teenagers on the verge of adulthood."
—*The Seattle Times*

"French . . . writes beautifully."
—*The Boston Globe*

"*The Secret Place* is an absorbing take on a hot subgenre by one of our most skillful suspense novelists."
—*Popmatters.com*

"[Tana French] simply nails it. . . . I just could not put it down!"
—*BookPage*

"*The Secret Place* simmers and seethes with skillfully crafted suspense, and French's prose often shines with beauty. But her strongest point is her characters who are sharply observed and layered into complex and surprising people, revealed both in the wild memories of the flashback sequences and the crushing pressure of the interrogations in the present."
—*Tampa Bay Times*

PENGUIN BOOKS

THE SECRET PLACE

Tana French is the author of *In the Woods*, *The Likeness*, *Faithful Place*, *Broken Harbor*, *The Secret Place,* and *The Trespasser*. Her books have won awards including the Edgar, Anthony, Macavity, and Barry awards, the *Los Angeles Times* Award for Best Mystery/Thriller, and the Irish Book Award for Crime Fiction. She lives in Dublin with her family.

To access Penguin Readers Guides online,
visit our Web site at www.penguin.com.

BY TANA FRENCH

TANA FRENCH

The Secret Place

PENGUIN BOOKS

PENGUIN BOOKS

An imprint of Penguin Random House LLC
375 Hudson Street
New York, New York 10014
penguin.com

First published in the United States of America by Viking Penguin,
a member of Penguin Group (USA) LLC, 2014
Published in Penguin Books 2015

THE LIBRARY OF CONGRESS HAS CATALOGED THE HARDCOVER EDITION AS FOLLOWS:
French, Tana.
The secret place / Tana French.
pages cm
ISBN 978-0-670-02632-6 (hc.)
ISBN 978-0-14-312751-2 (pbk.)
1. Detectives—Ireland—Dublin—Fiction. 2. Murder—Investigation—Fiction. I. Title.
PR6106.R457S44 2014
823'.92—dc23   2014004500

Printed in the United States of America
5 7 9 10 8 6 4

For Dana, Elena, Marianne and Quynh Giao,

who luckily were nothing like this

The Secret Place

PROLOGUE

There's this song that keeps coming on the radio, but Holly can only ever catch bits of it. *Remember oh remember back when we were,* a girl's voice clear and urgent, the fast light beat lifting you up off your toes and speeding your heart to keep up, and then it's gone. She keeps trying to ask the others *What is it?* but she never catches enough to ask about. It's always slipping in through the cracks, when they're in the middle of talking about something important or when they have to run for the bus; by the time things go quiet again it's gone, there's just silence, or Rihanna or Nicki Minaj pounding silence away.

It comes out of a car, this time, a car with the top down to dragnet all the sunshine it can get, in the sudden explosion of summer that could be gone tomorrow. It comes over the hedge into the park playground, where they're holding melting ice creams away from their back-to-school shopping. Holly—on the swing, head tipped back to squint up at the sky, watching the sunlight pendulum across her eyelashes—straightens up to listen. "That song," she says, "what's—" but just then Julia drops a glob of ice cream in her hair and shoots up on the roundabout yelling "Fuck!," and by the time she's got a tissue off Becca and borrowed Selena's water bottle to wet it and cleaned the sticky off her hair, bitching the whole time—to make Becca blush, mostly, says the wicked sideways glance at Holly—about how she looks like she gave a blow job to someone with bad aim, the car's gone.

Holly finishes her ice cream and hangs backwards by the swing chains, just keeping the ends of her hair from brushing the dirt, watching the others upside down and sideways. Julia has lain back on the roundabout and is turning it slowly with her feet; the roundabout squeaks, a lazy regular sound, soothing. Next to her Selena sprawls on her stomach, stirring idly through her shopping bag, letting Jules do the work. Becca is threaded through the climbing frame, dabbing at her ice cream with the tip of her tongue, seeing how long she can make it last. Traffic noises and guys' shouts seep over the hedge, sweetened by sun and distance.

"Twelve days left," Becca says, and checks to see if the rest of them are happy about that. Julia raises her cone like a toast; Selena clinks it with a maths notebook.

The huge paper bag by the swing-set frame hangs in the corner of Holly's mind, a pleasure even when she's not thinking about it. You want to drop your face and both hands into it, get that pristine newness on your fingertips and deep into your nose: glossy ring binder with unbumped corners, matched graceful pencils with long points sharp enough to draw blood, geometry set with every tiny measuring line clean and unworn. And other stuff, this year: yellow towels, ribbon-wrapped and fluffy; a duvet cover, striped in wide yellow and white, slick in its plastic.

Chip-chip-chip-churr, says a loud little bird out of the heat. The air is white and burns things away from the edges in. Selena, glancing up, is only a slow toss of hair and an opening smile.

"Net bags!" Julia says suddenly, up to the sizzling sky.

"Hmmm?" Selena asks, into her fanned handful of paintbrushes.

"On the boarders' equipment list. 'Two net bags for in-house laundry service.' Like, where do you get them? And what do you do with them? I don't think I've ever even seen a net bag."

"They're to keep your stuff together in the wash," Becca says. Becca and Selena have been boarding since the start, back when they were all twelve. "So you don't end up with someone else's disgusting knickers."

"Mum got mine last week," Holly says, sitting up. "I can ask her where," and as the words come out she smells laundry at home rising warm from the dryer, her and Mum shaking out a sheet to fold between them, Vivaldi bouncing in the background. Out of nowhere for one hideous swooping moment the thought of boarding turns into a vacuum inside her, sucking till her chest's caving in on itself. She wants to scream for Mum and Dad, fling herself on them and beg to stay at home forever.

"Hol," Selena says gently, smiling up as the roundabout takes her past. "It's going to be great."

"Yeah," Holly says. Becca is watching her, clutching the bar of the climbing frame, instantly spiky with worry. "I know."

And it's gone. There's just a residue left, graining the air and gritting the inside of her chest: still time to change your mind, do it fast before it's too late, run run run all the way home and bury your head. *Chip-chip-churr*, says the loud little bird, mocking and invisible.

"I dibs a window bed," Selena says.

"Uh-uh, you do not," says Julia. "No fair dibsing now, when me and Hol don't even know what the rooms are *like*. You have to wait till we get there."

Selena laughs at her, as they turn slowly through hot blurred leaf-shadows. "You know what a window's like. Dibs it or don't."

"I'll decide when I get there. Deal with it."

Becca is still watching Holly under pulled-down eyebrows, rabbit-gnawing absently on her cone. "I dibs the bed farthest from Julia," Holly says. Third-years share four to a room: it'll be the four of them, together. "She snores like a buffalo drowning."

"Bite my big one, I totally do not. I sleep like a dainty fairy princess."

"You do too, sometimes," Becca says, turning red at her own daring. "Last time I stayed over at yours I could actually *feel* it, like vibrating the entire room," and Julia gives her the finger and Selena laughs, and Holly grins at her and can't wait for Sunday week again.

Chip-chip-churr, the bird says one more time, lazy now, blurred with doziness. And fades.

1

She came looking for me. Most people stay arm's length away. A patchy murmur on the tip line, *Back in '95 I saw*, no name, *click* if you ask. A letter printed out and posted from the wrong town, paper and envelope dusted clean. If we want them, we have to go hunting. But her: she was the one who came for me.

I didn't recognize her. I was up the stairs and heading for the squad room at a bounce. May morning that felt like summer, juicy sun spilling through the reception windows, lighting the whole cracked-plaster room. A tune playing in my head, me humming along.

I saw her, course I did. On the scraped-up leather sofa in the corner, arms folded, crossed ankle swinging. Long platinum ponytail; sharp school uniform, green-and-navy kilt, navy blazer. Someone's kid, I figured, waiting for Daddy to bring her to the dentist. The superintendent's kid, maybe. Someone on better money than me, anyway. Not just the crest on the blazer; the graceful slouch, the cock of her chin like the place was hers if she could be arsed with the paperwork. Then I was past her—quick nod, in case she was the gaffer's—and reaching for the squad-room door.

I don't know if she recognized me. Maybe not. It had been six years, she'd been just a little kid, nothing about me stands out except the red hair. She could have forgotten. Or she could have known me right off, kept quiet for her own reasons.

She let our admin say, "Detective Moran, there's someone to see you," pen pointing at the sofa. "Miss Holly Mackey."

Sun skidding across my face as I whipped around, and then: of course. I should've known the eyes. Wide, bright blue, and something about the delicate arc of the lids: a cat's slant, a pale jeweled girl in an old painting, a secret. "Holly," I said, hand out. "Hiya. It's been a long time."

A second where those eyes didn't blink, took in everything about me and gave back nothing. Then she stood up. She still shook hands like a little girl, pulling away too quick. "Hi, Stephen," she said.

Her voice was good. Clear and cool, not that cartoon squeal. The accent: high-end, but not the distorted ugly-posh. Her dad wouldn't have let her away with that. Straight out of the blazer and into community school, if she'd brought that home.

"What can I do for you?"

Lower: "I've got something to give you."

That left me lost. Ten past nine in the morning, all uniformed up: she was mitching off, from a school that would notice; this wasn't about a years-late thank-you card. "Yeah?"

"Well, not *here*."

The eye-tilt at our admin said *privacy*. A teenage girl, you watch yourself. A detective's kid, you watch twice as hard. But Holly Mackey: bring in someone she doesn't want, and you're done for the day.

I said, "Let's find somewhere we can talk."

I work Cold Cases. When we bring witnesses in, they want to believe this doesn't count: not really a murder investigation, not a proper one with guns and cuffs, nothing that'll slam through your life like a tornado. Something old and soft, instead, worn fuzzy round the edges. We play along. Our main interview room looks like a nice dentist's waiting room. Squashy sofas, Venetian blinds, glass table of dog-eared magazines. Crap tea and coffee. No need to notice the video camera in the corner or the one-way glass behind one set of blinds, not if you don't want to, and they don't. This won't hurt a bit, sir, just a few little minutes and off you go home.

I took Holly there. Another kid would have been twitching all the way, playing head tennis, but none of this was new on Holly. She headed down the corridor like she lived there.

On the way I watched her. She was doing a grand job of growing up. Average height, or a little under. Slim, very slim, but it was natural: no starved look. Maybe halfway through getting her curves. No stunner, not yet anyway, but nothing ugly there—no spots, no braces, none of her face stuck on sideways—and the eyes made her more than another blond clone, made you look twice.

A boyfriend who'd hit her? Groped her, raped her? Holly coming to me instead of to some stranger in Sex Crime?

Something to give you. Evidence?

She shut the interview-room door behind us, flick of her wrist and a slam. Looked around.

I switched on the camera, casual push of the switch. Said, "Have a seat."

Holly stayed put. Ran a finger over the bald-patch green of the sofa. "This room's nicer than the ones before."

"How're you getting on?"

Still looking around the room, not at me. "OK. Fine."

"Will I get you a cup of tea? Coffee?"

Shake of her head.

I waited. Holly said, "You've got older. You used to look like a student."

"And you used to look like a little kid who brought her doll to interviews. Clara, wasn't it?" That turned her head my way. "I'd say we've both got older, here."

For the first time, she smiled. Little crunch of a grin, the same one I remembered. It had had something pathetic in it, back then, it had caught at me every time. It did again.

She said, "It's nice to see you."

When Holly was nine, ten, she was a witness in a murder case. The case wasn't mine, but I was the one she'd talk to. I took her statement; I prepped her to testify at the trial. She didn't want to do it, did it anyway. Maybe her da the detective made her. Maybe. Even when she was nine, I never fooled myself I had the measure of her.

"Same here," I said.

A quick breath that lifted her shoulders, a nod—to herself, like something had clicked. She dumped her schoolbag on the floor. Hooked a thumb under her lapel, to point the crest at me. Said, "I go to Kilda's now." And watched me.

Just nodding made me feel cheeky. St. Kilda's: the kind of school the likes of me aren't supposed to have heard of. Never would have heard of, if it wasn't for a dead young fella.

Girls' secondary, private, leafy suburb. Nuns. A year back, two of the nuns went for an early stroll and found a boy lying in a grove of trees, in a back corner of the school grounds. At first they thought he was asleep, drunk maybe. Revved up to give him seven shades of shite, find out whose precious virtue he'd been corrupting. The full-on nun-voice thunder: *Young man!* But he didn't move.

Christopher Harper, sixteen, from the boys' school one road and two extra-high walls away. Sometime during the night, someone had bashed his head in.

Enough manpower to build an office block, enough overtime to pay off mortgages, enough paper to dam a river. A dodgy janitor, handyman, something: eliminated. A classmate who'd had a punch-up with the victim: eliminated. Local scary non-nationals seen being locally scary: eliminated.

Then nothing. No more suspects, no reason why Christopher was on St. Kilda's grounds. Then less overtime, and fewer men, and more nothing. You can't say it, not with a kid for a victim, but the case was done. By this time, all that paper was in Murder's basement. Sooner or later the brass would catch some hassle from the media and it would show up on our doorstep, addressed to the Last Chance Saloon.

Holly pulled her lapel straight again. "You know about Chris Harper," she said. "Right?"

"Right," I said. "Were you at St. Kilda's back then?"

"Yeah. I've been there since first year. I'm in fourth year now."

And left it at that, making me work for every step. One wrong question and she'd be gone, I'd be thrown away: got too old, another useless adult who didn't understand. I picked carefully.

"Are you a boarder?"

"The last two years, yeah. Only Monday to Friday. I go home for weekends."

I couldn't remember the day. "Were you there the night it happened?"

"The night Chris got killed."

Blue flash of annoyance. Daddy's kid: no patience for pussyfooting, or anyway not from other people.

"The night Chris got killed," I said. "Were you there?"

"I wasn't *there* there. Obviously. But I was in school, yeah."

"Did you see something? Hear something?"

Annoyance again, sparking hotter this time. "They already *asked* me that. The Murder detectives. They asked all of us, like, a thousand *times*."

I said, "But you could have remembered something since. Or changed your mind about keeping something quiet."

"I'm not *stupid*. I know how this stuff works. Remember?" She was on her toes, ready to head for the door.

Change of tack. "Did you know Chris?"

Holly quieted. "Just from around. Our schools do stuff together; you get to know people. We weren't close, or anything, but our gangs had hung out together a bunch of times."

"What was he like?"

Shrug. "A guy."

"Did you like him?"

Shrug again. "He was there."

I know Holly's da, a bit. Frank Mackey, Undercover. You go at him straight, he'll dodge and come in sideways; you go at him sideways, he'll charge head down. I said, "You came here because there's something you want me to know. I'm not going to play guessing games I can't win. If you're not sure you want to tell me, then go away and have a think till you are. If you're sure now, then spit it out."

Holly approved of that. Almost smiled again; nodded instead.

"There's this board," she said. "In school. A noticeboard. It's on the top floor, across from the art room. It's called the Secret Place. If you've got a secret, like if you hate your parents or you like a guy or whatever, you can put it on a card and stick it up there."

No point asking why anyone would want to. Teenage girls: you'll never understand. I've got sisters. I learned to just leave it.

"Yesterday evening, me and my friends were up in the art room—we're working on this project. I forgot my phone up there when we left, but I didn't notice till lights-out, so I couldn't get it then. I went up for it first thing this morning, before breakfast."

Coming out way too pat; not a pause or a blink, not a stumble. Another girl, I'd've called bullshit. But Holly had practice, and she had her da; for all I knew, he took a statement every time she was late home.

"I had a look at the board," Holly said. Bent to her schoolbag, flipped it open. "Just on my way past."

And there it was: the hand hesitating above the green folder. The extra second when she kept her face turned down to the bag, away from me, ponytail tumbling to hide her. The nerves I'd been watching for. Not ice-cream-cool and smooth right through, after all.

Then she straightened and met my eyes again, blank-faced. Her hand came up, held out the green folder. Let go as soon as I touched it, so quick I almost let it fall.

"This was on the board."

The folder said "Holly Mackey, 4L, Social Awareness Studies," scribbled over. Inside: clear plastic envelope. Inside that: a thumbtack, fallen down into one corner, and a piece of card.

I recognized the face faster than I'd recognized Holly's. He had spent weeks on every front page and every TV screen, on every department bulletin.

This was a different shot. Caught turning over his shoulder against a blur of autumn-yellow leaves, mouth opening in a laugh. Good-looking. Glossy brown hair, brushed forward boy band–style to thick dark eyebrows that sloped down at the outsides, gave him a puppy dog look. Clear skin, rosy cheeks; a few freckles along the cheekbones, not a lot. A jaw that would've turned out strong, if there'd been time. Wide grin that crinkled his eyes and nose. A little bit cocky, a little bit sweet. Young, everything that rises green in your mind when you hear the word *young.* Summer romance, baby brother's hero, cannon fodder.

Glued below his face, across his blue T-shirt: words cut out of a book, spaced wide like a ransom note. Neat edges, snipped close.

I know who killed him.

Holly watching me, silent.

I turned the envelope over. Plain white card, the kind you can buy anywhere to print off your photos. No writing, nothing.

I said, "Did you touch it?"

Eyes to the ceiling. "Course not. I went into the art room and got that"— the envelope—"and a balsa knife. I pulled out the tack with the knife, and I caught the card and the tack in the envelope."

"Well done. And then?"

"I put it up my shirt till I got back to my room, and then I put it in the folder. Then I said I felt sick and went back to bed. After the nurse came round, I sneaked out and came here."

I asked, "Why?"

Holly gave me an eyebrows-up stare. "Because I thought you guys might want to *know.* If you don't care, then you can just throw it away, and I can get back to school before they find out I'm gone."

"I care. I'm only delighted you found this. I'm just wondering why you didn't take it to one of your teachers, or your dad."

A glance up at the wall clock, catching the video camera on the way. "Crap. That actually reminds me. The nurse comes round again at break time, and if I'm not there, they will *freak out.* Can you phone the school and say you're my dad and I'm with you? Say my granddad's dying, and when you rang to tell me, I did a runner without telling anyone because I didn't want to get sent to the guidance counselor to talk about my *feelings.*"

All worked out for me. "I'll ring the school now. I'm not going to say I'm your dad, though." Exasperated explosion of sigh from Holly. "I'll just say you had something you wanted to pass on to us, and you did the right thing. That should keep you out of hassle. Yeah?"

"Whatever. Can you at least tell them I'm not allowed to talk about it? So they won't bug me?"

"No problem." Chris Harper still laughing at me, enough energy running in the turn of those shoulders to power half Dublin. I slid him back in the folder, closed it over. "Did you tell anyone about this? Your best friend, maybe? It's grand if you did; I just need to know."

A shadow sliding down the curve of Holly's cheekbone, turning her mouth older, less simple. Layering something under her voice. "No. I didn't tell anyone."

"OK. I'm going to make this call, and then I'll take your statement. Do you want one of your parents to sit in?"

That brought her back. "Oh, Jesus, no. Does someone have to sit in? Can't you just do it?"

"What age are you?"

She thought about lying. Decided against it. "Sixteen."

"We need an appropriate adult. Stop me intimidating you."

"You don't intimidate me."

No shit. "I know, yeah. Still. You hang on here, make yourself a cup of tea if you fancy one. I'll be back in two minutes."

Holly thumped down on the sofa. Coiled into a twist: legs curled under, arms wrapped round. Pulled the end of her ponytail round to the front and started biting it. The building was boiling as per usual, but she looked cold. She didn't watch me leave.

Sex Crime, two floors down, keeps a social worker on call. I got her in, took Holly's statement. Asked your woman, in the corridor afterward, would she drive Holly back to St. Kilda's—Holly gave me the daggers for that. I said, "This way your school knows for definite you were actually with us; you didn't just get a boyfriend to ring in. Save you hassle." Her look said I didn't fool anyone.

She didn't ask me what next, what we were going to do about that card. She knew better. She just said, "See you soon."

"Thanks for coming in. You did the right thing."

Holly didn't answer that. Just gave me the edge of a smile and a little wave, half sarcastic, half not.

I was watching that straight back move away down the corridor, social worker duck-footing along beside her trying for a chat, when I copped: she'd never answered my question. Swerved out of the way, neat as a Rollerblader, and kept right on moving.

"Holly."

She turned, hauling her bag strap up her shoulder. Wary.

"What I asked you earlier. Why'd you bring this to me?"

Holly considered me. Unsettling, that look, like the follow-you stare off a painting.

"Back before," she said. "The whole year, everyone was *tiptoeing*. Like if they said one single wrong word, I'd have a nervous breakdown and get taken away in a straitjacket, *foaming*. Even Dad—he pretended to be totally not bothered, but I could see him worrying, all the time. It was just, *ahhh!*" A gritted noise of pure fury, hands starfished rigid. "You were the only one who didn't act like I was about to start thinking I was a *chicken*. You were just like, *OK, this sucks, but big deal, worse stuff happens to people all the time and they survive. Now let's get it done.*"

It's very very important to show sensitivity to juvenile witnesses. We get workshops and all; PowerPoint presentations, if our luck's really in. Me, I remember what it was like, being a kid. People forget that. A little dab of sensitive: lovely. A dab more, grand. A dab more, you're daydreaming throat punches.

I said, "Being a witness does suck. For anyone. You were better able for it than most."

No sarcasm in the smile, this time. Other stuff, plenty, but not sarcasm. "Can you explain to them at school that I don't think I'm a chicken?" Holly asked the social worker, who was plastering on extra sensitive to hide the baffled. "Not even a little?" And left.

One thing about me: I've got plans.

First thing I did, once I'd waved bye-bye to Holly and the social worker, I looked up the Harper case on the system.

Lead detective: Antoinette Conway.

A woman working Murder shouldn't rate scandal, shouldn't even rate a mention. But a lot of the old boys are old school; a lot of the young ones, too. Equality is paper-deep, peel it away with a fingernail. The grapevine says Conway got the gig by shagging someone, says she got it by ticking the token boxes—something extra in there, something that's not pasty potato-face Irish: sallow skin, strong sweeps to her nose and her cheekbones, blue-black shine on her hair. Shame she's not in a wheelchair, the grapevine says, or she'd be commissioner by now.

I knew Conway, to see anyway, before she was famous. Back in training college, she was two years behind me. Tall girl, hair scraped back hard. Built like a runner, long limbs, long muscles. Chin always high, shoulders always back. A lot of guys buzzed round Conway, her first week: just trying to help her settle in, nice to be friendly, nice to be nice, just coincidence that the girls who didn't look the same didn't get the same. Whatever she said to the boys, after the first week they stopped giving her come-ons. They gave her shite instead.

Two years behind me, in training. Got out of uniform one year behind. Made Murder the same time I made Cold Cases.

Cold Cases is good. Very bleeding good for a guy like me: working-class Dub, first in my family to go for a Leaving Cert instead of an apprentice-ship. I was out of uniform by twenty-six, out of the General Detective Unit and into Vice by twenty-eight—Holly's da put in a word for me there. Into Cold Cases the week I turned thirty, hoping there was no word put in, scared there was. I'm thirty-two now. Time to keep moving on up.

Cold Cases is good. Murder is better.

Holly's da can't put in a word for me there, even if I wanted one. The Murder gaffer hates his guts. He's not fond of mine, either.

That case when Holly was my witness: I took the collar. I gave the cau-tion, I clicked the handcuffs, I signed my name on the arrest report. I was just a floater, should have handed over anything worthwhile that came my way; should have been back in the incident room, like a good boy, typing seen-nothing statements. I took the collar anyway. I had earned it.

Another thing about me: I know my shot when I see it.

That collar, along with the nudge off Frank Mackey, got me out of the General Unit. That collar got me my chance at Cold Cases. That collar locked me out of Murder.

I heard the click, with the click of the handcuffs. *You are not obliged to say anything unless you wish to do so*, and I knew that was me on Murder's shit list for the foreseeable. But handing over the collar would have put me on the dead-end list, staring down the barrel of decades typing up other people's seen-nothing statements. *Anything you do say will be taken down in writing and may be used in evidence.* Click.

You see your shot, you take it. I was sure that lock would open again, somewhere down the line.

Seven years on, and the truth was starting to hit.

Murder is the thoroughbred stable. Murder is a shine and a dazzle, a smooth ripple like honed muscle, take your breath away. Murder is a brand on your arm, like an elite army unit's, like a gladiator's, saying for all your life: *One of us. The finest.*

I want Murder.

I could have sent the card and Holly's statement over to Antoinette Conway with a note, end of story. Even better behaved, I could have rung her the second Holly pulled out that card, handed the both of them over.

Not a chance. This was my shot. This was my one and only.

The second name on the Harper case: Thomas Costello. Murder's old workhorse. A couple of hundred years on the squad, a couple of months into retirement. When a spot opens on the Murder squad, I know. Antoinette Conway hadn't picked up a new partner yet. She was still flying solo.

I went and found my gaffer. He didn't miss what I was at, but he liked what it would do for us, being involved in a high-profile solve. Liked what it would do for next year's budget. Liked me, too, but not enough to miss me. He had no problem with me heading over to Murder to give Conway her Happy Wednesday card in person. No need to hurry back, said the gaffer. If Murder wanted me on this, they could have me.

Conway wasn't going to want me. She was getting me anyway.

Conway was in an interview. I sat on an empty desk in the Murder squad room, had the crack with the lads. Not a lot of crack, now; Murder is busy. Walk in there, feel your heart rate notch up. Phones ringing, computers clicking, people going in and out; not hurried, but fast. But a few of them took time out to give me a poke or two. You want Conway? Thought she was getting some, all right, she hasn't bust anyone's balls all week; never thought she was getting it off a guy, though. Thanks for taking one for the team, man. Got your shots? Got your gimp suit?

They were all a few years older than me, all dressed that bit snappier. I grinned and kept my mouth shut, give or take.

"Never would've guessed she went for the redsers."

"At least I've got hair, man. No one likes a baldy bollix."

"I've got a gorgeous babe at home who does."

"That's not what she said last night."

Give or take.

Antoinette Conway came in with a handful of paper, slammed the door with her elbow. Headed for her desk.

Still that stride, keep up or fuck off. Tall as me—six foot—and it was on purpose: two inches of that was square heels, crush your toe right off. Black trouser suit, not cheap, cut sharp and narrow; no effort to hide the shape on those long legs, the tight arse. Just crossing that squad room, she said *You want to make something of it?* half a dozen ways.

"He confess, Conway?"

"No."

"Tsk. Losing your touch."

"He's not a suspect, fuckhead."

"You let that stop you? Good kick in the nads and Bob's your uncle: confession."

Not just the normal back-and-forth. A prickle in the air, a slicing edge. I couldn't tell if it was about her, or just the day that was in it, or if it was the squad. Murder is different. The beat goes faster and harder; the tightrope is higher and narrower. One foot wrong, and you're gone.

Conway dropped into her chair, started pulling up something on her computer.

"Your boyfriend's here, Conway."

She ignored that.

"Does he not get a snog, no?"

"What're you shiteing on about?"

The joker jerked a thumb at me. "All yours."

Conway gave me a stare. Cold dark eyes, full mouth that didn't give a millimeter. No makeup.

"Yeah?"

"Stephen Moran. Cold Cases." I held out the evidence envelope, across her desk. Thanked God I wasn't one of the ones who'd sleazed her up in training. "This came in to me today."

Her face didn't change when she saw the card. She took her time looking it over, both sides, reading the statement. "Her," she said, when she got to Holly's name.

"You know her?"

"Interviewed her, last year. Couple of times. Got fuck-all out of her; snotty little bitch. All of them are, in that school, but she was one of the worst. Like pulling teeth."

I said, "You figure she knew something?"

Sharp glance, lift of the statement sheet. "How'd you end up with this?"

"Holly Mackey was a witness in a case I worked, back in '07. We got on. Even better than I thought, looks like."

Conway's eyebrow went up. She'd heard about the case. Which meant she'd heard about me. "OK," she said. Nothing in her tone, either way. "Thanks."

She swung her chair away from me and punched at her phone. Clamped the receiver under her jaw and leaned back in her chair, rereading.

Rough, my mam would have called Conway. *That Antoinette one*, and a sideways look with her chin tucked down: *a bit rough*. Not meaning her personality, or not just; meaning where she came from, and what. The accent told you, and the stare. Dublin, inner city; just a quick walk from where I grew up, maybe, but miles away all the same. Tower blocks. IRA-wannabe graffiti and puddles of piss. Junkies. People who'd never passed an exam in their lives but had every twist and turn of dole maths down pat. People who wouldn't have approved of Conway's career choice.

There's people who like rough. They think it's cool, it's street, it'll rub off and they'll be able to pull off all the good slang. Rough doesn't look so sexy when you grew up on the banks of it, your whole family doggy-paddling like mad to keep their heads above the flood tide. I like smooth, smooth as velvet.

I reminded myself: no need to be Conway's best bud. Just be useful enough to get on her gaffer's radar, and keep moving.

"Sophie. It's Antoinette." Her mouth loosened when she talked to someone she liked; got a ready-for-anything curl to the corner, like a dare. It made her younger, made her into someone you'd try and chat up in the pub, if you were feeling gutsy. "Yeah, good. You? . . . I got a photo coming your way . . . Nah, the Harper case. I need fingerprints, but can you have a look at the actual pic for me, too? Check out what it was taken on, when it was taken, where, what it was printed out on. Anything you can give me." She tilted the envelope closer. "And I got words stuck on it. Cutout words, like ransom-note shite. See can you figure out where they got cut out of, yeah? . . . Yeah, I know. Make me a miracle. See you round."

She hung up. Pulled a smartphone out of her pocket and took shots of the card: front, back, up close, far off, details. Headed over to a printer in the corner to print them off. Turned back to her desk and saw me.

Stared me out of it. I looked back.

"You still here?"

I said, "I want to work with you on this one."

A slice of a laugh. "I bet you do." She dropped back into her chair, found an envelope in a desk drawer.

"You said yourself you got nowhere with Holly Mackey and her mates. But she likes me enough, or trusts me enough, that she brought me this. And if she'll talk to me, she'll get her mates talking to me."

Conway thought about that. Swung her chair from side to side.

I asked, "What've you got to lose?"

Maybe the accent did it. Most cops come up from farms, from small towns; no love for the smart-arse Dubs who think they're the center of the universe, when everyone knows that's Ballybumfuck. Or maybe she liked whatever it was she'd heard about me. Either way:

She scrawled a name on the envelope, slid the card inside. Said, "I'm going down the school, take a look at this noticeboard, have a few chats. You can come if you want. If you're any use to me, we can talk about what happens next. If you're not, you can fuck off back to Cold Cases."

I knew better than to let the *Yes!* show. "Sounds good."

"Do you need to ring your mammy and say you're not coming home?"

"My gaffer knows the story. It's not a problem."

"Right," Conway said. She shoved her chair back. "I'll get you up to speed on the way. And I drive."

Someone wolf-whistled after us, low, as we went out the door. Ripple of snickers. Conway didn't look back.

2

On the first Sunday afternoon of September, the boarders come back to St. Kilda's. They come under a sky whose clean-stripped blue could still belong to summer, except for the V of birds practicing off in one corner of the picture. They come screaming triple exclamation marks and jump-hugging in corridors that smell of dreamy summer emptiness and fresh paint; they come with peeling tans and holiday stories, new haircuts and new-grown breasts that make them look strange and aloof, at first, even to their best friends. And after a while Miss McKenna's welcome speech is over, and the tea urns and good biscuits have been packed away; the parents have done the hugs and the embarrassing last-minute warnings about homework and inhalers, a few first-years have cried; the last forgotten things have been brought back, and the sounds of cars have faded down the drive and dissolved into the outside world. All that's left is the boarders, and the Matron and the couple of staff who drew the short straws, and the school.

Holly's got so much new coming at her, the best she can do is keep up, keep a blank face and hope that, sooner or later, this starts to feel real. She's dragged her suitcase down the unfamiliar tiled corridors of the boarders' wing, the whirr of the wheels echoing up into high corners, to her new bedroom. She's hung her yellow towels on her hook and spread the yellow-and-white-striped duvet, still neatly creased and smelling packet-fresh of plastic, on her bed—she and Julia have the window beds; Selena and Becca let them have first dibs, after all. Out the window, from this new angle, the grounds look different: a secret garden full of nooks that pop in and out of existence, ready to be explored if you're fast enough.

Even the canteen feels like a new place. Holly's used to it at lunch hour, boiling to the ceiling with gabble and rush, everyone yelling across tables and eating with one hand and texting with the other. By dinnertime the arrival buzz has worn off and the boarders clump in little knots between long stretches of empty Formica, sprawled over their meatballs and salad, talking in murmurs that wander aimlessly around the air. The light feels dimmer than at lunch and the room smells stronger somehow, cooked meat and vinegar, somewhere between savory and nauseating.

Not everyone is keeping it to a murmur. Joanne Heffernan and Gemma Harding and Orla Burgess and Alison Muldoon are two tables away, but Joanne takes it for granted that everyone in any room wants to hear every word she says, and even when she's wrong it's not like most people have the balls to tell her. "Hello, it was in *Elle*, don't you read? It's supposed to be totes amazeballs, and let's face it, I mean not being mean but you could do with an amazeballs exfoliator, couldn't you, Orls?"

"Jesus," Julia says, grimacing and rubbing her Joanne-side ear. "Tell me she's not that loud at breakfast. I'm not a morning person."

"What's an exfoliator?" Becca wants to know.

"Skin thing," Selena says. Joanne and the rest of them do every single thing the magazines say you have to do to your face and your hair and your cellulite.

"It sounds like a gardening thing."

"It sounds like a weapon of mass destruction," Julia says. "And they're the droid exfoliation army, just following orders. We will exfoliate."

Her Dalek voice is deliberately loud enough that Joanne and the others whip around, but by that time Julia is holding up a forkful of meat and asking Selena if it's actually supposed to have eyeballs in it, like Joanne has never occurred to her. Joanne's eyes scan, blank and chilly; then she turns back, with a hair toss like paparazzi are watching, to poking through her food.

"We will exfoliate," Julia drones, and then instantly in her own voice: "Yeah, Hol, I meant to ask, did your mum find those net bags?" They're all fighting giggles.

Joanne snaps, "Excuse me, did you *say* something to me?"

"In my suitcase," Holly tells Julia. "When I unpack, I'll— Who, me, you mean?"

"Whoever. Is there a *problem*?"

Julia and Holly and Selena look blank. Becca stuffs potato into her mouth, to keep the ball of fear and thrill from exploding out in a laugh.

"The meatballs suck?" Julia offers. And laughs, a second late.

Joanne laughs back, and so do the rest of the Daleks, but her eyes stay cold. "You're funny," she says.

Julia crinkles up her nose. "Awww, thanks. I aim to please."

"That's a good idea," Joanne says. "You keep aiming," and goes back to her dinner.

"We will exfoli—"

This time Joanne almost catches her. Selena comes in just in time—"I've got extra net bags, if you guys need them"; her whole face is knotted with giggles, but she's got her back to Joanne and her voice is peaceful and sure, no hint of a laugh. Joanne's laser stare sweeps over them and around the tables, searching for someone who would have the nerve.

Becca has shoveled her food down too fast: an enormous burp explodes out of her. She turns bright red, but it gives the other three the excuse they're desperate for: they're howling with laughter, clutching at each other, faces practically down on the table. "My God, you're totally disgusting," Joanne says, lofty lip curling, as she turns away—her gang, well trained, promptly match the turn and the lip-curl. They just make the laughing fit worse. Julia gets meatball down her nose and turns bright red and has to try and blow it noisily into a paper napkin, and the others almost fall out of their seats.

When the laughter finally fades, their own daring sinks in. They've always got on fine with Joanne and her gang. Which is a very smart thing to do.

"What was *that* about?" Holly asks Julia, low.

"What? If she didn't quit yowling about her stupid skin thing, my eardrums were going to melt. And hello: it worked." The Daleks are huddled over their trays, shooting suspicious glances around and keeping their voices ostentatiously low.

"But you're going to piss her off," Becca whispers, big-eyed.

Julia shrugs. "So? What's she going to do, execute me? Did I miss where someone made me her bitch?"

"Just take it easy, is all," Selena says. "If you want a fight with Joanne, you've got all year. It doesn't have to be tonight."

"What's the big deal? We've never been best buddies."

"We've never been *enemies*. And now you have to live with her."

"Exactly," Julia says, spinning her tray around so she can reach her fruit salad. "I think I'm going to enjoy this year."

A high wall and a stretch of leafy street and another high wall away, the Colm's boarders are back too. Chris Harper has thrown his red duvet onto his bed, his clothes into his strip of wardrobe, singing the dirty version of the school song in his new rough-edged deep voice, grinning when his roommates join in and add the gestures. He's stuck a couple of posters over his bed, put the new framed family photo on his bedside table; he's wrapped that packed-with-promise plastic bag in a ratty old towel and tucked it deep in his suitcase, shoved the case far back on top of the wardrobe. He's checked the swoop of his fringe in their mirror and he's galloping down to dinner with Finn Carroll and Harry Bailey, the three of them all shouts and extra-loud laughs and taking up the whole corridor, dead-arming and wrestling experimentally to find out who's got strongest over the summer. Chris Harper is all ready for this year, he can't wait; he's got plans.

He has eight months and two weeks left to live.

"Now what?" Julia asks, when they've finished their fruit salad and put their trays on the rack. From the mysterious inner kitchen comes the clatter of washing up, and an argument in some language that might be Polish.

"Whatever we want," Selena says, "till study time. Sometimes the shopping center, or if the Colm's guys have a rugby match we can go watch that, but we can't leave the grounds till next weekend. So we can go to the common room, or . . ."

She's already drifting towards the outside door, with Becca beside her. Holly and Julia follow them.

It's still bright out. The grounds are layers of green, unrolling on and on. Up until now they've been a zone Holly and Julia aren't really supposed to enter; not off-limits, not exactly, but the only chance day girls get is during lunch hour and there's never time. Now it feels like a sheet of foggy glass has fallen away from in front of them: every color is leaping, every birdcall is separate and vivid on Holly's ear, the furls of shadow between branches look deep and cool as wells. "Come on," Selena says, and takes off running down the back lawn like she owns it. Becca is already after her. Julia and Holly run, throwing themselves into the whirl of green and whistle, to catch up.

Past the curly iron gate and into the trees, and all of a sudden the grounds are a swirl of little paths that Holly never knew about, paths that don't belong just a corner away from a main road: sunspots, flutters, crisscrossing branches overhead and splashes of purple flowers catching in the corners of your eyes. Up and off the path, Becca's dark plait and Selena's stream of gold swinging in unison as they turn, up a tiny hillside past bushes that look like they've been clipped into neat balls by elf gardeners, and then: out of the light-and-dark dapple, into clean sun. For a second Holly has to put her hands around her eyes.

The clearing is small, just a circle of short grass ringed by tall cypresses. The air is instantly and utterly different, still and cool, with tiny eddies moving here and there. Sounds drop into it—a wood dove's lazy coo, the fizz of insects about their business somewhere—and disappear without leaving a ripple.

Selena says, only a little out of breath, "We come here."

"You never showed us this place before," Holly says. Selena and Becca glance at each other and shrug. For a second, Holly feels almost betrayed—Selena and Becca have been boarding for two years, but it never occurred to her that they would have separate stuff together—until she realizes that now she's part of it too.

"Sometimes you feel like you're going to go crazy if you don't go somewhere private," Becca says. "We come here." She drops down on the grass in a spider-tangle of skinny legs and looks up anxiously at Holly and Julia. Her hands are cupped together tight, like she's offering them the glade for their welcome present and isn't sure it's going to be good enough.

"It's great," Holly says. She smells cut grass, the rich earth in the shadows; a trace of something wild, like animals trot silently through here on their road from one nighttime place to another. "And nobody else ever comes?"

"They've got their own places," Selena says. "We don't go there."

Julia turns, head tilted back to watch birds wheeling in the circle of blue, in and out of their V. "I like it," she says. "I like it a lot," and she drops down on the grass next to Becca. Becca grins and lets her breath out, and her hands loosen.

They stretch out, shift till the slipping sun is out of their eyes. The grass is dense and glossy, like some animal's pelt, good to lie on. "God, McKenna's *speech*," Julia says. " 'Your daughters already have such a wonderful head start in life because you're all so *literate* and *health-conscious* and *cultured* and just super-awesome all over, and we're so totally thrilled to have the chance to continue your good work,' and pass the puke bag."

"It's the same speech every year," Becca says. "Every single word."

"In first year my dad almost took me straight home because of that speech," Selena says. "He says it's elitist." Selena's dad lives on some commune place in Kilkenny and wears handwoven ponchos. Her mum picked Kilda's.

"My dad was thinking the same thing," Holly says. "I could see it. I was terrified he was going to say something smart-arsed when McKenna finished, but Mum stood on his foot."

"It totally was elitist," Julia says. "So? There's nothing wrong with elitist. Some stuff is better than other stuff; pretending it's not doesn't make you open-minded, it just makes you a dick. What made me want to puke was the fawning. Like we're these *products* our parents shat out, and McKenna's patting all their heads and telling them what a *good job* they did, and they're wagging their tails and licking her hand and just about peeing on the floor.

How does she even know? What if my parents never read a book in their lives, and they feed me deep-fried Mars bars for every meal?"

"She doesn't care," Becca says. "She just wants to make them feel good about spending a load of money to get rid of us."

There's a snip of silence. Becca's parents work in Dubai most of the time. They didn't make it back for today; the housekeeper brought Becca in.

"This is good," Selena says. "You being here."

"It doesn't feel real yet," Holly says, which is only sort of true but is the best she can do. It feels real in flashes, between long grainy stretches of dizzy static, but those flashes are vivid enough that they throw every other kind of real out of her head and it feels like she's never been anywhere else but here. Then they're gone.

"Does to me," Becca says. She's smiling up at the sky. The bruise has faded out of her voice.

"It will," says Selena. "It takes a while."

They lie there, feeling their bodies sink deeper into the glade and change rhythm to blend with the things around them: the *tink tink tink* of a bird somewhere, the slow slide and blink of sunbeams through the thick cypresses. Holly realizes she's flipping through the day, the way she does every afternoon on the bus home, picking out bits for telling: a funny story with a bit of boldness in it for Dad, something to impress Mum or—if Holly's pissed off with her, which it seems like she mostly is these days—something to shock her into letting a reaction slip out: *Sweet Lord, Holly, why would anyone want to say such a . . .* while Holly rolls her eyes to heaven. It hits her that there's no point in doing that now. The picture each day leaves behind isn't going to be given its shape by Dad's grin and Mum's lifting eyebrows, not any more.

Instead it'll be shaped by the others. Holly looks at them and feels today shifting, fitting itself into the outlines she'll remember in twenty years' time, fifty: the day Julia came up with the Daleks, the day Selena and Becca brought her and Julia to the cypress glade.

"We better go in soon," Becca says, without moving.

"It's early," Julia says. "You said we're allowed to do whatever we want."

"We can, mostly. When you're new, though, they get hyper about being able to see you all the time. Like you might run away otherwise."

They laugh, softly, into the circle of still air. That flash hits Holly again— thread of wild-goose calls strung high across the sky, her fingers woven deep into the cool pelt of grass, flutter of Selena's lashes against the sun and this has been forever, everything else is a daydream falling away over the horizon. This time it lasts.

A few minutes later Selena says, "Becs is right, though. We should go. If they come looking for us . . ."

If a teacher came into the glade: the thought squirms in their spines, pokes them up off the grass. They brush themselves off; Becca picks fragments of green out of Selena's hair and finger-combs it into place. "I need to finish unpacking anyway," Julia says.

"Me too," Holly says. She thinks of the boarders' wing, the high ceilings that feel ready to fill up with cold airy nun-voice harmonies. It seems like there's someone new hovering by the yellow-striped bed, waiting for her moment: a new her; a new all of them. She feels the change seeping through her skin, whirling in the vast spaces between her atoms. Suddenly she understands what Julia was doing at dinner, poking Joanne. This flood was rocking her on her feet, too; she was kicking into its current, proving that she had a say in where it took her, before it could close over her head and bowl her away.

You know you can come home any time you want, Dad said, like eighty thousand times. *Day or night: one phone call, and I'll be there inside the hour. Got it?*

Yeah I know I get it thanks, Holly said eighty thousand times, *if I change my mind I'll call you and come straight back home.* It didn't occur to her, up until now, that it might not work like that.

3

She liked her cars, Conway. Knew them, too. In the pool, she went straight for a vintage black MG, stunner. A retired detective left it to the force in his will, his pride and joy. The fella who runs the pool wouldn't have let Conway touch it if she hadn't known her stuff—transmission's playing up, Detective, sorry 'bout that, lovely VW Golf just over here . . . She waved, he tossed her the keys.

She handled the MG like it was her pet horse. We headed southside, where the posh people live, Conway nipping fast around corners in the whirl of laneways, laying into the horn when someone didn't scarper fast enough.

"Get one thing straight," she said. "This is my show. You got problems taking orders from a woman?"

"No."

"They all say that."

"I mean it."

"Good." She braked hard, in front of a wheat-bran-looking café where the windows needed washing. "Get me coffee. Black, no sugar."

My ego's not that weak; it won't collapse without a daily workout. Out of the car, two coffees to go, even got a smile out of the depressed waitress. "There you go," I said, sliding into the passenger seat.

Conway took a swig. "Tastes like shit."

"You picked the place. Lucky they didn't make it out of beansprouts."

She almost smiled, clamped it back. "They did. Bin it. Both of them; I don't want that stink in my car."

The bin was across the road. Out, dodge traffic, bin, dodge traffic, back into the car, starting to see why Conway was still flying solo. She hit the pedal before I had my leg in the door.

"So," she said. A little thawed out, but only a little. "You know the case, yeah? The basics?"

"Yeah." Dogs on the street knew the basics.

"You know we got no one. Grapevine say anything about why?"

The grapevine said plenty. Me, I said, "Some cases go that way."

"We hit a wall, is why. You know how it works: you've got the scene, you've got whatever witnesses you can pick up, and you've got the victim's life, and one of those better give you something. They gave us a fuckton of nothing." Conway spotted a bike-sized gap in the lane she wanted, maneuvered us in with a spin of the wheel. "Basically, there was no reason anyone would want to kill Chris Harper. He was a good kid, by all accounts. People say that anyway, but this time they might've actually meant it. Sixteen, in fourth year at St. Colm's, boarder—he's from down the road, practically, but his da figured he wouldn't get the *full benefit of the Colm's experience* unless he boarded. Places like that, they're all about the contacts; make the right friends at Colm's, and you'll never have to work for less than a hundred K a year." The twist to Conway's mouth said what she thought about that.

I said, "Kids cooped up together, you can get bad situations. Bullying. Nothing like that on the radar, no?"

Over the canal, into Rathmines. "Nada. Chris was popular at school, plenty of mates, no enemies. The odd fight, but boys that age, that's what they do; nothing major, nothing that took us anywhere. No girlfriend, not officially anyway. Three exes—they start young, nowadays—but we're not talking true love, we're talking a couple of snogs at the cinema and then everyone moves on; all the breakups were more than a year back and no hard feelings, as far as we could find out. He got on fine with the teachers—they said he got rowdy sometimes, but it was just too much energy, not badness. Average brains, no genius, no idiot; average worker. Got on fine with his parents, the little he saw of them. One sister, a lot younger, got on well with her. We pushed all of them—not because we thought there was anything there; because they were all we'd got. Nothing. Not a sniff of anything."

"Any bad habits?"

Conway shook her head. "Not even. Mates said he'd had the odd smoke at parties, both kinds, and he got pissed every now and then when they could get their hands on drink, but there was no alcohol in him when he died. No drugs in his system, either, and none in his stuff. No links to gambling. A couple of porn sites in his computer history, at his parents' gaff, but what do you expect? That's the worst he ever did, far as we could establish: few puffs of spliff and a bit of online minge."

The side of her face was calm. Eyebrows a little down, focused on the driving. You'd have said, anyway, she was fine with her fuckton of nothing: just the way the dice roll, nothing to take to heart.

"No motive, no leads, no witnesses; after a while we were chasing our tails. Interviewing the same people over and over. Getting the same answers. We had other cases; we couldn't afford to spend another few months hitting ourselves over the head with this one. In the end I called it quits. Stuck it on the back burner and hoped something like this would turn up."

I said, "How'd you end up as the primary?"

Conway's foot went down on the pedal. "You mean, how'd a little girlie end up with a big case like this. I should've stuck to domestics. Yeah?"

"No. I mean you were a newbie."

"So *what*? You saying that's why we got nowhere?"

Not fine with it. Covering well enough to keep the squad lads off her back, but a long way from fine. "No, I'm not. I'm saying—"

"Because fuck you. You can get out right here, get the fucking bus back to Cold Cases."

If she hadn't been driving, she'd have had a finger in my face. "*No.* I'm saying a case like this, a kid, a posh school: yous had to know it'd be a big one. Costello had seniority. How come he didn't put his name on top?"

"Because I'd earned it. Because he knew I'm a fucking good detective. You got that?"

Needle still sliding up, over the limit. "Got it," I said.

Bit of quiet. Conway eased off the pedal, but not a lot. We had hit the Terenure Road; once the MG got some space, it started showing what it could do. I said, once I'd left enough silence, "The car's a beauty."

"Ever drive it?"

"Not yet."

Backwards nod, like that matched what she already thought of me. "A place like St. Kilda's, you have to come in up here." Hand higher than her head. "Get the respect."

That told me something about Antoinette Conway. Me, I'd have picked out an old Polo, too many miles, too many layers of paint not quite hiding the dings. You come in playing low man on the totem, you get people off guard.

"That kind of place, yeah?"

Her lip pulled up. "Jesus fuck. I thought they were gonna put me through a decontamination chamber, get rid of my accent. Or throw me a cleaner's uniform and point me at the tradesmen's entrance. You know what the fees are? They *start* at eight grand a year. That's if you're not boarding, or taking any *extracurricular activities*. Choir, piano, drama. You have any of that, in school?"

"We had a football in the yard."

Conway liked that. "One little geebag: I go into the holding room and call out her name for interview, and she goes, 'Em, I can't exactly go *now*, I've got my clarinet lesson in five?'" That curl rising at the corner of her mouth again. Whatever she'd said to the girl, she'd enjoyed it. "Her interview lasted an hour. Hate that."

"The school," I said. "Snobby and good, or just snobby?"

"I could win the Lotto, still wouldn't send my kid there. But . . ." One-shouldered shrug. "Small classes. Young Scientist awards everywhere. Everyone's got perfect teeth, no one ever gets up the duff, and all the shiny little pedigree bitches go on to college. I guess it's good, if you're OK with your kid turning out a snobby shite."

I said, "Holly's da's a cop. A Dub. From the Liberties."

"I know that. You think I missed that?"

"He wouldn't send her there if she was turning into a snobby shite."

Conway edged the MG's nose past a red light. Green: she floored it. Said, "She fancy you?"

I almost laughed. "She was just a kid: nine when we met, ten when it went to trial. I didn't see her after that, till today."

Conway shot me a look that said I was the kid here. "You'd be surprised. She a liar?"

I thought back. "She didn't lie to me. Not that I caught, anyway. She was a good kid, back then."

Conway said, "She's a liar."

"What'd she say?"

"Dunno. I didn't catch her out either. Maybe she didn't lie to me. But girls that age, they're liars. All of them."

I thought about saying, *Next time you've got a trick question, save it for a suspect.* Said, instead, "I don't give a damn who's a liar, as long as she's not lying to me."

Conway shifted up a gear. The MG loved it. "Tell us," she said. "What did your little pal Holly say about Chris Harper?"

"Not a lot. He was just a guy. She knew him from around."

"Right. You think she was telling the truth?"

"I haven't worked that out yet."

"You go ahead and let me know when you do. Here's why we paid special attention to Holly and her mates. There's four of them that hang out to-gether, or did back then: Holly Mackey, Selena Wynne, Julia Harte and Rebecca O'Mara. They're like that." Crossed fingers. "Another girl in their class, Joanne Heffernan, she said the vic had been going out with Selena Wynne."

"So you figure that's what he was doing in St. Kilda's. Snuck in to meet her."

"Yeah. Here's something we didn't release, so try not to blab it in interview: he had a condom in his pocket. Fuck-all else, no wallet, no phone—those were back in his room—just a condom." Conway craned her neck, spun the wheel, whipped us round a VW snail and out of the way of a lorry just in time. The lorry wasn't happy. "Fuck you, you want to start with me? . . . And there were flowers on the body—that wasn't released either. Hyacinths—those blue curly ones, real strong sweet smell? Four stems of them. They came from a flower bed on the school grounds, not far from the scene, so the killer could've put them there, but . . ." Shrug. "Guy in his girlfriend's school after midnight, with a condom and flowers? I'm gonna say he was on a promise."

"The school was definitely the primary scene, yeah? He wasn't dumped there after he died?"

"Nah. The blow split his head right open, shitloads of blood. The way it flowed, the Tech Bureau worked out he stayed still after he was hit. No dump job, no trying to crawl for help, he didn't even reach up and touch the wound—no blood on his hands. Just bang"—she snapped her fingers—"and down he went."

I said, "I'm betting Selena Wynne said she'd had no plans to meet him that night."

"Oh, yeah. The three mates said the same. Selena wasn't meeting him, she wasn't going out with him, she only knew him from around. Shocked, they were, that I'd suggest anything like that." A dry edge on Conway's voice. Not convinced.

"What did Chris Harper's mates say?"

Snort. " 'Urgh, dunno,' mostly. Sixteen-year-old boys, you'd get more sense going down the zoo and interviewing the chimp cage. There was one that could make sentences—Finn Carroll—but it's not like he had much to tell us. They're not staying up all night having heart-to-hearts, the way the girls are. They said yeah, Chris fancied Selena, but he fancied a lot of girls, and a lot of girls fancied him. As far as the guys knew, him and Selena never went further than that."

"Anything to contradict that? Contact on their phones, on Facebook?"

Conway shook her head. "No calls or texts between them, nothing on Facebook. These kids all have Facebook accounts, but the boarders mostly only use them during the holidays; both the schools block social networking sites on their computers, don't allow smartphones. God forbid little Philippa runs off with some internet pervert she met on school time. Or even worse, little Philip. Imagine the lawsuit."

"So it's just Joanne Heffernan's evidence."

"Heffernan didn't *have* evidence. All she had was 'And then I saw him look at her, and then I saw her look at him, and then he said something to her this other time, so they were definitely shagging.' Her mates all swore they thought the same, but they would. She's a poison bitch, Heffernan is. Her gang, they're the cool crowd, and she's the queen bee. The rest are petrified of her. Any of them blink without her say-so, they'll be out in the cold, taking nonstop shit from her and the posse till they leave school. They say what they're told."

I said, "Holly and her lot. Cool crowd or not?"

Conway watched another red light and tapped two fingers on the steering wheel, in time to her blinker. "Odd crowd," she said, in the end. "Not the boss bitches; not part of Heffernan's gang. But I wouldn't say Heffernan gives them any hassle, either. She dropped Selena in the shit when she got the chance, nearly wet her knickers with the thrill, but she wouldn't take them on face-to-face. They're not the top of the totem pole, but they're high enough."

Something in my face, start of a grin.

"What?"

"You're talking like these are girl gangs from East LA. Razor blades in their hair."

"Close," said Conway, and swung the MG off the main road. "Close enough."

The houses turned bigger, set farther back off the street. Big cars, sparkly new ones; not a lot of those about, these days. Electric gates everywhere. One front garden had a statue thing made of polished concrete, looked like a five-foot mug-handle.

I said, "So you fancied Selena for it? Or someone who was jealous of her going out with Chris, on one side or the other?"

Conway slowed down—not a lot, for a residential area. Thought.

"I'm not saying I fancied Selena. You'll see her; I wouldn't've said she could get the job done, not right. Heffernan was jealous as fuck—Selena's twice the looker Heffernan is—but I'm not saying I fancied her either. Not even saying I believed her. I'm just saying there was something. Just something."

And there it was, probably: the reason she had let me come along.

Something in the corner of her eye, gone when she looked at it straight. Costello hadn't been able to pin it down either. Conway thought maybe a fresh pair of eyes; maybe me.

I said, "Could a teenage girl have done the job? Physically, like?"

"Yeah. No problem. The weapon—and this wasn't released either—the weapon was a hoe out of the groundskeepers' shed. One blow, right through Chris Harper's skull and into his brain. The Bureau said, with the long handle and the sharp blade, it wouldn't have taken a lot of strength. A kid could've done it, easy, if she got a good swing."

I started to ask something, but Conway spun the car into a turn—so sudden, no blinker, I almost missed the moment we crossed over: high black-iron gates, stone guardhouse, iron arch with "St. Kilda's College" picked out in gold. Inside the gates she braked. Let me take a good look.

The drive swung a semicircle of white pebbles around a gentle slope of clipped green grass that went on forever. At the top of that slope was the school.

Someone's ancestral home, once, someone's mansion with grooms holding dancing carriage horses, with tiny-waisted ladies drifting arm in arm across the grass. Two hundred years old, more? A long building, soft gray stone, three tall windows up and more than a dozen across. A portico held up by slim curl-topped columns; a rooftop balustrade, pillars curved delicate as vases. Perfect, it was; perfect, everything balanced, every inch. Sun melting over it, slow as butter on toast.

Maybe I should have hated it. Community-school me, classes in rundown prefabs; keep your coat on when the heating went every winter, arrange the geography posters to cover the mold patches, dare each other to touch the dead rat in the jacks. Maybe I should have looked at that school and wanted to take a shite in the portico.

It was beautiful. I love beautiful; always have. I never saw why I should hate what I wish I had. Love it harder. Work your way closer. Clasp your hands around it tighter. Till you find a way to make it yours.

"Look at that," said Conway. Leaning back in her seat, eyes narrow. "This is the only time I'm sorry I'm a cop. When I see a shitpile like this and I can't petrol-bomb it to fuck."

Watching me, for my reaction. A test.

I could've passed, easy. Could've given out some stink about spoiled rich brats and my council-house life. Mostly I would've. Why not? I'd been wishing for the Murder squad for a long time. Work your way closer, make it yours.

Conway wasn't someone I wanted to bond with.

I said, "It's beautiful."

Her head going back, mouth twisting sideways, what could have been a grin if it hadn't been something else. Disappointment?

"They're gonna love you in here," she said. "Come on; let's find you some West Brit arse to lick." She gunned it and we went shooting up the drive, pebbles flying out from under the wheels.

The car park was round to the right, screened off by tall dark-green trees—cypress, I was pretty sure; wished I knew trees better. No sparkly Mercs here, but no wrecks, either; the teachers could afford to drive something decent. Conway parked in a "Reserved" space.

Odds were, no one at St. Kilda's was going to see the MG, not unless they'd been looking out a front window when we came in the gate. Conway had picked it for herself; for how she wanted to go in, not how she wanted people to see her go in. I re-wrote what I thought of her, again.

She swung herself out of the car, threw her bag over her shoulder—nothing girly, black leather satchel, more butch than most of the Murder lads' briefcases. "I'll take you round the scene first. Let you get your bearings. Come on."

Through the cool curtain of shade under the screening trees. A sound like a sigh, above us; Conway's head snapped up, but it was just wind nosing through the dense branches. On our left, when we came out into the sun again: the back of the school. Right: another great down-slope of grass, bordered by a low hedge.

The main building had wings, one stretching out to the rear from each end. Built on later, maybe, but built to match. Same gray stone, same light hand on the ornaments; someone going for line, not for frills.

Conway said, "Classrooms, hall, offices, all the school stuff, they're in the main building. That"—the near wing—"that's the nuns' gaff. Separate entrance, no connecting door to the school; the wing's locked up at night, but all the nuns have keys, and they've got their own rooms. Any of them could've snuck out and bashed Chris Harper. There's only a dozen of them left, most of them are about a hundred and none of them's under fifty; but like I said before, it didn't take a bodybuilder."

"Any motive?"

She squinted up at the windows. Sun flashed off them into our eyes. "Nuns are fucked up. Maybe one of them saw him stick his hand up some girl's jumper, figured he was a minion of Satan, corrupting the innocent."

She headed across the smooth lawn at a diagonal, away from the building. Nothing said KEEP OFF THE GRASS, but it looked it. Two heads like us in a place like this: I was waiting for a gamekeeper to burst out of the trees and chase us off the grounds, attack dogs chewing the arses out of our trousers.

"The other wing, that's the boarders. Locked down tight as a nun's gee at night; the girls don't have keys. Bars on the ground-floor windows. Door at the back there, but it's alarmed at night. Connecting door to the school on the ground floor, and that's where it gets interesting. The school windows don't have bars. And they're not alarmed."

I said, "The connecting door isn't kept locked?"

"Yeah, course it is. Day and night. But if there's something important, like if some boarder forgets her homework in her room, or if she needs a book from the library to get some project done, she can ask for a key. The school secretary and the nurse and the Matron—I'm not joking you, there's a *Matron*—they've got one each. And January last year, four months before Chris Harper, the nurse's key went missing."

"They didn't change the lock?"

Conway rolled her eyes. Not just her face was on the edge of foreign; something in the way she moved, too, in the straight back and the swing of her shoulders, the quick-fire expressions. "You'd think, right? Nah. The nurse kept the key on a shelf, right above her bin; she figured it'd just fallen off, got dumped with the rubbish. Got a new one cut and forgot the whole thing, tra-la-la, everything's grand, till we came asking questions. Honest to Jaysus, I don't know who's the most naïve in this place, the kiddies or the staff. If a boarder had that key? She could go through the connecting door into the school any night, nip out a window, do whatever she wanted till she had to show for breakfast."

"There's no security guard?"

"There is, yeah. Night watchman, they call him; I think they think it sounds classier. He sits in that gatehouse we passed coming in, does the rounds every two hours. Dodging him wouldn't be a problem, though. Wait'll you see the size of the grounds. Over here."

A gate in the hedge, wrought-iron curlicues, long soft squeak when Conway swung it open. Beyond it was a tennis court, a playing field, and then: more green, this time carefully organized to look that bit less organized; not wild, just wild enough. Mishmash of trees that had taken centuries, birch, oak, sycamore. Little pebbled paths twisting between flowerbeds mounded with yellow and lavender. All the greens were spring ones, the ones so soft your hand would go right through.

Conway snapped her fingers in my face. "Focus."

I said, "What do the boarders sleep in? Dorms or single rooms?"

"First- and second-years, six to a dorm. Third- and fourth-years, four to a room. Fifth- and sixth-years, two to a room. So yeah, you'd have at least one roommate to worry about, if you were sneaking out. But here's the thing: from third year up, you get to choose who you share with. So whoever's in your room, chances are they're already on your side."

Down the side of the tennis court—nets loose, couple of balls rolled into a corner. I still felt the school windows staring at my back. "How many boarders are there?"

"Sixty-odd. But we narrowed it down. The nurse gave some kid the key on a Tuesday morning, kid brought it straight back. Friday lunchtime, someone else asks for it and it's gone. The nurse's office is locked when she's not there—she swears she managed to get that right, at least, stop anyone from mainlining Benylin or whatever she keeps in there. So if someone nicked the key, it was someone who was in to the nurse between Tuesday and Friday."

Conway shoved a branch out of her way and headed down one of the little paths, deeper into the grounds. Bees working away at apple blossom. Birds up above, not rattly magpies, just little happy birds getting the gossip.

"The nurse's log said there were four of those. Kid called Emmeline Locke-Blaney, first-year, boarder; she was so petrified of us she practically wet herself, I don't see her being able to keep anything back. Catríona Morgan, fifth-year, day girl—which doesn't rule her out, she could've passed the key on to a mate who boarded, but they clique up pretty tight; day girls and boarders don't really mix, don'tchaknow." A year on, every name off by heart, easy as that. Chris Harper had got to her, all right. "Alison Muldoon, third-year, boarder—one of Heffernan's little bitches. And Rebecca O'Mara."

I said, "Holly Mackey's gang again."

"Yeah. See why I'm not convinced your little buddy's telling you everything?"

"Their reasons for going to the nurse. Did they check out?"

"Emmeline was the only one with a verifiable reason: sprained her ankle playing hockey or polo or whatever, needed it strapped. The other three had headaches or period cramps or dizzy fits or some bullshit. Could've been legit, or they could've just wanted to get out of class, or . . ." A lift of Conway's eyebrow. "They got a couple of painkillers and a nice lie-down, right by the shelf with the key."

"And they all said they didn't touch it."

"Swore to Jesus. Like I said, I believed Emmeline. The rest . . ." The eyebrow again. Sun through the leaves striped her cheeks like war paint. "The headmistress swore none of her girls would yada yada and the key had to have gone in the bin, but she changed the lock on the connecting door all the same. Better late than never." Conway stopped, pointed. "Look. See that over there?"

Long low building, off to our right through the trees, with a bit of a yard in front. Pretty. Old, but all the faded brick was scrubbed clean.

"That used to be the stables. For my lord and lady's horses. Now it's the shed for their highnesses' groundskeepers—takes three of them, to keep this place up. In there's where the hoe was."

No movement in the yard. I'd been wondering for a while now; wondering where everyone was. Few hundred people in this school, minimum, had to be, and: nothing. A thin *tink tink tink* somewhere far away, metal on metal. That was it.

I said, "Is the shed kept locked?"

"Nah. There's a cupboard inside, where they keep the weed killer and wasp poison and whatever; that's locked, all right. But the actual stables? Walk right in, help yourself. Never occurred to this shower that practically everything in there is a *weapon*. Spades, hoes, shears, hedge trimmers; you could wipe out half a school with what's in there. Or get good money from a fence." Conway jerked her head away from a cloud of midges, started moving again, down the path. "I said that to the headmistress. Know what she said? 'We don't attract the type who think in those terms, Detective.' With a face on her like I'd shat on her carpet. Fucking *idiot*. Kid's lying out here, bashed to death, and she's telling me their whole world's made of frappuccinos and cello lessons and no one here ever has bad thoughts. See what I mean about naïve?"

I said, "That's not naïve. That's deliberate. And a place like this, things come from the top down. If the headmistress says everything's perfect, and no one's allowed to say it's not . . . That's not good."

Conway's head turning to look at me, full on and curious, like she was seeing something new. It felt good, walking side by side with a woman whose eyes met mine level, whose stride was the same length as mine. Felt easy. For a second I wished we liked each other.

She said, "Not good for the investigation, you mean? Or just not good?"

"Both, yeah. But I meant just not good. Dangerous."

I thought I had a slagging coming, for being dramatic. Instead she nodded. She said, "Something was that, all right."

Round a bend in the path, out from thick trees and into a dapple of sun. Conway said, "That over there. That's where the flowers came from."

Blue, a blue that changed your eyes like you'd never seen blue before. Hyacinths: thousands of them, tumbling down a soft slope under trees, like they were being poured out of some great basket with no bottom. The smell could have set you seeing things.

Conway said, "I put two uniforms on that flowerbed. Going through every stalk, looking for broken-off ones. Two hours, they were there. Probably they still hate my guts, but I don't give a fuck, 'cause they found the stems. Four of them, right about there, near the edge. The Bureau matched the break patterns to the flowers on Chris's body. Not a hundred percent definite, but near enough."

That brought it home to me, that bed. Here, in this place that looked like nothing bad could ever happen in all the world: just last time those flowers bloomed, Chris Harper had come here looking for something. He must have smelled this, clearest thing in the dark around him. Last thing left, when everything else had dissolved away.

I asked, "Where was he?"

Conway said, "There." Pointed.

Maybe thirty feet off the path, up the slope, across short grass and past bushes clipped into neat balls: a grove of those same tall maybe-cypress trees, dense, dark, circled round a clearing. The grass in the middle had been left to grow long and wild. Haze of seed-heads, floating over it.

Conway took us around the side of the flowerbed and up. The slope pulled in my thighs. The air in the clearing was cooler. Deep.

I said, "How dark was it?"

"Not. Cooper—you know Cooper, yeah? the pathologist?—Cooper said he died around one in the morning, give or take an hour or two either way. It was a clear night, half moon, and the moon would've been highest a little after one. Visibility was about as good as it gets, for the middle of the night."

Things moved in my head. Chris straightening with his hands full of blue, squinting to make out the quick shape in the moonlight glade, his girl, or . . . ? And side-by-side with that, slip-sliding in and out, the opposite. Someone stock-still in a shadow with their feet among flowers, her feet? his feet?, watching Chris's face turn from side to side in the white among the cypress trees, watching him wait, waiting for him to stop watching.

Meanwhile, Conway was waiting and watching me. She reminded me of Holly. Neither of them would've liked that, but the narrowed slant to the eye, like a test, like a game of Snakes and Ladders: go careful: right move and you'll be let in one more little step, wrong move and you're back to square one.

I said, "What angle did the hoe hit him at?"

Right question. Conway took me by the arm, moved me a couple of yards nearer the middle of the clearing. Her hand was strong; not I'm-detaining-you cop, not I-fancy-you girl, just strong; well able to fix a car, or punch someone who needed punching. She turned me facing down to the flowers and the path, my back to the trees.

"He was about here."

Something buzzed, a bumblebee or a faraway lawnmower, I couldn't tell; the acoustics were all swirl and ricochet. Seed-heads waved around my shins.

"Someone came up behind him, or got him to turn away. Someone standing about here."

Close behind me. I twisted my head around. She lifted the imaginary hoe over her left shoulder, two-handed. Brought it down, her whole body behind it. Somewhere behind the chirpy spring sounds, the swish and thud shivered the air. Even though she was holding nothing, I flinched.

The corner of Conway's mouth went up. She held up her empty hands.

I said, "And he went down."

"Got him here." She put the edge of her hand against the back of my skull, high up and to the left of the center line, slanting up from left to right. "Chris was a couple of inches shorter than you: five foot ten. The killer wouldn't've had to be tall. Over five foot, under six, was all Cooper could say from the angle of the wound. Probably right-handed."

Her feet rustling, as she moved back from me. "The grass," I said. "Was it like this back then?"

Right question again, good boy. "Nah. They let it grow afterwards—some kind of memorial thing or the place spooks the groundskeepers, I don't know. No one sees this part, so I guess it doesn't ruin the school's *image*. Back then, though, the grass was like the rest: short. If you had soft shoes, you could sneak across it without getting heard, no problem."

And without leaving shoeprints, or at least none that the Bureau could use. The paths were pebbled: no prints there, either.

"Where'd you find the hoe?"

"Back in the shed, where it belonged. We spotted it because it matched what Cooper said about the weapon. The Bureau took about five seconds to confirm it. She—he, she, whatever—she'd tried to clean off the blade, smacked it into the earth over there a couple of times"—the ground under one of the cypresses—"rubbed it on the grass. Smart; smarter than wiping it down with a cloth, then you've got the cloth to get rid of. But there was still plenty of blood left."

"Any prints?"

Conway shook her head. "The groundskeepers'. No one else's epithelials, either, so no touch DNA. We figured she wore gloves."

"'She,'" I said.

Conway said, "That's what I've got. A load of shes and not a lot of hes. Back last year, one theory was it was some pervert, snuck in here to crack one off watching the girls' windows or playing with their tennis rackets or whatever; Chris came in to meet someone, caught the guy out. Doesn't fit the evidence—what, the guy had his mickey in one hand and a hoe in the other?—but a lot of people liked it anyway. Better than thinking it was some cute little rich girl. From a *beautiful* school like this."

The slant to the eye again. Testing. A crossbeam of sun lightened her eyes to amber, like a wolf's.

I said, "It wasn't an outsider. Not with that postcard. If it had been, why all the secrecy? Why wouldn't the girl just ring you up and tell you what she knew? If she's not making up the lot, then she knows something about someone inside the school. And she's scared."

Conway said, "And we missed her first time round."

A grim layer stamped on her voice. Not just hard on other people, Conway.

"Maybe not," I said. "They're young, these girls. If one of them saw something, heard something, she might not have copped what it meant; not at the time. Specially if it had to do with sex, or relationships. This generation know all the facts, they've seen the porn sites, probably they know more positions than you and me put together; but when it comes to the real thing, they're miles out of their depth. A kid could see something and know it was important, but not understand why. Now she's a year older, she's got a bit more of a clue; something makes her look back, and all of a sudden it clicks together."

Conway thought about that. "Maybe," she said. But the grim layer stayed put: not letting herself off that easy. "Doesn't matter. Even if she didn't know she had info, it's our job to know for her. She was right in there"— backwards flick of her head, to the school—"we sat there and interviewed her, and we let her walk away. And I'm not fucking happy about it."

It felt like the end of the conversation. When she didn't say anything else I started to turn towards the path, but Conway wasn't moving. Feet apart, hands in her pockets, staring into the trees. Chin out, like they were the enemy.

She said, without looking at me, "I got to be the primary because we thought this was a slam dunk. That first day, the morgue boys hadn't even taken away the body, we found half a kilo of E in the stables, back of the poison cupboard. One of the groundskeepers came up on the system: prior for supply. And St. Colm's, back at the Christmas dance they'd caught a couple of kids with E; we never got the supplier, the kids never squelt. Chris wasn't one of the ones who had the E, but still . . . We figured it was our lucky day: two solves for the price of one. Chris snuck out to buy drugs off the groundskeeper, some fight over money, bang."

That long sigh again, above us. This time I saw it, moving through the branches. Like the trees were listening; like they would've been sad about us, sad for us, only they'd heard it all so many thousand times before.

"Costello . . . He was sound, Costello. The squad used to slag him off, call him a depressing fucker, but he was decent. He said, 'You put your name on this one. Mark your card.' He must've known then, he was gonna put in his papers this year; he didn't need a big solve. I did."

Her voice was indoors-quiet, small-room quiet, falling through the wide sunshine. I felt the size of the stillness and green all round us. The breadth of it; the height, trees taller than the school. Older.

"The groundskeeper alibied out. He'd had mates round to his gaff for poker and a few cans; two of them kipped on his sofa. We got him for possession with intent, but the murder . . ." Conway shook her head. "I should've known," she said. She didn't explain. "I should've known it wasn't gonna be that simple."

A bee thumped into the white of her shirt front; clung on, addled. Conway's head snapped down and the rest of her went still. The bee crawled past the top button, reached over the edge of the cloth, feeling for skin. Conway breathed slow and shallow. I saw her hand come out of her pocket and rise.

The bee got its head together and took off, into the sunlight. Conway flicked some speck off her shirt where it had been. Then she turned and headed down the slope, past the hyacinths and back to the path.

4

The Court, the biggest and best shopping center within walking distance of Kilda's and Colm's, the wrapping of every moment in the world that doesn't have some sour-faced adult looming over it ready to pounce. The Court pulls like a towering magnet and everyone comes. Anything can happen here, in the sparkling slice of freedom between classes and teatime; your life could lift right off the ground and shimmer into something brand-new. In the dizzying white light all the faces glimmer, they mouth words and crack open in laughs you can almost catch through the cloud of sounds, and any one of them could be the heart-stopping one you've been waiting for; anything you can imagine could be waiting for you here, if you turn your head at just the right second, if you just catch the right eye, if the right song just comes spinning out of the speakers all around you. Sugar-smell of fresh doughnuts drifting out from the kiosk, lick it off your fingers.

It's the beginning of October. Chris Harper—scuffling with Oisín O'Donovan on the rim of the fountain in the middle of the Court, mouth wide in a laugh, the other Colm's guys around them whooping them on—has a little over seven months left to live.

Becca and Julia and Selena and Holly are on the opposite rim of the fountain, with four open packets of sweets in between them. Julia has one eye on the Colm's guys and is talking fast and snappy, telling some possibly mostly true story about how this summer she and this English girl and a couple of French guys blagged their way into a super-fancy nightclub in Nice. Holly is eating Skittles and listening, with one eyebrow at an angle that says *Yeah right*; Selena is lying on the battered black-marble edge of the fountain with her chin propped on her hands, so that her hair drapes over her shoulder almost to the floor. Becca wants to lean over and cup it in her hands, before it touches the grime and the ground-in gum.

Becca despises the Court. Back at the start of first year, when the new boarders had to wait a month before they were allowed off school grounds— until they were too worn down to run away, she figures—that was all she ever heard about: oh the Court the Court the Court, everything'll be so fab when we get to go to the Court. Glowing eyes, hands sketching pictures like it was shining castles and skating rinks and chocolate waterfalls. Older girls trailing back smug and sticky, wrapped with scents of cappuccino and tester lip gloss, one-finger-swinging bags packed with colors, still swaying to the dazing pump of glossy music. The magic place, the shimmering place to make you forget all about sour teachers, rows of dorm beds, bitchy comments you didn't understand. Vanish it all away.

That was before Becca knew Julia and Selena and Holly. Back then she was so miserable it astonished her every morning. She used to ring her mother sobbing, huge disgusting gulps, not caring who heard, begging to come home. Her mother would sigh and tell her how much fun she'd be having any day now, once she made friends to chat with about boys and pop stars and fashion, and Becca would get off the phone stunned all over again by how much worse she felt. So the Court sounded like the one thing to look forward to in the whole horrible world.

And then she finally got there and it was a crap shopping center. All the other first-years were practically drooling, and Becca looked up at this windowless nineties lump of gray concrete and wondered whether, if she just curled up on the ground right here and refused to move, they would send her home for being crazy.

Then the blond girl next to her, Serena or something—Becca had been too busy being wretched for much to stick in her mind—Selena took a long thoughtful look up at the top of the Court and said, "There actually is a window, see? I bet if you could find it, you could see half of Dublin."

Which it turned out you could. And there it was, spread out below them: the magic world they'd been promised, neat and cozy as storybooks. There was washing billowing on lines and little kids playing swing-ball in a garden, there was a green park with the brightest red and yellow flower beds ever; an old man and an old lady had stopped to chat under a curly wrought-iron lamppost, while their perky-eared dogs wound their leads into a knot. The window was in between a parking pay-station and a huge bin, and adults paying their parking tickets kept giving Becca and Selena suspicious looks, and in the end a security guard showed up and threw them out of the Court even though he didn't seem sure exactly why, but it was a million kinds of worth it.

Two years on, though, Becca still hates the Court. She hates the way you're watched every second from every angle, eyes swarming over you like bugs, digging and gnawing, always a clutch of girls checking out your top or a huddle of guys checking out your whatever. No one ever stays still, at the Court, everyone's constantly twisting and head-flicking, watching for the watchers, trying for the coolest pose. No one ever stays quiet: you have to keep talking or you'll look like losers, but you can't have an actual conversation because everyone's thinking about other stuff. Fifteen minutes at the Court and Becca feels like anyone who touched her would get electrocuted.

And at least back when they were twelve they just put on their coats and went. This year, everyone gets ready for the Court like they're getting ready for the Oscars. The Court is where you bring your bewildering new curves and walk and self so people can tell you what they're worth, and you can't risk the answer being *Nothing zero nothing.* You like so totally *have* to have your hair either straightened to death or else brushed into a careful tangle, and fake tan all over and an inch of foundation on your face and half a pack of smoky eyeshadow around each eye, and super-soft super-skinny jeans and Uggs or Converse, because otherwise someone might actually be able to tell you apart from everyone else and obviously that would make you a total loser. Lenie and Jules and Holly are nowhere near that bad, but they still redo their blusher four times and check the mirror from twenty angles, while Becca fidgets springy-footed in the doorway, before they can actually leave. Becca doesn't wear makeup to the Court because she hates makeup and because the idea of spending half an hour getting ready to sit on a wall in front of a doughnut shop makes her brain short out with stupid.

She goes because the others do. Why they want to is a total mystery to Becca. They always act like they're having an amazing time, they're louder and high-pitched, shoving each other and screaming with laughter at nothing. But Becca knows what they're like when they're happy, and that's not it. Their faces on the way home afterwards look older and strained, smeared with the scraps of leftover expressions that were pressed on too hard and won't lift away.

Today she's even more electric than usual, checking the time on her phone every two minutes, shifting like the marble hurts her bones. Julia's already said to her twice, "Jesus, will you settle *down?*" Becca mutters, "Sorry," but a minute later she's shifting again.

It's because like two meters down from them on the fountain edge are the Daleks. Becca hates everything about the Daleks, in detail. She hates them separately—the way Orla's mouth hangs open, the way Gemma wiggles her bum when she walks, Alison's poor-ickle-scared-baby look, the fact that

Joanne exists—and as a unit. She hates them extra today because three of the Colm's guys across the fountain have come over to sit with them, so the Daleks are even more everything than usual. Every time one of the guys says something, all four of them have to shriek with laughter and pretend they're almost falling off the fountain so the guys will catch them. Alison keeps lolling her head right over to one side to look up at this blond guy, and sticking out the tip of her tongue between her teeth. She looks brain damaged.

"So," Julia is saying, "Jean-Michel points at me and Jodi and he's all, 'This is Candy Jinx. They just won the Irish *X Factor*!' Which was kind of smart, because since that doesn't exist it's not like the bouncers were going to know the actual winner, but not *that* smart, because I could've told him exactly where this was going to fucking go." Julia is trying out swearing. It still only sort of works. "And yeah, surprise, the bouncers are like, 'OK, let's hear them sing.'"

"Uh-oh," Becca says. She's trying to ignore the Daleks and concentrate on Julia. Julia's stories are always good, even if you have to subtract ten or twenty percent and Becca's never completely sure she's subtracting enough.

Julia's eyebrow shoots up. "Thanks a bunch."

Becca flinches. "No, I just meant—"

"Chillax, Becs. I know I can't sing for shit. That's the whole point." Becca blushes, and goes for another handful of Skittles to hide the blush. "So I'm like, we're so fucked, what are me and Jodi even supposed to sing? We both like Lady Gaga, but what are we going to do, say Candy Jinx's first single is 'Bad Romance'?"

Selena is laughing. The Colm's guys are looking over.

"Luckily, though, Florian is smarter than Jean-Michel. He goes, 'Are you joking? They're under contract. If they sing a note, we'll all get our arses sued off.'"

Holly isn't laughing. She looks like she hasn't heard. Her head's tucked sideways, listening to something else.

"Hol?" says Selena. "You OK?"

Holly nods backwards, at the Daleks.

Julia leaves the rest of her story for later. The four of them pretend to be fascinated by picking out exactly the right sweets from the packets, and listen.

"He is," Joanne says, and nudges Orla's leg with her foot.

Orla snickers and cringes her chin down between her shoulders.

"Look at him. He's so into you, it's pathetic."

"He is not."

"OMG, he so is? He told Dara and Dara told me."

"No way does Andrew Moore like *me*. Dara was just messing."

"Um, excuse me?" Joanne's voice has an instant cold edge that sets Becca shifting on the fountain again. She hates being this scared of Joanne, but she can't stop. "You think Dara's going to make an idiot out of *me*? Hello, I don't *think* so?"

"Jo's right," Gemma says lazily. She's lying with her head in one of the guys' lap, with her back arched so that her chest sticks up at him. The guy is desperately trying to look like he's not trying to look down her top. "Andrew's totally drooling over you."

Orla squirms delightedly, bottom lip sucked in between her teeth.

"He's just too shy to tell you," Joanne says, sweet again. "That's what Dara said. He doesn't know *what* to do." To the tall brown-haired guy next to her: "Isn't that right?"

The guy says, "Yeah. Totally," and hopes he's getting it right. Joanne gives him a good-boy smile.

"He thinks he hasn't got a chance with you," Gemma says. "But he does, right?"

"You *do* like him, don't you?"

Orla makes some kind of mewing noise.

"OMG, of *course* you do! It's Andrew *Moore*!"

"He's, like, the biggest babe *ever*!"

"*I'm* into him."

"Me too." Joanne nudges Alison. "You are too, right, Ali?"

Alison blinks. "Um, yeah?"

"See? I'm *so* jel."

Even Becca knows who Andrew Moore is. Over on the other side of the fountain, he's the center of the Colm's guys: blond head, rugby shoulders, loudest of all, shoving. Andrew Moore's dad flew in Pixie Geldof to DJ at his sixteenth birthday party last month.

Orla manages to get out, "I guess I kind of like him. I mean—"

"Course you do."

"Everyone does."

"You lucky cow."

Orla's grinning from ear to ear. "So can you . . . ? OhmyGod. I mean, can you, like, tell Dara and then he can tell Andrew?"

Joanne shakes her head regretfully. "That wouldn't work. He's still going to be too shy to actually come over to you. You're going to have to say something to him."

That sends Orla into a paroxysm of wriggles and giggles, hands splayed over her face. "OhmyGod, I can't! I just, like—Ohmy*God*!"

Joanne and Gemma are all earnestness, Alison looks confused, but the guys are jaw-clamping down sniggers. Holly, with her back to them, does an eye-widening *Do you believe this?* grimace.

"Fuck me gently," Julia says to the M&Ms, too low for Joanne to hear. "With friends like those . . ."

It takes Becca a second. "You think they're *lying*?" Joanne has always been the kind of person who doesn't even have to hate you to be horrible to you: she says vicious things out of nowhere, for no reason at all, and then smirks at your stunned face. But this is different. Orla is Joanne's friend.

"Hi. Welcome to the world. Of course they're lying. You think Andrew Moore would go for *that*?" Julia tilts her head at Orla, who is bright red and gummy with hysterical giggles and in fairness not looking her best.

"That's disgusting," Becca says. Her hand is clenched around the Skittles packet and her heart is thudding. "You can't *do* that."

"Yeah? Watch them."

"They're doing it to impress them," Holly says, and nods at the three guys. "Showing off."

"And they're impressed? Like, they *want* girls to do that? To their own *friends*?"

Holly shrugs. "If they thought it was so terrible, they'd say something."

"This is the perfect chance," Joanne says, throwing a private smirk to the tall guy. "Just go over and say to him, 'Yes, I like you too.' That's all you have to do."

"I *can't*, ohmyGod, I soooo can't—"

"Course you can. Hello, it's the twenty-first century? Like, girl power? We don't have to wait for guys to ask us out any more. Just do it. Think about how happy he'll be."

"Then he'll take you back behind the Court," Gemma says, body moving languidly on the fountain edge, "and he'll put his arms around you, and he'll start kissing you . . ." Orla twists herself into a knot and snorts with giggles.

Julia says, "A fiver says she actually does it. Anyone on?"

Selena says quietly, glancing over at Andrew Moore, "If she does, he's going to be horrible."

"A total dick," Julia agrees. She throws a couple of Mentos into her mouth, like she's at the cinema, and watches with interest.

"Let's go," Becca says. "I don't want to see this. This is awful."

"Tough. I do."

"Better hurry up," says Joanne, singsong, nudging Orla's leg with her toe again. "He's not going to wait forever, no matter how much he fancies you. If you don't get in there fast, he'll go off with someone else."

"I could use a fiver," Holly says. She turns around. "Hey! Orla!" And when Orla unrolls herself enough to look over, red and grinning like an idiot: "They're just messing with you. If Andrew Moore wants to be with someone, you think he's too shy to chat her up? Seriously?"

"Ex*cuse* me?" Joanne snaps, sitting up straight and shooting Holly a vile look. "I don't actually remember asking you what you think?"

"Excuse *me*, you're screaming in the middle of the *Court*. If I have to listen to it, I get to have an opinion about it. And my opinion is, he doesn't even know Orla exists."

"And *my* opinion is that you're an ugly skanger who should be in some community school where normal people wouldn't have to listen to your stupid *opinions*."

"Whoa," says the guy with Gemma's head in his lap. "Catfight."

"Ohhh yeah," says the tall guy, grinning. "Bring it on."

"Holly's dad's a detective," Julia explains, to the guys. "He arrested Joanne's mum for hooking. She's still holding a grudge."

The guys start to laugh. Joanne draws herself up and opens her mouth to come back with something terrible—Becca is already flinching—when, across the fountain, the noise level goes up. Andrew and three of his mates are holding another one over the water, swinging him by his wrists and his ankles while he shouts and struggles. They all have one eye on the girls, to make sure they're noticing.

"OhmyGod!" Joanne nudges Orla so violently she almost goes into the fountain. "Did you see that? He was looking straight at you!"

Orla's eyes go to Holly. Holly shrugs. "Whatever."

Orla stares, paralyzed. Her head is obviously spinning so hard she can't think, even by her standards.

"What are you looking at me for?" Julia wants to know. "I'm just here for the show."

Selena says gently, "Holly's right, Orla. If he likes you, he'll say something."

Gemma is watching, amused, from her guy's lap. She says, "Or else you're just jel."

"Um, obviously? Because Andrew Moore wouldn't touch any of them with someone else's," Joanne snaps. "Who are you going to believe? Us, or *them*?"

Orla's mouth is hanging open. For a second her eyes meet Becca's, stupid and desperate. Becca knows she has to say something—*Don't do it, he'll rip you to pieces in front of everyone . . .*

"Because if you trust them more than us," Joanne says, cold enough to freeze Orla's face off, "maybe they should be your best friends from now on."

That snaps Orla out of her daze. Even she understands when to be scared. "I don't! I mean, I don't trust them. I trust you." She gives Joanne a wet smile, belly-up dog. "I do."

Joanne keeps up the cold stare for a moment, while Orla twists with anxiety; finally she smiles back, graciously, all forgiveness. She says, "I know you do. I mean, hello, you're not *stupid*. So off you go." She shoves Orla's leg with her foot, pushing her off the fountain edge.

Orla gives her one last agonized look. Joanne and Gemma and Alison nod encouragingly. Orla heads off around the fountain, so tentatively that her walk turns into a half-tiptoe mince.

Joanne looks up at the tall guy, with her head dropping to one side, and smirks. He grins back. His hand slides onto the side of her waist, and down, as they watch Orla get closer to Andrew Moore.

Becca lies on her back on the cold sticky marble and looks up at the domed ceiling of the Court, four high stories above them, so she won't have to see. The people scurrying upside down on the balconies look tiny and precarious, like any second they're going to lose their footing and go plummeting, arms outspread, smash headfirst into the ceiling. From the other side of the fountain she hears the rising predator roar of laughter, the mocking shouts—*Wahey Moooore scooore!*—*Go for it, Andy, the ugly ones give the best head*—*Pity fuck! Pity fuck!* And, nearer, the high insane screams of laughter from Joanne and Gemma and Alison.

"I'll have my fiver now," Julia says.

Becca looks up at the top floor, at the corner where the car-park pay stations are hidden away. Next to them is a thin slice of daylight. She hopes a couple of first-years are up there, craning their necks out the window, all of this greasy mess windblown out of their minds by the sweet wide world rolled out below them. She hopes they don't get kicked out. She hopes as they're leaving they light a piece of paper on fire, toss it in the bin and burn the Court to the ground.

5

The front door was heavy wood, dark and battered. For a second after Conway pushed it open, the deserted stillness stayed. Empty dark-wood staircase sweeping upwards. Sun across worn checkerboard tiles.

Then a bell went off, everywhere. Doors flew open and feet came drumming out, floods of girls in that same navy-and-green uniform, all talking at once. "Fucking *hell*," said Conway, raising her voice so I could hear her. "Timing. Come on."

She headed up the stairs, shouldering through the wave of bodies and books. Her back was set like a boxer's. She looked like this was Internal Affairs and root canal rolled into one.

I went after her, up those stairs. Girls poured round me, flying hair and flying laughs. The air felt full and glossy, felt high, felt shot through with sun at mad-dash angles; sun swirling along the banisters like water, snatching colors and spinning them in the air; lifting me, catching me everywhere and rising. I felt different, changing. Like today was my day, if I could just figure out how. Like danger, but my danger, conjured up by a high-tower wizard specially for me; like my luck, sweet tricky urgent luck, tumbling through the air, heads or tails?

I'd never been anywhere like this before, but it felt like it took me back. It had that pull, all down the length of your bones. It made me think words I hadn't thought since I was a young fella reading my way through the Ilac Centre library, thinking that would get me in between walls like these. Deliquescent. Numinous. Halcyon. Me, long-legged and clumsy and daydreaming, far off my patch so no one would see me, giddy with thrill like I was doing something bold.

"We'll start with the headmistress," Conway said, on the landing, when we could get side by side again. "McKenna. She's a cow. First thing she asked me and Costello, when we got on the scene? Could we stop the media naming the school. Do you believe that? Fuck the dead kid, fuck gathering info to catch whoever did it: all she cared about was that this made her school *look bad*."

Girls dodging past us, "'Scuse me!" high and breathless. A couple of them threw looks back over their shoulders at one of us, or both; most were moving too fast to care. Lockers banging open. Even the corridors were lovely, high ceilings and plaster moldings, soft green and paintings on the walls.

"Here," Conway said, nodding at a door. "Put your game face on." And pushed the door open.

A curly blonde turned around from a filing cabinet, hitting the big-smile button, but Conway said, "Howya," and kept walking, past her and through the inner door. She closed it behind us.

Quiet, in there. Thick carpet. The room had been done up with plenty of time and money, to look like someone's old-fashioned study: antique desk with green leather on top, full bookshelves everywhere, heavy-framed oil painting of a nun who was no oil painting. Only the fancy executive chair and the sleek laptop said *office*.

The woman behind the desk put down a pen and stood up. "Detective Conway," she said. "We've been expecting you."

"No flies on you," Conway said, tapping her temple. She picked up two straight chairs from against a wall, spun them both to the desk and sat down. "Nice to be back."

The woman ignored that. "And this is . . . ?"

"Detective Stephen Moran," I said.

"Ah," said the woman. "I believe you spoke to the school secretary earlier today."

"That was me."

"Thank you for keeping us informed. Miss Eileen McKenna. Headmistress." She didn't put out her hand, so I didn't either.

"Sometimes we like to bring in a fresh pair of eyes," Conway said. Her accent had got rougher. "A specialist. Yeah?"

Miss McKenna raised her eyebrows, but when no one gave her more, she didn't ask. Sat down again—I waited to sit till she had—and folded her hands on the green leather. "And what can I do for you?"

Big woman, Miss Eileen McKenna. Not fat, just big, the way some women get in their fifties after years of being the boss: all out front, hoisted up high and solid, ready to sail through anything and not get wet. I could see her in a break-time corridor, girls skittering away in front of her before they even knew she was coming. Lots of chin; lots of eyebrow. Iron hair and steely glasses. I don't know women's gear but I know quality, and the greeny tweed was quality; the pearls weren't from Penney's.

Conway said, "How's the school getting on?"

Leaning back in her chair, legs sprawled, elbows out. Taking up as much of the office as she could. Prickly as fuck. History there, or just chemistry.

"Very well. Thank you."

"Yeah? Seriously? 'Cause I remember you telling me the whole place was about to go . . ." Nose-dive move with her hand, long whistle. "All those years of tradition and whatever, down the tubes, if us plebs insisted on doing our jobs. Here was me feeling guilty. Nice to see it all turned out grand after all."

Miss McKenna said—to me, leaving Conway out—"As I'm sure you can imagine, most parents were disturbed by the thought of letting their daughters stay in a school where a murder had been committed. The fact that the murderer remained uncaught didn't improve matters."

Thin smile at Conway. Nothing back.

"Ironically, neither did the ongoing police presence and the constant interviews—possibly they should have helped everyone to feel that the situation was under control, but in fact they prevented any return to normality. The persistent media intrusion, which the police were too busy to curb, exacerbated the problem. Twenty-three sets of parents removed their daughters from the school. Almost all the others threatened to, but I was able to persuade them that it would not be in their daughters' best interests."

I bet she had. That voice: like Maggie Thatcher turned Irish, shoulder-barging the world into its place with no room for argument. Made me feel like I should apologize quick, if I could work out what for. It'd take a parent with balls of steel to contradict that voice.

"For several months it was touch and go. But St. Kilda's has survived more than a century of various ups and downs. It has survived this."

"Lovely," said Conway. "While it was surviving, anything come up that we should know?"

"If anything had, we would have contacted you immediately. On which note, Detective, I should be asking you the same question."

"Yeah? Why's that?"

"I assume," Miss McKenna said, "that this visit is connected to the fact that Holly Mackey left school without permission, this morning, to speak to you."

She was talking to me. I said, "We can't go into details."

"I wouldn't expect you to. But, just as you have the right to know anything that might be crucial to your job—hence the fact that I have al-ways given consent for you to speak with the students—I have a right, even an obligation, to know anything that might be crucial to mine."

Just the right amount of threat. "I appreciate that. You can be sure I'll tell you if anything relevant comes up."

Glint off the glasses. "With all due respect, Detective, I'm afraid I'll have to be the judge of what is and isn't relevant. It's impossible for you to make that decision for a school and a girl about which you know nothing."

That test-vibe drilling in from both sides, this time. Miss McKenna lean-ing in to see if I could be pushed; Conway watching, leaving me to it, to see the same thing.

I said, "It's not the perfect answer, no. But it's the best we can do."

Miss McKenna eyed me up some more. Copped there was no point in push-ing harder. Smiled at me instead. "Then we shall have to rely on your best."

Conway shifted, getting comfortable. Said, "Why don't you tell us about the Secret Place."

Outside, the bell exploded again. Faint yelps, more running feet, class-room doors closing; then silence.

Wariness curling like smoke in Miss McKenna's eyes, but her face hadn't changed. "The Secret Place is a noticeboard," she said. Took her time, picked her words. "We established it in December, I believe. The students pin cards on it, using images and captions to convey their messages anonymously—many of the cards are very creative. It gives the students a place to express emotions that they don't feel comfortable expressing elsewhere."

Conway said, "A place where they get to slag off anyone they don't like, no worries that they'll get in hassle for bullying. Spread any rumor they want, no tracing it back. Maybe I'm just too thick to get it, maybe your young ladies would never do anything that common, but this seems like one of the worst ideas I've heard in a long time." Piranha grin. "No offense."

Miss McKenna said, "We felt it was the lesser of two evils. Last autumn, a group of girls set up a website that fulfilled the same function. The kind of behavior you describe was, in fact, rife. We have one student whose father took his own life a few years ago. The site was brought to our attention by her mother. Someone had posted a photo of the girl in question, with the caption 'If my daughter was this ugly I'd kill myself too.'"

Conway's eye on me: *Razor blades in their hair. Still beautiful now?*

She was right. It startled me more than it should have, a shock like a splinter jamming under a nail. That hadn't come in from outside, like Chris Harper. That had grown inside these walls.

Miss McKenna said, "Both the mother and the daughter were, under-standably, very upset."

"So?" Conway said. "Block the site."

"And the new one twenty-four hours later, and the next one, and the next? Girls need a safety valve, Detective Conway. Do you recall, a week or so after the incident"—small snort of laughter from Conway: *incident*—"a group of students claimed to have seen Christopher Harper's ghost?"

"In the girls' jacks," Conway said sideways, to me. "Fair enough; first place a young fella would go if he was invisible, am I right? A dozen young ones screaming their lungs up, hanging on to each other, shaking. I almost had to do the old slap in the face before they could tell me what was going on. They wanted me to go in with my gun and shoot it. How long'd it take to settle them, in the end? Hours?"

"After that," Miss McKenna said—to me, again—"we could, of course, have forbidden any mention of Christopher Harper. And the 'ghost' would have reappeared every few days, possibly for months. Instead, we arranged group counseling sessions for all the girls, with emphasis on grief manage-ment techniques. And we set up a photograph of Christopher Harper on a small table outside the assembly hall, where students could say a prayer or leave a flower or card. Where they could express their grief in an appropri-ate, controlled fashion."

"Most of them hadn't even *met* him," Conway told me. "They didn't *have* any grief to express. Just wanted an excuse to go mental. They needed a kick up the hole, not a pat on the head and poor-little-you."

"Possibly," said Miss McKenna. "But the 'ghost' never made another ap-pearance."

She smiled. Pleased with herself. Everything back on track, nice and neat.

Not stupid. From what Conway had said, I'd been expecting some half-wit snob dyed certain-age-blond, starved into a size zero and stitched into a frozen grin, running the school on big talk and hubby's contacts. This woman was no half-wit.

"So," she said, "we followed the same approach with the noticeboard. We diverted the impulse into a controllable, controlled safety valve. And, again, the results have been highly satisfactory."

She hadn't moved since she sat down. Straight-backed, hands folded. Massive.

"'Controlled,'" Conway said. She flipped a pen off the desk—Montblanc, black and gold—and started playing with it. "How?"

"The board is monitored, obviously. We check it for any inappropriate material before the first class, again at break time, again at lunch and again after classes end for the day."

"Ever find any inappropriate material?"

"Of course. Not often, but occasionally."

"Like what?"

"Usually some variation on 'I hate So-and-So'—So-and-So being either another student or a teacher. There is a rule against using names, or making another person identifiable, but of course rules do get broken. Generally in harmless ways—naming a boy the writer finds attractive, or declaring eternal friendship—but sometimes in crueler ones. And, in at least one case, in order to help, rather than to hurt. A few months ago, we found a card with a photograph of a bruise and the caption 'I think So-and-So's dad hits her.' Obviously we removed the card immediately, but we raised the issue with the girl involved. Discreetly, of course."

"Of course," said Conway. She tossed the pen spinning in the air, caught it easily. "Discreetly."

I asked, "Why the actual physical board? Why not just set up an official website of your own, with a teacher to moderate it? Anything that could hurt someone's feelings, it never gets posted. Safer."

Miss McKenna looked me over, picking out details—good coat but a couple of years old, good haircut but a week or two past its best—and wondering what kind of specialist, exactly. Unfolded and refolded her hands. Not wary of me, not that far, but being careful.

"We considered that option, yes. Several teachers were in favor of it, for exactly the reason you mention. I was against. In part because it would have excluded our boarders, who have no unsupervised internet access; but primarily because young girls slip between worlds very easily, Detective. They lose their grasp on reality. I don't believe they should be encouraged to use the internet more than necessary, let alone to make it the focus of their most intense secrets. I believe they should be kept firmly rooted in the real world as much as possible."

Conway's eyebrow was right up: *The real world, this?*

Miss McKenna ignored her. That smile again. Satisfied. "And I was right. There have been no more websites. The students actually enjoy the complications of the real-world process: the need to wait for a moment when no one can see them pin up a card, to find an excuse to visit the third floor without being noticed. Girls like to reveal their secrets, and they like to be secretive. The board provides the perfect balance."

I asked, "Do you ever try and trace who put up a card? Like, if there was one that said 'I'm on drugs,' you'd want to work out who wrote it. How would you go about that? Is there a CCTV camera on the board, anything like that?"

"CCTV?" Drawn out like a foreign word. Amusement, real or put on. "This is a school, Detective. Not a prison. And the students here don't tend to be heroin addicts."

I said, "How many students have you got?"

"Almost two hundred and fifty. First year through sixth, two classes in each year, roughly twenty girls in each class."

"The board's been up around five months. Statistically, in that amount of time, a few of your two hundred and fifty have had something in their lives that you'd want to know about. Abuse, eating disorders, depression." The words came out of my mouth strange. I knew I was right, but in that room they made a flat splat like I'd spit on the carpet. "And like you just said, girls want to tell their secrets. You're telling me you never find anything more serious than 'French class sucks'?"

Miss McKenna looked down at her hands, hiding behind her eyelids. Thought.

"When identifying a writer is necessary," she said, "we have found that it can be done. We had one card that showed a pencil drawing of a girl's stomach. The drawing had been sliced in a number of places by a sharp blade. The caption said, 'I wish I could cut the whole thing off of me.' Obviously, we needed to identify the student. Our art teacher offered suggestions based on the style of the drawing, other teachers offered suggestions based on the handwriting of the caption, and within the day we had a name."

"And was she cutting?" Conway asked.

Eyes hooded over again. Meaning yes. "The situation has been resolved."

No drawing on our card, no handwriting. The cutter had wanted to be found. Our girl didn't, or didn't want to make it easy.

Miss McKenna said—to both of us, now—"I think this makes it clear that the board is a positive force, not a negative one. Even the 'I hate So-and-So' cards are useful: they identify the students whom we need to watch for signs of bullying, in one direction or the other. This is our window into the students' private world, Detectives. If you know anything about young girls, then you'll understand just how invaluable that is."

"Sounds deadly all round," said Conway. Tossed the pen again, whipped it out of the air. "Did the invaluable board get checked after school finished up yesterday?"

"After classes end every day. As I told you."

"Who checked it yesterday?"

"You would have to ask the teachers. They decide amongst themselves."

"We will. Do the girls know when it's checked?"

"I'm sure they're aware that it is monitored. They see teachers looking at it; we don't attempt to conceal the fact. We haven't announced the precise schedule, however, if that is your question."

Meaning our girl wouldn't have known we could narrow it down. She would have thought she could vanish, into the stream of bright faces tumbling down that corridor.

Conway said, "Were any of the girls in the main school after classes ended?"

Silence again. Then: "As you may know, Transition Year—fourth year—involves large amounts of practical work. Group projects. Experiments. So forth. Often, fourth-years' homework requires access to school resources. The art room, the computers."

Conway said, "Meaning there were fourth-years here yesterday evening. Who and when?"

The full-on headmistress stare. Full-on cop stare coming back. Miss McKenna said, "Meaning no such thing. I have no knowledge of who was in the main building yesterday. The Matron, Miss Arnold, holds a key to the door connecting the school to the boarders' wing, and makes a note of any girl who is given permission to enter the main building after hours; you would need to ask her. I am simply telling you that, on any given evening, I would expect at least a few fourth-years to be here. I understand that you feel the need to find sinister meaning everywhere, but believe me, Detective Conway, there will be nothing sinister about some poor child's Media Studies project."

"That's what we're here to find out," Conway said. She stretched, big, back arching, arms going over her head and out. "That'll do for now. We'll need a list of girls who had access yesterday after school. Fast. Meanwhile, we're taking a look at this invaluable board."

She flipped the pen back onto the desk, neat snap of her wrist like skimming a stone. It rolled across the green leather, stopped an inch from Miss McKenna's clasped hands. Miss McKenna didn't move.

The school had gone quiet, the kind of quiet made out of a hundred different low buzzes. Somewhere girls were singing, a madrigal: just snippets, layered up with sweet high harmonies, cut off and started over every couple of lines when the teacher corrected something. *Now is the month of maying, when merry lads are playing, fa la la la la . . .*

Conway knew where we were headed. Top floor, down the corridor, past closed classroom doors (*If tall dominates short, then . . . Et si nous n'étions pas allés . . .*). Open window at the end of the corridor, warm breeze and green smell pouring in.

"Here we go," Conway said, and turned in to an alcove.

The board was maybe six foot across by three high, and it came leaping out of that alcove screaming straight in your face. Like a mind gone wrong, someone's huge mad mind racketing out every-colored pinballs full speed, with no stop button. Every inch of it was packed: photos, drawings, paintings, jammed in on top of each other, punching for space. Faces blacked out with marker. Words everywhere, scribbled, printed, sliced.

A sound from Conway, quick breath through her nose that could've been a laugh or the same shock.

Across the top: big black letters, fantasy-book curlicues. *THE SECRET PLACE.*

Under that, smaller, no fancy font here: *Welcome to The Secret Place. Please remember that respect for others is a core school value. Do not alter or remove others' cards. Cards that identify anyone, as well as offensive or obscene cards, will be removed. If you have any concerns about a card, speak to your class teacher.*

I had to shut my eyes for a second before they could start splitting the frenzy into individual cards. Black Labrador: *I wish my brothers dog would die so I could get a kitten.* Index finger: *STOP PICKING YOUR NOSE AFTER LIGHTS OUT I CAN HEAR YOU!!!* Cornetto wrapper stuck down with Sellotape: *This was when I knew I love u . . . and I'm so scared u know too.* Tangle of algebra equations, cut out and glued on top of each other: *My freind lets me copy cos I'm never goin 2 understand dem.* Colored-pencil drawing of a soother-faced baby: *Everyone blamed her brother but I'm the one who taught my cousin to say F*** off!*

Conway said, "'The card was pinned over one that has half a postcard of Florida on top and half a postcard of Galway on the bottom. It says, "*I tell everyone this is my favorite place 'cause it's cool . . . This is my actual favorite place 'cause no one here knows I'm supposed to be cool.*" I like Galway too, so sometimes I look at it when I go past. That's why I noticed the picture of Chris.'"

It took me a second to cop. Holly's statement; word for word, near as I could make out. Conway caught the startled look, gave me a sarky one back. "What, you thought I was thick?"

"Didn't think you had a memory like that on you."

"Live and learn." She leaned back from the board, scanning.

Big red-lipsticked mouth, teeth bared: *My mother hates me because I'm fat.* Darkening blue sky, soft green hillsides, one golden-lit window: *I want to go home I want to go home I want to go home.* Downstairs, the same delicate curve of madrigal, over and over.

"There," said Conway. She nudged aside a photo of a man cleaning an oil-stained seagull—*You can keep telling me to be a solicitor but I'm going to do THIS!*—and pointed. Half Florida, half Galway. Left-hand side of the board, near the bottom.

Conway bent close. "Pinhole," she said. "Looks like your little pal didn't make the whole thing up."

If she had, she wouldn't have forgotten the pinhole; not Holly. "Looks like."

No point taking it for prints; anything proved nothing. Conway said, quoting again, " 'I didn't look at the Galway card yesterday evening when we were in the art room. I don't remember when was the last time I looked at it. Maybe last week.' "

"If the teachers on monitoring duty did their job, we're down to whoever was in the building after class. Otherwise . . ."

"Otherwise, a mess like this, a card could sit for days without getting noticed. No way to narrow it down." Conway let the seagull drop back into place, stepped back to take in the whole board again. "Your woman McKenna can yap on about safety valves all she wants. Me, I think this is fucked up."

Hard to argue with that. I said, "We're gonna have to check the lot."

I saw her think it: ditch me with the scut work, go do the good stuff herself. She was the boss.

She said, "Quickest way would be to take them down as we go. That way we can't miss any."

"We'll never get them back right. You OK with the girls knowing we've been through them?"

"Fuck's *sake*," said Conway. "The whole case was like this. Fiddly pain-in-the-hole walking-on-eggshells bullshit. Better leave them where they are. You start from that side, I'll take this one."

It took us the guts of half an hour. We didn't talk—lose your place in that tornado, you'd be banjaxed—but we worked well together, all the same. You can tell. The rhythms match up; the other person doesn't start to annoy you just by existing. I'd been all ready to put in the work, make sure this went smooth as butter—straight back to Cold Cases for me, if I held Conway up or mouth-breathed into her ear—but there was no need. It was easy; effortless. Another surge of that lifting feeling I'd got on the stairs: *your day, your luck, catch it if you can.*

By the time we were finishing up, the good had gone out of that. I'd a taste in my mouth and a turn in my stomach like gone-off cider, fizzy and strong and wrong. Not because it was such bad stuff up there, it wasn't; they were right, Conway and McKenna in their different ways, we were a long way from my old school. Someone had done a bit of shoplifting (box off a mascara, *I stole this + I'm not sorry!!*); someone was well pissed off with someone else (photo of a laxative packet, *I wish I could put this in your stupid herbal tea*). Nothing worse than that. A lot of it was sweet, even. A little young fella from the grin down, squeezing a worn-to-bits teddy: *I miss my bear!! But this smile is worth it.* Six bits of different-colored ribbon twisted together in a tight knot, each trailing end sealed to the card with thumb-printed wax: *Friends forever.* Some was dead creative; art, near enough, better than you see in some galleries. One card was cut out in the shape of a window frame full of snowflakes—fine as lace, must have taken hours; scraps of a girl's face behind the frame, too snowed over to recognize, screaming. Tiny letters cut out of the edge: *You all think you see the whole of me.*

That there was what was giving me the off-cider feel. That gold air transparent enough to drink, those clear faces, that happy flood of chatter: I had liked all that. Loved it. And underneath it all, hidden away tight: this. Not just one messed-up exception, not just a handful. All of them.

I wondered, hoped, maybe most of it was bollix. Girls bored, having a mess about. Then thought maybe that was just as bad. Then thought: no.

"How much of this do you figure is true?"

Conway glanced at me. We'd worked our way in close, from the edges; if she'd been wearing perfume, I could've smelled it. All I smelled was soap, unscented. "Some. Most. Why?"

"You said they're all liars."

"They are. But they lie to get out of trouble, or to get attention, or to look cooler than they are. Shit like that. Not much percentage in that if no one knows it's you."

"But you figure some of it's bollix anyway."

"Oh, God, yeah." She flipped a fingernail off a photo of your man out of *Twilight*. The caption said, *I met him on holiday and we kissed it was amazing we're meeting again next summer.*

I said, "So where's the percentage in that?"

"That one there, I'd say your one's dropping hints to all her mates every time they go past; that way everyone's convinced it's her, but she doesn't have to come out with a bollix story upfront, so she can't get called on it. Other stuff . . ." Conway's eyes moved across the board. She said, "If someone liked making trouble, some of these could make plenty."

The madrigal had come together, skipping along, clean and perfect. *The spring, clad all in gladness, doth laugh at winter's sadness, fa la la la la . . .*

"Even with the monitoring?"

"Even with. The teachers can look all they want; they don't know what to look for. Girls are smart: if they want to start trouble, they'll find ways that adults can't spot. A mate tells you a secret, you stick it up here. You don't like someone, you make something up and put it up like it's hers. That?" Conway tapped the lipsticked mouth. "Quick shot of the mammy photo that someone keeps on her bedside table, and away you go, you can tell her that her ma thinks she's a pig and hates her for it. Bonus points if everyone else recognizes the photo and thinks she's spilling her guts."

"Nice," I said.

"I warned you."

Fie, then, why sit we musing, youth's sweet delight refusing, fa la la la la . . .

I said, "Our card. What do you think are the odds there's anything in it?"

I'd wondered from the start. Didn't want to say it; didn't want to think about all this ending a couple of hours in, with some crying kid getting suspended and me getting sent back to Cold Cases with a pat on the head.

"Fifty-fifty," Conway said. "Maybe. If someone wanted to make trouble, this is doing the job, all right. But we get to treat it like gospel anyway. You about done, yeah? Any second now that bleeding bell's going to go again and we'll be mobbed."

"Yeah," I said. I wanted to move. My feet hurt from standing in the one place. "I'm done."

We had two cards that needed keeping. Photo of a girl's hand underwater, pale and blurred: *I know what you did.* Photo of bare ground under a cypress tree, deep-dug ballpoint X marking the spot, no caption.

Conway dropped them into evidence envelopes out of her satchel, tucked them away. She said, "We'll talk to whoever was meant to check this yesterday. Then we'll get that list of the girls who were in here, have the chats. And the list better be ready, or there's gonna be hassle."

When we turned to go the corridor looked a mile long, after that cramped alcove. Under the hum of classrooms and the trill of *fa la la la la* I thought I could hear the board behind us, boiling.

6

Out behind the Court there's a field, or sort of; people call it that, at least, the Field, with a dab of snigger on top because of what goes on there. It's where another wing of the Court was supposed to get built—there was going to be an Abercrombie & Fitch—but then the recession happened. Instead there's a wire-fenced expanse of tall raggedy weeds, with raw patches of hard earth still showing through like scars where the bulldozers had started work; a couple of stacks of forgotten breeze blocks, sliding to heaps because people are always climbing them; a piece of mysterious machinery gone rusty. One corner of the wire fencing has been worked loose from its pole; bend it out of your way and you can slide through, if you're not fat, and fat people mostly wouldn't come here anyway.

The Field is the Court's shadow side, the place where all the stuff happens that can't happen in the Court. Colm's guys and Kilda's girls wander round the side of the Court, so innocent they're practically whistling, and slip in here. The emos who think they're too deep for a shopping center, mostly—there's always a gang of them down by the back fence playing Death Cab for Cutie on their iPod speakers, even when it's freezing or lashing rain—but sometimes other people, too. If you've no-blink bluffed a bottle of vodka off some shopkeeper or nicked half a pack of smokes off your dad, if you've got a couple of joints or a handful of your mum's tablets, this is where you bring them. The weeds grow high enough that no one outside the fence can see you, not if you're sitting down or lying down, and you probably are.

At night other things happen. Some afternoons people come in and find like a dozen condoms, used ones, or a scatter of syringes. Once someone found blood, a long splashed trail of it across the bare ground, and a knife. They didn't tell. The next day the knife was gone.

Late October, a sudden blond smiling afternoon that popped its head up in the middle of a string of shivering wet days, and it set the Field stirring in people's minds. A gang of Colm's fourth-years got someone's big brother to buy them a few two-liters of cider and a couple of packs of smokes; word spread, till now there are maybe twenty people sprawled in the tangle of chickweed or perched on the breeze blocks. Dandelion seeds drift, spiky ragwort is flowering yellow. The sun melts over them, fools the wind-chill away.

The makeup hall in the Court is pimping a new line, so all the girls have had their makeup done. Their faces are stiff and heavy—they're afraid to smile, in case something cracks or slips—but the new way they feel is worth it. Even before they got a first swig of cider or breath of smoke, they were sashaying bold, their new careful head-high walk turning them haughty and inscrutable, powerful. Next to them the boys look bare and young. To make up for it, they've gone louder and they're calling each other gay more often. A few of them are throwing rocks at a loll-tongued grinning face that someone spray-painted on the back wall of the Court, roaring and punching the air when anyone gets a hit; a couple more are shoving each other off the rusty machine. The girls, to make sure everyone knows they're not watching, get out their phones and take photos of each other's new looks. The Daleks pout and thrust on a pile of breeze blocks; Julia and Holly and Selena and Becca are down among the weeds.

Chris Harper is behind them, blue T-shirt against the blue sky as he balances arms-out on top of another pile of breeze blocks, crinkling his eyes down at Aileen Russell as he laughs about something she's said. He's maybe eight feet away from Holly and Selena wrapping their arms around each other and puckering up their new lipstick ready for a dramatic smooch, Becca rounding her heavy lashes and her Fierce Foxxx mouth at the camera in fake shock, Julia hamming up the photographer act—"Oh yeah, sexayyy, gimme more"—but they barely know he's there. They feel someone, the green fizz and force of him, the same way they feel hot patches of it pulsing all across the Field; but if you closed their eyes and asked them who it was, none of them would be able to name Chris. He has six months, three weeks and a day left to live.

James Gillen slides in next to Julia, holding a bottle of cider. "Oh, come on," he says to her. "Seriously?"

James Gillen is a babe, in a dark slicked way, with a curl to his mouth that puts you on the defensive: he always looks amused, and you can never tell whether it's at you. Plenty of girls are into him—Caroline O'Dowd is so in love with him that she actually bought a can of Lynx Excite and she puts it on a piece of her hair every morning, so she can smell him whenever she wants to. You look over at her in Maths and she's there sniffing her hair, with her mouth hanging open, looking like she has an IQ of about twenty.

"Hi to you too," Julia says. "And: what?"

He flicks her phone. "You look good. You don't need a photo to tell you that."

"No shit, Sherlock. I don't need you, either."

James ignores that. "I know what I'd like a few pics of," he says, and grins at Julia's boobs.

He obviously expects her to blush and zip up her hoodie, or squeal and get outraged—either one would be a win for him. Becca is blushing for her, but Julia isn't about to give him the satisfaction. "Believe me, buddy," she says. "You couldn't handle these."

"They're not that big."

"Neither are your hands. And you know what they say about guys with small hands."

Holly and Selena are getting the giggles. "Jesus," says James, eyebrow lifting. "You're pretty fucking forward, aren't you?"

"Better than being backward, dude," Julia tells him. She clicks her phone shut and puts it back in her pocket, ready for whatever's going to happen next.

"You're so disgusting," Joanne says from her breeze block, wrinkling her nose cutely. To James: "I actually can't believe some of the stuff she actually says?"

But Joanne's out of luck: James has his eye on Julia, not on her, for today anyway. He gives Joanne a grin that could mean anything and turns his shoulder to her. "So," he says to Julia. "You want some?" and holds out the bottle of cider.

Julia feels a quick puff of triumph. She shoots Joanne a super-sweet smile, over James's shoulder. "Sure," she says, and takes the bottle.

Julia doesn't like James Gillen, but that's not the point, not out here. In the Court, back in the Court any eye you catch could be Love peal-of-bells-firework-burst Love, all among the sweet spray of the music and the rainbowing prisms of the lights, this could be the one huge mystery every book and film and song is sizzling with; could be your one-and-only shoulder to lean your head on, fingers woven with yours and lips gentle on your hair and Our Song pouring out of every speaker. This could be the one heart that will open to your touch and offer up its never-spoken secrets, that has spaces perfectly shaped to hold all of yours.

Out here in the Field it's not going to be Love, it's not going to be the mystery everything talks about; it's going to be the huge mystery everything talks around. The songs try so hard to pump it in your face, but they're just throwing the right words into the air and hoping they sound dirty enough to fuzz your mind till you can't ask questions any more. They can't tell you what it's going to be like, someday when; they can't tell you what it is. It's not in the songs; it's out here, in the Field. In the apple and smoke of everyone's breath, in the reek of ragwort and the milk of broken dandelion stems sticky on your fingers. In the emos' music, rising up through the earth to pound at the bottom of your spine. Everyone says the reason Leanne Naylor didn't come back for fifth year is because she got pregnant in the Field and she didn't even know which guy it was.

So Julia not liking James Gillen is beside the point. The point out here is the hard handsome curve of his lips, the flecks of stubble along his jaw; the tingle sparking down her wrist veins when their fingers touch on the bottle. She holds his eye and licks a leftover drop off the rim of the bottle, with the tip of her tongue, and grins when his eyes widen.

"Do we get some of that?" Holly wants to know. Julia passes her the bottle without looking at her. Holly rolls her eyes and takes a good swig before she passes it on to Selena.

"Want a smoke?" James asks Julia.

"Why not."

"Oops," says James—he doesn't even bother patting his pockets first. "I must've dropped my smokes over there. My bad." He stands up and holds out his hand to Julia.

"Well," Julia says, only a tenth of a breath of hesitation. "Then I'll just have to come help you find them." And she catches James's hand and lets him pull her up. She takes the cider bottle off Becca and winks while she's got her back to James, and they walk away side by side, into the tall bobbing weeds.

The sunlight opens to receive them and blinks closed again behind them; they're lost in its dazzle, vanished. Something between loss and pure panic shoots through Becca. She almost screams after them to come back, before it's too late.

"James Gillen," Holly says, half wry, half impressed. "For God's sake."

"If she starts going out with him," Becca says, "we'll never see her again. Like Marian Maher: she doesn't even talk to her friends any more. She just sits there texting Whatshisname."

"Jules isn't going to go out with him," Holly says. "With James *Gillen?* Are you joking?"

"But what . . . ? Then what . . . ?"

Holly shrugs, one-shouldered: too complicated to explain. "Don't worry. She's just snogging him."

Becca says, "I'm never doing that. I'm not getting off with some guy unless I actually care about him."

There's a silence. A shriek and an explosion of laughter, somewhere down the Field, and a girl from fifth year leaps up to chase after a guy waving her sunglasses over his head; a victory howl as someone gets a bull's-eye on the graffiti face.

"Sometimes," Holly says suddenly, "I actually wish it was still like it used to be fifty years ago. Like, no one shagged anyone till they got married, and it was this huge big deal if you even kissed a guy."

Selena is lying back with her head on her jacket, scrolling through her photos. She says, "And if you did shag a guy, or even if you just acted like you might someday think about it, you could end up locked in a Magdalen laundry for the rest of your life."

"I didn't say it was so totally perfect. I just said at least everyone knew what they were supposed to do. They didn't have to figure it out."

"Then just decide you're not going to shag anyone till you get married," Becca says. Usually she likes cider, but this time it's left her tongue coated in a thick stale layer. "And then you'll know, and you won't have to figure it out."

"That's what I mean," Selena says. "At least we've got the choice. If you want to be with someone, you can. If you don't want to, you don't have to."

"Yeah," Holly says. She doesn't sound convinced. "I guess."

"You don't."

"Right. Except if you don't, hello, you're a total frigid freak."

Becca says, "I'm not a total frigid freak."

"I know you're not. I didn't say that." Holly is stripping the lobes off a ragwort leaf, carefully, one by one. "Just . . . why *not* do it, you know? When it's hassle if you don't, and there's no reason why not? Back then, people didn't because they thought it was wrong. I don't think it's wrong. I just wish . . ."

The ragwort leaf is coming apart; she rips it in half and tosses the pieces into the undergrowth. "Forget it," she says. "And that dick James Gillen could've at least left us the cider. It's not like they're going to be drinking it."

Selena and Becca don't answer. The silence settles and thickens. "I dare you," Aileen Russell's high overexcited voice yelps behind them, "I so dare you," but it skims off the surface of the silence and fizzles away into the sunlight. Becca feels like she can still smell Lynx Sperminator or whatever it's called.

"Hi," says a voice beside her. She looks around.

This little spotty kid has edged up next to her in the weeds. He needs a haircut and he looks about eleven, both of which Becca knows she does too, but she's pretty sure this kid actually is in second year, maybe even first. She decides this is OK: he's presumably not looking for a snog, and he might even be all right with the two of them getting some rocks and joining the guys throwing stuff at the graffiti face.

"Hi," he says again. His voice hasn't broken.

"Hi," Becca says.

"Was your dad a thief?" he asks.

Becca says, "What?"

The kid says, in one fast gabble, "Then who stole the stars and put them in your eyes?"

He looks at Becca hopefully. She looks back; she can't think of a single thing to say. The kid decides to take this as encouragement. He scoots closer and tries to find her hand among the weeds.

Becca takes her hand away. She says, "Has that ever worked for you?"

The kid looks injured. He says, "It works for my brother."

It hits Becca: he thinks she's the only girl out here who might be desperate enough to snog him. He's decided she's the only one on his level.

She wants to leap up and do a handstand, or get someone to race her fast and far enough to wreck them both: anything that will turn her body back into something that's about what it can do, not all about how it looks. She's fast, she's always been fast, she can cartwheel and backflip and climb anything; that used to be good, but now all that matters is that she has no tits. Her legs stretched out in front of her look limp and meaningless, made out of a bunch of lines that add up to exactly nothing.

Suddenly the spotty kid leans in. It takes Becca a second to realize he's trying to snog her; she turns just in time to give him a mouthful of hair. "No," she says.

He sits back, looking crestfallen. "Ahhh," he says. "Why not?"

"Because."

"Sorry," the kid says. He's gone scarlet.

"I think your brother was taking the piss out of you," Holly tells him, not being mean. "I don't think that line's ever worked for anyone. It's not your fault."

"I guess," the kid says miserably. He's obviously still there only because the walk of shame back to his mates is too horrible to contemplate. Becca wants to curl up like a bug and pull weeds over herself till she disappears. The makeup feels like someone held her down and painted HAHAHAHA across her face.

"Here," Selena says. She hands the kid her phone. "Take a photo of us. Then you can head back to your friends, and it'll look like you were just here doing us a favor. OK?"

The kid shoots her a look of pure animal gratitude. "Yeah," he says. "OK."

"Becs," Selena says, and holds out an arm. "Come here."

After a second Becca shuffles herself closer. Lenie's arm wraps tight around her, Holly leans in against her other shoulder; she feels the warmth of their skin straight through tops and hoodies, the solidity of them. Her body breathes it in like it's oxygen.

"Say cheese," says the spotty little kid, kneeling up. He sounds a lot more cheerful.

"Hang on," Becca says. She drags the back of her hand across her mouth, hard, smearing Fierce Foxxx super-matte long-lasting lipstick across her face in a wide war-paint streak. "OK," she says with a great big smile, "cheese," and hears the fake click-whirr of the phone as the kid presses the button.

Behind them, Chris Harper shouts out, "OK, here I go!" To the soundtrack of Aileen Russell's squeal he straightens, high on the breeze blocks, and launches himself up and over in a backflip against the sky. He lands staggering; his momentum takes him skidding through ragwort, onto his back in a patch of shuddering green and gold. He lies there, splayed and breathless, looking up at the cheating blue sky and laughing his heart out.

7

The between-classes rush was different, this time round. Huddles against walls, shiny heads tucked close. Low thrumming of a hundred top-speed whispers going at once. Buzz sliced off and girls scurrying when they whipped round and saw us coming. Word had got around.

We caught a bunch of teachers on the early lunch in the staff room—nice staff room, espresso machine and Matisse posters, bit of niceness to keep the mood happy. The PE teacher had been on board-check duty the day before, and she swore she'd checked straight after classes and checked right. Two new cards, she'd spotted, the black Labrador and one about some girl saving her pocket money towards a boob job. Par for the course, she said: back when the board first went up it had been hopping, dozens of new cards a day, but the rush had died down. If there'd been a third new one, she would have noticed.

Wary eyes following us out of the staff room; wary eyes and cozy beef-stew smell, and just too soon, one step before we got out of earshot, a surge of low voices and shushing.

"Thank Jesus," Conway said, ignoring. "That ought to narrow it down."

I said, "She could've put it up herself."

Conway took the stairs two at a time, back up towards McKenna's office. "The teacher? Not unless she's an idiot. Why get herself on the list? Throw the card up there someday when you're not on duty, let someone else find it: no connection to you. She's out, or as near as it gets."

McKenna's curly secretary had the list ready for us, all typed up and printed off, service with a smile. *Orla Burgess, Gemma Harding, Joanne Heffernan, Alison Muldoon—given permission to spend first evening study period in art room (6:00–7:15 p.m.). Julia Harte, Holly Mackey, Rebecca O'Mara, Selena Wynne—given permission to spend second evening study period in art room (7:45–9:00 p.m.).*

"Huh," Conway said, taking the list back off me and leaning one thigh against the secretary's desk to have another read. "Who woulda thought. I'll need to talk to the eight of them, separately. And I want them all pulled out of class right now and supervised, nonstop, till I'm done." No point in letting them match up stories or move evidence, on the off chance they hadn't already. "I'll have the art room, and a teacher to sit in with us. Whathername, teaches French: Houlihan."

The art room was free and Houlihan would be with us momentarily, as soon as someone was found to take over her class. McKenna had given orders: what the cops want, the cops get.

We didn't need Houlihan. You want to interview an underage suspect, you need an appropriate adult present; you want to interview an underage witness, it's your call. If you can skip the extra, then you do: there are things kids might tell you that they won't say in front of Mammy, or in front of a teacher.

If you get in an appropriate adult, then it's for reasons. I got the social worker in with Holly because I was on my own with a teenage girl, and because of her da. Conway wanted Houlihan for reasons.

Wanted the art room for reasons, too. "That," she said, at the door, jerking her chin at the Secret Place across the corridor. "When our girl walks past that, she's gonna look."

I said, "Unless she's got serious self-control."

"If she did, she wouldn't've put up that card to begin with."

"She had enough self-control to wait a year."

"Yeah. And now it's cracking." Conway pushed open the art-room door.

The art room was cleaner-fresh, blackboard and long green tables washed bare. Gleaming sinks, two potter's wheels. Easels, wooden frames stacked in a corner; smell of paint and clay. The back of the room was tall windows, looking out over the lawn and the grounds. I felt Conway remembering art class, one roll of paper and a handful of hairy paints.

She spun three chairs into an aisle, in a rough circle. Pulled a handful of pastels out of a drawer and went between tables scattering them, shoving chairs off-kilter with her hip. Sun turned the air bright and hot-still.

I stayed by the door, watching. She said, like I'd asked, "I fucked up, last time. We did the interviews in McKenna's office, had McKenna be the appropriate adult. Three of us sitting in a row behind her desk like a parole board, staring some kid out of it."

A last glance down the aisles. She turned to the blackboard, found a piece of yellow chalk and started scribbling nothing.

"Costello's idea. Make it formal, he said, make it like being called in to the headmistress, only way worse. Put the fear of God into them, he said. Sounded right, made sense—just kids, just little girls, used to doing what they're told, crank up the authority high enough and they'll crack, right?"

She tossed the chalk on the teacher's desk and rubbed out the scribbles, leaving snippets and swipe marks. Specks of chalk dust whirled in the sun all round her. "Even then, I knew it was wrong. Me sitting there like I'd a poker up my arse, knowing every second a little more of our chance was going out the window. But it went fast, I couldn't put my finger on how to do it any different, then it was too late. And Costello . . . even if it was my name on the case, wasn't like I could tell him to shove it."

She ripped bits off a roll of blank paper, crumpled them, threw them without checking where they landed. "In here, they're on their own turf. Nice and chilled, nothing formal, no need to get the guard up. And Houlihan's the type, kids spend the whole class asking her the French for 'testicle' to make her blush—that's if they can be arsed noticing she's there. She's not gonna put the fear of God into anyone."

Conway tugged open a window with a thump, let in a smooth sweep of cool and mown grass.

"This time," she said, "I fuck up, I'm fucking up my way."

There was my shot, lined up all ready to pot. I said, "If you want them relaxed, let me do the talking."

That got me a stare. I didn't blink.

Conway leaned her arse on the windowsill. Chewed her cheek, looked me over from hair to shoes. Behind her, faint urgent calls from the playing field, football flying high.

"OK," she said. "You talk. I open my mouth, you shut yours till I'm done. I tell you to close the window, that means you're out, I'll take it from there, and you don't say Word One till I tell you to. Got it?"

Click, and into the pocket. "Got it," I said. Felt the soft gold air move up the back of my neck and wondered if this was it, this room riddled with echoes and shining with old wood: if this was the place where, finally, I got the chance to fight that door unlocked again. I wanted to memorize the room. Salute someone.

"I want their accounts of yesterday evening. And then I want them hit with the card, out of nowhere, so we can see their reactions. If they say, 'Wasn't me,' I want to know who they think it was. Can you do that?"

"I'd say I can just about handle it, yeah."

"Jesus," Conway said, shaking her head like she couldn't believe herself. "Just try not to get down on the floor and start licking anyone's boots."

I said, "We hit them with the card, it'll be all round the school before home time."

"You think I don't know that? I *want* that."

"You're not worried?"

"That our killer'll get spooked and come after the card girl."

"Yeah."

Conway tapped the edge of the window blind, light one-fingered tap, sent a shake and a sway running down the slats. She said, "I want something to happen. This is gonna get things happening." She pushed herself off the windowsill. Went to the three chairs in the aisle, turned one of them back to its table. "You're worried about the card girl? Find her before someone else does."

There was a one-knuckle knock at the door, and had-to-be-Houlihan stuck a worried rabbity face round the edge and lisped, "Detectives, you wanted to see me?"

Joanne Heffernan's lot had been the first ones buzzing around the Secret Place: we started with them. Orla Burgess, we kicked off with. "That'll put Joanne's designer knickers in a twist," Conway said, when Houlihan had gone to find her, "not getting top billing. If she's pissed off enough, she'll get sloppy. And Orla's got the brains of roadkill. We catch her off guard, we lean on her: if she's got anything, she'll spill. What?"

She'd snared me trying not to smile. "Thought this time we were going for relaxation. Not intimidation."

"Fuck you," Conway said, but there was the corner of a grin there too, bitten back. "Yeah, yeah. I'm a hard bitch. Be glad. If I was a sweetheart, you'd be out of a gig."

"I'm not complaining."

"Better not," Conway said, "or I bet there's some no-hoper case from the seventies that could use your relaxation techniques. You want to do the talking, take a seat. I'll watch Orla coming in, see if she looks for her card."

I settled myself on one of the chairs in the aisle, nice and casual. Conway went to the door.

Fast double trip-trap of steps down the corridor, and Orla was in the doorway, wiggling, trying not to giggle. No beauty—no height, no neck and no waist, plenty of nose to make up for it—but she tried. Hard-work straight blond hair, fake tan. Something done to her eyebrows.

Conway's quick fraction of a headshake, behind her back, said Orla hadn't clocked the Secret Place. "Thanks for that," she told Houlihan. "Why don't you have a seat over here," and she had Houlihan swept to the back of the room and planted in a corner before Houlihan could manage more than a gasp.

"Orla," I said, "I'm Detective Stephen Moran." That made a bit of the giggle burst out. Comic genius, me. "Have a seat." I stretched out a hand to the chair opposite me.

Conway propped herself against a table, near my shoulder, not too near. Orla gave her a vacant look, on her way over. Conway's the type that makes an impression, but this kid barely recognized her.

Orla sat down, squirmed her skirt down over her knees. "Is this about Chris Harper again? OhmyGod, did you find out who . . . ? You know. Who . . . ?"

Snuffly voice. Pitched high, all ready for a squeal or a simper. That accent you get these days, like a bad actor faking American.

I said, "Why? Is there something you want to tell us about Chris Harper?"

Orla practically jumped back out of the chair. "Huh? No! No way."

"Because if you've got anything new to add, now's the time. You know that, right?"

"Yeah. I totally do. If I knew anything, I'd tell you. But I don't. Honest to God."

Tic-smile, involuntary, wet with hope and fear.

You want in with a witness, you figure out what she wants. Then you give her that, big handfuls. I'm good at that.

Orla wanted people to like her. Pay attention to her. Like her some more.

Stupid, it sounds; is. But I felt let down. Thrown down, with an ugly splat like puke. This place had had me expecting something, under these high ceilings, in this turning air that smelled of sun and hyacinths. Expecting special, expecting rare. Expecting a shimmering dappled something I had never seen before.

This girl: the same as a hundred girls I grew up with and stayed miles from, exact shoddy same, just with a fake accent and more money spent on her teeth. She was nothing special; nothing.

I didn't want to look at Conway. Couldn't shake the feeling that she knew exactly what was going on in my head, and was laughing at it. Not in a good way.

Big warm crinkly grin, I gave Orla. Leaned in. "No worries. I was just hoping. On the off chance, you know the way?"

I held the grin till Orla smiled back. "Yeah." Grateful, pathetically grateful. Someone, probably Joanne, used Orla for kicking when the world pissed her off.

"We've just got a few questions for you—routine stuff, no big deal. Could you answer those for us, yeah? Help me out?"

"OK. Sure."

Orla was still smiling. Conway slid backwards onto the table. Got out her notebook.

"You're a star," I said. "So let's talk about yesterday evening. First study period, you were here in the art room?"

Defensive glance at Houlihan. "We'd got permission."

Her only worry about yesterday evening: hassle from teachers.

I said, "I know, yeah. Tell us, how do you go about getting permission?"

"We ask Miss Arnold. She's the Matron."

"Who asked her? And when?"

Blank look. "It wasn't me."

"Whose idea was it to spend the extra time up here?"

More blank. "That wasn't me either." I believed her. I got the feeling most ideas weren't Orla.

"No problem," I said. More smile. "Talk me through it. One of you got the key to the connecting door off Miss Arnold . . ."

"I did. Right before first study period. And then we came up here. Me and Joanne and Gemma and Alison."

"And then?"

"We just worked on this project we have. It has to be art and another subject, like mixed—ours is art and computer studies. That's it over there."

She pointed. Propped in a corner, five foot high, a portrait of a woman—a pre-Raphaelite I'd seen before, somewhere, but I couldn't place her. She was only half made, out of small glossy squares of colored paper; the other half was still an empty grid, tiny code in each square to tell them what color to stick on. The change had twisted the woman's dreamy gaze, turned her wall-eyed and twitchy-looking, dangerous.

Orla said, "It's about, like, how people see themselves differently because of the media and the internet? Or something; it wasn't my idea. We turned the picture into squares on the computer, and now we're cutting up photos from magazines to stick in the squares—it takes forever, that's why we needed to use the study period. And then at the end of first study we went back to the boarders' wing and I gave the key back to Miss Arnold."

"Did any of you leave the room, while you were up here?"

Orla tried to remember, which took some mouth-breathing. "I went to the toilet," she said, after a bit. "And Joanne did. And Gemma went into the corridor because she rang someone and she wanted to talk in *private*." Snigger. A guy. "And Alison went out for a phone call too, only hers was her mum."

Every one of them. "In that order?"

Blank. "What?"

Sweet Jesus. "Do you remember who went out first?"

Think, think, mouth-breathe. "Maybe Gemma? And then me, and then Alison, and then Joanne—maybe, I'm not sure."

Conway moved. I snapped my mouth shut, but she didn't open hers; just pulled a photo of the postcard out of her pocket, handed it to me. Sat back on the table again, foot up on a chair, went back to her notebook.

I flipped the photo back and forth against my finger. "On your way here, you passed the Secret Place. You passed it again on your way to the toilet and back. And again when you left at the end of the evening. Right?"

Orla nodded. "Yeah." Hardly a glance at the photo. Not making any connection.

"Did you stop for a look, any of those times?"

"Yeah. When I was coming back from the toilet. Just to see if there was anything new. I didn't touch anything."

"And was there? Anything new?"

"Uh-uh. Nothing."

Labrador and boob job, according to the PE teacher. If Orla had missed them, she could have missed one more.

"What about you? Have you ever put up cards on the board?"

Orla did a coy squirm. "Maybe."

I grinned along with her. "I know they're private. I'm not asking for the details. Just tell me: when was the last one?"

"Like a month ago?"

"So this isn't yours."

I had the photo in Orla's hand, face up, before she realized it was coming. Prayed it wasn't hers.

I needed to show Conway what I could do. Five minutes and an easy answer would get me nothing, except maybe a lift back to Cold Cases. I needed a fight.

And, somewhere in a locked back corner, detectives think old ways. You take down a predator, whatever bleeds out of it flows into you. Spear a leopard, grow braver and faster. All that St. Kilda's gloss, that walk through old oak doors like you belong, effortless: I wanted that. I wanted to lick it off my banged-up fists along with my enemy's blood.

This fool, smelling of body spray and cheap gossip: not what I'd had in mind. This would be like taking down some kid's fat hamster.

Orla stared, while the photo sank in. Then squealed. High flat wail, like air squeezed out of a squeaky toy.

"Orla," I said. Sharp, before she could work herself up. "Did you put that up on the Secret Place?"

"No! OhmyGod, I swear to God, *no*! I don't know anything about what happened to Chris. Swear to *God*."

I believed her. The photo at arm's length, like it could hurt her; the bug-eyed stare zipping from me to Conway to Houlihan, looking for help. Not our girl. Just the detective gods throwing me an easy one, to start me off.

I said, "Then one of your friends did. Who was it?"

"I don't *know*! I don't know anything about this. I totally *swear*."

"Any of them ever mention any ideas about Chris?"

"No way. I mean, we all think it was that groundskeeper guy—he used to smile at us all the time, he was totally creepy, and you guys arrested him for having drugs, right? But we don't *know* anything. Or anyway I don't. And if any of the others do, they never told me. Ask them."

"We will," I said. Nice and soothing. Smile. "Don't worry. You're not in trouble."

Orla was calming down. Gawping at the photo, starting to like having it in her hand. I wanted to whip it off her. I let her hang on to it, have her fun.

Reminded myself: the ones you don't like are a bonus. They can't fool you as easy as the ones you do.

Twenty watts went on over Orla's head. "Probably it wasn't even any of us. Julia Harte and all them were in here right after us. Probably they did it."

"You figure they know what happened to Chris?"

"Not even. I mean, maybe, but no? Like, they could've just made it up."

"Why would they?"

"Because. They're, ohmyGod, *so weird*."

"Yeah?" Me leaning forward, hands clasped, all confidential and ready for a gossip. "Seriously?"

"Well, they used to be OK, like *ages* ago. Now we're just like, 'What*ever*,' you know?" Orla's hands flapping upwards.

"What kind of weird are they?"

Too much to ask. Short-circuited stare, like I was looking for calculus. "Just like weird."

I waited.

"Like they think they're so special." The first zip of something, bringing Orla's face alive. Malice. "Like they think they can do whatever they want."

I gave it intrigued. Waited more.

"I mean, just for example, right? You should have *seen* them at the Valentine's dance. They looked totes insane. Like Rebecca had on *jeans*, and Selena was wearing I don't even know *what* it was, it looked like she was in a *play*!" That high sharp giggle shot out again, jabbed me in the ear. "Everyone was like, hello, what are you *like*? I mean, there were *guys* there. The whole of *Colm's* was there. They were all staring. And Julia and all of them acted like that didn't even *matter*." Jaw-dropped face. "That was when we realized, um, hello, *weirdos*?"

I gave her the crinkly grin again. "And that was February?"

"Last February. Last year." Before Chris. "And I swear to God they've got worse and *worse*. This year Rebecca didn't even *come* to the Valentine's dance. They don't wear makeup—I mean, we're not allowed to in school"—virtuous glance at Houlihan—"but sometimes they don't even wear it to hang out at the Court—the shopping center. And this one time, like just a few weeks ago, there's a load of us down there? And Julia says she's going back to school? And one of the guys is there, 'How come?' And Julia says, she says her stomach is killing her because . . ."

Orla shot me a look. Sucked in her bottom lip, did a cringe like she was trying to disappear into her shoulders.

Conway said, "She had period cramps."

Orla collapsed in giggles, scarlet and snorting like goodo. We waited. She got it together.

"But, I mean, she just *said* it. Straight out. All the guys were like, 'OMG, ew! Way TMI!' And Julia just waved and left. See what I mean? They act like they can say anything they want. None of them have boyfriends—duh, surprise?—and they act like that's not even a big deal." Orla was hitting her stride. Face lit up, lip curling. "And did you *see* Selena's *hair*? OhmyGod. You know when she cut it off? Like, right after Chris got killed. How much of a show-off can you actually *be*?"

I was getting the head spins again. "Hang on. Her haircut is showing off, yeah? About what?"

Orla's chin vanished into where her neck should have been. New look on her, sly, careful. "About how she was going out with Chris. Like she's in *mourning* or something. We're all, 'Hello, who cares?' "

"What makes you think she was going out with Chris?"

Slyer. More careful. "We just do."

"Yeah? Did you see them kissing? Holding hands?"

"Um, *no*? They wouldn't exactly have been that *obvious* about it."

"Why not?"

Flash of something: fear. Orla had slipped up, or thought she had. "I don't know. I just mean, if they'd been OK with everyone seeing they were going out, they wouldn't have kept it a secret. I mean, that's all I mean."

"But if they kept it so secret that they never actually acted like they were together, how come you think they were together to begin with?"

That blown-fuse gawp again. "What?"

Jesus. Head-desk territory. I rewound. Nice and slow: "Why do you think Chris and Selena were going out together?"

Empty stare. Shrug. Orla wasn't taking any more risks.

"Why would they keep it a secret if they were?"

Empty stare. Shrug.

"What about you?" Conway asked. "You got a boyfriend?"

Orla sucked in her bottom lip, let out a breathy titter through it.

"Do you?"

Squirm. "Sort of. It's, ohmyGod, complicated?"

"Who?"

Titter.

"I asked you a question."

"Just this guy from Colm's. He's called Graham, Graham Quinn. But we're not exactly going *out* out—I mean, ohmyGod, don't go to him and say he's my *boyfriend*! Like, he sort of is, but—"

"I get it," Conway said, final enough to get through even to Orla, who shut up. "Thanks."

I said, "If you could pick just one thing to tell me about Chris Harper. What would it be?"

The stare. I was less and less in the humor for the stare. "Like what?"

"Like anything. Whatever you think is most important."

"Um, he was gorgeous?"

Giggle.

I took the photo away from her. "Thanks," I said. "That helps."

I left a second. Orla said nothing. Conway said nothing. She was sitting back on the table, writing or doodling, I couldn't tell which out of the corner of my eye. I wasn't going to look at her, like I was looking for a hand.

Houlihan cleared her throat, a compromise between asking and keeping schtum. I'd forgotten her.

Conway shut her notebook.

I said, "Thanks, Orla. We might need to talk to you again. Meanwhile, if you think of anything that might help us, anything at all, here's my card. Ring me any time. Yeah?"

Orla gave the card a look like I'd asked her to jump into my white van. Conway said, "Thanks. We'll talk soon." To Houlihan, who jumped: "Gemma Harding next."

I gave Orla more smiles. Got the two of them out the door.

Conway said, "Like, totes OMG?"

I said, "Like, OMG, WTF?"

We almost looked at each other. Almost laughed.

Conway said, "Not our girl."

"Nah."

I waited. Didn't ask, wouldn't give her the satisfaction, but I needed to know.

She said, "That went all right."

I almost caught a huge breath, crushed it back in time. Stuck the photo away in my pocket, ready for the next go-round. "Anything you figure I should know about Gemma?"

Conway grinned. "Thinks she's a sex bomb, kept leaning over to show Costello her cleavage. Poor bastard didn't know where to look." The grin went. "But this one's not thick. Not by a long way."

Gemma was like looking at Orla stretched. Tall, slim—trying hard for thin, only she didn't have the build for it. Pretty, top end of pretty, but that jaw was going to give her man-face before she was thirty. Hard-work straight blond hair, fake tan, skinny eyebrows. No glance at the Secret Place, but then Conway had said she wasn't stupid.

She took the walk to the chair like a catwalk. Sat down and crossed one long leg over the other, slow flourish. Arched her throat.

Even after what Conway had said, it took me a second to see it, through the school uniform and the sixteen. Gemma wanted me to fancy her. Not because she fancied me; that hadn't even crossed her mind. Just because I was there.

I went to school with dozens like that, too. I didn't play their game.

Conway's eye like a hot pin burning through the back of my jacket, into my shoulder blade.

I told myself again. Nothing special means nothing you can't handle.

I offered Gemma a slow grin, lazy. Appreciative. "Gemma, right? I'm Detective Stephen Moran. It's *very* nice to meet you."

She soaked it up. Tiny smile tucked in the corners of her mouth, almost hidden, not quite.

"We've just got a few routine questions for you."

"No problem. Anything you want."

A little too much weight on *Anything*. The smile swelled. That easy.

Gemma had the same story as Orla, in the same bad-actor American accent. Drawled off, bored, too cool for school. Foot swinging. Checking me out to make sure I kept checking her out. If talking about last night spiked her adrenaline, it didn't show.

Conway said, "You made a phone call while you were up here."

"Yeah. I rang my boyfriend." Gemma licked the last word. Threw Houlihan a glance—phone calls during study period obviously weren't allowed—to see if she was shocked.

Conway asked, "What's his name?"

"Phil McDowell. He's at Colm's."

Course he was. Conway sat back.

I said, "And you went outside to talk to him."

"I went out in the corridor. We had stuff to talk about. Private stuff." Puckered-up smile, slantwise to me. Like I was in on the secret, or could be.

I smiled back. "Did you have a look at the Secret Place, while you were out there?"

"No."

"No? You're not into it?"

Gemma shrugged. "It's mostly stupid. Basically all of it is 'Oh, everyone's mean to me and I'm so unique!' Which, hello, they totally never are? If anything juicy goes up, everyone's talking about it anyway. I don't need to look."

"Ever put up any cards of your own?"

Another shrug. "Back when they first put the board up. Just for the laugh. I don't even remember all of them. We made some of them up." Small flurry of concern from Houlihan's corner. Gemma gave herself a little slap on the wrist. "*Bad* girl." Amused.

I said, "How about this one?" Passed Gemma the photo.

Gemma's foot stopped swinging. Her eyebrows hit her hairline.

After a second, slowly: "Oh. My. God."

Real. Caught in the quickening of her breath, in the darkened eyes, slashing through all that carefully built sexiness: something true. Not our girl. Two down.

I said, "Did you put that up?"

Gemma shook her head. Still scanning the card, looking for sense.

"No? Just for the laugh?"

"I'm not stupid. My dad's a solicitor. I know this isn't a laugh."

"Any idea who might have?"

Headshake.

"If you had to guess."

"I don't know. Honest to God. I'd be surprised if it was Joanne or Orla or Alison, but I'm not swearing it wasn't, or anything. I'm just saying, if it was, they never told me."

Two out of two, now, ready to throw their mates in the shite so they could leap away unspattered. Lovely.

Gemma said, "But there were other people in here, yesterday evening. After us."

"Holly Mackey and her friends."

"Yeah. Them."

"Them. What are they like?"

Gemma's eye on me, wary. She held out the photo. "I don't know. We don't really talk to them."

"Why not?"

Shrug.

I gave her a grin with a glint. "Let me guess. I'd say your lot are pretty popular with the fellas. Holly and them, were they cramping your style?"

"They're just not our type." Arms folded. Gemma wasn't biting.

Something was there. Orla might believe all that about Selena wearing the wrong getup to the dance, might not, but Gemma knew better. Something else had got in between these two lots.

If Conway wanted any pushing done, she could do it herself. Not my job. Mr. Lovely, me; the one you can talk to. If I threw that away, Conway had no reason to keep me around.

Conway said nothing.

"Fair enough," I said. "Let's talk about Chris Harper. Got any ideas about what happened to him?"

Shrug. "Some psycho. Whatshisname, the groundskeeper, the one you guys arrested. Or some randomer. How would I know?"

Arms still folded. I leaned forward, gave her a grin out of a late-night bar. "Gemma. Talk to me. Try this: pick one thing to tell me about Chris Harper. One thing that mattered."

Gemma thought. Stretched out her long crossed leg, ran a hand up and down her calf; we were back. I watched, so she could catch me. Itched to push my chair back a few feet. I could have kissed Conway just for existing. Gemma was dangerous as fuck, and she knew it.

She said, "Chris was the total last person you would've expected to get killed."

"Yeah? How come?"

"Because everyone liked him. The whole school fancied him—some people said they didn't, but that was just because they wanted to look special, or because they knew they didn't have a chance of getting him anyway. And all of Colm's wanted to hang out with him. That's why I said it had to be a randomer who did it. No one would've gone after Chris on purpose."

I said, "You fancied Chris?"

Shrug. "Like I said: everyone did. It wasn't a big deal. I fancy a lot of guys." Small hooded smile, intimate.

I matched it. "Ever go out with him? Hook up with him?"

"No." Instant, definite.

"Why not? If you fancied him . . ." Little lean on the *you*. *Any guy you want, bet you get.*

"No reason. Me and Chris just never happened. End of."

Gemma was shutting down again. Something there, too.

Conway didn't push, I didn't push. Here's my card, if you think of anything, all the rest of it. Conway told Houlihan to bring us Alison Muldoon. I gave Gemma a grin that was one step from a wink, as she swayed out the door and glanced back to make sure I was watching.

Let out my breath, wiped my mouth to scrape that grin off. "Not our girl," I said.

Conway said, "What's all this with one thing about Chris?"

She had had a year to get to know him. I'd had a few hours. Anything I could get was good.

No reason why I should get to know Chris. Not my case, not my vic. I was just here to bat my eyelashes, come up with the right smiles, get girls talking.

I said, "What's all this about boyfriends?"

Conway came off the table, into my face, fast. "You questioning me?"

"I'm asking."

"I ask you. Not the other way round. You go to the jacks, I get to ask whether you washed your hands if I want. You got that?"

That almost-laugh was well gone. I said, "I need to know how they felt about Chris. No point me talking up how lovely he was and how a guy like that deserves justice, if I'm talking to someone who hated his guts."

Conway stared me out of it for another minute. I kept steady, thought about six girls left and how far Conway would get without me. Hoped to God she was thinking the same thing.

She eased back onto the table.

"Alison," she said. "Alison's petrified of bleeding everything. Me included. I'm gonna be keeping my mouth well shut, unless you fuck up. Don't fuck up."

Alison was like looking at Gemma shrunk. Short little thing, scrawny, shoulders curled in. Fidgety fingers, twisting at her skirt. Hard-work straight blond hair, fake tan, skinny eyebrows. No glance at the Secret Place.

This one recognized Conway, anyway. Conway got out of the way fast as Alison came through the door, tried to disappear, but Alison did a body-swerve away from her all the same. "Alison," I said, quick and smooth, to distract her. "I'm Stephen Moran. Thanks for coming in." Smile. Reassuring, this time. "Have a seat."

No smile back. Alison perched the edge of her backside on the edge of the chair and stared at me. Pinched little features, gerbil, white mouse. I wanted to hold out my fingers, do tongue-clicky noises.

Instead, I said gently, "Just a few routine questions; it'll only take a few minutes. Can you tell me about yesterday evening? Starting with your first study period?"

"We were in here. But we didn't *do* anything. If anything got, like, stolen or broken or whatever, it wasn't me. I *swear*."

Pinched little voice to match, rising towards a whine. Conway was right, Alison was scared: scared that she was screwing up, that everything she said and did and thought was wrong. She wanted me to reassure her that she was doing things right. Seen it in school, seen it in a million witnesses, patted it on the head and said all the right words.

I said, soothing, "Ah, I know that. Nothing's gone missing, nothing like that. No one's done anything wrong." Smile. "We're just checking something out. All I need you to do is run through your evening. That's it. Could you do that for me, yeah?"

Nod. "OK."

"Beautiful. It'll be like a test where you know all the answers and you can't get anything wrong. How's that?"

Tiny smile back. Tiny step towards relaxing.

I needed Alison relaxed, before I whipped out that photo. That was what had got me my answers from Orla and from Gemma: the ease I had made for them, and the fast shove out of it.

Alison gave me the same story again, but in chips and snippets that I had to coax out of her, like playing pickup sticks. Telling it made her tense up even more. No way to know if there was a good reason, a bad reason or none.

She backed Orla on who had left the art room when—Gemma, Orla, her, Joanne—and she sounded a lot more sure than Orla had. "You're very observant," I said. Approving. "That's what we like to see. I came in here praying we'd get someone exactly like you, you know that?"

Another scrawny smile. Another step.

I said, "Can you make my day? Tell me you had a look at the Secret Place, somewhere along the way."

"Yeah. When I went out to the . . . On my way back, I had a look." Quick glance at Houlihan. "I mean, only for a second. Then I came straight back in to do the project."

"Ah, lovely. That's what I was hoping to hear. Spot any new cards up there?"

"Yeah. There was one with this dog that was, like, *so* adorbs. And someone put up one of . . ." Nervous smirk, duck. "*You* know."

I waited. Alison twisted.

"Just a . . . a lady's, like, her chest. In a *top*, I mean! Not . . ." High painful giggle. "And it said, 'I'm saving up so the day I turn eighteen I can buy ones like this!'"

Observant, again. It went with the fear. Prey animal, watching everything for a threat. "That's it? Nothing else new?"

Alison shook her head. "Those were it."

If she was telling the truth, that backed what we thought already: Orla and Gemma were out. "Well done," I said. "That's perfect. Tell us: have you ever put up any cards?"

Eyes skittering. I said, "Nothing wrong with it if you did. Sure, that's what the board's for; it'd be a waste if no one used it."

That twitch of a smile again. "Well . . . yeah. Just a couple. Just . . . when something was bothering me and I couldn't talk about it, sometimes I . . . But I stopped ages ago. I had to be so careful, and then I was always scared someone would guess they were mine and get angry 'cause I put it up there instead of telling her? So I stopped. I took mine down."

Someone. One of her own gang, Alison had been scared of.

She was as relaxed as she was ever going to get: not a lot. I said, easily, "Is this one of yours?"

The photo. Alison gasped. Clapped her free hand over her mouth. A high humming noise came out through it.

Fear, but no way to read it: fear that she had been caught, that there was a killer out there, that someone knew who it was, reflex response to any surprise, take your pick. *Petrified of bleeding everything*, Conway had said. It blurred her like streaming rain on a windscreen, turned her opaque.

I said, "Did you put that up?"

"No! No no no . . . I didn't. Honest to God—"

"Alison," I said, soothing, rhythmic. Leaned forward to take the photo back off her, stayed leaning. "Alison, look at me. If you did, there's nothing wrong with it. Yeah? Whoever put this up was doing the right thing, and we're grateful to her. We just need to have a chat with her."

"It wasn't me. It wasn't. I didn't. Please—"

That was all I was getting. Pushing would do nothing but lose my next chance as well as this one.

Conway off in a corner, still playing invisible, watching me. Gauging.

"Alison," I said. "I believe you. I just have to ask. Just routine. That's all. OK?"

Finally I got Alison's eyes back. I said, "So it wasn't you. Any ideas about who it might have been? Anyone ever mention having suspicions about what happened to Chris?"

Headshake.

"Any chance it was one of your mates?"

"I don't think so. I don't know. No. Ask them."

Alison was sliding back towards panic. "That's all I needed to know," I told her. "You're doing great. Tell us something: you know Holly Mackey and her friends, yeah?"

"Yeah."

"Tell me about them."

"They're just weird. *Really* weird."

Alison's arms tightening around her middle. Surprise: she was afraid of Holly's lot.

I said, "That's what we've heard, all right. But no one's been able to tell us what kind of weird. I figure if anyone can put a finger on that, it's you."

Her eyes on mine, torn.

"Alison," I said gently. I thought strong, thought protective, thought myself into all her wishes. Didn't blink. "Anything you know, you need to tell me. They'll never find out it came from you. No one will. I swear."

Alison said—hunched forward, a whisper, shrunk so as not to reach Houlihan—"They're *witches*."

Now that was new.

I could hear *What the fuck?* inside Conway's head.

I nodded. "Right," I said. "How did you find that out?"

Houlihan, in the corner of my eye, leaning half off her chair. Too far away to hear. She wouldn't come closer. If she tried, Conway would stop her.

Alison was breathing faster, with the shock of having said it. "They used to be, like, normal. Then they just went *weird*. Everyone noticed."

"Yeah? When?"

"Like the start of last year? A year and a half ago?" Before Chris; before that Valentine's dance when even Orla had spotted something. "People said all kinds of stuff about why—"

"Like what?"

"Just stuff. Like they were gay. Or they were abused when they were kids, I heard that. But we thought they were witches."

Glance at me, fearful. I asked, "Why's that?"

"I don't know. Just because. We just thought it." Alison hunched down farther, over whatever she was hiding. "Probably I shouldn't have told you."

Her voice was tamped down to a whisper. Conway had stopped writing, in case she drowned it out. Took me a second to cop: Alison figured she'd just put herself in line for a good cursing.

"Alison. You're doing the right thing, telling us. That's going to protect you."

Alison didn't look convinced.

I felt Conway shift. Keeping her mouth shut, like she'd promised, but doing it loudly.

I said, "Just a couple more questions. Are you going out with anyone?"

A surge of blush that nearly drowned Alison. A muffled clump of words I couldn't hear.

"Say again?"

She shook her head. Huddled right down, eyes on her knees. Braced. Alison thought I was going to point and laugh at her for not having a fella.

I smiled. "Not met the right guy, no? You're dead right to wait. Plenty of time for that."

Something else muffled.

I said—fuck Conway, she had her answer, I was getting mine—"If you had to pick just one thing to tell me about Chris, what would it be?"

"Huh? . . . I barely even knew him. Can't you ask the others?"

"I will, of course. But you're my observer. I'd love to hear what you remember most."

The smile was automatic this time, a reflex spasm with nothing behind it. Alison said, "People noticed him. Not just me; everyone noticed him."

"How come?"

"He was . . . I mean, he was *so* good-looking. And he was good at everything—rugby, and basketball; and talking to people, making everyone laugh. And I heard him sing once, he was really good, everyone was telling him he should do the *X Factor* auditions . . . But it wasn't just that. It was . . . He was just more than everyone else. More *there*. You could walk into a room with like fifty people in it, and the only one you'd see would be Chris."

A wistful something in her voice, in the droop of her eyelids. Gemma was right: everyone had fancied Chris.

"What do you think happened to him?"

That made Alison shrink. "I don't know."

"I know you don't. That's OK. I'm only asking for guesses. You're my observant one, remember?"

A thin ghost of the smile. "Everyone said it was the groundskeeper."

No thoughts of her own, or else a dodge. "Is that what you think?"

Shrug. Not looking at me. "I guess."

I let the silence grow. So did she. That was all I was getting.

Card, speech, smile. Alison dove out the door like the room was on fire. Houlihan flapped after her.

Conway said, "That one's still in the running."

Watching the door, not me. I couldn't read her. Couldn't tell if that meant *You fucked up*.

I said, "Pushing any harder wouldn't have done any good. I've set up the beginnings of rapport; if I talk to her again, I can move it on, maybe get an answer."

Conway's eye sliding sideways to me. She said, "If you talk to her again."

That sardonic corner of a grin, like my obviousness brightened her day. "Yeah," I said. "If."

Conway flipped to a clean page in her notebook. "Joanne Heffernan," she said. "Joanne's a bitch. Enjoy."

Joanne was like looking at all the other three averaged out. I'd been expecting something impressive, all the hype. Medium height. Medium thin. Medium looks. Hard-work straight blond hair, fake tan, skinny eyebrows. No glance at the Secret Place.

Only the way she stood—hip cocked, chin tucked, eyebrows up—said *Impress me*. Said *The Boss*.

Joanne wanted me to think she was important. No: admit she was important.

"Joanne," I said. Stood up for her. "I'm Stephen Moran. Thanks for coming in."

My accent. Whirr, went Joanne's filing system. Spat me out in the bottom drawer. Eyelid-flutter of disdain.

"I didn't exactly get a choice? And just by the way, I actually had things to *do* for the last *hour*. I didn't need to spend it sitting outside the office getting bored to death and not even allowed to *talk*."

"I'm really sorry about that. We didn't mean to keep you waiting. If I'd known the other interviews were going to take this long . . ." I rearranged the chair for her. "Have a seat."

Curl of her lip at Conway, on her way: *You*.

"Now," I said, when we'd sat down. "We've just got a few routine questions. We'll be asking a lot of people the same things, but I'd really appreciate hearing your thoughts. It could make a big difference."

Respectful. Hands clasped together. Like she was the Princess of the Universe, doing us a favor.

Joanne examined me. Flat pale-blue eyes, just a little too wide. Not enough blinks.

Finally she nodded. Gracious, honoring me.

"Thanks," I said. Big smile, humble servant. Conway moved in the corner of my eye, a sharp jerk; trying not to puke, probably. "If you don't mind, could we start with yesterday evening? Could you just run through it for me, from the beginning of first study period?"

Joanne told the same story over again. Slow and clear, small words, for the plebs. To Conway, scribbling away: "Are you getting this? Or do I have to slow down?"

Conway gave her a great big grin. "If I need you to do anything, you'll know. Believe me."

I said, "Thanks, Joanne. That's very considerate of you. Tell me: while you were up here, did you look at the Secret Place?"

"I had a little lookie when I went to the loo. Just to see if there was anything good."

"Was there?"

Joanne shrugged. "Same old stuff. Boring."

No Labradors, no boobs. I said, "Any of those cards yours?"

Glance flicked at Houlihan. "No."

"Are you sure?"

"Um, *yes*?"

"Just asking because one of your friends mentioned that you'd made up a few, early on."

Joanne's eyes chilled over. "Who said that?"

Spread my hands, humble. "I can't give out that information. Sorry."

Joanne was biting at the inside of her mouth, squashed her face up sideways. The others were all going to pay. "If she said it was just me, she's such a liar. It was all of us. And we took them down again. I mean, come *on*. You make it sound like some massive big deal. We were just having a laugh."

Conway had been right: lies on that board, as well as secrets. McKenna had put it up for her purposes; the girls used it for theirs.

I said, "How about this one?" Photo into her hand.

Joanne's jaw dropped. She recoiled in the chair. Squealed, "OhmyGod!" Clapped a hand over her mouth.

Fake as fuck.

It meant nothing. Some people are like that: everything comes out like a lie. Not that they're brilliant liars, just that they're useless at telling the truth. You get left with no way to tell what's the real fake and what's the fake one.

We waited for her to finish up. Caught her fast glance at us, between squealy noises, to check if we were impressed.

I said, "Did you put that up on the Secret Place?"

"Um, hell*o*, *no*? I mean, can't you see I'm literally in *shock*?"

The hand was pressed to her chest. She did a bit of gaspy breathing. Conway and I watched with interest.

Houlihan hovered, half out of her chair. Twittered.

Conway said, without looking, "You can sit down. She's grand."

Joanne shot Conway a poison look. Quit gasping.

I said, "Not for a laugh, no? There's nothing wrong with that; it's not like you're under oath to stick to real secrets. We just need to know."

"I told you. No. OK?"

Backing off meant good-bye to my shot at ruling out all but one, hearing that lock click open.

Joanne was giving me the shit-on-my-shoe stare. An inch from throwing me away in the same bin as Conway.

"Absolutely," I said. Took the photo back, tucked it away, all gone. "Just making sure. So which of your friends do you think it was?"

Something catching and flaring in Joanne's eye; something real. Outrage; fury. Then it died.

"Uh-uh." One finger wagging. Little smile. "No way any of them put this up."

A hundred percent positive. *They wouldn't dare.*

"Then who did?"

"Um, how is that my problem?"

"It's not. But you've obviously got your finger on the pulse of everything that happens in this school. If anyone's guess is worth hearing, it's yours."

Satisfied smile, Joanne accepting her due. I had her back. "If it's someone who was in the school yesterday evening, then it's the people who were in here after us. Julia and Holly and Selena and Whatshername."

"Yeah? You figure they know something about what happened to Chris?"

Shrug. "Maybe."

"Interesting," I said. Nodded away, grave. "Anything special making you think that?"

"I don't have *evidence*. That's your job. I'm just saying."

I said, "I'm going to ask for your opinion on one more thing. Any ideas you've got could help us. Who do you think killed Chris?"

Joanne said, "Wasn't it totally Groundskeeper Willy? I mean, I don't know his *name*, that's just what everyone called him because there was this rumor that he offered this girl some E if she would . . ." Glance at Houlihan, who was starting to look like today was an education and not in a good way. "I mean, *I* don't know if he was a pervert or just a drug dealer, but either way, *ew*. I thought you guys knew it was him but you didn't have enough evidence."

Same as Alison: could be what she actually thought, could be a smart screen. "And you think Holly and her friends might have that evidence? How?"

Joanne pulled a strand of hair out of her ponytail, examined it for split ends. "I guess you think they're all such angels, they'd *never* do drugs. I mean, God, *Rebecca*, she's just *so* innocent, right?"

"I haven't met her yet. Would they do drugs, yeah?"

Another quick look at Houlihan. Shrug. "I'm not saying they did. I'm not saying they'd have, like, *done* anything with Groundskeeper Willy." Smirk curling the corners of Joanne's mouth. "I'm just saying they're freaks and I don't know *what* they'd do. That's all."

She would've been delighted to play this game all day, drop hints like farts and mince away from the stink. I said, "Pick one thing to tell me about Chris. Whatever you think was most important."

Joanne thought. Something unpleasant pulling at her top lip.

Said, right on cue, "I wouldn't feel comfortable saying anything bad about him."

Under-the-lashes look at me.

I leaned forward. Grave, intent, eyebrows down while I focused on the noble young girl who held the secret that could save the world. Deepest voice: "Joanne. I know you're not the kind of person who speaks ill of the dead. But there are times when the truth matters more than kindness. This is one of those times."

I could almost hear my own soundtrack rising. I felt Conway, at my shoulder, wanting to laugh.

Joanne took a deep breath. Gearing herself up to be brave, sacrifice her personal conscience on the altar of justice. The fake spread out, the whole thing felt fake, Chris Harper felt like someone I'd made up.

"Chris," she said. Sigh. A little sad, a little pitying. "Poor Chris. For such a lovely guy, he had seriously crap taste."

I said, "Do you mean Selena Wynne?"

"Well. I wasn't going to name names, but since you already know . . ."

I said, "Thing is, no one says they saw Chris and Selena doing anything couple-y. No kissing, no holding hands, not even going off on their own together. So what makes you think they were going out?"

Lashes fluttering. "I'd rather not say."

"Joanne, I understand that you're trying to do the right thing, and I appreciate it. But I need you to tell me what you saw, or heard. All of it."

Joanne liked watching me work hard. Liked knowing that what she had was worth all that. She pretended to think, running her tongue around her teeth, which did nothing for her looks. "OK," she said. "Chris liked girls to like him. You know what I mean? Like, he was always trying to get every girl in the room to be all over him. And all of a sudden, like over-*night*, he's totally ignoring everyone except Selena Wynne. Who, I mean, I don't want to be a B or anything but I'm just being honest because that's who I am: she isn't exactly anything special? She acts like she is, but I'm sorry, most people really aren't into . . . you know." Joanne gave me a mean-ingful little smirk and mimed *large* with both hands. "I mean, hello? I thought maybe it was one of those stupid movie things where it's all a bet to embarrass someone, because if it wasn't, I could've literally cringed to *death* for Chris."

"That doesn't say they were going out, though. Maybe he was into her, but she wasn't having any of it."

"Um, I don't *think* so? She'd have been, like, *insanely* lucky to get him. And anyway, Chris wasn't the type to waste his time if he wasn't getting anywhere. If you know what I mean."

"Why would they keep it a secret?"

"Probably he didn't want people knowing he was with *that*. I wouldn't blame him."

I said, "Is that why you don't get on with Selena's lot? Because she and Chris got together?"

Wrong move. That flare in Joanne's eyes again, cold enough and violent enough that I nearly leaned back. "Um, ex*cuse* me? I didn't exactly care if Chris Harper was into hippos. I thought it was hilarious, but apart from that, *so* not my problem."

I did a string of fast humble nods: got it, been put in my place, won't be a bold boy again. "Right. That makes sense. Then why do you not get on with them?"

"Because there isn't a law that we have to *get on with* everybody. Because I'm actually choosy about who I hang out with, and hippos and weirdos? Yeah, um, no thanks?"

Just some little bitch, exact same as the little bitches in my school, in every school. Ten a penny, cheap at half the price, cheap anywhere in this world. No reason why this should be the one that made me sick. "Got it," I said, grinning away like a lunatic.

Conway said, "You got a boyfriend?"

Joanne took her time. A beat—*Did I hear something?*—then a slow sweep of her head to Conway.

Conway smiled. Not nicely.

"Excuse me, that's my private life?"

Conway said, "I thought you were all about helping the investigation."

"I am. I just don't see how my *private* life is the investigation's business. Do you want to explain that?"

"Nah," said Conway. "I can't be arsed. Specially when I can just go over to Colm's and find out."

I spread on a double helping of concerned. Said, "I can't imagine Joanne would make us do that, Detective. Especially since she knows that any information she's got could be very valuable to us."

Joanne thought that over. Got her virtuous face back on. Graciously, to me: "I'm going out with Andrew Moore. His dad's Bill Moore—probably you've heard of him." Property developer, one of the ones on the news for being bankrupt and a billionaire all at once. I looked properly impressed.

Joanne checked her watch. "Do you want to know anything else about my love life? Or are we *done*?"

"Bye-bye," Conway said. To Houlihan: "Rebecca O'Mara."

I walked Joanne to the door. Held it for her. Watched Houlihan scuttle after her down the corridor, Joanne not bothering to look.

Conway said, "And another one still in the running."

Nothing in her voice. No way, again, to tell if that was *You better up your game.*

I shut the door. Said, "There's stuff she's thinking about telling us, but she's holding back. That fits our card girl."

"Yeah. Or else she's just trying to make us think she's holding something back. Make us think she knows for sure that Chris and Selena were together, or whatever, when actually she's got nothing."

"We can call her back. Push harder."

"Nah. Not now." Conway watched me come back to my chair, sit down. Said, roughly, "You were good with her. Better than me."

"All that arse-licking practice. Came in useful in the end."

Wry glance from Conway, but a brief one. She was filing Joanne away for later, moving on. "Rebecca's the weak link in this bunch. Shy as fuck; went scarlet and practically tied herself in knots just being asked her name, never managed anything louder than a whisper. Get your kid gloves on."

Bell again, rush of feet and voices. It was past lunchtime. I could've murdered a dirty great burger, or whatever this canteen was into, probably organic fillet steak and rocket salad. I wasn't going to say it till Conway did. She wasn't going to say it.

Conway said, "And go careful with this lot, till you get the feel. They're not the same thing."

8

An evening in early November, the air just starting to flare with little savory bursts of cold and turf-smoke. The four of them are in their cypress glade, snug in the lovely pocket of free time between classes and dinner. Chris Harper (over the wall and far away, not even a whisper of a thought in any of their minds) has six months, a week and four days left to live.

They are scattered on the grass, lying on their backs, feet dangling from crossed knees. They have hoodies and scarves and Uggs, but they're holding out a last few days against winter coats. It's day and night at once: one side of the sky is glowing with pink and orange, the other side is a frail full moon hanging in darkening blue. Wind moves through the cypress branches, a slow soothing hush. Last period was PE, volleyball; their muscles are slack and comfortably tired. They're talking about homework.

Selena asks, "Did you guys do your love sonnets yet?"

Julia groans. She's drawn a dotted line across her wrist in ballpoint and is writing under it IN CASE OF EMERGENCY CUT HERE.

"'And if you don't feel that you have, em, adequate *experience* of, em, *romantic* love,'" Holly says, in Mr. Smythe's reedy simper, "'then perhaps a child's love for her mother, or, em, love for *God* would be, em, would be—'"

Julia mimes sticking two fingers down her throat. "I'm going to dedicate mine to vodka."

"You'll get sent to Sister Ignatius to get counseled," says Becca, not entirely sure whether Julia is serious.

"Whee."

"I'm stuck on mine," Selena says.

"Lists," says Holly. She pulls one foot to her face to examine a scuff mark on her boot. "'The wind, the sea, the stars, the moon, the rain; The day, the night, the bread, the milk, the train.' Instant iambic pentameter."

"Instant iambic craptameter," Julia says. "Thanks for the most boring sonnet in history, here's your F."

Holly and Selena glance at each other sideways. Julia has been a bitch for weeks now; to everybody equally, so it can't be something one of them did.

"I don't *want* to tell Smythe about anyone I love," Selena says, sliding past that. "Ew."

"Do it about a place or something," Holly says. She licks her finger and rubs it on the scuff mark, which fades. "I did my gran's flat. And I didn't even say it was my gran's, just a flat."

"I just made mine up," says Becca. "I did it about a girl who has this horse that comes under her window at night and she climbs out and rides him." She has her eyes unfocused so that the moon has turned into two, translucent and overlapping.

"What's that got to do with love?" Holly says.

"She loves the horse."

"Kinky," says Julia. Her phone beeps. She pulls it out of her pocket and holds it above her face, squinting against the sunset.

If it had been an hour earlier, when they were throwing off their uniforms in their room and singing Amy Winehouse, deciding whether to go across the road and watch the guys' rugby match. If it were an hour later, when they would be in the canteen, sprawled forward over the table, catching last crumbs of dry cake with licked fingertips. None of them would ever have imagined what they had brushed up against; what other selves, other lives, other deaths were careening ferocious and unstoppable along their tracks, only a sliver of time away. The grounds are pocketed with clusters of girls, all blazing and amazed with inchoate love for one another and for their own growing closeness; none of the others will feel the might of that swerve as the tracks switch and their own power takes them barreling into another landscape. When Holly thinks about it a long time afterwards, when things are starting to stay fixed and come into focus at last, she will think that probably there are ways you could say Marcus Wiley killed Chris Harper.

"Maybe I'll just do it about pretty flowers," Selena says. She stretches a lock of hair across her face—the last of the sun turns it to a web of gold light—and examines the trees through it. "Or ickle kittens. You think he'd care?"

"I bet someone does theirs about One Direction," Holly says.

"*Aah*," Julia says, sudden and too loud, disgusted and angry.

The others come up on their elbows. "What?" Becca asks.

Julia shoves her phone back in her pocket, clasps her hands behind her head again and stares up at the sky. Nostrils flaring as she breathes, too fast. She's red right down to the neck of her jumper. Julia never goes red.

The rest look at each other. Holly catches Selena's eye and tilts her chin at Julia: *Did you see what . . . ?* Selena shakes her head, just a millimeter.

"What?" Holly says.

"Marcus Wiley is a douchewipe, is what. Any more questions?"

"Duh, we knew *that*," Holly says. Julia ignores her.

Becca asks, "What's a douchewipe?"

"You don't want to know," Holly tells her.

"Jules," Selena says gently. She turns over onto her stomach to be side by side with Julia. Her hair is bright and messed, with bits of grass and cypress fans tangled here and there, and the back of her hoodie is ribbed with creases from lying on it. "What'd he say?"

Julia's head moves away from Selena, but she says, "He didn't *say* anything. He sent me a dick pic. Because he's a fucking douchewipe. OK? Now can we talk about the sonnets some more?"

"Oh my God," Holly says. Selena's eyes are massive. "Seriously?"

"No, I made it up. Yeah, seriously."

The sunset light feels different, a slow grind like fingernails across every bit of bare skin.

"But," Becca says, bewildered, "you don't even really know him."

Julia whips up her head and stares, teeth bared about to bite, but then Holly starts to laugh. After a second Selena joins in and at last even Julia, head falling back on the grass. "What?" Becca wants to know, but they're gone, their whole bodies are shaking with it and Selena is curled up to hold herself: "The way you said it!" And "The *face* on you," Holly gasps, "'You've barely been properly *introduced*, dahling, why to *goodness* would he share his little friend with you?'" and the fake English accent has Becca blushing and giggling too. Julia hoots up at the sky, "I don't believe we've even taken tea and . . . and . . . and cucumber sandwiches together . . ." and Holly manages, "Dicks should *never* be served until *after* the cucumber sandwiches . . ."

"Oh, God," Julia says, wiping her eyes, when it dies down. "Oh, Becsie baby, what would we do without you?"

"It wasn't *that* funny," Becca says, still red and grinning and not sure whether to be embarrassed.

"Probably not," Julia says. "But that's not the point." She props herself up on her elbow again and fishes in her pocket for her phone.

"Let's see," Holly says, sitting up and scooting over to Julia.

"I'm deleting it."

"So let's see first."

"You're a pervert."

"Me too," Selena says cheerfully. "If you're scarred for life, we want to be too."

"God, don't be so gay," Julia says. "It's a dick pic, not some kind of bonding experience." But she hits buttons, finding the picture.

"Becs," Holly says. "Coming?"

"Ew. No." Becca twists her head away, so she doesn't see by accident.

"Here you go," Julia says, and hits Open.

Holly and Selena lean in against her shoulders. Julia pretends to look, but her eyes slide past the phone, into the shadows. Selena feels her spine clamp up, and leans harder.

They don't giggle or scream, the way they did when they went looking online. Those were primped and plastic as Barbie, no way could you imagine a real guy attached. This is different: smaller; shoving itself up at them like a thick middle finger, like a threat, out of a mess of dark sticky hair. They can smell it.

"If that was the best I could come up with," Holly says coolly, after a moment, "I wouldn't exactly *advertise* it."

Julia doesn't look up.

"You should text him back," Selena says. " 'Sorry, can't tell what pic is, way too small.' "

"And get a close-up. Yeah, no thanks." But the corner of Julia's mouth twitches up.

"You can come on over, Becs," says Holly. "Totally safe, unless you've got a microscope." Becca smiles and ducks her head and shakes it, all at the same time. The grass squirms under her legs, prickling.

"Well," Julia says. "If you perverts have seen enough mini-dick for one day . . ." She hits Delete with a flourish and gives her phone a finger-wave. "Bye-bye."

Tiny beep, and it's gone. Julia puts the phone away and lies down again. After a bit Holly and Selena drift back to their places, looking around for the thing to say, finding nothing. The moon is strengthening, as the sky turns darker.

In a while Holly says, "Hey, you know where Cliona is? She's in the library, looking for a sonnet to copy that Smythe won't know."

"She's gonna get caught," Becca says.

"That's so typical," Selena says. "Wouldn't it be easier to just write the sonnet?"

"Well, totally," Holly says. "This always happens. She ends up working harder to get out of doing the thing than she would just doing the thing."

They leave space for Julia to say something. When she doesn't, the space gets bigger. The conversation falls into it and vanishes.

The photo isn't gone. The faint rank smell of it is still stained onto the air. Becca breathes shallowly, through her mouth, but it greases her tongue.

Julia says, up into the smeared watercolor sky, "How come guys think I'm a slut?"

The red is blotching her skin again. Selena says gently, "You're not a slut."

"Duh, I *know* I'm not. So why do they act like I am?"

"They want you to be," says Holly.

"They want all of us to be. But I don't see anyone sending any of you guys dick pics."

Becca moves. She says, "It's only the last while."

"Since I snogged James Gillen."

"Not that. Loads of people snog someone and the boys don't care. It's since before that. Since you started having a laugh with Finn and Chris and all them. Because you make jokes, because you say things . . ."

She trails off. Julia says, "You are shitting me."

But Holly and Selena are nodding, as it sinks in and clicks into place. "That," Selena says. "You say stuff like that."

"So you figure they want me to be some prissy hypocrite bitch like Heffernan, who let Bryan Hynes finger her at the Halloween dance because he had booze, but she acts totally OMG-so-outraged if you make a dirty joke. And then they'll *respect* me."

Holly says, "Just about, yeah."

"*Fuck* that. Fuck them. I'm not doing it. I'm not being it." Her voice is raw and older.

Thin clouds are running across the moon so it feels like the moon is moving, or like all the world is tilting under them.

Selena says, "Then don't."

"And just keep taking this kind of crap. Sounds great. Anyone got any more genius ideas?"

"Maybe that's not why," Becca says, wishing she had kept her stupid mouth shut. "Maybe I'm totally wrong. Maybe he was trying to text someone else with a J, Joanne or someone, and he hit the wrong—"

Julia says, "When I snogged James Gillen."

The dark condenses, under the cypresses, at her voice.

"He tried to put his hand up my top, right? Which I was expecting—I swear, I don't know why guys all have such a fixation with tits, did their mommies not breast-feed them enough or something?"

She isn't looking at the others. The clouds move faster, setting the moon speeding across the sky.

"So since I'm not actually interested in James Gillen feeling me up and let's be honest I'm only even snogging him because he's cute and I want the practice, I go, 'Whoa, I think this is yours,' and give him his nasty clammy hand back, right? And James, being a total gentleman, James decides the appropriate thing to do is to shove me back against the fence—like an actual *shove*, not just a little nudge or whatever—and stick his hand right back where it was. And he says something incredibly predictable along the lines of, 'You love it, don't act so pure, everyone knows about you,' blah blah whatever. Prince Charming or what?"

The air feels chilly and searing all at once, feverish.

They've had it spelled out a dozen times, in cringey classes, in cringey parent talks: when to tell an adult. The idea never comes near any of their minds. This thing opening in front of them is nothing to do with those careful speeches. This mix of roaring rage and a shame that stains every cell, this crawling understanding that now their bodies belong to other people's eyes and hands, not to them: this is something new.

"The little *shit*," Holly says, through her heartbeat and her breath running wild. "The little prick. I hope he dies of cancer."

Selena stretches out a leg so that her foot touches Julia's. This time Julia jerks her foot away.

Becca says, "What did you do? Did you, did he . . . ?"

"I kneed him in the balls. Which actually works, just in case you ever need to know. And then when we came back here I showered the living shit out of myself." They remember. They never thought to connect it up with James Gillen (Julia offhand, flipping a shoulder, *Shouldn't have bothered, like snogging a Labrador*). Now, in the seething space of their new knowledge, it feels slap-in-the-face obvious.

"And I don't know about you, but being the genius I am, I figure James Gillen didn't feel like telling the rest of Colm's that all he got out of his afternoon was a bruised ballsack, so he told them I was a slut who couldn't get enough. And that's why Marcus fucking Wiley feels I'd just love a photo of his dick. And it's just going to keep on coming, isn't it?"

Selena says, but there's a thread of uncertainty flawing her voice, "They'll forget about it. In a few weeks—"

"No. They won't."

Silence, and the watchful moon. Holly thinks about finding out some disgusting secret about James Gillen and spreading it till everyone laughs whenever he walks past and finally he kills himself. Becca tries to think of things to bring Julia, chocolate, funny poems. Selena pictures some yellowed book with curled writing, a low rhyming chant, knotted grass and the smell of burning hair; a shimmer closing around the four of them, turning them impermeable. Julia concentrates on finding animals in the clouds and digs her fingernails through the layers of grass into the ground, till clumps of dirt stab up into the quick.

They have no weapons for this. The air is bruised and swollen, throbbing in black and white, ready to split open.

Julia says, hard and final as a slamming door, "I'm not touching any guy from Colm's again. Ever."

"That's like saying you're never going near any guy ever," Holly says. "Colm's guys are all we meet."

"So I won't go near any guy ever, till college. I don't care. Better than having another of those stupid pricks telling the whole school exactly what my tits feel like." Becca goes red.

Selena hears it like a single *ding* of silver on crystal, shivering the air. She sits up. She says, "Then me neither."

Julia shoots her a ferocious stare. "I'm not just being all, 'Oh, my ickle feelings are hurt so I'm giving up men forever.' I *mean* it."

Selena says, unruffled and sure, "Me too."

In daylight it would be different. In daylight, in indoor light, this would never come to them. Powerless and stifled, the rage would turn ingrown. The stain on their skin would burn deeper, branding them.

The clouds are gone but the moonlight is speeding faster, turning around them. Becca says, "Same here."

Julia's eyebrow flicks, half wryly. Becca can't find how to tell her that it's not nothing and that she wants it to be more, she would bring the biggest thing in the world to put in the middle of their circle and set it on fire if she could, so that she'd deserve this; but then Julia gives her a small smile and a private wink.

All their eyes have gone to Holly. She has a flash of her dad, his grin as he sideslips when you try to pin him to an answer: never get tied down, not till you're beyond sure, not even then.

The others, blazing white against the dark trees, triple and waiting. The soft curve of shadow under Selena's chin, the narrow back-bend of Becca's wrist where she leans on her hand in the grass, the downward quirk at the corner of Julia's mouth: things Holly will know by heart when she's a hundred, when all the rest of the world has been scoured away from her mind. Something throbs in the palms of her hands, pulling towards them. Something shifting, the smoke-spiral ache of something like thirst but not, catching her in the throat and under the breastbone. Something is happening.

"Same here," she says.

"Oh, God," Julia says. "I can hear it now. They're gonna say we're some kind of lesbian orgy cult."

"So?" Selena says. "They can say what they want. We won't have to care."

A breathtaken silence, as that sinks in. Their minds race wild along its trail. They see Joanne wiggling and giggling and sneering in the Court to make the Colm's guys fancy her, they see Orla howling helpless into her sodden pillow after Andrew Moore and his friends ripped her apart, they see themselves trying desperately to stand right and dress right and say the right things under the guys' grabbing eyes, and they think: *Never, never ever, never never never again. Break that open the way superheroes burst handcuffs. Punch it in the face and watch it explode.*

My body my mind the way I dress the way I walk the way I talk, mine all mine.

The power of it, buzzing inside them to be unlocked, makes their bones shake.

Becca says, "We'll be like the Amazons. They didn't touch guys, ever, and they didn't care what people said. If a guy tried to do anything to them, he ended up . . ." A second that whirls with arrows and flares of blood.

"Whoa," Julia says, but the small smile is back and it's her own smile, the one that most people never get to see. "Chill. This isn't forever. It's just till we leave school and we can meet actual human guys."

Leaving school is years away and unimaginable, words that can never turn real. This is forever.

Selena says, "We need to swear it. Make a vow."

"Oh, come on," Julia says, "who does stuff like . . ." but she's only saying it out of reflex, it spins faint and dizzy away into the shadows, none of them hear.

Selena holds out her hand, palm down over the grass and the hidden trails of night insects. "I swear," she says.

Bats call, up in the dark air. The cypresses lean closer to watch, intent, approving. The rush and whisper of them lifts the girls, surges them on.

"OK," Julia says. Her voice comes out stronger than she meant it to, so strong it startles her; her heartbeat feels like it's going to lift her off the ground. "OK. Let's do it."

She brings her hand down on top of Selena's. The small slap echoes across the clearing. "I swear."

Becca, thin hand light as a dandelion on Julia's, wishing fiercely and too late that she had looked at the photo, that she had seen what the others were seeing. "I swear."

And Holly. "I swear."

The four hands twist into a knot wrapped with moonlight, fingers tangling, all of them trying to stretch wide enough to tighten round all the others at once. A breathless small laugh.

The cypresses sigh, long and sated. The moon stands still.

9

Rebecca O'Mara, in the art-room doorway, hovering on one foot with the other wrapped round her ankle. Long dark-brown hair in a ponytail, soft and straggly, no straighteners here. Maybe an inch taller than Holly; skinny, not scary-skinny but definitely could have done with a pizza. Not pretty—face still catching up with her features—but it was coming soon. Wide brown eyes, on Conway, wary. No glance at the Secret Place.

If Rebecca was low on the old confidence, the old self-esteem, I could bring that. Give it the sweet big brother, looking for help with the important adventure and shy Little Sis is the special one who can save the day.

"Rebecca, yeah?" I said. Smiled, not too big, just easy and natural. "Thanks for coming in. Have a seat."

She didn't move. Houlihan had to dodge past her, scurry off to her corner. "It's about Chris Harper. Isn't it?"

Not scarlet and tangled up this time, but her voice was barely over a whisper. I said, "I'm Stephen Moran—maybe Holly's mentioned me along the way, has she? She gave me a hand with some stuff, a few years back?"

Rebecca looked at me properly, for the first time. Nodded.

I held out a hand at the chair, and she pulled herself out of the doorway and came. That gangly teenage half prance, like it was only the heavy shoes bringing her feet back to the ground. She sat down, tied her legs in a knot. Wrapped her hands in her skirt.

Sucking feeling in my chest, like water draining: letdown. From knowing Holly, from Conway saying *Just something*, from all that wide-eyed shite about freaks and witches, I'd been expecting these to be more than the last lot. This was just Alison over again, a bundle of fidgety fears wrapped in a grow-into-it skirt.

I let my spine go loose like a teenager's, knees everywhere, and gave Rebecca another smile. Rueful, this one. "I need a hand again. I'm good at my job, I swear, but every now and then I need someone to help me out or I'll get nowhere. I've got a feeling maybe you might be able to do that for me. Would you give it a shot, yeah?"

Rebecca said, "Is it about Chris?"

Not too shy to dig in her heels a bit. I made a face. "I've gotta tell you, I'm still trying to work out what it's about. Why? Has something happened to do with Chris, yeah?"

She shook her head. "I just . . ." Gesture at Conway, with the bundle of hands and skirt. Conway was picking her nails with the cap of her pen, didn't look up. "I mean, because she's here. I thought . . ."

"We'll try and figure it out together. OK?"

I shot her the warm crinkly smile. Got a blank look back.

I said, "So let's start with yesterday evening. First study period: where were you?"

After a moment Rebecca said, "The fourth-year common room. We have to be."

"And then?"

"We get our break. Me and my friends, we went outside and sat on the grass for a while."

Her voice was still a scraped-down wisp, but it got stronger on that. *Me and my friends.*

I said, "Which friends? Holly and Julia and Selena, yeah?"

"Yeah. And some others. Most of us went out. It was warm."

"And then you had second study period. You were here in the art room?"

"Yeah. With Holly and Julia and Selena."

"How do you go about getting permission to spend a study period here? Like who asked who, and when? Sorry, I'm a bit . . ." I did shrug, head-duck, sheepish grin. "I'm new on this. Don't know the ropes yet."

More blank. Great with the young people, me, I'll get them relaxed, I'll get them talking . . . Lovely Big Bro was striking out.

Conway was squinting at a thumbnail against the light. Missing nothing.

Rebecca said, "We ask Miss Arnold—she's the Matron. Julia went and asked her day before yesterday, at teatime. We wanted to go for first study, but someone was already going then, so Miss Arnold said to go for second study instead. They don't like too many people being in the school after hours."

"So at break yesterday evening, yous got the key to the connecting door off the other girls who'd been up here?"

"No. We're not allowed to pass it around. Whoever signs the key out has to sign it back in, when they said they would. So the other girls gave it back to Miss Arnold, and then we went and got it off her."

"Who did that?"

I saw the instant where a streak of fear flew bright across Rebecca's face, and she thought about lying. No reason why she should, nothing there that could get her in trouble as far as I could see, but that was where she turned all the same. Conway was right about this one, anyway: a liar, at least when she was scared; at least when something pulled her separate from her friends, put her in the spotlight all alone.

Not stupid, though, scared or not. Took her half a second to realize there was no point. She said, "Me."

I nodded like I'd noticed nothing. "And then yous came up to the art room. All four of you together, yeah?"

"Yeah."

"And what did you do?"

"We have this project." She untangled one hand from her skirt, pointed at a table by the windows: bulky shape under a paint-spattered drop cloth. "Selena was doing calligraphy, and Holly was grinding up chalk for snow, and Julia and I were mostly making stuff out of copper wire. We're doing the school a hundred years ago—it's art and history together. It's complicated."

"Sounds it. So you put in the extra time," I said. Approving. "Whose idea was that?"

The approval did nothing for Rebecca. "Everyone's needed to use study time on the project. We did last week, too."

Which could have been when someone's light bulb switched on. "Yeah? Whose idea was it to come back last night?"

"I don't even remember. We all knew we needed to."

"And did all of yous stay here the whole time, till nine? Or did anyone go out of the room?"

Rebecca unwrapped her hands from her skirt and tucked them under her thighs. I was lobbing the questions fast and she was still wound tight and wary, and getting warier all the time, but the wariness was scatter-gun stuff, general cover; she didn't know where to point it. Unless she was good or I was thick, she didn't know about the card.

"Only for like a minute."

"Who went where?"

Fine dark eyebrows pulled down. Brown eyes ticking back and forth between me and Conway.

Conway traced over table graffiti with her ballpoint. I waited.

"How come?" Rebecca asked. "How come you need to know?"

I left a silence. Rebecca matched it. All those thin elbows and knees looked like sharp corners, not so frail any more.

Conway had got her far wrong, or a year had taken her a long way. Rebecca wasn't looking for a confidence boost, wasn't looking for me or anyone to make her feel special. She wasn't Alison, wasn't Orla. I was going wrong.

Conway's head had come up. She was watching me.

I binned the easy slouch, straightened my spine. Leaning forward, hands clasped between my knees. Adult to adult.

"Rebecca," I said. Different voice, direct and serious. "There are going to be things I can't tell you. And I'm going to sit here asking you to tell me everything you know just the same. I know that's unfair. But if Holly's ever said anything about me, I'm hoping she's told you that I'm not going to treat you like an idiot or a baby. If I can answer your questions, I'll do it. Give me the same respect. Fair enough?"

You can hear when you hit the right note, hear the ring of it. Rebecca's chin lost the stubborn tilt; some of the wariness in her spine shifted to readiness. "Yeah," she said, after a moment. "OK."

Conway quit messing with her pen. Sat still, ready to write.

"Grand," I said. "So. Who left the art room?"

"Julia went back to our room, to get one of our old photos that we'd forgotten. I went to the toilet; I think so did Selena. Holly went to get chalk—we ran out of white, so she went and got more. I think from the science lab."

"Do you remember what times? What order?"

Rebecca said, "We were in the building the whole time. We didn't even go off this floor, except Julia and she was only gone like a minute."

I said gently, "No one's saying you did anything wrong. I'm only trying to work out what you might have seen or heard."

"We didn't. See or hear anything. Any of us. We had the radio on, and we just did our project and then went back to the boarders' wing. And we all left together. In case you were going to ask."

Spark of defiance in there at the end, chin going up again.

"And you gave the key back to Miss Arnold."

"Yeah. At nine. You can check." We would. I didn't say it.

I took out the photo.

Rebecca's eyes hit it like magnets. I kept it facing me, did the flip back and forth against a fingertip. Rebecca tried to crane her neck without moving.

I said, "On your way here last night, you passed the Secret Place. You passed it again on your way to the toilet and back. And again when you left at the end of the evening. Right?"

That pulled her eyes away from the photo, back to me. Wide eyes, on guard, riffling through wild guesses. "Yeah."

"Did you stop for a look, any of those times?"

"No."

I gave it the skepticals.

"We were in a hurry. At first we were working on the project, and then I had to get the key back on time. We weren't thinking about the Secret Place. Why?" One hand coming out from under her leg, uncurling towards the photo; long thin fingers, she was going to be tall. "Is that—"

"The secrets on there. Any of them yours?"

"No."

No beat beforehand, no split-second decision. No lie.

"Why not? You don't have secrets? Or you keep them to yourself?"

Rebecca said, "I've got *friends*. I tell them my secrets. I don't need to go around telling the whole school. Even anonymously."

Her head had gone up; her voice had filled out all of a sudden, rang through the sunlight to the corners of the room. She was proud.

I said, "Do you figure your friends tell you all their secrets, too?"

A beat there; quarter of a second when her lips opened and nothing came out. Then she said, "I know everything about them."

Still that ring in her voice, like joy. A lift to her mouth that was almost a smile.

I felt it change my breathing. Right there, a flash like a signal: the something else I'd been looking for. Burning hotter, throwing off sparks in strange colors.

Not the same thing, Conway had said; not the same as Joanne's lot. No shit.

I said, "And you all keep each other's secrets. You'd never rat the others out."

"No. None of us would. Ever."

"So," I said, "this isn't yours?" Photo into Rebecca's hand.

Breath and a high whimper came out of her. Her mouth was open.

"Someone put that on the Secret Place yesterday evening. Was it you?"

All of her was sucked into the photo. It took a moment for the question to sink in enough that she said, "No."

Not lying: not enough of her attention was left for it. Another one down. "Do you know who did?"

Rebecca hauled herself out of the photo. She said, "It wasn't any of us. Me and my friends."

"How do you know?"

"Because none of us know who killed Chris."

And she put the photo back into my hand. End of story. She was pulled up straight-backed and head high, looking me in the eye, no blink.

I said, "Let's say you had to guess. Had to, no way out. What would you say?"

"Guess what? Who did the card, or . . . Chris?"

"Both."

Rebecca gave me the blank teenage shrug that sends parents apeshit.

I said, "The way you talk about your friends, it sounds like they mean a lot to you. Am I right?"

"Yeah. They do."

"People are going to know the four of you could have had something to do with this card. Fact. No way round that. If I had friends I cared about, I'd do whatever it took to make sure there wasn't a killer out there thinking they had info on him. Even if it meant answering questions I didn't like."

Rebecca thought about that. Carefully.

She moved her chin at the photo. "I think someone just made that up."

"You say it wasn't any of your mates. Which means it had to be Joanne Heffernan or one of her friends. They're the only other people who were in the building at the right time."

"You said it was them. I didn't. I don't have a clue."

"Would they? Make it up?"

"Maybe."

"Why?"

Shrug. "Maybe they were bored. They wanted something to happen. And now here you are."

Flare to her nostril: *They.* Rebecca didn't think much of Joanne's lot. Meek little thing, to look at. Not so meek inside.

"And Chris," I said. "Who do you think did that?"

Rebecca said—no pause—"Guys from Colm's. I think a bunch of them sneaked in here—maybe they were planning some kind of joke, like stealing something or painting something; a few years ago some of them came in one night with spray cans and sprayed a picture all across our playing field." Tinge of red running up her cheeks. She wasn't going to tell us what the picture had been. "I think they came in for something like that, but then they had a fight. And . . ."

Her hands spreading. Setting the image loose, to float away on the air.

I said, "Was Chris the kind of guy who would do that? Sneak out of his school, come in here on a prank?"

Some picture unfolded inside Rebecca's mind, taking her away from us. She watched it. Said, "Yeah. He was."

Something lying across her voice, a long shadow. Rebecca had had feelings about Chris Harper. Good or bad, I couldn't tell, but strong.

I said, "If you could tell me just one thing about him, what would it be?"

Rebecca said, unexpectedly: "He was kind."

"Kind? How?"

"This one time, we were hanging around outside the shopping center and my phone was doing something weird; it looked like I'd lost all my photos. A couple of the other guys were being total morons—like, 'Ooo, what did you have on there, were there photos of . . .'" The tinge of red again. "Just stupid stuff. But Chris went, 'Here, give me a look,' and he took the phone off me and started trying to fix it. The idiots thought that was *hilarious*, but Chris didn't care. He just fixed the phone and gave it back to me."

A small sigh. The picture in her mind folded away, slid into its drawer. She was looking at us again.

"When I think about Chris, that's what I think about. That day."

A girl like Rebecca, that day could have meant a lot. Could have rooted and grown, inside her mind.

Conway moved. Said, "You got a boyfriend?"

"No."

Instant. Almost scornful, like it was a stupid question: *You got a rocket ship?*

"Why not?"

"Do I have to?"

"A lot of people do."

Rebecca said flatly, "I don't."

She didn't give a fuck what either of us thought of that. Not Alison, not Orla. The opposite.

Conway said, "We'll see you around."

Rebecca left stuffing my card in her pocket, forgetting it already. Conway said, "Not our girl."

"Nah."

She didn't say it. I had to. "Took me a while to get off the ground."

Conway nodded. "Yeah. Not your fault. I steered you wrong."

She'd gone absent, eyes narrowed on something.

I said, "I think I got it right in the end. No harm done, that I could see."

"Maybe not," Conway said. "This fucking place. Trips you up every time you turn around. Whatever you do, turns out it was the wrong call."

Julia Harte. Conway didn't brief me on her, not after how Rebecca had gone, but I knew as soon as Julia walked in the door she was the boss of that outfit. Short, with dark curly hair fighting a ponytail. A bit more weight on her than the rest, a few more curves, a walk that showed them. Not pretty—roundy face, bump on her nose—but a good chin, small chin with plenty of stubborn, and good eyes: hazel, long-lashed, direct and smart as hell. No glance at the Secret Place, but there wouldn't have been either way, not with this one.

"Detective Conway," she said. Nice voice, deeper than most girls', more controlled. Made her sound older. "Did you miss us that much?"

A smart-arse. That can work for us, work nicely. Smart-arses talk when they shouldn't, say anything as long as it'll come out good and snappy.

Conway pointed at the chair. Julia sat down, crossed her knees. Looked me up, looked me down.

I said, "I'm Stephen Moran. Julia Harte, right?"

"At your service. What can I do for you?"

Smart-arses want a chance to be smart. "You tell me. Anything you think I should know?"

"About what?"

"You pick." And I grinned at her, like we were old sparring partners who'd missed each other.

Julia grinned back. "Don't eat the yellow snow. Never play leapfrog with a unicorn."

Ten seconds in, and it was a conversation, not an interview. The boy was back in town. I felt Conway ease back on the table; felt the whoosh of relief go through me.

"I'll make a note of that," I said. "Meanwhile, why don't you tell me what you did yesterday evening? Start with first study period."

Julia sighed. "Here I was hoping we could talk about something interesting. Any reason why we're going for, like, the most boring thing in the world?"

I said, "You'll get your info once I've got mine. Maybe. Till then, no fishing."

Twitch of her mouth, appreciative. "Deal. Here you go: boring storytime."

The same story as Rebecca's: the art project, the key, the forgotten picture and the toilet breaks and the chalk, the too busy to look at the board. No mismatches. It was true, or they were good.

I brought out the photo. Did the fingertip flip. "Have you put up any cards in the Secret Place?"

Julia snorted. "Jesus, no. Not my thing."

"No?"

Her eye on the photo. "Truly, madly, deeply no."

"So you didn't put up this one."

"Um, since I didn't put up any of them, I'm going to go with no?"

I held out the photo. Julia took it. Blank-faced, all set up to give away nothing.

She turned the photo towards her and went still. The whole room went still.

Then she shrugged. Handed the photo back to me, almost tossed it.

"You've met Joanne Heffernan, right? If you find anything she won't do for attention, I'd love to hear it. It probably involves YouTube and a German shepherd." Squeak from Houlihan. Julia's eyes went to her and flicked away again, insta-bored.

"Julia," I said. "Messing aside, just for a sec. If this was you, we need to know."

"I actually do know serious when I see it. That was totally, one hundred percent not me."

Julia wasn't out. Almost out; not quite. "You figure Joanne's behind it?"

Another shrug. "The only people you had waiting outside the office were us and Joanne's little poodles—plus you're asking about yesterday evening, so it has to be someone who was in the school then. It wasn't us, so that leaves them. And the other three don't scratch their arses unless Joanne says they can. 'Scuse my language."

I said, "How come you're so sure none of your mates put this up?"

"Because. I know them."

An echo of that note that had rung through Rebecca's voice. That signal-flash again, so bright it almost hurt my eyes. Something different. Something rare.

I shook my head. "You don't know them inside out. Trust me. Doesn't happen."

Julia looked back at me. One eyebrow raised: *Is there a question here?*

I could feel Conway, hot. Holding back.

I said, "Tell us. You have to have thought about who killed Chris. What's your guess?"

"Colm's guys. His friends. They're the type who'd think it was totally hilarious to climb in here to play some joke—steal something, paint SLUTS on a wall, whatever. And they're the type who'd think it was a wonderful idea to start messing about in the dark with sticks and rocks and anything else dangerous they could find. Someone got a little overexcited, and . . ."

Julia spread her hands. Same gesture as Rebecca. Same story as Rebecca, almost word for word. They'd talked it over.

I said, "Yeah, we heard something about Colm's boys spray-painting a picture on the grass, a few years back. Was that Chris and his mates?"

"Who knows. They didn't get caught, whoever they were. Personally, I'd say no. We were in first year when that happened, so Chris would've been in second year. I don't think a bunch of second-years would've had the guts."

"What was the picture of?"

Another squeak from Houlihan. Julia threw her a finger-wave. "Scientifically speaking, a great big penis and testicles. They're such imaginative boys, over at Colm's."

I said, "Any reason you think that's what happened to Chris?"

"Who, me? I'm just guessing. I leave the detecting to the professionals." Batted her eyelashes at me, chin tucked down, watched for a reaction. Not sexy, not Gemma. Mocking. "Can I go?"

I said, "You're in some hurry to get back to class. Studious type, yeah?"

"Don't I look like a good little schoolgirl to you?"

Little pout, mock-provocative. Still nudging for that reaction.

I said, "Tell me one thing about Chris. One thing that mattered."

Julia dropped the pout. She thought, eyes down. She thought like an adult: taking her time, not worried about letting us wait.

In the end she said, "Chris's dad is a banker. He's rich. Very, very rich."

"And?"

"And that's probably the most important thing I can tell you about Chris."

"He was flash with it? Always had the best stuff, used it to pull rank?"

Slow headshake, click of her tongue. "Nothing like that. He was a lot less of a show-off than most of his friends. But he *had* it. Always. And first. No waiting for Christmas or his birthday. He wanted it, he had it."

Conway moved. Said, "Sounds like you knew Chris's gang pretty well."

"I didn't have much choice. Colm's is like two minutes away, we do all kinds of activities together. We see each other."

"Ever go out with any of them?"

"God, give me some credit. No."

"You got a boyfriend?"

"No."

"Why not?"

Julia's eyebrow arching. "Since I'm such a total babe? All we meet is Colm's guys, and I'm holding out for someone who can actually have conversations in words of more than one syllable. I'm so picky."

Conway said, "OK. You can go. You think of anything, you ring us."

I passed Julia my card. She took it. Didn't stand up.

She said, "Can I ask you for a piece of that info? Now that I've been such a good girl and given you all mine."

"Go for it," I said. "Can't swear I'll answer, but go ahead and ask."

"How did you hear about that card?"

"How do you think?"

"Ah," Julia said. "I guess you did warn me. It's been fun, Detectives. See you around."

She stood up, automatically gave her waistband a quick roll so her skirt came above her knees. Walked out, without waiting for Houlihan.

I said, once Houlihan had skittered after her, "The card was a shock."

"That or she's good," Conway said. She was still watching the door, tapping her pen off her notebook. "And she's good."

Selena Wynne.

All gold and bloom. Huge sleepy blue eyes, cream-and-rosy face, full soft mouth. Blond hair—the real thing—curling in short raggedy ringlets like a little boy's. Nowhere near fat—Joanne had been talking out her hole—but she had curves, soft round ones, made her look older than sixteen. Lovely, Selena was; the kind of lovely that couldn't last. You could see that somewhere this summer, maybe even this afternoon, this was the loveliest she'd ever be.

You don't want to notice this stuff on a kid, your mind wants to jump away. But it matters, same as it would on a grown woman. Changes every day of her life. So you notice. Scrape the greasy feeling off your mind whatever way you can.

Posh girls' school: lovely and safe, I'd've thought, if I'd thought. Beats a council estate where buses won't go. But I was starting to see it, out of the corner of my eye: the shimmer in the air that says *danger*. Not aimed at me personally, no more than it would've been in that estate, but there.

Selena stood in the doorway, swinging the door back and forth like a little kid. Gazing at us.

Behind her Houlihan murmured, trying to nudge Selena forward. Selena didn't notice. She said, to Conway, "I remember you."

"Same here," said Conway. Her glance at me, as she headed back to her chair, said Selena hadn't clocked the Secret Place. Zero out of seven. Our card girl had self-control. "Why don't you have a seat."

Selena moved forward. Sat down, obedient and incurious. Examined me like I was a new painting on one of the easels.

I said, "I'm Detective Stephen Moran. Selena Wynne, am I right?"

She nodded. Still that gaze, lips parted. No questions, no what's-this-about, no wariness.

And no point in trying to bond with this one. I could burst my bollix trying, get the same answers as if I'd sent a list of questions by e-mail. Selena wanted nothing from me. She barely knew I was real.

Slow, I thought. Slow or sick or hurt, or whatever this year's approved words are. The first snip of why Joanne's lot thought these were freaks.

I said, "Can you tell me what you did yesterday evening?"

Same story as the other three, or bits of it. She wasn't sure who'd asked for permission, who'd left the art room; looked vague at me when I asked if she'd gone to the toilet. Agreed that she might've done, but agreed like she was saying it to make me happy, being kind because it didn't matter to her either way.

She hadn't looked at the Secret Place, any time during the evening. I asked, "Have you put up any cards there?"

Selena shook her head.

"No? Never?"

"I don't really get the Secret Place. I don't even like reading it."

"Why not? You don't like secrets? Or you figure they should stay secret?"

She wove her fingers together, watched them fascinated, the way babies do. Soft eyebrows pulling together, just a touch. "I just don't like it. It bothers me."

I said, "So this isn't yours." Slapped the photo into her hands.

Her fingers were so loose, the photo fell right through them, spun to the ground. She just watched it fall. I had to pick it up for her.

It got us nothing, this time. Selena held it and gazed at it for so long, not a budge in that sweet peaceful face, I started wondering had she copped what it meant.

"Chris," she said, in the end. I felt Conway twitch, *No shit Sherlock.*

I said, "Someone put that up in the Secret Place. Was it you?"

Selena shook her head.

"Selena. If it was, you're not in any trouble. We're only delighted to have it. But we need to know."

Another headshake.

She was mist-smooth, your hand went right through her without touching. No cracks to jimmy, no loose threads to pull. No way in.

I asked, "Then who do you think it was?"

"I don't know." Puzzled look, like I was a weirdo to ask.

"If you had to guess."

Selena did her best to come up with something; trying to make me happy again. "Maybe it was a joke?"

"Would any of your friends play a joke like that?"

"Julia and Holly and Becca? No."

"What about Joanne Heffernan and her friends? Would they?"

"I don't know. I don't understand most of what they do." The mention of them slid a faint frown across Selena's forehead, but a second later it had faded.

I said, "Who do you think killed Chris Harper?"

Selena thought about that for a long time. Sometimes her lips moved, like she was about to start a sentence but then it fell out of her mind. Conway at my shoulder, sizzling with impatience.

In the end Selena said, "I don't think anyone's ever going to know."

Her voice had turned clear, strong. For the first time, she was looking at us like she saw us.

Conway said, "Why not?"

"There are things like that. Where no one ever knows what happened."

Conway said, "Don't you underestimate us. We're planning on finding out exactly what happened."

Selena gazed at her. "OK," she said, mildly. Passed the photo back to me.

I said, "If you had to pick one thing to tell me about Chris, what would it be?"

Selena turned back to vague. Drifted off into the sunlight like the dust motes, lips parted. I waited.

What felt like a long time later, she said, "Sometimes I see him."

She sounded sad. Not scared, not trying to scare us, impress us, nothing. Just so sad.

Twitch from Houlihan. Sound of Conway clamping back a snort.

I said, "Yeah? Where?"

"Different places. On the second-floor landing, once, sitting on the windowsill texting someone. Running laps around the Colm's playing field, during a match. Once on the grass outside our window, late at night, throwing a ball up in the air. He's always doing something. It's like he's trying to get all the things done that he'll never have a chance to do, get them done as fast as he can. Or like he's still trying to be like the rest of us, like maybe he doesn't realize . . ."

A sudden catch of breath that lifted Selena's chest. "Oh," she said quietly, on the sigh out. "Poor Chris."

Not slow, not sick. I had practically forgotten even thinking that. Selena did things to the air, slowed it to her pace, tinted it her pearly colors. Brought you with her, strange places.

I said, "Any idea why you see him? Were you close, yeah?"

A flash across Selena's face, as she raised her head. Just that one flash, there and gone in a blink, too fast to catch and hold. Something sharp, shining through the haze like silver.

"No," she said.

That second, I would've sworn to two things. Somewhere, down some tangled thread we might never follow, Selena was at the heart of this case. And I was going to get my fight.

I did puzzled. "I thought you were going out with him."

"No."

Nothing more.

"Then why do you think you see him? If you weren't close."

Selena said, "I haven't worked that out yet."

Conway moved again. "When you figure it out, you go right ahead and let us know."

Selena's eyes shifted to her. "OK," she said, peaceably.

Conway said, "Have you got a boyfriend?"

Selena shook her head.

"Why not?"

"I don't want one."

"Why not?"

Nothing. Conway said, "What happened to your hair?"

Selena lifted a hand to her head, puzzled. "Oh," she said. "That. I cut it."

"How come?"

She considered that. "It felt like the right thing."

Conway said, again, "How come?"

Silence. Selena's mouth had gone loose again. She wasn't ignoring us; simpler. She had let go of us.

We were done. We gave her our cards, sent her drifting out the door with Houlihan, no backward glance.

Conway said, "Another one we can't rule out."

"Yeah."

"Chris Harper's ghost," Conway said, shaking her head, disgusted. "For fuck's *sake*. And there's McKenna upstairs, giving herself pats on the back because her and her shrine got rid of all that carry-on. I'd love to tell her, just to see her face."

And, last of all, Holly.

Holly had changed her angle—for Conway or for Houlihan, no way to tell. She was all good little schoolgirl, straight back, hands folded in front of her. When she came in the door, she practically curtsied.

It occurred to me, a bit late, that I had no clue what Holly wanted off me.

"Holly," I said. "You remember Detective Conway. We both really appreciate you bringing in that card." Solemn nod from Holly. "We've just got a few more questions to ask you."

"Course. No problem." She sat down, crossed her ankles. I swear her eyes had got bigger and bluer.

"Can you tell us what you did yesterday evening?"

Same story as the other three, only smoother. No nudging needed here, no going back to correct herself. Holly reeled it off like she'd been rehearsing. Probably she had.

I said, "Have you ever put any secrets up on the board?"

"No."

"Never?"

Quick spark, the impatient Holly I knew, through all that demure. "Secrets are *secret*. That's the point. And no way is it totally anonymous, not if someone really wants to track you down. Half the cards up there, everyone knows who they are."

Daddy's daughter: watch your back, always. "So who do you think put up this card?"

Holly said, "You've narrowed it down to us and Joanne's lot."

"Say we have. Who would you guess?"

She thought, or pretended to. "Well. It obviously wasn't me or my friends, or I'd have told you already."

"You sure you'd know?"

Spark. "*Yes*, I'm sure. OK?"

"Fair enough. Which of the others would you bet on?"

"It's not Joanne, because she'd have made a total incredible drama out of the whole thing—probably she'd have fainted in assembly and you'd have had to go talk to her in her hospital bed, or whatever. And Orla's way too stupid to think of this. So that leaves Gemma and Alison. If I have to guess . . ."

She was loosening, the longer we talked. Conway was staying well out, head down. I said, "Go for it."

"Well. OK. Gemma thinks her and Joanne run the universe. If she knew something, she probably wouldn't tell you at all, but *if* she did, it'd be straight out. With her dad sitting in—he's a solicitor. So I'd guess Alison. She's scared of basically everything; if she knew something, she'd never have the guts to go straight to you."

Holly snatched a glance at Conway, made sure she was writing this down. "Or," she said. "Probably you've thought of this. But someone could have got one of Joanne's gang to put that card up for her."

"Would they do it?"

"Joanne wouldn't. Or Gemma. Orla totally would, but she'd tell Joanne before she even did it. Alison might. If she did, though," Holly added, "she won't tell you."

"Why not?"

"Because. Joanne would be *way* pissed off if she found out Alison had put up that card and not told her. So she won't let on."

This was giving me the head-staggers, keeping it straight who would do what to who if which. Fair play to teenage girls; I'd never have been able for it.

Conway said, "If she put it up, we'll find out."

Holly nodded gravely. All faith in the big brave detectives, coming along to make everything OK.

I said, "What about Chris's death? Who would you guess was responsible for that?"

I was waiting for the prank-gone-bad story, rattled off nice and neat with Holly's own fancy twirls on top. Instead she said, "I don't *know*."

The clamp of frustration said it was true. "Not Colm's guys messing about, and it went wrong?"

"I know some people think that. But that would've probably been a whole bunch of them, and I'm sorry, at least three or four guys managing to keep their mouths shut and keep their stories straight and not slip up even once? I don't think so." Holly's eyes went to Conway. She said, "Not if you questioned them the way you questioned us."

I lifted the photo. Said, "Someone managed to keep her mouth shut this long."

That spark of irritation again. "Everyone thinks girls blab everything, yap yap yap, like idiots. That's total crap. Girls keep secrets. Guys are the ones who can't keep their mouths shut."

"There's a lot of girls blabbing on the Secret Place."

"Yeah, and if it wasn't there, they wouldn't blab. That's what it's for: to get us spilling our guts." A glance at Houlihan. Sweetly: "I'm sure it's very valuable in lots of ways."

I said, "Pick one thing to tell me about Chris. Something important."

I saw the breath lift Holly's chest, like she was bracing herself. She said, clear and cool, "He was a prick."

Protest noise from Houlihan. No one cared.

I said, "You know I'm going to need more detail on that one."

"He only cared about what he wanted. Most of the time that was fine, because what he wanted was for everyone in the world to *like* him, so he was all about being nice. But sometimes, like when he could make everyone laugh by slagging off someone who wasn't important? Or when he wanted something and he couldn't get it?" Holly shook her head. "Not so nice."

"Give me an example."

She thought, choosing. "OK," she said. Still cool, but an underline like anger in her voice. "This one time, a load of us were down at the Court, us and some Colm's guys. We're in line at this café, and this girl Elaine orders the last chocolate muffin, right? Chris is behind her, and he goes, 'Hey, I'm having that,' and Elaine's like, 'Uh-uh, too slow.' And Chris goes, loud, so everyone can hear him, 'Your arse doesn't need any more muffins.' All the guys start laughing. Elaine goes *scarlet*, and Chris pokes her in the arse and goes, 'You've got enough muffins in there to start your own bakery. Can I have a bite?' Elaine just turns around and practically *runs* out of the place. The guys are all yelling after her, 'Shake it, baby! Work the wobble!' and everyone's laughing."

Going by what Conway had said, this was the first time anyone had talked about Chris anything like this. I said, "Lovely."

"Right? Elaine wouldn't go anywhere she might see Colm's guys for, like, weeks, and I think she's still on a diet—and just by the way, she wasn't even fat to begin with. And the thing is, Chris didn't need to do that. I mean, it was just a *muffin*, it wasn't the last tickets to the rugby World Cup final. But Chris thought Elaine should've backed down the second he wanted it. So when she didn't"—twist of Holly's mouth—"he punished her. Like he figured she deserved."

I said, "Elaine what?"

A beat, but it was easy to check. "Heaney."

"Anyone else Chris was a prick to?"

Shrug. "It's not like I was taking notes. Maybe most people didn't notice it, because like I said, it was only sometimes, and mostly he made people laugh doing it. He made it seem like just messing, just fun. But Elaine noticed. And anyone else he did it to, I bet they noticed."

Conway said, "Last year you didn't say Chris was a prick. You said you hardly knew him but he seemed like an OK guy."

Holly examined that. Said, picking her words, "I was younger then. Everyone thought Chris was nice, so I figured probably he was. I didn't really get what he was doing, till later."

Lie: the lie Conway had been waiting for.

Conway pointed at the photo in my hand. "So why'd you bring us this? If Chris was such a prick, why do you give a damn if whoever killed him gets caught?"

Good-girl gaze. "My dad's a detective. He'd want me to do the right thing. Whether I liked Chris or not."

Lie again. I know Holly's da. Doing the good-boy thing for its own sake isn't on his horizon. He never did anything in his life without an agenda.

Got fuck-all out of her, Conway had said. *Like pulling teeth.* Last year, Holly hadn't wanted the killer caught, or hadn't cared enough to stick her neck out. This year, she cared. I needed to find why.

"Holly," I said. Leaned forward, close, held her eyes: *It's me, talk to me.* "There's a reason why you're so into getting this solved, all of a sudden. You need to tell me what it is. You have to know from your da: anything like that could help us out, even if you don't see how."

Holly said, straight on and no flinch, "I don't know what you mean. There's no *reason*. I'm just trying to do the right thing." To Conway: "Can I go?"

"You got a boyfriend?" Conway asked.

"No."

"Why not?"

Angel face. "I'm *so* too busy. With school and everything."

"Such a good little student," Conway said. "You can go." To Houlihan: "All eight of them. In here."

When they were gone, Conway said, "If Holly knew who killed Chris. Would she go to you or her da? Tell someone straight out?"

Or would she make up a card to bring me. I said, "Maybe not. She's been a witness before, it wasn't a great experience; she might not be on for doing it again. But if she had something she wanted to give us, she'd make good and sure we got it. Anonymous letter, probably, with all the details laid out nice and clear. Not a something-and-nothing hint like that card."

Conway thought, pen flicking between two fingers. Nodded. "Fair enough. Tell you what I noticed, but. Your Holly talks like, whoever put up the card, she wanted it to get to us. She's assuming this card wasn't just meant to get a secret off someone's chest; this girl wanted to tell us something, and this was the best way she could find."

She wasn't my Holly. That was getting obvious, to me anyway. I didn't say it.

I said, "Holly could be feeling bad about coming to me. That age, taking something to adults is a big deal; makes you a rat, and that's about the dirtiest thing you can be. So she's convincing herself the girl wanted her to do it."

"Could be. Or she could know for sure." Conway tapped her pen up and down between her teeth. "If she does, what's the odds of getting it out of her?"

Two hopes: Bob and no. Unless Holly wanted to tell us, and was waiting for a moment we couldn't see.

I said, "I'll get it out of her."

Conway's eyebrow said *We'll see*. She said, "I want you to see them together. I'll do the talking this time. You just watch."

I leaned on a windowsill, sun warming my back through my jacket. Conway moved, back and forth across the front of the art room in an even long-legged stroll, hands in trouser pockets, while the girls filed in.

They settled, like birds. Holly's lot by the windows, Joanne's lot by the door. No one looking across the gap.

Slouched and fidgeted in their chairs; batted looks, eyebrow-lifts, whispers back and forth. They had thought we were done with them, had dumped us out of their minds. Some of them, anyway.

Conway said, over her shoulder to Houlihan, "You can wait outside. Thanks for your help."

Houlihan opened and shut her mouth, made a small-animal noise, scuttled off. The girls had stopped whispering. Houlihan gone meant the fib of school protection gone; they were all ours.

They looked different, a blurry streak. Like the Secret Place, the strobe of it: I couldn't see the separate girls any more, just all those crests on blazers, all those eyes. I felt outnumbered. Outside.

"So," Conway said. "One of you lot lied to us today."

They stilled.

"At least one of you." She stopped moving. Pulled out the photo of the card, held it up. "Yesterday evening, one of you put up this card on the secrets board. Then sat here and gave us, 'Oh God no, wasn't me, never seen that before in my life.' That's fact."

Alison blinking like a tic. Joanne with her arms folded, bobbing a crossed foot, sliding a glance to Gemma that said *OMG can't believe we have to listen to this*. Orla sucking her lips, trying to kill a nerves-giggle.

Holly's lot were still. Not looking at each other. Their heads tilted inwards, like they were listening to each other, not to us. The lean of their shoulders into the center, like they were magnetized, like it would take Superman to pull one of them away.

Just something.

Conway said, "I'm talking to you. The girl who put up this card. The girl who's claiming to know who killed Chris Harper."

A twitch around the room, a shiver.

Conway started moving again, photo balanced between her fingertips. "You think lying to us is the same as telling your teacher you left your homework on the bus, or telling your parents you didn't sneak a drink at the disco. Wrong. It's nothing like that. This isn't small-time bullshit that'll vanish when you leave school. This is real."

All their eyes following Conway. Pulled by her; hungry.

She was their mystery. Not like me, not like guys, an alien mystery they were learning to barter and bargain with, a thing they knew to want but didn't know why. Conway was theirs. She was a woman, grown: she knew things. How to wear what suited her, how to have sex right or how to turn it down, how to get her bills paid, how to balance through the wild world outside the school walls. The water where they were dipping their toes, she was over her head in it and swimming.

They wanted to get closer to her, finger her sleeves. They were judging her hard, deciding did she come up to the mark. Wondering if they would, someday. Trying to see the precarious trail that led from them to her.

"I'm gonna spell this out for you: if you know who murdered Chris, then you're in serious danger. Danger like, you could get killed." She flicked the photo through the air, a sharp snap. "You think this card is gonna stay a secret? If the rest of this lot here haven't spread it round the school already, they will by the end of today. How long is it gonna take for word to get back to the killer? How long is it gonna take him or her to work out who his problem is? And what do you think a killer does about that kind of problem?"

Her voice was good. Straight, clipped, intent. Adult to adult: she'd been paying attention to what worked for me. "You're in danger. Tonight. Tomorrow. Every second, right up until you tell us what you know. Once you've done that, the killer's got no reason to go after you. But up until then . . ."

A shiver again, a ripple. Joanne's lot swapping those covert sideways checks. Julia scraping something off a knuckle, eyes down.

Conway pacing faster. "If you made up this card for the laugh, you're in just as much danger. The killer doesn't know you were mucking about. He, or she, can't afford to take risks. And as far as she's concerned, you're a risk."

She snapped the photo again. "If this card is bogus, probably you're worried about coming clean in case you get in hassle, with us or with the school. Forget that. Yeah, me and Detective Moran, we'll give you a lecture about wasting police time. Yeah, you'll probably end up in detention. That's a lot better than ending up dead."

Joanne leaned sideways to Gemma, whispered something in her ear, not even trying to hide it. Smirked.

Conway stopped. Stared.

Joanne still smirking. Gemma fish-faced, trying to work out whether to smile or not; work out who she was more afraid of.

It needed to be Conway.

Conway moved fast, right up to Joanne's chair, leaning in. She looked ready to head-butt.

"Am I talking to you?"

Joanne staring back, slack-lipped with disdain. "Ex*cuse* me?"

"Answer the question."

The other girls' eyes had come up. The arena eyes you get in classrooms when trouble starts, waiting to see who bleeds.

Joanne's eyebrows lifting. "Um, I have literally no clue what it even means?"

"I'm only talking to one person here. If that's you, then you need to shut up and listen. If it's not, then you need to shut up because no one's talking to you."

Round Conway's patch of rough and mine, someone disses you, you punch hard and fast and straight to the face, before they see weakness and sink their teeth into it. If they back off, you're a winner. Out in the rest of the world, people back off from that punch, too, but that doesn't mean you've won. It means they've filed you under Scumbag, under Animal, under Stay Far From.

Conway had to know that, or she'd never have got this far. Something—this girl, this school, this case—had thrown her. She was fucking up.

Not my problem. I swore it the day I got my acceptance to cop college: that kind of rough wasn't my problem any more, never again, not that way. Mine to handcuff and throw in the back seat of my car; not mine to give a damn about, not mine like we had anything in common. Conway wanted to fuck up, let her.

Joanne was still wearing that openmouthed sneer. The others were leaning in, waiting for the kill. The sun felt like a hot iron pressed against the back of my jacket.

I moved, on the windowsill. Conway swung round, midway through taking a breath to reef Joanne out of it. Caught my eye.

Tiny tilt of my chin, just a fraction. Warning.

Conway's eyes narrowed. She turned back to Joanne, slower. Shoulders easing.

Smile. Steady sticky voice, like talking to a stupid toddler.

"Joanne. I know it's hard for you, not being the center of attention. I know you're only dying to throw a tantrum and scream, 'Everybody look at me!' But I bet if you try your very best, you can hang on for just a few more minutes. And when we're done here, your friends can explain to you why this was important. OK?"

Joanne's face was pure poison. She looked forty.

"Can you manage that for me?"

Joanne thumped back in her chair, rolled her eyes. "What*ever*."

"Good *girl*."

The circle of arena eyes, appreciative: we had a winner. Julia and Holly were both grinning. Alison looked terrified and over the moon.

"Now," Conway said, turning back to the rest of them—Joanne was dismissed, done. "You; whoever you are. I know you enjoyed that, but fact is, you've got the same problem. You're not taking the killer seriously. Maybe because you don't actually know who it is, so he or she doesn't feel real. Maybe because you do know who it is, and he or she doesn't look all that dangerous."

Joanne was staring at the wall, arms twisted into a knot of sulk. The rest of the girls were all Conway's. She had done it: come up to the mark for them.

She held up the photo in a slash of sun, Chris laughing and radiant. "Probably Chris thought the same thing. I've seen a lot of people who didn't take killers seriously. Mostly I saw them at their post-mortems."

Her voice was steady and grave again. When she stopped, no one breathed. The breeze through the open window rattled the blinds.

"Me and Detective Moran, we're going to get some lunch. After that, we'll be in the boarders' wing for an hour or two." That got a reaction. Elbows shifting on desks, spines snapping straight. "Then we've got other places to be. What I'm telling you is, you've got maybe three hours left where you're safe. The killer's not gonna come after you while we're on the grounds. Once we leave . . ."

Silence. Orla's mouth was hanging open.

"If you've got something to tell us, you can come find us any time this afternoon. Or if you're worried someone'll notice you going, you can ring us, even text us. You've all got our cards."

Conway's eyes moving across the faces, coming down on each one like a stamp.

"You, who I've been talking to: this is your chance. Grab it. And until you have, you look after yourself."

She tucked the photo back into her jacket pocket; tugged down her jacket, checked to make sure the line fell just right. "See you soon," she said.

And walked out the door, not looking back. She didn't give me any heads-up, but I was right behind her all the same.

Outside, Conway tilted her ear towards the door. Listened to the urgent fizz of two sets of talk behind it. Too low to hear.

Houlihan, hovering. Conway said, "In you go. Supervise."

When the door closed behind Houlihan she said, "See what I meant about Holly's gang? Something there."

Watching me. I said, "Yeah. I see it."

Brief nod, but I saw Conway's neck relax: relief. "So. What is it?"

"Not sure. Not yet. I'd have to spend more time with them."

Sniff of a laugh, dry. "Bet you would." She headed off down the corridor, at that fast swinging pace. "Let's eat."

10

In the middle of the Court, the fountain has been shut off and the huge Christmas tree is up, stories high, alive with light twirling on glass and tinsel. On the speakers, a woman with a little-kid voice is chirping "I Saw Mommy Kissing Santa Claus." The air smells so good, cinnamon and pine and nutmeg, you want to bite into it, you can feel the soft crunch between your teeth.

It's the first week of December. Chris Harper—coming out of the Jack Wills shop on the third floor in the middle of a gang of guys, bag of new T-shirts over his shoulder, arguing about *Assassin's Creed II*, hair glossy as chestnuts under the manic white light—has five months and almost two weeks left to live.

Selena and Holly and Julia and Becca have been Christmas shopping. Now they're sitting on the fountain edge around the Christmas tree, drinking hot chocolate and going through their bags. "I still don't have anything for my dad," Holly says, rummaging.

"I thought he was getting the giant chocolate stiletto," says Julia, stirring her drink—the coffee shop called it a Santa's Little Helper—with a candy cane.

"Ha ha, hashtag: lookslikehumorbutnot. The shoe's for my aunt Jackie. My dad's impossible."

"Jesus," Julia says, examining her drink with horror. "This tastes like toothpaste-flavored ass."

"I'll swap," Becca says, holding out her cup. "I like mint."

"What is it?"

"Gingerbread something mocha."

"No, thanks. At least I know what mine is."

"Mine's delish," Holly says. "What would actually make him happy is for me to get a GPS chip implanted, so he can track me every second. I know everyone's parents are paranoid, but I swear, he's *insane*."

"It's because of his job," Selena says. "He sees all the bad stuff that happens, so he imagines it happening to you."

Holly rolls her eyes. "Hello, he works in an *office*, most of the time. The worst thing he sees is forms. He's just mental. The other week when he came to pick me up, you know the first thing he said? I come out and he's looking up at the front of the school, and he goes, 'Those windows aren't alarmed. I could break in there in under thirty seconds.' He wanted to *go find McKenna* and tell her the school wasn't *secure*, and I don't know, make her install fingerprint scanners on every window or something. I was like, 'Just kill me now.'"

Selena hears it again: that single note of silver on crystal, so clean-edged it slices straight through the syrupy music and the cloud of noise. It falls into her hand: a gift, just for them.

"I had to *beg* him to just take me home. I was like, 'There's a night watchman, the boarders' wing has alarms on all night, I swear to God I am not going to get human trafficked, and anyway if you go bugging McKenna I'll never talk to you again,' and finally he went OK, he'd leave it. I was like, 'You keep asking why I always take the bus instead of letting you pick me up? *This* is why.'"

"I've changed my mind," Julia says to Becca, making a face and wiping her mouth. "Swap. Yours can't be worse than this."

"I should just get him a lighter," Holly says. "I'm sick of pretending I don't know he smokes."

Selena says, "I've been thinking about something."

"Ew," Becca says, to Julia. "You were right. It's like little kids' medicine."

"Minty ass. Bin it. We can share this one."

Selena says, "I think we should start getting out at night."

The others' heads turn.

"Out like what?" Holly asks. "Like out of our room, like to the common room? Or *out* out?"

"Out out."

Julia says, eyebrows up, "*Why?*"

Selena thinks about that. She hears all the voices from when she was little, soothing, strengthening: *Don't be scared, not of monsters, not of witches, not of big dogs.* And now, snapping loud from every direction: *Be scared, you have to be scared,* ordering like this is your one absolute duty. Be scared you're fat, be scared your boobs are too big and be scared they're too small. Be scared to walk on your own, specially anywhere quiet enough that you can hear yourself think. Be scared of wearing the wrong stuff, saying the wrong thing, having a stupid laugh, being uncool. Be scared of guys not fancying you; be scared of guys, they're animals, rabid, can't stop themselves. Be scared of girls, they're all vicious, they'll cut you down before you can cut them. Be scared of strangers. Be scared you won't do well enough in your exams, be scared of getting in trouble. Be scared terrified petrified that everything you are is every kind of wrong. Good girl.]

At the same time, in a cool untouched part of her mind, she sees the moon. She feels the shimmer of what it might look like in their own private midnight.

She says, "We're different now. That was the whole point. So we need to be doing something different. Otherwise . . ."

She doesn't know how to say what she sees. That moment in the glade sliding away, blurring. Them dulling slowly back to normal.

"Otherwise it's just about what we *don't* do, and we'll end up going back to the way things were before. There needs to be something we actually *do*."

Becca says, "If we get caught, we'll get expelled."

"I know," Selena says. "That's part of the point. We're too good. We always *behave* ourselves."

"Speak for yourself," Julia says, and sucks gingerbread something mocha off her hand with a pop.

"You do too—yeah, Jules, you *do*. Snogging a couple of guys and having a can or a cigarette sometimes, that doesn't count. Everyone does that. Everyone *expects* us to do it; even adults, they'd be more worried about us if we *didn't* do it. Nobody except Sister Cornelius actually thinks it's a big deal, and she's insane."

"So? I don't actually *want* to rob banks or shoot up heroin, thanks. If that makes me a goody-goody, I'll live with it."

"So," Selena says, "we only ever do stuff we're supposed to do. Either stuff we're supposed to do because our parents or the teachers say so, or stuff we're supposed to do because we're teenagers and all teenagers do it. I want to do something we're not supposed to do."

"An original sin," Holly says, through a marshmallow. "I like it. I'm in."

"Oh, Jesus, you too? For Christmas I want friends who aren't freaks."

"I feel criticized," Holly says, hand to her heart. "Should I use my Ds?"

"Don't be Defensive," Becca drones, in Sister Ignatius's voice. "Don't be Despondent. Take a Deep breath and be a Dickhead."

"It's OK for you," Julia tells Holly. "If you get kicked out, your dad'll probably give you a *prize*. My parents will freak. The fuck. *Out*. And they won't be able to decide who was the bad influence on who, so they'll just play it safe and never let me see any of you again."

Becca is folding up a silk scarf that she already knows her mother will never wear. She says, "My parents would freak out too. I don't care."

Julia snorts. "Your mother would be *delighted*. If you can convince her that you were heading to a gang bang in a coke den, you'll make her *year*." Becca is not what her parents had in mind. Usually she practically curls into a ball when they come up.

"Yeah, but having to find me a new school would be hassle. They'd have to fly home and everything. And they hate hassle." Becca shoves the scarf back in her bag. "So they actually would completely freak out. And I still don't care. I want to go out."

"Look at that," Julia says, amused, leaning back on one hand to examine Becca. "Look who's got ballsy all of a sudden. Good for you, Becs." She raises the cup. Becca shrugs, embarrassed. "Look: I'm so on for an original sin. But could we please make it, like, a good one? Call me a pussy, but getting expelled in exchange for what, exactly? Getting a cold up my gee sitting on a lawn where I can already sit any day I want to? Not exactly my idea of a good time."

Selena knew Julia would be the hardest to convince. "Look," she says, "I'm scared of getting caught too. My dad wouldn't care if I got expelled, but my mum would lose her *mind*. But I'm so sick of being scared of stuff. We need to do something we're scared of."

"I'm not *scared*. I'm just not *stupid*. Can't we just, like, dye our hair purple or—"

"Totally original," Holly says, flicking an eyebrow.

"Yeah, fuck you. Or have a twitch every time we talk to Houlihan—"

Even to Julia it sounds weaksauce. "That's not scary," Becca says. "I want something scary."

"I liked you better before you grew a pair. Or, I don't know, Photoshop Menopause McKenna's head onto a still from 'Gangnam Style' and stick it on the—"

"We've already done stuff like that before," Selena points out. "It has to be *different*. See? It's harder than it sounds."

"What are we even going to *do* out there?"

Selena shrugs. "I don't know yet. Maybe nothing special. That's not even the point."

"Right. 'Sorry I got expelled, Mum, Dad, I actually don't have a clue what I was even doing out there, but dyeing my hair purple wasn't *original* enough—'"

"Hi," says Andrew Moore. He's grinning down at them from between two matching mates, like they were expecting him, like they beckoned him over. Becca realizes: it's the way they're all sprawled on the fountain edge, loose, legs outstretched, leaning back on their hands. It counts as an invitation.

And Andrew Moore answered, Andrew Moore Andrew Moore all rugby shoulders and Abercrombie and those super-blue eyes that everyone talks about. The rush comes first, the breathtaking tingling surge like sweetness and bubbles cascading onto their tongues. It's *Oh God does he could he is it me*, exploding up your spine. It's his broad hands glowing now that they could wind around yours, his hard-cut mouth electric with maybe kisses. It's you snapping to sit just right, offering up boobs and legs and everything you have, cool and casual and heart slamming. It's you and Andrew Moore sauntering hand in hand down the endless neon corridors, king and queen of the Court, every girl turning at once to gasp and envy. "Hi," they say up to him, dazzled, and shiver when he sits down on the fountain edge beside Selena, when his sidekicks flank Julia and Holly. This is it, this is the trumpet blast and all flags flying that ever since the first of first year the Court has been promising, this is its magic finally unveiled and theirs for the taking.

And then it's gone. Andrew Moore is just some guy who actually none of them even like.

"So," he says, smiling, and leans back to enjoy the adoration.

Holly says, before she knows she's going to, "We're in the middle of a conversation here. Give us a sec."

Andrew laughs, because obviously that was a joke. His sidekicks join in. Julia says, "No, seriously."

The sidekicks are still laughing, but it's dawning on Andrew that he's having a brand-new experience. "Whoa," he says. "Are you, like, telling us to get lost?"

"Come back in five minutes," Selena offers. "We just need to work something out."

Andrew is still smiling, but those super-blue eyes aren't nice any more. He says, "Group PMS, yeah?"

"OMG, that's so *weird*," Holly says. "We were just talking about originality. You're not into it, no?"

Julia snorts into Becca's gingerbread drink. "And we were just talking about how half of Kilda's is dykes," Andrew says. "You're not into guys, no?"

"Can we stay and watch?" one of the sidekicks asks, grinning.

"I'm so confused," Julia says. "You guys never want to actually have conversations with each other? You only hang out together so you can swap blow jobs?"

"Hey," the other sidekick says. "Fuck off."

"OhmyGod, great chat-up line," says, of all the people in the whole world, Becca. "I totally fancy you now."

Julia and Holly and Selena stare at her and start to laugh. After a stunned second, Becca does too.

"Who gives a fuck who you fancy?" the sidekick demands. "Ugly bitch."

"That's rude," Selena says, trying so hard to be serious through the giggles that she makes the others even worse.

"Shoo," says Julia, waving. "Bah-bye."

"You're freaks," Andrew tells them, with finality; he's much too secure to be wounded, but he disapproves deeply. "You need some serious attitude adjustment. Come on, guys."

And he and his sidekicks get up and stride off down the Court, with guys scattering and girls gazing in their wake. Even their arses look displeased.

"OhmyGod," Selena says, hand over her mouth. "Did you see his *face?*"

"Once we finally got through to him," Julia says. "I've explained things to *fish* faster," which hits them all with another tornado of laughter. Becca is clutching a branch of Christmas tree to stop herself falling off the fountain edge.

"The *walk,*" Holly manages, pointing after the guys, "look, look how they're walking, it's like *Our balls are just too huge for those chicks to handle, they don't even fit between our legs*—"

Julia jumps up and does the walk, and Becca actually does fall off the fountain edge, and they scream so loud with laughter that the security guard comes over to frown at them. Holly tells him Becca has epilepsy and if he throws her out he'll be discriminating against the disabled, and he drifts off again, still frowning over his shoulder but without a lot of conviction.

Finally the giggles ebb. They look at each other, still grinning, amazed at themselves, shaken by their own daring.

"Now that was original," Julia tells Selena. "You have to admit. And, let's face it, kind of scary."

"Exactly," Selena says. "Do you want to keep on being able to do that? Or do you want to go back to almost wetting yourself if Andrew Moore even notices you exist?"

The heliumy woman is finishing up "All I Want for Christmas Is My Two Front Teeth." In the second before "Santa Baby" kicks in, Holly catches a flash of another song, just half a brushstroke of it somewhere far away, maybe outside the Court: *I've got so far, I've got so far left to*—and gone.

Julia sighs and holds out her hand for Becca's gingerbread thing. She says, "If you think I'm sliding down a bedsheet out our window like some chick in a shit movie, you are so very fucking wrong."

"I don't," Selena says. "You heard what Hol's dad said. The front windows aren't alarmed."

Becca does it. The others were taking for granted it would be Holly or Selena, in case the nurse notices the key gone missing; Holly is the best liar, and no one ever thinks Selena's done anything wrong, while Julia is always one of the first people teachers think of, even for things that would never occur to her. When Becca says, "I want to do it," they're taken aback. They try to convince her—Selena gently, Holly delicately, Julia bluntly—that this is a bad idea and she should leave it to the experts, but she digs her heels in and points out that she's even less likely to be suspected than Selena, given that she genuinely never has done anything worse than sharing homework and everyone thinks she's a huge goody-goody lick-arse, and that might as well be useful for once. In the end the others understand that she's not budging.

They coach her, after lights-out. "You need to be sick enough that she keeps you in her office for a while," Julia says, "but not sick enough that she sends you back here. What you want is something she'll want to keep an eye on."

"But not too much of an eye," Selena says. "You don't want her hovering."

"Exactly," says Julia. "Maybe you think you're going to puke, but you're not sure. And you think probably you'll be fine if you just lie still for a while."

They've left their curtains open. Outside it's below freezing, frost patterning the edges of the windowpane, the sky a thin sheet of ice laid over the stars. The shot of cold air hits Becca like it's been fired straight through the glass from the huge outside, wild and magic, pungent with foxes and juniper.

Holly says, "But don't act like you want to puke. That looks fake. Act like you *don't* want to puke. Think about trying your hardest to hold it in."

"Are you sure about this?" Selena asks. She's propped up on one elbow, trying to see Becca's face.

"If you're not," Holly says, "no probs. Just say it now."

Becca says, "I'm doing it. Stop asking me."

Julia catches a glance and the tip of a smile from Selena: *See, our shy Becca, this is what I meant*—"Good for you, Becsie," she says, reaching across the space between the beds to high-five Becca. "Make us proud."

The next day, lying on the too-narrow bed in the nurse's office, listening to the nurse hum Michael Bublé as she does paperwork at her desk, Becca feels the wild cold of the key strike deep into her palm, and smells running vixens and berries and icy stars.

Before lights-out they lay out their clothes on their beds and start getting dressed. Layers of tops—outside the window, the night sky is clear and frozen; sweatshirts; heavy jeans; pajamas to go over it all, until the moment comes. They fold their coats away under their beds, so they won't need to rattle hangers or squeak wardrobe doors. They line up their Uggs by the door so they won't have to fumble.

Now that it's turning real, it feels like a game, some geeky role-playing thing where someone will give them fake swords and they'll have to run around smacking imaginary orcs. Julia is singing "Bad Romance," cocking a hip and whirling a jumper by one sleeve like a stripper; Holly joins in with a pair of leggings on her head, Selena whips her hair in circles. They feel stupid, and they're turning giddy to dodge that.

"Is this OK?" Becca asks, spreading her arms.

The other three stop singing and look at her: dark-blue jeans and dark-blue hoodie, the hoodie stuffed spherical with layers and the hood strings pulled so tight only the tip of her nose shows. They start to laugh.

"What?" Becca demands.

"You look like the world's fattest bank robber," Holly says, which makes them all worse.

"You're twice your size," Selena manages. "Can you even move in all that?"

"Or *see?*" says Julia. "That's just what we need: if you can't make it down the corridor without smacking into walls." Holly does Becca, lurching along blinded and unwieldy. The giggles have hold of all three of them, the helpless kind that keep going even after you run out of breath and your stomach muscles hurt.

Becca has gone red. She turns her back to them and tries to get the hoodie off, but the zip is stuck.

"Becs," Selena says. "We're only having a laugh."

"Whatever."

"Jesus," Julia says, rolling her eyes at Holly. "Chillax."

Becca yanks at the zip till it dents her fingers. "If it's just a great big joke, then why are we even bothering?"

No one answers. The laughter has faded to nothing. They glance at each other sideways on, eyes skidding away from meeting.

They're looking for a way to ditch the whole thing. They want to throw their clothes back in the wardrobe, bin the key and never mention it again, blush when they remember how near they came to making idiots of themselves. They're just waiting for someone to say the word.

Then one of the second-floor prefects slams their door open, snaps, "Stop lezzing it up and get changed, it's lights-out in like five seconds and I will so report you," and bangs the door closed again before any of them can shut their mouths.

She didn't even notice their entire outdoor wardrobes spread out on their beds, or the fact that Becca looks like an inflatable burglar. All four of them stare at each other for a second and then collapse on their beds, screaming with laughter into their duvets. And realizing they're actually going.

At lights-out they're in their beds like good little girls—if the prefect has to come back, she might be in a more observant mood. After the bell goes, the edgy giddiness starts to fade. Something else starts to show through.

They've never listened to the sounds of the school falling asleep before, not this way, ears stretched like animals'. At first the flickers are constant: a burst of giggles through the wall, a faraway squeal, a patter of slippers as someone runs to the toilet. Then they drift further apart. Then there's silence.

When the clock at the back of the main building strikes one, Selena sits up.

They don't talk. They don't flick on torches, or bedside lights: anyone going down the corridor would see the flicker through the glass above the transom. In the window the moon is enormous, more than enough. They strip off their pajamas and stuff their pillows under their sheets, pull on final jumpers and coats, deft and synchronized as if they'd been practicing. When they're ready they stand by their beds, boots dangling from their hands. They look at each other like explorers in the doorway of a long journey, all of them caught motionless in the moment before one of them takes the first step.

"If you weirdos are serious about this," Julia says, "let's do it."

No one leaps out at them from a doorway, no stair creaks. On the ground floor Matron is snoring. When Becca fits the key into the door to the main building, it turns like the lock's been oiled. By the time they reach the maths classroom and Julia reaches up to the fastening of the sash window, they already know the watchman is asleep or on the phone and will never look their way. Boots on and out the window, one two three four quick and slick and silent, and they're standing on the grass and it's not a game any more.

The grounds are still as a set for a ballet, waiting for the first shivering run of notes from a flute; for the light girls to run in and stop, poised perfect and impossible, barely touching the grass. The white light comes from everywhere. The frost sings high in their ears.

They run. The great spread of grass rolls out to greet them and they skim down it, the crackle-cold air flowing like spring water into their mouths and running their hair straight out behind them when their hoods fall back and none of them can stop to pull them up again. They're invisible, they could stream laughing past the night watchman and tweak off his cap as they went, leave him grabbing at air and gibbering at the wild unknown that's suddenly everywhere, and they can't stop running.

Into the shadows and down the narrow paths enclosed by dark spiky weaves of branches, past leaning trunks wrapped with years of ivy, through smells of cold earth and wet layers of leaves. When they burst out of that tunnel it's into the white waiting glade.

They've never been here before. The tops of the cypresses blaze with frozen fire like great torches. There are things moving in the shadows, things that when they manage to catch a hair-thin glimpse are shaped like deer and wolves but they could be anything, circling. High in the shining column of air above the clearing, birds whirl arc-winged, long threads of savage cries trailing behind them.

The four of them open their arms and whirl too. The breath is spun out of them and the world rocks around them and they keep going. They're spun out of themselves, spun to silver dust flying, they're nothing but a rising arm or a curve of cheek in and out of ragged white bars of light. They dance till they collapse.

When they open their eyes they're in the glade they know again. Darkness, and a million stars, and silence.

The silence is too big for any of them to burst, so they don't talk. They lie on the grass and feel their own moving breath and blood. Something white and luminous is arrowing through their bones, the cold or the moonlight maybe, they can't tell for sure; it tingles but doesn't hurt. They lie back and let it do its work.

Selena was right: this is nothing like the thrill of necking vodka or taking the piss out of Sister Ignatius, nothing like a snog in the Field or forging your mum's signature for ear piercing. This has nothing to do with what anyone else in all the world would approve or forbid. This is all their own.

After a long time they straggle back to the school, dazzled and rumple-haired, heads buzzing. *Forever*, they say, at the threshold of the window, with their boots in their hands and the moonlight turning in their eyes. *I'll remember this forever. Yes forever. Oh forever.*

In the morning they're sprinkled with cuts and scrapes they can't remember getting. Nothing that actually hurts; just tiny mischievous reminders, winking up from their knuckles and their shins when Joanne Heffernan flips something bitchy at Holly for taking too long in the breakfast queue, or when Miss Naughton tries to make Becca cringe for not paying attention. It takes them a while to realize it's not just people being annoying; they actually are spacy, Holly actually was staring at the toast for like ever, and none of them have a clue what Naughton was on about. Their foothold has shifted; it's taking them a while to get their balance back.

"Do it again soon?" Selena says, at break time, through her juice straw.

For a second they're afraid to say yes, in case it's not the same, next time. In case that can only happen once, and they try to get it back and end up sitting in the glade getting colds up their gees and staring at each other like a pack of tossers.

They say it anyway. Something's started; it's too late to stop it. Becca picks a sliver of twig out of Julia's hair and stashes it in her blazer pocket, to keep.

11

It was gone three o'clock. Conway knew where the canteen was, poked around till she found some drudge scrubbing spotless steel, told him to make us food. He tried a hairy look but Conway's beat his. I kept an eye on him while he slapped together ham and cheese sandwiches, make sure he didn't spit in them. Conway went to a coffee machine, hit buttons. Snagged apples out of a crate.

We took the food outside. Conway led, to a low wall off to one side of the grounds, overlooking the playing field and the gardens below it. On the playing field little girls were running around swinging hockey sticks, PE teacher keeping up a string of motivational shouts. Trees threw down shadows that stopped them spotting us. Between the branch-stripes, the sun heated my hair.

"Eat fast," Conway said, parking herself on the wall. "After this, we search their rooms for whatever book those words got cut out of."

Meaning she wasn't packing me back to Cold Cases, not yet. And she wasn't heading back to base either. *A look at the noticeboard, a few chats*, we'd come for. Somewhere along the line it had turned into more. Those glimpses of something peeking out at us from behind what we were being told: neither of us wanted to leave without pulling it out into the open, getting a proper look.

Unless our girl was thick, the book wasn't in her room. But a soft tip like this one—could be nothing, could be everything—it's a rock and a hard place. Call in a full team, swarm the school grounds with searchers, come out with nothing or with some kid's messing: you're the squad joke and the gaffer's budget-waster headache, can't be trusted to make the judgment calls. Stick to whatever you and one tagalong can get done, miss the clue stuffed behind a classroom rad, miss the witness who could steer you home: you're the fool who had it handed to you on a plate and threw it away, who didn't think a dead boy was important, can't be trusted to make the judgment calls.

Conway was playing it tight, playing it careful. Not that she'd care, but I agreed with that. If our girl was smart, and the odds said she was, we wouldn't find the book either way. Stuffed in a bush a mile away by now, into a city-center bin. If she was extra smart she'd made the card weeks ago, ditched the book then, waited till it was well gone before she set things moving.

We set out the food on the wall between us. Conway ripped the cling film open and went for her sandwich. Ate like it was fast fuel, no taste. Mine was better than I'd been expecting. Nice mayo and all.

"You're good," she said, through a mouthful. Not like it was a compliment. "Give them what they want. Tailor it special for each one. Cute."

I said, "Thought that was my job. Get them comfy."

"They were that, all right. Next time maybe you can give them a pedicure and a foot massage, how's that?"

I reminded myself: *Just a few days, make your mark with the gaffer, wave bye-bye.* Said, "I thought you were gonna come in, maybe. Push them a little."

Conway flashed me a stare that said, *You questioning me?* I thought that was my answer, but after a moment she said, out to the playing field, "I interviewed the shite out of them. Last time."

"Those eight?"

"All the kids. Those eight. All their year. All Chris's year. All of them who could've known anything. A week in, the tabloids were getting their kacks in a knot, 'Cops are going easy on the rich kids, there's strings being pulled, that's why there's been no arrest'—a couple of them said right out, practically, there was a cover-up. But there was nothing like that. I went at these kids same as I'd have gone at a bunch of knackers out of the flats. Exactly the same."

"I believe you."

Her head came round fast, chin out. Looking for snide. I stayed steady.

"Costello," she said, once she relaxed again, "Costello was only horrified. The face on him; like I was mooning the nuns. Almost every interview, he'd stop the questioning and pull me outside to give me shite about what did I think I was doing, did I want to kill my career before I even got started."

I kept my mouth full. No comment.

"O'Kelly, our gaffer, he was as bad. Called me into his office twice, for a bollocking: who did I think these kids were, did I think I was dealing with the same scum I grew up with, why wasn't I spending my time looking into homeless guys and mental patients, did I know how many phone calls the commissioner was getting from pissed-off daddies, he was gonna buy me a dictionary so I could look up 'tact' . . ."

I do tact. I said, mild, "They're a different generation. They're old-school."

"*Fuck* that. They're Murder. They're trying to get a killer. That's the only thing that matters. Or that's what I thought back then."

Bitter sediment, running along the bottom of her voice.

"By that time I'd no hassle telling Costello to shove it. O'Kelly, even. The whole case was going to fuck, with my name on it. I'd've done anything. But by that time it was too late. Wherever my shot was, in there, I'd missed it."

I made some kind of noise, *Been there*. Concentrated on my sandwich.

Some cases are like that: dirty bastards. We all get them. But get one straight out of the gate, and that's what people see when they look at you: bad luck walking.

Anyone got too close to Typhoid Conway, he'd get that taint all over him. People would stay away from him, too; the Murder lads would.

Just a few days.

"So," Conway said. Swigged her coffee, balanced it on the wall. "Boils down to I've got a file full of complaints from rich guys, I don't have Costello to back me up any more, and best of all, a year on I still don't have a solve. O'Kelly gets this much of an excuse"—finger and thumb, a hair apart—"he's gonna kick my arse off this case, give it to O'Gorman or one of that shower of tossers. The only reason he hasn't done it already is he hates reassigning: says the media or the defense can spin that as the initial investigation fucked up. But they're on at him, O'Gorman and McCann, dropping the little hints about a fresh pair of eyes."

That was why Houlihan. Not to protect the kids. To protect Conway.

"This time I'm playing the long game. Those interviews weren't a waste: we've narrowed it down. Joanne, Alison, Selena, Julia as an outside chance. It's a start. Yeah, maybe we'd've got further if I'd started *pushing them*. I can't afford to chance it."

One more snap at Joanne, and there it would've been: Daddy's phone call, O'Kelly's excuse, both of our arse-kick out the door.

I felt Conway think it too. Didn't want her thanking me. Not that she probably would have, but just in case:

I said, "Rebecca's changed, since you were here last. Yeah?"

"You mean I steered you wrong."

"I mean with all of Joanne's lot, what you told me was bang on. With Rebecca, it was out of date."

"No shit. Last time, Rebecca could hardly open her mouth. Acted like she'd be happy to curl up and die, if that'd make us leave her alone. Teachers said she was like that, just shyness, she'd outgrow it."

"She's outgrown it now, all right."

"Yeah. She's got better-looking—just bones and braces, last year, looked about ten; now she's starting to come into herself. That could've upped her confidence."

I nodded at the school. "How about the rest of that lot? Have they changed?"

Conway glanced at me. "Why? You figure whoever knows something, it's gonna show?"

This whole chat, this was a test; same as the interviews, same as the search. Half of working a case together is this, table-tennising it. If that clicks, you're golden. The best partners tossing a case around sound like two halves of the same mind. Not that I was aiming that high here—smart money said no one had ever partnered like that with Conway, even if anyone had wanted to—but the click: if that wasn't there, I was going home.

I said, "They're kids. They're not tough. You think they could live with that for a year, like it was nothing?"

"Maybe, maybe not. Kids, if they can't cope with something, they'll file it away, act like it never existed. And even if they've changed, so what? This age, they're changing anyway."

I said, "Have they?"

She chewed and thought. "Heffernan's gang, nah. Just more of the same old. Even bitchier, even more alike. Thick blond geebag, slutty blond geebag, nervy blond geebag, geebaggy blond geebag, end of story. And the three lapdogs, they're even scareder of Heffernan than they were."

"We said before: someone was scared, or she wouldn't be messing about with postcards."

Conway nodded. "Yeah. And I'm hoping she's scareder now." She threw back coffee, eyes on the hockey. One of the little girls took another one down, whack to the shins, vicious enough that we heard it. "Holly and her gang, though. Back before, there was something about them, yeah. They were quirky or whatever, yeah. Now, though, Orla's an idiot but she's right: they're weird."

It took me till then to put my finger on it, what was different about them, or some of it. This: Joanne and all hers were what they thought I wanted them to be. What they thought guys wanted them to be, grown-ups wanted them to be, the world wanted them to be.

Holly's lot were what they were. When they played thick or smart-arsed or demure, it was what they wanted to play. For their reasons, not mine.

Danger again, shimmering down my back with the sun.

I thought about saying it to Conway. Couldn't work out how, without sounding like a nutter.

"Selena," Conway said, "she's the one that's changed most. Last year, she was away with the fairies, all right—you could tell she had one of those dream-catcher things over her bed, or some unicorny shite that said 'Believe in Your Dreams'—but nothing that stuck out a mile. And I put half of the spacy down to shock, specially if Chris had been her boyfriend. Now . . ." She blew out a hiss of breath between her teeth. "I met her now, I'd say she was one rich daddy away from special school."

I said, "I wouldn't."

That got Conway's eyes off the hockey. "You think she's putting it on?"

"Not that." Took me a second to say it right. "The spacy's real, all right. But I think there's more underneath, and she's using the spacy to hide it."

"Huh," Conway said. Thought back. "What Orla said about her hair, Selena's? Last year that was down to her arse. Deadly hair, real blond, wavy, the rest would've killed for it. How many girls that age wear their hair that short?"

I'm not up on teen fashion. "Not a lot?"

"When we go back in there, keep an eye out. Unless someone's had cancer, bet you Selena's the only one."

I drank my coffee. Good stuff, would've been better if Conway had cared that not everyone takes it black. I said, "How about Julia?"

Conway said, "What'd you think of her? Hard little bitch, yeah?"

"Tough enough, for her age. Smart, too."

"She's both of those, all right." Corner of Conway's mouth going up, like at least part of her approved of Julia. "Here's the thing, but. Last year, she was tougher. Hard as nails. Preliminary interview, half the other girls are bawling their eyes out, or trying to. Whether they knew Chris or not. Julia walks in with a face on her like she can't believe we're wasting her valuable time on this shit. We get to the end of the interview, I ask her does she have anything we should know, right? And she tells me—her words, and this is in front of McKenna, remember—she doesn't give a fuck who killed Chris Harper, he was just another Colm's moron and it's not like there's a shortage. McKenna goes off on some big bullshit speech about respect and compassion, and Julia yawns in her face."

"Cold," I said.

"Ice. And I'd swear it was the real thing. This year, though: there's something else there. Usually a kid puts on the tough at first, till she gets tough for real. Julia, but . . ."

She shoved in the last of her sandwich. "Here's the difference," she said, when she could talk. "See the way most of them looked at us? Hardly saw us. Julia was the same, last year. Me and Costello, far as she was concerned, we weren't people; just grown-ups. Just this background noise that you have to put up with, so you can get back to stuff that matters. I remember that, that age, except I didn't bother putting up with it."

I believed it. "I used to tune it out. Smile, nod, do my own thing."

"Yeah. But this year Julia's watching us like we're actual people, you and me." Conway finished her coffee in one long gulp. "I can't work out if that's gonna be a good thing or a bad one."

I said, "Holly?"

"Holly," Conway said. "Back when you first met her, what was she like?"

"Sharp. Stubborn. Plenty going on."

Wry flip to the corner of her mouth. "No change there, anyway. The big difference, you already picked up on. Last year, we had to drag every word out of her. This year, Little Miss Helpful, card in one hand, theory in the other, motive up her sleeve. Something's going on there." She stuffed the cling film into her coffee cup. "What d'you think of her theory? Someone else got one of these eight to put up the card for her?"

"Not a lot," I said. "You're aiming to stay anonymous, so you get someone else in on the game? Someone who isn't even one of your best mates?"

"Nah. Your Holly's just spreading the love. She wants us looking at the whole school, not focusing on her gang. You know what that makes me want to do?"

"Focus on her gang."

"Too fucking right. Even though, say one of them knows something and Holly doesn't want us identifying her: why bring in that card at all? Why not bin it, give your mate the tip-line number, keep it anonymous?" Conway shook her head. Said, again, "Something's going on there."

The tip line gets you whoever's on duty. The card had got her me. I wondered.

Conway said, "If we keep talking to Holly and her lot. She going to call Daddy?"

The thought itched my back. Frank Mackey is hard core. Even if he's on your side, you need to be watching him from more angles than you've got eyes. He was the last thing I wanted in this mix.

"Doubt it," I said. "She basically told me she doesn't want him onboard. What about McKenna?"

"Nah. You joking? He's a parent. She's up there saying rosaries that none of the parents find out we're here till we're good and gone."

The itch went; not gone, but down. "She'll be lucky," I said. "One kid phones home . . ."

"Bite your tongue. We're on McKenna's side there. For once." Conway jammed the cling film down harder. "So how about Julia and Rebecca's theory? A gang from Colm's came in here, something went wrong."

I said, "That one could play. If the lads were planning on a bit of vandalism, maybe digging another cock and balls into the grass, they could've nicked the hoe out of the stables. They're messing about, fighting or pretending to fight—guys that age, half the time there's no difference. And someone gets carried away."

"Yeah. Which puts the card on Joanne, Gemma or Orla. They're the ones going out with Colm's guys." The boyfriend question, suddenly making sense. The sardonic slant to Conway's eye said she'd seen the penny drop.

I said, "Whatever happened to Chris, it's been bothering one of the guys who was there. He doesn't want to talk to an adult, but he opens up to his girlfriend."

"Or he tells her because he thinks it'll make him sound interesting, get him into her knickers. Or he makes the whole thing up."

"We've ruled out Gemma and Orla. That leaves Joanne."

"Her fella, Andrew Moore, he was matey enough with Chris. Arrogant little prick." Snap of anger. One of those complaints had come from Andrew's da.

I said, "Did you work out how Chris got out of Colm's?"

"Yeah. Security over there was even shittier than in this place—they didn't have to worry about any of their little princes coming back pregnant after a night on the tiles. The fire door in the boarders' wing was alarmed, supposedly, but one kid was an electronics whiz, worked out how to disable the alarm. Took some doing to get it out of him, but we got there in the end." Grim smile in Conway's voice, remembering. "He got expelled."

"When'd he disable it?"

"A couple of months before the murder. And the kid, Finn Carroll, he was good mates with Chris. He said Chris knew all about the door, had snuck out plenty of times, but he wouldn't name any other names. Not a chance him and Chris were the only two, though. Julia and Rebecca could be on to something: gang of Colm's boys on the prowl, they're going to think of this place." Conway rubbed her apple to a shine on her trouser thigh. "If Chris is out for a bit of vandalism with the lads, though, what's he doing with a condom?"

I said, "Last year. Did you ask the girls were they sexually active?"

"Course we asked. They all said no. Headmistress sitting right there, staring them out of it, what else are they gonna say?"

"You think they were lying?"

"What, you figure I can tell just by looking?"

But there was a grin at the corner of her mouth. I said, "Better than I can, anyway."

"Like being back in school. 'D'you think she's Done It yet?' All we talked about, when I was that age."

"Same here," I said. "Believe me."

The grin hardened over. "I believe you, all right. And for yous, if a girl did the business, she was a slut; if she didn't, she was frigid. Either way, yous had a perfect reason to treat her like dirt."

It was a bit true; not a lot, not for me. I said, "No. Either way, she got even more exciting. If she did the do, then there was a chance you might get to have sex, and when you're a young fella that's the biggest thing in the world. If she didn't, there was a chance she might think you were special enough to do it with. That's pretty big too, believe it or not. Having a girl think you're something special."

"Smooth talker, you. Bet that got you into a lot of bras."

"I'm only telling you. You asked."

Conway thought that over, chewing apple. Decided she believed me; enough, anyway.

"If I was guessing," she said, "back then, I'd've said Julia and Gemma had had sex, Rebecca'd never even had a snog, and the rest were somewhere in between."

"Julia? Not Selena?"

"Why? Because Selena's got bigger tits, she's the slapper?"

"Jaysus! No. I wasn't noticing their . . . Ah, fuck's sake, now."

But Conway was grinning again: winding me up, and she'd snared me. "You fuck," I said, "that's disgusting, that is," and she laughed. She had a good laugh, rich, open.

She was starting to like me, whether she liked it or not. People do, mostly. Not bragging here; just saying. You have to know your strengths, in this job.

The mad part was, a bit of me was starting to like her too.

"Here's the thing," Conway said, laugh gone. "If I was guessing now, I'd guess the same again about Holly's gang."

"So?"

"The four of them. Pretty girls, right?"

"Jesus, Conway. What do you take me for?"

"I'm not calling you a perv. I'm saying when you were sixteen. Would you have been into them? Asked them out, Facebooked them, whatever kids do these days?"

When I was sixteen, I would've seen those girls like polished things in museum cases: stare all you want, get drunk on the dazzle of them, but no touching, unless you've got the tools and the balls to smash through re-inforced glass and dodge armed guards.

They looked different, now I'd seen that board. I couldn't see pretty, any more, without seeing dangerous underneath. Splinters.

I said, "They're grand. Holly and Selena are good-looking, yeah. I'd say they get plenty of attention—not from the same guys, probably. Rebecca's going to be good-looking soon enough, but when I was sixteen I might not have copped that, and she doesn't seem like great crack, so I'd have kept moving. Julia: she's no supermodel, but she's not bad, and she's got plenty of attitude; I'd've looked twice. I'd say she does OK."

Conway nodded. "That's about what I'd've said. So why no boyfriends? If I'm guessing right, why've none of them got any action in the last year?"

"Rebecca's a late bloomer. Still at boys are icky and the whole thing's embarrassing."

"Right. And the other three?"

"Boarding school. No guys. Not a lot of free time."

"Hasn't stopped Heffernan's gang. Two yeses, one no, one sort-of: that's what I'd expect, give or take. Holly's gang: no, no, no, no, straight down the line. No one takes a second to decide what to say, no one says it's compli-cated, no one's giggling and blushing, nothing. Just flat-out no."

"You figure what? They're gay?"

Shrug. "All four of them? Could be, but the odds say no. They're a close bunch, though. Scare one of them off the fellas, you'd scare off the lot."

I said, "You think someone did something to one of them."

Conway threw her apple core. She had a good arm; it skimmed long and low between the trees, smashed into a bush with a rattle that sent a couple of small birds panicking upwards. She said, "And I think something's fucked up Selena's head. And I don't believe in coincidences."

She pulled out her phone, nodded at my apple. "Finish that. I'm gonna check my messages, then we move."

Still giving the orders, but her tone had changed. I'd passed the test, or we had: the click was there.

Your dream partner grows in the back of your mind, secret, like your dream girl. Mine grew up with violin lessons, floor-to-high-ceiling books, red setters, a confidence he took for granted and a dry sense of humor no one but me would get. Mine was everything that wasn't Conway, and I would've bet hers was everything that wasn't me. But the click was there. Maybe, just for a few days, we could be good enough for each other.

I shoved the rest of my apple in my coffee cup, found my mobile too. "Sophie," Conway told me, phone to her ear. "No prints on anything. The lads in Documents say the words came out of a book, medium quality, probably fifty to seventy years old going by the typeface and the paper. Going by the focus on the photo, Chris wasn't the main subject; he was just in the background, someone cropped out the rest. Nothing on the location yet, but she's running comparisons with photos from the original investigation."

When I turned on my phone, it beeped: a text. Conway's head came round.

A number I didn't recognize. The text was so far from what I was expecting, took my eyes a second to grab hold of it.

Joanne kept the key to the boarders wing/school door taped inside the Life of St Thérèse, third year common room bookshelf. It could be gone now but it was there a year ago.

I held the phone out to Conway.

Her face went focused. She held her mobile next to mine, tapped and flicked fast at the screen.

Said, "The number's none of our girls, or it wasn't last year. None of Chris's friends, either."

All their numbers, still on her phone a year later. No thread cut, not even the finest.

I said, "I'll text back. Ask who it is."

Conway thought. Nodded.

Hi—thanks for that. Sorry, I don't have everyone's numbers, who's this?

I passed it to Conway. She read it three times, gnawing apple-juice sticky off her thumb. Said, "Go."

I hit Send.

Neither of us said it; no need. If the text was true, then Joanne and at least one other girl, probably more, had had a way to get out of the school the night Chris Harper was killed. One of them could have seen something.

One of them could have done something.

If the text was true, then today had turned into something different. Not just about finding the card girl, not any more.

We waited. Down on the playing field, the rhythm of the hockey sticks had turned ragged: the girls had spotted us, they were missing easy shots craning over their shoulders trying to pick us out of the shadows. Little feisty birds clicking and wing-flipping in and out of the trees above us. Sun fading and blooming as thin clouds shifted. Nothing.

I said, "Ring it?"

"Ring it."

It rang out. The voice mail greeting was the default one, droid woman telling me to leave a message. I hung up.

I said, "It's one of our eight."

"Oh, yeah. Anything else is way too much coincidence. And it's not your Holly. She brought you the card, she'd bring you the key."

Conway pulled out her phone again. Rang one number after another: *Hello, this is Detective Conway, just confirming that we still have the correct phone number for you, in case we need to get in touch* . . . All the voices were recorded—"School hours," Conway said, tapping; "phones have to be switched off in class"—but all of them were the right ones. None of our girls had changed her number.

Conway said, "You got a pal at any of the mobile networks?"

"Not yet." Neither did she, or she wouldn't have asked. You stockpile useful pals, build yourself a nice fat list, over time. I felt it like a thump: us, two rookies, in the middle of this.

"Sophie does." Conway was dialing again. "She'll get us the full records on that number. By the end of the day, guaranteed."

I said, "It'll be unregistered."

"Yeah, it will. But I want to know who else it's been texting. If Chris was meeting someone, he arranged it somehow. We never found out how." She slid down off the wall, phone to her ear. "Meanwhile, let's go see if Little Miss Text's fucking us around."

McKenna came out of her office all ready to wave us good-bye, wasn't a happy camper when she found out we weren't good-byeing anywhere. By now we were front-page headlines all round the school. Any minute the day girls would be heading home to tell their parents the cops were back, and McKenna's phone would start ringing. She'd been banking on being able to say this little unpleasantness was over and done with: just a few follow-up questions, Mr. and Mrs., don't worry your pretty heads, all gone now. She didn't ask how long it would be. We pretended not to hear her wanting to know.

A nod from McKenna, and the curly secretary gave us the key to the boarders' wing, gave us the combinations to the common rooms, gave us signed permission for us to search. Gave us everything we wanted, but the smile had gone. Tight face, now. Tense line between her eyebrows. Not looking at us.

That bell went again, as we came out of her office. "Come on," Conway said, lengthening her stride. "That's the end of classes. The Matron'll be opening the connecting door, and I don't want anyone getting in that common room before we do."

I said, "Combination locks on the common rooms. Were those there last year?"

"Yeah. Years, they've had those."

"How come?"

Behind the closed doors, the classrooms had exploded into gabble and scraping-back chairs. Conway took the stairs down to the ground floor at a run. "The kids leave stuff there. There's no locks on the bedroom doors, in case of fire or lesbians; the bedside tables lock, but they're tiny. So a lot of stuff winds up in the common rooms—CDs, books, whatever. With the combination, anything gets robbed, there's only a dozen people who could've done it. Easy enough to solve."

I said, "I thought no one here did stuff like that."

Wry sideways glance from Conway. " 'We don't attract that type.' Right? I said that to McKenna, said had there been problems with theft? She did the face, said no, none *whatsoever*. I said not since the combination locks, anyway, am I right? She did the face some more, pretended she didn't hear me."

Through the connecting door, standing open.

The boarders' wing felt different from the school. White-painted, cooler and silent, a bright white silence floating down the stairwell. A tinge of some scent, light and flowery. The air nudged at me like I needed to back off, let Conway go on alone. This was girls' territory.

Up the stairs—a Virgin Mary in her nook on the landing gave me an enigmatic smile—and down a long corridor, over worn red tiles, between closed white doors. "Bedrooms," Conway said. "Third- and fourth-years."

"Any supervision at night?"

"Not so's you'd notice. The Matron's room's down on the ground floor, with the little kids. Two sixth-years on this floor, prefects, but they're asleep, what're they gonna do? Anyone who wasn't a massive klutz could sneak out, no problem."

Two oak doors at the end of the corridor, one on each side. Conway went for the left-hand one. Pushed buttons on the lock, no need to look at the secretary's piece of paper.

Cozy enough to curl up in, the third-year common room. Storybook stuff. I knew better, I'd seen it on the board in black and white and every slap-sharp color, but I still couldn't picture bad things here: someone being bitch-whipped out of a conversation into one of those corners, someone snug in one of the sofas longing to cut herself.

Big squashy sofas in soft oranges and golds, a gas fire. Vase of freesias on the mantelpiece. Old wooden tables, for doing homework. Girls' bits and bobs everywhere, hair bands, ice-creamy nail polish, magazines, water bottles, half rolls of sweets. A meadow-green scarf with little white daisies hanging off the back of a chair, fine as a Communion veil, rising in the soft breeze through the window. A motion-sensor light snapped on like a warning, not a welcome: *You. Watching you.*

Two alcoves of built-in bookshelves. Ceiling-high, every shelf layers deep in books.

"Fuck's *sake*," said Conway. "They couldn't just have a telly?"

A spill of high voices down the corridor, and the door banged open behind us. We both whipped round, but the girls were smaller than our lot: three of them, jammed in the doorway, staring at me. One of them giggled.

"Out," Conway said.

"I need my *Uggs*!"

The kid was pointing. Conway picked up the boots, tossed them over. "Out."

They backed away. The whispering started before I got the door closed.

"Uggs," Conway said, pulling out her gloves. "Fucking things should be banned."

Gloves on. If that book and that key existed, the prints on them mattered.

One alcove each. Finger along the spines, skim, scoop the front row of books onto the floor and start on the back one. Fast, wanting to see something solid rise to the surface. Wanting it to be me who found it.

Conway had spotted the stare and giggle, or felt the shove in the air. She said, "Watch yourself. I was taking the piss out of you, before, but you want to be careful around this lot. That age, they're dying to fancy someone; they'll practice on any half-decent fella they can get. See that staff room? You think it's a coincidence all the guy teachers are trolls?" She shook her head. "It's to keep the crazy level down. Few hundred girls, hormones up to ninety . . ."

I said, "I'm no Justin Bieber. I'm not gonna start any riots."

That got a snort. "It doesn't take Justin Bieber. You're not a troll and you're not sixty: good enough. They want to fancy you, great, you can use that. Just don't ever be alone with any of them."

I thought of Gemma, the Sharon Stone leg-cross. I said, "I'm not planning to be."

"Hang on," Conway said, and the sudden lift in her voice had me on my feet before I knew it. "Here we go."

Low shelf, back layer, hidden away behind slick bright colors. Old hardback, dust jacket gone tatty at the edges. *St. Thérèse of Lisieux: The Little Flower and the Little Way.*

Conway pulled it out, carefully, one fingertip. Dust came with it. Sepia young one in a nun veil on the front, pudgy-faced, thin lips curved in a smile that could have been shy or sly. The back cover didn't close right.

I put two fingers on the book, top and bottom, held it steady while Conway eased open the back. The corner of the jacket flap had been folded in, taped to make a triangular pocket. Inside, when Conway gently hooked it open, was a Yale key.

Neither of us touched.

Conway said, like I'd asked, "I'm not calling it in yet. We've got nothing definitive."

This was the moment to bring in the cavalry: the full search team scouring the school, the Forensics lads taking prints to match up, the social worker in the corner of every interview. This wasn't a scrap of card, fifty/fifty chance of a bored teenager playing attention games. This was one girl, probably four, maybe eight, who had had the opportunity to be at the murder scene. This was real.

If Conway rang for the cavalry, she would have to show O'Kelly all the shiny new good stuff that justified him blowing his budget on a case turned cold. And bang, fast enough to make our heads spin, I would be headed home and she would be paired up with someone with years under his belt, O'Gorman or some other hint-dropper who would find a way to put his name on the solve, if there was a solve. Thanks for your help, Detective Moran, see you around next time someone drops a big fat clue into your hand.

I said, "We don't know for sure that this was actually the key to the connecting door."

"Exactly. I've got a copy of the real thing back at HQ, I can match it against that. Till then, I'm not calling out half the force for the key to someone's ma's booze cupboard."

"And we've only got the text girl's word on who put it here and when. It might not even have been here last May."

"Might not." Conway let the pocket drop closed. "I wanted to take this place apart, top to bottom. The gaffer said no. Said there was no evidence that anyone inside Kilda's was involved. What he meant was, all the posh mummies and daddies would have a conniption about some dirty detective going through their little darlings' undies. So yeah: for all we know, the key wasn't there to find."

I said, "Why would Joanne's lot leave it here, all this time? Why not bin it when Chris got killed and people started asking questions?"

Conway shut the book. Delicate touch, when she needed it. "You should've seen this place, after the murder. The kids didn't get left on their own for a second, in case Hannibal Lecter jumped out of a wardrobe and ate their brains. None of them would go to the jacks without five of their mates in tow. Our lot everywhere, teachers patrolling the corridors, nuns flapping about, everyone going off like fire alarms if they spotted anything out of the ordinary. This"—she flicked a finger at the book, no touching—"would've been the smart thing to do: leave the key, don't risk getting caught moving it. And just a few weeks later, the school year finished up. When our girls came back in September, they were fourth-years. No code for this room, no good reason to be in it. Coming after the key would've been riskier than leaving it. How often do you think this book gets read? What's the odds of anyone finding the key, or knowing what it was if they did?"

"If Joanne or whoever didn't bin the key, it's a good bet she didn't wipe down the book."

"Nah. We'll get prints." Conway pulled a plastic evidence bag out of her satchel, shook it open with a snap. "Who d'you figure for the text? None of Holly's lot are mad about Joanne."

She held the bag open while I balanced the book into it, two-fingered. I said, "'Who' isn't the bit that's getting me. I'd love to know why."

Wry glance from Conway, as she tucked the bag back into her satchel. "My scare speech wasn't good enough for you?"

"It was good. But it wouldn't scare anyone into texting us about this.

What's to be scared of? Why would the killer come after her for knowing this key was here?"

"Unless," Conway said. She was pulling off her gloves, carefully, finger by finger. "Unless the killer's Joanne."

The first time we'd had a name to say. It sent a fine zing through the air, rippling the throws on the sofas, twitching the curtains.

I said, "You're the boss. But if it was me, I wouldn't go at her yet."

I half expected a slap-down. Didn't get one. "Me neither. If Joanne hid this, her buddies knew about it. Who d'you want to try? Alison?"

"I'd go for Orla. Alison's nervier, all right, but that's not what we need. One push and she'll run crying to Daddy, and we're bollixed." The *we* flicked Conway's eyebrow, but she said nothing. "Orla's more solid, and she's thick enough that we can run rings round her. I'd try her."

"Mm," Conway said. She was opening her mouth to say something else when we heard the sound.

Thin shrilling sound, dipping and rising like an alarm. Before I copped what it was, Conway was up and running for the door. The savage bright burst on her face as she passed me said *Yes*, said *Action*, said *At fucking last*.

Girls clotted halfway down the corridor, a dozen of them, more. Half of them out of their uniforms now, bright in hoodies and T-shirts, cheap bangles shaking; a few half changed, clutching buttons together, shoving into sleeves. All of them crowding and yammering, high and fast, *Whatwhatwhat?* In the middle of the clot someone was screaming.

We were taller than them. Over shining heads: Joanne and her lot, surrounded. Alison was the one screaming, back pressed against the wall, hands splayed in front of her face. Joanne was trying to do something, cradle her, ministering angel, who knows. Alison was too far gone even for that.

Holly, between heads, the only one not gawping at Alison. Holly was scanning faces, with eyes like her da's. Holly was watching for someone to give something away.

Conway grabbed the nearest kid by the arm, little dark girl who leapt and screamed. "What's the story?"

"Alison saw a ghost! She saw, she said, she said she saw Chris Harper, his ghost, she saw—"

The shrieks kept coming; the kid was jumping and rattling under them. Conway said, loud, so anyone who could hear anything could hear her: "You know why he's back, right?"

The kid stared, openmouthed. Other girls were starting to look at us, baffled, tennis-heading, trying to work out through the brain-battering noise why these adults weren't stepping in and getting control and turning everything back to sane.

"Because someone here knows who killed him. He's come back to make her talk. We see it all the time, on murder cases, all the time, amn't I right?"

Conway shot me a look like a dig. I nodded. Said, "This is just the start. It's gonna get worse."

"They know, murder victims do, they don't like it when someone keeps them from getting justice. Chris isn't happy. He won't be able to rest till everyone's told us everything they know."

The kid made a muffled whine. Gasps around us, a girl catching her friend's arm, "OhmyGod—" High, trembling right on the edge of a scream to join Alison's. "OhmyGod—"

"Murder victims, they're raging. Probably Chris was a lovely guy, when he was alive, but he's not like you remember him. He's angry now."

A shiver swayed them. Teeth and sharp shards of bone, they saw, coming to rip the warm flesh off them. "OhmyGod—"

McKenna, surging through the boiling girls, massive. Conway dropped the kid's arm like a hot snot, stepped back smooth and fast.

McKenna boomed, "Quiet!" and the jabber fizzled to nothing. Only Alison's shrieks were left, exploding like fireworks into the shocked air.

McKenna didn't look at us. She got Alison's shoulders and spun her, face-to-face. "Alison! *Quiet!*"

Alison swallowed a shriek, choked on it. Stared up at McKenna, gulping and red-faced. Swaying, like she was hanging from McKenna's big hands.

"Gemma Harding," McKenna said, not taking her eyes off Alison. "Tell me what happened."

Gemma found her jaw. "Miss, we were just in our room, we weren't doing anything—"

She sounded years younger, looked years younger, a shaken little girl. McKenna said, "I'm not interested in what you weren't doing. Tell me exactly what happened."

"Alison just went to the loo, and then we heard her screaming out here. We all ran out. She was . . ."

Gemma's eyes zipping around the others, finding Joanne, grabbing for signals. McKenna said, "Continue. At once."

"She was just—she was up against the wall and she was screaming. Miss, she said, she said she saw Chris Harper."

Alison's head fell back. She made a high whining noise. "Alison," McKenna said sharply. "You will look at me."

"She said he grabbed her arm. Miss, there's—there's marks on her arm. I swear to God."

"Alison. Show me your arm."

Alison scrabbled at the sleeve of her hoodie, limp-fingered. Finally managed to pull it up to her elbow. Conway swept girls out of our way.

First it looked like a grip mark, like someone had got hold of Alison and tried to drag her away. Bright red, wrapped around her forearm: four fingers, a palm, a thumb. Bigger than a girl's hand.

Then we got in close.

Not a grip mark. The red skin was puffy and bubbled, thick with tiny blisters. A scald, an acid burn, a poison weed.

The press of girls rippled, necks craning. Moaned.

McKenna said acidly, "Were any of you unaware that Alison suffers from allergies? Please, raise your hands."

Stillness.

"Did any of you somehow miss the incident last term when she required medical attention after borrowing the wrong brand of tanning product?"

Nothing.

"No one?"

Girls looking at sleeves twisted round their thumbs, at the floor, sideways at each other. They were starting to feel silly. McKenna was bringing them back.

"Alison has been exposed to a substance that triggered her allergies. Presumably, if she has just been to the toilet, it was either a hand soap or a product used by the cleaning staff. We will investigate this and make sure the trigger is removed."

McKenna still hadn't looked at us. Bold kids get ignored. Talking to us too, though, or at us.

"Alison will take an antihistamine and will be fully recovered within an hour or two. The rest of you will go to your common rooms and will write me a three-hundred-word essay on allergy triggers, to be done by tomorrow morning. I am disappointed in all of you. You are old enough and intelligent enough to deal with this kind of situation with good sense rather than silliness and hysteria."

McKenna took one hand off Alison's shoulder—Alison slumped against the wall—and pointed down the corridor. "You may go now. Unless any of you have anything *useful* to share?"

"Miss," Joanne said. "One of us should stay with her. In case—"

"No, thank you. Common rooms, please."

They went pressed together in clumps, arm-linking and whispering, throwing back glances. McKenna stared them out of sight.

Said to us, "I assume you realize what caused this."

"Haven't a notion," said Conway. She moved in, between McKenna and Alison, till McKenna let go. "Alison. Did anyone say something about Chris Harper's ghost, before you went to the toilet?"

Alison was white and purple-shadowed. She said faintly, "He was in that door. Doing pull-ups off the top of the frame. His legs were waving."

Always doing something, Selena had said. I don't believe in ghosts. Felt the shiver rise up between my shoulder blades anyway.

"I think maybe I screamed. Anyway he saw me. He jumped down and came running down the corridor, really fast, and he grabbed me. He was laughing right into my face. I screamed more and I kicked him, and he disappeared."

She sounded almost peaceful. She was wrung out, like a little kid after puking its guts.

"That will do," McKenna said, in a voice that could have scared grizzlies. "Whatever allergy trigger you touched, it caused a brief hallucination. Ghosts do not exist."

I said, "Is your arm sore?"

Alison gazed at her arm. "Yeah," she said. "It's really sore."

"Unsurprisingly," McKenna said coldly. "And will continue to be until it is treated. On which note, Detectives, please excuse us."

"He smelled like Vicks," Alison told me, over her shoulder as McKenna marched her off. "I don't know if he used to smell like Vicks before."

Conway watched them go. Said, "What's the betting the Ugg kids spread the word we were in their common room?"

"No takers. And it had plenty of time to get round."

"To Joanne. Who had to guess what we were after."

I nodded after Alison. Footsteps rattling around the stairwell, echoing; her and McKenna were taking the stairs at a snappy old pace. "That wasn't put on."

"Nah. Alison's suggestible, but. And she was half hysterical to start with, after the interview and all." Conway was keeping her voice down, head tilted backwards to listen to the popcorn crackle of voices from the common rooms. "She's headed for the jacks, Joanne gives it loads about Chris's ghost being all stirred up—she knows Alison inside out, remember, knows exactly how to get her going. Then she sticks fake tan on her hand, gives Alison's arm a squeeze. It's a decent bet Alison'll go mental over one thing or the other. Joanne's hoping there'll be enough chaos that we'll leg it out of the common room, leave the door open, she'll have a chance to nip in there and swipe the book."

Sixteen-year-old kid, I almost said: *would she be up to that?* Copped myself on in time. Said, instead, "Alison's wearing long sleeves."

"So Joanne got her before she put on the hoodie."

It could work; maybe, just about, with plenty of luck. I said, "Joanne didn't try to go for the common room, but. She stayed right here, in the middle of the action."

"Maybe she was betting we'd take Alison away, she could take her time."

"Or Joanne had nothing to do with it. The ghost was Alison's imagination and the arm's accidental, like McKenna said."

"Could be. Maybe."

The footsteps had faded out of the stairwell. That white silence was sifting down again, filling the air with corner-of-the-eye shapes, making it hard to believe that anything in here was as simple as imagination and accident.

I said, "Does McKenna live here?"

"Nah. Got more sense. But she's not going home till we do."

We. "Hope she likes canteen food."

Conway flipped her bag open, checked the book tucked away inside. "Things happening," she said. Didn't even try to hide the blaze of satisfaction. "Told you."

12

In a way they were right: it's not the same the second time they sneak out, or the third. It turns out that doesn't matter. The glade where they lie and talk always has that other one behind it, a promise waiting for the right moment to be kept. It colors everything.

I never thought I'd have friends like you guys, Becca says, deep inside the third night. *Never. You're my miracles.*

Not even Julia bats that away. Their four hands are twined together on the grass, loose and warm.

Late in January, half past ten at night. Fifteen minutes till lights-out, for third-years and fourth-years at Kilda's and at Colm's. Chris Harper— brushing his teeth, half thinking about the cold soaking into his feet from the tiled floor of the bathroom, half listening to a couple of guys giving a first-year hassle in a toilet cubicle and wondering whether he can be arsed stopping them—has just under four months left to live.

A breadth of darkness away in Kilda's, snow brushes at the dorm-room window, small fitful flakes, not sticking. Winter has clamped down hard: early sunsets, petty sleet and the streaming cold that's been going around mean it's been a week since Julia and Holly and Selena and Becca felt daylight, and they're jiggly with confinement and leftover sniffles. They're arguing about the Valentine's dance.

"I'm not going," Becca says.

Holly is lying on her bed in her pajamas, copying Julia's maths as fast as she can, throwing in the odd minor mistake for authenticity. "Why not?"

"Because I'd rather burn off my own fingernails with a lighter than wiggle myself into some stupid dress with a stupid micro–miniskirt and a stupid stuck-on low-cut top, even if I owned that kind of crap, which I don't and I'm not going to ever. Is why."

"You have to go," Julia says, from her bed, where she's facedown reading.

"No I don't."

"If you don't, you'll get sent to Sister Ignatius and she'll ask if you don't want to go because you were abused when you were little, and when you tell her you weren't, she'll say you need to learn self-esteem."

Becca is sitting on her bed with her arms around her knees, clenched into a furious red knot. "I *have* self-esteem. I have enough self-esteem that I'm not going to wear something stupid just because everyone else is."

"Well, fuck you very much. My dress isn't stupid." Julia has a shimmy of a dress, black with scarlet polka dots, that she spent months saving for and bought in the sales just a couple of weeks ago. It's the tightest thing she's ever owned, and she actually kind of likes the look of herself in it.

"Your dress isn't. Me in your dress would be. Because I'd *hate* it."

Selena says, through the pajama top she's pulling over her head, "Why don't you wear whatever you like best?"

"I like jeans best."

"So wear jeans."

"Yeah, *right*. Are you going to?"

"I'm wearing that blue dress that was my granny's. The one I already showed you." It's a sky-blue micro-minidress that Selena's granny wore back in the sixties, when she was a shopgirl in cool parts of London. It's tight on Selena's chest, but she's wearing it anyway.

"Exactly," Becca says. "Hol, are you wearing jeans?"

"Ah, bugger," Holly says, scrubbing at a mistake that turned out bigger than she expected. "My mum bought me this purple dress for Christmas. It's actually OK. I might wear that."

"So I'd be the only loser in jeans, or else I have to go buy some stupid dress I hate and be a total compromise coward liar. No thanks."

"Do the dress," says Julia, turning a page. "Give us all a laugh."

Becca gives her the finger. Julia grins and gives it right back. She approves of the new feisty Becca.

"It's not *funny*. You're going to let me sit here by myself that night doing Sister Ignatius's stupid self-esteem exercises, while you're all wiggling in stupid dresses for—"

"So *come*, for fuck's sake—"

"I don't *want* to!"

"Then what do you want? You want the rest of us to stay home just because you don't feel like wearing a dress?" Julia has ditched her book and is sitting up. Holly and Selena have stopped what they're doing at the snap in her voice. "Because yeah, no: fuck that."

"I thought the whole *point* was we don't have to do stuff just because everyone else does—"

"I'm not going because everyone else is, genius, I'm going because I actually *want* to. Because it's *fun*, you've heard of that, right? If you'd rather sit here doing self-esteem exercises, knock yourself out. I'm going."

"Oh, thanks, thanks a lot—you're supposed to be my *friend*—"

"Right, which doesn't mean being your bitch—"

Becca is up on her knees on the bed, fists clenched and hair crackling with fury. "I never *fucking* asked you to—"

The light bulb spits a furious sizzle, pops and goes out. They all scream.

"Shut up!" the second-floor prefects both yell from down the corridor. A breathless "Jesus—" from Julia, a thump and "Ow!" as Selena knocks her shin off something, and then the light flicks back on.

"What the *hell*," Holly says. "What happened?"

The bulb is burning innocently, not a flicker.

"It's a sign, Becs," Julia says, with that breathless note almost under control. "The universe wants you to quit whinging and go to the dance."

"Ha ha, so very funny," Becca says. Her voice isn't under control at all; it sounds like a kid's, high and wobbly. "Or the universe doesn't want *you* going, and it's annoyed because you said you were."

Selena says, to Becca, "Did you do that?"

"You are shitting me," Julia says. "Right?"

"Becsie?"

"Oh, *please*," Julia says. "Come *on*. Don't even go there."

Selena is still looking at Becca. So is Holly. In the end Becca says, "I don't know."

"Oh, God," Julia says. "I can't even." She falls flat on her stomach on her bed and slams her pillow over her head.

Selena says, "Do it again."

"How?"

"However you did it before."

Becca is staring at the light bulb like it might leap at her. "I didn't. I don't think. I don't know."

Julia groans, under her pillow. "Better do it fast," Holly says. "Before she suffocates."

"I just . . ." Becca holds up one thin palm, wavering. "I was upset. Because of . . . And I just . . ." She closes her fist. The light goes out.

This time none of them scream.

"Turn it back on?" Selena's voice says, quietly, in the darkness.

The light comes back on. Julia has taken the pillow off her head and is sitting up.

"Oh," Becca says. She has her back pressed against the wall and a knuckle in her mouth. "Did I . . . ?"

"No, you fucking didn't," Julia says. "It's some kind of electrical thing. Probably the snow."

Selena says, "Do it again."

Becca does it again.

This time Julia doesn't say anything. All around them the air is shivering, bending the light.

"Yesterday morning," Selena says. "When we were getting ready, and I was getting something off my bedside table. My hand went up against my reading light, and it turned on. When I stopped touching it, it went off."

"Cheapo piece of crap malfunctions," Julia says. "News at nine."

"I did it a bunch of times. To check."

They all remember Selena's light blinking on and off. The bad weather was already on the way, tarnished sky clashing with the electric lights to give the school a tense battened-down feel: they thought it was just that, if they thought about it at all.

"So how come you didn't say anything?"

"We were in a hurry. And I wanted to think about it. And I wanted to wait and see . . ."

If it happened to anyone else. Becca remembers to breathe out, in a quick burst.

Holly says, almost unwillingly, "This afternoon. When I went to the jacks, during Maths? The lights in the corridor: they turned off when I went under them, and then they turned back on again once I was past. Like, all of them. I thought it was just a thing. The snow, or whatever."

Selena lifts her eyebrows at Holly, and glances up at the light bulb.

"Oh for God's sake," says Julia.

"It won't work," Holly says.

Nobody answers her. The air still has that waver to it: heat over sand, mirage-ready.

Holly holds up her palm and makes a fist like Becca did. The light goes out. "Jesus!" she yelps, and it comes on again.

Silence, and the thrumming air. They don't have ways to talk about this.

"I'm not psychic," Holly says, too loudly. "Or whatever. I'm not. That thing in Science, remember, guessing the shapes on the cards? I was crap."

Becca says, "Me too. This is because of . . . you know. The glade. That's what's changed." Julia flops back down on her bed and bashes her forehead off her pillow a few times. "OK, so what do you think just happened, smarty?"

"I told you. There's snow in some transponster somewhere in Ballybum-crack. Now can we go back to fighting about how I'm not your real friend? Please?"

Selena does the light bulb. "Stop!" Julia snaps. "I'm trying to read."

"I thought you thought it was snow," Selena says, grinning. "Why are you telling me to stop it?"

"Shut up. I'm reading."

"You try it."

"Uh-huh, right."

"I dare you."

Julia gives Selena a withering look. "Scared?" Selena asks.

"There's nothing to be scared *of*. That's my whole *point*."

"Then . . . ?"

Julia is crap at turning down a dare. She sits up again, reluctantly. "I can't believe I'm doing this," she says. Lifts her hand, sighing noisily, and closes it. Nothing happens.

"Ta-da," Julia says. To her huge irritation, a part of her is viciously, pain-fully disappointed.

Selena says, "Doesn't count. You weren't concentrating."

"When the lights in the corridor did it," Holly says. "This afternoon. Naughton had been giving out to me, remember? Cliona was talking and she thought it was me? I was well pissed off. And . . ."

"Fuck's *sake*," Julia says. She focuses on Becca being a contrary cow about the dance, and tries again. It works.

Silence, again. Reality feels strange against their skin: it's rippling and bubbling around them, it's spinning little whirlpools and shooting up gey-sers in unexpected places just for fun. They don't want to move, in case it responds in ways they're not expecting.

"Too bad it's not something useful," Holly says, as casually as she can—she feels like making a big deal of this would be a bad idea; like it might draw attention, she's not sure whose. "X-ray vision. We could read the exam papers the night before."

"Or not even bother," Becca says. She wants to giggle; everything feels like she's being tickled. "If we could just change our marks when the results came in—like, whee, all As!—*that* would be useful."

"I don't think it's like that," Selena says. She's snuggled down in bed, wearing a huge contented grin. She wants to hug all three of them. "It's not *for* anything. It's just there. Like, it was there all along; we just didn't know how to get to it. Till now."

"Well," Julia says. She's still not at all happy about this. It seems to her for some reason that they should have put up more of a fight, collectively: run screaming, refused to believe this was happening, changed the subject and kept it changed. Just not acted like this is something they can look at, go *Oh, wow, totally weird!* and keep bouncing cheerfully along. Even if that didn't make a difference in the long run, it would have said they weren't complete pushovers. "At least that settles the Valentine's dance bullshit. Someone with superpowers had better not be too much of a wimp to wear jeans."

Becca starts to answer, but she gets hit by a flood of giggles. She falls backwards on her bed, arms spread, and lets the laughter jiggle her whole body like popcorn popping inside her.

"Nice to see you quit bitching," Julia says. "So are you going to the dance?"

"Course I am," Becca says. "You want me to go in my swimsuit? 'Cause I'll do it."

"Lights out!" one of the prefects yells, slamming her hand against the door. They all turn the light off at once.

They practice in the glade. Selena brings her little battery-powered reading light, Holly has a torch, Julia brings a lighter. The night is thick with clouds and cold; they have to grope their way down the paths to the grove, wincing each time a branch twangs or a clump of leaves crunches. Even when they come out into the clearing they're nothing but outlines, distorted and un-readable. They sit cross-legged in a circle on the grass and pass the lights around.

It works. Uncertainly at first: just small tentative flickers, half a second long, vanishing when they startle. As they get better the flickers strengthen and leap, snatching their faces out of the dark like gold masks—a little wondering sound, between a laugh and a gasp, from someone—and then dropping them again. Gradually they stop being flickers at all; rays of light arrow up into the high cypresses, circle and flitter among the branches like fireflies. Becca would swear she sees their trails scribbled across the clouds.

"And to celebrate . . ." Julia says, and pulls a pack of smokes out of her coat pocket—it's been years since anyone asked Julia if she's sixteen. "Who was saying this wouldn't come in useful?" She holds up the lighter between thumb and finger, brings up a tall stream of flame, and leans in sideways to light a cigarette without singeing her eyebrows.

They get comfortable and smoke, more or less. Selena's left her reading light on; it sets a vivid circle of bowed winter grass soaring in mid-darkness, bounces off to catch folds of jeans and slivers of faces. Holly finishes her smoke and lies on her stomach with an unlit one in the palm of her hand, focusing hard.

"What're you doing?" Becca asks, scooting closer to watch.

"Trying to light it. Shh."

"I don't think it works like that," Becca says. "We can't just set random stuff on fire. Can we?"

"Shut up or I'll set you on fire. I'm *concentrating*."

Holly hears herself and tightens, thinking she's gone too far, but Becca rolls sideways and pokes her in the ribs with a toe. "Concentrate on this," she says.

Holly drops the cigarette and grabs her foot; Becca's boot comes off, and Holly scrambles up and runs with it. Becca hop-gallops after her, giggling helplessly and yelping under her breath when her sock comes down on something cold.

Selena and Julia watch them. In the darkness they're just a trail of rustle and laughter, sweeping a circle round the edge of the clearing. "Is this still bothering you?" Selena asks.

"Nah," Julia says, and blows a line of smoke rings; they wander through stripes of light and shadow, vanishing and reappearing like odd little night creatures. She can't remember exactly why it bothered her to begin with. "I was just being a wimp. It's all good."

"It is," Selena says. "Honest to God, it is. You're not a wimp, though."

Julia turns her head towards her, the slice she can see, a soft eyebrow and a soft hank of hair and the dreamy sheen of one eye. "I thought you thought I was. Like, *Here's this super-cool thing happening, why's she going off on some big emo-fest and fucking it all up?*"

"No," Selena says. "I got why: it could feel dangerous. I mean, it doesn't to me. But I get how it could."

"I wasn't scared."

"I know that."

"I wasn't."

"I know," Selena says. "I'm just glad you decided to try it. I don't know what we'd've done if you hadn't."

"Gone for it anyway."

"We wouldn't, not without you. There'd be no point."

Becca has managed to wrestle her boot back and is hopping about, trying to get it on before Holly can shove her off-balance. Both of them are panting and laughing. Julia leans her shoulder up against Selena's—Julia doesn't do touchy-feely crap, but just every now and then she props her elbow on Selena's shoulder while they're looking at something, or leans back to back with her on the fountain edge in the Court. "You sap," she says, "you total sappy sap, get a grip," and feels Selena meet the weight of her so they balance each other, solid and warm.

They're moving down the corridor towards their room, boots in their hands, when:

"Uh-oh," someone singsongs in the shadows. "You're going to get in *trouble.*"

They leap and whirl, hearts pummeling their chests, Selena clenching the key deep in her fist, but the shadows are deep and they don't see her till she steps out into the corridor. Joanne Heffernan, monochrome in the low lights left on in case someone needs to go to the toilet, just folded arms and a smirk and a baby-doll nightie with big lips all over it.

"Jesus fucking *Christ,*" Julia hisses—Joanne swaps her smirk for her pious face, to show she disapproves of Language. "What are you doing, trying to give us heart attacks?"

Joanne dials up the holiness. "I was worried about you. Orla was going to the ladies' and she saw you heading downstairs, and she thought you might be going to do something dangerous. Like, involving drugs or drink or something."

A puff of laughter bursts out of Becca. Joanne's holy look freezes for a second, but she gets it back.

"We were in the Needlework room," Holly explains. "Sewing blankets for orphans in Africa."

Holly always looks like she's telling the truth; for a second, Joanne's eyes pop. Julia says, "I had a vision of Saint Fucktardius telling me the orphans needed our help," and her face goes lemon-sucking pious again.

"If you were indoors," she says, moving forward, "then what's this?" She makes a grab at Selena's hair—"Ow!" from Selena, jumping back—and holds something out in the palm of her hand. It's a sprig of cypress, rich green, still wrapped in frosty outside air.

"It's a miracle!" Julia says. "Praise Saint Fucktardius, patron of indoor gardening."

Joanne drops the twig and wipes her hand on her nightie. "Ew," she says, wrinkling her nose. "You smell of *cigarettes*."

"Sewing-machine fumes," Holly says. "Lethal."

Joanne ignores that. "*So*," she says. "You guys have a key to the outside door."

"No we don't. The outside door's alarmed at night," Julia says. "Genius."

Which Joanne may not be, but she's not thick either. "Then the door to the school, and you went out a window. Same difference."

"So?" Holly wants to know. "If we did, which we didn't, what do you care?"

Joanne is still being holy—some nun along the way must have told her she looks like some saint—which turns her faintly bug-eyed. "That's dangerous. Something could happen to you out there. You could get *attacked*."

That gets another stifled pop of laughter out of Becca. "Like you'd care," Julia says. They've all drawn close, so they can keep to whispers; the forced nearness prickles like they're about to fight. "Skip to the part where you tell us what you want."

Joanne drops the saint thing. "If you get caught this easy," she says, "you're obviously too stupid to have the key. You should give it to someone who's got the brains to use it."

"That leaves you out, then," says Becca.

Joanne stares at her like she's a talking dog who's said something revolting. "And you should really go back to being too pathetic to talk," she says. "At least then people felt sorry for you." To Julia and Holly: "Can you explain to that uggo why she needs to watch her nasty metal mouth?"

Julia says to Becca, "I've got this."

"Why bother?" Becca wants to know. "Let's go to bed."

"Oh. My. God," Joanne says, smacking her forehead. "How do you manage not to kill her? Hello, keep up: you need to bother because if I call Matron and she sees you dressed like that, she's going to know you've been outside. Is that what you want?"

"No," Julia says, standing on Becca's foot. "We'd all be delighted if you could just go to bed and forget you ever saw us."

"Right. So if you want me to do you a massive favor like that, you should actually probably be nice to me?"

"We can do nice."

"That's great. The key, please," Joanne says. "Thanks *so* much." And she holds out her hand.

Julia says, "We'll make you a copy tomorrow."

Joanne doesn't bother to answer. She just stands there, staring at none of them in particular and holding out her hand.

"Come *on*. For fuck's sake."

Her stare widens a fraction. Nothing else.

The silence twists tight. After a long time Julia says, "Yeah. OK."

"*We* might make *you* a copy someday," Joanne says graciously, as Selena's hand slowly comes up towards her. "If you remember to be nice, and if you can teach Little Miss Smarty over there what nice even means. Do you think you can manage that?"

It means weeks months years of smiling meekly when Joanne flicks bits of bitchiness their way, of asking pretty-please with a cherry on top can we have our key now, of watching her cock her head and consider whether they deserve it and decide regretfully that they don't. It means the end of these nights; the end of everything. They want to wrap the dark air around her neck and pull. Selena's fingers open.

Joanne touches the key and her hand leaps. The key skids and whirls away from her down the floor of the corridor and she's squawking like she doesn't have enough breath for a shriek, "*Ow!* OhmyGod, it *burned* me, owowow it *burned* what did you *do*—"

Holly and Julia are in her face and hissing violently, "Shut up *shut up*!" but not fast enough: at the end of the corridor one of the prefects calls, drowsy and annoyed, "What do you want?"

Joanne whips around to scream for her. "No!" Julia whispers, grabbing her arm. "Go; get in your room. We'll give you the key tomorrow. I swear."

"Get off me," Joanne snarls, terrified into pure fury. "You're going to be *so sorry* for this. Look at my hand, look what you *did*—"

Her hand looks totally fine, not even a mark on it, but the light is streaky and Joanne is moving; they can't tell for sure. Down the corridor, less drowsy and more annoyed: "If I have to come out there, I swear to God—"

Joanne's mouth opens again. "Listen!" Julia hisses, with all the force she can cram into it. "If we get caught, then nobody'll have the key. Get it? Go to bed; we'll sort it tomorrow. Just *go*."

"You are total freaks," Joanne spits. "Normal people shouldn't have to be in the same school as you. If my hand's scarred, I'm going to *sue* you." And she whirls back into her room in a nightie-flounce of gaping lip-prints.

Julia grabs Becca's arm and runs for their door, feeling the others behind them silent and speedy as down the paths to the glade, Selena barely breaking stride to scoop up the key. In, door closed, Holly presses her ear to it; but the prefect can't be arsed hauling herself out of bed, now that the sounds have stopped. They're safe.

Selena and Becca are giggling, wild and breathless, into their sleeves. "Her *face*—ohmyGod, did you see her *face*, I almost died—"

"Let me feel it," Becca whispers, "come here, let me feel—"

"It's not hot now," Selena says. "It's fine."

They find her, in the darkness, and sift among one another's reaching fingers to touch the key in her open hand. It's palm-warm; nothing more.

"Did you see it *jump*?" Becca says. She's almost dizzy with delight. "*Zooming* down the corridor, away from that cow—"

"Or it bounced," Julia says. "Because she dropped it."

"It *jumped*. Her face, that was beautiful, I'd give anything for a photo—"

"Who even did that?" Holly wants to know, switching on her reading light half hidden under her pillow so they can change without knocking anything over. "Was that you, Becs?"

"I think it was me," Selena says. She tosses Julia the key, its glint like a tiny meteor streaking between them. "It doesn't actually matter, though. If I can do it, you guys can too."

"Ah, *cool*," Becca says, wriggling out of all her layers at once and kicking them under her bed. She throws on her pajamas and bounces into bed, where she balances the cap off her water bottle on edge on her bedside table and starts trying to knock it over without touching it.

Julia is stashing the key back inside her phone cover. She says, "Next time, could you save that stuff for when it's not going to get us into huge amounts of shit? Like, please?"

"I didn't do it on purpose," Selena says, muffled in the hoodie she's pulling over her head. "It just happened, because I was getting all wound up. And if it hadn't, Joanne would've taken the key."

"Yeah, well, it's not like she's going to forget the whole thing. We'll have to deal with it tomorrow instead, is all. And now she's raging with us."

That cools the air. "Her hand's fine," Selena says. "She's just being a drama queen."

"Right. So she's a total drama-queen bitch who's raging with us. How is that better?"

"What do we do?" Becca asks, glancing up from her bottle cap.

"What do you think we do?" Holly says, tossing jumpers into the wardrobe. "We make her a copy of the key. Unless you actually want to get expelled."

"Why would we get expelled? She can't prove we did anything."

"OK: unless you want to never go out again. Because if we do, Joanne can go running to Matron and be all, 'Oo Matron I just *happened* to see them going downstairs and I'm so *worried* about them,' and then Matron waits and catches us coming back in and *then* we get expelled."

"I'll do it," Julia says, kicking into her pajama bottoms. "I'll talk to her. I think the hardware place beside the Court does keys."

"She's going to be a total bitch about it," Holly says.

"Yeah, no shit. I'm going to have to apologize to her for what you said, smart-arse." She means Becca. "You think I'm looking forward to groveling for that ass-faced cow?"

"You won't have to," Becca says. "She's scared of us now."

"For the next ten seconds, she is. Then she'll turn the whole thing into some drama in her head, like she's the heroine and we're the evil witches who tried to burn her to death but she was just too special. And I'll have to apologize for that, too. And convince her that the key just felt hot because Lenie'd been holding it and her hand was hot from running or whatever." Julia climbs into bed and throws herself hard onto her pillow. "Fun fun fun."

Selena says, "At least this way we get to keep our key."

"We would've anyway. We'd have talked her out of it, or just robbed another one. You didn't need to go all fucking *poltergeist* on her."

Becca says, and her voice is tightening up, "Better than going all *Yes Joanne no Joanne three bags full Joanne*, letting that stupid cow be the boss of us—"

The bottle cap hops on the bedside table and tumbles over. "Look!" Becca yelps, and claps a hand over her mouth as the others hiss "Shhh!" at her. "No, look! I did it!"

"Awesomesauce," Holly says. "I'm gonna try in the morning."

"What are we doing?" Julia demands, suddenly and vehemently. "All this shit; this, and the lights. What are we getting into here?"

The others look at her. In that light she's the unreadable silhouette from the glade again, propped on her elbows, a tense arc.

"I'm getting happy," Becca says. "That's what I'm getting into."

Holly says, "We're not blowing stuff *up*. It's not like it's about to go all horrible."

"You don't know. I'm not saying OMG we're going to unleash demons; I'm just saying this is weird shit. If it only worked in the glade, then fine: it's something separate, with its own separate place. But it's *here*."

Holly says, "So? If it gets too weird, we just stop doing it. What's the big deal?"

"Yeah? Just stop? Lenie, you didn't even want the key to get hot: it *just happened*, because you were stressing. Same with Becs, the first time she turned the light off: that was because we were fighting. So if Sister Cornelius gives me hassle about something, do I just go ahead and zoom a book into her fat face, which yeah would be lots of fun but probably not the greatest idea ever? Or do I have to watch myself the whole time to make sure I'm totally zen, man, so I can live like a normal person?"

"Speak for yourself," Holly says, through a yawn, as she wriggles down in her bed. "Me, I am normal."

"I'm not," Becca says. "I don't want to be."

Selena says gently, "It just takes getting used to. You didn't like the lights thing at first, right? And then tonight you said that was fine."

"Yeah," Julia says, after a moment. The glade leaps in her mind like a flame; if it weren't for Joanne, she'd get back into all her jumpers and get back out there, where everything feels clean and straightforward, nothing looks blur-edged and flashed with danger signs. "That's probably it."

"We'll go out again tomorrow night. You'll see. It'll be fine then."

"Oh, God," Julia says on a groan, flopping backwards. "If we want to do tomorrow, I'll have to sort that bint Heffernan. I was trying to forget about her."

"If she gives you any hassle," Holly says, "just get her own hand and smack her in the face with it. What's she going to do, tell on you?" and they're falling asleep before they finish laughing.

When the others are asleep, Becca reaches one arm out of bed into the cold air and eases her bedside table open. She takes out, one by one, her phone, a little bottle of blue ink, an eraser with a pin stuck in it, and a tissue.

She stole the ink and the pin from the art room, the day after they made the vow. Under the covers, she pulls up her pajama top and angles the phone to light the pale skin just below her ribs. She holds her breath—to make sure she doesn't move, not to brace herself against the pain; pain doesn't bother her—while she pricks the dot into the skin, just deep enough, and rubs in the ink. She's getting better at it. There are six dots now, arcing downwards and inwards from the bottom right edge of her rib cage, too small to notice unless someone was closer than anyone's going to get: one for each perfect moment. The vow; the first three escapes; the lights; and tonight.

What's been coming to Becca, since all this began, is this: real isn't what they try to tell you. Time isn't. Grown-ups hammer down all these markers, bells schedules coffee-breaks, to stake down time so you'll start believing it's something small and mean, something that scrapes flake after flake off of everything you love till there's nothing left; to stake you down so you won't lift off and fly away, somersaulting through whirlpools of months, skimming through eddies of glittering seconds, pouring handfuls of hours over your upturned face.

She blots the extra ink from around the dot, spits on the tissue and dabs again. The dot throbs, a warm satisfying pain.

These nights in the grove aren't degradable, they can't be flaked away. They'll always be there, if only Becca and the others can find their way back. The four of them backboned by their vow are stronger than anyone's pathetic schedules and bells; in ten years, twenty, fifty, they can slip between those stakes and meet in the glade, on these nights.

The dot tattoos are for that: signposts, in case she needs them someday, to guide her home.

13

The fourth-year common room felt smaller than the third-year one, darker. Not just the colors, cool greens instead of oranges; on this side the building blocked out the afternoon sun, gave the room an underwater dimness that the ceiling lights couldn't fight.

The girls were clumped tight and jabbering low. Holly's lot were the only quiet ones: Holly sitting on a windowsill, Julia leaning against it snapping a hair elastic around her wrist, Rebecca and Selena back to back on the floor below; all their eyes focused and faraway, like they were reading the same story written across the air. Joanne and Gemma and Orla were in a huddle on one of the sofas, Joanne whispering fast and ferocious.

That was only for a flash. Then everyone spun to the door. Sentences bitten off in mid-word, blank faces staring.

"Orla," Conway said. "We need a word."

Orla looked like she might be going pale, far as I could tell through the orange tan. "Me? Why me?"

Conway held the door open till Orla got up and came, widening her eyes over her shoulder at her mates. Joanne hit her with a stare like a threat.

"We'll talk in your room," Conway said, scanning the corridor. "Which one is it?" Orla pointed: down the far end.

No Houlihan this time. Conway was trusting me to protect her. Had to be a good sign.

The room was big, airy. Four beds, bright-colored duvet covers. Smell of heated hair and four clashing body sprays thickening the air. Posters of thrusting girl singers and smooth guys I half recognized, all of them with full lips and hair that had taken three people an hour. Bedside tables half open, bits of uniform tossed on beds, on the floor: when the screaming started, Orla and Joanne and Gemma had been changing into their civvies, getting ready to do whatever they did with their bite of freedom before teatime.

The scattered clothes gave me that shove again, stronger: *Out.* No good reason, no bras on show or anything, but I still felt like a pervert, like I'd walked in on the four of them changing and wasn't walking back out.

"Nice," Conway said, glancing around. "Nicer than we had in training, am I right?"

"Nicer than I've got now," I said. Only a bit true. I like my place: little apartment, half empty still because I'd rather save for one good thing than buy four crap ones straightaway. But the high ceiling, the rose molding, the light and green space opening wide outside the window: I can't save for those. My place looks straight into a matching apartment block, too close for any light to squeeze in between.

Nothing said whose bit of room was whose; it all looked the same. The only clue was the photos on the bedside tables. Alison had a little brother, Orla had a bunch of lumpy big sisters. Gemma rode horses. Joanne's ma was the image of her, a few fillers on.

"Um," Orla said, hovering by the door. She'd swapped her uniform for a light-pink hoodie and pink jeans shorts over tights, looked like a marshmallow on a stick. "Is Alison OK?"

We looked at each other, me and Conway. Shrugged.

I said, "Could take a while. After that."

"But . . . I mean, Miss McKenna said? Like, she just needed her allergy pills?"

Another look at each other. Orla trying to watch both of us at once.

Conway said, "I reckon Alison knows what she saw better than McKenna does."

Orla gawped. "You believe in ghosts?" Not what she'd expected; not what she'd been looking for.

"Who said anything about believing?" Conway flipped a magazine off Gemma's bedside table, checked out celebs. "Nah. We don't believe. We know." To me: "Remember the O'Farrell case?"

I'd never heard of the O'Farrell case. But I knew, it slid from Conway to me like a note passed in class, what she was at. She wanted Orla scared.

I shot her a wide-eyed warning grimace, shook my head.

"What? The O'Farrell case, me and Detective Moran worked that one together. The guy, right, he used to beat the shite out of his wife—"

"*Conway.*" I jerked my chin at Orla.

"*What?*"

"She's just a kid."

Conway tossed the magazine onto Alison's bed. "Bollix. You just a kid?"

"Huh?" Orla caught up. "Um, no?"

"See?" Conway said to me. "So. One day O'Farrell's giving the wife the slaps, her little dog goes for him—trying to protect its mistress, yeah? The guy throws it out of the room, goes back to what he's doing—"

I did an exasperated sigh, rubbed my hair into a mess. Started cruising round the room, see what I could see. Handful of tissues in the bin, smudged that weird orangey-pink that doesn't exist outside makeup. A bust pen. No scraps of book.

"But the dog's scrabbling at the door, whining, barking, O'Farrell can't concentrate. He opens the door, grabs the dog, smashes its brains out on the wall. Then he finishes off the wife."

"OhmyGod. *Ew.*"

Gemma's phone was on her bedside table, Alison's was on her bed. I couldn't see the other two, but Joanne's table door was an inch open. "OK if I have a look around?" I asked Orla. Not a proper search, that could wait; just having a look-see, and unsettling her a little extra while I was at it.

"Um, do you . . . ? Like, do you have to?" She fumbled for a way to say no, but my hand was halfway to the bedside table and her mind was halfway on Conway's fairy tale. "I guess it's OK. I mean—"

"Thanks." Not that I needed her permission; just staying the good cop. Cheerful smile, I gave her, and straight in. Orla opened her mouth to take it back, but Conway was moving in closer.

"We show up"—Conway gestured at the two of us—"O'Farrell swears it was a burglar. He was good; we nearly fell for it. But then we sit him down in his kitchen, start asking questions. Every time O'Farrell gives us some crap about his imaginary burglar, or about how much he loved his wife, there's this weird noise outside the door."

Joanne's bedside table: hair straightener, makeup, fake tan, iPod, jewelry box. No books, old or new; no phone. Had to be on her.

"This noise, it's like . . ." Conway raked her nails down the wall by Orla's head, sudden and violent. Orla jumped. "It's exactly like a dog clawing at the door. And it's making O'Farrell jumpy as hell. Every time he hears it, he whips round, loses his train of thought; he's looking at us like, *Did yous hear that?*"

"Sweating," I said, "dripping. White. Looked like he was gonna puke."

It was so easy, it startled me. Felt like we'd practiced for months, me and Conway, slaloming round the twists and kinks of the story side by side. Smooth as velvet.

It felt like joy, only a joy you didn't go looking for and don't want. That dream partner of mine, the one with the violin lessons and the red setters: this was what we were like together, him and me.

Orla's bedside table: hair straightener, makeup, fake tan, iPod, jewelry box. Phone. No books. I left the door open.

Orla didn't even notice what I was doing. Her mouth was hanging open. "Wasn't the dog dead?" she wanted to know.

Conway managed not to roll her eyes. "Yeah. It was very dead. The techs had taken it away and all. That's the point. Detective Moran here, he says to O'Farrell, 'You got another dog?' O'Farrell can't even talk, but he shakes his head."

Alison's bedside table: straightener, makeup, yada yada, no books, no extra phone. Gemma's bedside table: same story, plus a bottle of capsules of some herbal thing swearing to make her skinny.

"We go back to questioning him, but the noise keeps happening. We can't concentrate, right? Finally Detective Moran gets pissed off. Jumps up, heads for the door. O'Farrell practically comes off his chair, *roars* at Moran, 'Jesus God, *don't open that door!*'"

She was good, Conway. The room had changed, dark places stirring, bright ones pulsing. Orla was mesmerized.

"But it's too late: Moran's already opening the door. Far as we can see, me and him, the hall's empty. Nothing there. Then O'Farrell starts to scream."

One big wardrobe, all along one side of the room. Inside, it was split into four sections. Tangled bright things spilling out.

"We look around, O'Farrell's flying backwards off his chair, grabbing his throat. Howling like he's being killed. First we think he's putting it on, right, get out of being questioned? Then we see the blood."

Breathy whine bursting out of Orla. I tried to check drawers without touching anything girly. Wished Conway was doing this bit. There were Tampax in there.

"It's dripping out between his fingers. He's on the floor, kicking, howling, 'Get it off me! Get it off!' Me and Moran, we're like, *What the fuck?* We haul him outside—we don't know what else to do, figure maybe the fresh air'll help. He stops screaming, but he's still moaning, holding his throat.

We get his hands away. And I swear to God"—Conway was in close, eyes locked on Orla's—"I've seen dog bites. That, on O'Farrell's throat, that was a dog bite."

Orla asked faintly, "Did he die?"

"Nah. Few stitches."

"The dog was only little," I said. Worked around someone's bras. "Couldn't do too much damage."

"After the doctors got him cleaned up," Conway said, "O'Farrell spilled his guts. Full confession. When we took him off in cuffs, he was still screaming, 'Keep it away from me! Don't let it get me!' Grown man, begging like a kid."

"Never made it to trial," I said. "Wound up in a mental hospital instead. He's still there."

Orla said, and it came from the heart, "Ohmy*God*."

"So," Conway said. "When McKenna says there's no such thing as ghosts, excuse us if we have a laugh."

Nothing in the wardrobe drawers that didn't belong there, not on a quick check. Plenty that did; these four could have started their own Abercrombie & Fitch outlet. Nothing in the pockets of the hanging clothes. "We're not saying Alison actually saw Chris Harper's ghost," I said, reassuring. "Not for definite."

"Jaysus, no," Conway agreed. "She could've imagined the whole thing."

"Well," I said, poking through shoes. "She didn't imagine that arm." Nothing on the wardrobe floor.

"Nah, not that. I guess that could've maybe been allergies or whatever, though; who knows?" Shrug, unconvinced. "All I'm saying is, if I knew anything that had anything to do with Chris, and I kept it to myself, I wouldn't fancy turning out the lights tonight."

I dialed the number that had texted me. All the phones stayed dark. No ringing coming from under a bed, from a stack of clothes I'd skimmed over.

"Hate to admit it," I said. Glanced over my shoulder, did a shiver. "Me neither."

Orla's eyes skimming the room, hitting the corners, the shadows. Real fear.

Conway's story had hit the mark. And Orla wasn't the only one she'd been aiming at. The ghost story, or as much of it as Orla could remember, would be round the fourth-years inside half an hour.

"Speaking of which." Conway swept up her satchel, plopped herself down nice and comfy on Joanne's bed, right on top of her uniform—Orla's eyes widened, like Conway had done something daring. "You might want to take a look at this."

Orla edged closer. "Have a seat," Conway said, patting the bed. After a second Orla moved Joanne's skirt carefully out of the way and sat down.

I swung the wardrobe shut, leaned against it. Got out my notebook. Kept an eye on the door for flickers of shadow moving behind it, out in the hall.

Conway flipped open the satchel, whipped out the evidence bag and smacked it down on Orla's lap, all before Orla had a chance to work out what was going on. Said, "You've seen this before."

Orla took one look at the *Thérèse* book and bit down on both lips, hard. Hiss of in-breath through her nose.

Conway said, "Do us a favor. Don't try to tell us you don't know what's in there."

Orla tried to shake her head and shrug and look innocent, all at once. It came out like some kind of spasm.

"Orla. Pay attention. I'm not asking you if this was yours. I'm telling you we already know. You try to lie about it, all that'll happen is you'll get us pissed off and you'll get Chris pissed off. You want to do that?"

Trapped between thick and terrified, Orla dived for the only way out she could see. "It's Joanne's!"

"What is?"

"The key. That was Joanne's. It wasn't mine."

And bingo. Straight in there, our Orla, dobbing her mates in as quick as she could. The flare of Conway's nose said she smelled it too. "Same difference. Yous robbed it out of the nurse's office."

"No! Swear to God, we never stole anything."

"Then how'd you get it? You telling me the nurse gave it to you 'cause she couldn't resist your pretty faces?"

Orla's face lit up with that thin malice. "Julia Harte had it. Probably she stole it, or one of them did. We got a copy off her—Joanne got it, I mean. Not me."

Not bingo. All eight of them in the frame for the card, now all eight in the frame for eyewitnesses. And all eight in the frame, opportunity clicking into place, for the killer.

Conway's eyebrow was up. "Right. Joanne asked nicely, Julia said, 'No problem, anything for you, darling.' Yeah? 'Cause you're all best buddies?"

Orla shrugged. "I mean, I don't know. I wasn't there."

I hadn't been there either, but I knew. Blackmail: Joanne had spotted Julia on her way in or out, *Share or we tell.*

"When was that?"

"Like, for*ever* ago."

"When's forever?"

"After Christmas—*last* Christmas. I haven't even, ohmyGod, *thought* about it all year?"

"How many times did you use it?"

Orla remembered she could get in trouble here. "I didn't. I swear. I totally *swear.*"

"You gonna keep swearing when we find your prints all over it?"

"I got it out a few times, or put it back. But for Joanne, and Gemma. Not for me."

"You never snuck out? Not once?"

Orla went cagey. Ducked her head down.

"Orla," Conway said, close above her. "You need me to explain again why keeping your mouth shut is a bad idea?"

Another flash of that fear. Orla said, "I mean, I went one time. All four of us went. We were meeting some guys from Colm's out in the grounds, just for a laugh." And a can and a spliff and a snog. "But it was *so scary* out there. I mean, it was really dark; I hadn't realized it would be that dark. And there were all these noises in the bushes, like animals—the guys kept saying they were rats, *ew*? And we'd have been expelled if we got caught. And the guys . . ." A wiggle, uncomfortable. "I mean, they were weird, that night. Mean. They were, they kept . . ."

The guys had tried to push the girls. Drunk, maybe. Maybe not. No way to know how that had ended. Not our problem.

"So no thank you, no way was I going again. And I never went out on my own."

"Joanne did, though. And Gemma."

Orla sucked in her bottom lip and did the titter. That fear, forgotten, just like that: zapped away, the moment sex gossip came into the story. "Yeah. Only a few times."

"They were meeting guys. Who?"

Hunched-up shrug.

"Chris? No, hang on—" Conway's finger going up, warning. "Remember: you don't want to lie on this one."

Promptly: "Uh-uh. Not Chris. And they would've said if it was."

"Was he there the night yous all went out?"

Headshake.

I said, "Is that how you guys knew Selena and Chris were together, yeah? Saw them outside one night?"

Orla swayed forward towards me, wet-lipped smirk widening, loving her moment. "Gemma saw them. Right here in the grounds. They were, like, all *over* each other. She said, if she'd watched for another five minutes, they'd've been . . ." Breathy snigger. "See? They were *with* each other. You guys were all 'Oh, you're just making it up.' Obviously we couldn't tell you how we knew, but see? We totally did know."

This was some kind of triumph, apparently. "Fair play to yous," I said.

Conway said, "When was this?"

Blank look. "Like, last spring? Maybe March or April? Before Chris . . . you know."

My eye caught Conway's for a second. "Yeah, we figured that much," she said. "Did yous tell anyone you'd seen them?"

"We talked to Julia. We were like, 'Em, excuse me, hello, that needs sorting out?'"

"And? Did she sort it out?"

"I guess."

"Why?" I asked, all fascinated. "Why didn't yous want Selena going out with Chris?"

Orla's mouth popped open, popped shut. "Because. We just didn't."

"Did one of yous fancy him, yeah? Nothing wrong with that."

That cringe again, hunching down into her shoulders. Something was scaring her worse than us and Chris combined. Joanne; had to be. Joanne had wanted Chris.

Conway tapped the book. "When was the last time any of yous snuck out?"

"Gemma was out like a week before what happened to Chris. I mean, how creepy is that? We were all, 'OhmyGod, if there was like a *serial* killer stalking the school, he could totally have got her instead!'"

"You never went out after that? Any of yous? Ah-ah"—finger lifting again—"think about it before you go lying to us."

Orla was shaking her head so hard her hair whipped her in the face. "No. I swear. None of us. After Chris, we weren't exactly about to go wandering around out there. Joanne actually told me to go get that key and bin it or something, and I *tried*, but I was just taking the books out and oh! my God! one of the prefects came barging in? And she was all, 'What are you doing in here?' 'cause it was after lights-out 'cause I couldn't exactly do it while everyone was in the common room? I almost had a heart attack. So after that, no way was I trying again."

Conway lifted an eyebrow. "Joanne was OK with that?"

"Oh my God, she would've been *so furious*! I told her . . ." Snorty giggle from Orla, hand going over her mouth. "I told her I'd done it. I mean, it's not like anyone could tell it was ours anyway, or even what it was . . ." Something dawned on her. "How'd you guys know?"

"DNA," Conway said. "Go back to the common room."

"Selena and Chris," Conway said, watching down the corridor as the common-room door shut behind Orla. "Not bullshit after all."

She didn't sound happy about it. I knew why. Conway figured she should have got to this a year ago.

I said, "Unless Orla's lying. Or Gemma lied to her."

"Yeah. I don't think so, but." Neither did I. "Let's see what Selena has to say."

We'd get nothing out of Selena. I could feel it, in with that feeling that she was at the heart of the mystery: she was wrapped so deep in layers of it, we would never get through them to her. "Not Selena," I said. "Julia."

Conway started to give me the glare. Changed her mind—I'd been right about Orla—nodded instead. "OK. Julia."

Orla was at the center of the common-room gabble, flopped on a sofa with one hand on her chest like she had the vapors, eating up the attention. Joanne looked ready to kill: Orla had come clean about not binning the key. Holly's lot hadn't moved, but their eyes were on Orla.

A nun—civvies and headgear and a grim puggy underbite—was supervising from a corner, letting them talk but keeping a tough eye on where the chat was going. For a second I was surprised at McKenna, delegating this, but then I copped. Day girls had got home, boarders had rung home. McKenna's phone was going like goodo. She was up to her glasses in damage control.

Sooner not later, some pissed-off daddy with pull was going to ring the brass. The brass was going to ring O'Kelly. O'Kelly was going to ring Conway and take her head off.

"Julia," Conway said, past the nun. "Let's go."

A beat, and then Julia got up and came. No glance back at her mates.

Their room was two doors down from Orla's. It had that same feeling, left in a hurry: bedside tables open, clothes dropped in the dash. This time, though, I knew straight off what bit belonged to who, no need to check the bedside photos. Bright red bed linen, vintage poster of Max's Kansas City: Julia. Old-looking patchwork quilt, poem written out poster-size in careful art-project calligraphy: Rebecca. Hanging mobile made of curled silver forks and spoons, good black-and-white photo that looked like a rock against low sky, till you looked twice and it was an old man's profile: Holly. And Conway had been bang on about Selena: no dream catcher, but over her bed was a print of some medium-quality old oil, unicorn bending to drink at a dark lake by moonlight. Conway caught it too. Her eyes met mine, and the shadow of a private grin flipped back and forth between us. Before I knew it, it felt good.

Julia bounced down on her bed, propped herself up on her pillow, hands behind her head. Stretched out her legs—she was in jeans, a bright orange T-shirt with Patti Smith on, hair down—and crossed her ankles. Nice and comfy. "Hit me," she said.

Conway didn't fuck about with fairy tales this time. She whipped out the evidence envelope, dangled it from finger and thumb in front of Julia's face. Stood over her and watched. I got out my notebook.

Julia took her time. Let Conway hold the bag while she read the book's title. "Is this a hint? I should be more virtuous?"

Conway said, "Are we gonna find your prints on that?"

Julia pointed at the book. "You think this is my bedtime reading? Seriously?"

"Cute. Don't do that again. We ask, you answer."

Sigh. "No you are not going to find my prints on this OK thank you for asking. The only way I read about saints is when I'm forced to for essays. And even then I do, like, Joan of Arc. Not some simpering wimp."

"Wouldn't know the difference," Conway said. "You can explain it to me some other time. Inside that book there's a key to the connecting door between here and the school. Belonged to Joanne and her gang, last year."

One of Julia's eyebrows flicked; that was all. "OMG. I'm like totally shocked."

"Yeah. Orla says it's a copy of one you had."

Julia sighed. "Oh, Orla," she said to the air. "Who's a predictable little girl? You are! Yes you!"

"You're saying Orla's lying?"

"Um, duh? I've never had a key to that door. But Joanne isn't stupid. She knows that anyone who had that key could've been outside the night Chris died, plus anyone who had that key is in *huge* trouble with McKenna, like possibly *expelled* trouble. Of course she's going to share the love."

"Joanne didn't tell us. Orla did."

"Right. With Joanne's hand up her arse."

"Why would Joanne want to get you lot in hassle?"

Eyebrow. "You didn't notice that she's not exactly our biggest fan?"

"Yeah," Conway said. "We noticed. Why's that, again?"

Julia shrugged. "Who cares?"

"We do."

"So ask Joanne. Because I don't."

"If someone was pissed off enough with me to try and get me expelled and arrested, I'd care why."

"That is why. Because we don't care what Joanne thinks. In her tiny mind, that's like a mortal sin."

Conway said, "Not because Selena was going out with Chris."

Julia mimed banging her forehead off her palm. "Oh my God, if I have to hear that one more time I'm going to stick pens through my eardrums. It's a *rumor*. Like, *first*-years know not to believe everything they hear unless there's actual *proof*. You don't?"

"Gemma saw them. Snogging."

Flash of something, just the one: that had caught Julia off guard. Then a finger-wag. "Uh-uh. Orla says Gemma says she saw them. Which isn't the same thing."

Conway leaned back against the wall beside Julia's bed. Held up the bag and tapped it with a finger, watched it spin.

"What's Selena going to say, if I give up on you and go ask her? You know I don't ask nicely."

Julia's face pulled tight. "She's going to say the same thing she said when you asked her last year."

Conway said, "I wouldn't bet on it. You have to have noticed: Selena's not the same as she was last year."

That hit home. I saw Julia weigh something up, stacking and balancing. Saw her decide.

She said, "Selena wasn't the one going out with Chris. Joanne was."

"Right," Conway said. "You say she was, she says Selena was, me and Detective Moran get to play Here We Go Round the Rumor Bush till early in the morning."

Julia shrugged. "Believe it or don't, whatever. But Joanne was going out with Chris for a couple of months, before last Christmas. Then he dumped her flat on her arse. She didn't like that one little bit."

Conway and I didn't look at each other, didn't need to. Motive.

If it was true. This case was jammed with lies, couldn't grab hold of it without getting a handful.

Conway said, jaw hardening, "How come no one said anything about this last year?"

Shrug.

"Jesus fucking Christ." Conway didn't move, but the line of her spine said she was ready to shoot through the ceiling. "This wasn't about someone smoking in the jacks. This was a *murder* investigation. Everyone just decided not to mention this? Are yous all morons? What?"

Julia's eyes and her palms turning up to the ceiling. "Hello? Have you noticed where we are? You found out about Joanne's key, so the first thing she did was turn it around on me. If anyone had told you about her and Chris, she'd have done exactly the same thing: got back at them by dragging them into the shit with her. Who wants that?"

"So how come you're telling us now?"

Julia gave Conway the teen slouch-stare. "We did Civic Responsibility this year."

Conway had her temper back. She was focused on Julia the same way she'd been on that sandwich. "How do you know they were together?"

"I heard it around."

"From who?"

"Oh, God, I don't remember. It was supposed to be this big secret, but yeah, right."

"Rumor," Conway said. "I thought even first-years knew not to believe everything they hear. Got any proof?"

Julia scraped something off the frame of her Max's poster. Balancing things inside her head again.

She said, "Yeah, actually. Sort of."

"Let's hear it."

"I heard Chris gave Joanne a phone. A special phone, so they could text each other without anyone finding out."

"Why?"

Another shrug. "Ask Joanne. Not my problem. Then when he dumped her, I heard she made Alison buy the phone off her. I'm not swearing on my mother's life or anything, but Alison got a new phone after last Christmas, all right. And I'm pretty sure she hasn't changed it since."

"Alison got a new phone? That's your proof?"

"Alison's got a phone that Joanne was using to do whatever she and Chris did over the phone, which I don't even want to think about. Obviously I bet she erased all the texts after Chris died, but can't you guys do something about that? Get them back?"

"Sure," Conway said. "Why not. Just like on *CSI*. Did Civic Responsibility class remind you of anything else you should be sharing?"

Julia put a finger to her chin, gazed into space. "You know, I honest to God can't think of anything."

"Yeah," Conway said. "I figured. You let us know if you do." And opened the door.

Julia stretched, slid off the bed. "See you round," she said to me, with a little grin and a wave bye-bye.

We watched her down the corridor and into the common room. Julia didn't look back, but her walk said she felt our eyes. Her arse was mocking.

Conway said, "Joanne." The name fell into the silence. The room spat it back out, snapped tight shut after it.

"Means, opportunity, motive," I said. "Maybe."

"Yeah, maybe. If everything pans out. If Chris dumped Joanne, that'd explain why she was such a bitch about him liking Selena."

"Specially if he dumped her for Selena."

"It'd explain why Joanne's gang hate Julia's, too."

I said, "They're using us. Both lots."

"Yeah. To get at each other." Conway, hands shoved in her back pockets, still staring where Julia had been. "I don't like being some little rich kids' bitch."

I shrugged. "As long as they're giving us what we're after, I'm grand with them getting a bit of what they want as well."

"I would be, too. If I was positive we had a handle on what they want. Why they want it." Conway straightened up, took her hands out of her pockets. "Where's Alison's phone?"

"On her bed."

"I'll confirm with Alison where she got it. You search this."

The thought gave me the heebie-jeebies: left alone here, surrounded by teenage girls and knickers that said MAYBE on the arse. Conway was right, but: we couldn't leave Alison's phone for someone to get rid of it, couldn't leave this room till we'd searched it, and Conway was the one who knew her way around to look for Alison. "See you in five," I said.

"Any of them come in here, you go straight into the common room. Where you're safe."

She wasn't joking. I knew she was right, too, but the common room didn't feel like such a safe place either.

The door shut behind her. For a stupid split second, I felt like my mate had abandoned me in the shit. Reminded myself: Conway wasn't my mate.

I got my gloves back on, started searching. Selena's phone spilling out of her blazer pocket onto her bed, Julia's on her bedside table. Rebecca's on her bed. Holly's missing.

I started on the bedside tables. Something about the Julia interview was poking at me. It was stuck in a back corner of my mind, where I couldn't get my hands on it: something she'd said, that we'd let go by when we should have pounced.

Julia shaking info in front of us like a shiny dangle, to keep us from questioning Selena. I wondered how far she would go, to protect Selena or what Selena knew.

No extra phones in the bedside tables. This lot had books, in with the iPods and the hairbrushes and whatever else, but nothing old and nothing with bits cut out. Julia went for crime, Holly was reading *The Hunger Games*, Selena was halfway through *Alice in Wonderland*, Rebecca liked Greek mythology.

Liked old stuff. I didn't know the poem above her bed—I don't know poetry the way I wish I did, just whatever they had down the library when I was a kid, whatever I pick up when I get the odd chance—but it looked old, Shakespeare-old.

A Retir'd Friendship

Here let us sit and bless our Starres
Who did such happy quiet give,
As that remov'd from noise of warres.
In one another's hearts we live.

Why should we entertain a feare?
Love cares not how the world is turn'd.
If crouds of dangers should appeare,
Yet friendship can be unconcern'd.

We weare about us such a charme,
No horrour can be our offence;
For mischief's self can doe no harme
To friendship and to innocence.

Katherine Philips

A kid's pretty calligraphy, pretty trees and deer woven into the capitals; kid's need to blaze her love on walls, tell the world. Shouldn't have hit me, a grown man.

If I made a card to put up on the Secret Place: me, big grin, in the middle of my mates. Arms around their shoulders and heads leaning together, outlines melded into one. Close as Holly and her lot, unbreakable. The caption: *Me and my friends.*

They'd be holes in the paper. Cut out with tiny scissors, tiny delicate snips, perfect to the last loved hair—this guy's head thrown back laughing, this one's elbow locked round my neck messing, this one's arm shooting out as he overbalanced—and not there.

I said people mostly like me. True; they do, always have. Plenty of people ready to be my mates, always. That doesn't mean I want to be theirs. A few scoops, a bit of snooker, watch the match, lovely, I'm on. The more than that, the real thing: no. Not my scene.

It was these girls' scene, all right. They were diving a mile deep and swimming like dolphins, not a bother on them. *Why should we entertain a feare?* Nothing could hurt them, not in any way that mattered, not while they had each other.

The breeze made soft sounds in the curtains. I got my mobile out, dialed the number that had texted me. No answer, no ringing. The phones lay there, dark.

A sock under Holly's bed, a violin case under Rebecca's, nothing else. I started on the wardrobe. I was wrist-deep in soft T-shirts when I felt it: a shift, behind my shoulder, outside in the corridor. A change in the texture of the stillness, a blink across the light through the door-crack.

I stopped moving. Silence.

I took my hands out of the wardrobe and turned, nice and casual, just having another read of Rebecca's poem; not looking at the door or anything. The door-crack was in the corner of my eye. Top half bright, bottom half dark. Someone was behind the door.

I pulled out my phone, sauntered around messing with it, mind on other things. Got my back up against the wall by the door, out of eyeline. Waited.

Out in the corridor, nothing moved.

I went for the handle and had the door thrown open all in one fast move. There was no one there.

14

The Valentine's dance. Two hundred third- and fourth-years from Kilda's and Colm's, shaved and waxed and plucked, carefully anointed with dozens of substances in every color and texture, dressed up in their agonized-over best and sky-high on hormones and smelling of two hundred different cans of body spray, crammed into the Kilda's school hall. Mobile screens bob and flicker blue-white among the crowd, like fireflies, as people record each other recording each other. Chris Harper—there in the middle of the crowd, in the red shirt, shoulder-bumping and laughing with his friends to get the girls' attention—has three months, a week and a day left to live.

It's only half past eight and Julia is bored already. She and the other three are in a tight circle on the dance floor, ignoring the OMG LOL!!! mileage that Joanne's gang are getting out of Becca's jeans. Holly and Becca both love dancing so they're having a blast, and Selena looks happy enough, but Julia is about ready to fake epic period cramps to get out of this. The sound system is banging them over the heads with some love-based song that's been autotuned to a slick perky shine, Justin Bieber or possibly Miley Cyrus, someone smooth in front and jerking through all the motions of sexy. The lights are flashing red and pink. The committee—shiny-haired gold-star types already working on their CVs—has decorated the hall with lacy paper hearts and garlands and whatever, in predictable colors. The whole place is gloopy with romance, but there are two teachers guarding the door in case some couple decides to sneak out and do unspeakable things in a classroom, and if anyone is wild and crazy enough to start slow-dancing, like for example because a slow song is playing, then insane Sister Cornelius charges over and practically sprays them with a fire hose full of holy water.

Most people who aren't on the committee are keeping a careful eye on the hall doors. On the afternoon before a dance, Colm's guys go down the road behind Kilda's and throw booze over the corner of the wall into the bushes, where they pick it up later if they manage to sneak out of the dance. The next day, Kilda's girls scavenge anything that didn't get collected and get drunk in their dorm rooms. This has been a tradition for so long that Julia can't believe They haven't figured it out, specially since two of the teachers actually went to Kilda's and presumably did the same thing themselves. Miss Long and Miss Naughton both look like they were born forty-year-old Irish teachers in 1952 and haven't changed anything including their revolting tan tights since, so maybe if they actually ever were teenagers it's been wiped out of their memories, but just recently Julia has wondered if it's more complicated than that. If Miss Long and Miss Naughton might be ninety-nine percent dreary teacher and still somehow one percent fifteen-year-old muffling whiskey giggles, and loyal to that. If this is one of the secrets that grown-ups keep unmentioned: how long things last, invisible, inside. Either that or they were such losers back in school that they never heard about the booze bushes.

Julia dances on autopilot and checks furtively for pit-stains while she's got her arms up. Last year she enjoyed the Valentine's dance; or maybe "enjoyed" isn't the word, but it felt like it mattered. It felt knife-edge, last year, felt breathtaking, felt ready to boil over with its own momentousness. She was expecting it to feel the same way this year, but instead the dance feels like it matters considerably less than your average nose-picking session. This is pissing Julia off. Most of the stuff she does every day is blindingly pointless, but at least no one expects her to enjoy it.

"Back in a sec," she yells to the others, miming drinking, and drops out of the dance. She starts squeezing her way through the crowd towards the edge. The lights and the dancing and the crush of bodies have turned everyone sweaty. Joanne Heffernan's makeup is already melting, which doesn't surprise Julia given how much of it there is and which doesn't seem to bother Oisín O'Donovan who is trying to maneuver his hand inside Joanne's dress and getting frustrated because the dress is complicated and Oisín is thick as shite.

"OhmyGod, get off me, you lezzer," snaps Joanne over her shoulder, as Julia tries to slide past without brushing up against one molecule of Joanne's designer arse.

"In your dreams," Julia says, stepping on Joanne's heel. "Oops."

At the end of the hall is a long table of cupid-covered paper cups, arranged in rows around a big fake-glass punch bowl. The punch is a lurid baby-medicine shade of pink. Julia takes a cup. It's squash with food coloring.

Finn Carroll is leaning against the wall by the table. Finn and Julia know each other, sort of, from debating society; when he sees her he cocks an eyebrow, lifts his cup to her and shouts something she can't hear. Finn has bright red hair, long enough to flop into loose curls at the back of his neck, and he's smart. These would add up to social death for most guys, but Finn has the minimum of freckles to go with the hair, he's decent at rugby and he's getting height and shoulders faster than most of his class, so he gets away with it.

"What?" Julia yells.

Finn leans down to her ear. "Don't drink the punch," he shouts. "It's shit."

"To go with the music," Julia yells back.

"That's just *insulting*. 'They're teenagers, so they must love shitty chart crap.' It never occurs to them that some of us might have taste."

"You should've hotwired the sound system," Julia yells. Finn is good with electronics. Last term he wired up a frog in Bio so that when Graham Quinn went to dissect it, it jumped, and Graham and his stool both went over backwards. Julia respects that. "Or at least brought something sharp we could stick through our eardrums."

Finn says, close enough that he can stop shouting, "Want to see if we can get out?"

Finn is actually pretty sound, for a Colm's guy; Julia likes the idea of having an honest-to-God conversation with him, she thinks there's a decent chance he might be able to manage that without spending too much of the time trying to stick his tongue down her throat, and she can't see him bragging to all his moron buddies that they had hot monkey sex in the bushes. Someone will notice they're gone, though, and the hot-monkey-sex rumors will get going anyway. "Nah," she says.

"I've got a naggin of whiskey out the back."

"I hate whiskey."

"So we'll nick something else. There's a whole offie out in those bushes. Take your pick."

The colored lights slide across Finn's face, wide mouth laughing. It occurs to Julia, with a giddy rush, that she doesn't have to give one single fuck about hot-monkey-sex rumors.

She glances over at the other three: still dancing. Becca has her arms out and is twirling around with her head back like a little kid, laughing. Any minute she's going to get dizzy and fall over her own feet.

"Stick beside me," Julia says to Finn, and starts sauntering casually towards the hall door. "When I say 'Go,' go fast."

Sister Cornelius is being cuboid and grim in front of the door; Miss Long is off down the other end of the hall, unsticking Marcus Wiley from Cliona, who looks like she's not sure which of them she hates more. Sister Cornelius gives Julia and Finn a suspicious glare. Julia smiles back. "The punch is lovely," she shouts, raising her cup. Sister Cornelius looks even more suspicious.

Julia puts her cup down on a windowsill. Out of the corner of her eye she sees Finn, who apparently catches on fast, do the same thing.

Becca falls over. Sister Cornelius gets a wild missionary look and charges off down the hall, shoving dancers out of her way right and left, to interrogate Becca and breathalyze her and run tests for Young People's Drugs. Holly will deal with her, no problem; grown-ups believe Holly, maybe because of her dad's job, maybe just because of the total sincere commitment she puts into lying. "Go," Julia says, and zips out the door, hearing the slam behind her a split second later but she doesn't look round till she's down the corridor and into the dark maths room and the footsteps echoing behind her turn into Finn swinging around the door frame.

Moonlight stripes the room, tangles confusingly in chairbacks and desklegs. The music has turned into a distant hysterical pounding and shrieking, like someone has a tiny Rihanna locked in a box. "Nice," Julia says. "Shut the door."

"Fuck," Finn says, banging his shin off a chair.

"Shh. Anyone see us go?"

"Don't think so."

Julia is unscrewing the window bolt, moonlight slipping over her fast-moving hands. "They'll have someone patrolling the grounds," Finn says. "Or anyway they do at our dances."

"I know. Shut up. And get back; you want to get seen?"

They wait, backs against the wall, listening to the small tinny shrieking, keeping one eye on the empty sweep of grass and one on the classroom door. Someone's forgotten a uniform jumper, squiggled down the back of a chair seat; Julia grabs it and pulls it on, over her polka-dot dress. It's not exactly flattering—it's too big and it has boob dents—but it's warm, and they can feel the outdoors cold striking through the glass. Finn zips up his hoodie.

The shadows come first, sliding around the corner of the boarders' wing, long on the ground. Sister Veronica and Father Niall from Colm's, marching side by side, heads whipping back and forth while they scan every inch of cover.

When they stomp out of sight, Julia counts twenty to let them get around the corner of the nuns' wing, ten more in case they stopped to look at something, ten more just in case. Then she shoves up the window, braces her back against the frame, swings her feet around and slides out to drop on the grass: one move, smooth enough that if Finn's mind hadn't been occupied he would have copped this wasn't her first time. As she hears him land behind her she takes off, running fast and easy for the cover of the trees, her ears still ringing from the music, stars jingling overhead to the beat of her footsteps.

Red lights, pink, white, spinning strange crisscrossing patterns like coded signals gone too fast to catch. The beat in the floor and the walls and in all of their bones, pulsing through them like electric current, leaping from one lifting hand to the next all along the hall, never letting up for a second, go go go.

Selena's been dancing too long. The weaving lights are starting to look like living things, giddy and desperately lost. Selena's going watery at the edges, starting to lose hold of the boundary line where she leaves off and other things start. Over by the punch table Chris Harper tilts back his head to drink and Selena can taste it, someone bashes into her hip and she can't tell whether the pain belongs to her or them, Becca's arms rise and they feel like hers. She knows to stop dancing.

"You OK?" Holly yells, without breaking the beat.

"Drink," Selena yells back, pointing at the punch table. Holly nods and goes back to trying out some complicated hip-and-footwork. Becca is jumping up and down. Julia's gone, sneaked out somehow; Selena can feel the gap in the room where she should be. It throws things even more off balance. She puts her feet down carefully, trying to feel them. Reminds herself: *Valentine's dance.*

The punch tastes all wrong, grassy-cool long-ago summer afternoons running barefoot in and out of open doors, not right for this sweaty thumping dark tangle. Selena leans back against the wall and thinks about things with lots of weight and no give. The periodic table. Irish verb conjugations. The music has gone a notch quieter, but it's still getting in her way. She wishes she could put her fingers in her ears for a second, but her hands don't feel like hers and getting them to her ears seems too complicated.

"Hi," someone says, next to her.

It's Chris Harper. A while back this would have surprised Selena—Chris Harper is super-cool and she's not; she doesn't think she's ever had an actual conversation with him before. But the last few months have been their own place, lush and waving with startling things Selena knows she doesn't need to understand. At this point she expects them.

"Hi," she says.

Chris says, "I like your dress."

"Thanks," Selena says, looking down to remind herself. The dress is confusing. She tells herself: *2013.*

"Huh?" Chris says.

Crap. "Nothing."

Chris looks at her. "Are you OK?" he asks. And, like he thinks she might be dizzy, before she can move away, he puts out a hand to cup her bare arm.

Everything slams into focus, bright colors inside sharp outlines. Selena can feel her feet again, tingling fiercely like they've been asleep. The prickle of her zipper down her back is a tiny precise line. She's looking straight into Chris's eyes, hazel even in the dimness, but somehow she can see the hall as well and the lights aren't signals or lost things, they're lights and she never knew anything could be so red and so pink and so white. The whole room is solid, it's vivid and humming with its own clarity. Chris—light glossing his hair, warming his red shirt, catching the small puzzled furrow in between his eyebrows—is the realest thing she's ever seen.

"Yeah," she says. "I'm fine."

"Sure?"

"Totally."

Chris takes his hand off Selena's arm. Instantly that clarity blinks out; the hall turns jerky and messy again. But she still feels solid and warm all over, and Chris still looks real.

He says, "I thought . . ."

He's looking at her like he's never seen her before; like some ghost of what just happened found its way into him, too. He says, "You looked . . ."

Selena smiles at him. She says, "I felt weird for a second. I'm OK now."

"Some girl fainted earlier, did you see? It's boiling in here."

"Is that how come you're not dancing?"

"I was, before. I just felt like watching for a while." Chris takes a swallow of his punch and makes a face at the cup.

Selena doesn't move away. The handprint on her arm is shining red-gold, floating in the dark air. She wants to keep talking to him.

"You're friends with her," Chris says. "Right?"

He's pointing at Becca. Becca is dancing like an eight-year-old but the kind of eight-year-old who barely existed even back when they were eight, the kind who's never even seen a music video: no booty-shake, no hip-wiggle, no chest-thrust, just dancing, like no one's ever told her there's a right way; like she's doing it just for her own fun.

"Yeah," Selena says. Seeing Becca makes her smile. Becca looks totally happy. Holly doesn't; Marcus Wiley is dancing behind her, trying to rub up against her arse.

"Why's she wearing that?"

Becca is wearing jeans and a white camisole with lace at the edges, and she has her hair in a long plait. "She likes it," Selena explains. "She doesn't really like dresses."

"What, is she a lesbian?"

Selena considers that. "I don't think so," she says.

Marcus Wiley is still trying to rub up against Holly. Holly stops dancing, turns around, and spells something out in small words. Marcus's mouth opens and he stands there, blinking, till Holly gives him an off-you-go finger-wave; then he half dances off, trying to look like he just happens to be edging away, and manically checking whether anyone saw whatever just happened. Holly holds out her hands to Becca and they start spinning around. This time they both look happy. Selena almost laughs out loud.

"You should've talked to her," Chris says. "Got her to wear something normal. Or even something like what you're wearing."

"Why?" Selena asks.

"Because look." He nods at Joanne, who is wiggling to the music and gabbling something in Orla's ear at the same time. Both of them are wearing smirks and staring over at Becca and Holly. "They're slagging her off."

Selena asks, "How come you care?"

She's not being snippy, she just wonders—she wouldn't have guessed that Chris even knew Becca existed—but Chris glances around sharply. "I'm not *into* her! Jesus."

"OK," Selena says.

Chris goes back to watching the dance floor. He says something, but the DJ is fading up a song loaded with bass, and Selena can't hear. "What?" she yells.

"I said she reminds me of my sister." The DJ slides the volume up to earthquake level. "Jesus!" Chris yells, a sudden rush of irritation jerking his head back. "This fucking *noise!*"

Joanne's spotted them; her eyes snap away when she sees Selena looking, but the curl to her top lip says she's not pleased. Selena shouts, "Let's go outside."

Chris stares, trying to work out if she means what most girls would mean. Selena can't think of a good way to explain, so she doesn't try. "How?" he yells, eventually.

"Let's just ask."

He looks at her like she's mental, but not in a bad way. "Since we're not going to be snogging," Selena explains, "we don't need somewhere private, just somewhere quiet. We can sit right outside the doors. They might be OK with that."

Chris looks taken aback about five different ways. Selena waits, but when he doesn't come up with anything, she says, "Come on," and heads for the doors.

Most times people would be staring at them all the way, but Fergus Mahon just poured punch down Garret Neligan's collar so Garret Neligan tackled him and they fell over on top of Barbara O'Malley who has spent the last couple of weeks telling everyone that her dress is by Roksanda Somebody and who is screaming at the top of her lungs. Chris and Selena are invisible.

Something is on their side, smoothing the way for them. Even at the doors: if Sister Cornelius was there, they'd have no chance—even if Sister Cornelius wasn't crazy, this year the nuns take one look at Selena and get the urge to lock her up, for guys' sake or hers or the sake of morality in general, probably even they don't know—but it's Miss Long standing guard, while Sister Cornelius is off shouting at Fergus and Garret.

"Miss Long," Selena yells. "Can we go sit on the stairs?"

"Of course not," Miss Long says, distracted by Annalise Fitzpatrick and Ken O'Reilly huddled together in a corner, with one of Ken's hands out of view.

"We'll just be right out there. At the bottom of the steps, where you can see us. We just want to talk."

"You can talk here."

"We can't. It's too loud, and it's . . ." Selena spreads out her hands at the lights and the dancers and everything. She says, "We want to talk *properly*."

Miss Long takes her eye off Annalise and Ken for a second. She examines Selena and Chris skeptically. "'Properly,'" she says.

Something makes Selena smile at her, a burst of a smile, real and radiant. She doesn't mean to; it happens by itself, out of nowhere, because there's a pinwheel whirl deep in her chest telling her something amazing is happening.

For half a second, Miss Long almost smiles back. She presses her lips together and it's gone. "All right," she says. "At the bottom of those stairs. I will be checking on you every thirty seconds, and if you're not there, or if you're so much as holding hands, you will both be in *enormous trouble*. More trouble than you can even imagine. Is that clear?"

Selena and Chris nod, putting in every drop of sincerity they can find. "It'd better be," Miss Long says, with one eye on Sister Cornelius. "Now go on. Go."

As she turns away from them, her eyes sweep the hall like for that minute it's turned different, it's leapt up to meet her sparkling and strawberry-sweet and chiming with maybes. Selena, slipping out the door, understands that she and Chris weren't the ones who got the permission; that it was a decades-lost boy at some half-forgotten dance, his bright eager face, his laugh.

15

Conway banged the door open hard enough that I jumped a mile, hands leaping out of the wardrobe like I'd been doing something dirty. The corner of a grin, malicious, said she hadn't missed it.

She dumped her bag on Rebecca's bed. "How'd you get on?"

I shook my head. "Nothing. Julia's got half a pack of smokes and a lighter wrapped up in a scarf at the back of her bit of wardrobe. That's it."

"Good little girls," Conway said, not like a compliment. She was moving around the room, fast, tilting the frames on the bedside tables to glance at the photos; or to make sure the room looked good and searched. "Any of them come looking for you? Looking to talk, jump your bones, whatever?"

I shut my mouth on the slice of shadow at the door; maybe that grin, maybe the fact that I couldn't swear there had been anything there. "Nah."

"They'll come. The longer we leave them to it, the tighter they'll wind themselves. I listened outside the common room: they're up to ninety, the place sounds like a wasps' nest. Give them long enough and someone'll snap."

I shoved Selena's flute case back into the wardrobe, shut the door on it. "How's Alison getting on?"

Conway snorted. "Tucked up in the sick room like she's dying in some season finale. Little fadey voice on her and all. She's having a great old time. The arm's grand, almost; the mark's still there, but the blisters have gone down. I'd say she'd be back in the common room by now, only McKenna's hoping the mark'll go, doesn't want the rest of them gawping at it." She pulled Holly's book out of her bedside table, zipped a nail through the pages and tossed it back in. "I tried to get at whether Joanne put the whole stunt in Alison's head, but the minute she heard Chris's name she shut down, gave me the bunny stare. I don't blame her: McKenna and Arnold were right there, dying to jump on anything they didn't like. So I backed off."

I said, "How about the phone?"

Triumph lifted Conway's chin. Winning looked good on her. She flipped her satchel open, held up an evidence bag. The mobile I'd seen on Alison's bed: pretty pearly-pink flip-phone, small enough to fit in a palm, silver charm dangling. Chris had picked carefully.

"Alison got it off Joanne. She didn't like admitting it; tried to dodge, pretended she felt faint. I didn't fall for it, kept pushing, in the end she came clean. Joanne sold her the phone just after last Christmas, a year and a bit ago. Sixty quid, she charged her. Robbing bitch."

Conway threw the phone back in her satchel, started circling again. The triumph had worn off fast. "That's all Alison would give me, though. When I started asking about where Joanne got the phone, why she was selling it, Alison went whiny on me: 'I don't know I don't know my arm hurts I feel dizzy can I have a drink of water?' That helium voice girls do, what the fuck is that? Do guys think that's sexy?"

"Never thought about it," I said. Conway was still moving. Something had her wound tight. I stayed back against the wall, out of her way. "Does nothing for me, anyway."

"Makes me want to punch them in the mouth. There's nothing left on the phone from before last Christmas, no texts, no call logs: Joanne wiped it before she sold it. Here's the good part, though. Alison didn't swap her old SIM card into Joanne's phone. When she bought it, her old one was out of credit, and Joanne's one had twenty-odd quid left on it, so she just binned her old one and switched to using Joanne's number. Which means we don't need to track that number down, beg the network for the records, all that shit: we've got them already. Me and Costello pulled records on half the school, last year, including Alison. I rang Sophie; she'll have them e-mailed to me any minute."

"Hang on," I said. "I thought you said none of the girls' numbers linked up to Chris's."

"They didn't. But if Chris gave Joanne this phone"—Conway gave her bag a slap, as she paced past—"to keep the relationship secret, that means he thought people might go through their normal phones. Right?"

"Kids snoop."

"Kids, parents, teachers, whoever. People snoop. If Chris didn't want that, and he was loaded, like Julia said? I guarantee he had a dedicated girlie-phone of his own. We go through the records off Joanne's one"—another slap to the bag, harder—"what's the odds we find one number showing up for a couple of months before last Christmas, a shitload of contact back and forth?"

I said, "And then we check that number, Chris's secret number, for links to the phone that texted me today. If he did this with one girl, chances are he did it with a few. If Selena actually was with him, she might have her own spare phone lying around."

"We cross-check Chris's secret number for links to *everyone*. I knew, back last year, I *knew* it was weird he didn't have his phone on him. These kids, they don't take a shite without bringing their phones along. I should've— Jesus!" A savage kick to Rebecca's bedpost; it had to hurt, but Conway kept pacing circles like she felt nothing. "I should've fucking known."

There it was. Anything like reassurance—*No way you could know, no one could've*—would get me ripped apart. "If Joanne's our woman," I said, "she'd have a good reason to take Chris's phone off his body. It would've linked her to him."

Conway pulled open a drawer, raked through the neat stacks of knickers. "No shit. And it's probably landfill by now; no way we can prove he ever had it to begin with. We wave the records at Joanne, she says she was texting someone she met online or fuck only knows what she'll come up with. And there's nothing we can do."

I said, "Unless we track down someone else Chris was contacting on the secret phone. Get her to come clean."

Conway laughed, short and harsh. "Right. Get her to come clean. Easy as that. 'Cause that's how this case rolls."

"Worth a shot."

She slammed the drawer on the mess she'd made. "Jaysus, you're a little ray of sunshine, aren't you? Like working with bleeding Pollyanna—"

"What do you want me to say? 'Ah, fuck it, it's never gonna work, let's go home'?"

"Do I look like quitting to you? I'm going nowhere. But if I have to listen to you being fucking *chirpy*, I swear to God—"

Both of us glaring, Conway shoving her face and her finger in close, me still against the wall so I couldn't have backed off if I'd wanted to. We were on the edge of a full-on barney.

I don't argue, not with people who have my career in their hands. Not even when I should; definitely not over bugger-all.

I said, "You'd rather have Costello, yeah? Depressing fucker like him? How'd that work out for you?"

"You shut your—"

A buzz from Conway's jacket. Message.

She wheeled away instantly, grabbing for her pocket. "That's Sophie. Joanne's phone records. About bloody time." She hit buttons, watched the download, knee jiggling.

I stayed well back. Waited, heart going ninety, for *Fuck off home.*

Conway glanced up, impatient. "What're you doing? Come see this."

Took me a second to cop: the fight was over, gone.

I took a breath, moved in at her shoulder. She tilted the phone so I could see the screen.

There it was. October, November, a year and a half back: one number going back and forth with the phone that had been Joanne's, over and over again.

No calls, just messages. Text from the new number, text to it, media message from, text from, from, from, to. Chris chasing, Joanne playing it cool.

First week of December, the pattern changed. Text to the new number, text to, text to, text to, text to. Chris ignoring, Joanne pressing, Chris ignoring harder. Then, when she finally gave up, nothing.

Down the corridor outside, rattle of a trolley, clinking plates, warm smell of chicken and mushrooms making my mouth water. Someone—I pictured a frilly apron—was bringing dinner up to the fourth-years. McKenna wasn't going to have them heading down to the canteen, spreading stories and panic like flu, yammering away with no nun to listen in. She was keeping them corralled nice and safe in their common room, everything under control.

Joanne's phone records went blank till mid-January. Then a mix of other numbers, to and from, calls and texts. No sign of Chris's number. Just what you'd expect off a girl's normal phone; off Alison.

"Sophie, you fucking *star*," Conway said. "We'll get her on to the network, see if that number links to—"

I felt her go still. "Hang on a second. Two nine three—" She snapped her fingers at me, staring at the screen. "Your phone. Show me that text."

I pulled it up.

That triumph lifting Conway's head again, making her profile into something off a statue. "Here we go. I knew I'd seen that number." She held out the two phones, side by side. "Have a look at this."

That memory. She was right. The number that had told me where to find the key was the same number that had been playing phone footsie with Joanne.

"Fuck me," I said. "Didn't see that coming."

"Me neither."

"So either Joanne's secret romance wasn't with Chris at all, it was with one of our other seven—"

Conway shook her head. "Nah. A breakup would explain why the two gangs hate each other, yeah, but you can't tell me we wouldn't have got even one hint from somewhere. Gossip, or Joanne giving it loads of 'So-and-so's a big dyke, she tried to jump my sexy body,' trying to get the ex in shite. Nah."

I said, "—or else someone just texted me off Chris Harper's secret phone."

A moment of silence.

Conway said, "Looks like it." Something in her voice, but I couldn't tell whether it was exhilaration or anger, or smelling blood. Whether there was a difference, for her.

The day had changed again, shifted under our eyes into something new. We weren't looking for a witness, in that roomful of shining hair and restless feet and watching eyes. We were looking for a killer.

"The way I see it," I said, "there's three ways that could've happened. One: Joanne killed Chris, took his phone, she used it to text us about the key because she wants to get caught—"

Conway snorted. "She does in her arse."

"Yeah, me neither. Two: the killer—Joanne or someone else—took the phone, handed it on to someone else."

"The same way Joanne sold her own to Alison. That'd fit her."

"Three," I said. "Someone else killed Chris, took the phone, has it still."

Conway started pacing again, but steady this time, none of that restless looking for something to wreck. She was focusing. "Why, but? She has to know the phone's evidence. Hanging on to it is dangerous. Why not bin it, a year ago?"

"Dunno. But it mightn't be the actual phone she kept. She might've ditched the phone, just hung on to the SIM card. That's a lot safer. Then today, she needs an anonymous number to text us from, swaps Chris's SIM into her own phone . . ."

"Why hang on to any of it?"

I said, "Say it's Theory Two, the killer passed it on to someone else. Maybe the other girl had a feeling there was something dodgy about it, something to do with Chris; she hung on to the phone, or just the SIM card, in case she ever felt like turning it in to us. Or maybe she didn't cop there was a connection, just liked the idea of having an anonymous number stashed away. Or maybe it just had credit left on it, like the one Joanne sold Alison."

Conway nodded. "OK. That'll work with Theory Two. I don't see how it works with One or Three. Which means the girl who texted you isn't the killer."

I said, "That says the killer's got plenty of nerve. Handing Chris's phone off to someone else, instead of binning it, when it could put her in jail."

"Plenty of nerve, plenty of arrogance, plenty of stupid, take your pick. Or she didn't hand it off on purpose; she ditched it somewhere, the texter found it."

Voices, seeping down the corridor with the chicken-and-mushroom smell: the fourth-years talking over their dinner. Not happy girly chitchat. This was a low, flattened-out buzz, got into your ear and turned you edgy.

I said, "Did Sophie say when we'll get the records off it?"

"Soon. Her contact's working on it. I'll e-mail her now, tell her we need the actual texts, not just the numbers. We could be out of luck—some of the networks dump that stuff after a year—but we'll give it a shot." Conway was typing fast. "Meanwhile," she said.

It was gone five o'clock. *Meanwhile we go back to HQ, sort our paperwork, sign out. Meanwhile we get something to eat, get some kip, nice work today Detective Moran see you bright and early in the morning.*

No way we could leave Kilda's, not now. Inside, all those girls, all jittering to start swapping stories and matching up lies the second our shadow lifted. Outside, the Murder lads, jaws ready to snap shut on this case the minute O'Kelly heard it was live again. In the middle, us.

If we walked out of Kilda's empty-handed, we'd never come back or we'd come back to a blank wall.

But:

I said, "We stick around much longer, McKenna's going to get onto your gaffer."

Conway didn't look up from her phone. "I know, yeah. She said that to me, down in Arnold's room. Didn't even bother being subtle: told me if we weren't out by dinnertime, she'd ring O'Kelly and tell him we bullied her *students* into fits."

"It's dinnertime now."

"Chillax. I wasn't subtle either. I told her if she tries to throw us out before we're good and ready, I'll ring my journalist pal and tell him we've spent the day interviewing Kilda's students about Chris Harper." Conway shoved her phone into her pocket. "We're going nowhere."

I could've backslapped her, hugged her, something. I didn't want my nads kicked in. "Fair play to you," I said, instead.

"What, you thought McKenna was gonna make me her bitch? Thanks a bunch." But the big grin on me pulled one out of her, too. "So. Meanwhile . . ."

I said, "Joanne?"

Conway took a breath. Behind her, the curtains stirred; the cutlery mobile made a faint high ringing, soft and faraway.

She nodded, once. "Joanne," she said.

I said, "Witness or suspect?"

A suspect, you need to caution her, get her to sign a rights sheet, before you go asking any questions. A suspect, you take her down to HQ, get everything on video. A suspect, if she wants a solicitor, she gets one. An underage suspect, you have an appropriate adult present; you don't even think about dodging.

Just now and again, we fudge it. No one can prove what you're thinking inside your own mind. Once in a long while you keep it casual, just a chat with a witness, till your suspect gets in too deep for you, or him, to deny.

If you get caught out, if the judge gives you a filthy look and says any officer with half a brain would've suspected this person, then you're done. Everything you got, gone: thrown out.

We were on the line. Plenty of reasons to think it might be Joanne; not enough to believe it was.

"Witness," Conway said. "Be careful."

I said, "You too. Joanne's not about to forget that you took her down a peg in front of the rest."

"Ah, for fuck." Conway's head tossing up with irritation: she'd forgotten. "That's me stuck in the back seat again. Next time we need to piss someone off, I'm gonna make you do it."

"Ah, no," I said. "You do it. You've got a gift." The face she made at me looked like a friend's.

In the common room the girls were neat around tables, heads bent over plates, homey rhythm of clinking cutlery. The nun had one eye on her food and one on them.

Lovely and peaceful, till you looked hard. Then you saw. Runners jittering under tables, bared teeth gnawing at the edge of a juice glass. Orla curling in tight on herself, trying not to take up space. A heavy girl with her back to me looked like she was lashing into her food, but over her shoulder I caught a full plate of chicken pie chopped into tiny perfect squares, getting tinier with each vicious cut.

"Joanne," Conway said.

Joanne threw a tsk and a disgusted eye-roll at the ceiling, but she came. She was wearing the same outfit as Orla, give or take: short jeans shorts, tights, pink hoodie, Converse. On Orla they looked like she'd been dressed by someone with a grudge; on Joanne they looked like she'd been made that way, all in one mold.

We went back to her room. "Have a seat," I said, held out a hand to her bed. "Sorry we've no chair, but we'll only be a few minutes."

Joanne stayed standing, arms folded. "I'm actually eating dinner?"

In a bit of a fouler, our Joanne. Orla was in big trouble. "I know," I said, nice and humble. "I won't keep you. I have to tell you, I've got a couple of questions that you might not like, but I need answers, and I'm not sure anyone's got them but you."

That caught her in the curiosity, or in the vanity. Long-suffering sigh, and she dropped onto her bed. "OK. I guess."

"I appreciate it," I said. Sat down on Gemma's bed, facing Joanne, staying well away from the thrown-off clothes. Conway melted off into the background, leaning against the door. "First off, and I know Orla's already told you this: we've found your key to the connecting door between here and the main building. Yous were sneaking out at night."

Joanne had her mouth half open to deny it and her outraged face half on—autopilot—when Conway held up the *Thérèse* book. "Covered in fingerprints," she said.

Joanne put the outraged look away for later. "So?" she said.

I said, "So this is confidential. We're not about to pass it on to McKenna, get you in trouble. We're just sorting what's important from what's not. OK?"

"Whatever."

"Lovely. So what'd yous do, when you snuck out?"

A little reminiscent smirk, slackening Joanne's mouth. After a moment she said, "Some of the Colm's day boys came in over the back wall. I mean, I don't normally hang out with day boys, but Garret Neligan knew where his parents kept their drinks and . . . stuff, so whatever. We did that a couple of times, but then Garret's mum caught him and she started locking stuff up, so we didn't bother any more."

Stuff. Garret had been getting into Mammy's meds. "When was this?"

"Like last March? After that, we didn't actually use the key that much. At Easter Gemma met this student guy at a club, so she went out to hook

up with him a bunch of times—she thought she was totes amazeballs because she'd caught someone who was in OMG *college*, but of course he
dumped her the second he found out how old she actually was? And obviously after Chris they changed the lock, so it wasn't even any use any more."

I said, "You have to realize that this puts you and your mates front and
center for having put up that card on the Secret Place. Any of you could
have been out in the grounds when Chris was killed. Any of you could have
seen something. Seen it happen, even."

Joanne's hands shot up. "Excuse me, *whoa*? Can we put the brakes on
here? We weren't the only ones who had a key. We got ours from Julia
Harte."

I did dubious. "Yeah?"

"Yeah."

"So where would we find hers?"

"Like I'd know? Even if I had a clue where they kept it, which I don't
actually pay attention to what those weirdos do, this was a *year* ago. They
probably threw it away once the locks got changed. That's what I *told* Orla
to do, except she's too useless to even get that right."

"Julia says they never had a key."

Joanne's face was starting to pinch in, turn vicious. "Um, hello, she
would, wouldn't she? That's total crap."

"Could be," I admitted, shrugging. "But we can't prove it. We've got
proof that you and your mates had one, no proof that Julia and hers did.
When it's one person's word against another's, we've got to go with the evidence."

"Same as with Chris and Selena," Conway said. "You lot say they were
going out, she says they weren't, not one speck of evidence says they ever
went near each other. What do you expect us to believe?"

The viciousness congealed into something solid, a decision. "OK. Fine."

Joanne pulled out her phone, pushed buttons. Thrust it at me, arm's
length.

"Is this *proof*?"

I took it. It felt hot from her hand, clammy.

A video. Dark; the rustle and bump of footsteps through grass. Someone
whispering; a tiny snort of laughter, a hissed *Shut up!*

"Who's with you?" I asked.

"Gemma." Joanne was sitting back, arms folded, swinging her crossed
foot and watching us. Anticipating.

Faint gray shapes, jiggling as Joanne's movement jolted the phone.

Bushes in moonlight. Clumps of small whitish flowers, folded up for the night.

Another whisper. The footsteps stopped; the phone stilled. Shapes came into focus.

Tall trees, black around a pale clearing. Even in blurry dark, I recognized the place. The cypress grove where Chris Harper had died.

In the moonlit heart of it, two figures, pressed so close they looked like one. Dark jumpers, dark jeans. Brown head bent over a flood of fair hair.

A branch bobbed across the screen. Joanne shifted the phone out of its way, zoomed in tight.

Night smudged the faces. I glanced at Conway; tiny dip of her chin. Chris and Selena.

They moved apart like they could hardly bear to move at all. Pressed their palms together, shoulders rising and falling with their quick breathing. They were amazed by each other, stunned silent, all in the circle of stirring cypresses and night wind. The world outside was gone, nothing. Inside that circle the air was unfurling new colors, it was changing to something that cascaded and fountained pure gold and dazzle, and every breath changed them too.

I used to dream of that, when I was a young fella. Never had it. Even when I was sixteen years old and ninety percent dick, I kept away from the girls in my school; scared that if I went beyond the odd snog and grope, I'd wake up the next morning a daddy in a council flat, stuck to the sticky linoleum forever. Dreamed of it instead. Dreams I can still taste.

By the time I got away and found other girls, it was too late. When you stop being a kid, you lose your one chance at that too-tender-to-touch gold, that breathtaken everything and forever. Once you start growing up and getting sense, the outside world turns real, and your own private world is never everything again.

Chris wove his fingers in Selena's hair, lifted it so that it fell strand by strand. She turned her head to touch her lips to his arm. They were like underwater dancers, like time was holding still just for them and every minute gave them a million years. They were beautiful.

Close to the phone, Joanne or Gemma snickered. The other one made a tiny gagging noise. Something like that in front of them, feet away, the real thing, and they couldn't even see it.

Selena raised her fingers to Chris's cheek, and his eyes closed. Moonlight ran down her arm like water. They moved closer, faces tilting together, lips opening.

Beep, end of the video.

"So," Joanne said. "Is *that*, like, enough *evidence* that Selena and all of them had a key? And that she was doing it with Chris?"

Conway took the phone off me and messed with it, hitting buttons. Joanne flipped out a palm. "Ex*cuse* me, that's mine?"

"You'll get it back when I'm done." Joanne tsked and threw herself back against the wall. Conway ignored her. To me: "Twenty-third of April. Ten to one in the morning."

Three and a half weeks before Chris died. I said, "So you and Gemma saw Selena leaving her room, and you followed her?"

"Gemma saw them out in the grounds by accident the first time, like a week before—she was meeting some guy, I don't even remember who. After that, we took turns watching the corridor at night." Grim project-manager voice on Joanne; I could picture her going for the jugular if one of the others had the nerve to doze off at her post. "This night, Alison saw Selena sneak out of their room, so she woke me up and I followed Selena."

"You brought Gemma along?"

"Um, I wasn't exactly about to go out there by my*self*? And anyway, I needed Gemma to show me where they were having their little make-out sessions. By the time we got dressed, Selena was well gone. She couldn't wait to get the action started. Some people are just sluts."

More midnight traffic than a train station, these grounds. McKenna was in for a coronary if she ever heard this. "So you tracked them down," I said, "and you filmed this clip. Just the one?"

"Yeah. That's not enough for you?"

"What happened after you stopped filming?"

Joanne prissed up her mouth. "We went back in. I wasn't going to stand there and watch them *do* it. I'm not a perv."

Conway's phone buzzed. "Sent myself the video," she told me. To Joanne: "Here." She tossed the mobile over.

Joanne made a big deal of wiping off the working-class germs on her duvet. I asked, "What were you planning to do with this clip?"

Shrug. "I hadn't decided yet."

Conway said, "Wild guess. You used it to blackmail Selena into dumping Chris. 'Stay away from him, or this goes to McKenna.'"

Joanne's top lip pulled up, that near-animal snarl. "Um, excuse me, no I didn't?"

I said—leaning forward, move her off Conway—"It would've been for Selena's own good if you had. That there, that wasn't the healthiest way for her to be spending her nights."

Joanne thought that over, decided she liked it. Did something with her face that was meant to look virtuous, came out looking stuffed. "Well. I would've if I'd had to. But I didn't."

"Why not?"

"That"—Joanne flicked a finger at the phone—"that was the last time Selena and Chris met up. I'd already had a chat with Julia, and after this she sorted it out. End of."

"How did you know?"

"Well, I didn't, like, take Julia's *word* for it, if that's what you mean. I'm not stupid. That's why I got the video: just in case she needed a little nudgie. We watched the corridor for weeks after, and Selena never went out on her own. The four of them still went out together, to do whatever they did out there—I heard they're witches, so maybe they were like sacrificing a cat or something, I literally don't even want to *know*?" Exaggerated wiggle of disgust. "And Julia went out a couple of times—she had this thing with Finn Carroll, which, I mean, nobody actually *wants* to be with a ginger but I guess if you look like Julia you take whatever you can get. But Selena had stopped going. So obviously her and Chris had broken up. Like, surprise?"

"Any idea who did the breaking?"

Shrug. "Do I look like I care? I mean, obviously I hoped for Chris's sake that he'd suddenly got some *standards*, but . . . Guys: they only care about one thing. If Chris was getting it off Selena, and he didn't have to, like, be *seen* with her, why would he dump her? So I figure it had to be Selena. Either Julia knocked some sense into her, or else Selena copped that, hello, Chris was only using her for an easy you-know-what and a pig like her was never going to be his actual *girlfriend*."

Chris's face bent over Selena's, holy with wonder. He'd been good, but that good?

"Why didn't you want them going out together?" I asked.

Joanne said coolly, "I don't like her. OK? I don't like any of them. They're a bunch of freaks, and they act like that's totally OK; like they're so special, they can just do whatever they want. I thought Selena should find out that it doesn't work like that. Like you said, I was actually doing her a favor."

I did puzzled. "You were fine with Julia and Finn, but. Any particular reason why Selena and Chris was a problem?"

Shrug. "Finn was OK, if you go for that kind of thing, but he wasn't a big deal. Chris was. Everyone was into him. I wasn't going to let Selena think someone like her had a right to get someone like that. Hello, Earth calling whale: just because you do whatever disgusting stuff you did to even get Chris to *look* at you, that doesn't mean you get to keep him."

I said, "It wasn't because you'd been going out with Chris, just a few months earlier."

Joanne didn't miss a beat. Gusty sigh, eye-roll. "Hello, haven't we been *over* this already? Am I imagining things? Am I out of my mind? I never went out with Chris. Only in his dreams."

Conway lifted the evidence bag with Alison's phone, waggled it at Joanne. "Try again."

Half a second where Joanne went rigid. Then she turned her head away from Conway, folded her arms deliberately.

"Oh, ouch," Conway said, hand to her heart. "That's put me in my place."

"Joanne," I said, leaning in. "I know this is none of our business, or anyway it wouldn't be normally. But if you were close enough to Chris that he might have told you anything that could be important, then we need to know. Make sense?"

Joanne thought. I could see her trying out the star-witness seat, liking the feel.

I said, "That phone that my partner's got, that was yours till you sold it to Alison. And we've got records of a million texts back and forth between that number and Chris's secret phone."

Joanne sighed. "OK," she said. "All right."

She rearranged herself on the edge of the bed. Hands folded, ankles crossed, eyes down. She was getting into character: bereaved girlfriend. "Chris and I were together. For a couple of months, the autumn before last."

It practically exploded out of her. She'd been only dying to tell, for a year now. Held it in because it might get her suspected, because she didn't want to admit she'd been dumped, because we were adults and the enemy, who knew. Finally, we'd given her the excuse to talk.

"But he never said anything about, like, having an *enemy* or anything. And he would've told me. Like you said, we were really close."

"Is that what you used that key for?" I asked. "Going out at night to meet Chris, yeah?"

Joanne shook her head. "I only got the key after we split up. And anyway, he couldn't get out at night either. I mean, obviously he found some way later, because he was meeting that fat cow, but he couldn't when we were together."

"And he had a secret phone specially for texting you, as well?"

"Yeah. He said the guys at Colm's went through each other's phones all the time, looking for sexts or photos—you know, *photos*? From girls?" Meaningful stare. I nodded. "Chris said the priests did it too—some of them are such perverts, it's just *eww*. I was like, 'Hello, if you think you're getting pictures of my la-la, I'm sorry, but you're going to have to work a little harder than that?' But it wasn't like that; Chris just wasn't going to have anyone reading my texts. Anything I said meant too much to him to have some D-head leching over them."

I caught a glance off Conway. Chris had been good, all right. "What kind of phone was it?" I asked. "Did you ever see it?"

Misty smile, reminiscent. "Exactly like my one, only red. 'A matching pair,' that's what Chris said. 'Like us.'"

Conway's eye said *Puke*. "How come all the secrecy?" I asked. "Why not just tell everyone you were together?"

That made Joanne move, a defensive jerk: the secret hadn't been her idea. She took a breath and got back in character. "I mean, this wasn't just some stupid shallow teenage thing. We had something special, me and Chris. It was so intense, it was like, ohmyGod, something out of a *song*? People wouldn't have understood; they literally wouldn't have been able to get it. I mean, obviously we were going to tell them anyway, in a while. Just not yet."

Coming out too pat and brittle, learned off by heart. The lines Chris had given her, that she'd told herself over and over to make it feel OK.

I asked, "It wasn't because there was someone specific who Chris didn't want finding out? A jealous ex, something like that?"

"No. I mean . . ." Joanne thought about that, liked it. "There could've been. I mean, lots of people would've been *so* jel if they'd known. But he never mentioned anyone."

"How'd you manage to meet up in secret, if you couldn't get out at night?"

"At the weekends, mostly. Sometimes in the afternoons, between classes and study period, but it was hard finding a place where we wouldn't get spotted. This one time, you know the little park down past the Court? It was November, so it was dark early and the park was closed, but me and Chris climbed over the railings. There's this little roundabout, for kids; we sat on that and . . ."

Joanne was half smiling, unconsciously, remembering. "I was there, 'OhmyGod, I can't believe I'm doing this, climbing around in the dark like some skanger; you'd better buy me something nice after this,' but I was just joking. It was actually . . . fun. We were laughing so hard. We had fun, that day."

A wisp of a laugh. A frail thing, lost, drifting between the slick posters and the makeup-smeared tissues. Not a laugh she'd learned off some reality star and practiced; just her, missing that day.

Here was why she had needed to see Selena and Chris through a dirty snicker and a gagging noise. That was the only way she could stand to look.

I said, "So what happened? You were together a couple of months, you said. Why'd you split up?"

That slammed Joanne shut again. Fake stare clanging into place, vein of hurt vanished behind it. "I broke up with him. I feel sooo terrible about it now—"

"Ah-ah," Conway said, waving the bag again. "That's not what this says."

"You kept texting him and ringing him after he stopped answering," I explained. Joanne's mouth thinned. "What happened?"

She got on top of that one faster than I expected. With another sigh: "Well. Chris got frightened of his feelings. I mean, like I already told you, what we had was totally special? Like really intense?" Wide earnest eyes, parted lips, voice pitched high. She was being someone off the telly; I hadn't a clue who, don't watch the right stuff. "And a lot of guys can't cope with that. I think Chris was just kind of immature. If he was alive, then probably by now we'd be . . ." Another sigh. Gaze drifting off, at a picturesque angle, into the might-have-beens.

"You must've been well annoyed with him," I said.

Joanne flicked hair. With an edge to her voice: "Um, I *so* didn't care?"

I went puzzled. "Seriously? I wouldn't've thought you were used to being dumped. You are, yeah?"

More edge. The wide-eyed thing was wearing off fast. "No, I'm not. Nobody's ever dumped me."

"Except Chris."

"Well, I was about to dump him anyway. That's why I said—"

"How come? I thought the relationship was great, he just got overloaded 'cause he was immature. But you're not immature, are you?"

"No. I just—" Joanne was thinking fast. Hand going to her heart: "I knew it was more than he could handle. I was going to set him free. 'If you love something—'"

"Then why'd you keep texting him after he stopped texting you?"

"I was just telling him. That I understood, you know, how it was too intense? That, I mean, I wasn't going to wait for him or anything, but I hoped we could be friends. Stuff like that. I can't remember."

"Not giving out to him, no? Because we've got someone pulling the actual texts. We'll be able to read them any minute."

"I don't remember. I guess I could've been a teeny bit *startled*, but I wasn't *angry* or anything."

Conway shifted her back against the wall. Warning me: if I pushed this any harder, we were over that line and into inadmissible.

"I understand," I said. Leaned in, hands clasped. "Joanne. Listen to me." I put that epic ring back into my voice: a speech to inspire the brave young heroine. "You had the key. You believed your relationship with Chris wasn't over. You kept an eye on Chris when he came into the grounds at night. Do you see where I'm going with this?"

That flat stare turned wary. Joanne shrugged.

"I think you were out there the night he died, and I think you saw something. No"—I raised a hand, masterful—"let me finish. Maybe you're protecting someone. Maybe you're afraid. Maybe you don't want to believe what you saw. I'm sure you've got a good reason for saying you weren't there."

Conway, in the corner of my eye, giving me a sliver of a nod. We were back on safe ground. If Joanne repeated that speech to her counsel someday, it said *witness*, loud and clear. But if it worked, if she admitted to being at the scene, she crossed over the line to suspect, no leeway left.

"But I'm also sure, Joanne, I'm just as sure that you saw something, or heard something. *You know who killed Chris Harper.*" I let my voice rise. "Time to stop hiding it. You heard what Detective Conway said, earlier. It's time to tell us—before we find out on our own, or someone else does. Now."

Joanne wailed, "But I *don't*! Honest to God, I swear, I didn't go out that night! I hadn't been out in weeks."

"You're trying to tell me you didn't have anyone to meet? Almost six months after Chris dumped you, you were still single?"

"Not *still*—I went out with Oisín O'Donovan for a while, you can ask anyone, but I dumped him *weeks* before Chris happened! Ask him. I wasn't out that night. I don't know anything. I *swear*!"

Huge-eyed, hand-wringing, all the trimmings: the way she'd learned that innocent looked, off the telly or wherever. Truth or lie, it would look exactly the same.

Another minute and she'd be scrunching up her face, trying to cry. Conway's eye said *Kill it*.

I eased back, on the soft intimate squash of Gemma's bed. Joanne drew a long shaky breath, snatched a sideways glance at me to make sure I'd caught it.

"OK," I said. "OK, Joanne. Thank you."

Joanne and her shorts headed back to the common room. Her arse watched us watching her, same as Julia's, only not the same at all.

"That's one pissed-off little geebag," Conway said, tinge of enjoyment. She was leaning a shoulder against the wall of the corridor, hands in her pockets. "She can spin it however she wants: she was well fucked off with Chris Harper."

"Fucked off enough to kill him?"

"Sure. She'd've loved to. But . . ."

Silence. Neither of us wanted to say it.

"If she could've pushed a button," I said. "Stuck a pin in a voodoo doll. Then yeah."

"Yeah. Like *that*." Finger-snap. "But heading out there in the dark, smacking him in the head with a hoe . . . I can't see Joanne taking that kind of risk. She wouldn't even go after Selena without dragging Gemma along. Very careful of herself, our Joanne. And she doesn't step outside her comfort zone. *Fuck*."

"The card could still be her." I heard the silver-lining note in my voice, waited for another Pollyanna jab. Didn't get it.

"If it is, she's trying to steer us towards Selena. Now there's revenge. You rob my fella, I'll frame you for murder."

"Or towards Julia," I said. "She made sure to tell us Julia was sneaking out right up until the murder, did you notice?"

"Julia and Finn," Conway said. Forehead-smack. "I knew there had to be a reason why Finn decided to hotwire the fire door all of a sudden. He wouldn't say. I should've known. Same as everything fucking else today."

I said, "Why was everyone keeping their love lives secret, but? When I was a young fella, if you had a girlfriend, you told the world. Did girls keep this stuff under wraps, when you were that age?"

"Fuck, no. That was half the point of going out with someone to begin with: show everyone that you had a fella. That meant you were a success, not some pathetic single loser. You'd shout it from the rooftops."

"And this generation, they care a lot less about privacy than we did. Everything goes online, unless it's embarrassing or it'll get them in trouble."

A kid came out of the third-year common room and headed towards the jacks, frantically trying to check us out without looking at us. Conway swung back into Joanne and Company's room, kicked the door shut. "Even then. My cousin's kid had a pregnancy scare; what's the first thing she did? Put it on Facebook. Then got pissed off with her ma for finding out."

"And they weren't shy about telling us who they're going out with now," I said. "Joanne gave us the bit of hassle, but that was just to be a bitch to you, not because she actually wanted to keep it secret. So what was different last year?"

Conway had started pacing circles around the room again. Whatever poor bastard ended up partnered with her, he was going to spend a lot of his time dizzy. "That crap Joanne gave us, about her and Chris keeping it to themselves because they were sooo intense or whatever the fuck. You believe that?"

"Nah. Load of bollix." I leaned against the wall, one-shouldered so I could keep an eye on that line of light around the door. "I don't know about Julia and Finn, but the others: Chris was the one that wanted things on the down-low. I'd bet it was so he could keep a few girls on the go at once. Joanne started pressuring him to go public, he dumped her."

Nod. She nodded sideways, on a twist, street style. "Looks like your Holly might've been right about Chris. Not the sweetheart everyone said."

He only cared about what he wanted, Holly had said.

The face on Chris, looking at Selena. But that age: wanting beats loyalty so easily. Doesn't mean the loyalty isn't real. You know what you've got, but you know what you want, too. So you go after it. You see your chance, and you take it. Tell yourself it'll be grand in the end.

I said, "If he kept up the two-timing, and one of the girls found out . . ."

"If Selena found out, you mean."

"Probably not her. Selena and Chris were over, weeks before he died. If you're gonna smash your fella's head in for cheating, you do it when you find out, not weeks later. Could've been why she broke it off, though."

"Maybe." Conway kicked someone's clumpy uniform shoe out of her way. She didn't sound convinced. "That didn't go down the way Joanne said, anyway. She told Julia to get Selena away from Chris, Julia went, 'Yes, ma'am, straight away, ma'am,' and ran right off to do what she was told? You think Julia takes orders on her mates' love lives from Joanne?"

"She'd tell her to go fuck herself. Unless Joanne had something major on her."

"That video's major enough: could've got Julia and all her mates expelled. But Joanne didn't need to use it. Chris and Selena split up first."

"You believe her?"

"On that, I do."

I thought back. Realized I'd already forgotten Joanne's face. Hard to tell, but: "Yeah. I think I do too."

"Right. So maybe Selena did dump him because she caught him two-timing." Conway swept up Gemma's hair straightener on her way past, gave it a what-the-fuck grimace, tossed it on Orla's bed. "Or maybe it was something else."

"They just fizzled out?" I didn't believe it, not after that footage. But, trying it on for size: "That age, even a month or two is a long time to be with someone. That's when Chris got bored of Joanne. He could've got restless again, started feeling like it was too much commitment. Or Selena wanted to go public, same as Joanne did."

Conway had stopped moving. The sun was lowering; it came in through the window arrow-straight and level, turned her face into a light-and-shadow mask. "I'll tell you what else a month or two is, at that age. It's when guys start turning up the pressure. Put out or get out."

I waited. Silence, and the thick flower-chemical smell of body sprays burning the inside of my nose.

Conway said, "Someone did something to Selena that fucked up her mind and put all four of them off guys. And right around the same time, Selena and Chris broke up."

I said, "You think Chris raped her."

"I think we need to check out the possibility. Yeah."

"Running into temptation and two-timing a girl you really like, that's one thing. Raping her's another. That video: on there, he looks like . . ." Conway was withering me. I finished anyway. "He looks like he was mad about her."

"Course he does. So does any teenage guy who thinks he's got a shot at a shag. They'll be whatever they think the girl wants to see. Right up until they realize it's not getting them into her knickers."

"That looked like the real thing to me."

"You an expert, yeah?"

"Are you?"

Conway upped the stare. Couple of hours earlier, I would've blinked. I stared right back.

She left it. "Even if it was real," she said. "Even if he was genuinely mad about her. He could've raped her anyway. Grown adults don't do something that's obviously gonna hurt someone they love, not if they can help it, but that age; remember that age? They're not the same. They don't put things together. That's why half of what they do looks full-on certifiable, to you or me or any sane adult. Things don't make sense, when you're that age; you don't make sense. You stop expecting to."

A second of silence. Her being right, me wishing she was wrong.

When he wanted something and he couldn't get it? Holly had said. *Not so nice.*

"That night," I said. "The night Joanne videoed. That was the last time Chris and Selena met up. If he did something to her . . ."

"Yeah. It was that night."

Silence, again. Under the body spray, I thought I caught a whiff of hyacinths.

"What now?" I asked.

"Now we wait for Sophie to get us Chris's phone records. I'm not talking to anyone else till I see what he was at last spring. Meanwhile, we do a proper search in here."

In the corner of my eye: a flutter of darkness, behind the door-crack.

I had the door flung open before I knew I was moving. Alison squealed and leapt back, hands flapping wildly. In the background, McKenna took a protective pace forward.

"Can I help you?" I asked. My heart was going harder than it should have been. Conway eased away from the wall on the other side of the doorway—I hadn't even seen her go for it. Even with no clue what I was at, she'd been straight in there, ready to back me up.

Alison stared. Said, like someone had taught her the line, "I need to get my books to do my homework please."

"No problem," I said. I felt like an eejit. "In you come."

She sidled in like we might hit her, started pulling stuff out of her bag— her hands looked frail as water spiders, skittering over the books. McKenna stood in the doorway, being massive. Not liking us one little bit.

"How's the arm?" I asked.

Alison shifted it away from me. "It's OK. Thanks."

"Let's see," Conway said.

Alison shot a glance at McKenna: she'd been told not to show it. McKenna nodded, reluctantly.

Alison pulled up her sleeve. The blisters were gone, but the skin where they'd been still had a bumpy look to it. The handprint had faded to pink. Alison had her head turned away.

"Nasty," I said sympathetically. "My sister used to get allergies. Up her face and all, once. Turned out it was the washing powder our mammy was using. Did you figure out what did that, no?"

"The cleaners must have switched to a new brand of hand soap." Another glance at McKenna. Another line learned off by heart.

"Yeah," I said. "Must've done." Shared a look with Conway, let Alison catch it.

Alison tugged down her sleeve and started scooping up her books. Glanced once round the room, big-eyed, like we'd turned it into somewhere strange and untrustworthy, before she scuttled out.

McKenna said, "If you should wish to speak to me, Detectives—or to any more of the fourth-years—you will find us in the common room."

Meaning the nun had ratted us out. McKenna was taking over the fourth-years, damage control or no, and we were getting no more interviews without an appropriate adult.

"Miss McKenna," I said. Held out a hand to keep her back, while Alison straggled down the corridor towards the common room. Even on her own, the kid walked like she was trailing after someone. "We'll need to speak to some of the girls without a teacher present. There are elements of this case that they wouldn't be comfortable discussing in front of school staff. It's only background to the investigation, but we need them to speak freely."

McKenna was opening her mouth on *Absolutely not.* I said, "If unsupervised interviews are a problem, obviously, we can have the girls' parents come in."

And start last year's flap again, parents outraged, panicking, threatening to pull their daughters out of Kilda's. McKenna swallowed the *No.* I added, for good measure, "It would mean we'd have to wait till the parents can get here, but it might be a good compromise solution. The girls would probably be more comfortable discussing breaches of school rules in front of their parents than in front of a teacher."

McKenna shot me a look that said *You don't fool me, you little bastard.* Said, salvaging, "Very well. I will allow unsupervised interviews, within reason. If any girl becomes distressed, however, or if you receive any information that affects the school in any way, I expect to be informed immediately."

"Of course," I said. "Thanks very much." As she turned away, I heard the surge of voices from the common room, hammering around Alison.

"That arm's gone down some more," Conway said. She tapped Joanne's bedside table. "Fake tan in there."

I said, "Joanne didn't have any reason to create a diversion to get us out of the common room. She thought Orla had ditched the key a year ago."

It had only hit me when I looked at the arm again. "Huh," Conway said. Thought that over. "Coincidence and imagination, after all." She didn't look as pleased as she should've been. Neither was I.

It does that to you, being a detective. You look at blank space and see gears turning, motives and cunning; nothing looks innocent any more. Most times, when you prove away the gears, the blank space looks lovely; peaceful. But that arm: innocent, it looked just as dangerous.

16

By the time Julia and Finn get to the back of the grounds, the music seeping out of the dance is long gone behind them. The moon catches flashes of light and snippets of color strewn through the bushes, like a crop of sweets in a witch's garden. Finn pulls out the nearest one and holds it up to the light: a Lucozade bottle, full of something dark amber. He uncaps it and sniffs.

"Rum. I think. That OK for you?"

There are always rumors about some guy who put some drug in some booze some year and raped some girl. Julia figures she'll take the chance. "My favorite," she says.

"Where'll we go? There's going to be a lot more people headed here, if they can get out."

No way is Julia bringing him to the glade. There's a little rise among cherry trees, tucked away at the side of the grounds; the cherry blossom is out, which turns the place more romantic than Julia had in mind, but it has plenty of cover and a perfect view of the back lawn. "This way," she says.

No one else has got there first. The rise is still. When a breeze flits through, a cherry blossom falls like a shake of snow on the pale grass.

"Ta-da," Julia says, sweeping a hand out. "Will this do?"

"Works for me," Finn says. He looks around, the bottle swinging from one hand, the other tucked in the pocket of his navy hoodie—it's cold, but there's almost no wind, so it's a mellow, clean cold that they can ignore. "I never even knew this was here. It's beautiful."

"It's probably covered in bird crap," Julia says, dampeningly. He doesn't sound like he's just playing Mr. Sensitive to up his odds of getting into her bra, but you never know.

"The element of risk. I like it." Finn points to a patch of clear grass among the cherry trees. "Over here?"

Julia lets him sit down first, so she can get the distance right. He uncaps the bottle and passes it to her. "Cheers," he says.

She takes a mouthful and discovers she hates rum as well as whiskey. She has no idea how the human race found out you could actually drink this stuff. She hopes she doesn't just hate booze in general. Julia figures she's ruled out enough vices already; this is one she was planning to enjoy.

"Good stuff," she says, giving it back.

Finn takes a swig and manages to avoid making a face. "Better than the punch, anyway."

"True. Not saying much, but true."

There's a silence, question-marked, but not uncomfortable. The ringing in Julia's ears is starting to fade. Far away, maybe in the grove, an owl calls.

Finn lies back on the grass, pulling up his hood so he won't get dew or bird crap in his hair. "I heard the grounds are haunted," he says.

Julia is not about to snuggle up for protection. "Yeah? I heard your mum is haunted."

He grins. "Seriously. You never heard that?"

"Course I did," Julia says. "The ghost nun. Is that why you invited me out here? To look after you while you got your booze?"

"I used to be petrified of her. The older guys made sure we all were, back in first year."

"Us too. Sadistic bitches."

Finn hands her the bottle. "They'd come into our dorm last thing before lights-out, right, and tell us the stories? The idea was, if they scared us enough, some poor kid wouldn't have the guts to go to the jacks and he'd end up wetting his bed."

"Ever get you?"

"No!" But he's grinning too. "They got plenty, though."

"Seriously? What'd they tell you? She came after guys with garden shears?"

"Nah. They said she . . ." Finn glances sideways at Julia. "I mean, the way I heard it, she was kind of a slut."

The word comes out practically radioactive with self-consciousness. Julia inquires, "Are you trying to see if I'll get all shocked because you said 'slut'?"

Finn's eyebrows go up and he stares, half shocked himself. She watches him coolly, amused.

"Well," he says, in the end. "I guess. Sort of."

"Were you hoping I would or I wouldn't?"

He shakes his head. He's starting to smile, at himself, snared. "I don't know."

"Anything else you want to try shocking me with? You could go for 'shit.' Or even 'fuck,' if you're feeling really crazy."

"I think I'm done. Thanks, though."

Julia decides to let him off the hook. She lies back on the grass beside him and spins the cap off the bottle. "The way we heard it," she says, "the nun was shagging like half the priests from Colm's, and then some kid found out and ratted her out to the Father Superior. Him and the Mother Superior strangled the nun and hid her body somewhere in the grounds, nobody's totally sure where, so she's haunting both schools till she gets a proper burial. And if she catches anyone, she thinks it's the kid who ratted her out, so she tries to strangle them and they go insane. Does that about cover what you heard?"

"Well. Yeah. More or less."

"Saved you some trouble there," Julia says. "I think I've earned this." She has another sip. This one actually tastes OK. She decides, with relief, that she doesn't hate rum after all.

Finn reaches for the bottle, and Julia holds it out. His fingers skim over hers, tentative, light. Over the back of her hand, up to her wrist.

"Ah-ah," Julia says, shoving the bottle at him and ignoring the leap of something in her stomach.

Finn takes his hand back. "Why not?" he asks, after a second. He's not looking at Julia.

Julia says, "Got a smoke?"

Finn props himself up on an elbow and scans the back lawn; somewhere far off a high squeal falls into a giggle, but there's nothing that sounds like nuns on the hunt. He fishes in his jeans pocket and pulls out a very battered packet of Marlboro Lights. Julia lights up—she's pretty sure it looked expert—and hands the lighter back.

"So . . . ?" Finn says, and waits.

"Nothing personal," Julia says. "Believe me. Me and a Colm's guy is never going to happen, is all. No matter what you've probably heard." Finn tries to stay blank, but the eyelid-flicker tells her he's heard plenty. "Yeah. So if you want to go back inside and find someone who'll spend the evening with your hand up her top, feel free. I promise not to get my ickle feelings hurt."

She totally, no question, expects him to go. There are at least two dozen girls inside who would rugby-tackle the chance to have Finn Carroll's tongue down their throats, and most of them are prettier than Julia to begin with. Instead Finn shrugs and pulls out a smoke of his own. "I'm here now."

"I'm not kidding."

"I know."

"Your loss," Julia says. She lies back on the grass, feeling the damp tickle of it on the back of her neck, and blows smoke up at the sky. The rum is kicking in, making her arms go happily floppy. She considers the possibility that she underestimated Finn Carroll.

Finn uncaps the bottle and has a swig. "So the ghost nun," he says. "Do you believe in stuff like that?"

"Yeah, I do," Julia says. "Some of it. Maybe not the ghost nun—I bet the teachers just made her up to stop us doing this—but some stuff. How about you?"

Finn takes another swig. "I don't know," he says. "I mean, no, because there's no scientific evidence, but I actually think I'm probably wrong. You know?"

"More rum," Julia says, holding out her free hand. "I think I need to catch up."

Finn passes it over. "Like, OK: everyone in history's thought they were the ones who finally knew everything. In the Renaissance, right, they were positive they knew exactly how the universe worked, till the next set of guys came along and proved that they were missing like a hundred important things. And then *that* set of guys were sure they had it all down, till another set came along and showed them parts they were missing."

He glances at Julia, checking if she's laughing at him, which she isn't, and if she's listening. Which she is, completely.

"So," he says, "it's pretty unlikely, just mathematically, that we're living in the one single era that happens to finally have everything figured out. Which means there's a decent possibility that the reason we can't explain how ghosts and stuff could exist is because we haven't figured it out yet, not because they don't. And it's pretty arrogant of us to think it definitely has to be the other way round."

Finn takes a drag of his cigarette and squints at the blow of smoke like it's turned fascinating. Even in the moonlight, Julia can see the deeper color on his cheeks.

"Well," he says. "Probably that all sounded totally stupid. You can tell me to shut up now."

Julia notices something that she never had room to spot before, through the whirl of *Does he fancy me do I fancy him is he going to try would I let him how much would I let him*. She really likes Finn.

"Actually," she says, "since you mentioned it, it's one of the least stupid things I've heard in ages."

He gives her a quick sideways glance. "Yeah?"

Julia would love with all her heart to show him. Lift her hand, send the Lucozade bottle slowly rising through the rich moonlight. Upend it, set the falling droplets of rum spiraling like a tiny amber galaxy against the star-thick sky. See the slow sheer joy lighting his face right through. The thought of what would happen to her makes the back of her neck twitch.

"OK," she says. "Here's something I've never told anyone."

Finn turns his head to look at her properly.

"Stuff like that, ghosts and ESP and stuff? I used to say it was all total bullshit. Like, I was fanatical about it. Once I went *off* on Selena, just because she was telling us about this thing in some magazine, about clairvoyance? I told her to prove it or shut up about it. When she couldn't prove it, because *obviously* she couldn't, I called her an idiot and told her she should try reading *Just Seventeen* because at least it'd be a step up from that crap."

Finn's eyebrows are up.

"Yeah, I know. I was a bitch. I apologized. But it was because I *wanted* her to prove it was all true. I wanted it to be real, so *badly*. If I hadn't cared, I'd've been like, 'Yeah, whatever, maybe just possibly clairvoyance happens, probably not.' But I couldn't stand the idea of actually believing in all this amazing mysterious stuff, and then finding out that duhhh I was a big thicko sucker and there was nothing there."

It's true: she's never said this even to the others. With them she's the one who's always sure straight through—Julia figures Selena knows it's more complicated than that, but they don't talk about it. Something moves through her, unstoppable as the rum: tonight matters, after all.

"Then what happened?" Finn asks.

Wariness shoots up in Julia. "Huh?"

"You said, a minute ago: now you do believe in some of this stuff. So what changed?"

Her fucking mouth, always open one sentence too long. "So," she says, lightly, rolling over onto her stomach to put out her smoke in the grass. "You don't believe in the ghost nun, but you think she might be out here anyway. And I kind of believe in her, but I don't actually think she's here."

Finn is smart enough not to push. "Between the two of us, we're basically guaranteed to get haunted."

"Is that why you're hanging on here? In case she goes boo and gives me a heart attack?"

"You're not scared?"

Julia arches an eyebrow. "What, because I'm a girl?"

"No. Because you believe in it. Kind of."

"I'm out here every *day*. The ghost hasn't got me yet."

"You're out here in the daytime. Not at night."

Finn is testing; finding new ways to work out what he thinks of her, now that the normal ones are useless. They're in new territory. Julia realizes she likes it here.

"This isn't night," she says. "It's nine o-fucking-clock. *Babies* are still out playing. If it was summer, it'd be daylight."

"So if I got up right now and went inside, you'd be totally fine out here by yourself."

It occurs to Julia that actually she probably should be scared, here on her own with a guy who's already tried once. It occurs to her that a few months ago, after what happened with James Gillen, she would have been scared; she would have been the one leaving.

She says, "As long as you left me the rum."

Finn pulls himself up off the grass with a sit-up and a jump. He brushes off his jeans and lifts an eyebrow at Julia.

She waves up at him, from her nest. "Off you go and find yourself some nice tit. Have fun."

Finn pretends to start turning away. She laughs at him. After a minute he laughs back and drops down on the grass again.

"Too scary?" Julia asks. "All that way on your ownio, in the big bad dark?"

"It's nine o-fucking-clock. Like you said. If it actually was night, bet you'd be scared."

"I'm badass, baby. I can handle ghost nuns."

Finn lies back and passes Julia the bottle. "Right. Let's see you out here at midnight."

"Bring it on."

"Yeah. Right."

That grin, like a dare. Julia's never been any good at turning down a dare. Thin ice, she feels it, but the rum is dancing in her and what the hell, it's not like she's going to tell him anything. She says, "When's the next social?"

"What?"

"Come on. March?"

"Sometime in April. So?"

She points up at the fancy-hands clock on the back of the school. "So at the next social, I'll have a photo of that clock showing midnight."

"So you've done Photoshop. Fair play."

Julia shrugs. "Trust me or don't. Yeah, I want to own you, but not that badly. I'll get the photo straight up."

Finn turns his head, on the grass. Their faces are inches apart, and Julia thinks *Oh God no* because him trying to kiss her now would be more kick-in-the-teeth depressing than she wants to admit, but Finn is grinning, a wide-open wicked grin like a kid's. "Bet you a tenner you don't," he says.

Julia grins back, the way she grins at Holly when an idea's hit them both. "Bet you a tenner I do," she says.

Their hands come up at the same time, slap together, and they shake. Finn's hand feels good, strong, an even match to hers.

She picks up the bottle and holds it up above her face, to the stars. "Here's to my tenner," she says. "I'll put it towards ghost-hunting equipment."

In the entrance hall the huge chandelier is off, but the sconce lights on the walls turn the air a warm old-fashioned gold. Above their reach, floors of darkness stretch upwards, untouched, echoing with Chris and Selena's footsteps.

Selena sits on the staircase. The steps are white stone, veined with gray; once upon a time they were polished—there are still traces between the banisters—but thousands of feet have worn them down till they're velvety-rough, with dips in the middle.

Chris sits down next to her. Selena has never been this close to him before, close enough to see the scattering of freckles along the tops of his cheekbones, the faintest shading of stubble on his chin; to smell him, spices and a thread of something wild and musky that makes her think of outside at night. He feels different from anyone she's ever met: charged up fuller, electric and sparking with three people's worth of life packed into his skin.

Selena wants to touch him again. She slides her hands under her thighs to stop herself reaching out and pressing her palm against his neck. With a sudden leap of warning, she wonders if she fancies him; but she's fancied guys, back Before, even snogged a few of them. This isn't the same thing.

She shouldn't have let him touch her even that once, back in the hall. She understands that.

She wants the world to be that real again.

Chris says, "Are your friends going to wonder where you are?"

They will. Selena feels another nudge of unease: she never even thought of telling them. "I'll text them," she says, feeling for the pocket in the unfamiliar dress. "What about yours?"

"Nah." Chris's half smile says his friends expected him to go missing tonight.

To Holly: *Am just outside, wanted to get out for a few mins, back soon.* "There," Selena says, sending it.

The hall door opens, letting out a rush of thumping bass and squeals and hot air, and Miss Long sticks her head out. When she sees Chris and Selena, she nods and points a threatening finger: *Stay.* Someone shrieks behind her, she whips round and the door slams shut.

Chris says, "Back in there. I wasn't trying to tell you what you guys should wear."

"Yeah, you were," Selena says. "It's OK, though. I'm not mad."

"I was just saying. If you wear jeans to a dance and do your hair like that, people are going to laugh at you, end of. Your friend Becca—I mean, I know she has to be the same age as us, but she's like a kid. She doesn't get it. You can't just let her walk out there to get eaten alive by Joanne Heffernan."

"Joanne would say stuff anyway," Selena points out. "No matter what Becca was wearing."

"Yeah, because she's a total raving bitch. So don't give her extra excuses."

Selena says, "I thought you liked Joanne."

"I was with her a few times. That's not the same thing."

Selena thinks about that for a while. Chris bends over his shoelace, untying and retying it. His cheek glows. Selena can feel the heat of it, deep in her palm.

She says, "I think maybe Becca doesn't want to be that."

"So? It's not like those are the only two options. Be some bitch or be some freak. You can just be *normal*."

"I don't think she wants to be that either."

Chris's eyebrows pull together. "What, like she thinks she can't because she's not . . . ? I mean, with the braces, and the . . ." He nods downwards. "You know. She's flat. She's worried because of that? Jesus, that's no big deal. It's not like she's some total ditch-pig. She just has to make, like, *this* much effort and she'd be fine."

He was telling the truth about not being into Becca. He doesn't want anything from her. He's doing it all wrong, but all he wants is to build a castle around her and keep her safe.

"Your sister," Selena says. "Who you were talking about. What's her name?"

"Caroline. Carly." That brings up a smile on Chris's face, but it gets jammed with worry and breaks apart.

"How old is she?"

"She's ten. In a couple of years she's going to be coming here; Kilda's. If I was at home I could talk to her, you know? Prepare her or whatever. But I only see her for, like, a few hours every couple of weeks. It's not enough."

Selena says, "Are you worried she's not going to like it here?"

Chris sighs and rubs a hand up the side of his jaw. "Yeah," he says. "I worry about that a lot. She won't . . . aah. She does stuff like Becca: like she's actually *trying* to be weird. Wearing jeans to the Valentine's dance, that's totally something she'd do. Like, last year everyone in her class was wearing those stupid bracelets, right? The ones with the different-colored links and you all wear each other's colors to show you're friends, I don't know. And Carly's all pissed off because some girls slagged her for not having one. So I'm like, 'Get one, I'll buy you one if you've run out of pocket money,' right? And Carly turns around and tells me she'd cut off her arm before she'd wear one of those bracelets, because those girls aren't her boss and she's not their slave and she doesn't have to do anything just because they want her to."

Selena is smiling. "Yeah, that's like Becca. That's sort of why she's wearing jeans."

"Well, what the fuck?" Chris's hands fly up, frustrated. "I'm not *asking* her to cut her arm off. I'm like, who cares if you actually want a dumb bracelet? You *definitely* don't want to be that girl who no one will go near her and everyone's texting around stories about how she eats her snot and pees herself in class. So just do this one tiny thing that everyone else is doing."

"Did she?"

"No. I bought her the fucking bracelet, and she binned it. And if she pulls something like that in Kilda's? People like Joanne, if Carly swans in here like it doesn't matter what any of them think, they're going to . . . Jesus." He rakes a hand through his hair. "And I'll be in college by then; I won't even be around to do anything about it. I just want her to be happy. That's all."

Selena says, "Has she got friends?"

"Yeah. She's not super-popular or whatever, obviously, but she's got these two girls who've been her best friends since they were all in Junior Infants. They're coming to Kilda's too. Thank God."

"Then she'll be OK."

"You think? They're two people. What about everyone else? What about all them?" Chris jerks his chin at the hall doors, the muffled jumble of beats and screams. "Carly can't just ignore them and hope they leave her alone. It's not going to happen."

He sounds like they're one great bristle-backed creature, laser-eyed and dribbling for throats to rip out, never sated. Selena realizes that Chris is afraid. For his sister, for Becca, but bigger than that. Just afraid.

There are things stronger than that creature. There are things that could rip it limb from limb if they felt like it, spike its head a hundred feet high on a cypress tree and use its sinews to string their bows. For a second Selena sees the white arc of a hunting call flash across the sky.

"Not ignore them," she says. "Just . . . not let them matter."

Chris shakes his head. "It doesn't work that way," he says. For a second the full curves of his lips harden; he looks older.

Selena says, "Becca's happy in there, right? In her jeans."

"She can't exactly be happy about those geebags bitching about her."

"She's not. It just . . . like I said. It doesn't matter."

Chris stares. "If that was you. If they were bitching about your dress. That'd be fine with you?"

"I bet they are," Selena says. "I don't care."

He's turned towards her on the steps. His eyes are hazel, a cool hazel speckled with gold. Selena knows if she could just touch him she could draw out the fear like snake venom, roll it into a glistening black ball and throw it away.

He demands—like he's really asking, like he needs to know—"How? How can you not care?"

People talk to Selena. They always have. She doesn't talk to them, except Julia and Holly and Becca. She almost never even tries.

She says, slowly, "You have to have something else you care about more. Something so you know that some geebags bitching aren't the most important thing; you're not the most important thing, even. Something enormous."

It's just words, sounds, it doesn't come near what she means. This isn't something you can tell.

Chris says, "What? Like *God*?"

Selena considers that. "Probably that would work. Yeah."

He's openmouthed. "Are you guys going to be, like, *nuns*?"

Selena laughs out loud. "No! Can you see Julia being a nun?"

"Then what . . . ?"

The more she tries, the more she's going to get it wrong. She says, "I just mean: maybe, depending, Carly could be fine just the way she is. Better than fine."

Chris is looking at her, very close and very intent, and his eyes have warmed. He says, "You're a once-off. You know that?"

Selena wants to say nothing at all. The thing finding its shape in the space between them is so new, so precious, the wrong touch could burst it like a bubble. "I'm not anything special," she says. "It just worked out this way."

"Yeah, you are. I never talk to people about stuff like this. But this, talking to you, this is . . . I'm glad we came out here. I'm really glad."

Selena knows, like he's reached out and dropped the knowledge into her lap, that he's going to try to take her hand. The handprint on her arm burns, a painless gold fire. She wraps her fingers hard around the cold stone edge of the step.

The hall door flies open, and Miss Long points at them. "Your time's up. Back inside. Don't make me come out there and get you." And she slams the door.

Chris says, "I want to do this again."

Selena is still working to breathe. She can't tell if she's grateful or something else to whatever sent Miss Long. She says, "Me too."

"When?"

"Next week, after school? We can meet outside the Court and go for a walk."

Chris shifts on the step, like the stone hurts him. He presses his thumbnail into the wood of the banister. "Everyone'd see us."

"That's OK."

"They'd . . . you know. Like, they'd slag us. Both of us. They'd think we were going to . . ."

Selena says, "I don't care."

"I know," Chris says, and there's a wry laugh in his voice, like the joke's on him. "I know you don't. I do, though. I don't want people thinking that." He hears himself. "No, I mean— *Shit.* I don't mean I don't want people thinking we're together. I'd be totally fine with that, it's not like I'm embarrassed or—I mean, not just *fine,* it would be better than just—"

He's knotting himself up. Selena says, laughing at him, "It's OK. I know what you mean."

Chris takes a breath. He says simply, "I don't want it to be like that. Like me and Joanne going into the Field to . . . whatever. I want it to be like this."

His hand going up. The hall, smoky gold. The small flutters of air in the darkness, far above their heads.

"If we meet outside the Court after school, I'm going to make a balls of it. I'll say something stupid to make the guys laugh, or else we'll go somewhere to talk and everyone'll watch us go and I'll have, like, not one single thing to say. Or else the guys'll slag me, afterwards, and I'll say something . . . you know. Dirty. I wish I wouldn't, but I will."

Selena says, "Can you get out of school at night?"

She hears the hiss of caught breath in the air all around her. She wants to say back, *It's OK, I know what I'm doing,* but she knows it wouldn't be true.

Chris's eyebrows go up. "At night? No way. You can? Seriously?"

Selena says, "I'll give you my number. If you find a way, text me."

"No," he says, instantly. "Maybe it's different here, but the guys go through each other's phones all the time, looking for . . . well. Stuff. The Brothers do it too. I'll find a way to get in touch. Just not like that. OK?"

Selena nods. "About getting out," Chris says. "One of my mates. He might be able to figure something out."

"Ask him."

Chris says, "I'll *make* him."

Selena says, "Don't tell him why. And till then, don't talk to me. If we see each other around the Court or something, we'll act like we don't even know each other; like before. Otherwise it'll all get ruined."

Chris nods. He says, obscurely and out to the hall but Selena understands, "Thanks."

Miss Long bangs the door open. "Selena! You, whatsyourname! Inside. *Now.*" This time she stays there, staring.

Chris jumps up and holds out a hand to Selena. She doesn't take it. She stands up, feeling the movement spin little eddies up into the high darkness. She smiles at Chris and says, "See you soon." Then she moves around him, carefully so not even the hem of her dress brushes up against him, and goes back into the gym. The handprint, wrapped around her arm, is still glowing.

17

S earch time," Conway said. "And if we're stuck in here . . ." She shoved
the sash window up.

A whirl of breeze shot in, carried the mess of body sprays away.
Outside, the light was cooling and the sky was turning pale. It was almost
evening.

"One more second of that stink," Conway said, "I was gonna puke my
ring."

The stir-crazy was starting to needle at her. I felt it too. We'd been in
those rooms a long time.

Conway pulled the wardrobe open, said "Fuck me," at the amount or the
labels. Started running her hands down hanging dresses. I went for the
beds, Gemma's first. Pulled back the bedclothes, shook them out, patted
down the mattress. Not just checking for big lumps of phone or old book,
the way I had been the first time. This time we were after something that
could be as small as a SIM card.

"The door," Conway said. "What was up with that?"

I'd have only loved to leave that. But the way she'd been straight in there,
got my back on whatever I hadn't told her; I heard myself say, "When you
were off talking to Alison, I thought I saw someone behind the door.
Thought it could be someone trying to get up the guts to talk to us, but by
the time I opened the door there was no one there. So, when I saw something behind there again . . ."

"You went for it." I waited for the slagging—*And you went full-on, fair
play to you, you'd've been all ready to save the day if one of the kids had built
herself a nuke in Physics class*—but she said, "The first time, while I was out.
You positive there was someone there?"

I flipped the mattress up to check the bottom. Said, "Nah."

Conway squeezed her way down a puffy jacket. "Yeah. We had the same thing last year, a few times: thought we saw something, nothing there. Something about this place, I don't know. Costello had this theory about the windows being different in old buildings: they're not the same shapes and sizes as what you get now, not placed the same way. So the light comes in at different angles, and if you catch something in the corner of your eye, it's gonna look wrong." She shrugged. "Who knows."

I said, "If it's that, it could be why people keep seeing Chris's ghost."

"The kids are used to this light, but. And an actual ghost? Is that what you saw?"

"Nah. Bit of shadow, just."

"Exactly. They're seeing Chris because they want to. Feeding off each other, trying to impress each other, give each other something good." She shoved the jacket back into the wardrobe. "They need to get out more, this lot. They spend too much time together."

Nothing down behind Gemma's bedside table, nothing under the drawer. "At this age, that's what it's about."

"Yeah, they're not gonna be this age forever. When it hits them that there's a great big world out there, they're gonna get the shock of their lives."

The scraping of satisfaction on her voice, I didn't feel that. Instead I felt the wind that would hit you from every side, raw-edged and gritty, smelling of spices and petrol, whirling hot in your hair, when you stepped out of a place like this and the door slammed behind you.

I said, "I'd say Chris getting murdered made the great big world hard to miss."

"You think? Even that was all about each other, for these. 'Look, I cried harder than her, so I'm a better person.' 'We all saw his ghost together, look how close we are.'"

I moved on to Orla's bed. Conway said, "I remember you from training."

Her head was in the wardrobe, I couldn't see her face. I said—carefully, skimming back—"Yeah? Good or bad?"

"You don't remember, no?"

If I'd talked to her beyond "Howya" in corridors, I'd forgotten. "Tell me I didn't make you do push-ups."

"Would you remember if you had?"

"Ah, Jaysus. What'd I do?"

"Relax the kacks. I'm just wrecking your head." I could hear the grin in Conway's voice. "You never did anything on me."

"Thank fuck. You had me worried there."

"Nah, you were grand. I don't think we ever even talked. I only clocked you to start with because of the hair." Conway pulled something out of a hoodie pocket, grimaced: wad of tissues. "After that, but, I kept noticing because you did your own thing. You had mates, but you weren't hanging out of anyone. All the rest, fuck me: they spent the whole time crawling up each other's hole. Half of them trying to *network*, like the little bastards at Colm's: if I get all buddy-buddy with the commissioner's kid, I'll never have to do traffic duty and I'll make inspector by thirty. The other half trying to *bond*, like this lot here: oh, these are the best days of our lives and we'll all be best pals forever and tell these stories at our retirement dinners. I was like, what the fuck? You're grown adults; you're here to learn the job, not to swap friendship bracelets and do each other's eyeshadow." She shoved clothes down the crowded rail. "I liked that you didn't get sucked into that either."

I didn't tell her: a part of me watched my classmates bonding away like goodo, and wished. Just like Conway said, it was my own choice that I wasn't in there swapping friendship bracelets with the best of them. Mostly that made it OK.

I said, "If you think back, we were kids; only a couple of years older than this lot. People wanted to belong. Nothing strange there."

Conway thought, unrolling tights. "I'll tell you," she said. "It's not the making friends that gets on my tits. Everyone needs those. But I had mine back at home. Still do."

Glance at me. I said, "Yeah."

"Right. So you didn't need to go chasing more. If you make friends inside some bubble that's going to burst on you in a couple of years—like training, or like here—you're an idiot. You start thinking that's the whole world, nowhere else exists, then you end up with all this hysterical shite. Best friends forever, she-said-you-said-I-said wars, everyone working themselves into fits over they don't even know what. Nothing's just normal; everything's right up *here*, all the time."

Hand above head level. I thought of the Murder squad room. Wondered if Conway was thinking of it too.

"Then you head out into the big bad world," she said, "everything looks different all of a sudden, and you're fucked."

I ran a hand under the slats of Joanne's bed frame. "Orla and Alison, you mean? No way Joanne's going to be hanging out with them in college."

Conway snorted. "Yeah, not a chance. Here, they're useful; out there, they'll be gone. And they'll be devastated. I wasn't thinking of them, though. I meant the gangs that actually genuinely care about each other. Like your Holly and her mates."

"I'd say they'll still be mates on the outside." I hoped so. That something special, gilding the air. You want to believe it'll last forever.

"Could be. Probably, even. That's not the point. The point is, right now, they don't give a fuck about anyone except each other. Great, that's cute, I bet they're delighted with themselves." Conway threw a handful of bras back into a drawer, slammed it. "But when they get out there? That's not going to be an option any more. They won't be able to hang out of each other's hole twenty-four-seven, ignore everyone else. Other people are going to start mattering, whether these four like that or not. The rest of the world's gonna be *there*. It's gonna be real. And that's gonna fuck up their heads like they can't even imagine."

She pulled out another drawer, hard enough that it nearly fell on her foot. "I don't like bubbles."

Down the back of Joanne's headboard: dust and nothing. I said, "How about the squad?"

"What about it?"

"Murder's a bubble."

Conway flipped out a T-shirt with a snap. "Yeah," she said. Jaw set like she was seeing fights ahead. "Murder's a lot like here. The difference is, I'm there for good."

I thought about asking if that meant she was planning on making friends on the squad. Decided I had better sense.

Conway said, like she'd heard me anyway, "And I'm still not gonna get all buddy-buddy with the squad lads. I don't want to *belong*. I want to do my fucking *job*."

I did my fucking job—ran my hand over shiny posters; nothing—and thought about Conway. Tried to work out if I envied her, or felt sorry for her, or thought she was talking bollix.

We were finishing up when Conway's phone buzzed. Message.

"Sophie," she said, slamming the wardrobe door. "Here we go." This time I went to her shoulder without waiting for an invitation.

The e-mail said, *Records for the number that texted Moran. My guy's working on the actual texts, says they should still be in the system but might take him an hour or two. Probably all "OMGLOLWTFbwahaha!!!!" but you want them, you're getting them. Enjoy. S.*

The attachment was pages long; Chris had been getting plenty of use out of his special phone. He'd activated it at the end of August, just before he went back to school—good little Boy Scout, coming prepared. By the middle of September, two numbers were showing up. No calls, but plenty of texts and media messages back and forth with both, every day, a few times a day. "You were right," Conway said, hard-edged. I felt her think it: witnesses she should have found.

"Ladies' man, our Chris."

"And smart, too. See all these picture messages? Those weren't pics of fluffy kitties. If one of his girls started threatening to tell the world, these would keep her nice and quiet."

I said, "That'll be why none of them said it to you last year. They were hoping if they kept their mouths shut, no one would link these to them."

Conway's head came round, suspicious, ready to shove my comfort up my hole. I kept my eyes on the screen till she turned back to it.

October, both of Chris's girls got the boot—same MO we'd seen on Joanne's records: he ignored their texts, the flood of calls from one of them, till they gave up. As they faded, Joanne's number kicked in. By the middle of November, Chris was two-timing her; after Joanne faded away in December, the other girl hung on a couple more weeks, but by Christmas she was history. January, a new number swapped a handful of texts and vanished: something that never got off the ground.

Conway said, "I wondered all along. Why Chris hadn't had a girlfriend in a year. Popular guy like him, good-looking, did fine with the girls before; it didn't add up. I should've . . ." Quick jerk of her head, angry. She didn't bother finishing.

Last week in February, the next run of texts started. One a day, then two, then half a dozen. All the one number. Conway scrolled down: March, April, the texts kept coming.

She tapped the screen. "That'll be Selena."

I said, "And he wasn't two-timing her."

We left a second for what that meant. My theory, the girl who had caught Chris cheating, she was out. Conway's was getting stronger.

Conway said, "See that? No media messages, just texts. No tit pics here. Selena wasn't giving Chris what he was after."

"Maybe he dumped her for that."

"Maybe."

April twenty-second, Monday, the usual couple of texts back and forth during the day—setting up the meeting, probably. That night, Joanne had taken the video.

Early on April twenty-third, Chris texted Selena. She answered before school, he came straight back to her. No answer. Chris texted her again after school: nothing.

He tried three more times the next day. Selena didn't answer.

Conway said, "Something went wrong, anyway, that night. After Joanne and Gemma went inside."

I said, "And she's the one dumping him." Conway's theory swelled bigger.

It was the twenty-fifth, Thursday, when Selena finally got back to Chris. Just the one text. No answer.

Over the next few weeks, she texted him six times. He didn't answer any of them. Conway's eyebrows were pulled together.

Early on the morning of the sixteenth of May, Thursday, a text from Selena to Chris and, finally, one back. That night, Chris had been murdered.

After that, nothing into his phone or out, for a year. Then, today, the text to me.

Below the window, a tumble of high voices: girls outside, getting fresh air on their break between dinner and study. Nothing on our corridor. McKenna was keeping this lot where they were, under her eye.

Conway said, "It goes bad the night of the twenty-second. Next day, Chris tries to apologize, Selena tells him to fuck off. He keeps trying, she ignores him."

"Over the next few days," I said, "she comes out of shock, starts getting mad. She decides she wants to confront Chris. By that time, though, he's in a snot because she didn't accept his apology; he's decided to move on. Like that story Holly told us, with the muffin: he didn't like not getting what he wanted."

"Or it's started to sink in that this is serious shit, and he's scared Selena's going to tell. He figures the safest thing he can do is cut off contact; if she comes forward, he'll call her a liar, claim the person she was texting wasn't him, he never had anything to do with her."

"Finally," I said, "on the sixteenth of May, Selena finds a way to get him to meet up. Maybe he figures he needs to get the phone off her, in case there's a way it can be traced back to him."

The rest turned in the air between us. On the grass below the window a huddle of little girls were chattering, indignant as small birds: *She totally knew I wanted it and she like looked at me going for it and then she just barged right in front—*

Conway said, "I told you in the car I didn't fancy Selena for it, didn't think she could get the job done. I still don't."

I said, "Julia's very protective of Selena."

"You spotted that, yeah? I make noises about questioning Selena, say I don't play nice; Julia's straight in with the info about Joanne and Chris, throwing another ball for me to chase."

"Yeah. And I'd say it's not just Julia: all four of them look after each other. If Chris did something to Selena, or tried to, and the others found out . . ."

"Revenge," Conway said. "Or they saw Selena losing the plot, thought she'd go back to normal if Chris was gone and she felt safe again. And I'd say any of those three could get the job done just fine."

"Rebecca?" But I remembered it, that lift of her chin, the glint that had told me *Not so frail after all.* Thought of the poem on her wall, of what her friends meant to her.

"Yeah. Even her." After a second, carefully not looking at me: "Even Holly."

I said, "Holly's the one who brought me that card. She could've just binned it."

"I'm not saying she did anything. I'm just saying I'm not ready to rule her out yet."

Made me prickle, the carefulness; like Conway thought I was going to throw a full-on hissy, demand she take *my Holly* off the list, start making calls to my big daddy Mackey. I wondered all over again what Conway had heard about me.

I said, "Or it could be all three of them."

"Or all four," Conway said. She pressed her fingers to her nose, rubbed them along her cheekbones. "*Fuck.*"

She looked like today was starting to close over her head. She was longing to leave: go back to Murder and turn in her paperwork, sit in the pub with a mate till her head was wiped clear, start fresh in the morning.

She said, "This fucking place."

"Long day," I said.

"You want to go, go."

"And do what?"

"Do whatever you do. Go home. Get your glad rags on and go clubbing. There's a bus stop down the main road, or you can phone a taxi. Send me the receipt, I'll put it on expenses."

I said, "If I've got the choice, I'm staying."

"I'm gonna be here a while. I don't know how long."

"No problem."

Conway looked at me, eyebag to eyebag. Fatigue had rasped the coppery sheen off her skin, left her bare and hard and dusty.

She said, "Ambitious little fucker, aren't you?"

It stung, places where it shouldn't have, because it was true and because it wasn't all the truth. I said, "It's your case. No matter what I do, it's your name going on the solve. I just want to work it."

Second of silence, while Conway looked at me. She said, "If we get a suspect and we bring her back to base, the lads are gonna give me hassle. About the case, about you, whatever. I can deal with that. If you add to the hassle because you want to be one of the lads, you're gone. Clear?"

What I'd felt in the squad-room air that morning: not just your normal Murder-squad edge, fast Murder-squad pulse. Something more, beating faster and sharper around Conway. And not just today. Her every day had to be a fight.

I said, "I've ignored eejits before. I can do it again." Hoped to Jaysus the squad room would be empty whenever we walked in there. Last thing I wanted to do was pick between pissing off Conway and pissing off the Murder lads.

Conway kept up the stare for another moment. Then: "Right," she said. "You better be good at it." She clicked her phone to black, slid it back into her pocket. "Time to talk to Selena."

I glanced around the beds. Shoved Alison's bedside table back into place, pulled Joanne's duvet straight. "Where?"

"Her room. Keep it casual, keep her relaxed. If she comes out with it . . ."

If Selena said *rape*, then parent or guardian, support officer, video camera, all the bells and whistles. I asked, "Who does the talking?"

"I do. What're you looking at? I can do sensitive. And you think she'll talk to you about a rape? You stay back and try to disappear."

Conway slammed the window shut. Before we got out of the room, the smell of body sprays and hot hair was rising around us again.

To keep the girls occupied, God help them, McKenna had started a sing-along. Their voices straggled down the corridor to meet us, thin and thread-bare. *O Mary, we crown thee with blossoms today* . . .

The common room was too hot, even with the windows open. The dinner plates were scattered around, mostly barely touched; the smell of cooled chicken pie turned me starving and queasy at the same time. The girls' eyes were glazed and ricocheting, to each other, the windows, to Alison huddled in an armchair under a pile of hoodies.

Half of them were barely moving their lips. *Queen of the angels and queen of the may* . . . It took them a second to notice us. Then the voices faltered and died.

"Selena," Conway said, barely a nod to McKenna. "Got a minute?"

Selena had been singing along, absently, gazing into nowhere. She looked at us like she was trying to work out who we were, before she got up and came.

"Remember, Selena," McKenna told her, as she passed, "if at any point you feel in need of support, you can simply put a stop to the interview and ask to have me or another teacher present. The detectives are aware of that."

Selena smiled at her. "I'm fine," she said, reassuring.

"She is, of course," Conway said cheerfully. "Hang on for us in your room, yeah, Selena?"

As Selena wandered off down the corridor: "Julia," Conway said, beckoned. "Come here a sec."

Julia had her back to us, hadn't moved when we came in. In the second when she turned around, she looked wrecked: gray and tense, all the spark faded out of her. By the time she reached us she'd found a last bit of zip somewhere, gave us the smart eye again.

"Yeah?"

Conway pulled the door to behind her. Quietly, so as not to reach Selena: "How come you never told me you had a thing going with Finn Carroll?"

Julia's jaw tightened. "Bloody Joanne. Right?"

"Doesn't matter. Last year, I asked you about relationships with Colm's guys. How come you said nothing?"

"Because there was nothing to *say*. It wasn't a *relationship*; Finn and I never touched each other. We just *liked* each other. As actual human beings. And that's exactly why we didn't tell anyone we were hanging out, which we barely even were anyway, only for like two seconds. But we knew everyone would be like, 'OMG, hee-hee-hee, Finn and Julia sitting in a tree . . .' And we didn't feel like putting up with that bullshit. OK?"

I thought of Joanne and Gemma, snickering low in the darkness, and I believed her. So did Conway. "OK," she said. "Fair enough." And as Julia turned away: "What's Finn at these days? He doing OK?"

Just for a second, the slash of grief turned Julia's face into an adult's. "I wouldn't know," she said, and went back into the common room and closed the door.

Selena was waiting outside her room. The low sun through the window at the end of the corridor sent her shadow towards us, floating over the glowing red tiles. The singing had started up again. *O virgin most tender, our homage we render . . .*

Selena said, "It's break time. We should be outside. People are getting sort of fidgety."

"I know, yeah," Conway said, brushing past her and getting comfortable on Julia's bed. Sitting differently this time, one foot tucked under her, teenager curled up for a chat. "Tell you what: when we finish up with all this, I'll ask McKenna if she'd let yous have a late break outside. How's that?"

Selena glanced down the corridor, dubious. "I guess."

In danger defend us, in sorrow befriend us . . . Raggedy, splintering at the edges. I thought I saw that flash of wide-awake silver in Selena's face again, saw her seeing something we shouldn't miss.

If it was there, Conway didn't spot it. "Great. Have a seat." Selena sat on the edge of her bed. I shut the door—the singing vanished—and melted into a corner, got out my notebook to hide behind.

"Lovely." Conway pulled out her phone, tapped at the screen. "Have a look at this," she said, and passed it to Selena.

It hit her. Even if I hadn't been able to hear it—bumping footsteps, rustling branches—I'd've known what it was, by Selena.

She went white, not red. Her head reared back, away from the screen, and her face had a terrible, violated dignity to it. The shorn hair, nothing to hide behind, made her look stripped naked. I felt like I should look away.

"Who?" she said. She pressed her other hand down over the phone, palm covering the screen. "How?"

"Joanne," Conway said. "Her and Gemma followed you. I'm sorry for hitting you with this, it's a dirty trick, but it seems like it's the only way to get you to stop claiming you weren't going out with Chris. And I can't afford to waste any more time on that. OK?"

Selena waited, like she couldn't hear anything else, till the muffled sounds from under her palm ended. Then she loosened her hands—it took an effort—and passed the phone back to Conway.

"OK," she said. Her breath was still coming hard, but she had her voice under control. "I was meeting Chris."

"Thanks," Conway said. "I appreciate that. And he gave you a secret phone that you used to keep in touch. Why was that?"

"We were keeping things private."

"Whose idea was that?"

"Chris's."

Conway shifted an eyebrow. "You didn't mind?"

Selena shook her head. Her color was starting to come back.

"No? Me, I would've minded. I'd've figured, either this guy thinks I'm not good enough to take out in public, or he wants to keep his options open. Either way, I'm not happy."

Selena said simply, "I didn't think that."

Conway left a pause, but that was it. "Fair enough," she said. "Would you say it was a good relationship?"

Selena had herself back. She said, slowly, turning over the words before she let them out, "It was one of the most wonderful things I've ever had. That and my friends. Nothing's ever going to be like that again."

The words dissolved and spread into the air, turned it those still, back-lit blues. She was right; course she was. You don't get a second first time. It seemed like she shouldn't have had to know that, not yet. Like she should have had the chance to leave that glade behind, before she realized she could never go back.

Conway held up her phone. "So why'd you dump him after this night?"

Selena went vague, but I got that feeling again: she was wrapping the vague around her. "I didn't."

Conway tapped at her screen, quick and deft. "Here," she said, holding it out. "That's records of the texts going back and forth between you and Chris. See here? This is the couple of days after that night in the video. He's trying to get in touch, but you're ignoring him. You'd never done that before. Why after that night?"

Selena never even thought about denying the number was hers. She looked at the phone like it was alive and strange, maybe dangerous. She said, "I just needed to think."

"Yeah? About what?"

"Chris and me."

"Yeah, I figured that. I meant what specifically? Did he do something, that night, that made you rethink the relationship?"

Selena's eyes went away somewhere, for real this time. She said quietly, "That was the first time we kissed."

Conway gave her the skepticals. "That doesn't match our information. You'd been seen kissing at least once before."

Selena shook her head. "No."

"No? That doesn't match with anything we've learned about Chris. You'd met up, how many times?"

"Seven."

"And never laid a hand on each other. All pure and innocent, no bad thoughts, never anything the nuns couldn't've seen. Seriously?"

A faint pink had come up in Selena's cheeks. Conway was good; every time Selena tried to drift away into her cloud, Conway got a finger on her. "I didn't say that. We'd held hands, we'd sat there with our arms round each other, we . . . But we'd never kissed before. So I needed to think. Whether it should happen again. Stuff like that."

I couldn't tell if she was lying. As hard to gauge as Joanne, not for the same reasons. Conway nodded away, turning her phone between her fingers, thinking. "Right," she said. "So that means you and Chris weren't having sex?"

"No. We weren't." No wiggle, no giggle, none of that shite. That rang true. Score one for Conway's instincts.

"Was Chris OK with that?"

"Yeah."

"Really? A lot of guys his age would've been putting on the pressure. Did he?"

"No."

"Here's the thing," Conway said. Her tone was good: gentle, but direct, no talking down to the kiddie; just woman to woman, working through something tough together. "A lot of times, people who get sexually assaulted don't want to report it because the aftermath is so much hassle. Medical examinations, testifying in court, getting cross-examined, maybe watching the attacker walk away scot-free: they don't want to deal with any of that mess, they just want to forget the whole thing and move on. Hard to blame them for that, right?"

A pause to let Selena nod. She didn't. She was listening, though, eyebrows pulled together. She looked bewildered.

Conway said, a notch slower, "See, though, this is different. There's not gonna be any medical exam, since this happened a year ago; and there's not gonna be any trial, since the attacker's dead. Basically, you can tell me what happened, and it won't blow up into some huge big thing. If you want, you can talk to someone who's had a load of practice helping people deal with things like this. That's it. End of story."

"Wait," Selena said. The bewilderment had got bigger. "You mean me? You think Chris *raped* me?"

"Did he?"

"No! God, no way!"

It looked real. "OK," Conway said. "Did he ever make you do anything you didn't want to do?" You always rephrase this one, keep coming at it from different angles. Scary, how many girls think it doesn't count as rape unless it's a laneway stranger with a knife; how many guys do.

Selena was shaking her head. "No. Never."

"Keep touching you after you told him to stop?"

Still shaking her head, steady and vehement. "No. Chris wouldn't have done that to me. Never."

Conway said, "Selena, we know Chris wasn't an angel. He hurt a lot of girls. Slagging them, two-timing them, messing them around and then blanking them when he got bored."

Selena said, "I know. He told me. He shouldn't have done that."

"It's easy to romanticize someone who's dead, specially someone who meant a lot to you. Fact is, Chris had a cruel streak, specially when he didn't get what he wanted."

"Yeah. I know that; I'm not romanticizing."

"Then why're you telling me he wouldn't have hurt you?"

Selena said—not defensive, just patient—"That was different."

Conway said, "That's what all the other girls thought, too. Every one of them thought she had something special with Chris."

Selena said, "Maybe they did have. People are complicated. When you're a little kid, you don't realize, you think people are just one thing; but then you get older, and you realize it's not that simple. Chris wasn't that simple. He was cruel and he was kind. And he didn't like realizing that. It bothered him, that he wasn't just one thing. I think it made him feel . . ."

She drifted for long enough that I wondered if she'd left the sentence behind, but Conway kept waiting. In the end, Selena said, "It made him feel fragile. Like he could break into pieces any time, because he didn't know how to hold himself together. That was why he did that with those other girls, went with them and kept it secret: so he could try out being different things and see how it felt, and he'd be safe. He could be as lovely as he wanted or as horrible as he wanted, and it wouldn't count, because no one else would ever know. I thought, at first, maybe I could show him how to hold the different bits together; how he could be OK. But it didn't work out that way."

"Right," Conway said. No interest in the deep and meaningfuls, but I could feel her clocking that I had been right: no short bus for Selena. She skimmed a finger over her phone, held it out again. "See here? After that night on the video, you ignored Chris for a few days, but then you stopped. These here, these are texts from you to him. What changed your mind?"

Selena had her head turned away from the phone, like she couldn't look. She said, to the slowing light outside the window, "I knew the right thing to do was cut him off totally. Never be in touch again. I knew that. But . . . you saw that. The video." A bare nod towards the phone. "It wasn't just that I missed him. It was because that was special. We made it together, me and Chris, it was never going to exist anywhere else in the world, and it was beautiful. Wrecking something like that, grinding it up to nothing and throwing it away: that's evil. That's what evil is. Isn't it?"

Neither of us answered.

"It felt like a terrible thing to do. Like it might even be the worst thing I'd ever done—I couldn't tell for sure. So I thought maybe I could save just some of it. Maybe, even if we weren't going to be together, we could still . . ."

Everyone's thought that: *maybe even if, maybe we could still*, maybe small bits of precious things can be salvaged. No one with cop-on thinks it after the first try. But her voice, quiet and sad, shimmering the air into those pearly colors: for a second I believed it, all over again.

Selena said, "It would never have worked out like that. Probably I knew that; I think I might've. But I had to try. So I texted Chris a couple of times. Saying let's stay friends. Saying I missed him, I didn't want to lose him . . . Stuff like that."

"Not a couple of times," Conway said. "Seven."

Selena's eyebrows pulling together. "Not that many. Two? Three?"

"You were texting him every few days. Including the day he died."

Selena shook her head. "No." Anyone would've said that, anyone with half a brain. But the bewildered look: I would've nearly sworn that was real.

"It's right here in black and white." Conway's tone was turning. Not hard, not yet, but firm. "Look. Text from you, no answer. Text from you, no answer. Text from you, no answer. This time Chris was ignoring you."

Things moved in Selena's face. She was watching the screen like a telly, like she could see it all happening in front of her, all over again.

"That had to have hurt," Conway said. "Didn't it?"

"Yeah. It did."

"So Chris was prepared to hurt you, after all. Right?"

Selena said, "Like I told you. He wasn't just one thing."

"Right. So is that why you broke up with him? Because he did something to hurt you?"

"No. That, when he didn't answer my texts, that was the first time Chris ever hurt me."

"Must've made you pretty angry."

"Angry," Selena said. Turned the word over. "No. I was sad; I was so sad. I couldn't figure out why he'd do that, not at first. But angry . . ." She shook her head. "No."

Conway waited, but she was done. "And then? Did you figure it out in the end, yeah?"

"Not till afterwards. When he died."

"Right," Conway said. "So why was it?"

Selena said, simply, "I was saved."

Conway's eyebrows shot up. "You mean you—what? Found God? Chris broke it off because—"

Selena laughed. The laugh startled me: fountaining up into the air, full and sweet, like laughter out of girls splashing in some tumbling river, miles from any watcher. "Not saved like that! God, can you imagine? I think my parents would've had a heart attack."

Conway smiled along. "The nuns would've been delighted, though. So what way were you saved?"

"Saved from getting back with Chris."

"Huh? You said being with Chris was great. Why did you need saving?"

Selena examined that. Said, "It wasn't a good idea."

That flash again. Wrapped in the pearly mist was someone wide awake and careful, someone we'd barely met.

"Why not?"

"Like you said. He messed around all the other girls he was with. Going out with someone brought out his worst side."

Conway trying to box Selena in, Selena leading her in loops. Conway said, "But you said he never did anything bad on you till after you split. What bad side did being with you bring out?"

"It hadn't had time to, yet. You said it would've, sooner or later."

Conway dropped it. "Probably would've," she said. "So someone saved you."

"Yeah."

"Who?"

So smooth and easy, it slid out.

Selena thought. She thought without moving: no ankles twisting or fingers weaving, not even her eyes flicking; just still, gazing, one hand loose in the other.

Said, "That doesn't matter."

"It does to us."

Selena nodded. "I don't know."

"Yeah. You do."

Selena met Conway's eyes straight on. She said, "No, I don't. I don't need to."

"But you've got a guess."

She shook her head. Slow and adamant: the end.

"OK," Conway said. If she was pissed off, she didn't give any sign. "OK. The phone Chris gave you: where is it now?"

Something. Wariness, guilt, worry; I couldn't tell. "I lost it."

"Yeah? When?"

"Ages ago. Last year."

"Before Chris died, or after?"

Selena thought about that for a while. "Around then," she said, helpfully.

"Right," Conway said. "Let's try this. Where were you keeping it?"

"I'd cut a slit in the side of my mattress. The side that was against the wall."

"Good. So think hard, Selena. When's the last time you took it out?"

"By the end I knew he wasn't going to text me. So I only checked last thing at night, sometimes. Just in case. I tried not to."

"The night he died. Did you check?"

The thought of that night sent Selena's eyes skidding. "I don't remember. Like I said, I was trying not to."

"But you'd texted him that day. You didn't want to see if he'd answered?"

"I hadn't. I mean, I don't think so. Maybe I might've, but . . ."

"What about after you heard he'd died? Did you go for the phone, see if he'd sent you one last text?"

"I can't remember. I wasn't . . ." Selena caught her breath. "I wasn't thinking straight. A lot of that week doesn't . . . it's not really in my head."

"Think hard."

"I am. It's not there."

"OK," Conway said. "You keep trying, and if it comes back, you let me know. What'd the phone look like, by the way?"

"It was little, like this big. Light pink. It was a flip phone."

Conway's eye found mine. The same phone Chris had given Joanne; he must have got a job lot. "Did anyone know you had it?" she asked.

Selena said, "No." And flinched. The others, certain sure that there were no secrets in their holy circle: under cover of the night she had slipped out of that circle, left them sleeping and trusting. "None of them knew."

"You positive? Living in each other's pockets, it's not easy to keep a secret. Specially not one as big as that."

"I was super-careful."

Conway said, "They knew you were with Chris, though, right? It was
just the phone they didn't know about?"

"No. They didn't know about Chris." Flinch. "I only went out to him like
once a week, and I waited till I was completely sure the others were asleep.
Sometimes they take ages, specially Holly, but once they're asleep they don't
wake up for anything. I've always had trouble sleeping, so I knew."

"I thought yous were so close. Shared everything. Why didn't you tell
them?"

Another flinch. Conway was hurting her, on purpose. "We are. I just
didn't."

"Would they have had a problem with you seeing Chris?"

Vague look. The pain had her moving away again, taking refuge in her
mist. Another girl would have been shifting as the pressure went on, glancing at the door, asking if she could go; Selena didn't need to. "I don't
think so."

"So that's not why you dumped him? Someone found out you two were
seeing each other, didn't like it?"

"Nobody found out."

"You positive? Anything ever make you worry that you'd been sussed?
Like maybe one of the others said something that sounded like a hint, or
maybe you found the phone in the wrong position one night?"

Conway trying to go after her, haul her back. One flicker in Selena's eyes
and I thought she had her, but then the gauze came down again. "I don't
think so."

"After he died, though. You told them then, right?"

Selena shook her head. She was gone: gazing at Conway peacefully, the way
you gaze at a fish swimming up and down an aquarium, all the pretty colors.

Conway looked puzzled. "Why not? It's not like it could've done any
harm: Chris was the one who'd wanted privacy, and he wasn't around to
care. And you'd lost someone who meant a lot to you. You needed support
from your mates. It would've only made sense to tell them."

"I didn't want to."

Conway waited. "Huh," she said, when she got nothing else. "Fair
enough. They must've copped that something was up, though. I'd say you
were in tatters; anyone would've been. Even before Chris died: you said you
were upset that he was ignoring you. Your friends can't have missed that."

Selena gazing, tranquil, waiting for the question.

"Did any of them ever say it to you? Ask you what was up?"

"No."

"If you're all so close, how'd they miss that?"

Silence, and those peaceful eyes.

"OK," Conway said, in the end. "Thanks, Selena. If you remember when you last saw that phone, you tell me."

"OK," Selena said, agreeably. Took her a second to think of standing up.

As she drifted for the door, Conway said, "When all this is sorted, I'll e-mail you that video."

That turned Selena fast, in a quick rush of breath. For a second she was vivid, blazing at the heart of the room.

Then she switched it off, deliberately. "No," she said. "Thanks."

"No? I thought you said nothing bad happened that night. Why wouldn't you want the video? Unless it brings back bad memories?"

Selena said, "I don't need to have what Joanne Heffernan saw. I was there." And she went out, closing the door gently behind her.

18

In the Court the pink-and-red Valentine windows are gone, all the big-eyed furry things holding hearts, enticing and barbed: *For you or not for you, will you won't you dare you hope?* In their place Easter eggs are starting to pop up, surrounded by shredded green paper to remind you that, somewhere on the other side of the pissed-off-and-on drizzle, it's going to be spring. Outside, in the Field, crocuses have started in corners and people who stayed indoors for the winter have buttoned their jackets high and come out to see what they can find.

Chris Harper is sitting on a weed-grown heap of rubble, away from the rest, looking out over the bare Field. His elbows are leaning on his knees and a pick-and-mix bag is hanging forgotten from one hand, and something in the set of his shoulders makes him seem older than the yelping rest of them. It stabs Selena in her palms and her chest, like she's being hollowed, how much she wants the right to go to him: sit down by his side on the rubble, clasp his hand close, lean her head against his and feel him ease against her. For a flashing second she wonders what would happen if she did it.

She and Julia and Holly and Becca have been there half an hour, sitting among the weeds sharing a couple of cigarettes, and he hasn't said a word to her, hasn't even looked at her. Either he's doing exactly what they planned, or he's changed his mind about the whole thing; he wishes he'd never left the dance with her. *I'll find a way to get in touch,* he said. That was weeks ago.

Selena knows this is good, either way. When they slid through the gap into the Field and she saw Chris sitting there, she prayed he wouldn't come over. But she wasn't ready for how it would hurt, how every time his eyes skim past her would feel like the air being ripped out of her lungs. Harry Bailey keeps talking to her about the mock exams and she keeps answering, but she has no clue what she's said. The whole world is weighted and sliding towards Chris.

He has two months and three weeks left to live.

"My *photos*!" Becca bursts out, on a rising note that's almost a wail. For the last few minutes Selena's felt Becca winding tighter beside her, doing something more and more hyper with her phone, but Chris pushed that to the edge of her mind.

"Huh?" says Holly.

"They're *gone*! OhmyGod, all of them—"

"Breathe, Becs. They're in there."

"No they're not, I checked everywhere—I never backed them *up*! All my photos of *us*, like everything all *year*—oh Jesus—"

She's panicking. "Hey," says Marcus Wiley, eyes sliding up from his slouch among his mates and all over Becca. "What've you got on there that's such a big deal?"

Finbar Wright says, "Gotta be tit pics."

"Maybe she's sent them to all her contacts," says someone else. "Everyone check, quick."

"Fuck that, man," Marcus Wiley says. "Who wants to see those?"

Howls of laughter, exploding up like mines. Becca is scarlet—with fury, not embarrassment, but it silences her just as hard. "Nobody wants to see your mini-dick either," Julia points out coolly, "but that doesn't stop you."

Howls, even louder ones. Marcus grins. "You liked the pic, yeah?"

"It gave us a laugh. Once we figured out what it was supposed to be."

"I thought it was a cocktail sausage," Holly says. "Only smaller."

She bounces it Selena's way with a glance—*Your turn*—but Selena looks away. She remembers that day in the Court with Andrew Moore and his friends, just a few months ago, the wild gale of new strength whipping her breath away: *We can do this we can say this whether they want us to or not.* Now it feels stupid, like spending your afternoon hand-slapping some bratty snotty toddler that isn't even yours. The speed of things changing makes her feel carsick.

"Was it your baby brother's?" Julia asks. "Because kiddie porn is illegal."

"Man," says Finbar, shoving Marcus and grinning. "You told us it got her all wet."

They all sound like yammering nothing. Chris hasn't moved. Selena wants to go home and lock herself in a toilet cubicle and cry.

"Maybe he meant she wet herself laughing," says Holly, charitably. "Which she almost did."

Marcus can't think of anything to do to Julia and Holly, so he launches himself onto Finbar. They wrestle and grunt through the weeds, half showing off for the girls but meaning it anyway.

Becca, frantically jabbing buttons, is on the edge of tears. "Did you check if they're on your SIM card?" Selena asks.

"I checked *everywhere!*"

"Hey," says someone, and Selena feels the jolt slam through her even before she turns her head. Chris drops down to sit beside Becca and holds out his hand. "Give us a look."

Becca whips her phone out of reach and gives Chris a suspicious glare. *It's OK*, Selena wants to say, *you can give it to him, don't be scared.* She knows better, a whole bunch of different ways, than to say anything.

"Whoa, look at that!" Someone from Marcus's gang, whooping across Marcus and Finbar still rolling in the weeds. "Harper's into mingers!"

"You're wasting your time," Holly tells Chris. "She doesn't actually have tit pics."

"She doesn't actually have *tits*—"

Chris ignores them both. To Becca, gently, the way he'd coax a prickling cat: "I might be able to get your photos back. I used to have that phone; it does this weird thing sometimes."

Becca wavers. His face, clear and steady-eyed: Selena knows how it opens you. Becca's hand comes out, her fingers uncurl on the phone.

"Fucking *hell!*" Marcus yells, sitting up with a hand to his face and blood coming out between his fingers. "My fucking *nose!*"

"Yeah. Well." Finbar dusts himself off, half scared, half proud, glancing over at the girls. "You went for me, man."

"You were asking for it!"

"I started it," Julia points out. "Are you planning on punching me too? Or just sending me more mini-dick pics?"

Marcus ignores her. He pulls himself up and heads for the fence, with his head tipped back and his hand still over his nose. "Ahh," Julia says with satisfaction, turning her back to the guys. "You know something? I needed that."

"Here," Chris says, holding out Becca's phone. "Are these them?"

"OhmyGod!" Becca yelps, on a wild rush of relief. "Yeah, they are. That's them. How did you . . . ?"

"You just moved them to the wrong folder. I put them back."

"Thanks," Becca says. "Thank you." She's giving him the smile she never normally gives anyone but the three of them, a huge shining monkey-crunch. Selena knows why. It's because if Chris can do something like that, just out of niceness, then not all guys are Marcus Wiley or James Gillen. Chris has that knack: turning the world into a different place, one that makes you want to take a running dive right into the middle.

Chris smiles back at Becca. "No hassle," he says. "If it gives you any more grief, you come find me and I'll have a look, yeah?"

"Yeah," Becca says. She's mesmerized, face upturned to his, radiant in his light.

Chris gives her a tiny wink and turns away, and for a second Selena can't breathe, but his eyes go right over her like she's not there. "I like your new pet," he tells Julia, nodding at the front of her jumper, which has a stoned-looking fox woven into it. "Is he house-trained?"

"He's very well-behaved," Julia says. "Sit! Stay! See? Good boy."

"I think there's something wrong with him," Chris says. "He's not moving. When was the last time you fed him?" He throws a marshmallow at the fox, out of his pick-and-mix bag.

Julia catches the marshmallow and tosses it into her mouth. "He's fussy. Try chocolate."

"Yeah, right. He can buy his own."

"Uh-oh," Julia says, "I think you've pissed him off," and sticks a hand up her jumper to send the fox leaping at Chris, and he mock-yells and jumps up. And then somehow he's next to Selena and the air has turned into something you can feel on every inch of your skin, lifting you, irresistible. His smile feels like she's known it by heart forever.

"Want one?" he says, and holds out the pick-and-mix bag.

Something in his eyes tells Selena to pay attention. "OK," she says. She looks into the bag, and in with the powdery bonbons and the dried-out fudge is a small pink phone.

"Actually," Chris tells her, "you have the rest of them. I've had enough." And he leaves the bag in her hand and turns away to ask Holly what she's doing for Easter.

Selena puts a sherbet lemon in her mouth, rolls the top of the bag and shoves it deep into her coat pocket. Harry has given up on her and is telling Becca how his economics mock was a total 'mare, doing an impression of himself having a full-on cross-eyed wobbler in the middle of the exam room, and Becca is laughing. Selena looks up at the long strokes of light plummeting down between clouds straight at them all, and tastes exploding lemon and feels the insides of her wrists tingling.

During first study period Selena goes to the toilet. On the way, she slips into their bedroom, pulls the pick-and-mix bag out of her coat and shoves it into the pocket of her hoodie.

The phone is dusted with sugar and it's empty: nothing in the contacts folder, nothing in the photo album, even the time and date haven't been set. The only thing on it is one text, from a number she doesn't recognize. It says *Hi*.

Selena sits on the toilet lid, smelling cold and disinfectant and powdered sugar. Rain blows softly against the windowpane, shifts away again; footsteps slap down the corridor and someone runs into the bathroom, grabs a handful of toilet paper, blows her nose wetly and runs out again, slamming the cubicle door behind her. Upstairs, where the fifth-years and sixth-years are allowed to study in their own rooms if they want to, someone is playing some song with a fast sweet riff that catches in your heartbeat and tugs it speeding along: *Never saw you looking but I found what you were looking for, never saw you coming but I see you coming back for more* . . . After a long time Selena texts back, *Hi*.

By the first night they meet, the rain has stopped. No wind rattles the bedroom window to wake the others when Selena eases her way out of bed and slips the key, millimeter by millimeter, out of Julia's phone case. No cloud blocks the moonlight as she pushes up the sash window and slides out onto the grass.

She's barely taken two steps when she starts to realize: outside is a different place tonight. The shadowy spots are seething with things she can almost hear, scuttles and slow-rising snarls; the patches of moonlight stake her down for the night watchman, for Joanne's gang, for anyone or anything who happens to be on the prowl. It reaches her vividly that the usual protections aren't in place tonight, that anyone who wants her could walk up and grab her. It's been so long since she felt this, it takes her a moment to understand what it is: fear.

She starts to run. As she dives off the lawn into the trees it sinks into her that she's different tonight, too. She's not weightless now, not skimming over the grass and jackknifing between trees deft as a shadow; her feet snap great clusters of twigs, her arms snag branches that bounce back wildly through rustling bushes, every time she moves she's screaming invitations to every predator out there and tonight she's prey. Things pad and sniff behind her and are gone when she leaps around. By the time she reaches the back gate her blood is made out of white terror.

The back gate is old wrought iron, backed with ugly sheet metal to stop anyone getting ideas about climbing, but the stone wall is rough with age, handholds and footholds everywhere. Back in first year Selena and Becca used to climb up and balance along the top, so high that sometimes passersby on the lane outside walked right under them without ever realizing they were there. Becca fell off and broke her wrist, but that didn't stop them.

Chris isn't there.

Selena presses into the shadow of the wall and waits, trying to muffle her breathing to nothing. A fresh kind of fear is rising inside her, whirling and horrible: *What if none of those texts were him at all, what if he was setting me up with some friend of his and that's who shows up—what if the whole thing was one huge big joke and they're all waiting to jump out from somewhere and howl laughing, I'll never live it down ever—serve me right—* The sounds in the dark are still circling, the moon overhead is sharp-edged enough to slice your hands to separate bones if you dared lift them. Selena wants to run. She can't move.

When the shape rises over the top of the wall, black against the stars, pulling itself up to hunch above her, she can't scream. She can't even try to understand what it is; she only knows something has turned solid and come for her at last.

Then it whispers, "Hey," in Chris's voice. The sound zaps white lightning across her eyes. Then she remembers why she's there.

"Hey," she whispers back, shaking and hoping. The black shape rears up on top of the wall, miles high, stands tall and straight for a second and then soars.

He lands with a thud. "Jesus, I'm glad it's you! I couldn't see you properly, I was thinking it was a watchman or a nun or—"

He's laughing under his breath, brushing down his jeans where the leap landed him on his knees. Selena thought she remembered what he was like, how when he's there the world snaps into focus almost too real to bear, but he hits her like a searchlight to the face all over again. The vividness of him sends the circling things scuttling backwards into the darkness. She's laughing too, breathless and giddy with relief. "No! There is a watchman, though, he checks this gate when he does his rounds—we've seen him. We have to move. Come on."

She's already moving, backwards and beckoning down the path, with Chris bounding after her. Now that the terror's gone she can smell the air, rich and pulsing with a thousand signs of spring.

There are benches along the paths, and Selena's aiming for one of those, the one shadowed under a wide oak between two open stretches of grass, so you can see anyone coming before they see you. The best thing would be one of the deepest corners of the grounds, the ones where you have to fight through bushes and clamber over awkward undergrowth to find a tiny patch of grass to sit on—she knows them all—but you would have to sit close, almost touching already. The benches are wide enough to leave an arm's length between you. *See*, she says in her mind, *see, I'm being safe.* Nothing comes back.

As they pass the rise to the glade, Chris's head turns. "Hey," he says. "Let's go up there."

That dark prickle hits Selena's back again. She says, "There's a place just down here that's really nice."

"Just for a minute. It reminds me of somewhere."

She can't think of a reason to say no. She climbs the slope side by side with Chris and tells herself maybe it's on purpose to help her, maybe the glade is going to keep her untempted, but she knows: she's not getting help tonight. As they step into the clearing the cypress branches boil and hiss. This is a bad idea.

In the middle of the clearing, Chris turns, his face tipped up to the stars. He's smiling, a small private smile. He says, "It's good here."

Selena says, "Where does it remind you of?"

"There's this place. Near home." He's still turning, looking up at the trees; it catches at Selena, the way he looks at them like they matter, like he wants to remember every detail. "It's just an old house, Victorian or something, I don't know. I found it when I was a kid, maybe seven; it was empty, like you could tell it'd been abandoned for ages—holes in the roof, the windows were all broken and boarded up . . . It's got this big garden, and right in one corner there was a circle of trees. Not the same kind as these—I don't know what they are, I don't know that stuff—but still. It reminded me."

He catches her eye and pulls back into a shrug and a half laugh. In texts they've talked about stuff Selena doesn't even tell the others, but this is different; they're so close they make each other's skin fizz. "I mean, I don't go there now. Someone bought it a couple of years back; they started locking the gates. I climbed up and looked over the wall once, and there were a couple of cars in the drive. I don't know if they actually live there, or if they did it up, or what. Anyway." He heads over to the edge of the clearing and starts poking a foot into the undergrowth. "Do animals live in here? Like rabbits or foxes?"

Selena says, "Did you go there when you wanted to be on your own?"

Chris turns and looks at her. "Yeah," he says, after a moment. "When things weren't great at home. Sometimes I'd get up really early, like five in the morning, and I'd go there for a couple of hours. Just to sit there. Out in the garden, if it wasn't raining, or inside if it was. Then I'd go home, before anyone else was awake, and get back into bed. They never even knew I was gone."

In that instant it's him, the same guy whose texts she's cupped in her hands like fireflies. He says, "I never told anyone that before." He's smiling at her, half startled, half shy.

Selena wants to smile back and tell him how she and the others come to the glade, in exchange, but she can't; not till she's cleared away the thing pinching at her. She says, "The phone. The one you gave me."

"You like it?" But he's looked away again. He's peering back under the cypresses, even though there's no way he could see into that dark. "There could even be badgers in here."

"Alison Muldoon's got one exactly the same. So's Aileen Russell, in fourth year. So's Claire McIntyre."

Chris laughs, but it sounds like an attack and he doesn't feel like the guy she knows any more. "So? You can't have the same phone as any other girl? Jesus, I didn't think you were that type."

Selena flinches. She can't think of anything to say that won't make everything even worse. She says nothing.

He starts moving again, fast mean-dog circles round the clearing. "OK. I gave phones like that to some other girls. Not Alison Whatever, but the others: yeah. A couple more, too. And? You don't own me. We're not even going out. What do you care who else I text?"

Selena stays very still. She wonders if this is her punishment: this, like a whipping, and then he'll be gone and she can drag herself home through the dark and pray that nothing comes skulking to the smell of blood off her. And the whole thing will be over.

After a moment Chris stops circling. He shakes his head, almost violently. "Sorry," he says. "I shouldn't've . . . But those other girls, they were months ago. I'm not in touch with any of them any more. I swear. OK?"

Selena says, "That's not what I meant. I don't care about that." She thinks that's true. "Just: when you say you've never told anyone something before, I don't want to wonder if you've actually told the same story to a dozen other people and said 'I never told anyone this before' every time."

He opens his mouth and she knows he's going to rip her apart, rip this into shreds they can never put back together. Then he rubs his hands up the sides of his jaw, hard, clasps them behind his head. He says, "I don't think I know how to do this."

Selena waits. She doesn't know what to hope.

"I should go. We can keep texting; I'd rather just do that than try seeing each other and have the whole thing go tits-up."

Selena says, before she knows she's going to, "It's not like this *has* to go tits-up."

"Yeah? We've been here two seconds, and look at us. I shouldn't have come."

"That's just being dramatic. We were fine outside the dance. All we have to do is talk to each other. Properly."

Chris stares at her. After a moment he says, "OK: I meant it. I never told anyone about the house before."

Selena nods. "See?" she says, "How hard was that?" and grins at him, and gets a startled half laugh back. Chris blows out a long breath, and loosens.

"I survived."

"So you don't have to leave. It won't go tits-up."

He says, "I should've been straight with you about the phone. Instead of . . ."

"Yeah."

"Being a prick to you, and all. That was shit. Sorry."

"It's OK," Selena says.

"Yeah? We're OK?"

"We're fine."

"God. Phew." Chris does a big exaggerated forehead-swipe, but he means it. He crouches to feel the grass. "It's dry," he says, dropping down, and touches a spot beside him.

When Selena doesn't move, he says, "I'm not going to . . . I mean, don't worry, I know you're not—or we're not— *Jesus*. I can't *talk*. I'm not going to try anything. OK?"

Selena is laughing. "Relax," she says. "I know what you mean," and she goes over and sits down next to him.

They sit there for a while, not talking, not even looking at each other, just getting used to the shapes of them in the shape of the clearing. Selena feels the hidden things thinning away to black veils you could pop with a fingertip, puddling into harmless sleep on the ground. She's a foot away from Chris, but that side of her is rich with the warmth off him. He has his hands clasped around his knees—they're like a man's hands, strong-knuckled and wide—and his head tilted back to look at the sky.

"I'll tell you something else I've never told anyone before," he says quietly, after a while. "You know what I'm going to do? When I'm old enough, I'm going to buy that house. I'll fix up the whole place, and then I'll invite all my friends round and we'll have a party that lasts like a week. Great music, and lots of drink and hash and E, and the house is big enough that when people get tired they can just go off to one of the bedrooms and crash for a while and then come back to the party, right? Or if they want some privacy or just some quiet, there are all these empty rooms, there's the whole garden. Whatever mood you're in, whatever you need right then, this place will have it."

His face is glowing. The house flowers in the air above the clearing, every detail carved and shimmering, every corner ringing and fountaining with someday music and laughter. It's as real as they are.

"And we'll all remember that party for the rest of our lives. Like, when we're forty and have jobs and kids and the most exciting thing we ever do is *golf*, that party's what we'll think about when we need to remind ourselves what we used to be like."

It comes to Selena that Chris has never once thought it might not happen. What if when he's old enough the people who own the house don't want to sell it, what if it's been knocked down to build an apartment block, what if he doesn't have enough money to buy it: none of these have ever crossed his mind. He wants it; that makes it as simple and certain as the grass under their legs. Selena feels a shadow like a great bird's flit across her back.

She says, "It sounds incredible."

He turns towards her, smiling. "I'll invite you," he says. "No matter what."

"I'll come," she says. She hopes with every part of her that they're both right.

"Deal?" Chris asks, holding out his hand to shake on it.

"Deal," Selena says, and because she can't not, she stretches out her hand and shakes his.

When it's time to go, he wants to walk her back to the school building, see her safe in at the window, but she won't let him. The moment they started talking about separating, she felt the things in the shadows stir and raise themselves, hungry; felt the watchman get restless, legs twitching for a walk in the full spring air. If they take any chances, they'll get caught.

Instead she lets him watch her up the path towards the school till she knows she's blurred into the dapple. Then she turns and stays still, feeling the shadows thickening at her back.

He's thrumming in the center of the clearing, full to exploding. When he leaps, it's head back and punching the sky, and she hears the low jubilant burst of breath. He comes down grinning, and Selena feels herself smiling back. She watches while he runs down the rise to the path, in big bounds so he won't crush the starting hyacinths, and heads for the back gate at a jog like he can't keep his feet on the ground.

Last time he was the one who touched her, before she knew it was coming. This time she reached out to touch him.

Selena's ready for the punishment. She expects the others to be wide awake and sitting up when she slips into the bedroom, three pairs of eyes slamming her back against the door, but they're so floppy asleep they've barely moved since she went out—it feels like nights ago. She waits all the next day to be called into McKenna's office so the night watchman can say *Yes that's her*, but the only time she sees McKenna is sailing past in a corridor with her general-purpose majestic half smile. In a bathroom cubicle, she tries whether she can still flicker the lights, whether her silver ring will still spin above her palm. She does it on her own so the others won't see her fail and guess why, but everything works perfectly.

After that she realizes it'll be less obvious than that, more oblique, a blow from the side when she isn't braced. A phone call telling her that they've lost all their money somehow, and she'll have to drop out of Kilda's. Her stepdad losing his job and they all have to emigrate to Australia.

She tries to feel guilty about it, whatever it is, but there's no space in her mind. Chris is shining into every corner. His laugh, sliding higher than you'd expect from someone with such a deep voice, turning him suddenly young and mischievous. The chop of pain, *When things weren't great at home*, slicing off all his careful cheerful façade, turning his face taut and private. The narrow of his eyes against moonlight, the shift of his shoulders as he leans forward, the smell of him, he's in every moment. She can't believe the others don't taste her hot and cinnamony, don't see it spinning off her like gold dust every time she moves.

There's no phone call. She doesn't get hit by a lorry. Chris is texting her *When?* The next time Selena and the others go to the glade, she thinks up at the moon: *Please do something to me. Or I'm going to meet him again.*

Silence, cold. She understands that Chris is her battle; no one is going to fight it for her.

I'll tell him we can't meet up any more. I'll tell him he was right and we should just text. The thought of it knocks her breath out, like icy water. *If he's not OK with that, then I'll stop texting him.*

The next time they meet, in a grassy and moonless silence between two secrets, she takes his hand.

19

We went to the bedroom door, watched Selena down the corridor and safe to where she was supposed to be. The singsong was over; when Selena swung the common-room door open, the silence surged out at us, tight and brittle, thrumming.

Conway watched the door click shut. "So," she said. "You think Chris raped her?"

"Not sure. Gun to my head, I'd say no."

"Same. But there was more to the breakup than she's saying. Who dumps a guy because they kissed? What kind of reason is that?"

"Once we get those texts, they might give us something."

"If Sophie's guy's gone home for his dinner, I swear I'm gonna get his address and track the little bollix down." A couple of hours earlier, it would've come out like she meant it. Now it was auto-pitbull, too tired to clamp down. She checked her watch: quarter to seven. "Fuck's *sake*. Come *on*."

I said, "Even if Chris didn't rape Selena, someone could've thought he had."

"Yeah. They break up, she's all upset, crying into her unicorns. One of her mates knows she was seeing Chris, figures he did something to her . . ."

I said, "She thinks one of her mates killed him."

"Yeah. She's not sure, but she thinks so, yeah." This time Conway wasn't pacing: slumped against the corridor wall instead, head back, trying to rub the day out of her neck. "Which means she's out. Not officially, but out."

I said, "She's not *outside*, but. She's . . ." That vortex pull of Selena, things spinning round her axis, I didn't know how to say that. "When we get the story, she'll be in it."

Talking like an eejit, and in front of one of the Murder squad, but Conway wasn't sneering. Nodding. "If she's right and one of her mates did the job, it was because of Chris and Selena. One way or another."

"That's what she thinks, too. At least one of the mates knew all about her and Chris, and didn't like it. And Selena knew they wouldn't; that's why she didn't tell them to start with." I leaned on the wall beside Conway. Fatigue kicking in, me too, the wall felt like it was swaying. "Maybe they knew he was a player, thought he'd end up hurting Selena. Maybe he'd done something shite on one of them—just casually, like what Holly told us about— and he was the enemy. Maybe one of them was into him. Maybe one of them had already been with him, earlier in the year."

"OK," Conway said. Rolled her neck, winced. "Say we pull them back in, one by one. Tell them we think Selena did it, we're getting ready to arrest her. That should shake them loose."

"You think if one of them's our girl, she'll come clean to get Selena off the hook?"

"She might. That age, self-preservation isn't high on their list. Like we were saying before: nothing matters as much as your friends. Not even your life. You're practically *looking* for a good reason to sacrifice it."

Beat of pain at the base of my throat and in the crooks of my elbows, places where veins run near the surface. I said, "That cuts two ways. If one of them confesses, doesn't mean she did it."

"If they all go bloody Spartacus, I swear I'll take them up on it. Arrest the fucking lot, let the prosecutors sort it out." Conway pressed the heels of her hands into her eye sockets, like she didn't want to see the corridor any more. We'd been there long enough that the place was starting to look familiar, in a glitchy way, something you saw in a stuttering DVD or when you were too hammered to see straight. She said, "We'll go at the three of them as soon as we get those full texts. I want some clue what went down between Chris and Selena—the breakup, and after. See her face, when she looked at those records? The ones for just before the murder?"

I said, "Startled. Looked like the real thing to me."

"You think everything's the real thing. How you got this far . . ." She didn't have the energy. "It did, but. She didn't expect to see all those texts. She might've just flaked out and forgotten them; she's spacy enough to start with, and she says herself she's not too clear on those couple of weeks. Or else . . ."

"Or else someone else knew about her phone. Used it to send some of those texts."

Conway said, "Yeah. Joanne must've figured that Selena had a special Chris phone, same as she did. Julia must've, too, since she knew about

Joanne's. And did you see Selena clam up when I asked about finding the phone in the wrong position? Someone was at it, all right."

I said, "We need those texts. Even if they're not signed—"

"They won't be."

"Yeah, probably not. But there might be something that gives us a hint who wrote them."

"Yeah. And I want to ID the other girls Chris was texting, before he hooked up with Selena. If another one of our eight was in there, things are gonna get interesting—specially if she's the one he was juggling with Joanne. Bet you anything the special phones were never registered, but we could get lucky, find a name somewhere in the texts—or there could be something in the photos they sent, if we can get them. Any girl with the brains of pet food would've cropped out her face, but I'm gonna bet on at least one idiot. And someone might have a mole on her tit, a scar, something identifiable."

I said, "OK if I leave that part to you?"

Conway still had her hands on her eyes, but I saw the twitch of her mouth, what might have been a grin if she'd been less wrecked. "I'll look at the girls' pics, you look at Chris's. No one needs brain bleach."

"We hope."

"Yeah." The grin was gone. "OK: I'll go ask McKenna to let that lot outside for a while. Seeing as I promised Selena." I'd forgotten. "Then we'll head down to the canteen, see if we can find something to eat while we wait for Sophie's guy to pull his finger out. I could murder a dirty great burger."

"Two."

"Two. And chips."

We were straightening up, smoothing down, when it came: buzz from Conway's pocket.

She grabbed for the phone. "The texts." She was straight-backed and alert as morning, fatigue tossed away like a wet jacket. "Ah, yeah. Here we go. Swear to God, I'd marry Sophie."

This attachment was even longer than the last one. "Sit down for this," Conway said. "Over there," and jerked her chin towards the window alcove at the far end of the corridor, between the two common rooms. The window had gone a clear lit purple, dusk that looked like thunder. Fine clouds shifted, restless.

We pulled ourselves onto the sill and sat shoulder to shoulder. Started at the beginning of the attachment and skimmed fast, trying to pay attention to the early stuff. Kids on Christmas morning, able to think about nothing but the big shiny package we were saving for last. Silence drumming at us, from the doors on both sides.

Lots of flirting. Chris flattering, *Saw u down at d court 2day, u were looking gorgeous*; the girl coming back coy, *OMG cant beleive u saw me looking sooo crap my hair was a total mess lol*. Chris straight in there, *Wasn't looking at ur hair, not with the way ur tits looked in that top :-D*. You could practically hear the girl squealing. *U r so dirty!*

Bits of drama: some girl on a high-strung high horse, *Don't listen 2 what ppl r saying abt Fri evening they weren't there! Ne1 can make up whatever shit they want but there was only the 4 of us there so if u want to know the truth then just ASK ME!!!* Lots of making appointments, but all of them were legit, mostly after school at the shopping center or in the park; no one had been sneaking out at night, not back then. One chain text: *If you love your mother then text this to 20 people. A girl ignored this and 30 days later her mam died. Sorry I can't ignore this because I love my mother!*

You forget what it was like. You'd swear on your life you never will, but year by year it falls away. How your temperature ran off the mercury, your heart galloped flat-out and never needed to rest, everything was pitched on the edge of shattering glass. How wanting something was like dying of thirst. How your skin was too fine to keep out any of the million things flooding by; every color boiled bright enough to scald you, any second of any day could send you soaring or rip you to bloody shreds.

That was when I really believed it, not as a detective's solid theory but right in my gut: a teenage girl could have killed Chris Harper. Had killed him.

Conway had caught it, too. "Bloody hell. The *energy*."

I said, before I felt it coming out, "Do you ever miss that?"

"Being a teenager?" She glanced over at me, eyebrows pulling together. "Fuck no. All that drama, wrecking your own head over something you won't even remember in a month? What a waste."

I said, "It's got something, but. There's something beautiful there."

Conway was still watching me. That morning's tight hairdo was wearing out, glossy bits coming out of the bun to fall in front of her ear, and the sharp suit had wrinkles. Should've made her look softer, girlier, but it didn't. Made her look like a hunter and a fighter, ragged from a bare-knuckle round. She said, "You like things to be beautiful."

"I do, yeah." When she waited: "So?"

"So nothing. Good luck with that." She went back to the phone.

Bits of low-level smoochy talk, back and forth: *Cant wait 2 c u again. Had THE BEST TIME with u yesterday. U r something special u no that?*

"Gag," said Conway. "God rest, and all that shite, but what a sleaze he was."

I said, "Or he wanted to believe it. Wanted to find someone he felt that way about."

Conway snorted. "Right. Sensitive soul, our Chris. See these?"

One girl, back in October, had been scraped raw when Chris dumped her. The other one got the message quick enough, sent Chris a fast *Fuck you* and moved on, but this one: avalanche of texts, begging for answers. *Is it bcos of that time in the park???* . . . *Is it bcos your friends don't like me?* . . . *Was someone spreading rumors abt me?* . . . *Please please please I'll leave you alone I just need to know* . . .

Chris never got back to her. "Yeah," Conway said. "Just a poor lonely heart looking for love."

No name, but the girl would need ID'ing. No names anywhere. *OMG did you see Amy fall of the skateboard right on her ass thought I was going to get sick lauhging so hard!* That was it.

Conway had been right about the photos: not fluffy kitties.

Chris: *Send me a pic :-D*

Another girl we needed to find: *U already no what I look like lol*

Chris: *U no what I mean :-D So I have sthing nice to tink about til i see u again*

No way!!! + have it go round the whole of Colms?? Hello don't tink so???

Chris: *Hey I would NEVER do that. Thought you knew me better than that. If you think I'm such an arsehole then maybe we should call it quits*

OMG I was just messing! So soooo sorry, didn't mean that at all, I know ur not an arsehole :-(

Chris: *OK just thought you of all people would know I'm not like that. Thought you trusted me.*

I totally do!! [attachment: .jpg file]

"Go Chris," Conway said. Wry, but the undercurrent made me look up.

"He doesn't just get his tit pics; he gets an apology out of her for not sending them faster."

"He was good, all right."

"Always got what he wanted, Julia said."

I said, "He could've been telling this girl the truth, though. At least about keeping the pics to himself. Any of his mates mention them, last year?"

"Nah. Like they would've? In front of Father Whoever? 'Yeah, Chris was passing around underage tit shots, now please expel me and arrest me for kiddie porn thank you very much—'"

"They might've done, if they copped that one of the girls could've killed him over it. Chris was their mate. Maybe they wouldn't say it in front of Father Whoever, but all it would've taken was an anonymous text to you, an e-mail, whatever. And you said Finn Carroll was no thicko."

"He's not." Conway sucked her front teeth. "And him and Chris were close enough that if Chris had been sharing the pics, Finn would've seen them. Why would Chris keep them to himself?"

I said, "Selena said he was complicated."

"Yeah, girls always think arseholes are sooo complicated. Surprise, kids: they're just arseholes." Conway was flicking at her screen again. "If he didn't pass the pics around, it wasn't because deep down he was actually a knight in shining armor. It was because he figured the girls might find out, and his supply of wank material would dry up." She held the phone between us. "Here we go. Joanne."

Joanne started the same way as all the others. Chris playing cheeky, seeing how far he could go, Joanne slapping him down and loving it. Lots of meetings. He got pics off her, but she made him work hard for them: *Say please. Now say pretty please. Good boy lol now send me a pic of something nice youd like to buy me. Now send me a pic of where youd like to take me on holiday . . .* You could see her huddled snickering with her mates, working out the next demand.

"Fuck's sake," Conway said, lip curling. "High-maintenance little bint. Why didn't he give her the heave-ho right there? Plenty more tits in the sea."

"Maybe he liked a challenge," I said. "Or maybe Joanne was right, and he was genuinely into her."

"Right. Chris being sooo complex again. He wasn't all that into her. Look."

Pics, more flirting, more meetings, smoochy talk getting smoochier. Then Joanne started hinting hard about going public—*Cant wait 4 the xmas* *dance!! We can ask the DJ to play our song . . . I dont even care if Sister Cornelius throws us off the dance floor lol <3 <3 <3—*and Chris was gone.

Joanne: *Hey where were you this eve? We were suposd to meet!*

Joanne again: *Did u get my text?*

Hello?? Chris whats going on??

Just 2 let you know I had something special planned for this wk-end . . . If your curious text me quick ;-)

If someone said something to you then ask urself WHY . . . Plenty of ppl are mad jel of me . . . didnt think you were stupid enuf to fall for it

Excuse me I dont let guys treat me like this . . . Im not some stupid slut you can treat how ever you want . . . If you dont answer by 9.00 then we are OVER!!

Do you want me to tell everyone your gay?? I'll do it

Surprise I was about to dump your arse anyway. You cant kiss for shit . . . and I dont do it w guys who have tiny dxxxs!!! You make me want to puke I hope you get aids from some slapper

Chris if you dont answer this + apologize to me YOU WILL BE SORRY. I hope your reading carefully because this was a big BIG mistake . . . I dont care how long it takes YOU WILL BE SORRY.

OK you asked for it. Bye.

"Now there's a beauty of a hissy fit," Conway said.

Joanne again. Motive, opportunity and now mind-set.

I said, "This was five months before Chris got killed. You think she'd hold a grudge that long?"

" 'I don't care how long it takes . . .' " Conway shrugged. "Maybe not. Maybe. You heard her: still stings now, and it's been a year and a half."

I still didn't see Joanne in a midnight grove with a hoe in her hand. By the look on her face, neither did Conway. I said, "Any chance she got someone else to do the job for her?"

Conway shook her head, regretfully. "I was thinking the same thing. Great minds. I doubt it, but. It'd have to be one of her girls—if she'd shagged a guy into doing it, he'd never have managed to keep his gob shut this long—and who? Alison would've fucked it up, so would Orla, and even if somehow they managed to get the job done and not get caught the next day, they would've let it slip by now. Gemma could've got it done and kept her mouth shut, but Gemma's got plenty of cop-on and a healthy sense of self-preservation on her. She wouldn't do it to start with."

I said, "One of Holly's lot might."

Conway's eyebrows shot up. "Blackmail."

"Yeah. Joanne had that video. She could've got Selena expelled—probably the other three, too."

"Not without dropping herself in the shite as well."

"Sure she could. Put the video on a memory stick, post it to McKenna. Or upload it to YouTube some weekend, e-mail the school the link. McKenna might guess who made the video, but she couldn't prove it."

Conway was nodding, thinking fast. "OK. So Joanne gets the video, takes it to . . . who? Not Selena. Joanne's got more sense than to give a job like that to a spacer like her."

I said, "And Selena wouldn't've done it anyway. She was mad about Chris; she would've been grand with getting expelled for his sake."

"Right. Romeo and Juliet, middle-class version." Conway was concentrating too hard to get her snide on properly. "If I was Joanne, I wouldn't go for Rebecca, either."

"Nah. Too unpredictable; she looks all meek, but I'd say she'd be more likely to lose the head and tell Joanne to fuck herself than to take orders off her. And Joanne's good at gauging people, or she wouldn't be the boss bitch. Not Rebecca."

Silence, while the rest hung waiting in the air. Conway said, when someone had to, "Joanne said she had a chat with Julia, told her to make Selena back off. Maybe that's not all she told her to do."

Julia. The eyes of her, watchful. The way she'd jumped to protect Selena. The slam of stillness when she'd seen that postcard.

Conway said, "Julia knew about Joanne's secret phone. I can't see any reason why Joanne would let her in on that. Except to show her what to look for."

The silence came back bigger and stronger. Said it for us: neither of us wanted it to be her.

I said, "Julia's got better sense. Getting expelled isn't the end of the world."

"Wasn't where we came from, maybe. It is for most of this lot. You should've seen the faces on the Colm's guys when they heard Finn Carroll was out. They looked like he was *gone* gone, like they'd never see him again; they were practically as upset about him as they were about Chris. You know what they think? Schools like this are the whole civilized world. Outside, it's wilderness. Teenage mutant skanger smackheads selling your kidneys on the black market."

I could see it. Didn't say it to Conway, but I could see so clearly. Thrown out of here would feel like thrown over a wall into blackened rubble and air made of grime. Everything gone; everything golden and lit, everything silken, everything carved in delicate curlicues to welcome your fingertips, everything made to chime in sweet spacious harmonies: gone, and a flaming sword to bar your way back forever.

Conway leaning back against the wall and watching me at a slant, through those streaks of warrior hair. One dark eye, hooded.

I said, "Let's see the rest."

The texts between Chris and Selena started on the twenty-fifth of February, and they were different. No flirting, no sexy talk, no wheedling for pics; none of that feel, speed and fever.

Hi

Hi

That was it, their first conversation. Just feeling the other one there.

Over the next couple of days they started telling each other stories. Chris's class had made some gadget that beeped at random intervals, stuck it under a desk and watched their Irish teacher lose his mind. Selena's class had been messing with Houlihan's head by inching their desks forward, too gradually to spot, till she was practically pinned against the blackboard. Small stories, to make each other laugh.

Then—carefully, step-by-step, like they had all the time in the world—they moved into personal stuff.

Chris: *OK so this wknd I get home n my sister's cut her hair in one of those emo fringes. What do I do??*

Selena: *Depends, does it look good?*

Chris: *Actually not bad . . . or wouldn't be bad if she'd got it done at the hairdresser instead of doing it herself with nail scisors :-0*

Selena: *LOL! Then take her to the hairdresser + get it done right!*

Chris: *I might actually do it :-D*

Late-night texts, typoed, hurrying in the jacks or texting blind under covers. Chris's sister loved her pro haircut. He and his friends got locked at someone's brother's party, shouted insults at some girl on their way home, Chris felt guilty about it in the morning (*Sooo complex*, Conway's eye-roll said, *such a sensitive soul*). Selena wished her dad and her mum would talk when one of them dropped her off at the other's place; Chris wished his parents would stop talking, because they always ended up yelling. They were getting close.

Feeling their way closer. Chris: *Nothing intelligent to say, was just thinking about you*

Selena: *That's mental, I was just going to text you to say I was thinking about you*

Chris: *In fairness I think about you alot so not that crazy of a concidence*

Selena: *Don't be like that*

Chris: *I know sorry. I actully mean it. It just comes out sounding fake*

Selena: *Then don't say anything. You know you don't have to say stuff to me right?*

Chris: *Yeah. Just I don't want you thinking this doesn't matter to me*

Selena: *I won't. I promise*

Nothing like Chris's flirtations, overused words from telly scripts, with empty space underneath. This was something else; the real thing, confusing, thrilling, script going out the window. Sappy stuff, once-in-a-lifetime stuff, stuff to make you cringe and break your heart.

I said, "You think he's faking that?" Got that hooded dark eye again, and no answer.

Then, from Chris: *I wish we could talk properly. This is stupid.*

Selena: *Me too*

Chris: *We could try meeting after school in the field or in the park??*

Selena: *Wouldn't be the same. Like we said before. And someone would see us*

Chris: *Then somewhere else. Like we can find a cafe in the other direcion.*

Selena: *No. My friends would want to know where I was going. I'm not going to lie to them, this is bad enough*

Conway said, "This isn't like with Joanne and the others, where Chris wants to keep them under wraps and they're pushing to go public. Selena wants to stay on the down-low too."

"Like we said: she knows at least one of her gang wouldn't be happy."

"Julia knew Chris was a dog. And Holly didn't like him one little bit."

In the second week of March, Chris found the answer. *Ok guess what.*

Finn worked out a way we can get out at night. If you can still do it would you be on for meeting up? Don't want to get you in trouble, but I'd love to see you

Silence for a day, while Selena tried to decide. Then:

I'd love to too. Have to be late like 12:30. Meet me at the back gate of Kilda's and we can find somewhere to talk.

Chris, fast and bubbling over: *Yeahhhh!!! Thursday?*

Selena: *Yes thursday. I'll text you if I can't get out. Otherwise see you there Can't wait :-)*

Same :-)

The meetings started and the texts changed. Got shorter, less of them and less to them. No more stories, no families and friends and deep feelings and daydreams. *Hi :-)* and *Tonight same time same place?* and *Can't, thurs?* and *Yeah see you then.* That was it. The real stuff had grown too huge and too powerful to fit in little lit rectangles; it had come alive.

Noise from the fourth-year common room, roll of thuds like a heap of books tumbling. Conway and I whipped round, ready, but it vanished under a burst of laughter, spattering like bright flung paint, too hard.

And then the bit we'd been waiting for.

April twenty-second, Chris and Selena arranged to meet, just like we'd thought. *Same time same place. Can't wait.*

That night, the video. The kiss.

Early the morning of April twenty-third, Chris texted Selena. *I'm going to get in trouble cos I cant stop smiling :-)*

Before school, Selena got back to him. Epic text. *Chris I have to stop meeting you. I promise it's nothing you did. I should never have met up to start with but I genuienly thought we could be just friends. That was really really stupid. I am so sorry. I know you won't understand why, but if this hurts you, maybe it will help to know it hurts me so much too. I love you (another thing I should never have said).*

Conway said, "What the fuck is she on about?"

"That doesn't sound like a rape victim," I said.

She shoved stray hair out of her face with the heel of her hand, hard. "Sounds like a nutter. I'm starting to think Joanne and them were right about this lot."

"And it doesn't sound like Selena wanted time to think, the way she told us. The way that reads, she'd done all her thinking already."

"Why the fuck shouldn't she go out with Chris? You're so in love with each other, you go out together. Tell the world. Simple. What's *wrong* with these people?"

Chris came back fast and wild. *WTF?!!!!? Selena wgats going on??? If th4s isnt Selena then FUCK OFF. If it is then Selena we have to talk. Same time same place??*

Nothing.

After school: *Selena if you want to be just freinds then we can do that. I thought you wanted to or I would of never even tried you know that. Please can we meet tonite. I swear I won't even touch you. Same time same place I'll be there.*

Nothing.

Next day he was back. *I waited for you like a fucking plank til 3am. Swear to God I would of bet my life that you'd come. Still can't believe you didn't.*

A couple of hours later: *Selena are you serious about this? I don't get it what HAPPENED? If I did something wrnng I'll do whatever you want to aplogize. Just tell me what the fucks going on.*

That evening: *Selena you have to text me.*

Nothing.

The Thursday, the twenty-fifth of April, Selena finally texted Chris. *1 o'clock tonight. Usual place. DON'T text me back. Just come.*

"That," Conway said, and tapped her screen, "that's not Selena."

I said, "No. Selena would've said, 'Same time same place,' like they always did. And there's no reason why she wouldn't want him to text her back."

"Right. Someone else didn't want him answering, in case Selena saw the message."

"She didn't worry that Selena would spot her text? One night Selena gets a bit nostalgic, has a look back through her old chats with Chris, and all of a sudden she's going, *Hang on, I don't remember writing that.*"

"Mystery Girl didn't leave it on the phone. Wait for it to send, go into the Sent folder, delete."

"So," I said, "Selena's texts after the breakup, Chris wasn't ignoring them because he was in a strop with her. He was just doing what he was told."

Conway said, "Some of the time, he was. Not all. Look at this."

Five days later, thirtieth of April, Selena's phone to Chris's: *I miss you. I've been trying so hard not to text you and I don't blame you if you're raging with me but I wanted you to know I miss you.*

I said, "That's the real Selena again. Like she told us, she couldn't stand to cut him right off."

Conway said, dryly, "He's got no problem cutting her right off. No answer. He was ignoring her, all right. Chris hadn't got what he wanted, for once, and he wasn't happy."

I said, "Here's the other thing about that text. It says Mystery Girl didn't actually nick the phone. She used it when she needed it, then put it back in Selena's mattress."

Conway nodded. "Joanne and her lot didn't have that kind of access—even if they knew where Selena kept the phone, and how would they? Whoever set up that meeting lived in that bedroom."

Almost a week later, sixth of May, someone using Selena's phone texted Chris: *I'll be there.* No answer.

I said, "They'd already set up the appointment; Mystery Girl's just confirming. Chris must've shown up, the week before."

"Yeah. But that time, he went because he thought he was meeting Selena. This time, he knows he's not. And he's going along anyway."

"Why?"

Conway shrugged against the glass. "Maybe Mystery Girl says she's going to sort things out between him and Selena, or maybe he figures banging Selena's mate would make a great revenge. Or maybe he just thinks he's in with a chance at more tit pics. Chris liked chicks, any chicks. There's no 'why' there. The question is why she's meeting him."

The long day had my mind moving like porridge, bits of thought taking forever to find each other. The corridor stretching away in front of us looked unreal, tiles too red, lines too long, something we'd never be able to stop seeing.

I said, "If she was going to kill him, why not do it straight off? What were the extra meetings for?"

"Working up the guts. Or there's something she wants to find out, before she decides whether to do it—whether he actually raped Selena, maybe. Or she's got no plans to kill him, not at first; she's meeting him for some other reason. And then something happens."

Selena to Chris, the eighth of May, late at night: *I don't want us to be like this forever. Maybe this is completely stupid but there has to be some way we can be friends. Just hold on to each other till maybe if you're not too furious with me we can try again someday. I can't stand us losing each other totally.*

Conway said, "She's dying to get back with him. She can talk about just friends all she wants; that's what she's after."

I said, "She said she was saved from doing it. This is what she meant. If Chris had texted her back, no way she would've stayed hard-line about not meeting up. They would've been back together inside a couple of weeks. Maybe that's what Mystery Girl was at: keeping them apart."

"If you were a teenage girl," Conway said. "And you wanted to keep

Chris away from Selena, for whatever reason. And you were fairly sure she hadn't been shagging him. And you knew what Chris was like."

Silence, and the long red stretch of the corridor, tiles shifting queasily.

"He brought a condom."

I said, "Not Rebecca. She wouldn't think of it."

"Nah."

Julia would have thought of it.

Thirteenth of May: *I'll be there.*

Fourteenth of May, Selena again. *Don't worry, I know you're not going to answer this. I just like talking to you anyway. If you want me to stop, tell me and I will. Otherwise I'll keep texting you. We had a substitute today for Maths, when she smiled she looked exactly like Chucky—Cliona got mixed up and called her Mrs. Chucky and we all almost died laughing :-D*

Rewinding, back to the small stories for laughs, trying to bring Chris back with her to a safe place. I said, "For a while, Mystery Girl's able to convince Chris to stay away from Selena. Wouldn't be hard: he's pissed off with her anyway, and if Mystery Girl's giving him something Selena wasn't . . . But Selena keeps texting him. If he cared about her, if that was the real thing, then those texts had to get to him. After a while, it doesn't matter what Mystery Girl's bringing. Chris wants Selena back."

Conway said, "And Mystery Girl has to come up with a new plan."

Sixteenth of May, 9:12 a.m. The morning before Chris died.

Selena's phone to Chris's: *Can you meet tonight? 1 in the cypress clearing?*

4:00 p.m.—he must have checked his messages after school—Chris's phone to Selena's: *OK.*

Whoever had set up that meeting had killed Chris Harper. We had room for a crack of doubt—interception, coincidence. No more than that.

"Love to know who he thinks he's meeting," Conway said.

"Yeah. Not Mystery Girl's usual day, not her usual MO—this time she asks for an answer."

"It's not Selena. 'Cypress clearing,' Selena wouldn't've said that. That was their spot. 'Same time same place,' she'd've said."

Selena was out, again. I said, "But Chris could've thought it was her."

"Could be what Mystery Girl wanted him to think. By now, she's planning. She breaks the routine to get Chris wondering, make sure he shows up. Takes the risk of having him text her back—maybe she does nick the phone outright, this time. She knows no one's gonna be using it from now on."

Conway's voice was level and low, rough-edged with fatigue. Small eddies of air nosed around it, curious, carried it away down the corridor.

"Maybe Joanne's twisting her arm; maybe she's doing it off her own bat, for whatever reason. That night she sneaks out early, takes the hoe out of the shed—she's wearing gloves, so no prints. She heads for the grove, hides in among the trees till Chris arrives. When he's mooning around the clearing waiting for his twue wuv to show up, our girl hits him with the hoe. He goes down."

The lazy drone of bees, this morning, long ago. Seed-heads round my ankles, smell of hyacinths. Sunlight.

"She waits till she's sure. Then she wipes down the hoe, puts it back where she got it. She takes Chris's secret phone off his body and gets rid of it. Gets rid of Selena's, too. Maybe she does it that night, goes over the wall and ditches them in a bin; maybe she hides them somewhere in the school till the fuss dies down. Now there's nothing to link her or her mates to the crime—except maybe Joanne, and Joanne's got enough cop to keep her mouth shut. Our girl goes back inside. Goes to bed. Waits for the morning. Gets ready to squeal and cry."

I said, "Fifteen years old. You think any of them would have that kind of nerve? The murder, OK. But the wait? This whole last year?"

Conway said, "She did it for her friend. One way or another. For her friend's sake. That's got power. You do that, you're Joan of Arc. You've gone through fire; nothing's gonna break you."

Shiver building dark in my spine, the way it does when power comes near. That beat of pain again, deep in the palms of my hands.

"There's someone else who knows, but. And she hasn't been through fire for her mate; she hasn't got that kind of nerve. She holds in the secret as long as she can, but it finally gets to be too much. She cracks, makes the postcard. Probably she genuinely doesn't think it'll go further than that board, corridor gossip. The bubble again: you're inside it, the outside doesn't feel real. But your Holly's been to the outside before. She knows it's there."

Sound from the fourth-year common room, sharp and sudden. Something heavy thudding to the floor. A squeal.

I was half off the windowsill when Conway's hand clamped round my bicep. She shook her head.

"But—"

"Wait."

Murmur like bees, swelling and bristling.

"They're going to—"

"Let them."

A wail, rising above that murmur, high and trembling. Conway's hand tightened.

Words, a terrified cry too garbled to catch through the thick door. Then the screaming started.

Conway was down and hitting the combination lock before I realized her hand was gone off my arm. The door opened on a different world.

The noise punched me in the face, sent my vision skidding. Girls up and on their feet, hands and hair flying—I'd been seeing them through texts for so long, just narrow snippets of minds shooting through dark, it felt like a double take seeing them real and solid. And nothing like I'd seen them before, nothing. Those glossy gems, watching us cool-eyed and assessing with their knees perfectly crossed: gone. These were white and scarlet, wide-mouthed, clawed and clutching at each other, these were wild things.

McKenna was shouting something, but none of them heard her. Shrieks launched off them like birds, battering against the walls. I caught words, here and there, *I see him oh my God oh God I see him it's Chris Chris Chris—*

It was the high sash window they were fixed on, the one where Holly and her mates had been sitting an hour or two earlier. Empty now, blank evening sky. Heads back, arms open to that rectangle, they were screaming like it was a joy, a physical one. Like it was the one thing they'd been dying to do, for years and years, and the time had come.

It's him it's him look oh God look— Conway's ghost story had paid off.

Conway dived in. Aiming for Holly and her lot, pressed together in a far corner. They weren't screaming, weren't gone, but they were huge-eyed, Holly's teeth sunk into her forearm, Rebecca crouched in an armchair gasping, hands pressed over her ears. Get them now, we might get them talking.

I stayed put. To guard the door, I told myself. In case anyone made a break for it; the state those girls were in, one of them could do something stupid, down the stairwell before you know it and then we'd be in trouble—

Load of shite. I was afraid. Cold Cases takes you to bad motherfuckers, these were just little girls, but these were the ones that stopped me dead. These were the ones that would smell me stepping over their threshold and turn, hands rising, come for me in a rush of streaming hair and silence and rip me into a thousand bloody gobbets, one for each reason they had.

Oh God oh God oh—

The overhead bulb exploded. Sudden rush of dimness and slips of glass firing like golden arrows through the light of the standing lamps, a fresh burst of screams; a girl clapping her hand to her face, blood black in the shadows. The window burned pale, lit their upturned faces like worshippers'.

Alison was on her feet on the seat of a sofa, spindly and rocking. One skinny arm stretched out, finger pointing. Not at the window. At Holly's four: Rebecca head back and white-eyed, Holly and Julia grabbing at her arms, Selena glazed and swaying. Alison was screaming on and on, screams huge enough to rise up over all the rest: "Her it was her *I saw her I saw her I saw her*—"

Conway's head came round. She clocked Alison, scanned frantically for me. Caught my eye and gestured over the whirl of heads, yelled something I couldn't hear, but I saw it: *Fucking come on!*

I took a breath and I dived in.

Hair slicing across my cheek, an elbow ramming my ribs, a hand clawing at my sleeve and I wrenched away. My skin leapt at every touch, nails or for a second I thought teeth raked the back of my neck, but I was moving fast and nothing dug in. Then Conway's shoulder was against mine like protection.

We got Alison under the arms, lifted her off the sofa—her arms were rigid, brittle, sticks of chalk, she didn't struggle—had her back through the boiling mess and out the door before McKenna could do anything but see us go. Conway slammed the door behind us with her foot.

The sudden quiet and brightness almost turned me light-headed. We got Alison down the corridor so fast her feet barely touched the ground, dumped her on the landing at the far end. She collapsed, heap of arms and legs, still screaming.

Faces in the white stairwell, craning over the circling banister-rails above and below us, openmouthed. I called out, deep official voice, "Attention, please. Everyone go back to your common rooms. No one's been hurt; everything's fine. Go back to your common rooms immediately." Kept going till the faces pulled back, slowly, and were gone. Behind us McKenna was still shouting; the noise level was slowly going down, shrieks starting to crumble to sobs.

Conway was on her knees, up in Alison's face. Sharp as a slap: "Alison. You look at me." Snapping her fingers, over and over, in front of Alison's eyes: "Hey. Right here. Nowhere else."

"He's there don't let him please nonononoooo—"

"Alison. Focus. When I say, 'Go,' you're gonna hold your breath while I count to ten. Ready. *Go.*"

Alison cut herself off in mid-scream, with a sound like a burp. Almost made me start laughing. That was when I realized if I started, I might not stop. The scrapes down the back of my neck throbbed.

"One. Two. Three. Four." Conway kept the beat ruthlessly steady, ignored the noise still bubbling down the corridor. Alison stared at her, lips clamped shut. "Five. Six—" A swell of squealing in the common room, Alison's eyes zigzagged— "Hey. Over here. Seven. Eight. Nine. Ten. Now breathe. Slowly."

Alison's mouth fell open. Her breath came shallow and loud, like she was half hypnotized, but the screaming was gone.

"Nice," Conway said, easily. "Well done." Her eyes slid up over Alison's shoulder, to me.

I did a double-take out of a cartoon. *Me?*

Flare of her eyes. *Get a move on.*

I was the one who'd made it work with Alison earlier. I had the best chance. The biggest interview of the case, or it could be if I didn't fuck up.

"Hey," I said, sliding down to sit cross-legged on the tiles. Glad of the excuse: my knees were still shaking. Conway slipped away sideways, into a corner behind Alison, tall and black and raggedy against the smooth white wall. "Feeling better?"

Alison nodded. She was red-eyed, more white-mousey than ever. Her legs stuck out at mad angles, like someone had dropped her from a height.

I gave her my big reassuring smile. "Good. You're grand to talk, right? You don't need the Matron, more allergy medicine, anything like that?"

She shook her head. The chaos at the end of the corridor had ebbed to nothing; McKenna had the fourth-years under control at last. Any minute now, she was going to come looking for us.

"Lovely," I said. "You said, in there, that you saw one of Selena Wynne's gang do something. You were pointing at one of them. Which one?"

We braced and waited, me and Conway, to hear *Julia*.

Alison let out a little sigh. She said, "Holly."

That easy. On the corridors above us and below, the older girls and the younger ones had gone back into their common rooms and closed the doors. There was no sound anywhere, none at all. That white silence came sifting down again, piling into little drifts in the corners, slipping down our backs to collect in the folds of our clothes.

Holly was a cop's kid. Holly was my star witness. Holly was the one who had brought me that card. Even after I'd seen her here, deep in her own world, I had somehow thought she was on my side.

"OK," I said. Easy and loose, like it was nothing, nothing at all. Felt Conway's eyes, on me, not on Alison. "What'd you see?"

"After the assembly. The one where they told us about Chris. I was . . ."

Alison was getting that look again, the one from earlier: slack and dazed, like someone after a seizure. "Stick with me," I said, smiling away. "You're doing great. What happened after the assembly?"

"We were coming out of the hall, into the foyer. I was right beside Holly. She looked round, just quickly, like she was checking if anyone was watching her. So I noticed that, you know?"

Observant, just like I'd told her that morning. Prey animal's fast eyes.

"And then she stuck her hand down her skirt, like in the waist of her tights?" A snigger, limp and automatic. "And she pulled out this *thing*. Wrapped in a tissue."

Making sure she wouldn't leave prints. Just like Mystery Girl had done with the hoe. I nodded along, all interested. "That'd catch your eye, all right."

"It was just weird, you know? Like, what would you keep down your *tights*? I mean, ew? And then I kept looking because some of it was sticking out of the tissue, and I thought it was my phone. It was the same as mine. But I checked my pocket, and my phone was there."

"What did Holly do next?"

Alison said, "The lost-and-found bin's in the foyer, right at the door of reception. It's this big black bin with a hole at the top, so you can put things in but you can't get them out? You have to go to Miss O'Dowd or Miss Arnold and they have the key. We were going past reception, and Holly kind of ran her hand across the bin—like she was just doing it for no reason, she didn't even look at it, but then the phone wasn't in her hand any more. Just the tissue."

I saw Conway's eyes close for a second on the *Should've searched*. She said, from her corner, "How come you didn't say this to me last year?"

Alison flinched. "I didn't know it had anything to do with Chris! I never thought—"

"Course you didn't," I said soothingly. "You're grand. When did you start to wonder?"

"Just a couple of months ago. Joanne was . . . I'd done something she didn't like, and she said, 'I should call the detectives and tell them your phone used to text with Chris Harper. You'd get in *sooo* much trouble.' I mean, she was just saying it, she wouldn't have actually *done* it?"

Alison was looking anxious. "Course not," I said, all understanding. Joanne would've dropped Alison in a shredder feet first, if it had suited her.

"But I started thinking. Like, 'OhmyGod, what if they actually did look at my phone, they'd totally think I'd been with Chris!' And then I thought about that phone I saw Holly with. And I went, like, 'What if she was getting rid of it because she was scared of the same thing?' And then I was like, 'OhmyGod, what if she actually *was* with Chris?'"

I said, "Did you talk about it to Holly? Or anyone else?"

"OhmyGod, no way, not to Holly! I said it to Gemma. I thought she'd know what to do."

"Gemma's smart, all right." Which she was. Alison hadn't worked out that the phone might have been Selena's. Gemma would have. "What'd she say?"

Alison squirmed. Down to her lap: "She said it was none of our business. To just shut up and forget the whole thing."

Conway shaking her head, jaw clenched. I said, "And you tried. But you couldn't manage."

Headshake.

I said, "So you made that card. Put it up on the Secret Place."

Alison stared, bewildered. Shook her head.

"Nothing wrong with that. It was a good idea."

"But I didn't! I swear to God, I didn't!"

I believed her. No reason she would lie, not now. "OK," I said. "OK."

Conway said, "Well done, Alison. Probably you were right to begin with and it's nothing to do with Chris, but Detective Moran and I will have a chat with Holly, clear it up. First we'll take you back down to Miss Arnold. You're looking a bit pale."

Keep her isolated, so she couldn't spread the story. I stood up, kept my smile nailed in place. One of my feet had gone to sleep.

Alison pulled herself up by the banister rail, but she stayed there, holding onto it with both thin hands. In the white air her face looked greenish. She said, to Conway, "Orla told us about that case you did. With the—" A shudder twisted her. "The, the dog. The ghost dog."

"Yeah," Conway said. More hair had come out of her bun. "Nasty one, that was."

"Once the guy confessed. Did the dog—did it keep coming back for him?"

Conway examined her. Said, "Why?"

Alison's face looked bonier, fallen in. "Chris," she said. "In there, in the common room. He was there. In the window."

Her certainty hooked me in the spine, pulled a shiver. The hysteria rising up again, somewhere behind the air: gone for now, not for good.

"Yeah," Conway said. "I got that."

"Yeah, but . . . he was there because of me. Earlier, too, out here in the corridor. He came to get me, because I hadn't told you about Holly with the phone. In the common room"—she swallowed—"he was looking right at me. Grinning at—" Another shudder, rougher, wrenching at her breath. "If you hadn't come in then, if you hadn't . . . Is he . . . is he going to come back for me?"

Conway said, stern, "Have you told us everything? Every single thing you know?"

"I swear. I *swear*."

"Then Chris won't be coming back for you. He might hang around the school, all right, because there's plenty of other people keeping secrets that he wants them to tell us. But he won't be back for you. You probably won't even be able to see him any more."

Alison's mouth opened and a little rush of breath came out. She looked relieved, right to the bone, and she looked disappointed.

Far away down the corridor, through the silence, a long soft wail. For a second I thought it was coming from a girl, or something worse, but it was only the creak of the common-room door opening.

McKenna said, and I know a deeply fucked-off woman when I hear one, "Detectives. If it's not too much trouble, I would like to speak with you. Now."

"We'll be there in ten minutes," Conway said. To McKenna, but she was looking at me. Those dark eyes, and the silence falling like snow between us, so thick I couldn't read them.

To me: "Time to go."

20

An April afternoon, finishing up after-school volleyball. It's spring, the grounds are exploding with bluebells and daffodils in every corner, but the sky is thick and gray, and it's airless without actually being warm; the sweat won't dry off their skins. Julia flips her ponytail up to cool the back of her neck. Chris Harper has just under a month left to live.

They're picking up the volleyballs, taking their time because the showers will be full anyway by the time they get inside. Behind them, the Daleks are taking down the nets, slowly, bitching about something—Gemma calls, ". . . thighs like two walruses shagging, *disgusting* . . ." but it's not clear if she's talking about someone else or about herself.

Julia calls, "Saturday night. We're going, yeah?" It's the social evening at Colm's.

"Can't," Holly yells back, from a corner of the courts. "I asked. Family time blah blah."

"Same," Becca says, tossing a ball into the bag. "My mum's home. Although she'd actually probably be delighted if I put on an entire makeup counter and a miniskirt and went."

"Make her day," Julia says. "Come home drunk, E'd up and pregnant."

"I'm saving those for her birthday."

"Lenie?"

"I'm at my dad's."

"Well, fuck," Julia says. "Finn Carroll owes me that tenner, and I need it. My earbuds are going."

"I'll sub you," Holly says, spiking the last ball at the bag and missing. "It's not like I'm going to get any shopping in this weekend anyway."

"I want to rub it in, though. That smug bastard." Julia has just noticed how much she's looking forward to seeing Finn.

"He'll be at the debating next week."

For a second Julia considers going to the social on her own, but no. "I know, yeah. I'll catch him then."

They give the courts one more scan, and head off. "Water," Julia says, as they pass the tap by the gate, and peels off from the other three. Up ahead, Ms. Waldron calls, "Chop-chop, girls! Hup, two, three, four, march!" The others drift on, Becca spinning in circles swinging the bag of volleyballs, leaving Julia to catch up.

She drinks out of her hand, splashes her face and her neck. The water is underground-cold and gives her a quick, pleasurable shiver. A stream of geese pour overhead, honking, and Julia squints up to see them against the clouds.

She's turning away from the tap when the Daleks march up. Joanne stops right in front of Julia, folds her arms and stares. The other three fan out and stop one step behind Joanne, fold their arms and stare.

They're blocking Julia in. None of them say anything.

Julia says, "Are we doing something? Or is this it?"

Joanne's lip curls—Julia figures she thinks it makes her look superior, but if she did it in front of a mirror just once, she'd never do it again. She says, "Don't show off."

Julia says, "Bored already."

Joanne's pale flat stare gets paler and flatter. Julia remembers—amused, like it was a different person, some small silly cousin—how a few months ago that stare would have had her zinging adrenaline.

Joanne says, ominously, "We want to talk to you."

"They talk?" Julia inquires, nodding at the rest of them. "I thought they were your robot bodyguards."

Orla does an outraged noise, and Gemma throws Joanne a slantwise look. Joanne's face is pinching up. She says, tight as spitting, "You tell that fat slut Selena to stay *away* from Chris Harper."

Which is not what Julia was expecting. "Loser say what?"

"Don't act innocent. We know all about it." Nods from the robots.

Julia leans back against the wire fence and blots water off her face with the neck of her T-shirt. She's starting to enjoy herself. This is the problem with hoovering up gossip the way the Daleks do: every now and then, you're going to end up having an eppy over something totally imaginary. "What do you care what Selena does?"

"That's not your problem. *Your* problem is to make sure she backs off, before she ends up in big trouble."

Obviously this is meant to be terrifying. More impressive nods; Alison even says, "Yeah," and then cringes.

"You fancy Chris Harper," Julia says, grinning.

Joanne's chin jams out at a furious angle. "Ex*cuse* me, if I fancied him, I'd be going out with him? Not that it's any of your business."

"Then why do you care what Selena does with him?"

"Because. Everyone knows Chris Harper wouldn't even look at someone like her if she wasn't letting him *do* it to her. He is *way* out of her league. She needs to go find some spotty dickhead like Fintan Whatshisname who's always drooling at her."

Julia laughs, a real laugh, spontaneous, bubbling up towards the hanging gray cloud. "So you're here because she's getting uppity and she needs putting back in her place? Seriously?"

The more furious Joanne gets, the more bits of her stick out—elbows, tits, arse—and the uglier she gets. "Um, wake up and smell the coffee? We're doing you a favor. You seriously think a guy like Chris is actually going to go *out* with a mess like Selena? Hel*lo*? The second he gets bored of shagging her, he's going to dump her flat on her fat backside and send dirty photos to all the guys. Tell her to leave him alone or she'll be sorry."

Julia takes a swig of water and wipes drops off her chin. She'd love to bounce Joanne around for a while and then leave—Joanne is almost too easy to play with, once you notice that you're not afraid of her—but if she doesn't squash this before it takes off, they'll be stuck with the Daleks going after them for weeks, maybe months, maybe years, needling on and on like a cloud of mosquitoes till Julia's head blows off from the overload of stupid. "Chill," she says. "You need better quality tattletales. Selena wouldn't go near that wanker if you paid her."

Joanne snaps—she's getting shrill—"OhmyGod, you are *such* a liar. Do you think we're stupid?"

Julia raises her eyes to the thickening sky. "What, you think I'm saying it to make you happy? Newsflash: I don't give a fuck if you're happy or not. I'm just telling you. Selena doesn't even like Chris. She's hardly even talked to him. Whatever you heard, it's crap."

"Em, Gemma actually *saw* them? Totally wrapped around each other? So unless you want to try and convince me that Gemma's actually *blind*—"

Then Joanne sees something in Julia's face.

Joanne could taste one drop of power in an ocean. She eases back. "Oh. My. God," she says, drawing it out long and sweet and sticky, letting it drip all over Julia. "You actually didn't *know*?"

Julia has her face back to blank, but she knows it's too late. Coming from any of the other Daleks, this would have been just yak yak noise, it would never even have occurred to her to believe it. But Gemma; back in first year, when they were just kids, Julia and Gemma used to be friends.

A wide smirk is creeping over Joanne's face. "Oopsie," she says. "Em*barr*-assing." Orla sniggers.

Julia looks at Gemma. Gemma says, "Last night. I snuck out." Little smile that hints things. The other Daleks giggle. "I was heading down the path to the back wall, and the two of them were in that creepy place with the big trees where you guys hang out. I almost had a heart attack, I thought it was nuns or ghosts or something, but then I saw who it was. And they weren't there to talk about the weather, either; they were all over each other. I'd say if I'd watched for another few minutes . . ."

A scattering of snickers, falling like small grimy rain.

Gemma has perfect eyesight, and no one in school has hair like Selena's. On the other hand—Julia grabs for the other hand—Gemma lies like a rug. Julia scans her for bullshit, scans and scans. She can't tell. She can barely see Gemma, the solid dry-witted kid she used to share crisps and pens with, never mind read her.

Julia's heart is running crazy. She says coolly, "Whatever you and your little stud were smoking, can I have some too?"

Gemma shrugs. "Whatever. I was there. You weren't."

Joanne says, "Sort it out." Now that she knows she's in charge, all the twisted bits of her have gone back where they belong; she's smoothed to angelic, except for that curled lip. "We only bothered to warn you this once because we're being nice. We're not going to do it again."

She whisks around—she doesn't actually snap her fingers at the rest of the Daleks, but somehow it looks like she does—and struts off, out of the tennis courts and up the path towards the school. The others scuttle to keep up.

Julia turns the tap back on and moves her hand up and down between the water and her mouth, in case they look back, but she can't drink. Her heartbeat is jamming her throat. Her T-shirt sticks to her skin like some clammy sucker-footed thing, dragging. The sky presses down on her head.

Selena is in their room, alone; the others must still be in the showers. She's cross-legged on her bed, brushing out her wet hair and humming. When Julia comes in she glances up and smiles.

She looks the same. Just seeing her gentles Julia's heartbeat; one breath, and the layer of grime the Daleks left behind starts to blow away. So suddenly and overwhelmingly it nearly knocks her breath out, Julia wants to be touching Selena, pressing up hard against the familiar curve of her shoulder, the solid warmth of her arm.

Selena says, "You could text Finn to meet you."

It takes Julia's mind a minute to pull out what she's talking about. "Yeah," she says. "Maybe."

"Have you got his number?"

"Yeah. It doesn't matter. I'll see him whenever."

Julia sits on the floor, starts undoing her runners and fights with her mind. If Selena was with Chris, she'd have found a way to get to the social on Saturday, in case he hooked up with some other girl. If Selena had gone out last night, the rest of them would have woken up. If Selena had been with Chris, she wouldn't be first back from the showers; she'd want extra time to wash off the smell of him, of night grass, of guilt. If Selena had been with a guy, it would show, clear as suck marks blotched across her neck. If Selena had done that, she'd be staticky with it, she'd need to talk, need to tell, she'd need to somehow make it all—

"Lenie."

"Mmm?"

Selena looks up. Clear blue eyes, untroubled.

"Nothing."

Selena nods peacefully and goes back to brushing.

The whole vow thing was Selena's idea to begin with. If she hadn't wanted to do it, all she'd have had to do was keep her mouth shut. But getting the key, finding a way to get out at night, that was Selena's idea too—

There's a knot in Julia's shoelace. She digs her nails into it.

She feels Selena's eyes on the top of her head, hears her stop humming. She hears the quick indrawn breath as Selena braces herself to say something.

Julia doesn't look up. She tugs at the knot till a nail splits.

Silence. Then the long swish of the brush again, and Selena humming.

It has to be bullshit. If the Colm's guys had a way to get out of school, everyone would know. But if they don't, then who was Gemma meeting, unless Gemma was making up the whole thing—

"That song!" Holly yells, bouncing in smelling of strawberries, with her armful of PE gear flying everywhere and her hair turbaned up into a stripy ice-cream swirl. "What's that song? The one you're humming?" But neither of them can remember.

· · ·

Julia gets a text from Finn during first study period. *See you sat eve? Got a surprise for you.*

"Phones off," says the prefect supervising them, without looking up. The common room feels dim and dirty, light bulbs struggling against the murk outside and losing.

"Sorry, forgot." Julia slides the phone under her maths book and texts blind: *Not going sat.* After a moment she adds, *2moro after school? Got sthing for you too.*

She sets her phone on silent, sticks it in her pocket and goes back to pretending to care about maths. It's less than a minute before she feels the buzz against her leg. *The field, like 4.15?*

The thought of Finn hanging out in the Field gives Julia a twinge that's too stupid even to think about. *See you there,* she texts back, and switches her phone off. Across the table, Selena works quadratic equations in a steady, tranquil rhythm. When she feels Julia's eyes on her, she glances up.

Before she can help herself, Julia nods upwards, at the overhead bulb. Selena's eyebrows pull together: *Why?* Julia mouths, *Go on.*

Selena's hand tightens around her pencil. The light bulb flares; the common room leaps alive, instantly huge and rippling with colors. Around the tables people glance up, startled and golden, but it's already over; the air has turned muddy again, and their faces are sinking back into dimness.

Selena smiles across at Julia, like she's handed her a tiny sweet present. Julia smiles back. She knows she should feel better, and she does, but somehow not as much as she hoped.

When they slide past the wire fencing the next afternoon, the Daleks are already perched on their pile of breeze blocks, making squealy noises to get the attention of a handful of Colm's guys who are on the rusty machine, shoving each other to get the attention of the Daleks. Finn is sitting on another breeze-block heap, drawing on the side of his runner. It's a gray day, damp and chilly; against the solid skyful of cloud his hair looks like you could warm your hands at it. Seeing him feels even better than Julia expected.

"Back in a sec," she says to the others, and starts to speed up. It feels all wrong, wanting to get away from them snagging at her, to Finn where it's safe and easy.

Holly says after her, "Careful." Julia rolls her eyes and doesn't look back. She can feel Holly watching her all the way across the Field.

"Hey," she says, pulling herself up onto the breeze blocks next to Finn. His face lights up. He stops drawing and straightens. "Hi," he says. "How come you're not going Saturday?"

"Family shit." The Daleks have exploded into a flappy little whirlwind of sniggers and glances. Julia waves and blows them a kiss.

"Man," Finn says, putting his pen away in a jeans pocket. "They don't like you, do they?"

"No shit," Julia says. "And I don't like them, so it's all good. What've you got for me?"

"You first."

Julia has been looking forward to this for weeks. "Ta-da," she says, holding out her phone. She can't keep the grin off her face.

The photo shows her on the back lawn, which was dumb because any of the nuns could have looked out of their bedroom windows, but Julia was feeling daring. Duckface, hand on cocked hip, other hand flourished over her head pointing up at the clock. Midnight, bang on.

("Are you positive?" Holly asked, Julia's phone in her hand.

"Hell yes," Julia said, glancing up at the clock to make sure it would fit in the shot. "Why not?"

"Because he's going to know we sneak out, is why not." Behind Holly's head, Selena and Becca watched from under the trees, pale bobbing faces, waiting.

"We never said anything about not trusting guys," Julia said. "Just not touching them."

"Yeah, and we never said anything about, like, skipping around telling anyone who's a good laugh."

"Finn's not going to rat on us," Julia said. "I swear. OK?"

Holly shrugged. Julia struck a pose and pointed over her head at the clock. "Go," she said.

The flash blazed white lines of trees across their eyes like lightning and Holly and Julia ran for cover, ducking low, gasping with laughter.)

"I'll take my tenner now," Julia says. "And an apology. I like them with extra groveling."

"Fair enough," Finn says. "You want me to get down on my knees?"

"Tempting, but nah. Just make it good."

Finn puts one hand on his heart. "I apologize for saying you would be scared of anything in the universe. You're a fearless superhero who could kick my arse, or Wolverine's arse, or a mad gorilla's arse."

"Yeah, I am," Julia says. "You're forgiven. That was beautiful."

"Good pic," Finn says, having another look. "Who took it? One of your mates, yeah?"

"The ghost nun. Told you I was badass." Julia takes her phone back. "Tenner."

"Hold your horses," Finn says, pulling out his phone. "I've got a surprise for you, remember?"

If this is a photo of his dick, Julia thinks, *I will kill the fucker.* "Make my day," she says.

Finn hands her the phone and grins, that same straight-on wicked kid-grin, and Julia feels a rush of relief and guilt and warmth. She wants to touch him, hip-bump him off the breeze blocks or hook her elbow around his neck or something, to apologize for underestimating him all over again.

"Great minds," Finn says, and nods at the phone.

Him, on the back lawn, in almost exactly the same spot. Black hoodie pulled up over the red hair—he played it smarter than she did—and one hand above his head, just like her, pointing up at the clock. Midnight.

The first thing Julia feels is outrage: *Our place, at night that's our place, can't we even have—* Then she realizes.

"Still want your tenner?" Finn says. He's grinning away, like a Labrador bringing home something rotten, looking for pats and praise. "Or will we call it evens?"

Julia says, "How'd you get out of school?"

Finn doesn't notice the change in her voice; he's too pleased with his big surprise. "Trade secret."

Julia pulls it together. "Wow," she says. Big admiring eyes, sway in towards Finn. "I didn't know you guys could do that."

And this time she's not underestimating. He's delighted with himself, with how smart he is, dying to impress her even more. "I hotwired the fire-door alarm. Got the instructions online. It took me like five minutes. I can't open it from outside, obviously, but I stuck a piece of wood in to keep it open while I was out."

"OhmyGod," Julia says, hand over her mouth. It's so easy. "If someone had gone past and seen it, you'd have been in *so* much shit. You could've been *expelled*."

Finn shrugs, all fake-casual, leaning back with one foot up and his hands in his jeans pockets. "Totally worth it."

"When'd you do it? We could've run into each other." She giggles.

"Ages back. A couple of weeks after the dance."

Plenty of time for Chris to set up a meeting with Selena, a dozen meetings; if he knew. "On your own? Was that a selfie? Jesus, you really aren't scared of the nun, are you?"

"Live nuns, God, yeah: terrified. Dead ones, nah."

Julia laughs along. "So you went out there by yourself? Seriously?"

"Brought a couple of mates, for the laugh. I'd go on my own, though." Finn rearranges his feet and examines whatever he was drawing on his runner, like it's fascinating. "So," he says. "Seeing as we can both get out, and we're both not scared. Want to meet, some night? Just to hang out. See if we can spot the ghost nun."

This time Julia misses her chance to laugh along. A discreet distance away, among the ragwort and dandelions that are growing even taller and thicker this year, Selena and Holly and Becca are all trying to listen to something on Becca's iPod at the same time; Selena and Holly are elbowing each other for the earbud, laughing, hair in each other's face, like everything's that simple still. They make Julia want to shoot off the breeze blocks and explode. Any second now some mate of Finn's is going to show up and come bouncing over, and by then she needs to know. If Gemma wasn't lying, just if, Julia needs the weekend to figure out what to do.

"You're friends with Chris Harper," she says. "Right?"

Finn's face closes over. "Yeah," he says. He holds out a hand for his phone, shoves it back in his pocket. "So?"

"Does he know you've cut off the alarm?"

His mouth is getting a cynical curl to it. "Yeah. It was his idea. He's the one that took the photo."

Gemma wasn't lying.

"And if he's who you wanted to hook up with all along, you could've just said that to start with."

Finn thinks he's been played for a fool. Julia says, "He's not."

"I should've fucking known."

"If Chris disappeared off the earth in a puff of sleazebaggy smoke, I'd be celebrating. Believe me."

"Yeah. Whatever." Finn has changed colors, eyes gone dark, a raw burned red high on his cheeks. If she were a guy, he would punch her. Since she isn't, he's left stinging and helpless. "You're some piece of work, you know that?"

Julia understands that if she doesn't fix this right now, the chance will be gone and he will never forgive her. If they run into each other on the street when they're forty, Finn's face will get that burned look and he'll keep walking.

She doesn't have room to work out how to mend this. The other thing is spreading white and blinding across her mind, pushing Finn to the edges.

"Believe what you want," she says. "I have to go," and she slides off the breeze blocks and heads back to the others, feeling the Daleks' eyes scratching at her skin like needles, wishing she was a guy so that Finn could punch her and get it over with and then she could find Chris Harper and smash his face in.

Holly's eyes meet Julia's for a second, but whatever she sees warns her or satisfies her, or both. Becca glances up and starts to ask something, but Selena touches her arm and they go back to the iPod. Some game is sending little orange darts zipping across the screen; white balloons explode in slow motion, silent fragments fluttering down. Julia sits in the weeds and watches Finn walk away.

21

We didn't talk about Holly, me and Conway. We held her name between us like nitroglycerine and didn't look at each other, while we did what needed doing: handed Alison over to Miss Arnold, told her to hang on to the kid overnight. Asked her for the key to the lost-and-found bin, and the story on how long things stayed in there before they got dumped. Low-value stuff went to charity at the end of each term, but pricey things—MP3 players, phones—they got left indefinitely.

The school building was dim-lit for nighttime. "What?" Conway demanded, when the crack of a stair made me shy sideways.

"Nothing." When that wasn't enough: "A bit jumpy."

"Why?"

No way was I going to say *Frank Mackey*. "That light bulb was a bit freaky. Is all."

"It wasn't fucking *freaky*. The wiring in this place is a hundred years old; shit must blow up all the time. What's freaky about that?"

"Nothing. The timing, just."

"The *timing* was there'd been people in that common room all evening. The motion sensor's been working overtime, something overheated and the bulb blew. End of fucking story."

I wasn't going to fight her on it, not when I agreed with her and she probably knew it. "Yeah. I'd say you're right."

"Yeah. I am."

Even arguing, we were keeping our voices down—the place made you feel like someone could be listening, getting ready to jump out at you. Every sound we made flitted away up the great curve of the stairwell, settled to rest in the shadows somewhere high above us. Above the front door the fanlight glowed blue, delicate as wing-bones.

The bin was black metal, old, off in a corner of the foyer. I fitted the key—quietly as I could, feeling like a kid slipping through forbidden places, springy with adrenaline—and swung open the panel at the bottom. Things came tumbling out at me: a cardigan smelling of stale perfume, a plush cat, a paperback, a sandal, a protractor.

The pearly pink flip-phone was at the bottom. We'd walked past it on our way into the school, that morning.

I put on my gloves, eased it out between two fingertips like we might get prints. We wouldn't. Not off the outside, not off the inside of the cover, not off the battery or the SIM card. Everything would be shiny clean.

"Great," Conway said, grim. "A cop's kid. Beautiful."

I said, finally, "This doesn't mean for definite that Holly did it."

My voice sounded reedy and stupid, too weak to convince even me. Flick of Conway's eyebrow. "You don't think?"

"She could've been covering for Julia or Rebecca."

"Could've been, but we've got nothing that says she was. Everything else could point to any of them; this is the only thing we've got that's specific, and it points straight at Holly. She couldn't stand Chris. And from what I've seen of her, the kid's determined, independent, got brains, got guts. She'd make a great killer."

The cool of Holly, that morning in Cold Cases. Running the interview, glossy and sharp, throwing me a compliment to jump for at the end. Taking control.

"Anything I'm missing," Conway said, "feel free to point it out."

I said, "Why bring me the card?"

"I didn't miss that." Conway shook out another evidence envelope, spread it on top of the bin and started labeling. "She's got balls, too. She knew someone would come to us sooner or later, figured doing it herself would take her off the suspect list—and it worked, too. If there's trouble waiting for you, better to go out and meet it head-on, not stick your head in the sand and hope it doesn't find you. I'd do the same thing."

The look on Holly, that afternoon in the corridor when Alison lost the plot. Scanning faces. For a murderer, I'd thought then. For an informer had never crossed my mind.

I said, "That's a lot of balls for a sixteen-year-old."

"So? You don't think she's got them?"

No answer to that. It hit me like a mouthful of ice: Conway had had Holly in her sights all along. The second I had shown up in her squad room, all eager, with my little card and my little story, she had started wondering.

Conway said, "I'm not saying she definitely did the job all by herself.

Like we said before, it could've been her and Julia and Rebecca together; could've been the whole four of them. But whatever went down, Holly was up to her tits in it."

"And I'm not saying she wasn't. I'm just keeping an open mind."

Conway had finished labeling the envelope and straightened up, watching me. She said, "You think the same thing. You just don't like that your Holly had you fooled."

"She's not *my* Holly."

Conway didn't answer that. She held out the envelope for me to drop in the phone. Let it swing between her fingers. "If this interview is gonna be a problem for you," she said, "I need to know now."

I kept my voice even. "Why would it be a problem?"

"We're gonna have to get her da in."

No way to pretend Holly wasn't a suspect. The stupidest detective alive wouldn't bite on that. Holly's da isn't stupid.

I said, "Yeah. And?"

"Word on the street is that Mackey's done you a few favors. I'm not giving you hassle for that; you do what you need to do. But if the two of you are all buddy-buddy, or if you owe him, then you're not the guy to interrogate his kid for murder."

I said, "I don't owe Mackey anything. And he's not my buddy."

Conway watched me.

"It's been years since I even talked to the guy. I came in useful to him once, he's made sure to be useful to me since—he wants everyone knowing that helping him out pays off. That's it. End of."

"Huh," Conway said. Maybe she looked satisfied; maybe she just looked like she had decided it might soften Mackey up, having an ally in the room. She sealed off the envelope, shoved it in her satchel with the rest. "I don't know Mackey. Is he gonna give us hassle?"

"Yeah," I said. "He will. I wouldn't say he'll whip Holly straight off home, tell us to talk to his solicitor; he's not like that. He'll fuck with us, but he'll do it sideways, and he won't leave unless it looks like we're getting somewhere. He'll want to keep us talking till he works out our theory, what we've got."

Conway nodded. Said, "Got his number?"

"Yeah."

Next second I wished I'd said no, but all Conway said was, "Ring him."

Mackey picked up fast. "Stephen, my man! Long time no talk."

I said, "I'm at St. Kilda's."

The air sharpened, instantly, to a knifepoint. "What's happened."

"Holly's fine," I said, fast. "Totally fine. We just need to have a chat with her, and we figured you'd want to be there."

Silence. Then Mackey said, "You don't say Word One to her till I get there. Not Word One. Have you got that?"

"Got it."

"Don't forget it. I'm nearby. I'll be there in twenty." He hung up.

I put my phone away. "He'll be here in fifteen minutes," I said. "We need to be ready."

Conway slammed the panel of the lost-and-found bin, hard. The deep clang shot off into the shadows, took its time dissolving.

She said, loud, to the high darkness, "We'll be ready."

McKenna launched herself out of the common room at Conway's knock like she'd been waiting behind the door. The long day and the white light in the corridor weren't good to her. Her hair was still set solid and the expensive suit hadn't a crease, but the discreet makeup was wearing off, in clumps. Her wrinkles had got deeper since that morning; her pores looked the size of chicken-pox scars. She had her phone in her hand: still doing damage control, trying to patch leaking seams.

She was raging. "I have no idea whether your standard procedures involve sending witnesses into hysterics—"

"We weren't the ones who kept a dozen teenage girls cooped up all day," Conway said. Gave the common-room door a slap. "Lovely room and all, but after a few hours the most tasteful decor in the world won't stop them going stir-crazy. If I were you, I'd make sure they get a chance to stretch their legs before bed, unless you want them going off again at midnight."

McKenna's eyes closed for a second on the thought. "Thank you for your advice, Detective, but I think you've done enough already. The students have been *cooped up* in case you needed to speak with them, and that will no longer be an issue. I would like you to leave now."

"Can't be done," Conway said. "Sorry. We need a quick word with Holly Mackey. Just waiting for her da to get here."

That sent McKenna up another notch. "I gave you permission to speak to our students specifically so you would *not* need to request parental authorization. Involving the parents is completely unnecessary, it can only complicate the situation both for you and for the school—"

"Holly's da's going to hear all about this anyway, soon as he shows up for work in the morning. Don't worry: I wouldn't say he'll be straight on the phone to the mummy network to pass on the gossip."

"Is there any earthly reason why this needs to be done tonight? As you so cleverly pointed out, the students have already had more than enough of this pressure for one day. In the morning—"

Conway said, "We can talk to Holly in the main school building. Get us out of your hair, let the rest of the girls go back to the normal routine. How's the art room?"

McKenna was all monobosom, no lips. "Lights-out is at a quarter to eleven. By that time I expect Holly—and all the other students—to be in their rooms and in bed. If you have further questions for any of them, I assume they can wait until tomorrow morning." And the common-room door shut in our faces.

"You have to love the attitude," Conway said. "Doesn't give a shite that we could arrest her for obstruction; this is her manor, she's the boss."

I said, "Why the art room?"

"Keep her thinking about that postcard, remembering there's someone out there who knows." Conway tugged the elastic out of what was left of her bun. Hair came down around her shoulders, straight and heavy. "You start us off. Good Cop, nice and gentle, don't spook her and don't spook Daddy. Just set up the facts: she was getting out at night, she knew about Chris and Selena, she didn't like Chris. Try and fill in the details: why she didn't like him, whether she discussed the relationship with the others. When you need Bad Cop, I'll come in."

A couple of fast twists of her wrists, a snap of hairband, and the bun was in place, smooth and glossy as marble. Her shoulders had straightened; even the scoured look had fallen away from her face. Conway was ready.

The common-room door opened. Holly in the doorway, with McKenna behind her. Ponytail, jeans, a turquoise hoodie with sleeves that hid her hands.

I'd been thinking of her all snap and sheen, but that was gone. She was white and ten years older, daze-eyed, like someone had shaken her world like a snow globe and nothing was coming down in the same places. Like she had been so confident she was doing everything right, and all of a sudden nothing looked that simple any more.

It turned me cold. I couldn't look at Conway. Didn't need to; I knew she'd seen it too.

Holly said, "What's going on?"

I remembered her nine years old, so stiff with courage she would break your heart. I said, "Your dad's on his way. I'd say he'd rather we don't talk till he gets here."

That burned off the daze. Holly's head went back in exasperation. "You called my *dad*? Come *on*!"

I didn't answer. Holly saw the look on me and closed her mouth. Disappeared behind the smoothness of her face, innocent and secretive all at once.

"Thanks," Conway said to McKenna. To me and Holly: "Let's go."

The long corridor we'd walked down that morning, to find the Secret Place. Then it had been humming with sun and busyness; now—Conway passed the light switch without a glance—it was twilit and sizeless. Evening through the window behind us gave us faint shadows, me and Conway stretched even taller on either side of the straight slip of Holly, like guards with a hostage. Our steps echoed like marching boots.

The Secret Place. In that light it looked like it was rippling, just off the corner of your vision, but it had lost that boil and jabber. All you could almost hear off it was a long murmur made of a thousand muffled whispers, all begging you to hear. A new postcard had a photo of one of those gold living statues you get on Grafton Street; the caption said, *They terrify me!*

The art room. Not morning-fresh and rising with sunlight now. The overhead lights left murky corners; the green tables were smeared with shreds of clay, Conway's balls of paper were still tumbled under chairs. McKenna must have canceled the cleaners. Battening down the school as tight as she could, everything under control.

Outside the tall windows the moon was up, full and ripe against a dimming blue. On the table against them, that morning's drop cloth had been pulled away, not put back. Where it had been was the whole school in miniature, in fairy-tale, in the finest curlicues of copper wire.

I said, "That. Is that the project you were working on last night?"

Holly said, "Yeah."

Close up, it looked too delicate to stay standing. The walls were barely sketched, just the odd line of wire; you could look straight through them, to wire desks, ragged cloth blackboards scribbled with words too small to read, high-backed wire armchairs cozy around a fire of tissue-paper coals. It was winter; snow was piled on the gables, around the bases of the columns and the wine-jar curves of the balustrade. Behind the building, a lawn of snowdrift trailed off the edge of the base board into nothing.

I said, "That's here, yeah?"

Holly had moved in, hovering, like I might smash it. "It's Kilda's a hundred years ago. We researched what it used to be like—we got old photos and everything—and then we built it."

The bedrooms: tiny copper-wire beds, wisps of tissue paper for sheets. In the boarders' wing and the nuns', fingernail-length parchment scrolls swung in the windows, from threads fine as spider web. "What are the bits of paper?" I asked. My breath set them spinning.

"The names of people who were listed living here in the 1911 census. We don't actually know who had what room, obviously, but we went on what age they were and the order they were listed in—like probably friends would be one after the other, because they would've been sitting together. One girl was called Hepzibah Cloade."

Conway was spinning chairs into place around one of the long tables. One for Holly. One six feet down the table: Mackey. She brought them down hard, flat bangs on the lino.

I said, "Whose idea was it?"

Holly shrugged. "All of ours. We were talking about the girls who went to school here a hundred years ago—if they ever thought about the same things as us, stuff like that; what they did when they grew up. If any of their ghosts ever came back. Then we thought of this."

Chair across the table from Holly, for me. Bang. Chair opposite Mackey, for Conway. Bang.

Four scrolls hanging in the air above the main staircase. I said, "Who're those?"

"Hepzibah and her friends. Elizabeth Brennan. Bridget Marley. Lillian O'Hara."

"Where are they going?"

Holly reached between wires and touched the scrolls with the tip of her little finger, set them whirling. She said, "We don't even know for sure they were friends. They could've all hated each other's guts."

I said, "It's beautiful."

"Yeah," Conway said. Like a warning. "It is."

From behind us: "Fancy meeting you here."

Mackey, in the doorway. Leaning back on his heels, bright blue eyes scanning, hands in the pockets of his brown leather jacket. Barely changed from the first time I'd seen him; the long fluorescents picked out deeper crows' feet, more gray mixed in with the brown, but that was all.

"Hiya, chickadee," he said. "How's tricks?"

"OK," Holly said. She looked at least half glad to see him, which is pretty good for a sixteen-year-old's daddy. Another thing that hadn't changed much: Mackey and Holly made a good team.

"What've you been chatting about?"

"Our art project. Don't *worry*, Dad."

"Just making sure you haven't made mincemeat of these nice people while I wasn't there to protect them." Mackey switched to me. "Stephen. Too long no see." He came forward, held out his hand. Firm handshake, friendly smile. At least to start with, we were going to play this like everything was hunky-dory, all friends together, all on the same side.

I said, "Thanks for coming in. We'll try not to keep you too long."

"And Detective Conway. Nice to meet you, after all the good things I've heard. Frank Mackey." A smile that was used to getting a response, got none off her. "Let's step outside while you brief me."

"You're not here as a detective," Conway said. "We've got that covered. Thanks."

Mackey tossed me an eyebrow-lift and grin: *Who pissed in her cornflakes?* I got caught, not sure whether to smile back or not—with Mackey, you never know what he could turn into ammo. The paralyzed gawp on me just made his grin get bigger.

He said to Conway, "Then if I'm just here as a daddy, I'd like a quick chat with my daughter."

"We need to get started. You can have a chat when we take a break."

Mackey didn't argue. Probably Conway thought that meant she'd won. He wandered off around the room, past the chair we'd set out for him, having a look at the art projects. Gave Holly's hair a quick rub on his way. "Do us a favor, sweetheart. Before you answer any of the lovely detectives' questions, give me a fast rundown of what we're doing here."

Shutting her down would wreck the vibe right there. Conway's look said she was starting to see what I meant about Mackey. Holly said, "This morning I found a card on the Secret Place. It had a photo of Chris Harper and it said, 'I know who killed him.' I took it to Stephen, and they've been hanging around here all day. They just keep interviewing all of us and all of Joanne Heffernan's idiots, so I think they narrowed it down to one of us eight must've put the card up."

"Interesting," Mackey said. Leaned over, examined the wire school from different angles. "That's coming along nicely. Anyone else's parents get brought in?"

Holly shook her head.

"Professional courtesy," Conway said.

"Makes me feel all warm and squishy," Mackey said. He pulled himself up onto a windowsill, one foot swinging. "You remember the deal here, sweetheart, am I right? Answer what you want to, leave what you don't. You want to discuss something with me before you answer it, we'll do that. Anything upsets you or makes you uncomfortable, tell me and we'll make tracks. That all sound OK?"

"Dad," Holly said. "I'm *fine*."

"I know you are. Just laying out the ground rules, so everyone's clear." He winked at me. "Keeps everything nice, amn't I right?"

Conway swung a leg over her chair. Said, to Holly, "You are not obliged to say anything unless you wish to do so, but anything you do say will be taken down in writing and may be used in evidence. Got it?"

You try to keep it casual, the caution, but it changes the room. Mackey's face giving away nothing. Holly's eyebrows pulling together: this was new. "What . . . ?"

Conway said, "You've been keeping stuff to yourself. That makes us get careful."

I took my seat, opposite Holly. Held out a hand to Conway. She sent the lost-and-found phone, in its evidence bag, shooting down the table.

I passed it over to Holly. "Ever seen this before?"

A puzzled second; then Holly's face cleared. "Yeah. It's Alison's."

"No. She has one the same, but that's not it."

Shrug. "Then I don't know whose it is."

"That's not what I need to know. I'm asking if you've seen it before."

Longer puzzled look, slow headshake. "Don't think so."

I said, "We have a witness who saw you drop it in the lost-and-found bin, the day after Chris Harper died."

Total blank; then realization dawned across Holly's face. "Oh my God, that! I'd totally forgotten that. Yeah. We had a special assembly that morning, so McKenna could give us this big speech about a tragedy and assisting the police and whatever." Talky-mouth hand sign. "At the end we were all coming out of the hall into the foyer, and that phone was on the floor. I thought it was Alison's, but I couldn't see her; everything was a mess, everyone was talking and crying and hugging, the teachers were all trying to get us to shut up and go back to our classrooms . . . I just shoved the phone into the lost-and-found bin. I figured Alison could get it herself; not my problem. If it wasn't hers, then whose was it?"

Flawless, even better than the real thing. And—clever clever girl—her story kept the whole school in the frame for having owned the phone. Conway's jaded look said she'd spotted the same thing.

I took the phone back. Put it to one side, for later. Didn't answer Holly's question, but she didn't push.

I said, "Julia and Selena must've told you: we know you guys used to get out at night, last year."

Holly shot a fast glance at Mackey. "Don't worry about me, chickadee," he said, pleasant grin. "My statute of limitation's run out on that one. You're OK."

Holly said, to me, "So?"

"What'd yous do out there?"

Her chin was out. "Why do you want to know?"

"Come on, Holly. You know I have to ask."

"We just hung. Talked. OK? We weren't doing bath salts or having gang bangs or whatever you think the young people do these days. A couple of times we had a can, or a cigarette. Oh my God, shock horror."

"Don't smoke," Mackey said severely, pointing. "What've I told you about smoking?" Conway gave him a warning stare and he lifted his hands, all apologetic, all responsible dad who would never mess with the interview.

I ignored the pair of them. "Ever meet up with anyone? Guys from Colm's, maybe?"

"Jesus, no! We see enough of those morons already."

"So," I said, puzzled, "you were basically doing stuff you could've done indoors, or during the day. Why go to all that hassle, risk getting expelled?"

Holly said, "You wouldn't understand."

"Try me."

After a moment she sighed noisily. "Because out there in the dark was a better place to talk, is why. And because probably you never ever broke any rules in school, but not everyone always feels like doing everything exactly like they're supposed to. OK?"

"OK," I said. "That makes sense. I get that."

Thumbs-up. "Wahey. Good for you."

Almost four years of her teens left. I didn't envy Mackey. I said, "You know Selena was sneaking out on her own to meet Chris Harper. Right?"

Holly pulled out the teenage vacant stare, bottom lip hanging. Made her look thick as pig shite, but I knew better.

"We've got proof."

"Did you read it in your favorite gossip mag? Right under 'R-Patz and K-Stew broke up again'?"

"Behave," Mackey said, didn't bother looking up. Holly rolled her eyes.

She was being a bitch because, for this reason or that one, she was scared. I leaned forward, close, till against her will she caught my eye. "Holly," I said gently. "This morning, you came to me for a reason. Because I was never thick enough to patronize you, and because you thought there was a chance I might understand more than most people. Right?"

Twitch of her shoulder. "I guess."

"You're going to end up talking to someone about this stuff. I'd say you'd love to go back to your mates and pretend all this never happened—and I don't blame you—but you don't have that option."

Holly was slumped in her chair, arms folded, eyes on the ceiling, like I was boring her into an actual coma here? She didn't bother answering.

"You know that as well as I do. You can talk to me, or you can talk to someone else. If you want to stick with me, I'll do my best to live up to your good opinion. I don't think I've let you down yet."

Shrug.

"So. You want to stick with me, or you want someone else?"

Mackey was watching me, under his eyelids, but he kept his mouth shut, which couldn't be a compliment. Another shrug from Holly. "Whatever. Stick with you, I guess. I don't care."

"Good," I said, and gave her a smile: *We're a team*. Pulled my chair up closer to the table, ready for work. "So here's the story. Selena's already told us she was seeing Chris Harper. She's told us she had a phone matching this description, which she used to text him. We have the phone records between the two of them. We have the actual texts setting up late-night meetings." Fast glance from Holly, before she could stop herself. She hadn't known we could do that. "It's not like I'm asking you to tell us something we don't already know. I'm only asking for confirmation. So, one more time: did you know Selena was meeting Chris?"

Holly glanced at Mackey. He nodded.

"Yeah," she said. The teen-brat shtick was gone, that fast. She sounded older. More complicated; more careful. "I knew."

"When did you find out?"

"Last spring. Like a couple of weeks before Chris died, maybe? It was over by then, though. They weren't meeting any more."

"How'd you find out?"

Holly was meeting my eyes now, cool and under control. She had her hands folded together on the table. She said, "Sometimes, when it's hot, I can't sleep. This one night, it was boiling, I was going mental trying to find cool bits of the bed; but then I thought, *OK, maybe if I stay totally still I'll fall asleep*, right? So I made myself do it. It didn't work, but Selena must've thought I'd gone to sleep. I heard her moving around and I thought, *Maybe she's awake too and we can talk*, so I opened my eyes. She was holding a phone—I could see the screen, lit up—and she was kind of curled over it, like she didn't want anyone to see. She wasn't texting, or reading messages; just holding it. Like she was waiting for it to do something."

"And that made you curious."

Holly said, "There'd been something wrong with Lenie. She's always really calm, no matter what. Peaceful. But the last while before that night, she'd been . . ." Something rippling that cool, as she remembered. "She seemed like something terrible had happened to her. Half the time she looked like she'd been crying, or she was about to. We'd be talking to her and a minute later she'd go, 'What?' like she hadn't even heard us. She wasn't OK."

I was nodding along. "And you were worried about her."

"I was *crazy* worried. I figured nothing terrible could've happened at school, because we were all together all the time, we'd have known. Right?" Wry twist to Holly's mouth. "But at home, at the weekends—Selena's parents are split up, and they're both kind of weird. Her mum and her stepdad have these parties, and her actual dad lets weird hippie guys stay on his sofa . . . I thought something could've happened at one of their places."

"Did you talk to anyone about it? See if maybe Julia or Rebecca had any ideas?"

"Yeah. I tried talking to Julia, but she just went, 'Jesus, dial down the drama, everyone gets moods; like you don't? Give her a week or two, she'll be fine.' And then I tried Becca, but Becca can't really handle stuff like that—anything being wrong with any of us. She got so freaked out that in the end I told her it had just been my imagination, to get her to calm down."

Trying to sound like it was nothing. But something was blowing across Holly's face, just a wisp; something rain-colored, something flavored with sadness and with missing the long-lost. It startled me. Made her look older again, made her look like she understood things.

I said, "And she believed you? She hadn't noticed anything up with Selena?"

"Nah. Becca's . . . She's innocent. She figures as long as we've got each other, we're automatically OK. It wouldn't've occurred to her that Selena might not be."

"So Julia and Rebecca were no help to you," I said. Watched that wisp flicker again. "Did you talk to Selena?"

Holly shook her head. "I tried. Lenie's excellent at not having a conversation when she doesn't feel like it. She just does this dreamy look, and splat, conversation's dead. I barely even got as far as asking her what was wrong."

"So what did you do?"

Flash of impatience. "Nothing. Waited and kept an eye on her. What do you think I should've done?"

"Haven't a clue," I said peaceably. "So when you saw that phone, you figured it had something to do with whatever was bothering Selena?"

"Well, I didn't exactly have to be a hotshot detective for that. I kept my eyes like this"—slit open—"and watched till she put it away. I couldn't see where she put it exactly, but it was somewhere down the side of her bed. So the next day I made up some excuse to go to our room during school, and I found it."

"And read the texts."

Holly's crossed knee was bouncing. I was pissing her off. "Yeah. So? So would you have, if your friend was in that state."

I said, "They must've been a shock."

Eye-roll. "You think?"

"Chris wouldn't be the boyfriend I'd choose for my best mate."

"Obviously. Not unless your best mate liked them underage."

Mackey was grinning, not bothering to hide it. I said, "So what did you do about it?"

Her chin went out. "Um, hello, same as before: what was I supposed to do? Get her a Chris voodoo doll and some pins? I'm not actually *magic*. I couldn't wave my wand and make her feel all better."

Sore spot. I pressed it. "You could've texted him to leave her alone. Or arranged to meet up with him, tell him face-to-face."

Holly snorted. "Like that would've done any good. Chris didn't even like me—he could tell I didn't fall for his cute-little-puppy thing, which meant he was never going to get up my top, which meant I was a bitch and why would he bother even talking to me, never mind doing anything I asked him to?"

"You, young one. No one gets up your top till you're married." Mackey, from the windowsill.

I said, "I just can't get my head round the idea that you did nothing. This guy's making your best mate miserable, and you just went, 'Ah, well, stuff happens, it'll toughen her up'? Seriously?"

"I didn't *know* what to do! I feel like crap about it already, thanks very much, I don't need you telling me what a shit friend I was."

I said, "You could've talked to Julia and Rebecca, see if the three of you could come up with a plan together. That's what I'd've expected you to do. If yous are as close as you say."

"I'd already tried. Remember? Becca got upset, Julia didn't want to know. Probably I would've told Jules if Selena had been any worse, but it wasn't like I thought she was going to *kill* herself over that wanker. She was just . . . unhappy. There was nothing any of us could do about that." Something blowing across Holly's face again. "And she obviously really, like *really* didn't want any of us knowing. If she'd found out that I knew, it would've just made her feel worse. So I acted like I didn't."

The thing was it wasn't true, the little insomnia story, or not all the truth. I couldn't risk a glance at Conway to see if she'd spotted the lie. There had been no name attached to Chris's number, in Selena's phone; no names in the texts. No way a skim through the phone could have told Holly who Selena was texting.

Maybe the lie was Mackey reflex, always keep some nugget to yourself in case it comes in useful later on. Maybe not.

Holly moved like she felt that cold-rain something fingering the back of her neck, trailing across her shoulders. Said, "I wasn't just ignoring the whole thing. Back then, I thought the same as Becca: everything would be OK as long as we had each other. I thought, if we just stuck close to Lenie . . ."

"Did it work? Did she seem like she was snapping out of it?"

Holly said, quietly, "No."

I said, "That had to be scary. You're used to dealing with everything together with your friends, the four of yous: no secrets. All of a sudden, you're stuck dealing with this all on your own."

Holly shrugged. "I survived."

Trying hard for ice-cool, but that veil had wrapped her round. Those few days last spring had set things shifting, in the way the world looked to her. Left her lost, stripped raw in cold wind and no one's hands finding hers.

That was when I knew: Conway wasn't the only one who had Holly in her sights. Not any more.

"Course you did," I said. "You're well able; I know that from last time. But that doesn't mean you don't get scared. And being out on your own where your mates can't help, that's one of the scariest things around."

Slowly her eyes came up, met mine. Startled and clear, like this was more than she'd expected from me. A tiny nod.

"Hate to break up the little chat when it's going so nicely," Mackey said lazily, swinging himself off the windowsill, "but I'm gasping for a smoke."

"You told Mum you'd quit," Holly said.

"It's been a long time since I had your mum fooled about anything. See you in a few, chickadee. If these nice detectives say a word to you, you just stick your fingers in your ears and sing them something pretty." And he headed off, left the door swinging open behind him. We heard his footsteps down the corridor, him whistling a perky tune.

Conway and I looked at each other. Holly watched us, under those enigmatic curves of eyelid.

I said, "I could do with some fresh air."

In the foyer, the heavy wooden door was swinging wide. The rectangle of cold light spilling onto the checkerboard tiles was notched with a shadow that moved, one sharp flick, when my steps echoed. Mackey.

He was at the top of the steps, leaning against a column, smoke unlit between his fingers. His back was to me and he didn't turn. Above him, the sky was a blue aimed for night; it was gone quarter past eight. Faint and delicate, arcing somewhere in the great stretches of dimming air out there, bats' intent shrills and girls' intent chatter.

When I came up beside Mackey he raised the smoke to his lips, glanced at me over the click of the lighter. "Since when do you smoke?"

"Just needed some air." I loosened my collar, took a deep breath. The air tasted sweet and warm, night flowers opening.

"And a chat."

"Long time no see."

"Kid. You'll have to forgive me if I'm not in the mood for small talk."

"Nah, I know. I just wanted to say . . ." The squirm was real, and the red face. "I know you've been . . . you know. Putting in the odd good word for me, along the way. I just wanted a chance to say thanks."

"Don't thank me. Just don't fuck up. I don't like looking stupid."

"I'm not planning on fucking up."

Mackey nodded and turned his shoulder to me. Smoked like it was fuel and he was going to get every last inch to the gallon.

I leaned against the wall, not too near. Tilted my face up to the sky, just chilling.

Said, "I'm dying to ask, man. How'd you pick out St. Kilda's?"

"You figured I'd have Holly down the local community school?"

"Something like that, yeah."

"The tennis court wasn't up to my standards."

Narrowing his eyes against the smoke. Only one corner of his mind was on me.

"This place, but? When I saw it . . ." I blew out a half laugh. "Fuck me."

"It's something, all right. You didn't think I appreciated fine architecture?"

"Just didn't think it would be your scene. Rich kids. Holly living somewhere else most of the week."

I waited. Nothing, just the rise and fall of his cigarette. I said, "You wanted to get Holly away from home, yeah? Too much teen drama? Or you didn't like her mates?"

One corner of Mackey's mind was more than enough. Wolf-curl to his mouth, slow click of his tongue. "Stephen, Stephen, Stephen. Here you were doing so well. All the working-man-to-working-man stuff, I was really feeling that. And then you went and got impatient, and you went straight back into cop mode. Is your daughter a problem teen, sir? Does your daughter have any undesirable associates, sir? Did you ever see any sign that your daughter was shaping up to be a cold-blooded killer, sir? And just like that, the nice little bond we were building up: gone. Rookie mistake, sunshine. You need to practice your patience."

He lounged against the column, grinning at me, waiting to see what I'd come out with next. His eyes had turned alive; I had his attention now.

I said, "The school I can see, just about. Maybe Holly's ma went here, or maybe your local community school's a kip, Holly was getting bullied or offered drugs—most people's principles go out the window when it's their kid on the line. But boarding? Nah. I don't see it."

"Always fuck with people's expectations, sunshine. It's good for their circulation."

"Last time we worked together, you and Holly's ma were split up. Had been for a while, far as I could tell. You've already missed out on years of Holly, and now you send her off to boarding school so you can miss even more? It doesn't fit."

Mackey pointed his smoke at me. "That was cute, kid. 'Last time we worked together'; like we're working together now. I like that."

"You and Holly's ma are back together, that's your chance at being a family again. You wouldn't miss out on that unless there was a good reason. Either Holly was acting up and you needed her somewhere strict to straighten her out, or she was getting into bad company and you wanted her well away from that."

He was nodding away, doing a thinking face. "Not bad. It plays. Or maybe, just maybe, my wife and I felt we needed some time by ourselves to reconnect, after that whole nasty separation thing. Rekindle the romance. *Us time*, isn't that what I'm meant to call it?"

I said, "You worship the bones of that girl. You've never wanted less time with her in her life."

"My attitude to family is a little quirky, kid. I assumed you'd gathered that, last time we *worked together*." Mackey tossed his smoke onto the lawn. "Maybe the chance to be an adorable nuclear unit doesn't mean the same to me as it would to you. So sue me."

I said, "If Holly was getting into trouble at home, we'll find out."

"Good boy. I'd expect no less."

"I'm asking you to save us the time and hassle."

"No problem. The biggest trouble Holly ever got into was getting grounded for not tidying her room. Hope that helps."

We'd be checking. Mackey knew it. "Thanks," I said. Nodded.

He was going in. I said, before his hand reached the door handle, "I'd still love to know. The boarding, man. Why? It doesn't come cheap. Someone wanted it pretty bad."

Him watching me, amused, the way he used to seven years back, big dog watching feisty puppy. Seven years is a long time.

"I know it's nothing to do with our case, but it's going to keep at me. So I'm asking."

Mackey said, "Out of curiosity. Man to man."

"Yeah."

"Bollix. You're asking detective to suspect's father."

Unblinking, daring me to deny it: *God, no, she's not a suspect* . . . I said, "I'm asking."

Mackey examined me. Did some kind of maths behind his eyes.

He found his smokes again. Flipped one into the side of his mouth.

"Let me ask you this," he said, through it. Cupped his hand around the flame. "Just offhand, how much time would you guess Holly spends with my side of the family?"

"Not a lot."

"Good guess. She sees one of my sisters a couple of times a year. On Olivia's side there's a pair of Christmastime cousins, and there's Olivia's ma, who buys Holly designer shite and takes her to poncy restaurants. And, since Olivia and I were split up or splitting for most of the relevant time-frame, Holly's an only child."

He leaned back in the doorway, flicked the lighter and watched the flame. He was smoking this one differently, taking his time on every drag.

"You were right about how we picked St. Kilda's—well done there:

Olivia's alma mater. And you were right about me not being into the boarding idea. Holly asked at the beginning of second year, I said over my dead body. She kept begging, I kept saying hell no, but in the end I asked why she wanted it so badly. Holly said it was because of her mates—Becca and Selena were boarding already, Julia was running the same campaign on her folks. The four of them wanted to be together."

Flipped the lighter spinning into the air, caught it.

"She's smart, my girl Holly. The next few months, any day she had one of her mates over, she was a holy angel: helping around the house, doing her homework, never a complaint about anything, happy happy joy joy. When she wasn't having a mate round, she was a raging pain in the hole. Trailing round the house like something out of an Italian opera, giving us these accusing lip-trembly stares; ask her to do anything and she'd burst into tears and fling herself into her room—don't get overexcited there, Detective, they all throw drama fits, it's not a sign of juvenile delinquency. But after a while, Liv and me were dreading the days it was just the three of us. Holly had us trained like a pair of German shepherds."

"Stubborn," I said. "Must get it from your wife."

Wry sideways look. "Stubborn would've got her nowhere. If it was just that, I would've kept taking the piss out of her till she dropped the act; would've been a pleasure. But one evening Holly's throwing a full-on teen-queen strop—I can't even remember why, I think we'd said she couldn't go over to Julia's—and she yells, 'They're the only people I trust to be there no matter what. They're like my sisters! Because of you guys, they're the only sisters I'm ever going to have! And you're keeping me away from them!' And off she ran upstairs, to slam her door and sob into her pillow about how unfair it all was."

Another long drag on his ciggie. He tilted his head back, watched the stream of smoke spiral out between his teeth, up into the soft air.

"But the thing was, the kid had a point. It's a bitch when that happens. Family's important. And Liv and I haven't exactly done a bang-up job of providing Holly with one of those. If she's doing a better job of making her own, who am I to stand in her way?"

Fuck me. I would've bet a few pints that Frank Mackey only knew the meaning of guilt from the outside: something that came in useful for arm-twisting other people. Holly had him twisted into a reef knot.

I said, "So you decided to let her go for it."

"So we decided she could try boarding during the week for one term, see how she got on. Now we'd have to hire a tow truck to drag her away. I don't like it on principle, and I miss the little madam like hell, but like you said: when it's your kid at stake, everything else goes out the window."

Mackey slid his lighter back in his jeans pocket. "And there you go. A heart-to-heart with Uncle Frankie. Wasn't that fun?"

It was true. Maybe the whole truth, maybe not, but true.

"Does that answer all your questions?"

I said, "One left. I don't get why you'd tell me all that."

"I'm establishing interdepartmental cooperation, Detective. Showing the love, in a professional kind of way." Mackey flicked his smoke onto the ground, crushed it out in one heel-twist. "After all," he said over his shoulder with a great big grin, as he pushed the door open, "we're working together."

Holly was sitting where we'd left her; Conway was at the window, hands in her pockets, looking down at the gardens. They hadn't been talking. The air in the room, the fast turn from both of them when we came in, said they'd been listening hard to each other instead.

Mackey shifted his spot, keep us on our toes: sat on a table behind Holly, found himself a stray chunk of modeling clay to play with. I pulled Selena's phone towards me. Turned the evidence bag in circles on the table, between my fingertips.

"So," I said. "Let's go back to this phone. You say you found it on the foyer floor, the morning after Chris died. Let's stick with that for now. You'd seen Selena's secret phone; you knew what it looked like. You had to know this was it."

Holly shook her head. "I thought it was Alison's. Selena kept hers down the side of her bed; how would it get to the foyer?"

"You didn't even ask her?"

"No way. Like I told you, I didn't want to get into that with her. If I even thought about it—and I don't remember if I did—I would've figured, if it was somehow Selena's phone, then she'd rather go get it out of the lost-and-found than have to talk about how I knew it was hers and all that crap."

Smooth as butter. No one, not even Frank Mackey's kid, comes up with that kind of good stuff off the top of her head. Holly had been thinking this through, stuck in that common room with wild things zapping the air. Methodically going through everything we could know, working out her answers.

Some innocent people would do that. Not a lot.

"Makes sense," I said. Behind Holly, Mackey had flattened the clay into a disk, was trying to spin it on his finger. "Here's the thing, but. The way our witness tells the story, you didn't find the phone in the foyer. You had it tucked down your waistband, wrapped in a tissue."

Holly's eyebrows pulling together, baffled. "No I didn't. I mean, I might've had a tissue in my hand, everyone was crying—"

"You didn't like Chris. And you're not the type to fake a crying fit for someone you didn't like."

"I never said *I* was crying. I wasn't. I'm saying I *might* have been giving someone else a tissue, I don't remember. But I do know the phone was on the floor."

I said, "I think you took Selena's phone out from behind her bed and found a good way to ditch it. The lost-and-found bin, that was smart. It worked well. It almost worked for good."

Holly's mouth opened, but I held up my hand. "Hang on a sec. Let me finish first, before you tell me if I'm right or wrong. You knew there was a chance we'd search the school. You knew if we found the phone, we'd be talking to Selena. You knew what police questioning is like; let's face it, there's better ways to spend your day. You didn't want Selena put through that, not when she was already traumatized about Chris's death. So you binned the phone. Does that sound about right?"

It was an out: an innocent reason why she would have wanted the phone gone. Never take the out. It looks safe as houses. It takes you a step closer to where we want you.

Mackey said, without glancing up from his new toy, "You don't have to answer that."

I said, "No reason why you shouldn't. You think we're going to press charges against a minor for concealing something that might not even be evidence? We've got a lot more on our minds. Your da can tell you himself, Holly: if you're after something big, you're happy to let the small stuff slide. This is small stuff. But we need to clear it up."

Holly watched me, not her dad. Thought, or I thought she did, about that moment when she had seen me understand.

She said, "Selena didn't kill Chris. No way. I never worried that she did, not even for a second. She doesn't work like that." Straight-backed, straight-eyed, trying to shove it into my head. "I know you're thinking *Yeah, right.* But I'm not just being naïve. I *know* with most people you don't have a clue what they're capable of. I know that."

Mackey's piece of clay had gone still. It was true: Holly did know that.

"But with Selena I do. She wouldn't have hurt Chris. Ever. I swear to God, it's totally impossible."

I said, "Probably you'd have sworn to God that she wouldn't go out with Chris, either."

Twitch of impatience, I was losing cred again. "Like that's the same thing? Come *on*. Anyway, I don't expect you to just take my word about what kind of person she is. She actually physically couldn't have done it. Like I told you, sometimes I can't sleep. The night Chris died, I was having trouble sleeping. If Selena had gone out, I would've known."

It was a lie, but I left it. I said, "So you ditched the phone."

Not a blush on Holly, while she dumped the story she'd told me, all sincerity, about five minutes earlier; not a blink. Daddy's girl. "Yeah. So? If you knew that your friend was about to get in trouble for something she definitely hadn't even *done*, you mean you wouldn't try and get her out of it?"

I said, "I would, yeah. It's only natural."

"Exactly. Anybody would, who has any kind of *loyalty*. So yeah, I did."

I said, "Thanks. That clears that up. Except for one thing. When did you get the phone out of your room?"

Holly's face went still. "What?"

"The only thing that's confusing me. Chris's body was found at what time?"

"Little after seven-thirty a.m.," Conway said. Quietly, staying invisible. I was doing all right.

"And the assembly was when?"

Holly shrugged. "I don't remember. Before lunch. Noon?"

I said, "Did you have morning classes? Or did you get sent back to your rooms?"

"Classes. Well. Sort of. No one was paying any attention, even the teachers, but we still had to sit in the classrooms and act like we cared."

"So maybe you started hearing rumors around breakfast," I said. "At that stage it would've been just general stuff, police on the grounds; probably everyone thought it was about the groundskeeper who was dealing. Maybe a bit later, if someone saw the morgue van arriving and knew what it was, there might've been some talk about a dead person, but there's no way yous could've known who it was. When was Chris ID'd?"

"Eight-thirtyish," Conway said. "McKenna thought he looked familiar, rang up Colm's to see if they were missing anyone."

I balanced the evidence bag on one end, caught it when it fell. "So by noon, Chris's immediate family would've been notified, but we wouldn't have released his name to the media, not till the family got the chance to tell everyone who needed to know. You couldn't have heard it on the radio.

The assembly had to be the first time you heard what had happened, and who the victim was."

"Yeah. So?"

"So how did you know this phone could get Selena in trouble, in time to go get it before the assembly?"

Holly didn't miss a beat. "We were all watching out the windows, every chance we got—the teachers kept telling us not to, but yeah, right. We saw uniforms and Technical Bureau guys, so I knew there'd been a crime, and then we saw Father Niall from Colm's—he's like eight feet tall and he looks like Voldemort and he wears the robe, so it's not like you could get him mixed up for anyone else. So obviously something had to have happened to a Colm's boy. And Chris was the only one who I knew had been wandering around the grounds at night. So I guessed it had to be him."

Little cock of her eyebrow to me, as she finished up. Like a middle finger.

I said, "But you thought he and Selena had broken up. And you say you knew she hadn't been out that night, so it's not like you thought they'd got back together. What would Chris have been doing at Kilda's?"

"He could've got together with someone else. He wasn't exactly the deep type who'd spend months pining away for his lost true love. Him and Selena had been broken up for at *least* ten minutes; I'd've been amazed if he *hadn't* found someone else. And, like I said, he was the only one who I knew could get out of Colm's. I wasn't going to wait around till we found out for sure. I said I needed something from our room, I don't even remember what, and I got the phone."

"What did you figure would happen when Selena noticed it was gone? Specially if it turned out you were wrong, and Chris wasn't dead after all?"

Holly shrugged. "I figured I'd deal with that if it happened."

"At that point, you were just focusing on protecting your mate."

"Yeah."

I said, "How far would you go to protect your mates?"

Mackey moved. He said, "That's gibberish. She can't answer a question unless it means something."

Conway said, not invisible any more, "We're interviewing her. Not you."

"You're getting two for the price of one. You don't like it, tough shit. No one's under arrest; piss either of us off, and we'll walk."

"Dad," Holly said. "I'm OK."

"I know you are. That's why we're still here. Detective Moran, if you've got a specific question in there, ask it. If all you've got is the tag line for some teenybopper summer film, let's move on."

I said, "Specifically, Holly: Selena didn't tell the rest of yous that she was seeing Chris. Why do you think that was?"

Holly said coolly, "Because we didn't like him. I mean, Becca would've probably been fine with it—she thought Chris was OK; like I said, she's innocent. But Julia and I would've been like, 'Are you *serious*? He's an enormous tool, he thinks he's this big playa, he's probably three-timing you, what is *wrong* with you?' Selena doesn't like arguments—specially not with Julia, because Julia never ever backs down. I can totally see where Lenie would've been like, 'Oh, I'll tell them in a while, when I'm sure it's going somewhere, meanwhile I'll just try and get them to see he might not be a total prick after all, it'll all turn out fine in the end . . .' She'd still be doing that now, if they hadn't broken up. And if he hadn't died, obviously."

Something off there, just a notch. I wasn't one of Selena's best mates, what did I know, but all the same: the flinch, when she remembered leaving her best mates behind, sleeping and lied-to. That had hurt. She didn't seem like the type to do it for half a reason. Weather the argument and wait, gazing peacefully, let Julia storm herself out and Holly roll her eyes. Not squirm away, slice the others out of that crucial piece of her, just because they didn't fancy hers much.

Why lie about that?

I said, "So you figure she didn't tell you because she knew you'd want to protect her."

"If that's how you want to say it. Whatever."

Mackey, still pinching that clay about, still lounging, but watching me now, eyes hooded. I said, "But she was wrong. When you actually found out, you didn't feel any need to protect her after all, no?"

Holly shrugged. "From what? They were over. Happy ending."

"Happy ending," I said. "Only then Chris died. And you still didn't tell Selena you knew. Why not? You had to figure she was devastated. You didn't think she could use a bit of protecting then? A shoulder to cry on, maybe?"

Holly threw herself back in the chair, fists clenching, so sudden I jumped. "OhmyGod, I didn't *know* what she needed! I thought maybe she just wanted to be left alone, I thought if I said anything she'd be raging with me, I thought about it all the *time* and I couldn't work out what to do for her. Because I'm crap or whatever you're trying to say, yeah, you're right. OK? Just *leave me alone*."

I saw the little kid I remembered, furious with bafflement, red-faced and table-kicking. Behind her, Mackey's eyes closed for a second: she hadn't come to him. Then opened again. Stayed on me.

I said, "Your friendships: those mean a lot to you. Keeping them strong means a lot. Amn't I right?"

"*Duh.* So?"

"So that little prick Chris was after wrecking them. The four of you weren't acting like friends—Jesus, Holly, no you weren't. Selena's in love and doesn't even tell the rest of you. You're spying on her, but you don't mention that to the other two. Selena gets dumped flat on her arse, her first love gets *killed*, and you don't even give the poor girl a *hug*. Is that how you think friends act? Seriously?"

Good cop, Conway had said. In the corner of my eye I could see her leaning back in her chair, fake-easy, ready.

Holly snapped, "Me and my friends are none of your business. You don't have a clue about us."

"I know they're the most important things you've got. You burst your bollix getting your da and ma to let you board here, because of the three of them. You hung your whole *life* on your friends." My voice shoving at her, harder and harder. I couldn't tell why: prove to Conway I wasn't the Mackeys' bitch, prove it to the Mackeys, get back at Holly for thinking she could waltz in with her postcard and fold me into origami, get back at her for being right— "And then Chris came on the scene, and the four of yous went to pieces. Split apart, went to crumbs, easy as that—"

Holly was shooting sparks like an arc welder. "We *did not.* We're *fine.*"

"Someone wrecked me and my mates like that, I'd hate his guts. Anyone would, except a holy angel of God. You're a good young one, but unless you've changed a load in the last few years, you're no angel. Are you?"

"I never said I was."

"So how much did you hate Chris?"

Mackey said, "Aaand scene. Smoke break."

Mackey never minded being obvious, so long as you couldn't stop him. "Filthy habit," he said, sliding off the table and giving us a great big grin. "Need some more fresh air, young Stephen?"

Conway said, "You just had a smoke."

Mackey's eyebrow went up. He outranked the pair of us put together. "I want to talk to Detective Moran behind your back, Detective Conway. Was that not clear enough, no?"

"I got that, yeah. You can do it in a minute."

Mackey rolled his clay into a ball, tossed it to Holly. "Here you go, chickadee. Play with that. Don't be making anything that'll shock the detective; she looks like the pure-minded type."

To me: "Coming?" And he strolled out. Holly smashed the ball of clay flat on the table, viciously, with the heel of her hand.

I looked at Conway. She looked back. I went.

Mackey didn't wait for me. I watched him take the stairs a flight ahead of me, all the way down those long curves, watched him cross the hall. That dimness, that angle, he looked sinister, someone I didn't know and shouldn't be following, not that fast.

When I got to the door, he was leaning back against the wall with his hands in his pockets. He hadn't bothered to light a smoke.

He said, "I'm bored of playing games. You and Conway didn't get me out here because of professional courtesy. You got me out here because you need an appropriate adult. Because Holly's a suspect in the murder of Christopher Harper."

I said, "If you'd rather go back to HQ, get all this on video, we can do that."

"If I wanted to be somewhere else, we would be. What I want is for you to quit bullshitting me."

I said, "We think it's possible that Holly was involved in some capacity."

Mackey squinted past me, at the tree line ringing that sweep of grass. He said, "I'm a little surprised I need to point this out to you, sunshine, but what the hell, let's play. You're describing someone who's too thick to get her shoes on the right feet. Holly may be a lot of things, but she's not stupid."

"I know she's not."

"Yeah? Then let's just make sure I've got the theory straight. According to you, Holly's committed murder and got clean away with it. The Murder lads have done their little dance, got nowhere and buggered off. And now—a year later, when everyone's given up and moved on—Holly brings you that card. She *deliberately* drags the Murder boys back in. *Deliberately* puts herself in the spotlight. *Deliberately* points them towards a witness who can lock her up." Mackey hadn't moved from the wall, but he was looking at me now, all right. Those blue eyes, hot enough to brand you. "Talk to me, Detective. Tell me how that works, unless she's the level of moron that would make the baby Jesus swear. Am I missing something here? Are you just fucking with my head to prove you're a big boy now and I'm not the boss of you any more? Or are you honest to God standing there with a straight face and trying to tell me that makes one fucking iota of sense?"

I said, "I don't think for a second that Holly's thick. I think she's using us to do her dirty work."

"I'm all ears."

"She found that card and she needs to know who made it. She's narrowed it down, the same way we did, but that's where she's stuck. So she pulls us in to stir things up a bit, see who pops to the surface."

Mackey pretended to think that over. "I like it. Not a lot, but I like it. She's got no problem with the idea of us actually finding the witness and getting the goods, no? Landing in jail would just be a minor annoyance?"

"She doesn't think she'll land in jail. That means she knows the card girl won't rat her out. Either she knows it's one of her own, and Joanne Heffernan's bunch got mixed in along the way—by accident, or because Holly figured she might as well find out if they had any info while she was at it, since they were getting out at night as well, or because she just liked the idea of giving them a scare. Or else she's got some hold over Heffernan's lot."

Mackey's eyebrow was up. "I said she's not thick, kid. I didn't say she was Professor fucking Moriarty."

I said, "Tell me that doesn't sound like something you would do."

"I might well. I'm a pro. I'm not a naïve teenage kid whose entire experience of criminal behavior is one unfortunate encounter seven years back. I'm flattered that you think I've raised some kind of evil genius, but you might want to save a little of that imagination for your online warcrafting time."

I said, "So is Holly a pro. So are all of them. If I've learned one thing today, it's that teenage girls make Moriarty look like a babe in the woods."

Mackey gave me that with a tilt of his chin. Thought. "So," he said. "In this pretty little story, Holly knows the card girl won't dob her in, but she's still willing to take major risks to find out who it is. Why?"

"If that was you," I said. "Starting to think about leaving school. Starting to realize that you and your friends are going to be heading out into the big wide world; this, what you've got now, it's not going to last forever, you're not always going to be bestest mates who'd die sooner than dob each other in. Would you want to leave a witness out there?"

I expected a punch, maybe. Got a startled snort of laughter that even sounded real. "Jesus, kid! Now she's a serial killer? You want to check her alibi on the OJ case, too?"

I didn't know how to say it, what I'd seen in Holly. Things turning solid, the world widening in front of her eyes. Dreams shifting to real, and the other way round, like a drawing sliding from charcoal to oil in front of your eyes. Words changing shape, meanings slipping.

I said, "Not a serial killer. Just someone who didn't realize what she was starting."

"She's not the only one. You've already got a bit of a name for—how do they put it?—not being a *team player*. Personally, I don't think that's necessarily a bad thing, but not everyone agrees with me. You go another step down that road, and plenty of people won't want to know you. And believe me, pal: arresting a cop's kid does not count as being a team player. You do that, you can wave bye-bye to your shot at Murder or Undercover. For good."

He wasn't bothering to be subtle about it. I said, "Only if I'm wrong."

"You think?"

"Yeah. I do. We solve this, and I'm at the top of the queue for Murder. Everyone might hate my guts, but I'll get my shot."

"At working there, maybe. For a little while. Not at being one of them."

Mackey watching me. He's good, Mackey; he's the finest. Finger straight on the bruise, pressing just hard enough.

I said, "I'll settle for working there. I've got enough buddies to last me."

"Yeah?"

"Yeah."

"Well," Mackey said. He shot his cuff, checked his watch. "Better not keep Detective Conway waiting any longer. She's not too happy about you coming out for private chats with me."

"She's grand."

"Come here," Mackey said. Beckoned. Waited.

In the end I moved in.

He cupped a hand round the back of my neck. Gentle. Intent blue eyes, inches from mine. "If you're right," he said—no threat there, not scaring me, just telling me—"I'm going to kill you."

He gave the back of my head a double pat. Smiled. Moved off, into the high-arched dark of the hall.

That was when I realized: Mackey thought all of this was his fault. He thought he had put today in Holly's blood. Mackey thought I was right.

22

Monday morning, early, the bus grinding through traffic in stops and starts. Chris Harper has three weeks and less than four days left to live.

Julia is at the back of the half-empty top deck, with her ankles bent around her holdall at uncomfortable angles and her science homework on her lap. She spent the weekend banging her head against what to do about Chris and Selena. Her main instinct is to grab hold of Selena, probably literally, and ask her what the fuck she thinks she's doing; but some other instinct, further back and twisting restlessly, tells her that the moment she says this out loud—to Selena, or to Holly or Becca—nothing will ever be the same again. She can smell the poison smoke as everything they've got roars into flame. So she ended up getting nowhere with that and nowhere with homework, and this week is starting off to be a total peach all round. Rain streaks down the bus windows, the driver has turned the heat up to a million and everything is covered in a clammy film of condensation.

Julia is scribbling fast, something about photosynthesis, with one eye on her textbook and one on her barely reworded page, when she feels someone standing in the aisle looking down at her. It's Gemma Harding.

Gemma lives like four houses from the bus stop, but Daddy always drops her to school on Monday morning, in his black Porsche that takes half an hour to turn in the narrow school drive. Everything factors into the pecking order: Porsche beats most cars, any car beats bus. If Gemma's on OMG *public transport*, there's a reason.

Julia rolls her eyes. "Selena hasn't been anywhere near Chris. 'Kthanksbye." She sticks her head back in her textbook.

Gemma dumps her weekend bag on the next seat and slides in next to Julia. She's wet, raindrops sparkling on her coat. "This bus stinks," she says, wrinkling her nose.

It does: sweat-marinated raincoats, steaming. "So get off and call Daddy to come save you. Please."

Gemma ignores that. She says, "Did you know Joanne used to be going out with Chris?"

Julia gives her the eyebrow. "Yeah. As if."

"She was. For like two months. Back before Christmas."

"If she'd managed to get Chris Harper, she'd have had it tattooed across her face."

"He didn't want them to tell anyone. Which should've tipped Joanne off—like, hello? But Chris kept giving her loads about how he was scared because he'd never felt this way about anyone before, and his feelings were so strong—"

Julia snorts.

"I know, right? I don't know what kind of TV he watches, but, like, *barf*? I said it to Joanne: the only reason a guy doesn't want to tell people is either because you're a swamp-monster and he's ashamed of you, which Joanne completely isn't, or else because he's keeping his options open."

Julia closes her book, but she keeps it on her lap. "So?" she says.

"So Joanne was all, 'OhmyGod, Gemma, you are so cynical, what is *wrong* with you, are you jealous or something?' Chris had her completely convinced this was some huge romance."

Julia mimes puking. A couple of Colm's guys, up towards the front of the bus, are turning around to look at them, grinning and talking louder and shouldering each other. Gemma doesn't smile back, or do that annoying thing where she pretends to ignore them and sticks her boobs out; instead she rolls her eyes and lowers her voice.

"Like, she was starting to wonder if he was the love of her *life*. She kept talking about how someday she could tell their *kids* how they used to sneak away for these little secret meetings."

"Adorable," Julia says. "So how come she's not showing off her engagement ring?"

Gemma says flatly, "She wasn't shagging him, so he dumped her. Not even face-to-face. One evening they were supposed to meet up in the park, and Chris just didn't show up and didn't answer his phone. She texted him like ten times, trying to figure out what happened—at first she thought he had to be in *hospital* or something. A couple of days later, we were down at the Court and he walked straight past us. Saw us and looked the other way."

Julia stashes away the image of Joanne's face, to enjoy later. "That's shitty."

"Yeah, you think?"

"How come she wouldn't shag him?" Julia's never thought of Joanne as the save-it-for-marriage type.

"Well, she was *going* to. She's not frigid or anything. She was just holding off so he wouldn't think she was a slut, and to make him more into her. She'd actually decided to go for it, she was just waiting for one of them to have a free gaff at the weekend—she wasn't about to do it in the Field like some skanger. Only she hadn't said that to Chris, because she wanted him on his toes. So he got sick of waiting and dumped her."

"So the point of this story is, basically," Julia says, "Joanne's still all into Chris, so that makes him her property and everyone else in the world should back off. Did I miss anything?"

"Yeah, actually," Gemma says, giving her a fish-eyed stare. "You did."

She waits till Julia says, with a noisy sigh, "OK. What?"

"Joanne's tough."

"Joanne's a bitch."

Gemma shrugs. "Whatever. She's not soft. But what Chris did, that totally wrecked her head. Afterwards, she had to pretend she was sick for a whole week, so she could stay in our room."

Julia remembers that. Back at the time she considered telling people Joanne had come out in huge pus-filled face boils, but she wasn't interested enough to put in the effort. "What was she, crying?"

"She couldn't *stop* crying. She looked like a total mess, and she wasn't going to have anyone see her like that—plus she was scared she'd burst into tears in the middle of, like, French, and people would guess. But mostly it was because she was like, if she saw Chris or any of his mates, she'd die right there of embarrassment. She was all, 'I can't ever go out again, ever, I'm going to have to get my parents to transfer me to a school in London or somewhere . . .' It took me a week to get it through her head that she *had* to go out and see him, and act like she barely even remembered his name, or he'd know how upset she was, and then he'd think she was pathetic. That's how guys work. If you care more about them than they do about you, they hate you for it."

Julia would give more than ever for a chance to punch Chris's teeth in. Not because he hurt Joanne's precious feelings, which from Julia's viewpoint is the only bright spot in this whole vile mess; because all this is happening over such a little piece of shit. Selena ruining everything, the look on Finn's face in the Field: all because of some fifth-rate wankstain who's never had a thought in his head beyond WANT PUSSY.

She says, "So how is this my problem?"

Gemma says, "So Selena's not tough."

"Tougher than you think."

"Yeah? Tough enough that when Chris pulls the same thing on her, she'll be totally fine? Which he definitely will. I guarantee you he's giving her all the same lovey-dovey crap he gave Joanne, and if Jo fell for it, Selena is too. In a couple of weeks she'll be positive they're going to get married. And even if she's shagging him—"

"She's not."

Gemma throws Julia a skeptical one. Julia says, "She's not shagging him. And not because she's *frigid*."

"Well," Gemma says. "Even if she is shagging him, and even more if she's not, sooner or later he'll get bored. So he'll vanish off her phone and treat her like she doesn't exist. How gutted is Selena going to be? Specially once she hears whatever Jo puts around about *why* she got dumped. Because you know that's going to be good. You think she'll get over it in a week? Or do you think she'll have an actual nervous breakdown?"

Julia doesn't answer. Gemma says, "Selena's already . . . I mean, not being a bitch, but let's face it, she doesn't seem like it'd take much to push her over the edge."

"I went through Selena's phone," Julia says. "There's nothing on there from Chris. Nothing that could be from him, even."

Gemma snorts. "Course not. When he was going out with Joanne? He *gave* her a special secret phone, just for texting him. You know Alison's new phone? The pink one? That was it—Joanne made Alison buy it off her, after they broke up. I can't even remember what his excuse was, but basically if you ask me he was scared her parents or the nuns or one of us would go through her actual phone and find out. He told her to keep it hidden."

When of course the first thing Joanne had done with that phone was show it to all her friends. Not just a fifth-rate wankstain; a thick-as-pig-shit fifth-rate wankstain.

Gemma says, "So I bet Selena's got a special super-secret phone stashed away somewhere."

"Jesus," Julia says. "How much pocket money does he get?"

"As much as he wants. I heard"—a smile slides across the corner of Gemma's mouth; she isn't telling where she heard it—"he's got a separate phone too, just for girls he's with. You know what the other guys call it? Chris's pussyphone."

That kind of shit right there is why they made the vow in the first place.

Julia wants to get a table-tennis racket and smack some sense into Selena's head. "Classy."

Gemma says, "He's good. You need to get this fixed before Selena has time to be seriously in love with him."

"If she was going out with him," Julia says, after a moment, "then yeah. It sounds like I would."

They sit there in a silence that feels strangely companionable. The bus bumps over potholes.

"I don't know Chris," Julia says. "I've never even really talked to him. If you wanted to get him to dump someone fast, how would you do it?"

"Good luck with that. Chris . . ." Gemma mimes it, one hand coming down edge-first to point straight ahead: single-minded. "He knows what he wants, and he goes for it. Forget him. Work on Selena, get her to dump him. Not the other way around."

"Selena's not with him. Remember? I'm just asking *if*. For the laugh. *If* working on the girl was out, how would you work on Chris?"

Gemma pulls pink lip gloss and a mirror out of her weekend bag and puts it on, taking her time, like it helps her think. She says, "Joanne told me to tell him Selena's got gonorrhea. Which would probably do it."

Julia changes her mind: bright spot or no bright spot, she wishes Joanne and Chris had stayed together. They're perfect for each other.

She says, "Do it and I'll tell Holly's dad you buy speed off the grounds-keeper to lose weight."

"Whatever." Gemma rubs her lips together and examines them in the mirror. "You seriously figure Selena's not shagging him?"

"Yeah. And she's not going to."

"Well," Gemma says. She screws the lip gloss shut and drops it back into her bag. "You could try telling him that. Probably he won't believe you, because he thinks he's just so irresistible only a crazy person would actually say no to him. But if you can convince him, then he'll dump Selena for the first girl who does it. *That* fast."

"So why doesn't Joanne go for it? Tell him she wants his sexy body, but only if he breaks it off with Selena?"

"I said that. She said no way, he had his chance and he missed it."

In other words, Joanne is terrified Chris would turn her down. "You're her little sidekick," Julia says. "You're not going to do her dirty work?"

A slow, wet smile opens Gemma's mouth, but she shakes her head. "Um, yeah, no?"

"Like you're not into him? I didn't think you'd even need an excuse."

"He's totes yum. Not the point. Joanne would have a coronary."

Julia says, suddenly, "If you're that scared of her, why do you hang out with her?"

Gemma inspects her mouth in the mirror, dabs away a smear with the tip of her little finger. "I'm not *scared* of her. I just don't piss her off."

"She'd be *seriously* pissed off if she found out you'd told me about Chris dumping her."

"Yeah, I'd rather she didn't find out. Obviously."

Julia is turned in her seat, watching Gemma straight on. She says, "So how come you told me? It's not like you care if Selena gets her heart broken."

Gemma lifts one shoulder. "Not a lot."

"So?"

"Because fuck him. Probably you're right and Joanne's a bitch, but she's my friend. And you didn't see the state she was in, afterwards." Gemma clicks the mirror shut and slides it back into her bag. "We already started a rumor that she dumped him because he wanted to wear a nappy and have her change it for him—"

"Ew," Julia says, impressed.

Gemma shrugs. "It's an actual thing. There's guys who are into that. It didn't work, though; nobody believed it. We should've just said he couldn't get it up, or he had a tiny dick or something."

"So," Julia says, "since you didn't manage to fuck him up, you want me to do it for you. I get Selena to dump him, then you'll make sure everyone knows he got dumped, embarrass him the same way he embarrassed Joanne."

"Basically," Gemma says, unfazed. "Yeah."

"OK," Julia says. "Here's the deal. I'll get them split up. Fast." She has no idea how. "But you make sure Joanne and whatstheirnames don't tell anyone he was ever with Selena. You guys can say Joanne dumped him or something, if you want to embarrass him. Selena doesn't come into it. *Ever.* None of that gonorrhea crap, nothing. Deal?"

Gemma thinks it over. Julia says, "Or I'll tell Joanne you told me she thought she was going to marry Chris and have his ickle babies."

Gemma makes a wry face. "OK," she says. "Deal."

Julia nods. "Deal," she says, almost to herself. She wonders if there's any chance Gemma will stay there, not talking, just being solid and smelling of sticky lip gloss, till they get to school.

The bus pulls up at a stop, rocks under the rush of feet getting on. High excited voices, girls—"OhmyGod, you did *not* just say that, you did not—"

"See you around," Gemma says. She gets up and heaves her weekend bag onto her shoulder. Up front the Colm's guys see her stand up, and get louder. Just before Gemma swings her hips down the aisle towards them, she smiles at Julia and lifts her hand in a little wave.

23

The art room was turning chilly. Conway had pulled her chair up the table, next to mine. Bad Cop in the house.

This time she didn't turn round when Mackey and I came in. Neither did Holly, just kept gouging deep fingernail-curves in her ball of clay and thinking her own things. They hadn't been listening to each other, not this time; they'd been checking their armor, their weapons, preparing for the moment when we walked back in. Over by the window, the copper-wire school bloomed with a cold shimmer. The moon was high, staring in at us all.

Mackey leaned back on his table again. Every time he shifted, I twitched. All I could think about: what it was, that he was waiting to do. His look, cold and amused, said he hadn't missed it.

Conway caught my eye, as I sat down beside her. Hers said: *Ready. Steady. Go.*

She didn't rewind to where we'd been, to how Holly had to have hated Chris. No point: Mackey had wrecked that moment, nice and thorough. Instead she said, "You were right: we've narrowed the card down to the eight of you. One of the other seven knows who killed Chris."

Holly rolled the clay along the table, from hand to hand. "Yeah, well. Or at least she says she does."

"How do you feel about that?"

Incredulous face. "How do I *feel*? What is this, Guidance? You want me to draw a picture of my feelings in colored pencil?"

"Are you worried?"

"If I was worried, I wouldn't have *brought* you the card to begin with. Duh."

Too brazen, that hair-flick. Holly was putting it on.

That morning, she'd been grand with the card. Since then, something had happened.

I said, "That just means you weren't worried this morning. How about now?"

"What would I worry about?"

Conway said, "That one of your friends knows something that could put her in danger. Or that someone knows something that you might not want us to find out."

Holly threw herself back in her chair, hands flying up. "Oh my God, *look*. Nobody in school knows what happened to Chris. Joanne invented the card because she was looking for attention. OK?"

Conway lifted an eyebrow. "How come you didn't say this to Detective Moran when you brought him the card? 'Here you go, and by the way, it's a load of bollix, this girl Joanne Heffernan made it up.' Or did something happen since this morning, to make Joanne into your favorite theory?"

"Joanne keeps trying to get us into shit, is what's happened. When you guys showed up, obviously she totally freaked out—she probably wasn't expecting actual *police*, because she's an actual idiot. So she's spent all day frantically trying to make you look at us, so you won't figure out what she did and she won't get in trouble for wasting your time. Why would she be arsed, unless she had something she didn't want you noticing?"

Conway said, "If she wanted to make us look at you and your mates, she's done a good job."

"Yeah, *ob*viously. Or I wouldn't be sitting here. It never even occurred to you that she might be a huge liar?"

"I'd say she is, all right. But we don't need to take her word for anything. Selena meeting Chris, for example: when all we had was Joanne's word for it, we weren't too impressed. But then she showed us video. Of the two of them together."

Something skidding across Holly's face. Not surprise.

That video was how Holly had known about Chris and Selena.

She said, coolly, "What a pervert. I'm not even surprised."

Conway said, and I felt her mind right there next to mine, "Did she show it to you?"

Snort. "Yeah, no. Joanne and I don't share stuff."

Conway shook her head. "I wasn't thinking about sharing and caring. I was thinking about blackmail."

Blank. "Like how?"

"Joanne went out with Chris for a while. Before he was with Selena."

Holly's eyebrows went up. "Yeah? Shame it didn't work out."

Still no surprise. I asked, "You think Joanne was happy that he dumped her for Selena?"

"I doubt it. I hope it gave her a brain aneurysm."

"Just about," Conway said. "You know Joanne better than I do. You think it would piss her off enough that she'd want him dead?"

"Oh yeah. Definitely. Can I go now, and you can bother her instead?"

"Thing is," I said, "we're pretty sure Joanne didn't actually kill Chris. We're wondering if she got someone to do it for her."

"Orla," Holly said promptly. "Any dirty work Joanne wants done, she gets Orla to do it."

Conway was shaking her head. "Nah. We've got solid evidence that it was one of your four."

Still nothing out of Mackey, not yet, but his eyes were fixed on Conway. Holly had the same look on her. No more messing with the clay, that was over. She knew: this was the heart of it. She said, "Evidence like what?"

"We'll get to that. We think maybe Joanne showed that video to one of you four. Told her, 'Get rid of Chris for me, or this goes to McKenna and you all get expelled.'"

Conway was leaning in, picking up the rhythm. I eased back, put my head down over my notebook. Left her to it.

Holly's eyebrows were up. "And we just went, 'Uhhh, OK, anything you say'? Seriously? If we were that terrified of being expelled, we wouldn't've snuck out to begin with. We'd've stayed inside like good little girls."

"Not just because you were scared of being expelled. Joanne picked carefully. She picked someone who'd do a lot to protect her mates, who was already frantic about the damage Chris was doing, already hated his guts—"

Conway was ticking off finger after finger, relentless. Holly snapped, "I'm not *stupid*—Dad, leave me alone, I want to say this! If I was going to kill someone, which I didn't, no way would I do it in some kind of conspiracy with Joanne *Heffernan*. And be stuck for the rest of my life with that bitch holding that over my head? Do I look brain-dead? No fucking *way*. No matter *what* she had on video."

"Language," said Mackey lazily. Eyes still sparking alert, but there was a twitch at the corner of his mouth. His kid was holding her own.

"Whatever. And before you even *start* to say, oh, then it could've been Julia or Selena or Becca, the exact same thing goes for them. Did we do something to make you think we're the biggest idiots you've ever met? Or what?"

Conway was giving Holly her head, let her get it out of her system. Mackey said, "And while we're on the subject, ignore me if you want, but you're making this Joanne out to be a pretty big idiot herself. She wants a murder committed, so she asks a cop's kid? The person most likely to send her straight to jail, do not pass go? Holly: this Joanne, she have any head injuries?"

"No. She's a bitch, but she's not stupid."

Mackey spread his hands at us: *There you go.* Conway said, "We're not married to the blackmail motive. There's plenty of other possibilities."

She left it till Holly rolled her eyes. "Like *what?*"

"You told Detective Moran that when you found out what was wrong with Selena, you just stuck your head in the sand and hoped it'd go away. That rings my bullshit alarm. I don't see you being that much of a wimp. Are you a wimp, yeah?"

"No. I just didn't know what to do. Sorry I'm not some kind of *genius.*"

I'd got to Holly before, from this angle; Conway was banking on getting to her again. Mackey was paying attention.

"Like you just said, though, you're not some kind of idiot, either. You wouldn't freeze up just because you had to deal with something all by yourself. You're not a baby. Are you?" It was working. Holly had her arms folded, starting to knot into a furious ball. "I think you went to Selena, told her you knew about Chris. I think she told you she was planning on getting back with him. And I think you went, *Fuck no.* Made a chance to get hold of Selena's phone, texted Chris to meet up. Probably you just wanted him to leave Selena alone, did you?"

Holly had her face turned away from Conway, staring out the window.

"How'd you try to convince him? You said before, Chris wasn't happy that he was never going to get anywhere with you. Did you offer him a swap: leave Selena alone, I'll make up for it?"

That almost lifted her out of the chair. "I'd rather have my skin peeled off than do anything with Chris. *Jesus!*"

Nothing from Mackey. Holly hadn't even clocked him on that, and she would have, if she'd hooked up with Chris: talking about your sex life in front of Daddy, that had to get some reaction. She was telling the truth: she'd never touched Chris.

Conway said, "Then how'd you go at him?"

Holly bit down on her lip, angry at herself: she'd been got. Turned her face away again, started the ignoring from scratch.

"Whatever you tried, you gave it a few shots, it didn't work. Finally you made one more appointment with him. For the sixteenth of May."

Holly biting her lip harder, stop herself answering. Mackey didn't move, but he was pulled like a crossbow on the edge of it.

"This time you weren't planning on any persuading. You got out early, you got your weapon ready, and when Chris showed up—"

Holly whipped round on Conway. "Are you *stupid*? I *didn't kill Chris*. We can stay here all night and you can come up with four million different reasons I could've killed him, and I still won't have *done* it. Do you actually think I'm going to get confused enough that in the end I'll just be like, 'OhmyGod, you know what, maybe I totally *did* climb up a tree and drop a piano on his head because I hated his poncy haircut'?"

Mackey was grinning. "Nicely put," he told her.

Holly and Conway didn't even hear him, too focused on each other. "If you didn't," Conway said, "then you know who did. Why did you hide that phone?"

"I told you. I didn't want Selena—"

"You said she hadn't been in touch with Chris for weeks before he died. The phone would've showed that. What's incriminating there?"

"I didn't say it was *incriminating*, I said you'd have given her *hassle*. Which you would have."

"You're a cop's kid, you know better than to conceal evidence in a murder case, but you do it to save your mate a bit of *hassle*? Nah. No way." Holly tried to say something, but Conway's voice came down hard on top of hers. "One of you four had been texting Chris from that phone, after he split up with Selena. Arranging meetings with him. One of you four had arranged to meet him *the night he died*. Now that's incriminating, amn't I right? That's something you'd want to cover up."

"Whoa whoa whoa," Mackey said, lifting a hand. "Hang on a minute there. *That's* your evidence? Texts sent from someone else's phone?"

Conway said, to Holly, "A hidden phone, that you had access to. You and no one else that we know of, except Selena, and we're satisfied Selena didn't send the texts."

Mackey said, "A phone kept in a room that four girls share. Are the texts signed in Holly's handwriting, yeah? Got her prints on them?"

I copped, finally, why Mackey had told me that touching little tale about how Holly wound up boarding. He had been telling me how much she loved her friends. Anything we got out of her, there was how he was going to shoot it down: *Holly's protecting her friends. Prove she's not.*

Hard to be sure of anything, ever, with Mackey. I was sure of this: he would throw an innocent sixteen-year-old under a bus without thinking twice, if it would save his kid.

A hundred percent positive of this: he'd throw me and Conway.

Conway kept ignoring him. Said to Holly, "You're the one who knew the phone needed to disappear. None of the others: just you. And the killer had been deleting the meeting texts as she went; you'd never have known they existed, unless you were the one who sent them."

Mackey said, "Or unless someone told her, or unless she guessed, or unless she overreacted to what she already knew—God forbid a teenage girl should overreact, am I right?"

Conway looked at him then. Said, "I'm done interviewing you. You answer one more question, we're getting a different appropriate adult."

Mackey thought her over. Glint in his eye, raking her, would've had me twitching; Conway didn't notice or didn't care. Just waited for him to finish up and answer her.

"Seems to me," he said, and stood up, "that you and I both need a moment to clear our heads. I'm going out for a smoke. I think you should join me."

"I don't smoke."

"I'm not looking for a chance to give you shite about your attitude, Detective. That I could do right here. I'm suggesting that a deep breath and a bit of fresh air might do us both good; get us back on the right foot. When we come back, I promise not to answer any more questions for Holly. How's that?"

I moved. This was it; I couldn't tell what or how, but I could feel it, yelling warnings. Conway glanced at me; I thought *Careful*, loud as I could. She glanced at Mackey's smile—open, straightforward, just the right bit sheepish.

Said, "Smoke fast."

"You're the boss."

I followed them to the doorway. When Mackey arched an eyebrow at me, I said, "I'll wait out here."

His grin said *Good boy, you protect yourself from the scary little girl.* I didn't bite. He matched Conway's pace down the corridor, so their steps fading away sounded like one person's. Shoulder to shoulder, they looked like partners.

Holly hadn't watched them go. Every muscle of her was still clamped tight; there was a ferocious crease between her eyebrows. She said, "Do you honest to God think I killed Chris?"

I stayed in the doorway. "What would you think, if you were me?"

"I *hope* I'd be good enough at my job that I could tell when someone's not a murderer. *Jesus.*"

Her adrenaline was firing, touch her and the electric zap would've kicked you across the room. I said, "You're hiding something. That's all I know. I'm not good enough to telepathically guess what it is. You need to tell us."

Holly threw me a look I couldn't read, maybe scorn. Jerked her ponytail tight, hard enough to hurt. Then she shoved back her chair and went over to the model school. Unwound a length, expertly, from a spool of fine copper wire; chopped it off with a little pair of wire cutters, *snick* in the bleached air.

She leaned one hip against the table, flipped tweezers out of an empty bedroom. Twirled the wire deftly around the end of a thin pencil, adjusted with the tip of a fingernail when it slid out of true. Her fingers moved like a dancer's, tucking, swirling, weaving, like a spell-caster's. The rhythm and the focus steadied her, smoothed that forehead crease away. Steadied me along with her, till part of me even forgot to tense against whatever Mackey was trying to do with Conway.

In the end Holly held out the pencil towards me. Perched on top of it: a hat, wide-brimmed, barely big enough for a fingertip, decorated with one copper-wire rose.

I said, "Beautiful."

Holly smiled, a small detached smile, down at the hat. Spun it on the pencil.

She said, "I wish I'd never brought you that fucking postcard." Not angry, not wishing for an excuse to kick me in the nuts, not any more. Things that went too deep to leave room for that.

I said, "Why? You knew there'd be hassle; you had to expect all this. What's changed?"

Holly said, "I'm not allowed to talk to you till my dad gets back." She slipped the hat off the pencil, edged it between wires and dropped it over a tiny bedpost. Then she went back to her chair and sat down. Pulled her hoodie sleeves down over her hands and watched the moon.

Fast feet on the stairs: Conway, stepping out of the layers of shadow down the corridor, cool evening caught on her clothes. She said to me, "Mackey's hanging on for another smoke—in case it's a while before his next chance, he says. He says you can join him if you want. You might as well; he's not going to come in till you do."

She wasn't looking at me. Gave me a bad feeling, couldn't put my finger on it. I waited a second, trying to catch her eye, but all I got was Holly alert and scanning back and forth between the two of us, trying to snatch something. I left.

The tree line had turned black, swooping and dipping like a bird's flight line against deep blue sky. I'd never seen it in that light before, but it looked familiar all the same. The school was starting to feel like I'd been there forever, like I belonged.

Mackey was leaning against the wall. He lit his smoke, waggled it at me: *Look, see, I really did need one!*

"So," he said. "Interesting strategy you've got going on here, young Stephen. Some might say downright insane, but I'm willing to give you the benefit of the doubt."

"What strategy?"

Double-take, amused. "Hello? Remember me? We've met before. We've *worked together.* Your aw-shucks-little-old-me act won't fly here."

I said, "What strategy are we talking about?"

Mackey sighed. "OK. I'll play. Hooking up with Antoinette Conway. I'd love to know: what's your plan there?"

"No plan. I got the chance to work a murder, I took it."

Mackey's eyebrow went up. "I hope for your sake you're still playing innocent, kid. How much do you know about Conway?"

"She's a good D. Works hard. Going places, fast."

He waited. When he realized I was done: "That's it? That's all you've got?"

I shrugged. Seven years on and Mackey's eye could still make me squirm, still turn me into a kid gone insta-thick at an oral exam. "Up till today, I didn't spend a lot of time thinking about her."

"There's a grapevine. There's always gossip. You're above that kind of thing?"

"Not above it. Just never picked up anything about Conway."

Mackey sighed, shoulders sagging. Ran a hand through his hair, shook his head. "Kid. Stephen." His voice had gone gentle. "In this gig, you need to make friends. Have to. Otherwise you won't last."

"I'm lasting grand. And I've got friends."

"Not the kind I'm talking about. You need *real* friends, kid. Friends who have your back. Who tell you the things you need to know. Who don't let you prance straight into a shit tornado without even giving you a heads up."

"Like you?"

"I've done OK for you so far. Haven't I?"

"I said thanks."

"And I'd like to think you meant it. But I don't know, Stephen. I'm not feeling the love."

"If you're my best buddy," I said, "go ahead and tell me what you think I need to know about Conway."

Mackey leaned back against the wall. He wasn't bothering to smoke his fag; it had done its job. He said, "Conway's a leper, kid. She didn't mention that?"

"Hasn't come up." I didn't ask why she was a leper. He was going to tell me anyway.

"Well, she's not a whiner, anyway. I suppose that's one plus." He flicked ash. "You're no thicko. You had to have some clue that Conway's never going to win Miss Congeniality. You didn't mind teaming up with that?"

"Like I said. I'm not looking for a new best friend."

"I'm not talking about your social life. Conway: her first week on Murder, she's bending over writing something on the whiteboard, and this idiot called Roche smacks her arse. Conway whips round, grabs his hand, bends one finger back till his eyes pop out. Tells him next time he touches her, she'll break it. Roche calls her a bitch. Conway gives his finger one more jerk, Roche yells, Conway lets go of him and goes back to the whiteboard."

"I can see how that would make Roche into a leper. Not Conway."

Mackey laughed out loud. "I missed you, kid. I really did. I'd forgotten how cute you are. You're right: in a perfect squad, that's how it should work. And in some squads, in some years, it actually would. But Murder's not a cuddly place right now. They're not bad lads, most of them, in their own way; just a bit rugby-club, bit in-crowd, bit no-neck. If Conway had said something smart, or laughed along, or grabbed Roche's arse the next time she caught him bending, she'd've been grand. If she'd just made *this* much effort to fit in. But she didn't, and now the rest of the squad thinks she's an uppity ball-breaking humorless bitch."

"Sounds lovely in there. Are you trying to turn me off Murder?"

He spread his hands. "I'm not saying I approve; I'm just telling you the facts of life. Not that you need telling. That little speech about blaming the harasser and not the victim, that was pretty, but tell me the truth: say you walk into Murder tomorrow, someone calls you a ginger skanger, tells you to fuck off back onto the dole where you belong. You gonna break his fingers? Or are you gonna play along: have a laugh, call him a sheep-shagging bog-monster, do what it takes to get what you want out of the situation? The truth, now."

Mackey's eyes on mine, opaque and knowing in the last of the light, till I looked away. "I'm gonna play along."

"Yeah, you are. But don't say that like it's a bad thing, sunshine. I'd do exactly the same. That kind of accommodation, that's what keeps the world turning. A little bit of give. When someone like Conway decides she doesn't have to play along, that's when things go to shite."

I heard Joanne. *They act like they can do whatever they want. It doesn't work like that.* Wondered what Mackey thought about his Holly and her friends giving the world the finger.

"Their gaffer isn't an idiot; when the atmosphere in his squad room turned to poison, he noticed. He pulls people in, asks them what's the story; they all clam up, tell him everything's just dandy and everyone's the best of friends. Murder's like that: bunch of schoolkids, no one wants to be the telltale. The gaffer doesn't believe them, but he knows he's never getting the real story. And he knows the day things went south is the day Conway walked in. So as far as he's concerned, she's the problem."

"So he's going to drop her," I said. "First excuse he gets."

"Nah. They won't boot her out of Murder, because she's the type to sue for discrimination and they don't want the publicity. But they can make damn sure she quits. She'll never get a partner. She'll never get a promotion. She'll never get invited to join the lads for a pint after work. She'll never get another good case; once she gives up on this, there'll be nothing on her desk but D-list drug dealers till the day she hands in her papers." Smoke curling up between us from his hand, a warning taint on the sweet air. "That'll wear you down, after a while. Conway's got spine, she'll last longer than most would, but she'll crack in the end."

I said, "Conway's career is her problem. I'm here for mine. This is my shot at showing Murder what I can do."

Mackey was shaking his head. "No it isn't. It's a six-bullet round of Russian roulette. If you don't get on with Conway, you're back to Cold Cases: bye-bye, see you round, everyone remembers that Moran couldn't hack it in the big leagues even for one day. If you do get on with her, then you're her bitch-boy. No one else on Murder, and that includes the gaffer, is ever going to touch you with a ten-foot pole. Shit rubs off, kid. If you honestly haven't got a strategy, I suggest you get one. Fast."

I said, "You're trying to stir shite. You get me and Conway looking over our shoulders at each other, means we take our eyes off the ball. Next thing we know, our case's got away from us."

"I might well be. It sounds like something I'd do. Ask yourself this, though: does that mean I'm wrong?"

The nettle edges to the air in the Murder squad room, fine and poisonous, when Conway walked in. Tiny barbs, sticky, working deep.

I said, "What've you been saying to Conway about me?"

Mackey grinned. "Same as I've been saying to you, sunshine: just the truth. And nothing but the truth. So help you God."

And there it was. I could've kicked myself for asking. I knew what Mackey had told Conway. Didn't need to hear it, from either of them.

Interesting strategy, letting young Stephen onboard. Some might say downright insane, but I'm willing to give you the benefit of the doubt . . .

"Ahhh," said Mackey, stretching. Glanced at his smoke, burned down to long ash. Tossed it on the ground. "I needed that. Shall we?"

Conway was leaning against the outside of the door, hands in her trouser pockets, not moving. Waiting for us. I knew then.

You're no idiot, Detective Conway; I'm betting you know the story on how Holly and I met Moran. Some of it, anyway. Want to hear the rest?

She straightened up as we got close. Opened the door, held it for Mackey. Caught my eye. As she closed the door behind Mackey, he flicked a winner's grin over his shoulder at me.

Conway said, "I'll take it from here."

Moran was brand-new out of uniform, doing floater work on a murder case. The D in charge was called Kennedy. Kennedy was good to young Stephen. Very good. Pulled him out of the deep end of the floater pool, gave him a shot at the big time. Most Ds wouldn't've done it; most Ds would've stuck to tried and true, no newbies need apply. Bet Kennedy wishes he had . . .

I only did what Mackey wanted me to do, back then. It never hit me, and it should've, that he would keep it tucked away in his back pocket: something he could use against me someday, if he ever needed to.

I said—keeping it down: his ear was pressed to the back of that door—"Mackey's trying to fuck with us."

"There's no *us.* There's me and my case, and then there's some guy who's been useful for the day and isn't any more. Don't worry: I'll write your gaffer a nice note about what a good boy you were."

Like a punch in the jaw. It shouldn't've hit me; she was right, it had only been one day. Got me goodo.

It must've shown. The face on me pulled some fleck of guilt out of Conway. She said, "I'll give you a lift back to HQ—give me your mobile number, I'll text you when I'm done here. Till then, get a sandwich. Go for a nice walk, admire the grounds. See if you can get Chris's ghost to pop up for you. Whatever."

The second your boy Moran saw his chance, he shagged Kennedy up the arse with no Vaseline. Fuck loyalty, fuck gratitude, fuck doing the right thing: all young Stephen cared about was his glorious career.

I said, and I'd stopped caring about keeping it down, "You're doing exactly what Mackey wants you to do. He wants me gone because he's scared Holly'll talk to me. You can't see that?" Nothing on Conway's face. "He tried it on me, too: bitched about you, hoped I'd walk. You think I took any notice?"

"Course you didn't. You want to shake your booty in front of O'Kelly; doesn't matter whose case you piggyback on to get there. Me, I've got something to lose here. And I'm not having you lose it for me."

Kennedy never saw it coming. At least you won't get blindsided like he did. If you honestly haven't got a strategy, you might want to get one fast . . .

I gave Conway my phone number. She swung the door closed in my face.

24

O ne of Julia's more impressive talents has always been the ability to barf at will. It was cooler back in primary school, before anybody noticed that public puking might not be particularly dignified—it even earned her a decent chunk of dosh, one way and another—but it hasn't totally lost its usefulness since then. She just saves it for special occasions, these days.

Tuesday morning, April twenty-third, Chris Harper has just over three weeks left to live. Julia eats the biggest and most varied breakfast she can handle, because an artiste has her pride, then waits till the middle of Home Economics and barfs pyrotechnically all over the classroom floor. Orla Burgess is within range, but Julia resists temptation: her plan doesn't include Orla being sent back to the boarders' wing to change. As Miss Rooney shoos her towards the nurse's office, Julia—clutching her stomach—catches a flash of Holly and Becca baffled, Selena gazing out the window like she hasn't even noticed anything happening; Joanne's flat-eyed smirk while she plans how to spread the word that that slut Julia Harte is pregnant; and Gemma giving her a look like a wink, amused and approving.

She does wobbly legs and some mild gagging for the nurse, answers the usual questions about her period—you could break your leg and the nurse would still want to know when your last period was; Julia suspects that being a day overdue would get you ratted out to the nuns for interrogation—and a few minutes later she's all tucked up in bed with a glass of flat ginger ale and a pathetic look. And the nurse leaves her alone.

Julia works fast. She has it planned out: first Selena's part of the wardrobe, then her bed, if she doesn't score there she'll pop out the bottom of Selena's bedside table—they figured out how to do it last term, when Becca lost her key—and if she still comes up blank then she doesn't know what the fuck she's going to do.

It doesn't get that far. When she slides her hand along the side of Selena's mattress, between the bed and the wall, she finds a lump. Neat little slit in the mattress cover, and inside, surprise surprise, a phone. An adorable itsy-bitsy pink one, just like the one Alison bought off Joanne. Chris must have stocked up by the armful, one for each of the lucky babes he was planning on honoring with his glorious dick. Up until she saw that phone in her hand, Julia still thought there was a chance Gemma was lying.

Selena hasn't put a lock code on it, which might give Julia a flicker of guilt if she had room for that. Instead she goes to Messages and starts reading.

Still thinking abt the dance wd love to see you again— It punches a hiss of breath out of her. She's been wondering when and how Chris ever hooked Selena, been going over every trip to the Court, looking for just ten minutes when Lenie was unshielded, but it's actually almost creepy how close the four of them stick together; she couldn't put her finger on once when any-one even went to the loo alone. And all the time: the fucking Valentine's dance. While Julia was outside, getting reckless on rum and Finn's grin and the sparking cold-air newness in every breath, Selena was exploring a little new territory of her own. And something watched and—without any anger, or any mercy—started considering what their punishment would have to be.

She keeps reading. Chris is excellent; Julia is almost impressed. He had Selena sussed dead on, right from the start. One sext, one hint of romance even, and she'd have been gone; so smart boy Chris never went near there. Instead he went for long texts about his emo sister's problems, or how his parents didn't understand him, or how it wounded him that he couldn't show his true sensitive self to his shallow friends. Julia is glad she's already puked herself empty.

Selena is a sucker for anyone who needs her. Maybe some people would call it arrogance, thinking she's so super-special she can help where no one else could, but the thing is sometimes she can. Julia should know. You can say anything to Selena and she, unlike apparently everyone else in the world, will never come back with something that makes you want to hit her and yourself for having opened your big stupid mouth. So people who never talk to anyone talk to her. That's what she's used to. That's what Chris Harper smelled off her. And that's what he used to wiggle his way close enough to shove his hand down her top.

Because Selena was talking to him, too. *Yesterday there was this drawing i wantd to show my dad when he dropd me off at my mums and he wouldnt*

even come inside for 1 sec to see it, he waitd in the car while i got it. Sometimes
i feel like they wish i didnt exist cause then they wouldnt have to see each other.

She has never said anything like that to Julia. Julia never had a clue that
she felt that way.

They've been meeting for more than a month. It gets more obvious with
every text that Selena is gaga about Chris, gooey, stupid in love. Julia has a
hard time deciding who is the world's biggest moron: the one who's fallen
in love with Chris the Sleaze Harper, or the three who pranced along next
to her while she did it without noticing one single thing. She grits her teeth
and mashes her elbow along the wall next to her till it's scraped raw.

And then Julia gets to this morning. No wonder Selena looks spaced out.
She just dumped Chris's nasty arse.

The rush of relief almost throws Julia flat on her back on the bed, but a
second later it drains away. This won't last. Selena can't even get through the
dump text without babbling about how much she loves Chris, and he's already come back with a wild text demanding to know WTF and begging
her to meet him tonight. Selena hasn't answered, but another few days of
oh-please-I-need-you-so-much and she will.

Julia hears it clear as tapped bronze. *Your chance. Your choice.*

It takes her a long humming minute to understand what that means. To
hold in one hand what will happen if she does, and in the other what will
happen if she doesn't.

Julia can't breathe. She thinks like a howl: *That's not fair it's not fair it's*
not fair, whatever I do I'm going to get—I didn't get off with Finn. I barely
fucking touched him. I didn't do anything I should have to pay for. The silence
that meets her teaches her: this is not McKenna's office. You don't get to play
with nitpicks, dodge whining around the edges of But-Miss-I-never-exactly-
actually, not here. Unfair means nothing. She has been weighed up and the
decision has been made. She has these few days before Selena takes Chris
back, one last gift, in which to choose.

Julia thinks about throwing the phone at the wall and lining the pieces
up neatly on Selena's bed. She thinks about going to Matron and telling her
she needs to swap to a different room, today. She thinks about getting under
the covers and crying. In the end she just sits there on Selena's bed, watching
the sunlight slide across her lap and her arm and the phone in her hand,
waiting for ringing bells and brisk feet to make her move.

"So?" Holly wants to know, tossing her bag on the bed. "What were you
doing?"

"What did it look like? Puking my guts up."

"That was for real? We thought you were faking."

Julia glances at Selena before she can stop herself, but Lenie doesn't look suspicious; she's flopped down on her bed, still in her uniform, and is curled up staring at the wall. Julia is obviously the last thing on her mind.

"What for? So I could be bored off my tits all day? I have a virus."

Becca is pulling clothes out of the wardrobe and singing to herself. She breaks off to say, "Want us to stay here with you? We were going to the Court, but that was 'cause we thought you'd come too."

"Go. I'd be shit company anyway."

"I'll stay," Selena says, to the wall. "I don't want to go anywhere."

Holly makes a face at Julia, tilts her head: *What's with her?* Julia shrugs: *How would I know?*

"Oh, yeah, I meant to ask—" Becca's head pops out of her uniform jumper, flyaway hair everywhere. "Tonight?"

"Hello?" Julia says. "I feel like crap. Remember? I just want to sleep."

Please can we meet tonite, Chris texted Selena. *Same time same place I'll be there.*

"OK," Becca says, not bothered by the edge on Julia's voice. A year ago she would have flinched like she'd been hit. *At least that,* Julia thinks. *At least one good thing.* "Maybe tomorrow?"

"I'm on," Holly says, throwing her blazer at the wardrobe. Julia says, "Depends how I feel." Selena is still staring at the wall.

That night Julia doesn't go to sleep. She curls up in a loose ball the way she usually sleeps, keeps her eyes shut and her breathing long and even, and listens. She has the back of her hand up against her mouth, where she can bite into it if she feels herself drowsing off.

Selena isn't asleep either. Julia's back is to her, but she can hear her moving around, restless. Once or twice her breath has a wet sound, like she might be crying, but Julia can't tell for sure.

After a few hours, Selena sits up, very slowly, one move at a time. Julia hears her hold her breath, listening for the rest of them, and forces herself to stay slack and easy. Becca snores, a tiny delicate noise.

After a long time, Selena lies down again. This time she's definitely crying.

Julia thinks of Chris Harper waiting in their grove, probably throwing rocks at rustles and pissing on the cypress trunks. She wants to pray for a tree to drop a branch on his head and smash his slimy brain all over the grass, but she knows it's not going to work that way.

. . .

On Wednesday afternoon, as they get their books ready for study period, Julia says, "Tonight."

"You're over your virus, yeah?" Holly asks, tossing a copybook on her pile. The sideways slant of her eye says she's still not convinced.

"If it comes back, I'll make sure and aim for you."

"Whatever. I just don't want you puking your guts when we're right outside Matron's room and getting us all caught."

"You're all heart," Julia says. "Becs, you on?"

"Course," Becca says. "Can I borrow your red jumper? I got jam on my black one, and it's going to be freezing out."

"Sure." It's nowhere near cold, but Becca loves borrowing things, lending things, all the small rituals that blur the four of them into one warm space. If she had the choice they'd all live in each other's clothes. "Lenie," Julia says. "Tonight?"

Selena looks up from her study schedule. She's shadowy and thinner, the way she's been all the last two days, like she's in dimmer light than the rest of the room, but the thought of a night has raised a spark of what looks like hope. "Yeah. Definitely yeah. I need that."

"God, me too," Julia says. *One more*, she thinks. *One last night.*

They run. Julia takes off the second her feet hit the grass below the window, and feels the rush of the others build behind her. They stream down the great front lawn like wild birds thrown across the sky. In front of them the guardhouse glows yellow, but they're safe as houses: the night watchman never takes his eyes off his laptop except to do his rounds at midnight and again at two, and anyway they're invisible, they're soundless, they don't cast shadows; they could sneak up close enough to touch him, they could press their faces against the glass and singsong his name, he'd never blink. They've done it before, when they wanted to see what he did in there. He plays on-line poker.

They swing right, white pebbles fly up under their feet and they're in under the trees, faster and faster down the paths, chests burning, ribs aching, Julia running like she wants to take them skimming right off the surface of the path and up, into the cartwheel moon. By the time they collapse in the clearing, she's run everything else out of her mind.

They're all laughing, with what little breath they've got left. "Jesus," Holly says, doubling over with her hand pressed to a stitch. "What was *that*? Are you, like, going out for cross-country next year?"

"You just pretend Sister Cornelius is coming up behind you," Julia says. The moon is almost full, just one blurred edge for the next night to fill in, and she feels like she could leap the waist-high bushes from a standing start, up and over with her feet pedaling slow underwater circles in midair, down on her toes as light as a dandelion seed. She isn't even out of breath. "*Girls!* I have told you and informed you and let you know that you should never run on grass and herbaceous plants and—and verdant pastures—'"

That explodes them. "'The Bible tells us that our Lord Jesus *never* ran or jogged or galloped—'" Becca is helpless with panting and laughter.

Holly stabs a finger. "'—and who are you to think or believe that you are better than Our Lord? Well?'"

"'You, Holly Mackey—'"

"'—whatever class of a name that is, there's no saint named Holly, I think we'll have to call you Bernadette from now on—'"

"'—you, Bernadette Mackey, stop running this instant—'"

"'—and moment and minute—'"

"'—and tell me what Our Lord would have thought of you! Well?'"

Julia realizes Selena hasn't joined in. She's sitting up, with her arms clasped round her knees and her face tilted up to the sky. The moonlight hits her full on, burning her out to something you can only half see, a ghost or a saint. She looks like she's praying. Maybe she is.

Holly is watching Selena too, and she's stopped laughing. She says, quietly, "Lenie."

Becca props herself up on one elbow.

Selena doesn't move. She says, "Mm."

"What's wrong?"

Julia throws it at the side of Selena's head like a rock: *Shut up. This is my night my last night ever don't you dare wreck it.*

Selena turns her head. For a second her eyes, still and tired, meet Julia's. Then she says, to Holly, "What?"

"Something's up. Isn't it?"

Selena watches Holly tranquilly, like she's still waiting for the question, but Holly is sitting up straight and she's not backing down. Julia's nails dig into the earth. She says, "You look like you've got a headache. Is that it?"

Those tired eyes move back to her. After a long moment: "Yeah," Selena says. "Becs, do my hair?"

Selena loves having someone play with her hair. Becca scoots over behind her and carefully takes out her elastic; hair spills down her back almost to the grass, a hundred kinds of white-gold, glinting. Becca shakes it out like delicate fabric. Then she starts running her fingers through it, in a steady, confident rhythm. Selena sighs. She's left Holly's question behind.

Julia's hand is clamped around a smooth oval pebble that her nails dug out of the ground. She rubs damp dirt off it. The air is warm, flickering with tiny moths and with smells: a million hyacinths, the deep-water tang of the cypresses, the earth on her fingers and the cold stone in her palm. By now they have noses like deer. If someone tried to sneak up on them, he wouldn't get within twenty meters.

Holly has lain back, one knee crossed over the other, but her hanging foot is bobbing restlessly. "How long have you had a headache?"

"*Jesus*," Julia says. "Leave her alone."

Becca stares over Selena's shoulder, big-eyed, like a little kid watching her parents fight. Holly says, "Well, excuse *me*. She's been like this for days, and if you have a headache that lasts that long, you're supposed to go to a *doctor*."

"You're giving *me* a headache."

Becca says, in a too-loud burst, "I'm scared of the exams!"

They stop and look at her.

"Duh, you're supposed to be," Holly says.

Becca looks like she half wishes she'd kept her mouth shut. "I know that. I mean really scared. Like terrified."

"That's what the Junior Cert's *for*," Holly says. "To make us so scared that we'll behave. That's why it's this year, right when everyone starts going out and doing stuff. All that blahblah about how if you don't get all As you'll be working in Burger King for the rest of your life? The idea is, we'll be so petrified we won't do anything like have boyfriends or go to discos or for example get out at night, in case it distracts us and oh noooo! Whopper with fries please!"

Becca says, "It's not Burger King. It's . . . Like, what if I fail, I don't know, Science, and they won't let me do Honors Biology for the Leaving?"

Julia is surprised enough that she almost forgets about Holly and Selena. Becca's never said anything about what comes after school, ever. Selena's always wanted to be an artist, Holly's been thinking about sociology, Julia likes the idea of journalism more and more; Becca watches those conversations like they have nothing to do with her, like they're in a language she doesn't speak and doesn't want to learn, and is prickly for hours afterwards.

Holly is thinking the same thing, apparently. "So?" she wants to know. "It's not like you *have* to have Honors Biology because you want to do medicine or something. You don't know what you want to be. Do you?"

"I don't have a clue. I don't care. I just . . ." Becca's head is down, over her hands moving faster and faster. "I just can't be in all different classes from you guys, next year. I'm not going to be stuck in, like, Ordinary Level everything when you're all doing Honors and we never see each other and I have to sit next to Orla Stupid Burgess for the rest of my life. I'll kill myself."

Holly says, "If you fail Science, me and Lenie are too—no offense, Lenie, you know what I mean." Selena nods, carefully so her hair won't tug. "We'll all be sitting next to Orla Stupid Burgess together. It's not like we're all smarter than you."

Becca shrugs, without looking up. "I practically failed it in the mocks."

She got a C, but that's not the point. She's electric because there's something in the air, scraping at her even though she can't figure out what or where it is, and she needs to feel the four of them holding tight because she believes that's what will make everything OK again. Julia knows what she wants to hear. *It doesn't matter what marks we get. We'll pick our subjects together, we'll pick ones we can all do. Who cares about college? That's a million years away . . .*

Selena is the one who says stuff like that. Then Julia tells her to quit being such a sap and anyone who fails English is on her own, because personally she'd rather snog Orla Burgess with tongues than do Ordinary Level English and be forced to listen to Miss Fitzpatrick sniffing up her nose-drip every ten seconds like clockwork.

Selena says nothing. She's drifted away again, eyes on the sky, swaying with the rhythm of Becca's fingers.

Julia says, "If you fail Science, we'll all do Ordinary Level together. I'll survive without my world-famous-neurosurgeon career."

Becca glances up, startled, looking for the snide edge, but Julia smiles at her, a real full-on smile. One confused second and then Becca smiles back. Selena's swaying eases as her hands gentle.

"I don't want to do Honors Bio anyway," Holly says. She stretches her legs out luxuriously and clasps her hands behind her head. "They make you dissect a sheep heart."

"Eww," all round, even Selena.

Julia tucks the pebble into her pocket and stands up. She bends her knees, swings her arms, and leaps; hovers above the bush for a second, arms outspread, head back and throat bared to the sky; and floats down to land, one-toed like a dancer, on the grass.

On Thursday Julia barfs at the beginning of Guidance, right when Sister Cornelius is winding up for a long bewildering rant involving nightclubs and self-respect and what Jesus would think of Ecstasy drugs. She figures she might as well get something out of all this.

Selena's phone is still in the same place. Chris has been sending her predictable texts. She hasn't answered them.

Julia texts him: *1 o'clock tonight. Usual place. DON'T text me back. Just come.* Once the text has gone through, she deletes it out of Selena's Sent box.

She's planning to lie in bed and study, because the real world still exists, whether that prick Chris and that fool Selena like it or not, the Junior Cert is still going to need taking, and today that actually feels comforting. Instead she falls asleep, too instantly and intensely even to fight it.

She wakes up because the others are banging into the room and there are people shrieking in the corridor. "Oh my *God*," Holly says, slamming the door behind them. "You know what that's about? Rhona heard that somebody's cousin queued up somewhere for something and the one with the stupid hair out of One Direction touched her hand. Not, like, *married* her; just touched her. That's *it*. I think my *ear* died. Hi."

"I had a relapse," Julia says, sitting up. "If you want me to prove it, come over here."

"Whatever," Holly says. "I didn't ask." This time she doesn't sound like she cares. Her eyes are on Selena, who is rummaging in the wardrobe, head down so that her hair hides her face. Selena's hands move through the drawer in slow motion, like this is taking almost more concentration than she's got.

Holly is no idiot. "Hey," Julia says, shaking her arm that's gone to sleep. "If you guys are going down to the Court, can you get me earbuds? Because I'm going to die of boredom if I'm stuck here any more without music."

"Use mine," Becca says. Becca is no idiot either, but all this is zooming straight past her; it's outside her horizon. Julia wants to shove her deep into bed and tuck the duvet tight over her head, stash her in a warm safe place till all of this is over.

Holly is still watching Selena. "I don't want yours," Julia says—there's nothing she can do about the leap of hurt on Becca's face. "They hurt. My ears are the wrong shape. Hol? Will you sub me that ten squid after all?"

Holly wakes up. "Yeah, sure. What earbuds do you want?"

Her voice sounds fine, normal. Julia holds on to the thread of relief. "Those little red ones like I had before. Get me a Coke, too, OK? I'm sick of ginger ale."

That should keep them busy. There's only one place in the Court that carries the red earbuds: a tiny gadget shop at the back of the top floor, last place the others will look. With any luck, they'll be back just in time to grab their books for study, and Julia won't have to see them for more than a few seconds.

The realization that she's trying to dodge her best friends slams her with another tsunami of sleep. Sounds spiral away from her, Holly saying something and the slam of Becca's bedside table, Rhona still gibbering far away and a song playing down the corridor, sweet and light and fast, *I've got so far, I've got so far left to*—and Julia's gone.

That night, after lights-out, Julia realizes what the knockouts were for: now she's wide awake, couldn't doze off if she tried. And the others, wrecked after last night, are out for the count.

"Lenie," she says softly, into the dark room. She's got no clue what she'll say if Selena answers, but none of the others even move.

Louder: "Lenie."

Nothing. Their breathing, rhythmic and dragging, sounds drugged. Julia can do whatever she wants. No one is going to stop her.

She gets up and gets dressed. Jeans shorts, low-cut top, Converse, cute pink hoodie: Julia does drama club, she knows about dressing the part. She doesn't bother to be quiet.

The corridor light gives the glass panel above the transom a faint gray glow. Julia flares it to a blaze and looks down at the others. Holly is sprawled on her back, Becca is one neat curve like a kitten; Selena is a whirl of gold and a loose curl of fingers on the pillow. Their steady breathing has got louder. In the second before she opens the door and slips out into the corridor, Julia hates all of their guts.

Outside is different tonight. The air is warm and restless, the moon is enormous and too close. Every noise sounds sharper, focused on her, testing: twigs crack in the bushes to see if she'll jump, leaves rustle behind her to make her whip round. Something is circling among the trees, making a high rising call that runs down her spine like a warning—Julia can't tell if it's warning something about her, or the other way round. It's been so long since she was afraid of anything the grounds could hold, she'd forgotten it was possible. She moves faster and tries to tell herself it's just because she's on her own.

She is at the grove early. She slides behind one of the cypresses and leans against it, feeling her heart pound at the bark. The thing has followed her; it lets out its rising call, high up in the trees. She tries to get a look, but it's too fast, it's just the shadow of a long thin wing in the corner of her eye.

Chris is early too. Julia hears him coming a mile away, or at least she hopes to Jesus it's him, because otherwise something else the size of a deer is crashing down the paths like it doesn't care who hears. Her teeth are in the bark of the cypress and she tastes it on her tongue, acrid and wild.

Then he steps into the clearing. Tall and straight-backed, listening.

The moonlight changes him. Daytime, he's just another Colm's rugger-bugger, cute if you have cheap chain-restaurant tastes, charming if you like knowing every conversation before it begins. Here he's something more. He is beautiful the way something that lasts forever is beautiful.

It goes through Julia like the punch off an electric fence: he shouldn't be here. Chris Harper, half-witted teenage tit-hound, could come here and do his half-witted teenage tit-hound stuff and wander away safe and oblivious, no different from a mating fox or a spraying tomcat; the grove wouldn't shift a twig to take notice of something so small and so common, just doing what its kind do. But this boy: the grove has taken notice of him. This boy like white marble, lifted head, parted lips: the grove has a part for him to play.

Julia understands that the only smart thing to do here is get the fuck out. She is way out of her depth. Head very very quietly back to her bed, hope Chris thinks Selena was messing him around and flounces off in another snot. Hope the grove will allow him to walk back to his daytime self. Hope it all goes away.

It won't. What got her here hasn't changed: if she doesn't do this tonight, Selena will do it tomorrow, or next week, or the week after that.

Julia steps out onto the grass, and feels cold moonlight pour down her back. Behind her, the cypresses shiver into readiness.

Her movement sends Chris whirling towards her, bounding forward with his hands out, his face blazing up with what looks like sheer joy—the guy's even better than she thought, no wonder Lenie fell for it. When he sees who it isn't, he screeches to a stop like something in a cartoon.

"What are you doing here?" he demands.

"That's flattering," Julia says, before she can stop herself. She knows better than to be a smart-arse tonight. She knows exactly what to be; she's watched enough girls force themselves into the right shapes, pull the strings tighter till they can barely breathe. She does a lash-bat and giggle that's pure Joanne. "Who were you expecting?"

Chris shoves floppy fringe out of his face. "No one. None of your business. Are you meeting someone? Or what?"

His eyes are everywhere but on her, leaping to the path, to every rustle. All he wants from her is a fast exit, before Selena comes.

"I'm meeting *you*," Julia says, ducking her head coyly. "Hi."

"What are you talking about?"

"Hello? I'm the one who texted you?"

That gets Chris's attention. "Are you fucking serious?"

Julia does some combination of a shrug and a wiggle and a giggle.

Chris's head goes back and he moves, a tight fast circle around the clearing. He's furious with her, for not being Selena and for seeing that look on him, and Julia knows she should have planned for this.

She sends her voice up an octave, coaxing little whine, good and submissive to the big important boy. "Are you mad at me?"

"For fuck's *sake*."

"I'm sooo sorry for . . . you know. Fooling you. I just . . ." Julia tucks her head down and looks up at him sideways. Itsy-bitsy voice: "I wanted to meet you. In private. *You* know what I mean."

And just like that, Chris has stopped moving and he's looking at her. The edge has fallen off his anger; he's interested now.

"You could've just come up and talked to me. At the Court, or wherever. Like normal people do."

Julia pouts. "Excuse me, if you weren't so *popular*? There's always, like, literally a *queue* to get near you."

And there's the beginning of a gratified grin, at the corner of Chris's mouth. This is so easy, Julia can hardly believe it; suddenly she can see why everyone else has been doing it all along. "Sooo," she says, doing a boob-stretch. "Can we, like, sit down and talk?"

Chris says, suddenly wary, "How did you . . . ? That phone you texted me off. How did you . . . ?"

He wants to know if Selena was in on this. For a second, Julia considers letting him think she was. But then he might go off on Selena about it, and that would complicate everything. She goes with the truth, or part of it. "Me and Selena share a room. I found her phone and I read your texts."

"Whoa," Chris says. He steps back, hands going up. "You know about us?"

Julia does a winsome giggle. "I'm smart."

"Jesus," Chris says, face curling up in undisguised disgust. "Isn't she your friend? I mean, I know girls can be bitches, but this is, like, something special."

"You have no idea," Julia says. She doesn't bother to put a cutesy twist on it, and for a second Genius Boy's brow furrows, but before he can start to wonder if this is some elaborate scheme to take the piss out of him, she takes a condom out of her hoodie pocket and holds it up.

That knocks everything else out of Chris's head. His eyes pop. He was expecting a snog and a bra-based struggle. This never entered his mind. After a moment he says, "Seriously? I mean . . . like, we've talked, what, three times?"

Julia manages a giggle. "Come on. James Gillen must've told you about me. Right?"

Chris shrugs uncomfortably. "Well. Yeah. But James talks a load of bullshit. I thought you'd told him to get lost, and he was just being a prick."

For one second, Julia feels that shake her. Here she thought everyone believed shitty little James Gillen, and all the time Chris, the last guy she would ever have thought of— The creature calls a warning in the cypresses again and things pelt at her, if Chris was actually serious about Selena, meant the things he texted, if he was someone she might actually like instead of— They're chipping her away, battering her soft. Another second and she'll be cracking apart, gone.

She says, "James is a total prick. But he's not a total liar. Hello, it's the twenty-first century? Girls are actually allowed to like sex too? You're a babe, and I heard you're a great kisser. That's all I need to know. I'm not looking to *marry* you."

And Chris can't have been all that in love with Selena, after all, or else the condom has him hypnotized. He steps forward.

"Whoa, slow down there," Julia says, and flat-palms him, giving her nose a cute little scrunch to soften it. "Just one thing. I'm not sharing a guy with my best friend. I don't care who else you want to do, but starting now, Selena's off your menu. Deal?"

"Wha . . . ?" Most of Chris's mind is still on the condom, but his eyebrows pull together. "You said you didn't care that I was with her."

"Hey. Pay attention. I'm serious. If you try to play us both, I'll find out like *that*. I'm going to be watching Selena and watching that phone—I'll keep texting you off it, just so you know I'm not kidding. If you try anything cute, I'll tell Selena, and you'll never get another shot with either of us. But if you leave her alone—like, *alone* alone, no texts or anything—then every time we get a chance . . ."

Julia shakes the condom, dry little rattle in the air. In the end it turned out to be easy, getting away from the others down at the Court, where all the toilets have machines covered in pregnancy-related posters and graffiti. *Just going to the jacks back in a sec*, already moving away from the fountain, and gone before any of the others could stand up. Easy as that, escaping, if you wanted to. Just none of them had ever wanted to before.

Chris hasn't moved. Julia says, "Hello? Is there a problem? Because the only reason a guy's going to turn down a deal like this is if he's gay. Which I don't have a problem with, but you could at least *tell* me, so I can find someone else to play with."

He says, "I'm just not sure this is a good idea."

He knows something's wrong here. The poor bastard probably thinks he's going to figure out what. There aren't enough small words in the world. "Who cares?" Julia says. "It's not like you've got anything to lose: Selena doesn't want to see you ever again, or she'd have answered your texts. And anyway, even if you turn around and go home right now, I'm going to tell her we did it. So we might as well."

She gives Chris a big perky smile and unzips her hoodie. She can read every thought scrolling through his head, clear as print. She can see all the red-raw places where Selena used to be, the bruise-black hole where he thought she was going to be tonight, the bright flashes of him hating Selena and every girl he's been with and Julia most of all. She can see the moment when he decides. He smiles back at her and reaches out a hand for the condom.

Julia knows what to expect. The wind in the cypresses rising to a roar like a hunting pack, the warning call screaming across the black sky. The clearing heaving and rolling under her. The moon smashing to shards, the sharpest of them all arrowing down to rip her open from groin to throat, the smell of hot dark blood spilling from deep inside. The pain, bright enough to blind her forever.

Nothing happens. The clearing is just a patch of prissily trimmed grass; the cypresses are just trees that some gardener figured would be low maintenance. The calling sound is still circling, but all the spookiness has leached out of it; it's just some bird, yelping mindlessly because that's all it knows how to do. Even the pain is nothing special, just a dull unemphatic rasp. Julia shifts her arse off a sharp pebble and grimaces over Chris's bobbing shoulder. The moon has flattened to a disk of paper pasted to the sky, lightless.

25

I stood there in the corridor, just stood, my stupid gob hanging open and a big cartoon bubble saying "!!??!!" bouncing over my fat head. Stood till I copped that Mackey or Conway might come out and find me there. Then I moved. Past the Secret Place, cards jostling and hissing. Down the stairs. Caught myself moving slow and careful, like I'd taken a kicking and something hurt like fuck, if I could work out where.

The foyer was dark, I had to grope my way to the main door. It felt heavier or the strength had gone out of me, I had to lean my shoulder on it and heave, feet slipping on the tiles, picturing Mackey watching and grinning from the stairs. I half fell outside sweating. Let the door slam behind me. I didn't know any other way back into the school, but I wasn't going to need one.

I thought about ringing a taxi to take me home. The picture of Mackey and Conway coming out and finding me gone, flounced off to have a little cry on my pillow, turned me red in the twilight. I left my phone in my pocket.

Twenty to ten, and nearly dark. Outdoor lights were on, turning the grass whitish without actually illuminating it, doing strange eye-bending things in among the trees. I looked at that tree line and saw it the way the sixth-years had to see it, outline sharpened to slicing by the knowledge that it was about to sift away down the sky like a flower-fall, out of view. Something that would be there forever and ever; for other people, not for me. I was almost gone.

I picked my way down the steps—that light turned them depthless, treacherous—and started walking, along the front of the school and down the side of the boarders' wing. My feet crunched in pebbles, and that morning's jumpy reflex—head turning, checking for the gamekeeper siccing the hounds on the unwashed—was back.

I scrabbled through the mess for something good somewhere, couldn't find it. Told myself if Mackey was right about Conway—course he was, Mackey has something on everyone, no need to invent it—then she had just done me a favor: better out than in. I told myself I'd be relieved in the morning, when I wasn't wrecked and starving, when I hadn't used up everything I had. Told myself in the morning I wouldn't feel like something priceless had landed in my hand, been robbed away and smashed before I could close my fingers.

Couldn't make it stick. Cold Cases waiting for me outside these walls and Mackey had been right, the smirky fucker: now I was the kid who couldn't hack twelve hours in the big leagues, and he and Conway between them would make sure everyone knew that. Cold Cases had looked so shiny to me, my first day, such a wide glittering sweep of step up. Now it looked like a dingy dead end. This here, this was what I wanted. One day, and gone.

The only smudge of silver lining I could come up with: it was almost over. Even before Mackey's backstabbing break, we'd been starting to go in circles. If he didn't pull the plug soon, Conway would. I just had to wait out the last of their patience, then I could go home and try to forget today had ever happened. I'd've only loved to be one of those blokes who drink till days like this dissolve. Better: one of those blokes who texts his mates, days like this, *Pub.* Feels their circle click closed around him.

Everyone knows a wife and kids tie you down. What people miss somehow is that mates, the proper kind, they do the same just as hard. Mates mean you've settled, made your bargain: this, wherever you are together, this is as far as you're going, ever. This is your stop; this is where you get off.

Not just where you are: they tie you down to who you are. Once you have mates who know you, right down under the this-and-that you decide people want to see today, then there's no room left for the someday person who'll magic you into being all your finest dreams. You've turned solid: you're the person your mates know, forever.

You like things to be beautiful, Conway had said, and been right. Over my own dead body was I going to stake myself down somewhere, being someone, that didn't have all the beautiful I could cram into me. For ugly I could've stayed where I started, got myself a career on the dole and a wife who hated my guts and a dozen snot-faced brats and a wall-sized telly playing twenty-four-seven shows about people's intestines. Call me arrogant, uppity, me the council-house kid thinking I deserved more. I'd been swearing it since before I was old enough to understand the thought: I was going to be more.

If I had to get there without friends, I could do it. Had been doing it. I'd never met anyone who brought me somewhere I wanted to stay, looked at me and saw someone I wanted to be for good; anyone who was worth giving up the more I wanted down the line.

It landed inside me then, there under the dead weight of the shadow of Kilda's, too late. That light I had seen on Holly and her mates, so bright it hurt, the rare thing I had come into that school looking to find and to envy: I had thought it came to them showering down with the echoes from high ceilings, reflected onto them in the glow of old wood. I had been wrong. It had come from them. From the way they gave things up for each other, stripped branches off their futures and set them ablaze. What had felt like beautiful to me on the other side of today, balustrades and madrigals, those were nothing. I had been missing the heart of it, all along.

Mackey had taken one sniff of me, known the whole story. Seen me in school turning down a spliff and a laugh, in case getting caught cost me my chance at getting out; seen me at training college, big friendly smile and vague excuse to wander away from the big friendly guys who were going to be in uniform for life. Watched me fuck Kennedy over, and known exactly what was missing out of a person who would do that.

And Conway must have smelled it off me too. All day, when I'd been thinking how we clicked, thinking we were getting on like a house on fire. Thinking against my own will that this tasted like something brand-new.

Out the back of the school. Clusters of dark shapes tossed across the green-white grass, restless and stirring, for a moment my eye went wild trying to make sense of them—I thought big cats released for the night, thought another art project, thought ghosts got loose from Holly's model school—before one threw back her head, floodlight glossing long hair, and laughed. The boarders. Conway had told McKenna to let them out before bedtime. McKenna had been smart enough to do it.

Rustles under the trees, a shake in the hedge. They were everywhere, watching me. A trio on the grass glanced across, chins turning over shoulders, huddled in tight to whisper. Another laugh, this one fired straight at me.

Half an hour, maybe, till someone called time on the interview and I got to hunch in Conway's passenger seat like a kid caught spray-painting, for the long silent drive home. Spend that half hour standing here like a spare prick, with teenage girls giving me the sideways once-over and the snide commentary: bollix to that. Do a legger back round to the front of the school like this lot had terrified me off, hang around hoping no one would see me waiting for the big kids to give me my lift home: bollix to that, too.

"And fuck Conway anyway," I said, out loud, not loud enough for any of the glancing girls to hear. If we weren't working together, then I was flying solo.

I didn't know where to start looking. I didn't have to: they called to me. Voices out of the black-and-white dazzle, untwisting themselves from the breeze-rustles and the bats: *Detective, Detective Moran! Over here!* Silvery, gauzy, everywhere and nowhere. I turned like blindman's buff. Heard giggles whirl like moths among the leaves.

Off in the tree-shadows, across the slope of lawn: pale flutters, hands waving, beckoning. *Detective Stephen come here come here!* I went, weaving between the watching eyes. Could've been anyone, I would've gone.

They grew outlines and features out of nothing, like Polaroids. Gemma, Orla, Joanne. Propped on their elbows, legs stretched out, hair hanging to the grass behind them. Smiling.

I smiled back. That I could do, at least. That I was great at. Beat Conway any day.

"Did you miss us?" Gemma. Neck arched.

"Here," Joanne said. Shifted closer to Gemma, patted the grass where she'd been. "Come talk to us."

I knew to run. I had better sense than to be in a lit room alone with Holly Mackey, never mind out here with these three. But them looking at me like they actually wanted me around, that made a nice change; that was sweet as cool water on burns.

"Are we allowed to call you Detective Stephen?"

"Duh, what's he going to do, arrest us?"

"You'd probably enjoy it. Handcuffs—"

"Can we? Your card said Stephen Moran."

"What about Detective Steve?"

"Ew, please! That's like a porn name."

I kept smiling, kept my mouth shut. They were different, out in the wild and the night. Skittery, slanty-glanced, swaying with breezes I couldn't feel. Powerful. I knew I was outnumbered, back of my neck, the way you know it when three guys with a bad walk roll around the corner and pick up the pace towards you.

"Come on. We're bored." Joanne, crossed ankles rocking. "Keep us company."

I sat down. The grass was soft, springy. The air under the trees smelled richer, seething with spores and pollen.

"What are you doing still here?" Gemma wanted to know. "Are you staying here tonight?"

"Um, duh, exactly where would he stay?" Joanne, rolling her eyes.

"Gems wants him to share with her." Orla, giggling hard.

"Hello? Was I asking you?" No being a bitch around here without Joanne's say-so. "It's not like he could share with you, anyway. He'd have to be like a *midget* to fit in with your massive fat thighs."

Orla cringed. Joanne laughed: "OhmyGod, you should see your face! Chill out, it was a joke, ever heard of them?" Orla cringed smaller.

Gemma ignoring them, eyeing me, corner of smile. "He could share with Sister Cornelius. Make her night."

"She'd bite it off him. Offer it up to the Child of Prague."

Three feet deeper into the trees, we would've been in darkness. Here in the borderlands the light was mixed and moving, edges of moonlight, over-spill from the lawn floodlights. It did things to their faces. That throwaway cheapness that had turned my stomach earlier, all artificial colorings and flavorings: it didn't look throwaway now, not out here. It looked harder, chilled to something solid and waxy. Mysterious.

I said, "We'll be heading soon. Just finishing up a few things."

"It talks." Gemma, smiling wider. "I thought you were giving us the silent treatment."

Joanne said, "You don't look like you're finishing anything up."

"Taking a break."

She smirked like she knew better. "Did you get in trouble with Detective Bitchface?"

To them I wasn't a detective any more, big bad authority. I was something else: something to play with, play for, dance for. Strange thing dropped into their midst out of the sky, who knew what it might do, what it might mean. They were circling me.

I said, "Not that I know of."

"OhmyGod, her *attitude*? It's like, hello, just because you managed to save up for one suit that isn't from Penney's, it doesn't *actually* make you queen of the world?"

Gemma said, "Do you have to work with her all the time? Or sometimes, if you're good, do they let you work with someone who doesn't eat live hamsters for fun?"

All of them laughing, beckoning me or daring me to laugh back. I heard the small dull thud of Conway closing the door in my face. Watched those three faces dancing, every spark of it all for me.

I laughed. I said, "Jesus, have a heart. She's not my partner. I'm only working with her for the day."

Pretend collapses from relief, all of them fanning themselves: "Phew! OhmyGod, we were wondering how you survived, like if you were on *Prozac . . .*"

I said, "Another few days of this and I will be." We laughed harder. "That's one reason I'm out here. I needed a chat and a laugh with people who won't have my head melted."

They liked that. Arched like cats, gratified. Orla—she bounced back fast; used to getting hit—she said, "We decided you're a way better detective than her."

"Lick-arse," said Gemma.

"It's true, though," said Joanne. Eyes on me. "Someone should tell your boss that Whatshername being such a B means she can't actually do her job. She'd get a lot further if she had some basic *manners*. When she asks a question, it's like, whoa, anyone got a lump of raw meat to throw, and maybe it'll back off?"

Orla said, "We wouldn't tell her the *time* unless we had to."

"When you ask us stuff," Joanne said, and twisted her head to one side to smile at me, "we *want* to talk to you."

Last time I talked to her, we hadn't been best buds, not like this. They wanted something from me, wanted to give me something, I couldn't tell which. I said, sniffing my way, "Glad to hear it. You've been a lot of help to me so far; I don't know what I'd've done without you."

"We like helping you."

"We'd be your spies any day."

"Undercover."

"We've got your phone number. We could text you anything suspicious we see."

I said, "If you seriously want to give me a hand, you know how. You three, I'd say you know everything that happens in this school. Anything that could have to do with Chris, I'd only love to hear it."

Orla hunching forward, glint of moonlight on her wet mouth: "Who's in the art room?"

A zap of "Shhh!" from Joanne. Orla shrank back.

Gemma, amused: "Oops. Too late." To me: "We weren't going to just *ask* like that."

"But since Genius here did," said Joanne. Leaned back, throat arching. Pointed. "Who's that?"

The art room, a flare of chilly white across the heavy slab of the school. Above it the stone balustrade was silhouetted against the sky, a ghost's walk, black on near-black. In one window the wire school soared. In the next one was Mackey, slouching back, arms folded.

"That," Joanne said.

I said, "Another detective."

"Ooo." Wrist-shake, mocking eyes. "I knew you'd got thrown out."

"Sometimes we change things up while we're working. Keep everyone fresh."

"Who're they talking to?"

"Is it Holly Mackey?"

"We *told* you they were weird."

The glow on their faces, all eager and fascinated. Like I could be the one thing they'd been hoping to see. It made you want to be that, everything they were looking for, all at the same time. Chris Harper must have wanted the same thing.

Up in the art room, Conway strolled across the window, all long stride and sharp shoulders. I said, "Yeah. It's Holly." Conway would've eaten the head off me; fuck Conway.

Hiss of in-breath. Glances circling, but I couldn't catch them as they zipped past.

Orla breathed, "Did she kill Chris?"

"OhmyGod."

"Here was us thinking it was Groundskeeper Willy."

"Well, up until today we did."

"But once you started asking us and them all those questions—"

"Obviously we knew it wasn't *us*—"

"But we didn't think—"

"It was *Holly Mackey*?"

I would've only loved to have an answer for them. See their mouths pop open and their eyes go wide, see them overwhelmed by me, The Man, pulling out fountains of answers like a magician. I said, "We don't know who killed Chris. We're working hard on finding out."

"But who do you *think*?" Joanne wanted to know.

Holly, slouched at that table, all blue eyes and bite and something hidden. Maybe Mackey had been right, not wanting her talking. Maybe he had been right and she would've talked to me.

I shook my head. "Not my job." Skeptical looks. "Seriously. I can't go around with an idea stuck in my head, not till I've got evidence."

"Ahh." She pouted. "That's so not fair. Here you're asking us to—"

"OhmyGod!" Orla, shooting upright, clapping a hand over her mouth. "You don't think it was *Alison*, do you?"

"Is that where she is?"

"Is she under *arrest*?"

They were openmouthed. "No," I said. "She's just a bit upset. The thing with Chris's ghost, that got to her."

"Well, hello, yeah? It got to *all* of us, actually?" Joanne, cold: I'd forgotten to put her top of the list. Bad boy.

"Bet it did," I said, good and awed. "Did you see him?"

Joanne remembered to shiver. "Course I did. Probably he came back to talk to me. He was looking straight at me."

It hit me then: every girl who had seen Chris's ghost would've sworn the same. He had been looking at her. He had come because he wanted something from her, only her.

"Like I told you"—Joanne had her bereaved face on again—"if he hadn't died, we would've been together again. I think he wants me to know he still cares."

"Ahhh." Orla, head to one side.

I asked her, "Did you see him?"

Her hand shot to her chest. "OhmyGod, yes! I almost had a heart attack. He was literally right there. I swear."

I said, "Gemma?"

Gemma shifted on the grass. "I don't know. I'm not sure about ghosts."

Joanne said, an edge on it, "Excuse me, I know what I saw?"

"I'm not saying that. I'm just saying *I* didn't see him. I saw like a blur in the window, like when you get something sticky in your eye. That's it."

"Well. Some people are more *sensitive* than others. And some people were *closer* to Chris. Excuse me if I don't think it actually matters what you saw."

Gemma shrugged. Joanne said, to me, "He was there."

I couldn't tell whether she meant it. Back in the common room, I would've sworn all their terror was real: started as playacting, maybe, for notice or to blow off steam, but then snowballed into something too big and too true for them to control. But now, the shiver, the face on her, I couldn't tell; could've been just that plastic layer over her, blurring whatever was real underneath; could've been plastic straight through. Probably even they didn't know.

I said, "Then that's another reason why, whatever you know, you need to tell me. Chris would want you to."

"How would we know anything?" Joanne, blank and slick as cellophane. They were giving up nothing till I earned it.

But I knew the answer to that one. After Selena and Chris broke up, Joanne had posted her guard dogs on night watch, to make sure.

I said, "Let's say someone other than Selena was meeting up with Chris at night, the couple of weeks before he died. Who would you say it was?"

Joanne's face didn't change. "Was there someone?"

"I'm only saying *if*. Who would you guess?"

Sliding looks at each other, under their lashes. If the fear had ever been real, it had leaked out of them. Something else had risen, forced it out: power.

Joanne said, "Tell us if he was meeting someone, and we'll tell you something good."

I said I know my shot when I see it. Sometimes you don't even have to see it. Sometimes you feel it coming, screaming down the sky towards you like a meteor.

I said, "He was, yeah. We've found texts between them."

More looks. Gemma said, "Texts like what?"

"Texts arranging meetings."

"But there wasn't any name?"

"No," I said. "It wasn't one of you, was it?"

Joanne said sharply, "No. It wasn't." Didn't say, *Or she'd've been in deep shit*. We all heard it.

"But you've got a fair idea who it might've been."

And I waited to hear *Holly Mackey*.

Joanne stretched out on her back, arms behind her head, arching her chest up. Said, "Tell us what you think about Rebecca O'Mara."

Took my ear a second even to hear the question, past the burst of *what-thefuck?* Then I slammed my jaw shut and thought fast—there had to be a right answer. Said, "I haven't thought about her much at all, to tell you the truth."

Skitter of hooded glances, little smirks. Good answer.

Joanne said, "Because she's sooo totally *harmless*."

"Such a *good* girl," Orla breathed.

"So *pure*."

"So *shy*."

"I bet she acted like she was totally terrified of you, right?" Joanne dipping her head, doing fake-simpery doe-eyes up at me. "Rebecca'd never do anything bold. She's probably never even had a sip of booze in her life. Never even OMG *looked* at a guy."

Gemma laughed, low.

I said, "That's not true, no?" My heart was starting a slow hard pound, jungle drums, carrying a message.

"Well, I don't know if she's ever had booze—I mean, who cares. But she's looked at a guy, all right."

Orla sniggered. "You should've *seen* the way she looked at him. It was pathetic."

I said, "Chris Harper."

Slowly, Joanne started to smile. She said, "Ding. You win the prize."

Orla said, "Rebecca was *gooey* for Chris."

I said, "And you think in the end they got together?"

Joanne's lip curled. "OMG, excuse me while I barf? No *way*. She was on a total loser there. Chris could've had anyone he wanted; he wasn't going to go near some boring stick insect. They could've been stuck on a desert *island* and he'd've literally found a better-looking *coconut* to shag."

I said, "So that means she wasn't the one meeting him. Right? Or . . . ?"

The looks strobing again. "Well," Joanne said. "Not for *looove*. And not for you-know-what, either. She probably wouldn't even know *how*."

"For what, then?"

Titters. Orla sucking in her bottom lip. They weren't going to say it unless I did first.

That meteor, howling closer. All I had to do was get in the right place, hold out my hands.

That morning. Smell of chalk and grass; me tying myself in knots like a balloon animal, trying to make myself into whatever eight different girls and Conway wanted—lot of good that had done me. Joanne, lip pulled up: *I guess you think they're all such angels, they'd never do drugs. I mean, God, Rebecca, she's just so innocent . . .*

I said, "Drugs."

A change. I felt them tense up, waiting while I fumbled my way into place.

"Rebecca was on drugs."

A hysterical giggle burst out of Orla. Joanne smiled at me, teacher at a good boy. Ordered, "Tell him."

After a moment Gemma sat up. Folded her legs under her, picked bits of grass off her tights. She said, "You're not recording this or anything, are you?"

"No."

"Good, because this is totally off-the-record. Like, if you ever tell anyone I said any of this, I'm going to say it's all bullshit and you made it up to get back in Detective Dildo's good books."

Like I was a journalist. I was halfway through thinking *naïve* when she added, "And my dad'll ring your boss and tell him the same thing. Which, trust me, you don't want."

Not so naïve. I said, "Not a problem."

Joanne said, "Go on. Tell him."

"Well," Gemma said. Touched her tongue to her top lip, but it was autopilot, buying time while she got her head straight. "OK. You know about Ro, right? Ronan, who used to be a groundskeeper here?"

"You guys arrested him," Orla put in helpfully. She was bright-eyed, loving it. "For selling drugs."

I said, "I know the story, yeah."

Gemma said, "He dealt a *lot* of stuff. Like, mostly hash and E, but if you wanted something else, he could usually get it."

Still messing with bits of grass snagged in her tights. I couldn't tell for sure in the flexing light, but it looked like she'd gone red.

Joanne said, "Gems's diet wasn't exactly working." Gave Gemma's waist a malicious little pinch.

"I just wanted to lose like a couple more pounds. Big deal; doesn't everyone? So I asked Ronan if he could get me something to help."

Flicker of a glance, Gemma looking for something from me, badly scared of not getting it. I said, hoping, "Must've worked. You definitely don't need to be losing any weight now."

Relief curving her mouth. This was a whole other world: admitting you had hassle getting thin was scarier than telling a cop you'd bought speed. "Yeah, well. Whatever. Anyway. How you bought stuff from Ronan was, right, Wednesday and Friday afternoons he was the only groundskeeper on shift, so you went down to the shed after school and you hung around outside till you saw him. Then you went in and he got the stuff out of this cupboard. You totally weren't supposed to go into the shed unless you saw him there; he said he'd bar you if he caught you inside on your own. I guess in case someone robbed his stash."

Joanne and Orla were wiggling themselves along the grass, in closer to me. Openmouthed, starry-eyed.

"So this one Wednesday," Gemma said, "it's pissing rain, and I go down and I can't see Ro. I wait under the trees for a while, but in the end, come *on*, I'm not going to stand there all day freezing my nips off? So I head into the shed. I figure Ronan can just deal with it. He knew me by then; I wasn't some randomer."

Shiver from the other two, anticipating.

Gemma said, "And there's Rebecca O'Mara. Like, the *last* person you'd expect? She jumped a mile—I swear to God I thought she was going to faint. I start laughing and I'm like, 'Oh my God, what are *you* doing here? Looking for your crack fix?' "

Swirl of laughter, in the dark teeming air.

"Rebecca's all, 'Oh, I was just getting out of the rain,' and I'm there, 'Yeah, OK.' The school's like half a minute away, and she's wearing her coat and her hat, meaning she actually deliberately came out *into* the rain. And if she's so shy, how come she's hiding somewhere she's going to run into big scary groundskeepers?"

Gemma had herself back. The story was coming out easy, confident. It sounded true. "So I go, 'Planning on doing some gardening?'—there were all these shovels and stuff in the corner where she was; she had one of them in her hand, like she'd grabbed it when I came in, in case I was a psycho rapist and she had to fight me off. And she actually goes, 'Um, um, I guess, sort of, I was thinking about—' till I decide to put her out of her misery. I'm there, 'Puh-*lease*, you didn't think I was serious?' And she just stares at me for a moment, like, *Bwuh?* and then she goes, 'I have to go,' and she runs out into the rain and heads back to the school."

She must have put down the shovel, before she ran out. Shovel, or spade, or hoe. Left it there to come back for, now she knew what she wanted.

The meteor in the palm of my hand. Beautiful. Burning me through, with a welcome white fire.

If there was anything in my face, the tricky light would hide it for me. I made sure my voice stayed easy. "Did Ronan see her?"

Shrug from Gemma. "Don't think so. He didn't get there till a few minutes later—he'd been waiting somewhere for the rain to ease off. He was kind of pissed off that I was inside, but he got over it." Smile, reminiscent.

Joanne was close to me. "See? All that pure-and-innocent stuff, that is ohmyGod such *crap*. Everyone else totally falls for it, but we knew *you* wouldn't."

I said, "Did Ronan sell anything else besides drugs? Booze? Cigarettes?" Sometimes they'd had the odd smoke, Holly had said; and the packet hidden in Julia's bit of wardrobe. Rebecca could still have had an innocent reason for being in that shed; guilty kind of innocent, but innocent all the same.

Gemma snorted. "Right. And fizzy lollies."

Orla was giggling. "Phone credit."

"Mascara."

"Tights."

"Tampax."

That exploded the two of them, shrieking laughter, Orla fell over backwards onto the grass kicking her legs up. Joanne cut through it. Coldly: "He wasn't a *supermarket*. Rebecca wasn't buying chocolate chip cookies."

Gemma got herself together. "Yeah. He just sold the bad stuff." Lascivious curl on *bad*. "I'd love to know what she actually was buying."

Joanne shrugged. "Not diet pills, anyway. Unless she's anorexic, and I don't think she even has enough self-respect to bother. She doesn't even wear makeup."

"Probably hash." Orla, knowing.

"What kind of loser does hash by herself? OhmyGod, that's so *sad*."

"She could've been buying for all four of them."

"Hello, like they'd send *her*? If they were all in on it, they'd send Julia or Holly. Rebecca was there because *she* wanted something."

"Ro's hot body."

"Ew ew ew, pass the brain bleach?"

They were on the edge of getting the giggles again. I said, "When was this?"

That brought them back. Quick spatter of glances under their lashes. Joanne said, "We were wondering when you'd ask."

"Last spring?"

Another fizzle of glances. Gemma said, "The next night, Chris got killed."

A second of silence, while that spread up and out, into the branches.

"*So*," Joanne said. "See?"

I saw.

"You said someone was meeting up with Chris, after him and Selena broke up. Like I told you, no way would he meet up with Rebecca O'Mara because he was *into* her. But if she was buying something for him? She would totally have done it; she would've done anything for him. And he would've met up to get it. He might even have thrown her the odd charity snog, give her something to dream about."

Orla's snuffly laugh.

I said, "Did you ever see Rebecca going out on her own at night?"

"No. So? We stopped watching the corridor like *weeks* before Chris got killed."

Chris's tox screen had come back clean, Conway had said. No drugs in his gear.

"And then," Joanne said. Sliding in closer, her legs brushing up against mine. I couldn't see her eyes, through the floodlights glittering on their surfaces. "Maybe Rebecca thought they were like *together* or something. And when she found out they weren't . . ."

Moths whirling, out over the lawn.

I said, carefully, "Rebecca's only a little thing. Chris was a big strong guy. You think she could've . . . ?"

Gemma said, "She's a stroppy cow, is what she is, when she feels like it. If he really pissed her off . . ."

"The papers said head injuries," Joanne said. "If he was sitting down, then it wouldn't matter that she was smaller than him."

Orla said, practically lifting up off the grass with the thrill, "She could've hit him with a *rock*."

"Ew." Joanne, reproving. "We don't actually know it was a rock. The papers never said." And looked at me, question marks popping out all over. Gemma and Orla watched too, eager, bubbling with curiosity.

Not faking. None of them knew about the hoe.

More than that: no shake in their voices, no shadow sliding under their faces, when they talked about the moment that had robbed Chris Harper's life away. They could've been talking about cheating on an exam. Till then, one snip of me had wondered if they were making up the Rebecca story to steer me away from one of them, but no. None of these had ever touched murder.

I said, "That's great. Thanks a million for telling me." Smiled at them all.

"I wasn't about to say it in front of Detective Bitchface," Gemma said. "I'd probably be in jail right now. You're not going to get me in trouble, right? Because like I said—"

"No trouble. I might ask you to give me a statement at some stage, if I really need one—no, hang on, it won't get you in hassle. You can just say you went into the shed to get out of the rain, which is true, right? You won't need to explain why you were outside to start with. Yeah?"

Gemma didn't look convinced. Joanne didn't care about her. Leaning closer, fizzing with excitement: "So you think Rebecca *did it*. Right? That's what you think."

I said, "I think I'd like to know what Rebecca was doing in there. That's all."

Knelt up, dusted dirt and grass off my trousers. Kept it casual, but I was rattling with it, how badly I wanted to shoot up off that grass and leg it. I could have Rebecca. I could grope my way through streaks of light and whirling moths till I found her and Julia and Selena, dark eyes watching for me out of the dark under cypresses. I could ring the locals for a marked car and a social worker and have Rebecca in an interview room before Conway let go her pit-bull grab on Holly. If I worked it just right and kept my phone off, I could have a confession on O'Kelly's desk before Conway tracked me down. By morning I could be the hotshot who, in twelve hours, had solved the big one that had stumped Conway for a year.

Joanne said, "Stay and talk with us. We'll have to go inside soon anyway; you can go talk to boring Rebecca then."

"Yeah," Orla said. "We're way more interesting than her."

For a second I thought—the stupid swelled head on me—they might still be scared, want the big strong man to protect them. But they were comfy as cats on the grass. All the fear had run right out of them, once they were the powerful ones taking me where they wanted me, to whisper their saved-up secret in my ear.

I said, smiling, "I'd say you are, all right. But I'd better get this sorted out."

Joanne pouted. "We helped you. Now that you've got what you want off us, you're just going to dump us and run?"

"Typical guy," said Gemma, up to the branches, shaking her head.

Joanne said, "I told you before. I don't let guys treat me like crap."

Some first warning got to me, through the *Go go go* drumming in my ears. I said, "I'm under a bit of time pressure, is all. It's not that I don't appreciate what you've done for me. Believe me."

Joanne said, "Then stay." Lifted one finger and laid it on my knee. Cute nose-wrinkle smile, like a joke, but half a second too late. Orla sucked in breath, shocked, and giggled it out.

Somehow I stopped myself from leaping and running. If I fucked up now, I was fucked a dozen ways.

Gemma said, "Don't look so terrified. We're fun. Honest."

Smiling at me, her too. It looked friendly, but she was written in a code I couldn't begin to read. They all were. That bad-alleyway prickle that had faded for a bit, while they had me busy feeling like something they wanted and loving it; that was rising hard up the back of my neck again.

Joanne's fingernail ran an inch higher up my thigh. All of them giggling, tongues nipped between sharp little teeth. It was a game, and I was part of it, but I couldn't tell what part. I tried laughing. They laughed back.

"So," Joanne said. Another inch. "Talk to us."

Smack her hand away, leg it back to the school like my arse was on fire, bang on the art-room door and beg Conway to let me back in if I promised to be good. Instead I said, "Let's think this through for a second. Shall we?"

Put on my stuffiest voice. Thought teacher, thought McKenna, thought everything they didn't want. Picked them out one by one, looking them in the eye, separating them out: not triple and dangerous; just schoolgirls being very silly.

"Gemma, I realize that it took a lot of courage for you to give me this information. And Joanne, I realize that Gemma probably wouldn't have plucked up that courage without your support—and yours, Orla. So, after you've gone to considerable trouble to bring me this potentially valuable material, I'm not inclined to waste it."

They were looking at me like I'd gone flash-bang and turned two-headed. Joanne's finger had stopped moving.

"If I don't have an opportunity to interview Rebecca O'Mara before all of you students are called inside, then I'll have to liaise with Detective Conway, and I'll have no option but to bring her into the loop. I assume you gave me this information because you wanted me to utilize it. Not because you wanted to hand the credit for any results to Detective Conway. Am I correct?"

Three identical pairs of eyes, staring. Not a move, not a blink.

"Orla? Am I correct?"

"What? Um, yeah? I guess?"

"Very good. Gemma?"

Nod.

"Joanne?"

Finally, finally, a shrug, and her hand came off my leg. Conway's smack-down, way back in the art room, was paying off. "Whatever."

"Then I think we're all agreed." I handed out a thin smile for each of them. "Our top priority is for me to speak to Rebecca. Our chat will have to wait."

Nothing. Just those eyes, still staring.

I stood up, evenly, no sudden moves. Brushed myself down, straightened my jacket. Then I turned around and walked away.

It was like turning my back on jaguars. Every inch of me was waiting for the claws, but nothing came. Behind me I heard Joanne say, pompous and pitched just loud enough for me to hear, "*Potentially valuable material*," and a triple spurt of giggles. Then I was out, on the endless white-green lawn.

My heart was going like bongos. That drunken dizzy rushed up and over me; I wanted to let my knees fold, sink down on the cool grass.

I didn't do it. Not just the watchers all round. What I had told the three of them was true: somewhere out there, in the dapple of black and white and murmurs, was Rebecca. She was now or never.

It was exactly what Conway would expect out of me. It was what Mackey would put money on.

The white glare of the art room, staring down at me. Laughter, joyful, somewhere far away among the trees.

I owed Conway fuck-all. I'd brought her the key to her make-or-break case, she'd used me while I was useful and then kicked me out of the car going ninety.

The moon pinwheeling above the school. I felt like I was dissolving, fingers and toes sifting away.

She was everything Mackey had warned me about. She was the lifetime kibosh on my daydream partner, the one with the red setters and the violin lessons. She was edge and trouble, everything I had always wanted far from.

I know my shot when I see it. I saw it bright as day.

I found my phone.

Text, not ring. If Conway saw my number come up, she'd think I wanted to whinge about the wait; she'd let it ring out.

I could feel something happening to me. A change.

Message icon on my screen. Conway, a few minutes back, while I'd been too busy to notice. She must have pulled the plug, or Mackey had. I was just in time.

Got anything yet? Stalling him long as I can but lights out is 1045 get a move on

"What the *fuck*," I said out loud.

The grin came on top of it, grin like my face was splitting open and every color of light bursting out.

Idiot, me, supersize idiot and I could've punched myself in the head for it. For a second there I forgot all about Rebecca, didn't care.

Go for a nice walk, admire the grounds, Conway had said to me outside the door of the art room. *See if you can get Chris's ghost to pop up for you.* Meaning *Get outside and talk to those girls, stir them up as hard as you can, see what you can get out of them.* Clear as day, if I'd been looking. I'd been

so busy staring at how Mackey could've used me to fuck me up, I'd missed
what she was waving in front of my face.

Conway had trusted me: not just trusted me through all Mackey's doom-
peddling, but trusted me to know she would. I could've punched myself all
over again for not doing the same for her. Made my stomach turn cold, how
close I had come to too late.

I texted her back. *Meet me out the front. Urgent. Don't let Mackey come.*

26

May comes in restless, fizzing in the warm air. Summer is almost close enough to touch and so are the exams, and the whole of third year is wound too tight, laughing too loud at nothing and exploding into ornate arguments full of slammed desks and tears in the toilets. The moon pulls strange hues out of the sky, a tinge of green you can only see from the corner of your eye, a bruised violet.

It's the second of May. Chris Harper has two weeks left to live.

Holly can't sleep. Selena still has her fake headache, and Julia is being a bitch; when Holly tried to talk to her about whatever's up with Lenie, Julia blew her off so viciously that they're still only kind of speaking. The bedroom is too hot, overintimate heat that sends waves of itch across your skin. Things feel wrong and getting wronger, they twist and pull at the edges, drag the fabric of her all askew.

She gets up to go to the toilet, not because she needs to but because she can't lie still another second. The corridor is dim and even hotter than their room. Holly is halfway down it and thinking cold water when the shadow of a doorway convulses, only a foot or two away. She leaps back against the wall and grabs a breath ready to yell, but then Alison Muldoon's head shoots openmouthed out of the shadow, vanishes in a burst of urgent squeaky noises, and pops back out again.

"Jesus!" Holly hisses. "You almost gave me a heart attack! What is your *problem?*"

"OhmyGod, it's *you*, I thought— *Jo!*" And she's gone again.

By this point Holly is getting curious. She waits and listens; the rest of the corridor is silent, everyone deep under the weight of the night.

After a minute Joanne appears in the doorway, frizz-haired and wearing pale-pink pajamas that say OOH BABY across the chest. "Um, that's Holly

Mackey?" she snaps, examining Holly like something in a display case. "Are you retarded or what? I was *asleep*."

"Her *hair*," Alison bleats, just above a whisper, behind her. "I just saw her hair, and I thought—"

"OhmyGod, they're both blond, so is like everybody? Holly doesn't look anything like her. Holly's *thin*."

Which is the biggest compliment Joanne knows. She smiles at Holly, and rolls her eyes so they can share a laugh at how thick Alison is.

The thing about Joanne is you never can tell. Today she could be your snuggled-up best friend, and she'll get all wounded if you don't play along. It puts you at a disadvantage: she knows who she's dealing with; you have to figure it out from scratch, every time. She makes Holly's calf muscles go twitchy.

Holly says, "Who did she think I was?"

"She came out of the right room," Alison whines.

"Which means she was going the wrong way, duh," Joanne says. "Who cares if she goes to the loo? We care if she goes out. Which, hello, is *that* way?" Alison chews a knuckle and keeps her head down.

Holly says, "You thought I was Selena? Going out*side*?"

"*I* didn't. Because *I'm* not retarded."

Holly looks at Joanne's tight face, too hard for the cutesy pajamas, and it occurs to her that Joanne is kicking Alison because she's some strange combination of relieved and disappointed. Which is crazy. She says, feeling her way, "Where would Selena be going?"

"Don't you wish you knew?" Joanne says, tossing Alison a smirk. Alison lets out an obedient sharp giggle, too loud. "Shut *up*! Do you actually want to get us caught?"

Holly's heartbeat is changing, turning deeper and violent. She says, "Selena doesn't go out on her own. Only when we all do."

"OhmyGod, you guys are so *cute*," Joanne says, with a nose-crinkle that doesn't thaw her eyes. "All this blood-sisters-tell-each-other-everything stuff; it's like an old TV show. Did you actually do the blood-sisters thing? Because that would be so totes adorbs I could just die."

Not bessie mates, not tonight. "Just give me a sec," Holly says. If Joanne shows you her teeth, you bite first and hard. "I'm trying to look like I actually care what you think about us."

Joanne stares, hand on her hip, in the thin dirty light. Holly catches the moment when she starts seeing a more interesting football than Alison. "If you're such perfect little buddies," she says, "how come you don't know where your friend goes at night?"

Holly reminds herself that Joanne is a lying cow who would do anything for notice, while Selena is her best friend. She can't picture Selena's face.

"You've got trust issues," she says. "If you don't do something about them, you're going to turn into one of those crazy women who hire private investigators to follow their boyfriends around."

"At least I'll *have* a boyfriend. One of my own, not one I had to steal."

"Yay you?" Holly says, turning away. "I guess everyone has to be proud of something?"

"Hey!" Joanne snaps. "Don't you want to know what I'm talking about?"

Holly shrugs. "Why? It's not like I'm going to believe you." She starts for the toilets.

The hiss flicks after her: "*Come back here.*"

If things were normal, Holly would wave over her shoulder and keep walking. But they're not, and Joanne's clever in her own special way, and if she actually knows any of the answers—

Holly turns. Joanne snaps her fingers at Alison. "Phone."

Alison scurries back into the sleep-smelling cave of their room. Someone heaves herself over in bed and asks a drowsy question; Alison lets out a wild shush. She comes back carrying Joanne's phone, which she hands over like an altar boy at the offertory. Part of Holly's head is already hamming up the story for the others, snorting into her palm with laughter. The other part has a bad feeling.

Joanne takes her time pressing buttons. Then she hands the phone to Holly—the curl of her mouth is a warning, but Holly takes it anyway. The video is already playing.

It hits her in separate punches, with no room to get her breath in between. The girl is Selena. The guy is Chris Harper. That's the glade. It's turned into something Holly has never seen it be; something gathered and dangerous.

Joanne feels closer, licking up anything Holly lets out. Holly makes herself start breathing again and says, with no blink and her dad's amused half-grin, "OMG, some blond chick is snogging some guy. Call Perez Hilton quick."

"Oh, please, don't act stupider than you can help. You know who they are."

Holly shrugs. "It could be Selena and Chris Whatshisname from Colm's. Sorry to ruin your big moment here, but so?"

"So oopsie," Joanne says, pursed-up and cute. "I guess you're not bessie blood sisters after all."

Bite fast and hard. *Not one I had to steal*— "What do you even care?" Holly says, lifting an eyebrow. "You were never with Chris Harper. Just fancying him doesn't make him your *property*."

Alison says, "She was *too*."

"*Shut up*," Joanne hisses, whirling around on her. Alison gasps and vanishes into the shadows. To Holly, icy again: "That's none of your business."

If Chris actually dumped Joanne for Selena, Joanne is going to take Selena's throat out. "If Chris cheated on you," Holly says, carefully, "he's a prick. But why be pissed off with Selena? She didn't even know."

"Oh, don't worry," Joanne says, "we'll get him." Her voice calls up a sudden cold gleam, away in the thick dark corners of the corridor; Holly almost steps back. "And I'm not pissed *off* with your friend. It's over between them, and anyway I don't get pissed off with people like her. I get rid of them."

And with that video, she can do that any time she wants. "Clichés give me a rash," Holly says. She hits the Delete button, but Joanne is watching for that: she grabs the phone back before Holly can confirm. Her nails scrape down Holly's wrist.

"Ex*cuse* me, don't even think about it?"

"You need a manicure," Holly says, shaking her wrist. "With, like, garden shears."

Joanne slaps her phone back into Alison's hand, and Alison scuttles off to put it away. "You know what you and your pals need?" Joanne says, like it's an order. "You need to stop acting like you're such super-special amazing bessie friends. If you were, that manatee wouldn't be lying to you about shagging Chris Harper; and even if she did, you'd like *know* telepathically, which you so didn't. You're exactly the same as everyone else."

Holly has no comeback to that. *It's over between them.* That scraped-out look to Selena, ice wind ripping right through her: this is why. This, the most obvious typical clichéd reason in the world, so typical she never even thought of it. Joanne Heffernan got there first.

Holly can't take one more second of her face, swollen fat with all the delicious *gotcha* she was after. The corridor lights flicker, make a noise like paint spattering and pop out. Through the surge of chicken-coop noises from Joanne's room, Holly feels her way back to bed.

She says nothing. Not to Becca who would freak out, not to Julia who would tell her she was talking bullshit, not to Selena; especially not to Selena. When Holly can't sleep a few nights later, when she opens her eyes to Selena's whole body one curve of concentration over something cupped glowing in her palms, she doesn't sit up and say softly *Lenie tell me.* When a long wait later Selena takes a shivery breath and shoves the phone down the side of her mattress, Holly doesn't start making up excuses to be on her own in the bedroom. She lets the phone stay where it is and hopes she never sees it again.

She acts like Selena is totally fine and everything's totally fine and the biggest problem in the world is Junior Cert Irish which OMG is going to destroy her brain and turn her whole life into a total failure. This makes Becca chill out and cheer up, at least. Julia is still a bitch, but Holly decides to think this is because of exam stress. She spends a lot of time with Becca. They laugh a lot. Afterwards Holly can't remember about what.

Sometimes she wants to punch Selena right in the soft pale daze of her face and keep punching. Not because she got off with Chris Harper and lied to them and broke the vow that was her idea to begin with; those aren't even the problem. But because the whole point of the vow was for none of them to have to feel like this. The point was for one place in their lives to be impregnable. For just one kind of love to be stronger than any outside thing; to be safe.

Becca is not stupid and, no matter what people sometimes think, she's not twelve. And a place like this is riddled with secrets but their shells are thin and it's crowded in here, they get bashed and jostled against each other; if you're not super-careful, then sooner or later they crack open and all the tender flesh comes spilling out.

She's known for weeks that something is wrong and spreading. That night in the grove, when Holly was going on at Lenie, Becca tried to think it was just Holly having a mood; she does that sometimes, digs into something and won't let go, all you need to do is pull her attention somewhere else and she's fine. But Julia doesn't care about Holly's moods. When she jumped in to make everything all sweet and smooth, that was when Becca started knowing something real was wrong.

She's been trying hard not to know. When Selena spends the whole of lunchtime staring into her hand wrapped in her hair, or when Julia and Holly snap like they hate each other, Becca digs her heels into the ground, stares at her beef casserole and refuses to get pulled in. If they want to act like idiots, that's their problem; they can fix it themselves.

The thought of something they can't fix sends her mind wild, yipping with terror. It smells of forest fires.

It's Holly who corners her into knowing. The first time Holly

asked—*Does Lenie seem, like, weird to you, the last while?*—all Becca could
do was stare and listen to her own crazy heartbeat, till Holly rolled her eyes
and switched to *Never mind it's probably all fine.* But then Holly starts sticking to her harder and harder, like she can't breathe right around the others.
She talks too fast, she makes smart-arsed jabs at everything and everyone
and keeps going till Becca laughs to make her happy. She tries to get Becca
to do things just the two of them, without Julia and Selena. Becca realizes
that she wants to get away from Holly; that, unbelievably, for the first time
ever, they all want to get away from each other.

Whatever's wrong, it won't go away by itself. It's getting worse.

A year ago Becca would have kept slamming doors and turning keys
between her and this. Got a load of books out of the library, never stopped
reading even when someone talked to her. Pretended to be sick, stuck fingers
down her throat to puke, till Mum showed up tight-jawed to take her home.

Now is different. She's not a little kid any more, who can hide on her
friends when something bad is happening. If the others can't fix this, then
she needs to try.

Becca starts watching.

One night she opens her eyes on Selena sitting up in bed, texting. The
phone is pink. Selena's phone is silver.

The next day Becca wears last term's outgrown kilt to school, and gets
sent back to her room to change into something that doesn't show the world
her legs. It takes her like thirty seconds to find the pink phone.

The texts turn every soft part of her to water, spilling away between her
bones. She's crouched on Selena's bed and she can't move.

This little thing, harmless, this is what's turned everything wrong. The
phone feels black and hot in her hand, denser than rock.

It takes a long spinning time before she can think. The first thing her
mind holds up: there's no name in the texts. *Who who who*, she thinks, and
listens to the lonely hoot of it through her mind. *Who?*

Someone from Colm's; that's obvious, from the stories about teachers
and rugby matches and other guys. Someone cunning, to fracture a crack
into their high white wall and wiggle his sly way through. Someone smart,
to guess how Selena would sway to all these poor-sensitive-me stories with
her arms out, how she would never abandon anyone so special who needs
her so much.

Becca keeps watching. Down at the Court, as they wander through the
chilled hollow air and the candy-colored neon, she watches for some guy
who looks over their way too much or too little, for some guy who changes

Selena just by walking past. Marcus Wiley's eyes ferret down Selena's top but even if he wasn't disgusting Selena would never, not after he sent Julia that picture. Andrew Moore checks if they're looking as he dead-arms one of his friends and howls with lunatic laughter; Becca is about to think *Yeah right, a no-personality moron like that, she would never*, when she realizes like a punch in the gut she has no clue what Selena would never.

Andrew Moore?

Finn Carroll, head flicking away too sharply when he sees Becca see him looking across the doughnut stand? Finn is smart; he could do it. Chris Harper, crossing them on the escalators with a red slash on his cheek that might not be just sunburn, Selena's eyelashes flickering fast as she bends her head low over her carrier bag full of colors? The thought of Chris fishhooks Becca under the breastbone in weird sore ways, but she doesn't flinch: it could be. Seamus O'Flaherty, everyone says Seamus is gay but someone cunning could start that rumor himself, to get close to girls off guard; François Levy, beautiful and different, different could make Selena feel like it didn't count; Bryan Hynes, Oisín O'Donovan, Graham Quinn, for a second every one of them leaps out with a wet red grin like it's him him him. He's everywhere; he's claiming everything.

The air in the Court has been processed to something so thin and chilly that Becca can hardly breathe it. Next to her Holly is talking too fast and insistent to notice that Becca's not answering. Becca pulls her cardigan sleeves down over her hands and keeps watching.

She watches at night, too. It's Selena she's guarding—not that she knows what she would do if—but when she finally sees the slow rise and unfurl of bedclothes, it's on the wrong bed. Becca can tell by the delicacy of every movement, the wary flash of eyes before Julia straightens, that she's not going to the toilet.

The sound comes out before Becca can stop it, rips out of her gut, dirty and raw. This guy is running all through them, like an infection looking for the next place to erupt, he's everywhere—

Julia freezes. Becca turns and flops, doing bad-dream mutters; lets them subside, breathes deep and even. After a long time she hears Julia start moving again.

She watches Julia sneak out, watches her sneak in an hour later; watches her change fast into her pajamas and jam her clothes deep into the wardrobe. Watches her disappear to the bathroom, come back a long time later in a thick fog of flowers and lemon and disinfectant.

There's no phone down the side of Julia's bed, the next evening during second study when Becca finds an excuse. There's a half-empty packet of condoms.

It scalds Becca's fingers like hot grease; even after she shoves it back it keeps scalding, corroding right into her blood and pumping all through her body. Julia isn't Selena; no one could sweet-talk her into this, no amount of puppy-dog eyes and sensitive stories. This had to be something vicious, clotted with cruelty, a hard jerk of her arm up behind her back: *Do it or I'll tell on Selena, get her expelled, I'll send tit shots of her to every phone in the school*— Someone more than cunning. Someone evil.

Becca, kneeling on the floor between the beds, bites into the meat of her palm to keep that sound from wrenching out of her again.

Who who?

Someone who doesn't understand the immensity of what he's done. He thinks this is nothing. Turning girls from what they are into what he wants them to be, twisting and forcing till they're nothing but his desires, that's no big deal: just what they were there for, to begin with. Becca's teeth make deep dents in her hand.

Those moments in the glade that were supposed to last forever, that were supposed to be theirs to reclaim no matter how far away and apart the four of them travel: he's robbing those. He's scrubbing away the glowing maplines that were supposed to lead each of them back. Selena's and then Julia's, he'll go after Holly next, he's a crow gobbling their crumb-trails and never full. The road of dots across Becca's belly leaps with fresh pain.

Who who whose smell in the air of her room, whose fingerprints all over her friends' secret places—

Outside the window the moon is a thin white smear behind purple-gray clouds. Becca unclenches her teeth and holds out her palms.

Save us

The clouds pulse. They bubble at the edges.

Julia broke the vow; even if she was forced to, that doesn't matter, not to this. So did Selena, whatever she did or didn't do with him. If she danced along the line, if she broke up with him before they went right over, this doesn't care. None of those things change the punishment.

Forgive us. Burn this out of us turn us pure again. Get him out get us back to how we used to be

The sky simmers and thrums. The answers heave under a thin skin of cloud.

Something is required.

Whatever you want. You want blood I'll cut myself open

The light dims, rejecting. Not that.

Becca thinks of poured wine, clay figurines, flash of a knife and scatter of feathers. She has no clue where she would get a bird, or wine actually, but if—

What tell me what

With a vast silent roar the sky bursts open, the clouds explode to fragments that dissolve before they hit the ground. Out of the white and enormous blaze it drops into her open palms:

Him.

She was thinking like a stupid little kid. Booze nicked from Mum's wine rack, chicken blood; baby stuff, for eyelinered idiots playing witch games they don't understand.

In old times, there were punishments for forcing a girl who had made a vow. Becca's read about them: buried alive, flayed, clubbed to death—

Him. No other sacrifice could ever be enough, not to purify this.

Becca almost gets up and runs, back to the common room and French homework. She knows she could, if she wanted. Nothing would stop her.

Selena staring into her palmful of hair, the hunch of Julia's shoulders when she came back in from the seething dark, the fast desperate beat of Holly's voice. The moments, over the last few weeks, when Becca's hated all three of them. Any day now it'll be too late for them to find their way back, ever again.

Yes. Yes I'll do it. Yes I'll find a way.

The ferocity of celebration that rises to meet that, outside her and inside, almost throws her across the room. The dots across her belly drum wild rhythms.

But I don't know who I need to

Not Chris Harper. Chris didn't need to be kind to Becca, he didn't do it to get something—Becca knows perfectly well that a guy like Chris isn't after someone like her—and free kindness doesn't go with evil. But that leaves Finn Andrew Seamus François everyone, how can she—

It comes to her like the curve of a great smile: she doesn't have to know who. All she has to know is where and when. And she can choose those for herself, because she's a girl, and girls have the power to call guys running any time they want.

Becca knows how to be super-careful. Nothing is going to crack open her secret.

All the sky streams with white, great joyous cool sheets of it pouring down over her hands and her upturned face and her whole body, filling her open mouth.

On Thursday morning Becca wears her outgrown kilt again, and this time Sister Cornelius loses the head and bangs her desk with the ruler and gives the whole class a hundred lines of *I will pray to the Blessed Virgin to grant me modesty.* And then she sends Becca back to her room to change.

There's no way to know what time this guy and Selena were meeting, but at least Becca knows one place where they met. *Tonight in that clearing place?* one text said, way back in March. *Same time?*

In the last place in the world where she should have brought him. For a second, zipping up her too-long new kilt, Becca's afraid this guy must have power of his own behind him, to turn Selena into such a total lobotomized idiot. She spots a dropped scrap of paper on the carpet, launches it spinning like a moth around the light fixture to remind herself: she has power too.

The phone doesn't feel black and hot any more; it's turned foam-light and nimble, buttons pressing themselves almost before Becca's thumb can find them. She redoes the text four times before she's positive it's OK. *Can you meet tonight? 1 in the cypress clearing?*

She might not get the chance to check for an answer, but it doesn't matter: he'll be there. Maybe Julia's already set up a meeting for tonight—Becca doesn't know how she contacts him—but he'll blow Julia off, if he thinks Selena's beckoning. It rises off his texts like heat: what he really wants is Selena.

He can't have her.

Becca leaves soon after midnight, to give herself time to prepare. In the mirror on their wardrobe door, she looks like a burglar: dark-blue jeans and her dark-blue hoodie, and her designer black leather gloves that Mum gave her for Christmas and she's never worn before. Her hood strings are pulled so tight that just her eyes and nose stick out. It makes her grin—*You look like the world's fattest bank robber*—but the grin doesn't show; she looks solemn, almost stern, balanced on the balls of her feet ready for battle. Around her the others breathe slow and deep as enchanted princesses in a fairy tale.

The night glows like some strange daytime, under a huge low half-moon packed tight in stars. Over the wall and far away music is playing, just a tantalizing thread of it, a sweet voice and a beat like running feet. Becca freezes in a shadow and listens. *Never thought that everything we lost could feel so near, found you on a*—and it's gone, faded on a change of wind. After a long time she starts moving again.

The groundskeepers' shed is dark, thick earth-smelling dark and she's not about to turn on the light, but she prepared for this. Two steps forward, face left, five steps, and her outstretched hands hit the stack of tools propped against the wall.

The hoe is at the far right of the stack, where she left it yesterday. Spades and shovels are too heavy and too clumsy, anything short-handled would mean getting too close, but one hoe had a blade so sharp it almost split her fingertip like ripe fruit. Gemma came in and saw her choosing, but Becca's not worried about her. This isn't balconette bras and low-carb foods; this is a thousand miles outside what Gemma's mind can reach.

She sets branches parting like swinging doors in front of her, to leave her path clear. In the center of the glade she practices, swinging the hoe up behind her head and down; getting used to the heft of it, the reach. The gloves mean she needs to hold it extra tight, to stop her fingers sliding. The swish of it is fast and strong and satisfying. Low under the trees, here and there, luminous eyes watch her, curious.

One more go because it feels good, and Becca stops: she doesn't want her arms to get tired. She spins the hoe between her palms and listens. Only the comfortable, familiar sounds of the night: her own breathing, the undergrowth-rustles of small things about their business. He's nowhere near.

He'll come from the back of the grounds. The path, under arching branches, is an endless black cave flecked with snippets of white light. She pictures different guys stepping out of it: Andrew, Seamus, Graham. She pictures, carefully and methodically, everything that needs to come after that.

The hoe has stopped spinning between her hands. She hears its swish again, and this time the splintering thud and squelch at the end.

Her whole body would love it to be James Gillen—the thought opens her mouth in almost a smile—but that at least she knows Selena would never. She hopes it's Andrew Moore.

Becca feels lucky, so lucky she could lift right off the ground and somersault amid the whirling stars, to have been chosen for this. The beauty of the glade turns her heart over. All the clearing is lavish with every glory it can call up; the air is drenched with moonlight and the sweetness of hyacinths, owls sing like nightingales and hares dance and the cypresses are pearled in silver and lavender, for the celebration.

In the crosshatched dark away down the path, something cracks. The cypresses catch one deep breath and shiver on tiptoe. He's here.

For one second Becca is terrified, bones jackhammered to jelly by the same terror that Julia must have felt as she lay down for him, that Selena must have felt in the instant before she said *I love you*. It comes to her that, afterwards, she'll be different from everyone else. Her and this guy: that thud will take them both across one-way borderlines, into worlds they can't imagine.

She bites down on her cheek till she tastes blood, and with one arc of her hand she sweeps a long rustle like a black wing all around the tops of the cypresses. The other place has been there all along; for months now the borders have been turning porous, sifting away. If she wanted to be frightened, if she wanted to run, the moments for that were a long time ago.

The terror is gone, as fast as it came. Becca moves back into the shadows under the trees and waits for him like a girl waiting for a secret lover, lips parted and dark blood thrumming in her throat and her breasts, all her body reaching out for the moment when at long last she'll see his face.

27

I went round to the front of the school. My feet crossing the grass felt strange, too solid, sinking down and down like the lawn was made of mist. Girls still watching as I passed, still whispering. This time it didn't matter.

I waited at the corner of the boarders' wing, pressed back into the shadow. *If we're taking a break, Detective Conway, I think I'll walk down with you, have a quick smoke . . . No? Any reason why not?* With Mackey around, you need to stay ahead.

I felt like someone else, waiting there for Conway. Someone changed.

She came fast. One minute the oak door looked shut forever; the next she was poised at the top of the steps, scanning for me. Floodlights on her hair. Took me a second to feel the big grin right across my face.

No Mackey behind her. I stepped out of the shadow, lifted an arm.

The matching grin lit her up. She came striding across the white pebbles, held out a hand for a high five. It whipcracked out into the night, pure triumph, left a hard clean sting on my palm. "We did all right there."

I was glad of the half light. "Would you say Mackey bought it?"

"I'd say so, yeah. Hard to tell for definite."

"What'd you tell him?"

"Now? Just looked pissed off, said I had to sort out some shite and it'd only take me a minute, don't go anywhere. I'd say he thinks you're bitching about having to wait around." She glanced back at the door, a dark crack open. We started moving, into the shadow and round the boarders' wing, out of sight.

I asked, "Getting anywhere with Holly?"

Conway shook her head. "I threw around possible motives for a while, but nothing looked like it clicked. Went back to how she wasn't there for Selena, what she would've done to make up for it; the kid got stroppy, but she didn't give me anything new. I didn't want to push too hard: if she started going to bits, Mackey would've walked, and I wanted to give you time. What've you got?"

I said, "Rebecca was going through the shovels and spades in the grounds-keepers' shed. The day before the murder."

Conway went still. Stopped breathing.

After a moment: "Who said?"

"Gemma. She was looking to buy diet pills, walked in on Rebecca. Rebecca jumped a mile, did a legger."

"Gemma. Joanne's lapdog Gemma."

"I don't think she was bullshitting me. They weren't covering for themselves, anyway. They didn't cop that there was anything dodgy about Rebecca being at the tools. They thought the suss bit was her being in there at all—thought she was buying drugs off the groundskeeper to give to Chris, because she was into him, and then he turned her down and she lost it. I said Rebecca was too small to do the job; they said if Chris was sitting down, she could've hit him with a rock. If they knew the weapon was a hoe, no way could they have stopped themselves bringing it up. They don't have that kind of self-control. They don't know."

Conway still hadn't moved: feet braced, shoulders braced, hands dug in her pockets. Things going fast behind her eyes. She said, "I don't see it. The drugs thing, maybe that could play; Rebecca could've been bribing Chris to stay away from Selena. But remember the condom? Chris went out there expecting a ride. You think Rebecca'd been shagging him? Seriously?"

I said, "I don't think the earlier meetings were Rebecca. Remember what Holly said? When she realized something was up with Selena, she tried to talk to Julia about it. Julia didn't want to know: told her to forget it, Selena'd get over it sooner or later. Does that sound like Julia to you? She's a scrapper. One of her mates is in trouble, she's just going to stick her fingers in her ears, hope it goes away?"

Conway moved then. Her head went back, moonlight on the whites of her eyes. "Julia was already on it."

"Yeah. She didn't want Holly getting involved, making things more complicated. So she told her to leave it."

"*Fuck*," Conway said. "Remember what Joanne told us? She put her bitches on night duty, make sure Selena had stopped sneaking out to see Chris. No sign of Selena, but they saw Julia, all right. They thought she was meeting Finn Carroll. And we went along with that. Pair of fucking fools."

I said, "No way to keep a secret for long, in a room that size. Somewhere in there, Rebecca found out—either about Chris and Selena, or about Chris and Julia."

"Yeah. And Holly said even the thought of anything being wrong with any of them made Rebecca go mental."

"The thought of the four of them not being enough to make everything OK. She couldn't handle that." I saw the poster, the calligraphy that had taken hours, weeks, a fresh start for every finger-slip. *If crouds of dangers should appeare, yet friendship can be unconcern'd.*

Conway said, "This doesn't mean Holly's out."

She didn't say it the way she would have an hour or two before, a sideways eye checking me for a flinch or a flicker. Just said it. Eyes narrowed up at the school building, like it was daring her.

I said, "Right. Doesn't rule out Julia, either, or the whole three of them: for all we know it was one to find the weapon, one to lure Chris to the grove, one to do the job when he had his mind on other things. All we know for sure is Rebecca's in."

"Get anything else?"

After a moment I said, "That's it."

Conway's face came round to me. "But what?"

"But." I wanted to twist away from it, but she needed to know. "Joanne and them, they weren't pleased when I said I had to head. They were trying to do something, I don't even know what. Flirt with me, get me to stay. Something like that."

"Any touching?"

"Yeah. Joanne put her finger on my leg. I talked them down, she took the hand away, I got the fuck out of Dodge."

Conway watched me. "Is this you saying I shouldn't have thrown you into the shark tank all on your ownio?"

"No. I'm a big boy. If I hadn't've wanted to talk to them, I wouldn't have."

"'Cause I would've done it myself, if I could. But I'd have got nothing. It had to be you."

Me, the perfect bait, whatever whoever wanted. "I know. I'm only telling you. I figure you should know."

She nodded. "Don't worry about it." She saw me shift, *Easy for you to say.* "Seriously. They won't say anything. The amount we've got on them, they'd have to be mental to try and fuck with us. You think they want McKenna knowing about the diet pills? The sneaking out at night?"

"They might not think that far."

Conway snorted. "They're experts on thinking that far. That's what they do." More seriously, whatever she saw in my face: "They're scary fuckers, but we've got them pinned down. OK?"

"Yeah," I said. The way she said it—*scary fuckers*—like she knew, like she'd been there: that was what helped, more than the reassurance. "OK."

"Good." Conway clapped me on the shoulder. Awkward as a boy, but her hand felt strong and steady. "Fair play to you."

I said, "It's not enough. We've got enough to arrest Rebecca, but the DPP won't charge her on this. If she doesn't confess—"

Conway was shaking her head. "Not even enough for an arrest. If she was some skanger kid, then yeah, sure, haul her in and see how far we get. But a girl from Kilda's? We arrest her, we have to be able to charge her. No ifs. Otherwise we're fucked. O'Kelly's gonna pop a vein, McKenna's gonna pop a vein, the commissioner's phone's gonna be ringing off the hook, the media'll scream cover-up, and we'll be sharing a desk in Records till we retire." That bitter curl to her mouth. "Unless you've got friends in high places."

"That was the best I'd got." I nodded upwards, towards the art room. "And I'd say that's well scuppered now."

That got part of a laugh. "Then we need more on Rebecca. And we need it fast. We have to get her in custody tonight, or we're fucked. Julia and Holly, they're both smart enough to figure out where this is going—if they don't already know."

I said, "Holly knows."

"Yeah. We leave the four of them together overnight, they'll talk. We'll come back tomorrow morning and they'll have their stories all nice and matched up, butter won't melt, they'll have worked out exactly where to lie and where to keep their mouths shut. Not a chance in hell we'll crack them."

I said, "We won't crack Holly now. She's given us everything she's going to."

Conway was shaking her head again. "Forget her. And Selena. We need Julia."

I remembered what she had said earlier: *This year Julia's watching us like we're actual people, you and me.* And then: *I can't work out if that's gonna be a good thing or a bad one.*

"Mackey and Holly," I said. "Leave them where they are, yeah?"

"Yeah. We might need them again, and we don't want them running around getting in our way. If they don't like it—"

This time we both froze. Only a few yards behind us, round the front of the boarders' wing, someone's foot had slid on pebbles.

Conway's eyes met mine. She mouthed *Mackey*.

We moved fast and silent, swung round the corner together. The carriage sweep was wide and white, empty. The grass was bare. In the dark crack of the door, nothing moved.

Conway cupped a forearm round her eyes, blocking out the floodlights, and squinted into the trees. Nothing.

"D'you know where Julia is?"

"Didn't see them. They're not on the back lawn."

She eased back into the shadow. Said, for no one farther than me, "They'll be in that glade."

We were both half thinking about sneaking up on them, having a quick eavesdrop, see if they were talking hoes and texts and Chris. Not a hope. That pretty little woodlandy path, the one we'd walked that morning: the trees touching above it slashed the light to scraps, left us fumbling. We went crashing along like Land Rovers, twigs snapping, branches flapping, birds losing the head everywhere.

"*Jesus*," Conway hissed, when I went in a bush up to my knee. "Did you never do Boy Scouts, no? Go camping?"

"Where I'm from? No, I bleeding didn't. You want me to hotwire a car, no problem."

"I can do that myself. I want some woodcraft."

"You want some posh bastard who went pheasant-shooting every—" I caught my foot in something, shot forward flailing. Conway grabbed my elbow before I went on my snot. We snorted with giggles like a pair of kids, sleeves over our mouths, trying to glare each other silent.

"Shut up—"

"Fuck's *sake*—"

Only made us worse. We'd gone giddy: the moon-stripes swirling the ground under our feet, the spin of rustles spreading out all around us; the hard weight of what we were going to have to do at the end of the path. I was only waiting to see Chris Harper leaping widemouthed like a wildcat off a branch in front of us, couldn't tell if we'd scream like teenage girls or whip out our guns and blow his ghostly arse away—

"State of you—"

"Look who's talking—"

Around a bend, out from under the trees.

Smell of hyacinths.

Up the little rise, in the clearing among the cypresses, the moonlight came down full and untouched. The three of them leaned shoulder to shoulder, legs curled among the bobbing seed-heads; for a second they looked like one triple creature that made my hair lift. Still as an old statue, as smooth and white and as blank-faced. Watching us, three pairs of bottomless eyes. We had stopped laughing.

None of them moved. The hyacinth-smell rose over us like a wave.

Rebecca, shoulder against Selena's. Her hair was down and she was all patches of black and white, like an illusion. Like one blink would turn her into moonlight on grass.

Beside me Conway said, just loud enough to reach them, "Julia."

They didn't move. I had time to wonder what we would do if they never did; I knew better than to get any closer. Then Julia straightened, away from Selena's side, brought her legs under her and stood up. She came down the rise to us without a glance at the others, came swishing through the hyacinths with her back straight and her eyes on something behind us. My neck itched.

Conway said, "Let's walk down this way. We'll only need a few minutes."

She headed on down the path, deeper into the grounds. Julia fell into place behind her. The other two watched, side pressed to side, till I turned away. At my back, nearly made me leap, came the deep sigh of the cypress trees.

Even Julia's walk was different, out here. No mocking arse-sway now; she took the path deft as a deer, barely shifted a twig. Like this was her territory, she could've crept up on a sleeping bird and taken it in her hand.

Conway said, without looking over her shoulder, "I'm gonna assume Selena's updated you. We know yous were getting out at night, we know she had something going with Chris, we know they'd split up. And we know you were meeting Chris. Right up until he died."

Nothing. The path broadened out, wide enough for the three of us to walk abreast. Julia's legs were shorter than ours, but she didn't speed up; left us to slow to her pace or leave her behind, whichever. We slowed.

"We've got your texts. On the special super-secret phone he gave Selena."

Her silence felt unbreakable. She had put on a red jumper, no jacket, and the air was turning cold. She didn't seem to notice.

Conway said, "Is that why Selena broke it off with Chris, yeah? We couldn't work that out. Was it because she knew you were into him, didn't want him getting between you?"

That got to Julia. "I was never *into* Chris. I have *taste*."

"Then what were you doing with him out here at midnight? Algebra?"

Silence, and her silent steps. Time running out was pounding at me: Rebecca waiting behind us, Mackey and Holly waiting above us, McKenna waiting to ring the bell that would end the day. Rushing this would only slow it down.

Conway said, "How many times did you meet him?"

Nothing.

"If it wasn't you, it was one of your mates. Had Selena got back together with him?"

Julia said, "Three times. I met him three times."

"Why'd you stop?"

"He got killed. It put a damper on the relationship."

"Relationship," I said. "What kind?"

"Intellectual. We talked world politics."

The sarcasm was heavy enough to be all the answer we needed. Conway said, "If you weren't into him, then why?"

"Because. You never did anything stupid, when it came to guys?"

"Plenty. Trust me." The quick look between the two of them startled me: a matched look like understanding, a wry edge of smile on Conway. *Like we're actual people.* "But I always had a reason. A shite one, but it was there."

Julia said, "It seemed like a good idea at the time. What can I say: I was dumber then."

I said, "You were keeping him away from Selena. You knew he was trouble—you knew what he'd done to Joanne, knew Selena wasn't strong enough to handle the same thing happening to her. Selena had broken it off with him, but you read her texts; you knew all Chris had to do was snap his fingers and she'd come running. So you had to make sure he didn't snap them."

"You're tougher than Selena," Conway said. "Tough enough to take whatever a fool like Chris could dish out. So you took the bullet for her."

Julia walked, hands in her pockets. Watched something off in the trees ahead. The slice of her face I could see reminded me of Holly. That grief.

Conway said, "You think Selena killed Chris. Don't you?"

Julia's head snapped sideways like Conway had flicked her in the face. I hadn't realized till I heard the words fall into the air. This was what Julia had been thinking, all day; all year.

And that was her out. Julia out, Selena out, Rebecca in. Holly flickering on the line.

Conway said, "We say we're going to talk to Selena: bang, you throw us a stick to chase, send us dashing off after Joanne. I say maybe Selena had got back with Chris: bang, all of a sudden you're talking to us, coming clean about meeting him. You wouldn't need to protect her unless you thought she had something to hide."

We were speeding up. Julia was walking faster, smashing twigs and rattling pebbles, not caring.

I said, "You think Selena found out you were hooking up with Chris. Is that it? She was so angry, or so jealous, or so gutted, she lost the head and killed him. That makes it your fault. So it's up to you to protect her."

Only a pace or two ahead of us, she was already smudging away into the dark, just the red slash of her jumper glowing. "Julia," Conway said, and stopped walking.

Julia stopped too, but the line of her back pulled like a leashed dog's. Conway said, "Sit down."

In the end Julia turned. A pretty little wrought-iron bench, overlooking tidy flowerbeds—closed up for the night, now, all the daytime colors and petal-flourishes turned in tight on themselves. Julia aimed for the end of the bench. Conway and I boxed her into the middle.

Conway said, "Listen to me. We don't suspect Selena."

Julia rolled her a look. "Uh-huh. I'm so reassured, I might need to fan myself."

"All our evidence says she hadn't been in touch with Chris for weeks before he died."

"Right. Until you turn around and say, 'Oops, actually, we've decided those texts were from her, not from you! Sorry!'"

"Bit late for that," I said. "And we've had a lot of practice figuring out when people are lying. We both think Selena's telling us the truth."

"Great. Glad to hear it."

"So if we believe her, why don't you? She's meant to be your mate; how come you think she's a murderer?"

"I don't. I think she's never done anything worse than talking during study period. OK?"

The defenses shooting up in Julia's voice, I'd heard those before. That was when it clicked: the interview in her room that afternoon, that note in her voice, something left snagged in my mind. I said, "You're the one who texted me."

Off Chris's phone.

Her profile tightening. She didn't look at me.

"To tell me where Joanne kept the key to the connecting door. That was you."

Nothing.

"You said to us, this afternoon: *When you found out about Joanne's key, she turned it around on me. If anyone had told you about her and Chris, she'd have got back at them the same way.* Meaning Joanne was getting back at you, for telling us about the key."

I got one corner of Julia's eye. It said, *Good catch. Now prove it.*

Conway turned on the bench, pulled up one leg so she could face Julia straight on. "Listen. Selena's in bad shape. You know that. You thought it was because she couldn't handle being a killer, had to hide in cloud-cuckoo land. It's not that. You want me to swear? I'll swear on anything you want: it's not."

She said it clear and warm, the way she'd have said it to a friend, a best friend, to her closest sister. She was holding out a hand and beckoning Julia to cross that river. Go from the lifelong-familiar side where grown-ups were faceless mentallers trying to wreck everything, no point trying to understand them, over to this new strange place where we could talk face-to-face.

Julia looking at Conway. Things moving across her face said she knew the crossing was one-way. That you can never tell who'll still be beside you, on the other side, and who'll be left behind.

I kept quiet. This was theirs. I was outside.

Julia took a long breath. She said, "You're sure. It wasn't her."

"We don't suspect her. You've got my word."

"Lenie's not just naturally crazy, though. You don't know her; I do. She wasn't like this before Chris got killed."

Conway nodded. "Yeah, I know. But what's wrecking her head isn't that she killed him. It's that she knows something she can't handle. She's spacing out so she doesn't have to deal with it."

It was getting colder. Julia pulled her jumper tight at her neck. She said, "Like what?"

"If we knew, we wouldn't need to be having this conversation. I've got ideas, no proof. All I can tell you for sure is: you're not gonna get Selena in hassle by telling me the truth. I swear. OK?"

Julia tugged her sleeves down, the pale smudges of her hands vanishing into the red. She said quietly, "OK. I texted you about the key."

Conway said, "How'd you know where Joanne and them kept it?"

"I'm the one who gave her the idea about the book."

I said, "And the one who gave her the key."

"You make it sound like it was her birthday present. Actually, they saw us heading out one night, and Joanne said she'd tell McKenna what bad girls we'd been if we didn't make her a copy of the key. So I did."

"And gave her advice on where to keep it?" Conway raised an eyebrow. "You're very helpful altogether."

Julia matched the eyebrow. "When someone could get me expelled, yeah, I am. She wanted to know where we kept ours, which I wasn't going to tell her because fuck the bitch—"

"Which was where? While we're at it."

"Down the inside of my phone case. Simple, and it was always on me. Like I said, though, I wasn't about to give the Heifer Heffernan any more than I had to. So I told her the only way to be safe was to keep it in the common room, so if it got found no one could connect it to her, right? I was like, 'Pick a book no one ever reads. Who'd you do your saint essay on?'— the common rooms are all full of saint biogs, no one ever looks at them except once a year for essays, and we'd just handed ours in. She went, 'Thérèse of Lisieux. The Little Flower'—she actually got this *holy* face on, like that somehow made her into Joanne of Lisieux." Conway was grinning. "So I went, 'Perfect. No one's going to look at the book again till at least next year. Stick the key in there, you're sorted.'"

"And you figured she'd taken your word for it?"

"Joanne has zero imagination, except about herself. No way could she have come up with a place. Anyway, I checked. I thought it might come in useful."

"And it did," Conway said. "How come you decided to tell us?"

Julia hesitated. The small noises all around were moving deeper into night: flurries in leaves said hunting, the laughter from the lawn was long gone. I wondered how little time we had. Didn't look at my watch.

I said, "The interviews, earlier on. Did Selena come out of hers upset?"

After a moment: "I mean, she wouldn't have looked upset to most people. Just spacy; well, spacier than usual. But that is upset, for Selena. That's how she gets."

I said, "You were afraid we'd shaken her up enough that she might let something slip, maybe even confess. You needed us looking in another direction, at least till you could get her settled down again. So you threw us Joanne's key, to keep us occupied. And it worked. You've got a gift for this, you know that?"

"Gee, thanks."

Conway said, "And if you're the one who texted us, that means you've got Chris Harper's secret phone."

Julia went still. Her face was a new kind of wary.

"Ah, come on. Records say that text came from that phone. There's not a lot of point in mucking about."

A tilt of the head, acknowledging. Julia leaned back and wriggled a phone out of her jeans pocket, slim little thing in a snappy orange case. "Not his phone. Just his SIM card."

She pulled the case away from the back of the phone and tapped a SIM card into her palm. Handed it to Conway.

Conway said, "We're going to need to hear the story."

"There's no story."

"Where'd you get it?"

"Don't I have the right to an attorney, or something? Before I start telling you where I got a dead guy's SIM?"

I knew. I said, "You got his phone off Selena, after he died. She gave it to you, or you found it in her stuff. That's why you think she killed Chris."

Julia's eyes flicked away from me. Conway said, "We still don't. And it's pretty obvious you didn't do the job, or you wouldn't be climbing the walls thinking she did." That got a faint one-sided grin. "So dial down the paranoia and talk to me."

The night was turning that red jumper the color of a banked fire, compressed and waiting. Julia said, "I was actually trying to get rid of Selena's phone, the one we'd both used to text Chris. Imagine my surprise when this showed up."

Conway said, "When was this?"

"The day after Chris got killed."

"What time?"

An unconscious grimace, as she remembered. "Jesus. I started trying before *noon*—they had this big high-drama assembly to tell us about The Tragedy, we had to say a prayer or something . . . All I could think was I had to get Selena's phone out of our room. Before you guys decided to search the place."

"What were you going to do with it?"

Julia shook her head. "I hadn't even thought that far. I just wanted it out. But I could not get a fucking *second* alone in there. I guess McKenna had given orders that none of us were allowed to be alone in case a maniac was roaming the corridors, I don't know. I said I'd forgotten my French homework in my room, and they sent a prefect up with me—I had to pretend the shock had turned me into an airhead, ooo it was in my bag all along! Then I said I'd got my period, but they wouldn't let me go to my room, they sent me to the nurse instead. And then when school ended, McKenna made this announcement—'All students will please report immediately to their activity groups, while remaining calm and blah blah blah stiff upper lip school spirit . . .' "

She did a good McKenna, even if the wank mime was out of character. "I do drama group, so we had to go to the hall and pretend we were rehearsing. It was a *mess*, no one knew where they were supposed to be and all the teachers were trying to take like four groups at once and people were still crying—well, you were there."

That was to Conway, who nodded. "Loony bin," she said, to me.

"Exactly. So I thought maybe I could just slide out and sneak up to my room, seeing as I had the key on me, right? But nooo, the corridors were riddled with nuns and I got sent back to the hall. I tried again during study, said I needed some book, and Sister Patricia came *with* me. And then it was practically lights-out, you guys were still doing whatever down in the grounds, and I still hadn't got that *fucking* phone out of the way."

Julia's voice was tightening towards something. "So Holly and Becca go to brush their teeth, and I'm messing around hoping Selena goes too. But she's sitting on her bed, just sitting there staring into space. She's not going anywhere, and Holly and Becs are gonna be back any minute. So I say, 'Lenie, I need that phone.' She looks at me like I just landed in a UFO. I go, 'The phone Chris gave you. We don't have time to dick around. Come on.'

"She's still staring, so I'm just like, *OK, forget this.* I shove past her and I stick my hand down the side of her bed, where she kept the phone—it was this little foofoo pink thing, just like Alison's; I guess that's what Chris thought was appropriate for girls. I'm hoping to Jesus she hasn't moved it, 'cause I don't have time to try and figure out where, so I'm a happy girlie when I feel it there, right? Only then I pull it out, and it's red."

The memory made Julia take a hard in-breath through her nose, bite down on her lip. She wasn't someone you could pat on the head with the old *You're doing great.* Conway gave her a second before she said, "Chris's."

"Yeah. I'd seen it on him; it fell out of his pocket once, when we were . . . I go, 'Lenie, what the *fuck?*' She looks at me and she's like, 'Huh?' I swear I nearly shoved the phone up her arse. I went, 'Where did you get this? And where's your one?' She looks at the phone and after a second she says—this is it, this is all she says—'Oh.' "

Julia shook her head. "Just like that. 'Oh.' I still feel sick thinking about it."

Conway said, "You figured she'd killed Chris."

"*Duh*, yeah, I did. I just— What was I supposed to think? I thought she'd been out meeting him and he told her about me, and she— And then when she was legging it back inside, she grabbed the wrong phone somehow. If they'd, I don't know, if they'd taken off their clothes and their phones had ended up—"

I said, "Or she might have taken it so we couldn't link her to Chris."

"Yeah, no. Selena? Wouldn't even occur to her. What freaked me out was where was *her* phone, like had she left it wherever Chris was? But I figured I couldn't worry about that. I just grabbed the phone and I was out of there."

It jibed with Holly's story, or partway. Holly had thought faster: like her dad, always on top of the just-in-case, never let the off chance sneak up on her. She had swiped Selena's phone early in the morning, before the full story got through to McKenna and the school went into lockdown. Between then and study time, someone else had found a way into that room.

Conway said, "Where'd you put it?"

"Locked myself in a toilet cubicle, deleted the shit out of the message folders, took out the SIM and stuck the phone in a cistern. I figured even if you found it, you couldn't link it to us, and without the SIM you probably couldn't link it to Chris either. That weekend when I went home, I left the phone on the bus. If no one stole it, it's probably in the Dublin Bus lost and found."

She had guts, Julia. Guts and enough loyalty for a dozen. She was good stuff. I wished I knew how badly we were going to break her heart.

"Why keep the SIM card?" I asked.

"I thought it could come in useful. I was pretty sure Selena was about to get arrested—even if by some miracle she hadn't left evidence all over the place, I figured she'd go to pieces and confess. Do you even remember what a wreck she was?"

"So was everyone else," Conway said. The sharp point on her voice said *Should've known.* "She wasn't bawling or fainting: she looked to be in better nick than most."

Julia's eyebrow flicked. "Yeah, if only you'd told me that back then. I was there expecting you guys to come for her any minute. I thought if there was at least a way to show you that she was the one who'd dumped Chris, and that he was a total dickhead to girls, Lenie might get—I don't know, a lighter sentence or whatever. Otherwise everyone would just think he dumped her and she went psycho, lock the evil bitch up and throw away the key. I don't know, I wasn't exactly thinking clearly; I just figured keeping it couldn't hurt, at least for now, and it might help."

If Julia had talked to any of the others, she would have known that the story had tangles, that not everything pointed straight to Selena. No way to guess what they would have done next, but they would have done it together.

It had been months too late for that to happen. Chris had cracked the four of them right across. Even after he was gone, the fault line he made had kept widening, deep under the surface, while everything up on top shone beautiful as new. We were just finishing the job he had begun.

I said, "Can you remember if anyone did manage to go up to the boarders' wing before study period that day? We'll check the logbook, but while we have you here: anything come to mind?"

I had Julia's attention. She was watching me hard. "What? You think someone else put that phone down behind Selena's bed?"

"If Selena didn't take that phone off Chris, someone else did. And then somehow it got to where you found it."

"Like, someone tried to *frame* her?"

Behind her shoulder, Conway's eyes said *Careful.* I shrugged. "We can't say that yet. I'd just like to know if anyone had the opportunity."

Julia thought. Shook her head, reluctantly. "I don't think so. I mean, obviously I'd love to say yeah, but actually there's not a chance in hell anyone would've got up there without a really good excuse. And even then, no way would she have been allowed on her own. Seriously, when I asked could I go get my French homework, Houlihan acted like I'd asked to go into a drug den and buy heroin."

The violin under Rebecca's bed. The flute in Selena's bit of wardrobe. I said, "What about during activities? Anyone go missing then?"

"Seriously? You think I'd've noticed? If you'd seen the mess the place was in . . . Plus I was concentrating on trying to get that phone. Joanne and Orla do drama too, and I know they were both there because Joanne kept trying to burst into tears"—Julia mimed puking—"and Orla had to comfort her and shit. But they're the only ones I remember."

"We'll try asking your mates." I said it nice and casual. The moonlight blazed into my face, felt like it was stripping me naked. I tried not to turn away. "Do they do drama as well, yeah? Or would they be able to tell us about other groups?"

"We're not actually surgically attached. Holly does dance. Selena and Becca do instrument practice."

So they would have had to go back to their room to get their instruments. Two of them together, to protect each other from the brain-eating maniac; they would have been allowed.

"Right," I said. "How many people in those, do you know?"

Julia shrugged. "Lots of people do dance. Like forty? Instruments, maybe like a dozen."

The odds said the rest had been day girls. We would check the logbook, but if the numbers held, Rebecca and Selena had been the only ones through that door.

The sudden quiet, all the day's jabbering and wailing fizzled away into that white silence. Rebecca holding out the phone she had taken to make sure that Selena was safe, that no one could ever link her to Chris. Holding it out like a gift, priceless. Like salvation.

Or: Selena burrowing in the wardrobe for her flute, slow with shock and grief. Behind her back, Rebecca, light as a ghost and just as urgent, leaning over her bed. Selena was the one who had started keeping secrets. She was the one who had let Chris in, to start things cracking apart. It had been her fault.

I looked at Conway, across that lone gallant slash of red. She was looking at me.

"Right," I said. "Your mates might remember someone leaving. Worth a shot, anyway."

"I'd say Selena was too upset to do much noticing," Conway said. "Let's ask Rebecca." And she stood up.

Mostly people look relieved. Julia looked taken aback. "What, that's it?"

"Unless there's something else you want to tell us."

Blank second. Headshake, almost reluctant.

"Then yeah, that's it. Thanks very much."

I stood up too, turned towards the path. Julia said, "What did I give you?"

She was looking at nothing. I said, "Hard to tell at this point. We'll have to see as we go."

Julia didn't answer. We waited for her to stand up, but she didn't move. After a minute we left her there, looking out over what used to be her kingdom; black hair and white face and that ember of red, and the white grass spread all around her.

28

They're eating breakfast when Holly feels the thread-tug of something gone wrong, deep in the weave of the school. Too many footsteps tumbling too fast, down a corridor; nun-voices too shrill outside the window, snapping to hushed too suddenly.

No one else notices. Selena is ignoring her muesli and twisting at a loose pajama button, Julia is eating cornflakes with one hand and doing her English homework with the other. Becca is gazing at her toast like it's turned into the Virgin Mary, or maybe like she's trying to lift it off the plate without touching it, which would be a hugely stupid idea but Holly doesn't have time to worry about it right now. She nibbles her toast in circles, and keeps one eye on the window and the other on the door.

Her toast is down to thumb-sized when she sees the two uniformed cops, hurrying down the edge of the back lawn, trying for out of sight but getting it just wrong.

Someone says at another table, wide awake all of a sudden, "OhmyGod! Were those *policemen*?" A suck of breath sweeping across the canteen, and then every voice rising at once.

That's when Matron comes in and tells them breakfast is over, and to go up to their rooms and get ready for school. Some people complain automatically, even if they've already finished their breakfast, but Holly can tell from Matron's face—slanted towards the window, no time to hear whinge—that they're on a loser. Whatever's happening isn't small.

While they get dressed Holly watches the window. One movement and she's there, face to the glass: McKenna and Father Voldemort, in a smoke-whirl of black robe, heading down the grass at charge speed.

Whatever's happened, it's happened to a Colm's boy.

Something blue-white zips along Holly's bones. The face on Joanne as she held out that screen, tongue-tip curling, wet-fanged at the delicious thought of doing damage. The way she licked up the shock Holly couldn't help showing, every drop. Joanne would do bad stuff, stuff that comes from places most people would never know how to imagine.

Don't worry. We'll get him.

Holly knows how to imagine the places where bad stuff begins. She's had practice.

"What the fuck?" says Julia, craning against her shoulder. "There's people in the bushes, look."

Off in the haze of layered greens beyond the grass, a flick of white. Like Technical Bureau boiler suits.

"They look like they're looking for something," Selena says, leaning in at Holly's other side. Her voice has that floppy, hard-work sound it's had for the last couple of weeks; it gives Holly the plunk of guilt she's starting to get used to. "Are they police too? Or what?"

Other people have noticed: excited jabber is filtering through the walls, feet go thumping down the corridor. "Maybe some guy was running away from the cops and he threw something over the wall," Julia says. "Drugs. Or a knife he used to stab someone, or a gun. If only we'd been out last night. Now that would've made life more interesting."

They don't feel it, what's prickling at Holly's scalp. The tug in the air has hooked them—Lenie is buttoning her shirt too fast, Jules is bouncing on her toes as she leans against the window—but they don't understand what it means: bad things.

Trust your instincts, Dad always says. If something feels dodgy to you, if someone feels dodgy, you go with dodgy. Don't give the benefit of the doubt because you want to be a nice person, don't wait and see in case you look stupid. Safe comes first. Second could be too late.

All the school feels crammed with dodgy, like cicada noises zizzing through a hot green afternoon, so shrill and many that you've got no chance of picking out any single one and seeing it straight. Joanne would go a long long way to get Selena in bad trouble.

I don't get pissed off with people like her. I get rid of them.

The bell for school goes. "Come on," Becca says. She hasn't come to the window; she's been plaiting her hair in a calm methodical rhythm, like there's a pearly bubble of cool air between her and that fizz. "You guys aren't even ready. We're going to be late."

Holly's heartbeat has reared up to match the cicada pulse. Selena's made it so easy for Joanne. Whatever Joanne's done, she did it knowing: all it'll take is one sentence to a teacher or to the detectives who'll be patient in the corner of everything from now on, one fake slip of the tongue, and oopsie!

"Shit," Holly says, when they reach the bottom of the stairs. Through the open connecting door they can hear the net of school noise, pulled tighter and higher today. Someone squeals, *And a police car!!* "Forgot my poetry book. Hang on—" and she's squeezing back up the stairs against the flow and yammer, hand already outstretched to dive down the side of Selena's mattress.

Two hundred and fifty of them bundle whispering into the hall. They settle instantly like good girls, hands all demure, like they're not sucking up every detail of the two plainclothes police being bland in back corners, like that eager boil isn't simmering just below their smooth eyes. They're jumping to know.

That groundskeeper guy Ronan you know how he you-know-what, I heard cocaine I heard gangsters came looking for him I heard there were cops with guns right out there on the grounds! I heard they shot him I heard the shots I heard I heard . . . Selena catches Julia's sideways grin—*the grounds*, like it's some scary jungle full of drug lords and probably aliens—and manages to come up with one back. Actually she barely has the energy to pretend she cares about whatever pointless drama is going on here. She wishes she knew how to puke on demand like Julia, so she could go back to their room and be left alone.

But McKenna coming up behind the podium has her mouth and her eyebrows rearranged into her special solemn face, carefully mixed stern and sad and holy. Back when they were in first year and a fifth-year got killed in a car crash over the Christmas break, they all came back in January to that face. They haven't seen it since.

Not Ronan the groundskeeper. People are twisting to see if they can spot anyone missing. *Lauren Mulvihill isn't in ohmygod I heard she was going to fail her exams I heard she got dumped ohmygod—*

"Girls," McKenna says. "I have some tragic news to share with you. You will be shocked and grieved, but I expect you to behave with the good sense and dignity that are part of the St. Kilda's tradition."

Straining silence. "Someone found a used condom," Julia guesses, on a breath too low for anyone but the four of them to hear.

"Shh," Holly says, without looking at her. She's sitting up high and straight, staring at McKenna and wrapping a tissue around and around her hand. Selena wants to ask if she's OK, but Holly might kick her.

"I am sorry to tell you that this morning a student from St. Colm's was found dead on our grounds. Christopher Harper—"

Selena thinks her chair's spun over backwards, into nothing. McKenna's gone. The hall has turned gray and misty, tilting, clanging with bells and squeals and distorted scraps of music left over from the Valentine's dance.

Selena understands, way too late and completely, why she wasn't punished after that first night. She had some nerve, back then, thinking she had any right to hope for that mercy.

Something hurts, a long way away. When she looks down she sees Julia's hand on her upper arm; to anyone watching it would look like a shock-grab, but Julia's fingers are digging in hard. She says, low, "Don't fucking faint."

The pain is good; it pushes the mist back a little. Selena says, "OK."

"Just don't break down, and keep your mouth shut. Can you do that?"

Selena nods. She's not sure what Julia's talking about, but she can remember it anyway; it helps, having two solid things to hold on to, one in each hand. Behind her someone is sobbing, loud and fake. When Julia lets go of her arm she misses the pain.

She should have seen this coming, after that first night. She should have spotted it seething in every shadow, red-mouthed and ravenous, waiting for a great golden voice to give it the word to leap.

She thought she was the one who would be punished. She let him keep coming back. She asked him to.

The splinters of music won't stop scraping at her.

Becca watches the assembly through the clearest coldest water in the world, mountain water full of movement and quirky little questions. She can't remember if she expected this part to be difficult; she thinks probably she never thought about it. As far as she can tell she's having the easiest time of anyone in the whole room.

McKenna tells them not to be afraid because the police have everything under control. She tells them to be very careful, in any telephone calls to their parents, not to cause needless worry with foolish hysteria. There will be group counseling sessions for all classes. There will be individual counseling sessions for anyone who feels she may need it. Remember that you can talk to your class teacher or to Sister Ignatius at any time. At the end she tells them to return to their homerooms, where their class teachers will join them to answer any questions they may have.

They foam out of the gym into the entrance hall. Teachers are positioned ready to herd them and hush them, but the jabber and the sobs can't be tamped down any longer; they surge up, careening around the high ceiling-space and up the stairwell. Becca feels like she's taken her feet off the ground and she's being carried along effortlessly, floated from shoulder to shoulder, all down the long corridors.

The second they're through the homeroom door, Holly has a hand clamped round Selena's wrist and she's force-fielding the whole four of them past sobbing hugging clumps, into a back corner by the window. She grabs them into a fake hug and says, hard, "They're going to be talking to everyone, the Murder detectives are. Don't tell them *anything*. No matter what. Specially don't tell them we can get out. Do you get that?"

"OhmyGod, look," Julia says, holding up a cupped palm, "it's a great big handful of duhhhh. Is it all for us?"

Holly hisses into her face, "I'm not joking. OK? This is *real*. Someone's going to actual *jail*, for *life*."

"No, seriously, are they? Do I look handicapped?"

Becca smells the acrid electrical-short urgency. "Hol," she says. Holly's all jammed-out angles and staticky hair; Becca wants to stroke her soft and smooth again. "We know. We won't tell them anything. Honestly."

"Right, that's what you think now. You don't know what it's like. This isn't going to be like Houlihan going, 'Ooh dear, I smell tobacco, have you girls been smoking cigarettes?' and if you look innocent enough she believes you. These are *detectives*. If they get one clue that you know anything about anything, they're like *pit* bulls. Like, eight hours in an interview room with them interrogating you and your parents going apeshit, does that sound like fun? That's what'll happen if you even *pause* before you answer a question."

Holly's forearm is steel, pressing down across Becca's shoulders. "And the other thing is: they lie. OK? Detectives make stuff up all the time. So if they're all, 'We know you were getting out at night, someone saw you,' *don't fall for it*. They don't actually know anything; they're just hoping you'll get freaked out and give them something. You have to look stupid and go, 'Nuh-uh, they must've got mixed up, it wasn't us.' "

Someone behind them sobs, "He was sooo full of life," and a wavering wail rises above the fug of the room. "Jesus Christ, someone shut those dumb bitches up," Julia snaps, shouldering Holly's arm away. "Fucking *ow*, Holly, that hurts."

Holly jams her arm back where it was, clamping Jules in place. "*Listen.* They'll make up mental stuff. They'll be like, 'We know you were going out with Chris, we've got proof—' "

Becca's eyes snap wide open. Holly is looking straight at Selena, but

Becca can't tell why, if it's just because they're opposite each other or if it's because much more. Selena doesn't feel staticky. She feels too soft, bruised to jelly.

Julia's face has gone sharp. "They can do that?"

"OhmyGod, here, have some more duh. They can say whatever they *want*. They can say they've got proof that you *killed* him, if they want, just to see what you do."

Julia says, "I have to talk to someone." She shrugs Holly's arm off and heads across the classroom. Becca watches. There's a high-pitched huddle around Joanne Heffernan, who's draped artistically over a chair with her head back and her eyes half shut. Gemma Harding is in the huddle, but Julia says something close to her and they move a step away. Becca can tell by the angles of their heads that they're keeping their voices down.

Holly says, "Please tell me you get that."

She's still looking at Selena, who, without the tight brace of the fake hug on both sides, rocks a little and comes down on someone's desk. Becca's pretty sure she hasn't heard any of it. She wishes she could tell Lenie how utterly OK everything is, shake out a great soft blanket of OK and wrap it round Lenie's shoulders. Things will run their own slow dark ways, down their old underground channels, and heal in their own time. You just have to wait, till you wake up one morning perfect again.

"I got it," she says to Holly, comfortingly, instead.

"*Lenie.*"

Lenie says obligingly, from somewhere way off outside the window, "OK."

"No. Listen. If they say to you, 'We've got total proof that you were with Chris,' you just say, 'No I wasn't,' and then you shut up. If they show you an actual *video*, you just say, 'That's not me.' Do you get it?"

Selena gazes at Holly. Eventually she asks, "What?"

"Oh, Jesus," Holly says up to the ceiling, hands in her hair. "I guess that could work. It'd better."

Then Mr. Smythe comes in and stands in the doorway looking skinny and petrified at the soggy heaving hugging mess in front of him, and starts flapping his hands and bleating, and gradually everyone unweaves themselves and brings the sobs down to sniffles, and Smythe takes a deep breath and starts in on the speech that McKenna made him memorize.

Probably Holly is right; what with her dad and everything else, she would know. Becca figures she should really be terrified. She can see the terror right there, like a big pale wobbly lump plonked down on her desk, that she's supposed to hold on to and learn by heart and maybe write an essay about. It's a little bit interesting, but not enough that she can be bothered picking it up. She pokes it off the edge of her mind and enjoys the squelchy cartoon splat it makes hitting the floor.

By mid-afternoon the parents start showing up. Alison's mum is first, throwing herself out of a mammoth black SUV and running up the front steps in spike heels that send her feet flying out at spastic angles. Alison's mum has had a lot of plastic surgery and she wears fake eyelashes the size of hairbrushes. She looks sort of like a person but not really, like someone explained to aliens what a person is and they did their best to make one of their own.

Holly watches her from the library window. Behind her the trees are empty, no flashes of white or fluttering crime-scene tape. Chris is out the back, somewhere, with efficient gloved people picking over every inch of him.

They're in the library because nobody knows what to do with anybody. A couple of the tougher teachers have managed to get the first- and second-years under control enough to do some kind of classes, but the third-years have outgrown their little-kid obedience and they actually knew Chris. Every time anyone tried to jam them down under a lid of algebra or Irish verbs, they boiled up and burst out at the cracks: someone started crying and couldn't stop, someone else fainted, four people got into a shrieking row over who owned a pen. When Kerry-Anne Rice saw demon eyes in the chem supplies cupboard, they were basically done. The third-years got sent to the library, where they've reached an unspoken agreement with the two teachers supervising them: they manage not to lose it, and the teachers don't make them pretend to study. A thick layer of whispering has spread over the tables and shelves, pressing down.

"Awww," Joanne says, low, next to Holly's ear. She's big-eyed and pout-lipped, head to one side. "Is she OK?"

She means Selena. Who is skew-shouldered in a chair like she was tossed there, hands dumped palms-up in her lap, staring at an empty patch of table.

"She's fine," Holly says.

"Really? Because it just totally breaks my heart to think about what she must be going through."

Joanne has one hand over her heart, to demonstrate. "They were over ages ago, remember?" Holly says. "But thanks."

Joanne crumples up her sympathy face and tosses it away. Underneath is a sneer. "OhmyGod, are you literally retarded? I'm never going to care about anything any of you feel. Just *please* tell me she's not going to start acting like she just lost her true love. Because that would be so pathetic I might have to puke, and bulimia is so over."

"Tell you what," Holly says. "Give me your mobile number. The second you get any say about how Selena acts, I'll give you a text and let you know."

Joanne examines her, flat eyes that suck in everything and put nothing back out. She says, "Wow. You actually are retarded."

Holly sighs noisily and waits. Being this close to Joanne is trickling cold oil down her skin. She wonders what Joanne's face would do if she asked, *Did you do it yourself, or did you make someone do it for you?*

"If the cops find out what Selena was doing with Chris, she'll be a total suspect. And if she goes around acting like some big tragedy queen, then they're going to find out. One way or another."

Since Holly is not in fact retarded, she knows exactly what Joanne means. Joanne can't take the Chief Mourner seat that she'd love, because she can't afford to have the cops start paying special attention to her, but no one else is getting it either. If Selena acts too upset, then Joanne will upload that phone video online and make sure the cops get a link.

Holly knows Selena didn't kill Chris. She knows that killing a person does almost-invisible things to you; it leaves you arm-linked with death, your head tilted just a degree that way, so that for the rest of your life your shadows mix together. Holly knows Selena down to her bones, she's been watching Selena all day, and if that tilt had happened since yesterday she would have seen it. But she doesn't expect the detectives to know Selena that way, or to believe her if she tells them.

Holly won't be asking whether Joanne did it herself. She's never going to be able to give Joanne, or anyone else, one hint that the thought has crossed her mind.

Instead she says, "Like you know so much about how detectives work? They're not going to suspect *Selena*. They've probably arrested someone by now."

They both hear it in her voice: Joanne's won. "Oh, that's right," Joanne says, flicking one last sneer at her and turning away. "I forgot your dad's a *Guard*." She makes it sound like a sewage sorter. Joanne's dad is a banker.

Speaking of whom. Dealing with Joanne has taken Holly's attention off the window; the first she knows about Dad arriving is when there's a tap on the door and his head pokes round it. For one second the rush of helpless gladness blows away everything else, even embarrassment: Dad will fix it all. Then she remembers all the reasons why he won't.

Alison's mum must have got snared by McKenna for a de-panicking session, but Dad doesn't get snared unless he wants to be. "Miss Houlihan," he says. "I'm just borrowing Holly for a minute. I'll bring her back safe and sound, cross my heart." And gives Houlihan a smile like she's a movie star. She never thinks of saying no. The fog-layer of whispers stops moving to let Holly pass underneath, watched.

"Hiya, chickadee," Dad says, in the corridor. The hug is one-armed, casual as any weekend hello, except for the convulsive gripe of his hand pressing her head into his shoulder. "You OK?"

"I'm fine," Holly says. "You didn't need to come."

"I wasn't doing anything else, figured I might as well." Dad is never doing nothing else. "Did you know this young fella?"

Holly shrugs. "I've seen him around. We talked a couple of times. He wasn't my *friend*. Just some guy from Colm's."

Dad holds her away and scans her, blue eyes lasering right through hers to scour the inside of her skull for scraps. Holly sighs and stares back. "I'm not devastated. Swear to God. Satisfied?"

He grins. "Smart-arsed little madam. Come on; let's go for a walk." He links her arm through his and strolls her down the corridor like they're headed for a picnic. "How about your pals? Did they know him?"

"Same as me," Holly says. "Just from around. We saw the detectives during the assembly. Do you know them?"

"Costello, I do. He's no genius, but he's sound enough, gets the job done. Your woman Conway, I only know what I've heard. She sounds OK. No idiot, anyway."

"Were you talking to them?"

"Checked in with Costello on my way up. Just to make it clear that I won't be stepping on their toes. I'm here as a dad, not a detective."

Holly asks, "What'd they say?"

Dad takes the stairs at an easy jog. He says, "You know the drill. Anything they tell me, I can't tell you."

He can be a dad all he wants; he's always a detective too. "Why? I'm not a witness."

This time, says the space in the air when she stops.

"We don't know that yet. Neither do you."

"Yeah, I do."

Dad lets that lie. He holds the front door open for her. The air spreading its arms to them is soft, stroking their cheeks with sweet greens and golds; the sky is holiday-blue.

When they're down the steps and crunching across the white pebbles, Dad says, "I'd like to believe that if you knew anything—anything at all, even something that was probably nothing—you'd tell me."

Holly rolls her eyes. "I'm not *stupid*."

"Furthest thing from it. But at your age, going by what I remember from a few hundred years ago, keeping your mouth shut around adults is a reflex. A good one—nothing wrong with learning to sort stuff out by yourselves— but it's one that can go too far. Murder isn't something you and your mates can sort. That's the detectives' job."

Holly knows it already. Her bones know it: they feel slight and bendy as grass stalks, no core to them. She thinks of Selena, rag-dolled in that chair. Things need doing, things she can't even get hold of. She wants to lift Selena up, put her in Dad's arms and say *Take good care of her.*

She feels Joanne behind her, high in the library window. Her stare zipping through the sunlit air to fingernail-pinch the back of Holly's neck, twisting.

She says, "I've actually known that for a while. Remember?"

She can tell by Dad's head rearing back that she's taken him off guard. They never talk about that time when she was a kid.

"OK," he says, a second later. Whether he believes her or not, he's not going any farther down that trail. "I'm relieved to hear it. In that case, I'll have a word with Costello, ask him to interview you now, get it out of the way. Then you can pack up your stuff, nice and discreetly, and come home with me."

Holly was expecting this, but she still feels her legs go rigid against it. "No. I'm not going home."

And Dad was expecting that; his stride doesn't change. "I'm not asking you, I'm telling you. And it's not forever. Just for a few days, till the lads get this sorted."

"What if they don't? Then what?"

"If they don't have their man locked up by Monday, we'll review the situation. It shouldn't come to that, though. From what I hear, they're pretty close to an arrest."

Their man. Not Joanne. Whatever the detectives have against this guy, sooner or later it's going to crumble in their hands, and they're going to go hunting again.

"OK," Holly says, turning docile. "Lenie and Becs can come with me, right?"

That gets Dad's attention. "Say what?"

"Their parents are away. They can come home with us, right?"

"Um," Dad says, rubbing the back of his head. "I'm not sure we're equipped for that, sweetheart."

"You said it's only for a couple of days. What's the big deal?"

"I *think* it's only for a few days, but this gig doesn't come with guarantees. And I don't have their parents' permission to haul them away for the duration. I don't fancy being had up for kidnapping."

Holly doesn't smile. "If it's too dangerous for me to stay here, it's too dangerous for them."

"I don't think it's dangerous at all. I think I'm a paranoid bastard. Professional deformation, they call it. I want you at home so that any time I start getting panicky, I can stick my head in and look at you and take a few deep breaths. It's for my sake, not yours."

His smile down at her and the weight of his hand on her head make Holly want to let every muscle go floppy: shove her face back into his shoulder, fill herself up with his smell of leather and smoke and soap, daydream there sucking her hair and say yes to whatever he tells her. She'd do it, except for the things Selena's got stashed in her head, ready to spill out ping-ponging all over the floor if Holly isn't there to keep them battened down.

She says, "If you take me home, everyone's going to think it's because you know something. I'm not leaving Selena and Becca here thinking a murderer could come after them any time and there's nowhere they can get away. If they're stuck here, they need to know it's safe. And the only way they're going to know that is if you say it's safe enough for me."

Dad's head goes back and he snaps a chunk off a laugh. "I like the way you work, chickadee. And I'll happily sit your mates down and tell them I'd bet a lot of money they're safe as houses, if you want me to. But much as I like Selena and Becca, they're their own parents' responsibility, not mine."

He means it: he doesn't think anyone's in danger. He wants Holly home, not in case she gets murdered, but in case being around another murder traumatizes her poor fragile ickle mind all over again.

Holly doesn't want a lovely Daddy-cuddle any more. She wants blood.

She says, firing it at him, "They're my responsibility. They're my *family*."

Score: Dad's not laughing any more. "Maybe. I'd like to think I am too."

"You're a grown-up. If you're paranoid for no reason, that's your problem to deal with. Not mine."

The tightened muscle in his cheek tells her she might be winning. The thought scares her so she wants to take it all back, swallow it down in a great gulp and go running into the school to pack her things. She stays silent and stretches her steps to match his. Pebbles grind together.

"Sometimes I think your ma's right," Dad says, on a wry one-sided grin. "You're my comeuppance."

Holly says, "So I can stay?"

"I'm not happy about it."

"Yeah, hello? Nobody's *happy* about any of this?"

That brings up the other side of the grin. "OK. I'll make you a deal. You can stay, if you give me your word that you'll tell me or the investigating officers anything that could conceivably be relevant. Even if you're positive it isn't. Anything you know, anything you notice, anything that just happens to occur to you as a vague possibility. Can you live with that?"

It occurs to Holly that this might be what he was after all along, or at least his backup plan. He's practical. If he doesn't get his dad wish, at least he can get his detective one.

"Yeah," she says, giving him all the straight look he could want. "I promise."

Selena's in the bedroom and Becca wants to give her this red phone. It comes with a long explanation that Selena can't keep hold of, but it lights a grave holy shine all round Becca and almost lifts her off her toes, so probably it's good. "Thanks," Selena says, and puts the phone down the side of her bed since that's where a secret phone belongs, except her own one isn't there any more. She wonders if maybe Chris came and took it, and left this red one with Becca so he can text her later when he gets a chance because right now he has to be busy, only then that sounds wrong but she can't track down why because Becca is looking at her, this look that dives down inside Selena and lands right on the place that's trying hard to hurt. So she just says "Thanks" again and then she can't remember what they came up here for. Becca gets her flute out of the wardrobe and puts it into her hands and asks, "What music do you need?" and for a moment Selena wants to laugh because Becca looks so calm and grown-up, riffling through her music case neat as a nurse. She wants to say *That's what you should be after school, you should be a nurse*, but the thought of the look Becca would give her makes the knot of laughter swell bigger and harder at the bottom of her throat. "The Telemann," she says. "Thanks."

Becca finds it. "There," she says, and clicks Selena's music case shut. Then she leans in and presses her cheek to Selena's. Her eyelashes moth-wing against Selena's skin and her lips are stone-cool. She smells like ripped green and hyacinths. Selena wants to hold her tight and breathe her all in, till her blood feels erased to pure again, like none of this ever happened.

After that Selena stays as still as she can and listens to how her heartbeat's changed, gone slow and rolling in underwater dark. She thinks maybe if she follows it far enough down the tunnel she'll find Chris. Probably he's dead if they all say so, but there's no way he's gone. Not the taste of his skin, not the hot mountaintop smell of him, not the upward curl of his laugh. She thinks if she concentrates hard enough she'll at least find what direction he's in, but people keep interrupting her.

People ask her questions in McKenna's office. She keeps her mouth shut and doesn't break down.

Just like Holly said, they get called into McKenna's office one by one. There's McKenna, there's a woman with black hair, and there's a fat old guy, all sitting in a row behind the long battered gloss of McKenna's desk. Becca never noticed before—the couple of times she was in here, she was too panicky to notice anything—that McKenna's chair is extra tall, to make you feel little and helpless. Actually, with three of them back there and only one tall chair, it just looks funny, like the woman detective's feet must be dangling in mid-air, or like McKenna and the guy detective are midgets.

They start with the stuff they ask everyone. Becca thinks back to what she was just a few months ago and does that, huddling up and tangling her legs and answering into her lap. If you're shy enough, no one sees anything else. The guy detective takes notes and bites down on a yawn.

Then the lady detective says—examining an unraveling thread in her jacket cuff, like this is no big deal—"What did you think about your friend Selena going out with Chris?"

Becca frowns, bewildered. "Lenie never went out with him. I think maybe they talked to each other a couple of times at the Court, but that was ages ago."

The detective's eyebrows go up. "Nah. They were a couple. You mean you didn't know?"

"We don't have boyfriends," Becca says disapprovingly. "My mum says I'm too young." She likes that touch. Looking like a kid might as well come in useful for once.

The lady detective and the man detective and McKenna all wait, staring at her from behind the sun-patterns slanted across the desk. They're so huge

and meaty and hairy, they think they'll just squash her down till her mouth
pops open and everything comes gushing out.

Becca looks back at them and feels her flesh stir and transform silently
into something new, some nameless substance that comes from high on
pungent-forested mountain slopes. Her borders are so hard and bright that
these lumpy things are being blinded just by looking at her; she's opaque,
she's impermeable, she's a million densities and dimensions more real than
any of them. They break against her and roll off like mist.

That night Holly stays awake as long as she can, watching the others like just
by watching she can keep them safe. She's sitting up with her arms around
her knees, too electric to lie down, but she knows none of them will try to
start a conversation. Today has gone on long enough.

Julia is sprawled and far away. Becca daydreams, eyes dark and solemn
as a baby's, flicking back and forth as she watches something Holly can't see.
Selena is pretending to be asleep. The light over the transom does bad things
to her face, turns it puffy and purple in tender places. She looks pounded.

Holly remembers that time back when she was a kid, how everything felt
ruined, around her and inside her. Slowly, when she wasn't looking, most of
that washed away. Time does things. She tells herself it'll do them for Selena.

She wants to be in the grove. She can feel it, how the moonlight would
pour over them all, calcify their bones to a strength that could take this
weight. She knows they would be insane even to think about trying it tonight, but she falls asleep craving it anyway.

When Holly's breathing evens out, Becca sits up and takes her pin and her
ink out of her bedside table. In the faint light from the corridor the line of
blue dots swings across her white stomach like the track of some strange
orbit, from her rib cage down to her belly button and back up to the ribs on
the other side. There's just room for one more.

Selena waits till even Becca's finally gone to sleep. Then she looks to see if
there's a text for her on the red phone, but it's gone. She sits in the tangle of
sheets and wants to go frantic, scream and claw, in case it did come from
Chris. But she can't remember how—her arms and her voice seem like they've
been unhooked from her body—and anyway it would be too much work.

She wonders, like a retch, if she did see this waiting all along, and closed
her eyes because she wanted Chris so much. The more she tries to remember,

the more it slips and twists and leers at her. In the end she knows she's never going to know.

She goes back to staying still. She carefully cordons off enough of her mind to do the necessary stuff, like showers and homework, so people won't come bothering her. She puts the rest into concentrating.

After a while she understands that something destroyed Chris to save her.

After a while longer she understands that this means it wants her for its own, and that she belongs to it for good now.

She cuts her hair off, for an offering, to send the message that she understands. She does it in the bathroom and burns the soft pale heap in the sink—the glade would be better, but they haven't been back there since it happened, and she can't tell if that's because the others know some reason she hasn't figured out. Her hair takes the lighter flame with a fierceness she didn't expect, a *whump* and a widemouthed roar like faraway trees taking forest fire. She whips her hand away, but not fast enough, and her wrist is left with a small drumming wound.

The smell of burning stays. For weeks afterwards she catches it on her, savage and holy.

Chunks of her mind fall off sometimes. At first it frightens her, but then she realizes once they're gone she doesn't miss them, so it doesn't bother her any more. The burn scars red and then white.

When Chris has been dead for four days, Julia hears that Finn's been expelled for hotwiring the fire door, and starts waiting for the cops to come for her.

They gave her and the others some hassle about Selena going out with Chris, but it was the cunning mirage hassle Holly talked about, looked impressive till you got up close and saw there was nothing solid there. It dissolved after a few days of blank headshakes. Which means that Gemma couldn't keep Joanne from flapping her yap altogether—in fairness, nothing short of surgery could—but she must have managed to get it through Joanne's thick skull that, no matter how incredibly awesomesauce the drama would be, they need to keep the details quiet for their own sakes.

But Julia couldn't exactly get that through to Finn. (*Hi, Jules here! Remember how u thot i was usin u 2 shag ur mate? U no wat wd b totes amazeballs? If u cud not mention dat 2 d cops. Kthxbai!!*) All she could do was keep her fingers crossed he would somehow work out all the stuff Holly warned about, and this is the kind of situation that requires more than crossed fingers. A bunch of Colm's idiots versus those two detectives: of course someone slipped up, in the end.

She doesn't have a clue what she'll say when they come. As far as she can see, she has two options: spill her guts about how she wasn't the only one meeting Chris, or deny everything and hope her parents get her a good lawyer. A month ago she would have said she'd go to jail before she'd throw Selena under a bus, no question; but things have changed, in ferocious tangled ways she's having trouble getting a grip on. Lying awake late, she runs through each scenario in her head, tries to imagine each one playing out. They both feel impossible. Julia understands that doesn't mean they can't happen. The whole world has come apart and gone lunatic, gibbering.

By the end of the week she thinks the cops are playing mind games with her, waiting for the suspense to break her down. It's working. When she drops a binder—she and Becca are in the back of the library, collecting binders full of old Irish exams for the class to practice on—she almost leaps through the roof. "Hey," Becca says. "It's OK."

"I'm actually smart enough to decide for myself whether it's OK or not," Julia snaps in a whisper, scooping dusty pages off the staticky carpet. "And believe me, it fucking isn't."

"Jules," Becca says gently. "It is. I swear. It's all going to be totally fine." And she runs the backs of her fingers along Julia's shoulder, down her arm, like someone calming a spooked animal.

Julia, whipping upright to rip her a new one, finds Becca looking back with steady brown eyes and not a hint of a flinch, even smiling a little. It's the first time in weeks she's looked at Becca properly. She realizes that Becca is taller than her now, and that—unlike Selena and Holly and, Christ knows, Julia herself—she doesn't look like shit. The opposite: she looks smoothed, luminous, as if her skin's been stripped away and remade out of something denser and so white it's almost metallic, something you could shatter your knuckles on. She looks beautiful.

It makes Julia feel even farther away from her. She doesn't have the energy to rip anyone anything; she just wants to sit down on the disgusting carpet and lean her head against the bookshelves and stay there for a long time. "Come on," she says instead, heaving up her armful of binders. "Let's go."

After another week she realizes that the cops aren't coming. Finn hasn't given them her name. He could have used it to bargain down the expulsion into a suspension, thrown it to the cops to get them off his back, but he didn't.

She wants to text him, but anything she said would come out as *Ha-ha, you're in the shit and I'm not, sucker.* She wants to ask his friends how he's doing, but either he's told them everything and they hate her, or he hasn't and it would start rumors, or they'd tell him and he'd hate her even more, and the whole mess would just bubble up viler. Instead she waits till the others are asleep and bawls like a stupid whiny baby all night long.

After two and a half weeks the center of the world is starting to turn away from Chris Harper. The funeral is over; everyone's talked themselves tired of the photographers outside the church and who cried and how Joanne fainted during Communion and had to be carried outside. Chris's name has fallen off the front pages, into the occasional snippet in spare corners that need filling. The detectives are gone, most of the time. The Junior Cert is just a few days from pouncing, and the teachers get narky instead of guidance-y if someone messes up a class by bursting into tears or seeing Chris's ghost. He's drifted off to one side: there, all the time, but in the corner of your eye.

On the way to the Court, under trees puffed up with full summer green, Holly says, "Tonight?"

"Hello?" Julia says, eyebrows shooting up. "And walk straight into a dozen of your dad's buddies just waiting for someone to be that incredibly fucking stupid? Seriously?"

Becca is hopscotching over cracks, but Julia's whipcrack voice gets her watching. Selena keeps on walking with her head tipped back, face turned up to the sweet swirls of leaves. Holly has her elbow to make sure she doesn't smash into anything.

"There aren't any detectives. Dad's always complaining about how he can't even get surveillance authorized on, like, major *drug* dealers; no way would they authorize it on a *girls'* school. So duh, incredibly fucking stupid yourself."

"Well, isn't it just awesomesauce to have an expert on police procedure right here. I guess it never occurred to you that maybe your daddy doesn't tell you everything?"

Julia is giving Holly her fiercest better-back-down glare, but Holly's not backing anywhere. She's been waiting weeks for this; it's the only thing she can think of that might fix things. "He doesn't need to *tell* me. I have *brain* cells—"

"I want to go," Becca says. "We need it."

"Maybe you need to get arrested. I honest-to-God don't."

"We do need it," Becca says, stubborn. "Listen to you. You're being a bitch. If we have a night out there—"

"Oh, please, don't give me that crap. I'm being a bitch because this is a stupid idea. It's not going to get any less stupid if we—"

Selena wakes up. "What is?"

"Forget it," Julia tells her. "Never mind. Go think about pink fluff some more."

"Going out tonight," Becca says. "I want to go, so does Hol, Jules doesn't."

Selena's eyes float over to Julia. "Why not?" she asks.

"Because even if the cops don't have surveillance on the place, it's still a dumb idea. Have you even noticed that the Junior Cert *starts* this *week*? Have you even heard them, every single day: 'Oh you have to get sleep, if you don't get sleep you can't concentrate and you won't be able to study—'"

Holly's hands fly up and out. "Oh my God, since when do you care what Sister Ignatius thinks you should do?"

"I don't give a fuck about Sister Ignatius. I care if I end up stuck in, like, *needlework* class next year because I fail my—"

"Oh, yeah, *right*, because of one hour one night, you're totally going to—"

"I want to go," Selena says. She's stopped walking.

The rest of them stop too. Holly catches Julia's eye and widens hers, warning. This is the first time in weeks that Lenie has wanted anything.

Julia takes a breath like she's got another argument ready, the heaviest of all. Then she looks at the three of them and puts it away again.

"OK," she says. Her voice has dulled. "Whatever, I guess. Just, if it doesn't . . ."

"If what doesn't what?" Becca asks, after a moment.

Julia says, "Nothing. Let's do it."

"Woohoo!" Becca says, and jumps high to pull a flower off a branch. Selena starts walking and goes back to watching the leaves. Holly takes her elbow again.

They're almost at the Court; the warm sugary smell of doughnuts reaches out to make their mouths water. Something seizes Holly, in the tender space between where her breasts are growing, and drags downwards. At first she thinks she's hungry. It takes her a moment to understand that it's loss.

Outside their window the moon is slim and running wild with streaks of cloud. Their movements as they dress are filled up with every other time, with the first can't-believe-we're-doing-this half-joke, with the magic of a bottle cap floating above a palm, of a flame turning them to gold masks. As they pull up their hoods and take their shoes in their hands, as they slow-motion like dancers down the stairs, they feel themselves slowly turn buoyant again, feel the world flower and shiver as it waits for them. A smile is tipping the corner of Lenie's mouth; on the landing Becca turns her palms to the white-lit window like a thanksgiving prayer. Even Julia who thought she knew better is beating with it, the bubble of hope expanding inside her ribs till it hurts, *What if, maybe, maybe we really could—*

The key won't turn.

They stare at each other, wiped blank.

"Let me try," Holly whispers. Julia steps back. The rhythm in their ears is pounding faster.

It won't turn.

"They've changed the lock," Becca whispers.

"What do we do?"

"Get out of here."

"Let's go."

Holly can't get the key out.

"Come on come on come *on*—"

The terror leaps like wildfire among them. Selena has her mouth pushed into her forearm to keep herself quiet. The key rattles and grates; Julia shoves Holly out of the way—"Jesus, did you break it?"—and grabs it in both hands. In the second when it looks like it's really stuck, all four of them almost scream.

Then it shoots out, slamming Julia backwards into Becca. The thump and *oof* of breath and scrabble for balance sound loud enough to call out the school. They run, flailing clumsy in slipping sock-feet, teeth bared with fear. Into their room and the door closing too hard, clawing clothes off and pajamas on, leaping for their beds like animals. By the time the prefect drags herself awake and comes shuffling down the corridor to stick her head in at each door, they have themselves and their breathing all neatly arranged. She doesn't care if they're faking or not, as long as they're doing nothing that could get her in trouble; one glance around their smooth sleeping faces, and she yawns and closes the door again.

None of them say anything. They keep their eyes closed. They lie still and feel the world change shape around them and inside them, feel the boundaries set solid; feel the wild left outside, to prowl perimeters till it thins into something imagined, something forgotten.

29

The night had turned denser, ripening with little scurries and eddies of scent, things we couldn't trace. The moonlight was coming down thick enough to drench us.

I said, "You got that, what she gave us. Yeah?"

Conway was moving fast back along the path, mind already leaping up that slope to Rebecca. "Yeah. Selena and Rebecca go to their room for their instruments. Either Rebecca's pissed off enough with Selena that she hides Chris's phone to frame her, or she gives it to Selena—here you go, your dead fella's phone, just what you've always wanted—and Selena stashes it to deal with some other time."

We were keeping our voices down; girls could be hidden like hunters behind any tree. I said, "That, and Holly's out. Rebecca was working on her own."

"Nah. Holly could've stashed Chris's phone when she took Selena's."

I said, "Why, but? Say she had Chris's phone, or access to it: why not dump it in the lost-and-found bin along with Selena's, if she was trying to take suspicion off her lot? Or if she was trying to frame Selena, why not leave both phones behind her bed? There's no reason why she'd want to do different things with the two phones. Holly's out." A couple of hours too late. We had Mackey for an enemy now, not an ally.

Conway thought that through for two fast steps, gave it the nod. "Rebecca. All on her ownio."

I thought of that triple creature, still and watching. *All on her ownio* seemed like the wrong words.

Conway said, "We still don't have enough on her. It's all circumstantial, and the prosecutors don't like that. Specially when it's a kid. Extra-specially when it's a little rich kid."

"It's circumstantial, but there's a load of it. Rebecca had plenty of reasons to be pissed off with Chris. She was able to get out at night. She was seen with the weapon the day before the murder. She's one of the only two people who could've put Chris's phone where it was found—"

"*If* you believe a dozen stories from half a dozen other teenage girls who've all lied their little arses off to us. A decent defense barrister'll have reasonable doubt all over it inside five minutes. Plenty of girls had better reasons to be pissed off with Chris. Seven others could get out at night, and that's just the ones we know about; how do we prove no one else had found out where Joanne kept her key? Chris's phone: Rebecca or Selena could've found it wherever the killer dumped it, stashed it behind the bed while they worked out what to do with it."

"So what was Rebecca doing messing about with the murder weapon?"

"Gemma made that up. Or Rebecca was there to buy drugs. Or she actually was into gardening. Pick your favorite." Conway's stride was lengthening. By now I knew that was frustration. "Or she was scouting for Julia, or Selena, or Holly. We know they're out, but we've got nothing solid to prove it. Which means we've got nothing solid that proves Rebecca."

I said, "We need a confession."

"Yeah, that'd be great. You go pick us up one of those. Get next week's Lotto numbers, while you're at it."

I ignored that. "Here's what I've spotted about Rebecca: she's not scared. And she should be. Her situation, anyone but an idiot would be petrified, and she's no idiot. But she's still not scared of us."

"So?"

"So she must think she's safe."

Conway shoved a branch out of her face. "She fucking is, unless we come up with something amazing."

I said, "Tell you the one time I've seen her scared. In the common room, when everyone was losing the head about the ghost. We were so busy with Alison, we paid no attention to Rebecca, but she was terrified. We don't scare her; doesn't matter what we throw at her, evidence, witnesses, it won't shake her. Chris's ghost does."

"So what? You wanna dress up in a sheet and wave your arms at her from behind a tree? Because I swear to God, I'm almost that desperate."

I said, "I just want to talk to her about the ghost. Just talk to her. See where it goes."

It had hit me while I was on the grass with Joanne's lot: every girl in that common room had thought Chris was there specially for her. Rebecca had known it.

That made Conway glance my way. She said, "Thin ice."

If the ghost got something out of Rebecca, we were in for a fight, down the line. The defense would scream coercion, intimidation, scream about no appropriate adult present, try to get whatever she said ruled inadmissible. We would argue exigent circumstances: we needed to get Rebecca out of there, that night. Might work, might not.

If we didn't get something now, we were getting nothing, ever.

I said, "I'll be careful."

"OK," Conway said. "Go for it. Fuck knows I've got nothing better."

I knew the raw-scraped sound in her voice by now. Knew better than to try and soothe it. "Thanks," I said.

"Yeah."

Around the bend in the path, in under the trees—it felt like a drop into nothing, that step into the streaked black—and I smelled smoke. Could've been schoolgirl boldness, but I knew.

Mackey, leaning against a tree, all shoulder-slope and crossed ankles. "Nice night for it," he said.

We braked like kids caught snogging. I went red. Felt him see it through the dark, amused.

"Good to see you two crazy kids sorted out your problems. I wondered if you might. Been having fun?"

Behind his shoulder, the hyacinth bed. The flowers glowed blue-white like they were lit from inside. Behind that, up the slope, Selena and Rebecca had their heads bent close. Mackey was guarding them.

Conway said, "We'd like you to go inside and stay with your daughter. We'll be with you as soon as we can."

Cigarette caught between his knuckles, looked like the ember was blooming deep inside his black fist. He said, "It's been a long day. And these girls, in fairness to them, they're only kids. They're shattered, stressed-out, all the rest. Not trying to teach you two your job—God forbid—but I'm just saying: I wouldn't put too much stock in anything you get out of them at this point. A jury wouldn't."

I said, "We don't suspect Holly of the murder."

"No? That's nice to know."

Smoke curling through the stripes of moonlight. He didn't believe me.

"We've got new information," Conway said. "It points away from Holly."

"Well done. And in the morning, you can go galloping off wherever that information takes you. Now it's time to go home. Stop in the pub on the way, get yourselves a nice pint to celebrate the beginning of a beautiful friendship."

Behind him, a shadow slipped out of the trees, fitted itself into place beside Selena. Julia.

Conway said, "We're not done here yet."

"Yes, Detective. You are."

Gentle voice, but the glint of his eyes. Mackey meant it. "I've been picking up some information of my own. Three lovely girls saw me wandering around looking for you two, and they called me over." That dark hand with the burning core, lifting to point at me. "Detective Moran. You've been a bad boy."

Conway said, "If anyone's got a problem with Detective Moran, they need to take it to his superintendent. Not to you."

"Ah, but they've come to me now. I think I can convince them that Detective Moran didn't actually try to seduce their irresistible selves, and that one of them—blond, skinny, no eyebrows?—didn't actually feel her virtue was in imminent danger. But you're going to need to get out of my way and let me do it in peace. Is that clear?"

I said, "I can look after myself. Thanks all the same."

"I wish I agreed with you, kid. I really do."

"If I'm wrong, it's not your problem. And who we talk to isn't your call."

The words felt strange and strong, rising out of me, strong as trees. Conway's shoulder was against mine, level and solid.

Lift of Mackey's eyebrow, in a stripe of light. "Oo, get you. Did you grow those yourself, or did you borrow them off your new pal?"

"Mr. Mackey," Conway said. "Let me explain to you what's going to happen now. Detective Moran's going to talk to these three girls. I'm going to observe, with my mouth shut. If you think you can manage the same, feel free. If you can't, then fuck off and leave us to it."

The eyebrow stayed up. To me: "Don't say I didn't warn you."

About Conway, about what Joanne could do, about what he would do. He was right, on every one of them. And—what a guy—he was giving me one last chance, for old times' sake, to play nice.

"I won't," I said. "Word of honor, man: I'd never claim that."

Quick sniff of laughter from Conway. Then the two of us turned our backs on Mackey and moved through the miasma of hyacinths, up the slope towards the glade.

Under the cypresses Conway stopped. I heard Mackey's long leisurely stride catch up with her, felt her stretch out an arm: far enough.

He stopped because he'd been going to anyway. If anything led even an inch towards Holly, Conway wouldn't be able to hold him back.

I stepped out into the clearing and stood in front of those three girls.

The moon stripped my face bare to them. It turned them black-invisible, blazed their outline like a great white rune written on the air. Joanne and her lot were danger, bad danger. They were nothing compared to this.

I cleared my throat. They didn't move.

I said, "Do yous not have to head indoors for lights-out, no?"

My voice came out weak, a limp thread. One of them said, "We'll go in a minute."

"Right. Grand. I just wanted to say . . ." Foot to foot, rustling in the long grass. "Thanks for all your help. It's been great. Really made a difference."

A voice asked, "Where's Holly?"

"She's inside."

"Why?"

I twisted. "She's a bit shaken up. I mean, she's grand, but that thing back in the common room, with the . . . you know. Chris's ghost."

Julia's voice said, "There wasn't any ghost. That was just people looking for attention."

A shift, under the curves of that rune sign. Selena's voice said softly, "I saw him."

Another movement, quicker and cut off. Julia had elbowed Selena, kicked her, something.

I asked, "Rebecca? How about you?"

After a moment, from inside the dark: "I saw him."

"Yeah? What was he doing?"

Another ripple through that rune, changed the meaning in subtle ways I couldn't read.

"He was talking. Fast, like jabbering; like, he never stopped to breathe. I guess he doesn't need to."

"What was he saying?"

"I couldn't tell. I was trying to read his lips, but he was going too fast. One time he . . ." Rebecca's voice split on a shiver. "He laughed."

"Could you tell who he was talking to?"

Silence. Then—so soft, I would've missed it, only my ears were wide open as an animal's—"To me."

A tiny catch of breath, almost a gasp, from somewhere else in that condensation of darkness.

I asked, "Why you?"

"I told you. I couldn't hear."

"This morning you said you and Chris weren't close."

"We weren't."

"So it's not like he misses you so much, he had to come back and tell you that."

Nothing.

"Rebecca."

"Probably not. I guess. I don't know."

"Not like he was secretly in love with you, no?"

"No!"

I said, "You know how you looked, in there? Scared. Like, really scared."

"I saw a *ghost*. You'd be scared too."

The raw flick of defiance: she didn't sound like a mystery now, not like a danger. Sounded like a kid, just a teenage kid. The power was seeping out of her; fear was seeping in.

Julia said, "Don't talk to him any more."

I said, "Did you think he was going to hurt you?"

"How would I know?"

"Becs. *Shut up.*"

No way to tell if Julia was just wary, or if she was starting to understand. "But," I said, fast, "but Rebecca, I thought you liked Chris. You told us he was sound. Was that a lie? He was actually a dickhead?"

"No. He wasn't. He was *kind*."

That flare of defiance again, hotter. This mattered to her.

I shrugged. "Everything we've learned, he sounds like a dickhead. He used girls for whatever he could get, dumped them as soon as he wasn't getting it. A real prize."

"*No.* Colm's is full of those—they don't care what they wreck, they'll do anything to anyone as long as they get what they want. I know the difference. Chris wasn't like that."

The white outline moved. Things rising up underneath it, bubbling.

Rebecca felt them. She said, "I know the stuff he did. *Obviously* I know he wasn't perfect. But he wasn't like the rest of them."

A raw choke that could have been a laugh, out of Julia.

"Lenie. He wasn't. Was he?"

Selena moved. She said, "He was a lot of things."

"*Lenie.*"

They had forgotten me. Selena said, "He wanted not to be like them. He tried really hard. I don't know how much it worked."

"It did." Rebecca's voice was spiraling towards panic. "It worked."

That ugly twist of sound again, from Julia.

"It did. It *did*."

Something crunched behind me, a branch whipped. Something was happening. I couldn't tell what, couldn't afford to turn. Had to trust Conway and keep going.

I said, "So how come you were scared of his ghost? Why would it want to hurt you, if Chris never would've?"

Julia said, "Specially since it's *not fucking real*. Becca? Hello? They made you imagine it like some *Omen* thing. If you decide to imagine it as a purple turtle instead, then that's what you'll see. Hello?"

"Hello yourself, I *saw* him—"

"Rebecca. Why would it want to hurt you?"

"Because ghosts are angry. You guys said that, remember? This afternoon." But the panic was taking up more and more of Rebecca's voice. "And anyway, he *didn't* hurt me."

I said, "This time he didn't. What about next time?"

"Who says there'll be a next time?"

"I do. Chris had something to say to you, something he wants from you, and he didn't get through. He'll be back. Again and again, till he gets what he wants."

"He won't. It was because you were here, you got him all—"

"Selena," I said. "You know he was there. You want to tell us whether you think he'll be back?"

In the slow fall of silence, I heard something. Murmur of voices, away down at the bottom of the slope. A man. A girl.

Closer, in the cypresses behind me: a sound like the muted first breath of a roar. Conway, moving among the branches to cover the voices. "Selena," I said. "Is Chris going to be back?"

Selena said, "He's there the whole time. Even when I don't see him, I can feel him. I *hear* him, like this humming noise right inside the backs of my ears, like when the telly's on mute. All the time."

I believed her. Believed every word. I said, heard the hoarse note in my voice, "What does he want?"

"At first I was sure he was looking for me. Oh God I tried so hard but I could never make him see me, he never heard me, I was begging him *Chris I'm here I'm right here* but he just looked right past me and kept doing whatever he was doing, I tried to hold him but he just dissolved before I could—"

A high keening sound from Rebecca.

"I thought it was because we weren't allowed, like punishment, always looking for each other but we'd never be allowed to—But it's because it isn't me he wants. All that time—"

Julia said, "Shut up."

"All that time, he was never looking for—"

"Jesus Christ, can you shut *up*?"

Something like a sob, from Selena. Then nothing. The low roar among the cypresses wavered through the air and was gone, rock in a cold pool. The voices at the bottom of the slope sank with it.

Rebecca said, in the empty space, "Lenie. What's he want?"

Julia said, "Can we *please fucking please* talk about it later?"

"Why? I'm not scared of *him*." Me.

"Then *duh*, start paying attention. He's the only thing we need to be scared of. There isn't anything else. This ghost bullshit—"

"Lenie. What do you think he wants? Chris?"

"OhmyGod, he doesn't fucking *exist*, what do I have to *do*—"

Kids fighting, they sounded like. That was all. Not like Joanne's lot, cheap sneer-and-peck by numbers, every word and thought worn threadbare before it ever reached them, not that; but not the enchanted girls, soaring among tumbling arpeggios of gold, that I had come hoping for just that morning. What I had seen before, that triple power, that had been the last flicker of something lost a long time ago. Light from a dead star.

"Lenie. Lenie. Is it me he's after?"

Selena said, "I wanted it to be me so much."

The rune shimmered and crumpled. One fragment snapped off that solid dark mass, found a shape of its own: Rebecca. Sliver-thin, kneeling on the grass.

She said, to me: "I didn't think it was going to be Chris."

I said, "The ghost?"

Rebecca shook her head. She said, simply, "No, when I texted him to meet me here. I didn't know who it was going to be. I'd've bet anything it wouldn't be Chris."

"Oh, Becs," Julia said. She sounded folded over a gut-punch. "Oh, Becs."

In the cypress shadow behind me, Conway said, "You are not obliged to say anything unless you wish to do so, but anything you do say will be taken down in writing and may be used in evidence. Do you understand?"

Rebecca nodded. She looked frozen to the bones, too cold even to shiver.

I said, "So when you got here that night, you were expecting to meet one of the dickheads."

"Yeah. Andrew Moore, maybe."

"When you saw Chris, you didn't have second thoughts, no?"

Rebecca said, "You don't understand. It wasn't like that. I wasn't trying to figure it out, 'Oh am I right am I wrong what should I do?' I *knew*."

There it was: why she hadn't been frightened of Conway and Costello, why she hadn't been frightened of us. All the long way from that night until this evening—and this evening something had changed—she had known she was safe, because she had known she was right.

I said, "Even when you saw it was Chris? You were still positive?"

"*Specially* then. That's when I got it. Up until then, I had it backwards. All those stupid slimebags, James Gillen and Marcus Wiley, it could never have been them. They're nothing; they're totally worthless. You can't have a sacrifice that's worthless. It has to be something good."

Even in that light I saw the flicker of Julia's eyelids, hooding. The sad, sad smile on Selena.

"Like Chris," I said.

"Yeah. He wasn't worthless—I don't *care* what you guys say"—into the dark of Julia and Selena—"he wasn't. He was something special. So when I saw him, that was when I actually properly understood: I was getting it right."

Those voices again, down the bottom of the slope. Building.

I said, fast and a notch louder, "It didn't bother you? Some slimebag who deserved it, that's one thing. But a guy you liked, a good guy? That didn't upset you?"

Rebecca said, "Yeah. If I'd had the choice, I'd've picked someone else. But I would've been wrong."

Setting up for an insanity defense, I'd have thought, if she'd been older or savvier. If we'd been indoors, I'd've thought there was no setup about it, just plain insanity. But here, in the glowing spin and slipslide of her world, in the air thick with scents and stars: for a second I almost saw what she meant. Caught the edge of understanding, swung by my fingertips, before I lost hold and it soared up and away again.

Rebecca said, "That's why I left him the flowers."

"Flowers," I said. Nice and neutral. Like the air hadn't leapt into a hum around me.

"Those." Her arm rose, thin as a dark brushstroke. Pointed at the hyacinths. "I picked some of those. Four; one for each of us. I put them on his chest. Not to say sorry, or anything; it wasn't like that. Just to say good-bye. To say we knew he wasn't worthless."

Only the killer had known about those flowers. I felt, more than heard, a long sigh come out of Conway and spread across the clearing.

"Rebecca," I said gently. "You know we have to arrest you. Right?"

Rebecca stared, huge-eyed. She said, "I don't know how."

"That's OK. We'll walk you through everything. We'll find someone to look after you till your parents can get here."

"I didn't think this would happen."

"I know. Right now, all you need to do is come over here and we'll go indoors."

"I can't."

Selena said, "Give us a minute first. Just a minute."

I heard Conway breathe in for the *No*. I said, "We can do that. But it'll only be a minute."

"Becs," Selena said, so softly. "Come here."

Rebecca turned towards her voice, hands reaching, and her head bent back into that dark shape. Their arms folded around each other's shoulders like wings, drawing tighter, like they were trying to meld themselves into one thing that could never be prized apart. I couldn't tell which of them sobbed.

Footsteps behind me, running, and this time I could turn. Holly, hair spraying out of its ponytail, leaping up the slope in great desperate bounds.

Behind her, and making himself take his time, was Mackey. He had seen her coming, gone down to the path to keep her there as long as he could. He had left me and Conway up here, to do whatever we were going to do. In the end, for his own reasons, he had decided I was worth trusting.

Holly came past Conway like she was nothing, hit the edge of the clearing, and saw the other three. She pulled up like she'd smacked into a stone wall. Said, voice cracking wild, "What's happened?"

Conway kept her mouth shut. This was mine.

I said quietly, "Rebecca's confessed to killing Chris Harper."

Holly's head moved, a blind flinch. "Anyone can confess to anything. She said it because she was scared you were going to arrest me."

I said, "You already knew it was her."

Holly didn't deny it. She didn't ask what would happen to Rebecca next; didn't need to. She didn't throw herself on the others, didn't rush into Daddy's arms—he managed not to go to her. She just stood there, watching her mates motionless on the grass, with one hand braced against a tree like it was holding her up.

"If you'd known this morning," I said, "you'd never have brought me that card. Who did you think it was?"

Holly said, and she sounded way too tired and hollow for sixteen, "I always thought it was Joanne. Probably not actually her—I thought she made someone else do it, maybe Orla; she makes Orla do all her dirty work. But I thought it was her idea. Because Chris had dumped her."

"And then you figured Alison or Gemma found out, couldn't take the pressure, put up the card."

"I guess. Yeah. Whatever. Gemma wouldn't, but yeah, it's exactly the kind of hello-are-you-actually-that-thick thing Alison would do."

Conway asked, "Why didn't you just say all this to Detective Moran, straight up? Why make us dick around jumping through hoops all day?"

Holly looked at Conway like just the thought of all that stupid made her want to sleep for a year. She let her back slump against the tree trunk and closed her eyes.

I said, "You didn't want to be a rat."

Rustle behind her, sharp and then gone, as Mackey moved.

"Again," Holly said. Her eyes stayed closed. "I didn't want to be a rat again."

"If you'd told me everything you knew, you would've probably ended up testifying in court, and the rest of the school would've found out you'd squealt. But you still wanted the killer caught. That card was the perfect chance. You didn't have to tell me anything; just point me in the right direction, and keep your fingers crossed."

Holly said, "You weren't *stupid*, last time. And you didn't act like anyone under twenty had to be stupid. I thought if I could just get you in here . . ."

Conway said, "And you were right."

"Yeah," Holly said. The lines of her face, turned up to the sky, would have broken your heart. I couldn't look at Mackey. "Go me."

I asked, "How did you figure out it wasn't Joanne after all? When we came to take you to the art room, you knew. What happened?"

Holly's chest lifted and fell. "When that light bulb blew up," she said. "I knew then."

"Yeah? How?"

She didn't answer. She was done.

"Chickadee," Mackey said. His voice was a kind of gentle I'd never thought could come out of him. "It's been a long, long day. Time to go home."

Holly's eyes opened. She said to him, like no one else existed, "You thought it was me. You thought I killed Chris."

Mackey's face closed over. He said, "We'll talk about it in the car."

"What did I ever do to make you think I would kill someone? Like *ever*, in my whole life?"

"The car, chickadee. Now."

Holly said, "You just figured if anyone annoyed me I'd bash them over the head, because I'm your daughter and it's in our blood. I'm not just *your daughter*. I'm an actual *person*. Of my own."

"I know that."

"And you kept me down there so they could make Becca confess. Because you knew if I got up here, I'd shut her up. You made me leave her here till she . . ." Her throat closed.

Mackey said, "I'm asking you, as a favor to me: let's go home. Please."

Holly said, "I'm not going anywhere with you." She straightened, joint by joint, moved out from under the cypresses. Mackey took a fast breath to call after her, then bit it down. Conway and I both had better sense than to look at him.

In the center of the clearing, Holly dropped to her knees in the grass. For a second I thought the others were going to tighten their backs against her. Then they opened like a puzzle, arms unfurling, reached out to draw her in and closed around her.

A night bird ghosted across the top of the glade, calling high, trailing a dark spiderweb of shadow over our heads. Somewhere a bell grated for lights-out; none of the girls moved. We left them there as long as we could.

We waited in McKenna's office for the social worker to come take Rebecca away. For a different crime, we could have released her into McKenna's custody, let her have one last night at Kilda's. Not for this. She would spend the night, at least, in a child detention school. Whispers crowding around the new girl, eyes probing for clues to where she fit in and what they could do with her: deep down, under the rough sheets and the raw smell of disinfectant, it wouldn't be too different from what she was used to.

McKenna and Rebecca faced each other across the desk, Conway and I stood around in empty space. None of us talked. Conway and I couldn't, in case something came across like questioning; McKenna and Rebecca didn't, being careful or because they had nothing to say to us. Rebecca sat with her hands folded like a nun, gazing out the window, thinking so hard she sometimes stopped breathing. Once she shivered, all over.

McKenna didn't know what face to wear, for any of us, so she looked down at her hands clasped on the desk. She had layered up her makeup, but she still looked ten years older than that morning. The office looked older too, or a different kind of old. The sunlight had given it a slow voluptuous glow, packed every scrape with a beckoning secret and turned every dust mote into a whispering memory. In the stingy light off the overhead bulb, the place just looked worn out.

The social worker—not the one from that morning; a different one, fat in floppy tiers like she was made of stacked pancakes—didn't ask questions. You could tell from the fast sneaky glances that her job gave her more piss-sprayed blocks of flats than places like this, but she just said, "Well! Time we were getting some sleep. Off we go," and held the door open for Rebecca.

"Don't call me *we*," Rebecca said. She got up and headed for the door, not a glance at the social worker, who was clicking her tongue and tucking in her chins.

At the door she turned. "It's going to be all over the news," she said, to Conway. "Isn't it?"

"I haven't heard you caution her," the social worker said, pointing a waggy finger at Conway. "You can't use anything she says." To Rebecca: "We need to be very quiet right now. Like two little mice."

"The media won't use your name," Conway said. "You're a minor."

Rebecca smiled like we were the kiddies. "The internet isn't going to care how old I am," she pointed out. "Joanne isn't going to care, the exact second she gets online."

McKenna said to all of us, one notch too loud, "Every student and staff member in this school will be under the strictest instructions not to make any of today's events public knowledge. On or off the internet."

We all left a second for that to fall into. When it was gone Rebecca said, "If anyone goes looking for my name, like in a hundred years, they're going to find mine and Chris's. Together."

That shiver again, hard as a spasm.

Conway said, "It'll be headlines for a few days now, a few days later on." She didn't say *during the trial.* "Then it'll go off the radar. Online, it'll drop even quicker. One celebrity caught shagging the wrong person, and this is yesterday's news."

That curled the corner of Rebecca's mouth. "That doesn't matter. I don't care what people think."

Conway said, "Then what?"

"Rebecca," McKenna said. "You can speak to the detectives tomorrow. When your parents have arranged for appropriate legal counsel."

Rebecca, thin in the slanted space of the doorframe, where one sideways turn would vanish her into the immeasurable dark of the corridor. She said, "I thought I was getting him off us. Getting him off Lenie, so she wouldn't be stuck to him forever. And instead I am. When I saw him, there in the common room—"

"I've told her," the social worker said, through a tight little mouth. "You all heard me tell her."

Rebecca said, "So that has to mean I did the wrong thing. I don't know how, because I was sure, I was so—"

"I can't *force* her to be quiet," the social worker told whoever. "I can't *gag* her. That's not my job."

"But either I got it wrong, or else I got it right and that doesn't make a difference: I'm supposed to be punished anyway." The paleness of her face blurred its edges, bled her like watercolor. "Could it work like that? Do you think?"

Conway lifted her hands. "Way above my pay grade."

If crouds of dangers should appeare, yet friendship can be unconcern'd. That afternoon I had read it the same way Becca had. Somewhere along the way, it had changed.

I said, "Yeah, it could."

Rebecca's face turned towards me. She looked like I had lit something in her: a deep, slow-burning relief. "You think?"

"Yeah. That poem you have on your wall, that doesn't mean nothing bad can ever happen if you've got proper friends. It just means you can take whatever goes wrong, as long as you've got them. They matter more."

Rebecca thought about that, didn't even feel the social worker tugging at the leash. Nodded. She said, "I didn't think of that last year. I guess I was just a little kid."

I asked, "Would you do it again, if you knew?"

Rebecca laughed at me. Real laugh, so clear it made you shiver; a laugh that dissolved the exhausted walls, sent your mind unrolling into the vast sweet night. She wasn't blurry any more; she was the solidest thing in the room. "Course," she said. "Silly, course I would."

"*Right*," said the social worker. "That's *enough*. We're saying good night now." She grabbed Rebecca by the bicep—nasty little pinch off those stubby fingers, but Rebecca didn't flinch—and shoved her out the door. Their steps faded: the social worker's pissed-off clatter, Rebecca's runners almost too light to hear, gone.

Conway said, "We're going to head as well. We'll be back tomorrow."

McKenna turned her head to look at us like her neck hurt. She said, "I'm sure you will."

"If her parents get back to you, you've got our numbers. If Holly and Julia and Selena need anything else from their room, you've got the key. If anyone has anything to tell us, whatever time of night, you make sure they get the chance."

McKenna said, "You have made yourselves abundantly clear. I think you can safely leave now."

Conway was already moving. I was slower. McKenna had turned so ordinary; just one of my ma's mates, worn down by a drunk husband or a kid in trouble, trying to find her way through the night.

I said, "You told us earlier: this school's survived a lot."

"Indeed," McKenna said. She had one last punch left in her: that fisheye came up and hit me square on, showed me exactly how she smashed snotty teenagers into cringing kids. "And while I appreciate your belated concern, Detective, I am fairly sure that it can survive even such an impressive threat as yourselves."

"Put you in your place," Conway said, a safe distance down the corridor. "And serve you right for arse-licking." The dark took her face, her voice. I couldn't tell how much she was joking.

Us, leaving St. Kilda's. The banister-rail arching warm under my hand. The entrance hall, slants of white spilling through the fanlight onto the checkered tiles. Our footsteps, the clear bell-jingle of Conway's car keys hanging off her finger, the faint slow toll of a great clock striking midnight somewhere, all spiraling up through still air to the invisible ceiling. For one last second, the place we'd come to that morning materialized out of the dark for me: beautiful; whorled and spired of mother-of-pearl and mist; unreachable.

The walk to the car lasted forever. The night was wide open, full to dripping with itself, it smelled of hungry tropical flowers and animal scat and running water. The grounds had gone rogue: every flash of moonlight off a leaf looked like bared white teeth, the tree over the car looked dense with shadow-things hanging ready to drop. Every sound had me leaping around, but there was never anything to see. The place was only mocking or warning, showing me who was boss.

By the time I slammed myself inside the car I was sweating. I thought Conway hadn't noticed, till she said, "I'm only fucking delighted to get out of here."

"Yeah," I said. "Same."

We should've been high-fiving, high-stepping, high as kites. I didn't know how to find that. All I could find was the look on Holly's face and Julia's, watching the last shadow of something craved and lost; the distant blue of Selena's eyes, watching things I couldn't see; Rebecca's laugh, too clear to be human. The car was cold.

Conway turned the key, reversed out fast and hard. Pebbles flew up as she hit the drive. She said, "I'll be starting the interview at nine. In Murder. I'd rather have you for backup than one of those dickheads off the squad."

Roche and the rest of them, putting an extra spike in their jabs now that Conway had got her big solve after all. Ought to be backslaps and free pints, fair play to you and welcome to the club. It wouldn't be. If I wanted to be part of the Murder guy-love someday, my best bet was to leg it back to Cold Cases as fast as my tiny toesies would carry me.

I said, "I'll be there."

"You've earned it. I guess."

"Thanks a bunch."

"You managed a whole day without fucking up big-time. What do you want, a medal?"

"I said thanks. What do you want, flowers?"

The gates were closed. The night watchman had missed the long sweep of our headlights all the way down the drive; when Conway beeped, he did a double-take up from his laptop. "Useless bollix," Conway and I said, in unison.

The gates opened on one long slow creak. The second there was an inch to spare on either side, Conway floored it, nearly took off the MG's wing mirror. And Kilda's was gone.

Conway felt in her jacket pocket, tossed something on my lap. The photo of the card. Chris smiling, golden leaves. *I know who killed him.*

She said, "Who's your money on?"

Even in the dimness, every line of him was packed electric enough with life that he could've leapt off the paper. I tilted the photo to the dashboard light, tried to read his face. Tried to see if that smile blazed with the reflection of the girl he was looking at; if it said *love*, brand-new and brand-fiery. It kept its secrets.

I said, "Selena."

"Yeah. Same here."

"She knew it was Rebecca, from when Rebecca brought her Chris's phone. She managed to keep it to herself for a year, but in the end it was wrecking her head so badly she couldn't take it any more, had to get it out."

Conway nodded. "But she wasn't about to squeal on her mate. The Secret Place was perfect: get it out of your system, blow off the pressure, without telling anyone anything that mattered. And Selena's flaky enough, she never realized it'd bring us in. She thought it'd be a day's worth of gossip, then gone."

Streetlights came and went, flickered Chris in and out of existence. I said, "Maybe now she'll stop seeing him."

I wanted to hear Conway say it. *He's gone. We dissolved him right out of her mind. Left them both free.*

"Nah," Conway said. Hand over hand on the wheel, strong and smooth, arcing us round a corner. "The state of her? She's stuck with him for good."

The gardens we'd passed that morning were empty, deep under a thick fall of silence. We were meters from a main road, but among all that careful graceful leafiness we were the only thing moving. The MG's smooth engine sounded rude as a raspberry.

"Costello," Conway said, and left it, like she was deciding whether to keep talking. The people with the five-foot concrete mug-handle had it floodlit; make sure we could all appreciate it twenty-four-seven, or make sure no one nicked it to go with his eight-foot concrete mug.

Conway said, "They haven't replaced him yet."

"Yeah. I know."

"O'Kelly was talking about July; something about after the mid-year budget. Unless this goes tits-up, I should still be in the good books then. If you were thinking of applying, I could put in a word."

That meant partners. *You want him, Conway, you work with him* . . . Me and Conway.

I saw it all, clear as day. The slaggings from the butch boys, the sniggers rising when I found the gimp mask on my desk. The paperwork and the witnesses that took just that bit too long to reach us; the squad pints we only heard about the next morning. Me trying to make nice, making an eejit of myself instead. Conway not trying at all.

It means you can take whatever goes wrong, I had said to Rebecca. *As long as you've got your friends.*

I said, "That'd be deadly. Thanks."

In the faint glow of the car lights I saw the corner of Conway's mouth go up, just a fraction: that same ready-for-anything curl it had had when she was on the phone to Sophie, way back in the squad room. She said, "Should be good for a laugh, anyway."

"You've got a funny idea of a laugh."

"Be glad I do. Or you'd be stuck in Cold Cases for the duration, praying for some other teenage kid to bring you another ticket out."

"I'm not complaining," I said. Felt a matching curl take the corner of my mouth.

"Better not," Conway said, and she spun the MG onto the main road and hit the pedal. Someone smacked his horn, she smacked hers back and gave him the finger, and the city fireworked alive all around us: flashing with neon signs and flaring with red and gold lights, buzzing with motorbikes and pumping with stereos, streaming warm wind through the open windows. The road unrolled in front of us, it sent its deep pulse up into the hearts of our bones, it flowed on long and strong enough to last us forever.

30

They come back to school for fourth year in the rain, thick clammy rain that leaves your skin splashed with sticky residue. The summer was weird, disjointed: someone was always away on holiday with her parents, someone else always had a family barbecue or a dentist appointment or whatever, and somehow the four of them have barely seen each other since June. Selena's mum has taken her to have her new short hair cut properly—it makes her look older and sophisticated, till you get a proper look at her face. Julia has a hickey on her neck; she doesn't tell, and none of them ask. Becca has shot up about three inches and got her braces off. Holly feels like she's the only one who's still the same: a little taller, a little more shape to her legs, but basically just her. For a dizzy second, standing with her bag dragging at her shoulder in the doorway of the Windex-smelling room they'll be sharing this year, she's almost shy of the others.

None of them mention the vow. None of them mention getting out at night, not to talk about how cool it was, not to suggest they could find a new way. One tiny corner of Holly starts to wonder if for the others it was one big joke, just a way of making school or themselves more interesting; if she made a tool of herself, believing it mattered.

Chris Harper has been dead for three and a half months. No one mentions him; not them, not anyone. No one wants to be the first, and after a few days it's too late.

A couple of weeks into term the rain lets up a little, and on a restless afternoon the four of them can't face another hour of the Court. They slip on their innocent faces and drift round the back, into the Field.

The weeds are higher and stronger than last year; rockslides have taken down the heaps of rubble where people used to perch, turned them into useless knee-high jumbles. The wind scrapes wire against concrete.

No one's there, not even the emos. Julia kicks her way through the undergrowth and settles with her back against what's left of a rubble-heap. The others follow her.

Julia pulls out her phone and starts texting someone; Becca arranges pebbles in neat swirls on a patch of bare earth. Selena gazes at the sky like it's hypnotized her. A leftover spit of rain hits her on the cheekbone, but she doesn't blink.

It's chillier here than round the front, a wild countryside chill that reminds you there are mountains on the horizon, not that far away. Holly shoves her hands deep in her jacket pockets. She feels like she's itchy, but she can't tell where.

"What was that song?" she says suddenly. "It used to be on the radio all the time, last year? Some girl singer."

"What's it go like?" Becca asks.

Holly tries to sing it, but it's been months since she heard it and the words have gone; all she can find is *Remember oh remember back when . . .* She tries to hum the melody instead. Without that light speeding beat and the thrum of guitar, it sounds like nothing. Julia shrugs.

"Lana Del Rey?" Becca says.

"No." It's so totally not Lana Del Rey that even the suggestion depresses Holly. "Lenie. You know the one I mean."

Selena looks up, smiling vaguely. "Hmm?"

"That song. In our room one time, you were humming it? And I came in from the shower and asked you what it was, but you didn't know?"

Selena thinks about it for a while. Then she forgets it and starts thinking about something else.

"God," Julia says, shifting her arse on the dirt. "Where is everyone? Didn't this place use to be, like, *interesting*?"

"It's the weather," Holly says. Her itchy feeling has got worse. She finds a Crunchie wrapper in her pocket and twists it into a tight ball.

"I like it like this," Becca says. "All it used to be was dumb guys looking for someone to pick on."

"Which at least wasn't *boring*. We might as well have stayed inside."

Holly realizes what the itchy feeling is: she's lonely. Realizing makes it worse. "Then let's go in," she says. Suddenly she wants the Court, wants to stuff herself full to the seams with synthetic music and pink sugar.

"I don't *want* to go in. What's the point? We have to go back to school in like two minutes."

Holly thinks of going inside anyway, but she can't tell whether any of the others would come too, and the thought of dragging through the gray rain on her own swells the loneliness. Instead she launches the Crunchie wrapper into the air, spins it a couple of times and hovers it.

No one does anything. Holly floats the wrapper temptingly towards Julia, who bats it away like an annoying bug. "Stop."

"Hey. Lenie."

Holly practically bounces it off Selena's forehead. For a second Selena looks bewildered; then she gently plucks the wrapper out of the air and tucks it into her pocket. She says, "We don't do that any more."

The reasons hum in the air. "Hey," Holly says, too loud and ludicrous, into the wet gray silence. "That was mine."

No one answers. It comes to Holly, for the first time, that someday she'll believe—one hundred percent believe, take for granted—that it was all their imagination.

Julia is texting again; Selena has slid back into her daydream. Holly loves the three of them with such a huge and ferocious and bruised love that she could howl.

Becca catches her eye and nods at the ground. When Holly looks down, Becca skips a pebble through the weeds and lands it on the toe of Holly's Ugg. Holly has just time to feel a tiny bit better before Becca smiles at her, kindly, an adult giving a kid a sweetie.

It's Transition Year, things would be weird anyway. The four of them do their work-experience weeks in different places with different hours; when teachers split the class into groups to do projects about internet advertising or volunteer work with kids with handicaps, they break up gangs of friends on purpose, because Transition Year is all about new experiences. That's what Holly tells herself, on days when she hears Julia's laugh rise out of a crowd across the classroom, on days when the four of them finally have a few minutes together in their room at lights-out and they barely say a word: it's just Transition Year. It would have happened anyway. Next year everything will go back to normal.

This year when Becca says she's not going to the Valentine's dance, no one tries to change her mind. When Sister Cornelius catches Julia snogging François Levy right on the dance floor, Holly and Selena don't say a word. Holly isn't positive that Selena, swaying offbeat with her arms around herself, even noticed.

Afterwards, when they get back to their room, Becca is curled on her bed with her back to them and her earbuds in. Her reading light catches the flash of an open eye, but she doesn't say anything and so neither do they.

The next week, when Miss Graham tells them to get into groups of four for the big final art project, Holly grabs the other three so fast she almost falls off her chair. "Ow," Julia says, jerking her arm away. "What the hell?"

"Jesus, chillax. I just don't want to get stuck with some idiots who'll want to do a massive picture of Kanye made out of lipstick kisses."

"You chillax," Julia says, but she grins. "No Kanye kisses. We'll go with Lady Gaga made of tampons. It'll be a commentary on women's place in society." She and Holly and Becca all get the giggles and even Selena grins, and Holly feels her shoulders relax for the first time in ages.

"Hi," Holly calls, banging the door behind her.

"In here," her dad calls back, from the kitchen. Holly dumps her weekend bag on the floor and goes in to him, shaking a dusting of rain off her hair.

He's at a counter peeling potatoes, long gray T-shirt sleeves pushed up above his elbows. From behind—rough hair still mostly brown, strong shoulders, muscled arms—he looks younger. The oven is on, turning the room warm and humming; outside the kitchen window the February rain is a fine mist, almost invisible.

Chris Harper has been dead for nine months, a week and five days.

Dad gives Holly a no-hands hug and leans down so she can kiss his cheek—stubble, cigarette smell. "Show me," he says.

"*Dad.*"

"Show."

"You're so paranoid."

Dad wiggles the fingers of one hand at her, beckoning. Holly rolls her eyes and holds up her key ring. Her personal alarm is a pretty little teardrop, black with white flowers. Dad spent a long time searching for one that looks like a normal key ring, so she won't get embarrassed and take it off, but he still checks every single week.

"That's what I like to see," says Dad, going back to the potatoes. "I heart my paranoia."

"Nobody else has to have one."

"So you're the only one who'll escape the mass alien abduction. Congratulations. Need a snack?"

"I'm OK." On Fridays they use up their leftover pocket money on chocolate and eat it sitting on the wall at the bus stop.

"Perfect. Then you can give me a hand here."

Mum always makes dinner. "Where's Mum?" Holly asks. She pretends to focus on hanging up her coat straight, and watches Dad sideways. When Holly was little her parents split up. Dad moved back in when she was eleven, but she still keeps an eye on things, especially unusual things.

"Meeting some friend from back in school. Catch." Dad throws Holly a head of garlic. "Three cloves, finely minced. Whatever that means."

"What friend?"

"Some woman called Deirdre." Holly can't tell whether he knows she was looking for that, *some woman*. With Dad you can never tell what he knows. "Mince finely."

Holly finds a knife and pulls herself onto a stool at the breakfast bar. "Is she coming home?"

"Course she is. I wouldn't bet on what time, though. I said we'd make a start on dinner. If she gets back for it, great; if she's still off having girl time, we won't starve."

"Let's get pizza," Holly says, giving Dad the corner of a grin. When she used to go to his depressing apartment for weekends, they would order pizza and eat it on the tiny balcony, looking out over the Liffey and dangling their legs through the railings—there wasn't enough room for chairs. She can tell by the way Dad's eyes warm that he remembers too.

"Here's me giving my mad chef skills a workout, and you want pizza? Ungrateful little wagon. Anyway, your mammy said the chicken needed using."

"What are we making?"

"Chicken casserole. Your mammy wrote down her recipe, give or take." He nods at a piece of paper tucked under the chopping board. "How was your week?"

"OK. Sister Ignatius gave us this big speech about how we need to decide what we want to do in college and our whole entire lives depend on making the right decision. By the end she got so hyper about the whole thing, she made us all go down to the chapel and pray to our confirmation saints for guidance."

That gets the laugh she was looking for. "And what did your confirmation saint have to say?"

"She said I should be sure and not fail my exams, or I'm stuck with Sister Ignatius for another year and *aaahhh*."

"Smart lady." Dad tips the peelings into the compost bin and starts chopping the potatoes. "Are you getting a little too much nun in your life? Because you can quit boarding any time you want. You know that. Just say the word."

"I don't want to," Holly says, quickly. She still doesn't know why Dad is letting her be a boarder, especially after Chris, and she always feels like he might change his mind any minute. "Sister Ignatius is fine. We just laugh about her. Julia does her voice; once she actually did it all the way through Guidance, and Sister Ignatius didn't even realize. She couldn't work out why we were all cracking up."

"Little smart-arse," Dad says, grinning. He likes Julia. "The Sister's got a point in there, though. Been doing any thinking about what comes after school?"

It feels to Holly like the last couple of months that's all any adult ever talks about. She says, "Maybe sociology—we had a sociologist come in to talk to us in Careers Week last year, and it sounded OK. Or maybe law."

She's focusing on the garlic, but she can hear that the rhythm of her dad's chopping doesn't change, not that it would anyway. Mum is a barrister. Dad is a detective. Holly doesn't have a brother or a sister to go Dad's way.

When she makes herself look across, he's showing nothing but impressed and interested. "Yeah? Solicitor, barrister, what?"

"Barrister. Maybe. I don't know; I'm only thinking about it."

"You've got the arguing skills for it, anyway. Prosecution or defense?"

"I thought maybe defense."

"How come?"

Still all pleasant and intrigued, but Holly can feel the tiny chill: he doesn't like that. She shrugs. "Just sounds interesting. Is this minced enough?"

Holly's been trying to think of a time when her dad decided she shouldn't do something and she ended up doing it anyway, or the other way around. Boarding is the only one she could come up with. Sometimes he says no flat-out; more often, it just ends up not happening. Sometimes Holly even winds up, she's not sure how, thinking he's right. She wasn't actually planning to tell him about the law thing, but unless you concentrate you end up telling Dad stuff.

"Looks good to me," Dad says. "In here." Holly goes over to him and scrapes the garlic into the casserole dish. "And chop that leek for me. Why defense?"

Holly takes the leek back to her stool. "Because. There's like hundreds of people on the prosecution side."

Dad waits for more, eyebrow up, inquiring, until she shrugs. "Just . . . I don't know. Detectives, and uniforms, and the Technical Bureau, and the prosecutors. The defense just has the person whose actual life it is, and his lawyer."

"Hm," says Dad, examining the potato chunks. Holly can feel him being careful, looking over his answer from every angle. "You know, sweetheart, it's not actually as unfair as it looks. If anything, the system's weighted towards the defense. The prosecution has to build a whole case that stands up beyond a reasonable doubt; the defense only has to build that one doubt. I can swear to you, hand on heart, there's a lot more guilty people acquitted than innocent ones in jail."

Which isn't what Holly means, at all. She's not sure whether Dad not getting it is irritating or a relief. "Yeah," she says. "Probably."

Dad throws the potatoes into the casserole dish. He says, "It's a good impulse. Just take your time; don't get fixed on a plan till you're a hundred percent definite. Yeah?"

Holly says, "How come you don't want me to do defense?"

"I'd be only delighted. That's where the money is; you can keep me in the style to which I wish to become accustomed."

He's slipping away, the nonstick glint coming into his eyes. "Dad. I'm *asking.*"

"Defense lawyers hate me. I thought you were going to do your hating me around about now, get it out of your system, and by the time you were twenty or so we'd get on great again. I didn't think you'd be just getting started." Dad heads for the fridge and starts rummaging. "Your mother said to put in carrots. How many do you figure we need?"

"*Dad.*"

Dad leans back against the fridge, watching Holly. "Let me ask you this," he says. "A client shows up at your office, wanting you to defend him. He's been arrested—and we're not talking littering here; we're talking something way out on the other side of bad. The more you talk to him, the more you're positive he's guilty as hell. But he's got money, and your kid needs braces and school fees. What do you do?"

Holly shrugs. "I figure it out then."

She doesn't know how to tell her dad, only half of her even wants to tell her dad, that that's the whole point. Everything the prosecutors have, all the backup, the system, the safe certainty that they're the good guys: that feels lazy, feels sticky-slimy as cowardice. Holly wants to be the one out on her own, working out for herself what's right and what's wrong this time. She wants to be the one coming up with fast zigzag ways to get each story the right ending. That feels clean; that feels like courage.

"That's one way to do it." Dad pulls out a bag of carrots. "One? Two?"

"Put two." He has the recipe right there; he doesn't need to ask.

"How about your mates? Any of them thinking of law?"

A zap of irritation stiffens Holly's legs. "No. I actually can think all by myself. Isn't that amazing?"

Dad grins and heads back to the counter. On his way past he lays a hand on Holly's head, warm and just the right strength. He's relented, or decided to act like it. He says, "You'll make a good barrister, if that's what you decide on. Either side of the courtroom." He runs his hand down her hair and goes to work on the carrots. "Don't sweat it, chickadee. You'll make the right call."

The conversation's over. All his careful probing and all his deep serious speeches, and she slipped right past without him laying a finger on what she's actually thinking. Holly feels a quick prickle of triumph and shame. She chops harder.

Dad says, "So what do your mates have in mind?"

"Julia's going to do journalism. Becca's not sure. Selena wants to go to art school."

"Shouldn't be a problem. Her stuff's good. I meant to ask you: is she doing OK these days?"

Holly looks up, but he's peeling a carrot and glancing out the window to see if Mum's on her way. "What do you mean?"

"Just wondering. The last few times you've had her round, she seemed a little . . . spacy, is that the word I'm looking for?"

"She's like that. You just have to get to know her."

"I've known her a good while now. She didn't use to be this spacy. Anything been on her mind?"

Holly shrugs. "Just normal stuff. School. Whatever."

Dad waits, but Holly knows he's not done. She dumps the bits of leek into the casserole dish. "What'll I do now?"

"Here." He throws her an onion. "I know you and your mates know Selena inside out, but sometimes those are the last people to cop that something's wrong. A lot of problems can show up around your age—depression, whatever we're supposed to call manic depression these days, schizophrenia. I'm not saying Selena's got any of those"—his hand going up, as Holly's mouth opens—"but if something's up with her, even something minor, now's the time to get it sorted."

The balls of Holly's feet are digging into the floor tiles. "Selena's not *schizophrenic*. She *daydreams*. Just because she's not some stupid cliché teenager who goes around screaming about Jedward all the time doesn't mean she's *abnormal.*"

Dad's eyes are very blue and very level. It's the levelness that has Holly's heart banging in her throat. He thinks this is serious.

He says, "You know me better than that, sweetheart. I'm not saying she has to be Little Miss Perky Cheerleader. I'm just saying she seems a lot less on the ball than she did this time last year. And if she's got a problem and it doesn't get treated fast, it could do a pretty serious number on her life. Yous are going to be heading out into the big wide world before you know it. You don't want to be running around out there with an untreated mental illness. That's how lives end up banjaxed."

Holly feels a new kind of real all around her, pressing in. It squeezes her chest, makes it hard to breathe.

She says, "Selena's *fine.* All she needs is for people to leave her alone and quit annoying her. OK? Can you please do that?"

After a moment Dad says, "Fair enough. Like I said, you know her better than I do, and I know yous lot take good care of each other. Just keep an eye on her. That's all I'm saying."

A key rattling in the front door, impatient, and then a rush of cool rain-flavored air. "Frank? Holly?"

"Hi," Holly and Dad call.

The door slams and Mum blows into the kitchen. "My *God,*" she says, flopping back against the wall. Her fair hair is coming out of its bun and she looks different, flushed and loosened, not like cool good-posture Mum at all. "That was *strange.*"

"Are you locked?" Dad asks, grinning at her. "And me at home looking after your child, slaving over a hot cooker—"

"I am not. Well, maybe just a touch tipsy, but it's not that. It's—My God, Frank. Do you realize I hadn't seen Deirdre in almost thirty *years?* How on earth did that happen?"

Dad says, "So it went well in the end, yeah?"

Mum laughs, breathless and giddy. Her coat hangs open; underneath she's wearing her slim navy dress flashed with white, the gold necklace Dad gave her at Christmas. She's still collapsed against the wall, bag dumped on the floor at her feet. Holly gets that pulse of wariness again. Mum always kisses her the instant one of them gets through the door.

"It was wonderful. I was absolutely *terrified*—honestly, at the door of the bar I almost turned around and went home. If it hadn't worked, if we'd just sat there making small talk like acquaintances . . . I wouldn't have been able to bear it. Dee and I and this other girl, Miriam, back in school we were like you and your friends, Holly. We were inseparable."

One of her ankles is bent outwards above the high-heeled navy leather shoe, leaning her lopsided like a teenager. Holly says—*Thirty years, never, we'd never*—"So how come you haven't seen her?"

"Deirdre's parents emigrated to America, when we left school. She went to college there. It wasn't like now, there wasn't any e-mail; phone calls cost the earth, and letters took weeks. We did try—she's still got all my letters, can you imagine? She brought them along, all these things I'd forgotten all about, boys and nights out and fights with our parents and . . . I know I've got hers somewhere—in Mum and Dad's attic, maybe, I'll have to look—I can't have thrown them away. But it was college and we were busy, and the next thing we knew we were completely out of touch . . ."

Mum's long lovely face is transparent, things blowing across it bright and swift as falling leaves. She doesn't look like Holly's mum, like anyone's mum. For the first time ever, Holly looks at her and thinks: *Olivia.*

"But today—God, it was as if we'd seen each other a month ago. We laughed so *hard*, I can't remember the last time I laughed that hard. We used to laugh like that all the time. The things we remembered—we had this silly alternative verse for the school song, ridiculous stuff, dirty jokes, and we sang it together, right there in the bar. We remembered all the words. I hadn't thought of that song in thirty years, I'd swear it wasn't even *in* my mind any more, but one look at Dee and the whole thing came back."

"Getting rowdy in pubs at your age," Dad says. "You'll be barred." He's smiling, a full-on grin that makes him look younger too. He likes seeing Mum like this.

"Oh, God, people must have heard us, mustn't they? I didn't even notice. Do you know, Frank, at one stage Dee said to me, 'You probably want to get home, don't you?' and I actually said, 'Why?' When she said 'home,' I was picturing my parents' house. My bedroom when I was seventeen. I was thinking, 'Why on earth would I be in a hurry to get back there?' I was so deep in 1982, I'd forgotten all of this *existed.*"

She's grinning through a hand pressed over her mouth, ashamed and delighted. "Child neglect," Dad says to Holly. "Write it down, in case you ever feel like dobbing her in."

Something skitters across Holly's mind: Julia in the glade a long time ago, the tender amused curl of her mouth, *This isn't forever.* It snatches

Holly's breath: she was wrong. They are forever, a brief and mortal forever, a forever that will grow into their bones and be held inside them after it ends, intact, indestructible.

"She gave me this," Mum says, fishing in her bag. She pulls out a photo—white border turning yellow—and puts it down on the bar. "Look. That's us: me and Deirdre and Miriam. That's *us*."

Her voice does something funny, curls up. For a horrified second Holly thinks she's going to cry, but when she looks up Mum is biting her lip and smiling.

Three of them, older than Holly, maybe a year or two. School uniforms, Kilda's crest on their lapels. Look close and the kilt is longer, the blazer is boxy and ugly, but if it weren't for that and the big hair, they could be out of the year above her. They're messing, draped pouting and hip-jutting on a wrought-iron gate—it takes a strange twitch like a blink before Holly recognizes the gate at the bottom of the back lawn. Deirdre is in the middle, shaking a raggedy dark perm forward over her face, all curves and lashes and wicked glint. Miriam is small and fair and feather-haired, fingers snapping, sweet grin through braces. And over on the right Olivia, long-legged, head flung back and hands tangled in her hair, halfway between model and mockery. She's wearing lip gloss, pale candy-floss-pink—Holly can picture the mild distaste on Mum's face if she wore it home one weekend. She looks beautiful.

"We were pretending to be Bananarama," Mum says. "Or someone like that, I don't think we were sure. We were in a band that term."

"You were in a *band*?" Dad says. "I'm a groupie?"

"We were called Sweet and Sour." Mum laughs, with a little shake in it. "I was the keyboard player—well, barely; I played piano, so we assumed that meant I'd be good at the keyboard, but actually I was terrible. And Dee could only play folk guitar and none of us had a note in our heads, so the whole thing was a disaster, but we had a wonderful time."

Holly can't stop looking. That girl in the photo isn't one solid person, feet set solidly in one irrevocable life; that girl is an illusive firework-burst made of light reflecting off a million different possibilities. That girl isn't a barrister, married to Frank Mackey, mother of one daughter and no more, a house in Dalkey, neutral colors and soft cashmere and Chanel No. 5. All of that is implicit in her, curled unimagined inside her bones; but so are hundreds of other latent lives, unchosen and easily vanished as whisks of light. A shiver knots in Holly's spine, won't shake loose.

She asks, "Where's Miriam?"

"I don't know. It wasn't the same without Dee, and during college we grew apart—I was terribly serious back then, very ambitious, always studying, and Miriam wanted to spend most of her time getting drunk and flirting, so before we knew it . . ." Mum's still gazing down at the photo. "Someone told me she got married and moved to Belfast, not long after college. That's the last I heard of her."

"If you want," Holly says, "I'll have a look for her on the internet. She's probably on Facebook."

"Oh, darling," Mum says. "That's very kind of you. But I don't know . . ." A sudden catch of her breath. "I don't know if I could bear it. Can you understand that?"

"I guess."

Dad has a hand on Mum's back, just lightly, between her shoulder blades. He says, "Need another glass of wine?"

"Oh, God, no. Or maybe; I don't know."

Dad cups the back of her neck for a second and heads for the fridge.

"So long ago," Mum says, touching the photo. The fizz is fading out of her voice, leaving it quiet and still. "I don't know how it can possibly be so long ago."

Holly moves back to her stool. She stirs bits of onion with the point of the knife.

Mum says, "Dee isn't happy, Frank. She used to be the outgoing one, the confident one—like your Julia, Holly, always a smart answer for anything— she was going to be a politician, or the TV interviewer who asks the politicians the tough questions. But she got married young, and then her husband didn't want her to work till the children were out of school, so now all she can get is bits of secretarial stuff. He sounds like a dreadful piece of work— I didn't say that, of course—she's thinking of leaving him, but she's been with him so long she can't imagine how she would manage without him . . ."

Dad hands her a glass. She takes it automatically, without looking. "Her life, Frank, her life isn't anything like she thought it would be. All our plans, we were going to take the world by storm . . . She never imagined this."

Mum doesn't normally talk like this in front of Holly. She's cupping one cheek and looking into air, seeing things. She's forgotten Holly is there.

Dad asks, "Going to meet up with her again?" Holly can tell he wants to touch Mum, put his arms around her. She wants to as well, to press in against Mum's side, but she stays back because Dad is.

"Maybe. I don't know. She's going back to America next week; back to her husband, and the temp work. She can't stay any longer. And she's got all her cousins to see before then. We swore we'd e-mail this time . . ." Mum runs her fingers down her face, like she's feeling the lines around her mouth for the first time.

Dad says, "Maybe next summer we can think about taking a holiday over in that direction. If you want to."

"Oh, Frank. That's lovely of you. But she's not in New York or San Francisco, anywhere that . . ." Mum looks at the wineglass in her hand, bewildered, and puts it down on the counter. "She's in Minnesota, a smallish town there. That's where her husband's from. I don't know if . . ."

"If we headed to New York, she might come up and join us. Have a think about it."

"I will. Thank you." Mum takes a deep breath. She picks up her bag off the floor and tucks the photo back into it. "Holly," she says, holding out an arm and smiling. "Come here, darling, and give me my kiss. How was your week?"

That night Holly can't sleep. The house feels stuffed with heat, but when she kicks off the duvet a chill flattens itself along her back. She listens to Mum and Dad going to bed: Mum's voice still rising faster and happier, dropping suddenly now and then when she remembers Holly; the low rhythm of Dad adding in something that makes Mum laugh out loud. After their voices stop, Holly lies there in the dark on her own, trying to stay still. She thinks about texting one of the others to see if she's awake, but she doesn't know which one, or what she wants to say.

"Lenie," Holly says.

It feels like stretched hours before Selena, face down on her bed reading, looks up. "Mm?"

"Next year. How do we decide who shares with who?"

"Huh?"

"Senior rooms. Do you know who you want to share with?"

A thick skin of rain coats the window. They're stuck indoors; in the common room, people are playing a nineties edition of Trivial Pursuit, trying out makeup, texting. The smell of beef stew for tea has somehow made it all the way up from the canteen. It's making Holly feel slightly sick.

"For fuck's sake," Julia says, turning a page. "It's *February*. If you want something to worry about, how about that stupid Social Awareness Studies project?"

"Lenie?"

Senior rooms hang over the whole of fourth year. Friendships go down in flames and tears because someone picks the wrong person to share with. All the boarders spend most of the year edging carefully round the choice, trying to find some way to navigate it undamaged.

Selena gazes, lips parted, like Holly's asked her to fly a space shuttle. She says, "One of you guys."

A flutter of fear catches at Holly. "Well, yeah. Which one?"

Nothing out of Selena; empty space, echoes. Becca has felt something in the air and taken out her earbuds.

"Want to know who I'm going to share with?" Julia asks. "Because if you're going to start getting hyper about stuff that isn't even happening yet, it's definitely not you."

"I didn't ask you," Holly points out. "What'll we do, Lenie?" She wills Selena to sit up and think about it, come up with an idea that makes sure no one's feelings get hurt, that's what she's good at; names out of a hat maybe—*please Lenie please* . . . "Lenie?"

Selena says, "You do it. I don't mind. I'm reading."

Holly says, feeling her voice too loud and too sharp-edged, "We all have to decide together. That's how it works. You don't get to just make the rest of us do it."

Selena tucks her head down tight over her book. Becca watches, sucking the cord of her earbuds.

"Hol," Julia says, giving Holly the crinkle-nosed smile that means trouble. "I need something out of the common room. Come with me."

Holly doesn't actually feel like letting Julia boss her around. "What do you need?"

"Come on." Julia slides off the bed.

"Is it too heavy for you to carry by yourself?"

"Hahahaha, such a comedienne. Come on."

The force of her makes Holly feel better. Maybe she should have said something to Jules straight off; maybe the two of them together will come up with a decent answer. She swings her legs off the bed. Becca watches them out of the room. Selena doesn't.

The early darkness outside turns the light in the corridor a dirty yellow. Julia leans back against the wall with her arms folded. She says, "What the fuck are you doing?"

She doesn't bother keeping it down; the rain battering the landing window covers their voices from any listeners. Holly says, "I was just asking her. What's the big huge—"

"You were hassling her. Don't hassle her."

"Hello, how is that hassling her? We have to decide."

"It's hassling her because if you keep going on at her, she'll just get upset. The rest of us work it out, we tell her, she'll be happy with whatever we think."

Holly matches Julia's folded arms, and her stare. "What if I think Lenie should get a say too?"

Julia rolls her eyes. "Oh, for fuck's sake."

"What? Why not?"

"Did you have a lobotomy for lunch? You know why not."

Holly says, "You mean because she's not OK. That's why not."

Julia's face closes over. "She's fine. She's got shit she needs to sort out, is all. Doesn't everyone."

"It's not the same thing. Lenie can't *manage.* Like just normal stuff: she can't do it. What's going to happen to her when the rest of us aren't there every minute of every—"

"You mean, like, when we're in college? *Years* from now? Excuse me if I don't have a total drama attack over that. By then she'll be fine."

"She's not getting better. You know she's not."

It spins between them, razor-edged: she hasn't got better since then; since that; you know what. Neither one of them reaches out to touch it.

Holly says, "I think we need to make her go talk to someone."

Julia laughs out loud. "What, like Sister Ig*n*atius? Oh, yeah, that's totally going to make everything OK. Sister Ignatius couldn't sort out a broken fingernail—"

"Not Sister Ignatius. Someone real. Like a doctor or something."

"Jesus *Christ*—" Julia shoots off the wall pointing both forefingers at Holly. The angle of her neck is one degree off an attack. "Don't even fucking think about it. I am serious."

Holly almost slaps her hands away. The rush of fury feels good. "Since when are you the boss of me? You don't get to give me orders. Ever."

Neither of them has been in an actual fight since they were tiny kids, but they're eye to eye, on their toes and boiling for it, hands twitching for something soft to gouge and twist. Julia is the one who finally drops back, gives Holly her shoulder and sinks against the wall.

"Look," she says, to the landing window and the swollen streaks of rain. "If you care about Lenie, like even the tiniest bit, then you won't try and get her talking to a psychologist. You're going to have to take my word for it: that's like the absolute worst thing you could do for her, in the whole world. OK?"

The immensity of it is coiled tight inside every word. Holly can't get a hold on her, amid the relentless buzz of both their circling secrets, can't catch at what Julia knows or guesses. It's nothing like Julia to back down.

"I'm asking you as a favor here. Trust me. Please."

Holly wishes, right down into deep parts of herself that she didn't know existed, that it were still that simple. "I guess," she says. "OK."

Julia's face turns towards her. The layer of suspicion makes Holly want to do something, she can't tell what: scream it right off, maybe, or give it the finger and walk out the door and never come back. "Yeah?" Julia says. "You won't try and get her talking to anyone?"

"If you're sure."

"I'm *so* sure."

"Then OK," Holly says. "I won't."

"Good," Julia says. "Let's go get something out of the common room before Becs comes looking for us."

They head off down the corridor, in step, baffled and alone.

Holly isn't leaving it because Julia says so. She's leaving it because she has an idea.

It's the psychologist thing that made her think of it. She got sent to a counselor, that other time. He was kind of a moron and his nose sweated, and he kept asking questions that were none of his business so Holly just played with his stupid puzzles and ignored him, but he kept talking and he did come out with one thing that actually turned out to be true. He said it would get simpler once the trial was over and she knew exactly what was going on; either way, he said, knowing would make it easier to put the whole thing out of her head and concentrate on other stuff. Which it did.

It takes a few days before Julia lets go of the wary look and leaves Holly and Selena alone together. But one afternoon they're at the Court and Julia needs to get her dad a birthday card, and Becca remembers she owes her gran a thank-you card; and Selena holds up her bag from the art shop and starts drifting towards the fountain, and by the time Holly heads after her it's too late for Julia to change anything.

Selena arranges perfect tubes of paint in a fan on the black marble and strokes the color bands with a fingertip. Across the fountain a gang of guys from Colm's turn to eye her and Holly, but they won't come over. They can tell.

"Lenie," Holly says, and waits the long stretch till Selena thinks of looking up. "You know one thing that might make you better?"

Selena watches her like she's made of cloud-patterns, shifting gracefully and meaninglessly across a wide sky. She says, "Huh?"

"If you found out what happened," Holly says. Coming this close to it makes her heart skid fast and light, no traction. "Last year. And if someone got arrested for it. That would help. Right? Do you think?"

"Shh," Lenie says. She reaches over and takes Holly's hand—hers is cold and soft, and no matter how tight Holly squeezes, it doesn't feel solid. She lets Holly hang on to it and goes back to her paints.

Holly learned from her dad a long time back that the difference between caught and not is taking your time. She buys the book first, in a big second-hand bookshop in town on a busy Saturday; in a couple of months' time Mum won't remember *I have to get this book for school can I have ten euros I'll only be a sec*, no one at the till will remember some blond kid with a musty mythology book and a glossy art thing to wave at Mum. She finds a phone pic that has Chris in the background and prints it off a few weeks later, on a lunchtime dash for the computer room; in no time the others will have forgotten her taking a few minutes too long to get back from the toilet. She slices and glues on her bedroom floor that weekend, wearing gloves she stole from the chem lab, with the duvet ready to yank over the whole thing if Mum or Dad knocks; after long enough they'll forget any comforting play-school whiff of paper glue. She dumps the book in a bin in the park near home; within a week or two it'll be well gone. Then she slides the card down a slit in the lining of her winter coat, and waits for enough time to move past.

She wants a sign to tell her when the right day comes. She knows she won't get one, not for this; maybe not for anything after this, ever again.

She makes her own. When she hears the Daleks talking about OMG this stupid project taking forever have to go up on Tuesday evening so boooor-ing, Holly says, at the end of art class, *Study time again on Tuesday?* Watches the others nod, while they pour drifts of powdered chalk into the bin and coil copper wire away.

She is meticulous. She makes sure to chatter the others past the Secret Place, on their way into the art room and out again, so none of them see what isn't there. Makes sure to leave her phone out of sight, on a chair pushed under the table, so no one spots it for her. Makes sure to say, "Oh, *pants*, my phone!" after lights-out. Makes sure to run through every step, the next morning, up in the empty corridor: pin it, see it (quick gasp, hand to her mouth, like someone's watching), get the envelope and the balsa

knife, lever out the thumbtack as delicately as if there might actually be
fingerprints there. When she runs back down the corridor, the sound of each
footstep flies up into a high corner, slaps onto the wall like a dark handprint.

The others believe her when she says she has a migraine—she's had three
in the past two months, matching Mum's symptoms. Julia pulls out her
iPod, to keep Holly from getting bored. Holly lies in bed and watches them
leave for school like it's the last time she'll ever see them: already half gone,
Becca flipping through pages for her Media Studies homework, Julia hauling at a sock, Selena tipping a smile and a wave over her shoulder. When the
door slams behind them, there's a minute when she thinks she'll never be
able to make herself sit up.

The nurse gives her migraine pills, tucks her in and leaves her to sleep it
off. Holly moves fast. She knows what time the next bus into town leaves.

It hits her at the bus stop, in the cool-edged morning air. At first she
thinks she actually is sick, that what she's doing has called down some curse
on her and now all her lies come true. She hasn't felt it in so long and it tastes
different now. It used to be vast and dark-bloody; this is metallic, this is
alkaline, this is like scouring powder eating through your layers one by one.
It's fear. Holly is afraid.

The bus howls up like a stampeding animal, the driver eyes her uniform,
the steps sway precariously as she climbs to the top deck. Guys in hoodies are
sprawled along the back seat blasting hip-hop from a radio and they eye-strip
Holly bare, but her legs won't take her back down those stairs. She sits on the
edge of the front seat, stares out at the road diving under the wheels and
listens to the raw laughs behind her, tensed for the surge that would mean an
attack. If the guys come for her then she can push the emergency button. The
driver will stop the bus and help her down the stairs, and she can get the next
bus back to school and climb back into bed. Her heart punching her throat
makes her want to throw up. She wants Dad. She wants Mum.

The song starts so small, fading up through the hip-hop, it takes a minute to reach her. Then it hits her like a shock in the chest, like she's breathed
air made of something different.

Remember oh remember back when we were young so young . . .

It's crystal-clear, every word. It surges away the sound of the engine,
bowls away the hoodies' hooting. It carries them over the canal and all the
way into town. It soars the bus through chains of lights all flashing to green,
leaps it over speed bumps, slaloms it two-wheeled around jaywalkers. *Never
thought I'd lose you and I never thought I'd find you here, never thought that
everything we'd lost could feel so near . . .*

Holly listens to every word of it, straight through. Chorus, chorus again, again, and she waits for the song to fade. Instead it keeps going and it rises. *I've got so far, I've got so far left to travel . . .*

The bus skids towards her stop. Holly waves good-bye to the hoodies—openmouthed and baffled, looking for an insult, too slow—and flies down the rocking stairs.

Out on the street, the song is still going. It's fainter and tricky, flickering between traffic sounds and student-gang shouts, but she knows what to listen for now and she keeps hold of it. It spirals out in front of her like a fine golden thread, it leads her nimble and dancer-footed between rushing suits and lampposts and long-skirted beggarwomen, up the street towards Stephen.

Acknowledgments

I owe enormous thank-yous to more people every time: Clare Ferraro and Caitlin O'Shaughnessy at Viking, Ciara Considine at Hachette Books Ireland, and Sue Fletcher and Nick Sayers at Hodder & Stoughton, for the time and skill they put into making this book so much better; Breda Purdue, Ruth Shern, Ciara Doorley and everyone at Hachette Books Ireland; Swati Gamble, Kerry Hood and everyone at Hodder & Stoughton; Carolyn Coleburn, Ben Petrone, Angie Messina and everyone at Viking; Susanne Halbleib and everyone at Fischer Verlage; Rachel Burd, for another eagle-eyed copy edit; the amazing Darley Anderson and his crack squad at the agency, especially Clare, Mary, Rosanna, Andrea and Jill; Steve Fisher of APA; David Walsh, for not only answering all my questions on detective procedure but giving me the answers to questions I didn't know I needed to ask; Dr. Fearghas Ó Cochláin, as usual, for helping me kill off the victim as plausibly as possible; Oonagh "Better Than" Montague, for (among many, many other things) making me laugh at all the moments when I needed it most; Ann-Marie Hardiman, Catherine Farrell, Kendra Harpster, Jessica Ryan, Karen Gillece, Jessica Bramham, Kristina Johansen, Alex French and Susan Collins, for various wonderful combinations of seriousness, silliness and every kind of support; David Ryan, for being so very and so incomparably that without his endless I would never have; my mother, Elena Lombardi, for every single day; my father, David French; and, more than I'll ever be able to put into words, my husband, Anthony Breatnach.

Read on for a selection from
Tana French's new novel *The Trespasser*,
now available from Viking . . .

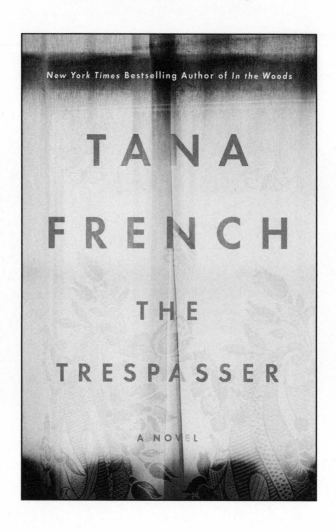

1

The case comes in, or anyway it comes in to us, on a frozen dawn in the kind of closed-down January that makes you think the sun's never going to drag itself back above the horizon. Me and my partner are finishing up another night shift, the kind I used to think wouldn't exist on the Murder Squad: a massive scoop of boring and a bigger one of stupid, topped off with an avalanche of paperwork. Two scumbags decided to round off their Saturday night out by using another scumbag's head as a dance mat, for reasons that are clear to no one including them; we turned up six witnesses, every one of whom was banjoed drunk, every one of whom told a different story from the other five, and every one of whom wanted us to forget the murder case and investigate why he had been thrown out of the pub / sold bad skunk / ditched by his girlfriend. By the time Witness Number 6 ordered me to find out why the dole had cut him off, I was ready to tell him it was because he was too stupid to legally qualify as a human being and kick all their arses out onto the street, but my partner does patience better than I do, which is one of the main reasons I keep him around. We eventually managed to get four of the witness statements matching not only each other but the evidence, meaning now we can charge one of the scumbags with murder and the other one with assault, which presumably means we've saved the world from evil in some way that I can't be arsed figuring out.

We've signed over the scumbags for processing and we're typing up our reports, making sure they'll be on the gaffer's desk all nice and tidy when he comes in. Across from me Steve is whistling, which out of most people would make me want to do damage, but he's doing it right: some old trad tune that I quarter-remember from singsongs when I was a kid, low and absent and contented, breaking off when he needs to concentrate and coming back with easy trills and flourishes when the report starts going right again.

Him, and the whispery hum of the computers, and the winter wind idling around the windows: just those, and silence. Murder works out of the grounds of Dublin Castle, smack in the heart of town, but our building is tucked away a few corners from the fancy stuff the tourists come to see, and our walls are thick; even the early-morning traffic out on Dame Street only makes it through to us as a soft undemanding hum. The jumbles of paperwork and photos and scribbled notes left on people's desks look like they're charging up, thrumming with action waiting to happen. Outside the tall sash windows the night is thinning towards a chilled gray; the room smells of coffee and hot radiators. At that hour, if I could overlook all the ways the night shift blows, I could love the squad room.

Me and Steve know all the official reasons we get loaded down with night shifts. We're both single, no wives or husbands or kids waiting at home; we're the youngest on the squad, we can take the fatigue better than the guys looking at retirement; we're the newbies—even me, two years in—so suck it up, bitches. Which we do. This isn't uniform, where if your boss is a big bad meanie you can put in a request for reassignment. There's no other Murder Squad to transfer to; this is the one and only. If you want it, and both of us do, you take whatever it throws at you.

Some people actually work in the Murder Squad I set my sights on, way back when: the one where you spend your day playing knife-edge mind games with psychopathic geniuses, knowing that one wrong blink could mean the difference between victory and another dead body down the line. Me and Steve, we get to rubberneck at the cunning psychopaths when the other lads walk them past the interview room where we're bashing our heads against yet another Spouse of the Year from our neverending run of domestics, which the gaffer throws our way because he knows they piss me right off. The head-dancing morons at least made a change.

Steve hits Print, and the printer in the corner starts its rickety wheeze. "You done?" he asks.

"Just about." I'm scanning my report for typos, making sure the gaffer's got no excuse to give me hassle.

He links his fingers over his head and stretches backwards, setting his chair creaking. "Pint? The early houses'll be opening."

"You must be joking."

"To celebrate."

Steve, God help me, also does positivity better than I do. I give him a stare that should nip that in the bud. "Celebrate what?"

He grins. Steve is thirty-three, a year older than me, but he looks younger: maybe the schoolboy build, all gangly legs and skinny shoulders; maybe the orange hair that sticks up in the wrong places; or maybe the relentless god-awful cheerfulness. "We got them, did you not notice?"

"Your granny could've got those two."

"Probably. And she'd've gone for a pint after."

"She was an alco, yeah?"

"Total lush. I'm just trying to live up to her standards." He heads for the printer and starts sorting pages. "Come on."

"Nah. Another time." I don't have it in me. I want to go home, go for a run, stick something in the microwave and fry my brain with shite telly, and then get some sleep before I have to do it all over again.

The door bangs open and O'Kelly, our superintendent, sticks his head in, early as usual to see if he can catch anyone asleep. Mostly he arrives all rosy and shiny, smelling of shower and fry-up, every line of his comb-over in place—I can't prove it's to rub it in to the tired bastards stinking of night shift and stale Spar danishes, but it would be in character. This morning, at least he looks ragged around the edges—eye bags, tea stain on his shirt—which I figure is probably my bit of satisfaction for the day used up right there.

"Moran. Conway," he says, eyeing us suspiciously. "Anything good come in?"

"Street fight," I say. "One victim." Forget the hit to your social life: the real reason everyone hates night shift is that nothing good ever comes in. The high-profile murders with complex backstories and fascinating motives might happen at night, sometimes, but they don't get discovered till morning. The only murders that get noticed at night are by drunk arseholes whose motive is that they're drunk arseholes. "We'll have the reports for you now."

"Kept you busy, anyway. You sort it?"

"Give or take. We'll tie up the loose ends tonight."

"Good," O'Kelly says. "Then you're free to work this." And he holds up a call sheet.

Just for a second, like a fool, I get my hopes up. If a case comes in through the gaffer, instead of through our admin straight to the squad room, it's because it's something special. Something that's going to be so high profile, or so tough, or so delicate, it can't just go to whoever's next on the rota; it needs the right people. One straight from the gaffer hums through the squad room, makes the lads sit up and take notice. One straight from the gaffer would mean me and Steve have finally, finally, worked our way clear of the losers' corner of the playground: we're in.

I have to close my fist to stop my hand reaching out for that sheet. "What is it?"

O'Kelly snorts. "You can take that feeding-time look off your face, Conway. I picked it up on my way in, said I'd bring it upstairs to save Bernadette the hassle. Uniforms on the scene say it looks like a slam-dunk domestic." He throws the call sheet on my desk. "I said you'll tell them what it looks like, thanks very much. You never know, you could be in luck: it might be a serial killer."

To save the admin the hassle, my arse. O'Kelly brought up that call sheet so he could enjoy the look on my face. I leave it where it is. "The day shift'll be in any minute."

"And you're in now. If you've got a hot date to get to, then you'd better hurry up and get this solved."

"We're working on our reports."

"Jesus, Conway, they don't need to be James bloody Joyce. Just give me what you've got. You'd want to get a move on: this yoke's in Stoney-batter, and they're digging up the quays again."

After a second I hit Print. Steve, the little lick-arse, is already wrapping his scarf around his neck.

The gaffer has wandered over to the roster whiteboard and is squinting at it. He says, "You'll need backup on this one."

I can feel Steve willing me to keep the head. "We can handle a slam-dunk domestic on our own," I say. "We've worked enough of them."

"And someone with a bit of experience might teach you how to work them right. How long did ye take to clear that Romanian young one? Five weeks? With two witnesses who saw her fella stab her, and the press and the equality shower yelling about racism and if it was an Irish girl we'd have made an arrest by now—"

"The witnesses wouldn't talk to us." Steve's eye says *Shut up, Antoinette*, too late. I've bitten, just like O'Kelly knew I would.

"Exactly. And if the witnesses won't talk to you today, I want an old hand around to make them." O'Kelly taps the whiteboard. "Breslin's due in. Have him. He's good with witnesses."

I say, "Breslin's a busy man. I'd say he's got better things to do with his valuable time than hand-holding the likes of us."

"He has, yeah, but he's stuck with ye. So you'd better not waste his valuable time."

Steve is nodding away, thinking at me at the top of his lungs, *Shut your gob, could be a lot worse*. Which it could be. I bite down the next argument. "I'll ring him on the way," I say, picking up the call sheet and stuffing it in my jacket pocket. "He can meet us there."

"Make sure you do. Bernadette's getting onto the techs and the pathologist, and I'll have her find you a few floaters; you won't need the world and his wife for this." O'Kelly heads for the door, scooping up the printer pages on his way. "And if you don't want Breslin making a show of the pair of ye, get some coffee into you. You both look like shite."

In the Castle grounds the street lamps are still on, but the city is lightening, barely, into something sort of like morning. It's not raining—which is good: somewhere across the river there could be shoe prints waiting for us, or cigarette butts with DNA on them—but it's freezing and damp, a fine haze haloing the lamps, the kind of damp that soaks in and settles till you feel like your bones are colder than the air around you. The early cafés are opening; the air smells of frying sausages and bus fumes. "You need to stop for coffee?" I ask Steve.

He's wrapping his scarf tighter. "Jaysus, no. The faster we get down there . . ."

He doesn't finish, doesn't have to. The faster we get to the scene, the more time we have before teacher's best boy pops up to show us poor thick eejits how it's done. I'm not even sure why I care, at this point, but it's some kind of comfort to know Steve does too. We both have long legs, we both walk fast, and we concentrate on walking.

We're headed for the car pool. It would be quicker to take my car or Steve's, but you don't do that, ever. Some neighborhoods don't like cops, and anyone who bottles my Audi TT is gonna lose a limb. And there are cases—you can never tell what ones in advance, not for definite—where driving up in your own car would mean giving a gang of lunatic thugs your home address. Next thing you know, your cat's been tied to a brick, set on fire and thrown through your window.

I mostly drive. I'm a better driver than Steve, and a way worse passenger; me driving gets us both where we're going in a much happier mood. In the car pool, I pick out the keys to a scraped-up white Opel Kadett. Stoneybatter is old Dublin, working class and never-worked class, mixed with handfuls of yuppies and artists who bought there during the boom because it was so wonderfully authentic, meaning because they couldn't afford anywhere fancier. Sometimes you want a car that's going to turn heads. Not this time.

"Ah, shite," I say, swinging out of the garage and turning up the heat in the car. "I can't ring Breslin now. Gotta drive."

That gets Steve grinning. "Hate that. And I've got to read the call sheet. No point us arriving on the scene without a clue."

I floor it through a yellow light, pull the call sheet out of my pocket and toss it to him. "Go on. Let's hear the good news."

He scans. "Call came in to Stoneybatter station at six minutes past five. Caller was a male, wouldn't give his name. Private number." Meaning an amateur, if he thinks that'll do him any good. The network will have that number for us within hours. "He said there was a woman injured at Number 26 Viking Gardens. The station officer asked what kind of injury, he said she'd fallen and hit her head. The station officer asked was she breathing; he said he didn't know, but she looked bad. The uniform started telling him how to check her vitals, but he said, 'Get an ambulance down there, fast,' and hung up."

"Can't wait to meet him," I say. "Bet he was gone before anyone showed up, yeah?"

"Oh yeah. When the ambulance got there, the door was locked, no one answering. Uniforms arrived and broke it in, found a woman in the sitting room. Head injuries. Paramedics confirmed she was dead. No one else home, no sign of forced entry, no sign of burglary."

"If the guy wanted an ambulance, why'd he ring Stoneybatter station? Why not 999?"

"Maybe he thought 999 would be able to track down his phone number, but a cop shop wouldn't have the technology."

"So he's a bloody idiot," I say. "Great." O'Kelly was right about the quays: the Department for Digging Up Random Shit is going at one lane with a jackhammer, the other one's turned into a snarl that makes me wish for a vaporizer gun. "Let's have the lights."

Steve scoops the blue flasher out from under his seat, leans out the window and slaps it on the roof. I hit the siren. Not a lot happens. People helpfully edge over an inch or two, which is as far as they can go.

"Jesus *Christ*," I say. I'm in no humor for this. "So how come the uniforms think it's a domestic? Anyone else live there? Husband, partner?"

Steve scans again. "Doesn't say." Hopeful sideways glance at me: "Maybe they got it wrong, yeah? Could be something good after all."

"No, it's fucking not. It's another fucking domestic, or else it's not even murder, she died from a fucking fall just like the caller said, because if there was a snowball's chance in *hell* that it was anything halfway decent, O'Kelly would've waited till the morning shift got in and given it to Breslin and McCann or some other pair of smarmy little—*Jesus!*" I slam my fist down on my horn. "Do I have to go out there and arrest someone?" Some idiot up at the front of the traffic jam suddenly notices he's in a car and starts moving; the rest get out of my way and I floor it, round onto the bridge and across the Liffey to the north side.

The sudden semi-quiet, away from the quays and the workmen, feels huge. The long runs of tall redbrick buildings and shop signs shrink and split into clusters of houses, give the light room to widen across the sky, turning the low layer of clouds gray and pale yellow. I kill the siren; Steve reaches out the window and gets the flasher back in. He keeps it in his hands: scrapes a smear of muck off the glass, tilts it to make sure it's clean. Doesn't go back to reading.

Me and Steve have known each other eight months, been partnered up for four. We met working another case, back when he was on Cold Cases.

At first I didn't like him—everyone else did, and I don't trust people who everyone likes, plus he smiled too much—but that changed fast. By the time we got the solve, I liked him enough to use my five minutes in O'Kelly's good books putting in a word for Steve. It was good timing—I wouldn't have been in the market for a partner off my own bat, I liked going it alone, but O'Kelly had been getting louder about how clueless newbies didn't fly solo on his squad—and I don't regret it, even if Steve is a chirpy little bollix. He feels right, across from me when I glance up in the squad room, shoulder to shoulder with me at crime scenes, next to me at the interview table. Our solve rate is up there, whatever O'Kelly says, and more often than not we go for that pint to celebrate. Steve feels like a friend, or something on the edge of it. But we're still getting the hang of each other; we still have no guarantees.

I have the hang of him enough to know when he wants to say something, anyway. I say, "What."

"Don't let the gaffer get to you."

I glance across: Steve is watching me, steady-eyed. "You telling me I'm being oversensitive? Seriously?"

"It's not the end of the world if he thinks we need to get better with witnesses."

I whip down a side street at double the speed limit, but Steve knows my driving well enough that he doesn't tense up. I'm the one gritting my teeth. "Yeah, it bloody well is. Oversensitive would be if I cared what Breslin or whoever thinks of our witness technique, which I don't give a damn about. But if O'Kelly thinks we can't handle ourselves, then we're going to keep getting these bullshit nothing cases, and we're going to keep having some tosser looking over our shoulders. You don't have a problem with that?"

Steve shrugs. "Breslin's just backup. It's still our case."

"We don't *need* backup. We need to be left the fuck alone to do our job."

"We will be. Sooner or later."

"Yeah? When?"

Steve doesn't answer that, obviously. I slow down—the Kadett handles like a shopping trolley. Stoneybatter is getting its Sunday morning under-

way: runners pounding along the footpaths, pissed-off teenagers dragging dogs and brooding over the unfairness of it all, a girl in clubbing
gear wandering home with goosebumps on her legs and her shoes in
her hand.

I say, "I'm not gonna take this much longer."

Burnout happens. It happens more in the squads like Vice and Drugs,
where the same vile shite keeps coming at you every day and nothing you
do makes any difference: you burst your bollix making your case and the
same girls keep on getting pimped out, just by a new scumbag; the same
junkies keep on buying the same gear, just from a new drug lord. You plug
one hole, the shite bursts through in a new place and just keeps on pouring. That gets to people. In Murder, if you put someone away, anyone else
he would've killed stays alive. You're fighting one killer at a time, instead
of the whole worst side of human nature, and you can beat one killer.
People last, in Murder. Last their whole careers.

In any squad, people last a lot longer than two years.

My two years have been special. The cases aren't a problem—I could take
back-to-back cannibals and kid-killers, never miss a wink of sleep. Like I
said, you can beat one killer. Beating your own squad is a whole other thing.

Steve has the hang of me enough to know when I'm not just blowing
off steam. After a second he asks, "What would you do instead? Transfer
back to Missing Persons?"

"Nah. Fuck that." I don't go backwards. "One of my mates from
school, he's a partner in a security agency. The big stuff, bodyguards for
high flyers, international; not nabbing shoplifters at Penney's. He says, any
time I want a job . . ."

I'm not looking at Steve, but I can feel him motionless and watching me.
I can't tell what's in his head. Steve's a good guy, but he's a people-pleaser.
With me gone, he could fit right into the squad, if he felt like it. One of the
lads, working the decent cases and having a laugh, easy as that.

"The money's great," I say. "And in there, being a woman would actually be a plus. That's what a lot of these guys want for their wives, daughters: women bodyguards. For themselves, too. Less obvious."

Steve says, "Are you gonna ring him?"

I pull up at the top of Viking Gardens. The cloud's broken up enough that light leaks through, a thin skin of it coating the slate roofs, the lean-ing lamppost. It's the most sunlight we've seen all week.

I say, "I don't know."

I already know Viking Gardens. I live a ten-minute walk away—because I like Stoneybatter, not because I can't afford anything fancier—and one of the routes I use for my run goes past the top of the road. It's less exciting than it sounds: a scruffy cul-de-sac, lined with Victorian terraced cottages fronting straight onto patched-up pavements. Low slate roofs, net curtains, bright-painted doors. The street is narrow enough that the parked cars all have two tires on the curb.

This is about as long as we can get away with not ringing Breslin, before he shows up at work and the gaffer wants to know what he's doing there. Before we get out of the car, I ring his voice mail—which may or may not buy us a few extra minutes, but at least it saves me making chitchat—and leave a message. I make the case sound boring as shite, which doesn't take much, but I know that won't slow him down. Breslin likes thinking he's Mr. Indispensable; he'll show up just as fast for a shitty domestic as he would for a skin-stripping serial killer, because he knows the poor victim is bollixed until he gets there to save the day. "Let's move," I say, swinging my satchel over my shoulder.

Number 26 is the one down the far end of the road, with the crime-scene tape and the marked car and the white Technical Bureau van. A cluster of kids hanging about by the tape scatter when they see us coming ("Ahhh! Run!" "Here, missus, get him, he robs Toffypops out of the shop—" "Shut the fuck up, you!") but we still get watched all the way down the road. Behind the net curtains, the windows are popping ques-tions like popcorn.

"I want to wave," Steve says, under his breath. "Can I wave, yeah?"

"Act your age, you." But the shot of adrenaline is hitting me, too, no matter how I fight it. Even when you know trained chimps could do your job that day, the walk to the scene gets you: turns you into a gladiator walking towards the arena, a few heartbeats away from a fight that'll make emperors chant your name. Then you take a look at the scene, your arena and your emperor go up in smoke, and you feel shittier than ever.

The uniform at the door is just a kid, long wobbly-looking neck and big ears holding up a too-big hat. "Detectives," he says, snapping upright and trying to work out whether to salute. "Garda J. P. Dooley." Or something. His accent needs subtitles.

"Detective Conway," I say, finding gloves and shoe covers in my bag. "And that's Detective Moran. Seen anyone hanging around who shouldn't be?"

"Just them kids, like." The kids will need talking to, and so will their parents. The thing about old neighborhoods: people still mind each other's business. It doesn't suit everyone, but it suits us. "We didn't do any door-to-door yet; we thought ye might want it done your own way, like."

"Good call," Steve says, pulling on his gloves. "We'll get someone onto it. What was that like when you got here?"

He nods at the cottage door, which is a harmless shade of blue, splintered where the uniforms bashed it in. "Closed," the uniform says promptly.

"Well, yeah, I got that," Steve says, but with a grin that makes it a shared joke, not the smackdown I would have pulled out. "Closed how? Bolted, double-locked, on the latch?"

"Oh, right, sorry, I—" The uniform's gone red. "There's a Chubb lock and a Yale. 'Twasn't double-locked, but. On the latch, only."

Meaning if the killer left this way, he just pulled the door closed behind him; he didn't need a key. "Alarm going off?"

"No. Like, there is an alarm system, like"—the uniform points at the box on the wall above us—"but it wasn't set. It didn't go off when we went in, even."

"Thanks," Steve says, giving him another grin. "That's great." The uniform goes scarlet. Stevie has a fan.

The door swings open, and Sophie Miller sticks her head out. Sophie has big brown eyes and a ballerina build and makes a hooded white boiler suit look some kind of elegant, so a lot of people try to give her shit, but they only try once. She's one of the best crime-scene techs we've got, plus the two of us like each other. Seeing her is more of a relief than it should be.

"Hey," she says. "About time."

"Roadworks," I say. "Howya. What've we got?"

"Looks like another lovers' tiff to me. Have you called dibs on them, or what?"

"Better than gangsters," I say. I feel Steve's quick startled glance, throw him a cold one back: he knows me and Sophie are mates, but he should also know I'm not gonna go crying on my mate's shoulder about squad business. "At least on domestics, you get the odd witness who'll talk. Let's have a look."

The cottage is small: we walk straight into the sitting-slash-dining room. Three doors off it, and I already know which is what: bedroom off to the left, kitchen straight ahead, shower room to the right of that—the layout is the same as my place. The decor is nothing like, though. Purple rug on the laminate flooring, heavy purple curtains trying to look expensive, purple throw artistically arranged on the white leather sofa, forgettable canvas prints of purple flowers: the room looks like it was bought through some Decorate Your Home app where you plug in your budget and your favorite colors and the whole thing arrives in a van the next day.

In there it's still last night. The curtains are closed; the overhead lights are off, but standing lamps are on in odd corners. Sophie's techs—one kneeling by the sofa picking up fibers with Sellotape, one dusting a side table for prints, one doing a slow sweep with a video camera—have their headlamps on. The room is stifling hot and stinks of cooked meat and scented candle. The tech by the sofa is fanning the front of his boiler suit, trying to get some air in there.

The gas fire is on, fake coals glowing, flames flickering away manically at the overheated room. The fireplace is cut stone, fake-rustic to go with the adorable little artisan cottage. The woman's head is resting on the corner of the hearth.